The Collected Novels of Conrad Aiken

Collections by Conrad Aiken

The Collected Novels of

CONRAD AIKEN

Blue Voyage   Great Circle   King Coffin

A Heart for the Gods of Mexico

Conversation

INTRODUCTION BY R. P. BLACKMUR

HOLT, RINEHART AND WINSTON

NEW YORK CHICAGO SAN FRANCISCO

Designer: Ernst Reichl
80190-0114
Printed in the United States of America

❲ Introduction

Aiken is all of a piece within his works, whether you think of his poems, his short stories, or his novels; and I think he is also personally deeply present in his works—of course, not all of him but only that part of him which he needs, or which clings to him, as an author aiming at a theme: the finding, declaration, and loss of the self or psyche among the melodramas of love and jealousy, death and immolation, personal power and the frustrate abyss which in their fragments assault his sensibility. The reader can pursue these relations and their phases in Jay Martin's admirable and useful book about Aiken,* which should invite him to the works themselves. Here I mean merely to assert the fact, which has made itself plain with a re-reading of his novels all at once, of the deep relatedness—the necessary reticulation—and the constant theme. Perhaps with this assertion I can divagate and return.

Aiken's novels and stories are full of observations of gesture, of fragmentary conversations, spots of scene, the accidents of itinerary—everything that can be overheard or spied out: everything (in a phrase he used in one of his poems) between the foremath and the aftermath, the early growth and the after growth of the intended harvest. In the novels these snippets of anecdote make minor *éclaircissements* of who-knows-what (a speculative version, two centuries or so further along in the study of what we cannot take hold of, though it takes careless sudden hold of us, the *je-ne-sais-quoi*), and become a part of the permanent ambience of everything we are up to and everything we flee from. It is the ambience of the vaudeville of the psyche. (It is worth while noting here that in Aiken the minor people are vaudeville or burlesque, while the major people go in for strip tease of the self with uncontrollable drums.) Whatever happens in the city invades and inspirits whatever happens to ourselves. Anyone who has dined often with Aiken must have been struck a livening blow by his restless percipience of the casual that was going on about him in the midst of no matter what genuine preoccupation—of money or marriage or career —concerned both of you. Whatever the roving eye or cocked ear could

* *Conrad Aiken: A Life of His Art*, Princeton, New Jersey, 1962.

5

report was in its circumfusion sponged into the preoccupation, and so becomes part of the declaration of the double self between you. The fresh observation gives ambience to that self.

The recapture—the retention by repetition—of the familiar locus—the place—the naming of buildings, streets, flowers is a strain similar to that of the fresh observation. It is like the dining. Every place is the scene of some crime, and if we can name it we reactivate the crime a little—even when we make mistakes of identity or direction now and then. There is a refuge from our present guilt in the old crime—or even our old guilt. Original sin is never ending. It is the precision (not the rightness or wrongness) of the observation that counts. Every observation must be made at least twice (though the second may be in memory only) before it presents itself as force, before it *works*. Observations made many times have the effect of creating something afresh that without our knowing it had already long been. There is thus an elegiac effect.

In Aiken's novels, Cambridge, Boston, and the Duxbury part of Cape Cod are full of such observations and recognitions. Anyone who has lived in these places between 1905 and 1940 (as I have myself) knows where he is, and knows within the harder knowledge of change; and each will add his own knowledges of contour and monument; and will perhaps complain because of a different and sometimes contradictory knowledge. My compass, for example, will not permit me to envisage, as Aiken's compass permits him, anything on the *south* side of Commonwealth Avenue near Massachusetts. I suppose Aiken means the side of Commonwealth toward the South End, which I would call the *east* side. Compass needles wobble and deviate upon their point, and the magnetic north is never the true north. Local knowledge is needed in these waters. I know where Aiken meant to place me, though it may not be exactly the same as where he placed himself; in either case I share the intense intimacy of his local knowledge and am therefore drawn along the pattern of physical movement in the Boston and Cambridge of his novels. I walk there, too.

Of course, most people don't dine with Aiken and most of his readers will not have lived in Boston and Cambridge the greater part of the years from 1905 to 1940. The point is, they will nevertheless be *placed*, and with intimacy, in Aiken's ambience of fresh and familiar observation. Local knowledge invites and commands general response reinforced and provisioned by the reader's own alien local knowledge. A "local habitation and a name" are among our most precious objects; possessed and tended they make a faith possible.

These remarks about Aiken's Boston and Cambridge would be an idle if agreeable commonplace if they were not, as I think, in analogy to the intense intimacy of his local knowledge and the flood of creative observation in the psychological territory—the strangely inhabited inscapes—of his novels. I do not mean that Aiken gives us the soul of Boston and Cambridge, only that he has a psychic territory—among many possible ones—of his own in which we find some part of ourselves, I will not say at home but in motion. We are in the two territories together, and as our awareness of one affects our awareness of the other, so the two territories act mutually upon each other's contours. They place each other and the place is a new place, and a place which is changing every minute. Every stop turns out to be a way station which we will reach again tomorrow or next year or in some more ancient repetition of pattern of memory and expectation than we yet know.

The place is changing every minute, whether in Cambridge or in the way stations of the psyche; and indeed the names of the novels insist on the change: *Blue Voyage, Great Circle, King Coffin, A Heart for the Gods of Mexico, Conversation.* All invoke journeys, and no pause may be more than a sojourn. Even a conversation, to be a good one, must be the intimate constant change in the exchanges of the speakers; the weaving of the inconsequential along the consequent pattern. The form is very old in our accounts of the novel. It is the combination of the form with the material that makes the innovation. The form is the picaresque, the material that of psychology, or the conditions of life which a particular psychology points at. Let us call the combination the Psychological Picaresque; it may not be the right name (for the right name is always receding, always secret), but it is an indication of what goes on in these novels. Depending on how your mind bends you will say either that you have in each of them a picaresque of conscience streams or, which I take to be the lesser mode, a picaresque of the stream of consciousness. Conscience would seem the better term because there is always in these novels a striking together, a clutching together, even if there is not a uniting, of what is known. It is conscience not consciousness that can make or follow a pattern; and it is conscience that estimates the lies we tell in our search for the truth of self or love in our blue voyage along the great circle of conversation. One does not know if it is the voyage or the great circle that never ends.

In *Blue Voyage* we have as windows to love and to the self, the psychology of virtual death and of virtual crucifixion, where, with the sea all around us, we have death as a condition of life and crucifixion as a specifically human condition. It is the story of the man with the love he cannot have because, or *as if,* it were out of his class, except when he ventures from his own second-class accommodations into the first class where his love, his Cynthia, is. It is a book where everything that is second class in us shrieks in self-crucifixion and everything that is out of class, or outclassed, in us looks for death. The blue voyage is where somebody, or anybody, or even everybody must die. *Amare* and *morire* or *aimer* and *mourir* become somehow *again* a single conjugation throughout to the supervening noise of the sea: *thalassa, thalassa:* to love is *not* to die. Demarest, the hero, is a logolater, an idolizer of his words, and the meanings of his words and of his visions change in him according to his desires—*come amor vuol* as Dante says of his dreaming pilgrim (*Purgatorio* XIX). The horror of identity and the horror of love lie somewhere along the great circle course of this change. No wonder the reaction is self-crucifixion and the coming action death, with damnation equally in acceptance or rejection. Demarest—play with the particles and syllables of this name in what psychology and what Latin of the heart you will—hears still and continuously what at least one of the Sirens sings: as if to love were *not* to die.

This is a vulgar translation, at best a barbarous Vulgate, of what every Aiken hero hears his siren sing: as if to love were *not* to die. It is the sirens, not the mermaids, sing the most human of all songs, and if the sirens fail or we have too hard a wax in our ears, it will be Circe we attend, for Circe we have always within us in Aiken's novels. In *Blue Voyage* Circe is perhaps Faubion, the young woman you can't take your eyes or your hands off, the young woman who haunts you before you have had her and whom you know, if only you get drunk enough, you will have.

In *Great Circle*, the hero, Andy Cather, is drunk enough both in liquor and in jealousy to create within himself—within his internal panic—the intolerable Circe voice. Memory and hope between them make a muck and in the muck there is Andy's life-long recurrent dream of the crucified pig—as if the pig were continuously stuck and continuously screaming. This is how the pig in us takes to crucifixion in the Aiken psychology that reeks catastrophe and creates disaster by prolonging, by "normalising" our moments of instinctive degradation beyond what the sleeping life can bear. In ordinary life we commonly wake up to our nightmares with a stifled scream, in Aiken's novels—particularly *Great Circle*—the nightmare is carried over and intensified in waking life. No wonder Bill the psychiatrist can listen no longer to Andy's waking nightmare but takes himself to sleep. Yet how tempting the Aiken psychology is to the frustrated or injured psyche as a providential occupation with our illusions. Reality is nothing, this psychology seems to say, anybody can cope with reality, but with our illusions we cannot cope, which is their blessing upon us: to satisfy our deep need for what we cannot cope with, except by martyrdom, crucifixion, degradation—all three in one nightmare.

How far Aiken's Circe psychology carries us in *Great Circle* is evident, I think, when in Sander's Theatre, Andy hears the other voice: Koussevitzky conducting the Boston Symphony in Mozart's overture to *The Magic Flute*. The listening is interspersed with a reading of the Program Notes (I like to think they were still Philip Hale's) and with a watching of his deserted and unfaithful wife far below him in the pit of the theatre with his own proper seat empty next to her. The last of the program notes quoted, to which Andy gives full assent, calls the overture "one of the most perfect instrumental compositions ever produced by human genius." To Andy god and the hurdy-gurdy speak to each other and then together. The Circe within listens to the siren without. This stands as preface to one of those intimate reconciliations that do not quite occur, but which may yet at another time and in an older place. I do not know that I read the end of the book right, and indeed I do not know that Aiken meant any one reading to prevail. Andy goes off to Duxbury, to the edge of the sea on Cape Cod, where as a child he had come on his first catastrophe and on his first knowledge of infidelity: when he found that his mother and his uncle were lovers, and had himself found them drowned. Now he must see for himself his own shattering daybreak on the old pattern repeated in himself; to see how "at a moment of discovery—one loses oneself in order to create oneself: the end that is still conscious of its beginnings. Birth that remembers death." This is of course the Great Circle. But how, in accepting it, does Andy qualify it? As "The wonderful nightmare, the wonderful and acceptable nightmare!" As if for the length of the next lap of the circle the crucified pig will scream again.

Certainly there is very little but that scream, subdued and muffled but penetrating, in *A Heart for the Gods of Mexico*, the scream in some one else not oneself, the scream in any silence listened to. It is in this case the scream in the willful nightmare of the young woman Noni, who has six months to live and eyes like the fringed gentian. Her lover, Gil, does not know of her coming death. Her confidant and as it were her lifetime hidden lover, Blomberg, knows it better than she. The three of them set off from Boston for Mexico—on the "great circle to Mexico," Mexico the death country, the murder country—so Noni can get a Mexican divorce and marry Gil before she dies. What do we say here? To love is *not* to die, as in *Blue Voyage*, or is it the older theme the gray horror where to love is altogether to die, a bloody heart on the altar of the Plumed Serpent? At any rate the only embrace we feel is of Noni in the arms of death, her own and other deaths surrounding. The book is a lyric fusion of several mythologies, and what the lyric cries, what it *implores*, is the manifest divination of death, and the voice is the voice of a sibyl (I here rearrange for compactness some of Aiken's own words). For the greater part of the book we are on the train, with its motion and pauses and changes, as a kind of parallel to the other motions and changes in the three travelers, each different from the others, each hurrying in its own way, never quite in time or key or gear. Each is on his own journey in the same train, which is on its own journey. It is a décalage on a Blue Train—a décalage of independent neuroses, which are all psychogenic, in a general neuritis, which is a condition of life whenever it chooses an individual form or commits a particularized self to experience. But it is a sibyl's book and I will not undertake to report her. Like Blomberg at the very end there is a misery that wants to laugh and especially when it is so very far from home.

Conversation is much nearer home, is indeed domestic in every detail. Even the screams in tenor and hope: the tenor of keeping things going, like the planting of a hundred lilacs by dusk and night; the hope of recovering—of recouping as they say so falsely on the market, truly in the soul—the accidental and unintelligent losses that constitute the history of a lifetime: the damages of the sojourn. This is Aiken's version of the two wars —or the warring which makes the conflict—of the journey and the pity of life which Dante announces (*Inferno* II) as the subject of his comedy, adding that such an account will show the nobleness of memory. What Aiken adds—what almost any modern poet without a future world in faith must add—is the other nobleness of expectation. In faithful days there was no bad end that might not be overcome. We cannot bank on heaven and must keep our expectations near, unless in desperation. Memory and expectation breed in our time, and in their hybrid we dream our safety. Hence our staying powers have shrunk. At the opening of *Conversation*, the man and wife, Timothy and Enid, are so shrunken that they have almost nothing to say to each other unless it can be converted into a quarrel. Looking at and listening to them we have a fresh instance of how so many marriages are only held together by the cement of fresh quarrels, so that if the quarrels stopped, the crazy glaze of the marriage would fall apart. Here is the dilemma for the marriage counselor (I mean the novelist): beware of the spouse who will not quarrel, but beware more of the spouse whose only enthusiasm is to quarrel. Timothy and Enid have not decided upon which horn to impale themselves; the only thing certain, as the story begins to unfold, is that both husband and wife are beginning to act against their own interests. Each informs upon himself to himself; each is marvellously equipped to find, nourish, and develop the evil in the self.

The informer is that blackguard in the soul who would justify only its shortcomings and who has nothing but contemptuous distrust, and even spite—diseased chagrin—for the importunate hope for magnanimity and compassion between persons. It is as if there were a heraldic motto for this family of mankind: Every Man and Woman their own Cad, as an apt translation of *Honi soit qui mal y pense*, or God angers Himself in Vain. We see this in dinners unprepared, in failing water pumps, in Earth closets that are no more, in falsified careers, in the waiting for contact in dark rooms, and in that anarchy between people which could not exist without the supervening order which the anarchy denies. This last perhaps needs translation. A shop-lifting anarchist has come to the Cape Cod town (another version of Duxbury) with a troupe of those who call themselves artists but who have no requirement of craft or talent, and the good fun of this anarchy becomes in argument the horror between man and wife. The man has brought them here, though there are no shops to lift, from love of the possibility; the wife cries out because they show up the strange fact of the impossibility. The scandal of that impossibility becomes the horror between them, as the possibility or impossibility of anarchy—of uncontrolled or uncontrollable life—is always the terror of people in deep relation. That the shoplifter and his friends are in themselves only freaks does not matter. The freaks that irritate are most easily made the monsters who sack our citadels. In *Conversation* husband and wife use the freaks to break each other's peace, but something else would have done as well; for the husband, a visit from the wife's family; for the wife, the discovery of her husband's affair with Nora, just now terminated by a lovely lyric letter of conscience from Nora. Indeed nothing at all but their sense of their martyred selves was needed; for their marriage had reached that stage, that interlude, where indifference becomes a malevolent force, which must end either in mutual hatred or new love, in the silent scream or the new conversation. I will not say that the conversation which ends the long quarrel of the book makes an affirmation; it may or may not, and if so it will have to be repeated; I would say rather than affirmation that it makes a compassionate annunciation. Annunciation is the everlasting possibility, and conversation is the compassion in which we feel it.

Thus in four of Aiken's five picaresque novels of the psyche, we have had differing but converging versions of his two themes: the declaration of the self and the accomplishment of love, with a teetering balance between the psychology of Circe and the psychology of the sirens, and with death a multivalent measure of every effort. All Aiken's people are in the troubles which we would like to be ours, or, even if we did not like them, into which we could slip as we slip into a vice or a heroism or a martyrdom or an ambition of love. Exactly in the middle comes *King Coffin*, in which love is discarded and the self asserted to the point of destruction. There the hero is megalomaniac, determined "to exist outside society" in "a deeper and darker world of which a pure terribleness would be the principle." This is the refuge we are all of us born to see when love fails and the self collapses and anonymous murder becomes the only possible act. If *King Coffin* must be taken in series with the other four novels, it is something like this which we must say about it: It is the lyric of our insane selves which frightens us out of the fear of love and the loving self.

Other than the insane self I would rather take the book as a splendid, gay, and entrancing venture (with the very best actual local topography) into the psychology of the gangster self (in Christian times more often the satanic self). Indeed, I am rather sorry that Jasper Ammen should be made explicitly insane, for it impairs the credibility of his thoughts and acts. I would, for the joy of reading, take him as one of the condottieri of the Psyche, a good companion on the domestic scene for Gide's Lafcadio, Dostoevsky's Stavrogin, Balzac's Vautrin, or even Mann's Felix Krull, with all of whom I feel much personal sympathy. Some part of us is most at home in the idea of pure crime. Which of us would not rejoice in the prospect, as Jasper Ammen did, of a pure and random murder as the most magnificent form of mastery available to us—magnificent because also spontaneous. Ammen was right when, once having conceived the idea of murder, he decided that neither an enemy nor a friend would do; the victim must be a stranger. Our purest intimacies are with strangers, especially those we spy on and never talk to, an intimacy without the taint of interest or conflict. And who has not seen, if by accident we meet the stranger, the instant pollution of intimacy with knowledge. No. Ammen was indeed right to master everything about his victim possible without acquaintance. In the anonymous is the truly communal, just as every ultimate action is a tour de force quite without love and altogether free of any notion of the shared self. Very few of us can maintain such purity to the end, but for those interested in pursuing the idea of such purity the venture of Jasper Ammen is exemplary if you stop short of the last pages. Regrettably, at the last, the mighty hero does not topple into insanity and kills himself instead of his victim. Or should we rather say that he relinquishes one mastery for the sake of another?

It is right, though, that *King Coffin* should stand as a reminder between the two pairs of the other novels. It comments both with the primitive and more terrifying form of the same psychology that inhabits those efforts of love and self. If you look over any human shoulder *King Coffin* is there, where the nightmares in human relations come from.

—R. P. BLACKMUR

Contents

Blue Voyage

E coelo descendit γνῶθι σεαυτὸν.

JUVENAL XI, 27.

What is there in thee, Man, that can be known?
Dark fluxion, all unfixable by thought,
A phantom dim of past and future wrought,
Vain sister of the worm——

COLERIDGE: *Self-Knowledge*

⟮ I

"Will you stop," said William Demarest, leaning his head out of the taxi window, "at the corner drug store?" Just like a cuckoo clock, he thought.

It had suddenly occurred to him that he had forgotten his sea sick pills—the little pink and green box was indispensable—oh, absolutely! A charm against sea serpents. As he stood on the marble floor, amid the thousand bottles and vials and jars, in a heavy smell of soap and disinfectant, watching the clerk wrap up and seal the box, the sound of the approaching voyage came loudly about him. Waves crashing against black portholes at midnight. Bugles blowing in sour corridors—red-carpeted corridors which suddenly, unaccountably, became hills to climb. O God, what a prospect! And the ship—what was the ship? A congregation of gigantic mushroomlike ventilators, red-throated, all belching a smell of hot oil and degenerate soup, with sounds of faint submarine clankings. Among them, a few pale stewards, faces like cauliflowers, carrying gladstone bags and hot-water bottles . . . He suddenly felt queasy. This would never do: it was all a matter of nerves. Day by day, and with every wave, the sea gets smoother and smoother. It might, in fact, be a regular yachting cruise—blue sky, blue sea, sunny decks, and a beautiful, mysterious young lady to talk to. Why not? It had happened before. "Thanks!" he said . . .

In the taxi, as they passed through Twenty-third Street, he lost fifteen years of his life, no less, and caught sight of himself (a very pale, sober-looking young man) mounting the stone steps of No. 421. The shy young widow was sitting in the garden watching her child. How had she managed to conceal so long from him, in their meetings in hall or on stairs, that she had only one hand? . . . And Stedman, the literary hack, came in at lunchtime to say, "Willst hog it with me over the way?"—his reference being to the free lunch at the saloon across the street. And the bedbugs! Stedman had left on his desk a small crystal vial, half full of bedbugs, alive, crawling, labeled, *"Take one before retiring. Dr. Stedman."*—A gay time, then! Now those people were all gone. Stedman, in his spare time (of which there was precious little), made models of ships—exquisite little things. He had gone into an insurance office. The old painter was dead. What had become of the detective? . . . and his thin submissive little wife, who never lifted her eyes from her plate.

"Here you are, sir!" said the taxi driver, turning his head.

And there he was. The wharf. An enormous, depressing place, cavernous, engulfing bales and trunks by the cartload, but with no sign of a ship anywhere. Where should he enter? The usual terror assailed him. Everywhere stood uncompromising officials, emblems of stupidity. He carried his bag into the great sounding gloom, which was itself, with its smells of oakum and hemp and slimy piles, like a vast ship; dodged his way among thumping trucks—trucks were everywhere, each pushed by a pirate; and at last, through a great sea door, caught sight of the black iron side of the vessel, streaked with filth and rust. A qualm came over him. What disgusting animals ships were! always fouling their sides with garbage. However, perhaps the lavatory would smell of antiseptic . . . "Second cabin? Next gangway" . . . He crawled up the next gangway, steep as a funicular, and stepped onto the resilient deck. O Thalassa! Thalassa! Unmerciful sea. He was already fairly launched into the infinite, the immense solitude, which seemed (to the steward who took his bag) to mean so little. Yes: alone. Alone with the sea for eight days: alone in a cage with a world of tigers roaring outside.

"Am I alone in this cabin?" he asked.

"I don't know, sir. You'll have to ask the cabin steward, after we start."

Now, Demarest, survey this cabin which will be your cell for eight days. Running water? Yes. Four berths. Ring once for Mr. Tomkins, twice for Mrs. Atherton. No porthole, of course. Red carpet, and the usual smell. He poured out a glass of water, and took two pills, as prescribed. The water was cloudy and tepid. Footsteps rang on the deck over his head. . . . And suddenly a feeling of unutterable desolation came over him, a nostalgia made only the more poignant by the echoes it brought of other voyages. Ah, that incurable longing for escape, for a spider's cable by which he might swing himself abruptly into space or oblivion! But this time, was it an escape or a return? . . . And the voices of his former fellow voyagers, fellow crawlers toward the infinite, came round him in melancholy chorus. "A safety razor? Just like a bally little lawn mower. And a thundering hot towel on your face." That was the "pynter and gilder" on the *Empress*. And his poverty-stricken roommate, who had got a Marconigram—for which he had to pay—saying, "Have a Guinness on us, at your expense." His comic fury, his bulging eyes! To make it worse, his only hat, left carelessly in a bunk, was a moment later sat upon and crushed beyond recognition . . . The German girl, with the long blue ribbons down the back of her skirt, deliciously fluttering as she walked, whom he had been too shy to speak to. She came and stood beside him while the stewards danced and sang below the hatch, stood very close to him, put her hands on the rope. "Curiously melancholy," he had thought of saying, "all this folk music is! . . ." Melancholy it was. But his courage had failed him; and next day, as he passed her (she was walking—how buoyantly she walked!—with the Professor), he heard her saying, "No, he vas afraid!" She laughed as she said it. And afterwards she had married the Professor. He had watched them pacing the deck, pacing the deck, looking more and more earnestly at each other. One time as he passed them the flying word was "*gymnasium.*" The next time it was "But SHAW!" Were they falling in love? Yes—as the voyage drew to its end they became inseparable; inseparable because they saw the inevitability of separation. They stood together at the railing, looking sadly at the gray waste of water. "Oh, how persuasive is the sound of the sea!" And he had felt curiously sorry for them, somehow—as if they had become in a sense, the sea's victims: nothing of them but doth change . . .

He edged his way along the corridor, past a continuous shuffling line of stewards carrying bags, and up the brass-edged stairs. The sun had come out; on the cool east wind sang the soft quarter bells of the Metropolitan; playing their melodius prelude to the solemn striking of the hour. Three o'clock. A few of his fellow passengers idled about on the deck, stood in groups talking, or watched the last trunks being swung in a great net over the opened hatch. A whistle blew, and the net, with its bulging catch of trunks, dropped soundlessly into the hold, the donkey engine emitting a rapid rattle. Stevedores pushed boxes down the polished gangway, caught them with hooks, and pulled them into the ship.

"Is this Mr. Demarest?" A young man stood before him, earnest, a little shy, deferential.

"Yes?"

"My name's Roscoe—I'm on the *News.* Helen Shafter told me you were on the ship, and I thought I'd look you up."

"How on earth did you know me?" (Demarest felt flattered.)

"Oh, I've seen photos of you! . . . I've spoken to the purser about you —hope he'll make you comfortable . . ."

"Helen Shafter? You know Helen Shafter?"

"Oh, I know Helen very well!"

One of Helen's mutton chops? Had he been in love with her? Well, he must be discreet himself: it would never do to betray too great an intimacy with Helen.

"I hope," said the young man, offering a cigarette, "you're not joining the expatriates over there. Are you coming back?"

"Good Lord yes. I'm just going over for a——" Demarest laughed.

"Drink?"

"Yes, a drink! put it that way. . . . No, I'm too old to transplant. Too many roots to be broken, too much underground bleeding. Ten years ago— well, that would have been a different story."

"I see . . . I'm glad to hear it. We don't like to see our best men running away from us."

"Oh! Best men!" Demarest felt a little idiotic.

"Your last book—I hope you don't mind my saying so—I liked enormously."

"I'm glad you liked it!"

"I certainly did . . . Hello! There's the bugle!"

The bright brass notes came from a steward, who blew solemnly, facing the dock. The donkey engine had become silent. There was a rattle of chains, an air of poised expectancy.

"Well, so long," said the young man, putting out his hand. "I hope you'll have a good trip."

"Thanks. So long!"

Roscoe disappeared down the deck stairs. Well, well—how remarkably pleasant. He was beginning to be a kind of celebrity. How fatuous it was! Pursers would bow to him, stewards would sing—Captains and second mates dance in a ring! . . . And all because he was slightly, but uncontrollably, mad. Damned decent of Helen, too. He wished now that he hadn't parted with her at eight o'clock on the subway stairs, last night—or had arranged to meet her later, at the hotel . . . Would she have come? . . . Perhaps not. An unaccountable, brooding, witty, perverse creature. "I'm becoming unduly agitated, Helen." "Very well, then!—I'll remove the immediate stimulus." And she had withdrawn her hand, which, under the restaurant table, lay on his knee . . . Just like her!

A devastating roar came from the siren: it was prolonged, shook the ship, and he noticed that the dock had begun to glide away. They were being blasted away from America. Handkerchiefs were waved, then dashed at tears; there were calls and cries; children were held up, their puppet arms wagged by enthusiastic parents. Good-by, New York, city of cigar shops and marble towers! The sight of the hysterical crowd was painful to him, and he walked to the other side of the deck.

They were not a very promising-looking lot of passengers. He might, after all, have to look up Dr. Purington in the first class—a snob, but intelligent. Two solid prelates, with kind eyes and soft beards, stood talking to a girl, perhaps their niece. She, at any rate, was pleasant to look at—tall, straight, graceful, with innocent gray eyes and a mouth just amiably weak. Still, one couldn't have a flirtation with the niece of two Irish prelates. Or was she merely a comparative stranger—traveling, by some remote arrangement, under their protection—and anxious, for other purposes, to be dissociated from them?

"Well, what kind of voyage we going to have?"

The old-middle-aged man with the gray mustache and cigar: he leaned on the railing, gently revolving the cigar in his mouth with thumb and finger, staring exophthalmically at Staten Island.

"Looks all right now," said Demarest, with a little laugh. "Still, you never know."

"No. You never know . . . Not very exciting, I guess—ship's half empty."

"Is that so?"

"That's what they say. Off season. . . . Can't go on too long for me though! Let her rip."

"Good God, don't suggest it."

"Don't you like a voyage? Nice ship, nice people?—just suits me. Yes, sir, it just suits me."

"No. I'd like to be chloroformed, and called when we get to Liverpool . . . You heard about the man who said he wanted the easiest job on earth —calling the stations on an Atlantic liner?"

"Ha, ha. That's good . . . Yes, that'd be a nice job for me . . . just let it go on forever."

The old-middle-aged man turned a humorous beam on Demarest. An oblique purple scar cleft his mustache near the left nostril.

"Only one thing I regret," he said.

"What's that?"

"Didn't get myself a cap. I meant to do it—remembered it, too, last night on the train, when I was taking off my shoes. 'Frank,' I said to my-self, 'don't forget that cap!' But I did. It went clean out of my head. I don't feel just right in this tweed hat. I hardly ever use it. Does it look all right?"

"Looks all right to me!"

"Well, guess it'll have to do . . . Been over before?"

"Yes. This is my tenth trip."

"Tenth! My Lord. You're a fish."

They both laughed lightly. A red ferryboat passed them, crowded with faces, the waves swashing under its blunt bow; a golden eagle flashed on the pilot house, where they could see the pilot shifting the easy wheel.

"Was that a reporter talking to you?"

"Yes."

"I thought so. I heard him mention the *News* . . . Well, there goes the Statue of Liberty—what's she waving at, I wonder? Long may she wave. It's about all she does . . . Fine piece of work, all the same . . . I'd like to have had the time to go out and see it."

A flock of gulls sailed in the blue high over the Goddess; the towers of Manhattan began to soften in the October haze. The ship throbbed more palpably, the wind freshened. How quickly one forgets the sound of sea, thought Demarest—the death of a wave, the melancholy chorus of sub-siding drops when wave breaks against wave, flinging white water into the air! There was Midland Beach—where he'd so often gone swimming, swim-ming among flotsam, old bottles and butter boxes. Was that the island he had swum across to? . . . Not so much of a swim after all. There, for the last time, he had seen Alan—Alan carrying a soiled towel, and grinning. Inconceivable vitality and charm: dead now, turned to ashes, fit to scatter on an icy sidewalk. He saw Alan leaning over the back of the sofa in the London boarding house, smiling amorously, with all his freckles, at the Welsh manageress. "What's your hurry, Bill? . . . Mrs. Porter wants to talk to me—don't you, Mrs. Porter!" And in the Underground, smirking ridiculously at the Great Lady, who blushed and smiled in answer. And in Piccadilly Circus, while waiting for a bus, bowing so elaborately to the girl who stood in the doorway. "Miss Simpkins, allow me to introduce my old friend Prince Schnitzkipopoff, sometime of Warsaw! . . ." Sometime of Warsaw! And where was Alan now, sometime of—life? Or was it Indiana?

"Have a cigar?" said Frank.

"Thanks! I don't mind if I do. Have you got plenty?"

"More than I can smoke. I bought two boxes myself, and then the Boss, Mr. Charlton, gave me another. Pretty decent of him, wasn't it? Havana too—expensive cigar. Well, it's only natural—I've been in his employ for thirty years: Yes, sir, thirty years. A long time." The old man looked wist-fully at the water. "Yes, sir, thirty years. I felt bad about leaving—guess everybody felt bad about it. The Charltons gave a farewell party for me—I know them well, like one of the family. They know I'm crazy about cigars —and they had a little practical joke on me. You know those cigars that are loaded—explode? They gave me one after dinner—*Bang!* Gee whillikins, I was startled. And you know, even Selina, the old nigger cook, had been tipped off. She came to the door to see me light it. You ought to have heard her laugh! . . . Well, you know, they're nice people, fine people, and New Orleans seems like home to me; but you can't go on forever. I thought I'd like to see the Old Country again . . . There goes Coney Island."

"You were born in England?"

"Devonshire. Left it thirty years ago; went straight to New Orleans; and been there ever since."

"You'll find England changed."

"You know, I'm sort of afraid, in a way—I don't believe I'll know a soul in my town."

"No relatives?"

"All dead . . . Isn't it funny? And yet I've got this craving to go back and walk round there. That's what I'd like to do—walk over the country. I was a great walker then—knew every stick and stone. And I may hate it— be lonely—come running back inside a month."

The wind whipped their coats about their knees. Green waves from the southeast, fluctuant pyramids of water tossing their points into the wind. The bow lifted gently, far ahead. The ship fell into a long leisurely swing, first greeting to the sea, the unvintagable sea . . . What was this strange passion for crucifixion that overcame the old man, as it overcame himself?

"You're like Ulysses, setting out at last to find the rim of the world, the Pillars of Hercules."

"Not much! No exploring for me. I want to get back, that's all."

The old man looked at him with brown eyes comically solemn, in which there was just a trace of something shy and fugitive. The arched gray eyebrows gave his eyes an odd startled roundness of appearance, childlike and charming.

"No, sir, I'm too old for any exploring!"

"But isn't that just what you're doing? You don't know what you're going to . . . I don't believe we're ever too old to explore—we're always exploring something. There was an old ex-Senator on a ship with me once— by George, he was a wonder. Eighty years old, with gout so bad that he could hardly walk, and had to keep one leg up in a chair when he sat in the smoking room. He'd outlived all his relatives except one son, who'd taken over his law practice—outlived his friends, his own generation, every damned one. He fought in the Civil War, was one of the first Government surveyors of Arkansas—surveyed it when it was a wilderness, hostile Indians. He knew Walt Whitman—Walt used to come and see his aunt, he said. He didn't have much use for Walt. 'Well,' he said, 'why should I hang around Washington? I can't live forever. There's nothing for me to do here. I might as well die with my boots on. Besides,' he said, 'I haven't seen Australia for thirty years, and I'd like to see it again. I hear it's changed.' So off he was going alone, eighty years old. A magnificent man, the kind we don't seem to produce any more: huge frame, head like a lion, face like Gibraltar. He sat and listened to the arguments in the smoking room. When he said anything, it settled the discussion. We didn't exist for him —were were just a lot of little yappers, still damp from the womb. I felt a sort of affection for him, and on the last morning as we were tying up, I hunted him out, on deck, to say good-by. 'Oh, good-by!' he said, sort of surprised, as if he'd never seen me before: and turned back to look at the landing stage . . . And you know, I don't believe he ever *had* seen me—never bothered to focus his eyes on me, though we'd been talking together for a week."

"Funny business," said the old man. "How soon do they open the bar, I wonder? I wouldn't mind a nice glass of Scotch."

Demarest laughed. "And let there be no moaning at the bar, when we put out to sea!"

"Too deep for sound or foam, eh? That's good—that's good!"

"Guess I'll go below and get a sweater. Maybe they'll be giving out the seats in the saloon. Shall I get you one?"

"Thanks! I wish you would. My name's Smith."

In the smoking room half a dozen men were sitting carefully apart; they smoked meditatively, eying one another askance. They were waiting for conversational openings, each of them eager to pour forth his story. When Demarest put his head in to look round, they all regarded him simultaneously with a mute interrogation, a dumb wistful invitation: perhaps he was the necessary solvent; and at any rate the feeling was manifest that acquaintance would become easier as the room became crowded. A steel-faced clock ticked briskly on the wall of fluted and varnished wood. The small windows, with screw fastenings, were of cheap stained glass, vicious mustard yellows and bilious greens hideously devised into marine patterns. Anemic crabs, pale-ribbed scallop shells, star fish, weeds, cornucopias. The bar steward, tall and thin, leaning against a chair back, gave him an ironic smile, meant to be friendly: Malvolio. "Bar not open?" said Demarest. "Not yet, sir: waiting for the keys." *Tick-tick-tick-tick*; and someone spat resonantly into a brass spittoon . . . Six tables . . . this would be his sitting room for eight days. The sound of the sea came softly here, muted, like the hush heard in a conch shell: *Sh—sh—sh*. A loose chair clicked gently as the floor inclined.

He descended the stairs into the main saloon, a wide, pillared room, red-carpeted, with long red-covered tables. Here the sound of the sea came fresher, through a long row of opened portholes. A palm tree stood by the pale piano, its branches faintly oscillating. Two bored-looking officers sat at the end of one of the tables with ship's papers before them. Demarest gave his name, and Smith's, to one of these. The other leaned forward and said in a subdued voice, "Oh—the Purser's table. Demarest." . . . So this is fame . . . A girl brushed his arm as he turned away. "Pardon ME!" she cried, drawling the "r" a little, and smiling. Then, to the bored officers, melodiously, extravagantly fluting—

"Are *you* giving out the seats? . . . 'Cause if you are, I want one! . . . Pauline Faubion!"

Demarest was amused. A wild little person, he thought: a baggage. Small, impertinent, pretty, with large dark eyes far apart and challenging, and the full mouth a little somber. An actress perhaps. As he went out of the saloon into the corridor he heard her laughing—a fine bold trill, by George! She was losing no time . . . Crucifixion. Why do we all want to

be crucified, to fling ourselves into the very heart of the flame? Empedocles
on Etna. A moment of incandescent suffering. To suffer intensely is to
live intensely, to be intensely conscious . . . Passionate, perverse refusal
to give up the unattainable—dashing ourselves blindly against the immortal
wall. "I *will* be crucified! Here are my hands! Drive nails through them—
sharp blows!" . . . He looked at his face in the cabin mirror, under the
caged electric light, and marveled that such madness could go on behind so
impassive a forehead, eyes so profoundly serene. He looked long into his
own eyes, so unfathomable, as if in an effort to understand himself, and—
through his own transparent elusiveness—the world. What was it he
wanted? What was it that was driving him back? What was this singular
mechanism in him that wanted so deliberately, so consciously, to break itself? A strange, a rich, a deep personality he had—it baffled and fascinated
him. Everybody of course, was like this,—depth beyond depth, a universe
chorally singing, incalculable, obeying tremendous laws, chemical or divine,
of which it was able to give its own consciousness not the faintest inkling
. . . He brushed the dark hair of this universe. He looked into its tranquil
black-pooled eyes. Its mouth was humorous and bitter. And this universe
would go out and talk inanely to other universes—talking only with some
strange minute fraction of its identity, like a vast sea leaving on the shore,
for all mention of itself, a single while pebble, meaningless. A universe that
contained everything—all things—yet said only one word: "I." A music, an
infinite symphony, beautifully and majestically conducting itself there in
the darkness, but remaining forever unread and unheard. "Do you like
cigarettes?" says one universe to another. "No, I prefer a pipe," says the
second. "And what is truth?" says one universe to another. "Truth is
pleasure," answers the second. Silence. The two universes smoke cigarettes
and pipes . . . And this universe sees another, far off, unattainable, and
desires passionately to approach it, to crash into it—why? To be consumed
in the conflagration, to lose its identity? . . . Ah—thought Demarest,
drawing on his sweater—if we stopped to consider, before any individual,
his infinite richness and complexity, could we be anything but idolatrous—
even of a fool? He looked again into his reflected eyes, but now with a long
melancholy, a mingling of pity and contempt. *Know thyself!* That was the
best joke ever perpetrated. A steaming universe of germ cells, a maelstrom
of animal forces, of which he himself, his personality, was only the collective gleam. A hurricane of maggots which answered to the name of
Demarest.

There was a knock at the door.

"Come in!"

"The bath steward, sir. Do you wish a bath in the morning?"

"What time is breakfast?"

"Eight o'clock, sir."

"Then let me have it at seven-thirty."

"Hot or cold, sir."

"Cold."

The footsteps went along the alley, another knock, the voice again,
farther off. "The bath steward, miss," a girl's voice answering. A girl next
door—that was good. Who was she? Another universe brushing its hair
under an electric light, calmly, with vanity. And all of them crowded to-

gether in this small ship. What was it for? Everything seemed senseless. The ship throbbed, the bed curtains vibrated on their rings. The woodwork creaked gently, slowly, as the long ship rose to the sea. Thalassa! Thalassa! The wine-dark sea.

As he went out of his room the girl next door came forth also—the Irish girl. Shutting her door she eyed him with a sort of tentative candor, a smile withheld. A brown woolen scarf, brown woolen stockings, nice ankles. He felt shy and turned stiffly away, his head lowered a little. He heard her steps behind him, apologetic, unobtrusive, oddly contriving to say, "We're not following you—no—no;" and his own steps, becoming lighter, replied, "We wouldn't dream of assuming it." Curious how such relations can spring into being! . . . He went fugitively up the stairs and onto the deck.

It had grown cloudy and cold. The clouds were bringing an early dusk. Whitecaps, on a dark gray sea:—lines of white on a sullen sea. Should he look up Purington? He walked to the companionway which led to the deck above, and there, of course, was the sign—"*Second Cabin Passengers Not Allowed on This Deck.*" Perhaps he would see Purington go by. He stood by the railing and watched a straggling procession of first-class men striding round the corner above. Their collars were turned up, hands in pockets. They eyed the sea with hostility. There was Purington. "Purington!" he called. But Purington didn't hear. The words had been blown overboard. Two old ladies, passing, looked at him curiously, looked up at the first cabin deck, and smiled, as much as to say "Harmless!" . . . Disgusting old toads . . . Well, there was no rush about seeing Purington: he could wait. Besides, would Purington want to see him—a second-cabin passenger whom he didn't know particularly well? . . . Perhaps not. He turned resolutely away and started to walk.

When he went down to dinner, he found himself sitting on the left of the Assistant Purser, who occupied the end seat. Old Man Smith was next to him, and opposite him were Mrs. Faubion (how delightful!) and another girl.

"No, sir," the old man was saying with bantering severity. "I think you girls are too young to be traveling alone like this. It isn't right." He supped his soup loudly and intently.

"Too young! Well, I don't know about Miss Dacey. But I'd like to tell you, Mr. Man, that *I'm married*; and if a married lady can't travel by herself I'd like to know who can! And what right have *you* got, anyway, to talk to us like that—huh?" She glared at him with a comic imitation of anger.

"Married, eh? She says she's married. I don't believe she's out of school . . . Besides, I'm old enough to be your father. I leave it to you, Mr. Captain, whether these girls aren't too young to be traveling alone like this."

The Assistant Purser, Mr. Barnes, red-faced and gray-eyed (sea-gazing eyes, thought Demarest—but they gazed for the most part at ledgers and passenger lists), was a little inclined to be stiff and pompous; reserved, perhaps. He laughed with uneasy amiability, looking from one face to another and crumbling his bread.

"But we mustn't have a quarrel, must we, on the very first night of the voyage—what? Besides, where could Mrs. Faubion and Miss Dacey be safer than on a ship?"

"There!" cried Mrs. Faubion, triumphantly.

"I don't know about a *ship* being so awfully safe though," said Miss Dacey, wriggling and grimacing in a manner intended to be arch. "We know all about these sailors with a wife in every port—ha ha! Of course, I don't mean *you*, Mr. Barnes!"

Mr. Barnes opened his mouth, a little taken back.

"Oh, of course not, Miss Dacey! How could you dream of such a thing!" He looked at Demarest, laughing. "The only 'ports' I know are New York, Liverpool and Southampton. So I suppose you credit me with three."

Miss Dacey blushed furiously and gave another desperate wriggle. She was blue-eyed, anemic, with a long, thin mouth. She wore a bangle. Not more than twenty, thought Demarest.

"Now you know I didn't mean that . . . How *mean* of you. I didn't mean it at all. Though, of course, these *handsome* men——!" She gave a peculiarly vapid little laugh, and eyed Mr. Barnes sidelong.

"Now! Now!" cried Mr. Smith. "That's enough! That'll do for you. We can't have our officers demoralized like this!"

"This is becoming a little *personal*," said Barnes.

"Highly," said Demarest. "You're elected."

Mrs. Faubion laughed absent-mindedly, looking rather hard at Demarest. She was handsome, saturnine, though her features were not particularly good. There was something brooding and dark about her which, combined with her extreme youth and brilliant vulgarity, intrigued him enormously. She was extraordinarily alive. And the fact that, although a mere girl, she was married, piqued him. What did she know? Certainly there was a good deal that was hard and blatant about her—and she had picked up, in America, an astounding vaudeville sort of accent. But at the same time there was something oddly unsophisticated in her somber eyes, a burning simplicity and candor. She looked now at Smith with amused suspiciousness, and asked him:

"Are you two traveling together?"

"Why, of course!" cried Demarest. "We're father and son."

"What! With different names! You're kidding me. Is *your* name Smith?"

"Well, now, father, that's a delicate question, isn't it . . . Shall we tell the lady the truth?"

Smith laughed. "Go on—go on!"

"Oh, don't be silly! I *know* you're not father and son."

She eyed him with a doubtful gleam, half smiling.

"Come now!" said Demarest, "don't you observe the startling resemblance? . . . You see, it was like this."

"*Yes*, it was!"

"Father, you see, had an unfortunate little affair some years ago—he has a peculiar psychological affliction—which caused him to spend two years in —er—jail. And when he came out, he changed his name."

"*Really!*" cried Miss Dacey, leaning forward intensely. "How exciting! And *what* is the affliction?"

"Are you sure we ought to know about this, Mr. Smith?" asked the Purser, with a fine, grave air of concern.

"Oh—among friends——!" laughed Smith, flourishing his fork.

"Yes, it's sad, it's sad," said Demarest, shaking his head. "No one knows what father has suffered—nor me either. You see, father is a kleptomaniac."

"A *what?*" Mrs. Faubion cried. "*What* did you say?"

"He has, every now and then, an uncontrollable impulse to steal. Spoons and forks are a great temptation to him. We can't let him go out to dinner alone—have to watch him every minute. And a restaurant or hotel! he goes simply cuckoo when he gets inside the door . . . It was a restaurant that undid him! A little restaurant on Sixth Avenue. And all for a couple of nickel-plated spoons!"

"Dear, dear," murmured the Purser, "a year for each spoon, too! How unfortunate!"

"Oh, but be serious! You *aren't* together, are you?"

She leaned back in the small swivel chair, and regarded him from an immense distance.

"Why, of course! . . . Don't you believe me?"

"No! I'm from *Missouri*," she replied savagely. "And I think you're real rude."

Smith poked Demarest with his elbow, not spilling the potato from his fork.

"Now see what you've gone and done—made the little girl mad. Just when I was getting on so well, too."

"*Who* was getting on so well?" . . . Mrs. Faubion glowered.

"Of all the *conceited* men——!" contributed Miss Dacey, bridling.

"Ah, father, you shouldn't blame *me* like this . . . Is it *my* fault? . . . Is the child father to the man . . . No; if you'd only *resisted* those nickel spoons—sternly—walked out proudly with empty pockets and a pure heart——"

"Well, you don't have to *tell* everybody, do you? . . . You've spoiled my chances. What hope is there for me now?" He looked sadly at Mrs. Faubion. "Me, an ex-convict, a kleptomaniac!"

"What a *lovely* word," said Miss Dacey. "Don't *you* think so, Mr. Barnes?"

Demarest thought she was about to lay her head on Mr. Barnes's plate —so yearningly did she gush forward. Mr. Barnes leaned back a little.

"Oh, a lovely word!" he agreed. "Still, as Purser of this ship, I suppose I ought to be careful—what? . . . I must warn you, Mr. Smith, that everything you say will be held against you. It's a beautiful word; but I'm a dutiful man."

Miss Dacey clapped her hands, jingling the bangle.

"Oh, doesn't he talk nicely! Beautiful—dutiful! Just like poetry! Do you like poetry, Mr. Barnes? Do you like poetry, Mr. Kleptomaniac? Do *you* like poetry, Mr. I-don't-know-your-name"?

"Demarest? . . . Certainly. If I can have a little beer and cheese with it, or a game of billiards after it!"

"How vulgar of you! . . . And you, Mr. Barnes?"

"Oh yes, yes!" cried Mr. Barnes.

"I don't," snapped Mrs. Faubion. "I think it's all tosh. Me for a good dance, or a nice show, and plenty of jazz. On the beach at Wy-kee-kee!"

She snapped her fingers lazily, dreamily, and gave a singular little "H'm'm!" like the dying-fall, cloying, of a ukelele.

"Twangle, twangle, little guitar!" said Smith. "I'm right with you, darling! Make it two!"

"Careful, father. Remember your years. Forgive him, Mrs. Faubion. He means well,—but you know—bubbles in the think-tank . . ."

"Yes, sir," said Smith. "I sure do like a little jazz. Give me a good nigger orchestra every time. I remember once, at the Starcroft Inn, a dance hall—but no. No, I can't tell it here. Too many ladies here."

"Well! If *that's* the way you feel about it!" . . . Mrs. Faubion folded her napkin, thrust it venomously into the ring, and rose. "Good *night!*" She walked away bristling. At the door she turned and looked hard at Demarest, who watching her. Their eyes met, then wavered apart. Smith laughed delightedly.

"That time, father, it was *you.*"

"*Don't* call me *father!*—makes me feel too old. *Brr!* . . . On the beach at Wai-ki-ki . . . Some girl! . . . Have a cigar, Mr. Purser? . . . Mr. Demarest?" He beamed, offering cigars. Then he walked solemnly away, pinching the end of a cigar between finger and thumb.

"Jolly old boy that!" said Mr. Barnes. "Have you know him long?"

"Never saw him till today."

"Jolly old boy! . . . Are you going, Miss Dacey? Have we fed you well enough?"

"Oh, beautifully, thank you, Mr. Barnes! Do you have to go and do that *awful* work now?"

"Yes, I'm afraid I do."

"Good night, then!"

"Good night!"

"Daisy Dacey," said Mr. Barnes to Demarest. "How's that for a name, eh? And look at her card, she gave it to me. 'Miss Daisy Dacey. England and the United States!' Isn't that a scream?"

"The Western Hemisphere and Mars," murmured Demarest.

Feeling suddenly that they had nothing more to say to each other, they drifted shyly apart. The orchestra, which had just come in from the first cabin, finished arranging its music on tripods, and struck loudly, coarsely into "My Little Gray Home in the West." Flute, violin, piano and double-bass. The flute player, a young man with a pale, fine girlish face and a blond cascade of hair, hooked his lip earnestly over the flute: uncous lip. How white his hands were, too, on the black flute. *My lit-tle gray ho-ome in the West.* A brick vault in the cemetery, overgrown, oversnarled, with gaudy trumpet vine, steaming in the tropic sun. Bones in the tropic dust. My little red house in the south. Bees and bones and trumpet flowers: nostalgia, Gauguin, heart of darkness . . . Mrs. Faubion passed him, singing "*My lit-tle gray ho'ome——*" her eyes wide and . . . *absorbent.* Demarest felt like turning up his coat collar against a draft. A tall, dark, romantic young man came after her, carrying her coat and a steamer rug. Victim No. 1. Daisy Dacey stood at the corridor door, engaged in lively conservation with the Chief Steward. She pirouetted, slid, waved her arms, giggled, and the Chief Steward looked down at her intently, preening his little black mustache abstractedly, as if he weren't so much listening as watching, wait-

ing. "Hello!" she cried to Demarest as he passed. "Hello!" sang Demarest
mockingly. After he had passed, he heard her crying, amid the harsh music,
"Never—never—*never!*" At the same time, thin and far away, he heard the
ship's bell hurriedly striking eight: *tin-tin, tin-tin, tin-tin, tin-tin.* What
watch was this—Dog Watch? No. The Watch of the Great Bear. The
Watch of the Lion. The Watch of the Sphinx. The Queen of Sheba would
be sitting in his stateroom, on a small golden chair, clawing a pomegranate
on a golden dish. "Naughty, naughty!" she cried to her Sphinx cub, wagging a finger. Then she put down her locked hands, crying, "Jump, Sphinx!"
and the little gray sphinx leapt, expressionless, over the alabaster hoop.
"Mad, mad. I'm completely mad."

He walked twice round the deck in the wind and dark. It was cold. The
deck was dimly lighted, and everything looked a little fantastic—enormous
ventilators, mysterious people stepping out of mysterious doors, a submarine murmur of ragtime. A cluster of tiny lights far away to port indicated Long Island. As he crossed the shelter deck behind the smoking room
he saw Pauline Faubion, and the Romantic Young Man, sitting, well
wrapped, in steamer chairs. The Young Man was leaning his head very
close to her, talking in a low confidential voice—she regarded him with
solemn probing indifference. Why was it not himself who sat beside her,
talking? Oh, he knew well enough why—though he knew also, with conviction, that Pauline would have preferred him to her present company
. . . The sea was black, with hints of white, and the wind brought unceasingly from it the fluctuatingly melancholy and savage sound of charging
waves.

The smoking room had become noisy and cheerful. Bottles stood on the
table with half-filled glasses, blue smoke drifted in long lazy-swirling parallels, like isobars on a weather chart. Four men played whist at the table in
the far corner—*bang!* went down a card; *knock!* went down another. Card
games as a form of physical exercise. In another corner, Smith sat back
alone, solemnly and appreciatively smoking. He tapped indicatively the seat
next to him, blowing a rich plume of smoke. Demarest sat down, feeling
relaxed and melancholy.

"Well," said Smith, after a pause. "I've told you what *I'm* going for—
what are *you* going for?"

Demarest laughed,—looking through Smith, through the wall, through
the sea, the night. He waved his hand weakly.

"Me?" he answered. "Oh, I'm going to see the chimera. The Great
Chimera."

"I didn't know it was in captivity."

"It isn't."

"A girl? I get you, Steve."

"Yes."

There was another pause, and Smith added humorously:

"Well, I'm an old man, but I keep my eyes open myself . . . Those
girls at our table—they have the stateroom opposite mine. There's some-
think funny about those girls—something queer." He eyed Demarest
provocatively. "Don't you think——"

Demarest thought, but did not answer . . . After a while they played
checkers.

⟨ II

It was manifest to Demarest that he had got into the wrong place. It was totally unfamiliar. He walked quietly along the side of the grape arbor and then, cautiously, passed under a fragrant trellis overgrown with roses. He emerged upon a wide lawn enclosed with trees and flowers, where a garden party was in progress. A score of glitteringly dressed men and women stood talking, sauntered here and there, or set cups down on flower-decked tables. How horrible! He felt out of place, furtive and shabby, an intruder. But how was he to escape? He couldn't recall where he had got in. Was it over a wall? . . . He turned back through the trellis, hearing behind him a mild laughter. He looked down, and saw that his shoes were covered with mud and that his trousers were torn. Passing this time to the left of the grape arbor, he hurried along the narrow path of deep, soft turf, and was horrified to encounter a group of ladies coming in. They looked at him with hard eyes. Perhaps they thought he was some kind of a gardener? . . . This, then, might be the way out? . . . A flunky in knee breeches eyed him suspiciously. Then he saw a green wooden gate; but just as he was about to open it, there came a loud knock at the other side, which was at once terrifyingly repeated, repeated——

"Bath's ready, sir."

He groaned with relief, waking . . . The ship, of course! he was on a ship. He relaxed, becoming conscious of the regular remote throbbing of the engines. His coat, hanging on the stateroom door, sidled a little . . . That curious dream! It was just a new version, nevertheless, of the familiar theme—his absurd "inferiority complex." Good God! Was he destined never to escape it? Why was it that he never could be at his ease with those who were socially his equals—only at ease with his "inferiors"? It was very strange. Formal occasions, polite people, froze him to the marrow: he couldn't remain himself . . . It was not that he hadn't had every opportunity to become accustomed to them—for all the rest of his family were happily and intensely social . . . Mary and Tom adored parties, and so had his mother . . . But he had always been instinctively hostile to such things; and while he recognized in himself a passionate attachment for the fine and rich—by way of environment—he wanted the fine and rich freed from the "social"; and moreover, every so often he wanted a good deep foaming bath in the merely vulgar. An occasional debauch was imperative —whether it was only a visit to a cheap vaudeville, with its jazz, its spangles, its coarse jokes, its "Chase me, boys—I issue trading stamps"—or a shabby little clandestine adventure of his own, in which his motive was largely, if not entirely, curiosity . . . It was precisely this damned inferiority complex that had put him at such an initial disadvantage with Cynthia. By the time he had succeeded in adjusting himself, psychologically, to her exquisite old-worldliness, the dim, deep constellations of refinements and manners amid which she so statelily moved, and by the time he had put out of his mind the feeling that he was a mere ugly duckling, and had scraped from his shoes (metaphorically speaking) the mud of the brief, violent, disgusting Helen Shafter affair: by this time Cynthia had left London and gone to the continent. Gone! and that was the end. . . . He shut his eyes in a spasm of pain.

Presently he put on his ancient slippers and his raincoat and shuffled along the corridor, inhaling a dreadful odor of coffee. The bath was green, deep, dazzling: electrically cold. He was inclined to yelp like a dog, as he emerged—or no—to blaff like a seal. Blaff! Superb word. It suggested the blowing away of the water from mouth and nostrils, and also a certain *joie de vivre*. Laughter. He overheard, as he was drying himself, a fragment of conversation.

". . . She says she's married to an American naval M.D."

"Oh, does she? Well, maybe she is . . . She looks to me like a wild one. You'd better be careful."

"Oh, I know the ropes . . . She told me last night she was going back to visit her family."

"She's English?"

"Yep . . . though you wouldn't guess it. That accent! You could cut it with a knife."

"I'd like to meet her—introduce me, will you?"

"Sure—if you like."

One of the men, Demarest saw as he came out, was the Romantic Young Man. The other was a short plump individual, swarthy and sleepy, with a walrus mustache and small green cupidinous eyes . . . He gathered that they were merely ship acquaintances.

"The Lord's Day," murmured the plump one through his lather. "Guess I'll go to church. They say there's a good stewards' choir quartet. Anything to pass the time."

"Well, put sixpense in the plate for me. I'll be among the missing."

"I'll pray for you—for those lost at sea."

"Do."

Demarest shaved, glancing now and then at the smoke-blue Atlantic framed in an open porthole. A glittering day. A pleasant, soft, surfy sound came through the port and filled the white-floored bathroom, giving it oddly the air of an aquarium. Pale water lights danced on the ceiling.

"And who's that other one—the girl with her?"

"Dacey, her name is. I haven't talked with her."

"A silly-looking cat of a girl."

"By Jove, she is."

Rasp, rasp—the bally little lawn mower. "*A pynter an' gilder, I am, an' I've been to Vancouver.*" . . .

❧

Walking the deck after his breakfast—at which he had sat alone—Demarest gave himself up, for the first time, to the enjoyment of the full salt flavor of sea voyage. The sun was hot, the breeze was cold, the sea was an immense disc of blue light, just sufficiently rough to escape monotony; and the bright ship burned and sparkled in the midst of the infinite, swaying its high yellow masts ever so slightly against a witch's fingernail of white moon, lifting and declining its bows against the cloudless horizon. The long white deck, polished like bone, rose and fell just perceptibly, and with immense leisure, to the soft irregular accompaniment of waves broken and falling; and with it rose and fell the promenading passengers. The sense of the infinite, and of being isolated in its garish and terrifying profundity, was beginning to work upon them. Delighted with the ship and the sea, inquisitive and explorative, nevertheless they were restless; they paced the deck, climbed the companionway, walked through the smoking room and out at the other side, as if driven by a secret feeling of being caged. It amused Demarest to watch them. It amused him to see them, like imprisoned animals, furtively try a bar, when none was looking, elaborately pretending all the while that no bars were there, that all was peace and freedom. They had put on their "old" clothes—supplemented here and there with grotesque white yachting caps, which the wind ballooned on their heads. Tweed suits were strangely accompanied by glaring white canvas shoes; and binoculars, obviously new, were extracted from strapped cases and leveled, with knit brows and a heavily professional air, at remote plumes of smoke which lay faint and supine along the horizon. Every slightest action betrayed their inordinate consciousness of one another. Those who walked, walked either more emphatically than was their wont, or more sheepishly, aware of the scrutiny, more or less veiled, of the row of sitters. Those who sat in deck chairs were conscious of their extended feet, their plaid rugs and shawls, and the slight physical and moral discomfort of having to look "up" at the walkers. The extraordinary feeling of kinship, of unity, of a solidarity far closer and more binding than that of nations or cities or villages, was swiftly uniting them; the ship was making them a community. How often Demarest had observed this process! He now felt, with almost physical vividness, its powerful, secret, and rapid operation. He felt it turning the head of one passenger to another, he felt the yearning confusion of friendliness, curiosity, loneliness, and love, which made them all puppets and set them bowing and nodding at one another; smiling mechanical smiles which concealed outrageous happiness; laughing a little too loudly or a little too politely; all like automatic performants of a queer primitive ritual. Every one of them wanted to be overheard or seen, wanted to be exposed, wanted even—it seemed to Demarest—to be stripped. Those who already knew each other, or were relatives, talked to each other in a tacit mutual conspiracy of unaccustomed emphasis, loudness, and good-nature, made humorous remarks, delivered themselves of aphorisms or scraps of knowledge, with the one aim of making, in all directions, a favorable impression. It was a grotesque sort of love-dance. The young women flaunted and fluttered their ribbons, loitered in the sunlight consciously and gracefully, leaned on the railing with a melancholy abstraction which was deliberately and beautifully an invitation. The young men, beginning to talk with one another, but as yet timid about extending their adventures to the realm of the other sex, tramped the deck, a little flustered and unsteady when they passed the young women. They all desired keenly to talk with the latter, but none wanted to be the first, fearing the eyes and laughter of the community. Only the ship's officers, coolly sauntering and smoking, were free from this singular spell. Demarest watched their adroit maneuvers, admiring their skill, and their deep social wisdom. He observed the doctor and the young wireless operator strolling appraisingly back and forth; imperturbably selecting, as they did so, the most promising fields for exploits. They were in no hurry—they felt no pressure. They were artists; and having selected their material with care, would manipulate it with the finest of tact and discretion. Ah! how admirable! They had stopped beside an old married couple and were lightly bantering with them. The wireless operator tucked up the old woman's feet, and the old woman laughed, delighted and flattered, at something he had said. An exquisite approach! They were now in touch with the new cargo of passengers, and in the best possible way—the way which would give them, later on, the greatest possible freedom. The pause was only for a second, the merest skimming of the water with swallow-wings, but much had been set in motion: eyes had seen them, ears had heard, they were marked and sealed now as "such nice young fellows." The young men among the passengers, who beheld this little maneuver, were frankly scornful and hostile, without knowing why; the young women were envious and reproachful, looking after the retreating officers with a faint momentary pang, soon forgotten, as of sorrow . . . Ah, these sea dogs, thought Demarest, what cunning devils they are! How well they know human nature! How he envied them their aplomb and cool sophistication, the effrontery with which they accomplished, in such fine publicity, the right thing! Why could he not do likewise, instead of slinking furtively along red-carpeted corridors, avoiding the too-crowded decks, or sitting for whole days at a time in the stuffy smoking room at games of chess or bridge, or vainly endeavoring to read? Why? Why? . . . Walking toward the smoking room, which was well aft, he passed the Irish girl, who stood with the two bearish prelates. Her eyes turned friendlily toward him, but he averted his face, pretending a distraction. Then he cursed himself. Nothing could have been simpler than to have smiled. Nor could anything, for that matter, have been easier! Her gray eyes, of an innocence not without daring, her kind mouth amiable and a little weak, her tall easy figure, the brown woolen scarf and rough brown stockings to match—he noticed sharply all these things—and noticed also the slight stiffening of shyness with which she observed his approach. Unconsciously, she had contrived to admit the fact that she was aware of him and liked him. The way in which she shifted her balance, at the same time lifting a little before her one of her brown slippers, and frowning at the bright buckle, and the way in which she broke rather emphatically into the middle of something that the older prelate was saying—ah! She would be friendly, she was prepared to like and be liked, and to make confessions by moonlight.

It was the brown woolen muffler and gray eyes which most disturbed him. Gray eyes, and brown muffler, on a ship's deck, in sunlight, at sea—this meant one thing to him: Cynthia. Cynthia, on the *Silurian*, had worn such a muffler: throwing it languidly over one shoulder and around her throat as she started forward, with that odd look of distance and somber detachment in her gray eyes, sea-gazing and imperious. Good God, what an absurd pang the mere visual thought of her still gave him after a year! A disgraceful weakness. He sank into the corner seat nearest the door of the smoking room, dropping his book on the table. The pianist of the ship orchestra sat next to him, a small golden harp embroidered on the sleeve of his soiled and stained blue coat. He was a pale, ill-shaven young man, with reddish hair slicked back from his clammy forehead and watery blue eyes behind thick spectacles. His mouth was small, curled and petulant, and his voice had a complaining quality. He was leaning forward on the table, talking to an extraordinary-looking young woman whom Demarest had not noticed before.

"You're Welsh aren't you?"

The young woman looked at him sidelong in a manner intended to be vampirine. Her green eyes were by nature narrow and gleaming under long black lashes, and she deliberately over exaggerated this effect. An extraordinarily lascivious face, thought Demarest—the eyes cunning and treacherous, and the mouth, which might have been beautiful had it been more moderate, extravagantly red and rich and extravagantly and cruelly curved downward at the corners. A vampire, a serpent, a lamia, a carrion flower— yes, a mouth like a carrion flower, and giving out poisonous juices; for as she laughed, Demarest noticed that the lower lip, which was undershot, was wet with saliva. She lifted her strange face to laugh, giving only two short musical sounds, then lowered her face again and wiped her mouth with a crumpled handkerchief.

"Welsh? Why do you think I'm Welsh? . . . You ought to be Welsh, with a harp on your sleeve!"

She gave another laugh, eying Demarest; and Demarest noticed, as she again lifted and dropped her head, that her throat was singularly beautiful. The pianist turned to look at Demarest, smiled, and went on:

"Well, I don't know if you look Welsh: except that you're dark. But you asked if I had any Welsh songs, so what could be simpler? Eh? . . . What could be simpler? . . ." The pianist smiled oilily, showing three gold teeth. He knitted his white plump fingers together before him on the table. "What's your name?" he then went on.

The young woman assumed an air at the same time injured and arch. She drew back a little, narrowed her eyes at the pianist's thick spectacles, then directed suddenly at Demarest a serpentine smile, at the same time giving him a gleaming wink quick as the eye of a Kodak.

"Isn't he smart? . . . And personal! . . . sweet hour."

Demarest smiled, lighting his pipe. He was taken aback, but somewhat excited. The creature was so obviously— What? While she turned, half rising, to look out of a porthole at the sea (again wiping her juicy mouth) he tried to analyze the effect she had on him. Tropical. He had never encountered at such close quarters so scarlet-flowering and rank a growth. The invitation, certainly, was tremendous. Here, close at hand, was the rich jungle—poisonous and naïve, treacherous and rich, with its tenacious creepers, its bright voracious birds, and its fleshlike fruit. Should he enter? He recognized, also, the pressure exerted upon him to do so by the mere fact of the pianist's presence, the pianist's prior pursuit and inquisitiveness. His impulse was to compete with the pianist: to be at the same time more tactful, more humorous, and more charming: to snatch the scarlet flower from under his very nose.

Against all this—ah! the manifold complications! For it was easy to foresee that this girl would be swarmed about by the men on the ship; swarmed about as by flies; would be talked about by every one, sniggeringly —"Yes, sir, she's a warm baby!"—and would be signally avoided by the women. To attach one's self to her too publicly—and *any* attachment would inevitably involve a publicity sufficiently rank—would be to make one's self conspicuous and a little ridiculous . . . Smiling, he picked up his book and opened it. He would neither refuse nor accept.

"Oh well," he murmured, more to the pianist than to the girl. "We're all personal on a ship! What else is there to do?"

"Right!" beamed the pianist. "What the devil can we do if we don't talk?"

"Talk!" sneered the vampire. "A lot of good talking does."

"What's wrong with it? There are worse things than talking."

"Ha—ha!" She laughed, lifting her throat. This amused her intensely, and she contrived without much subtlety to suggest that it was a little wicked of her to be amused. Her chief means to this end was another rapid green wink at Demarest. "Worse things—I should hope so!"

The pianist grinned sharply, eager to take her up on this.

"What do you mean?" he said, leaning toward her.

"Mean?" She drew back, her face becoming hard and distant. She was rebuking him. The rebuke, however, seemed to grow with difficulty in her mind, and before it had flowered into speech (as for a moment Demarest thought it would) she relented, changed her purpose, and again gave her short empty musical laugh.

"What's he talking about?" she said to Demarest. "I mean worse things, that's all! . . ."

"He's got an evil mind," said Demarest. "He thought you meant a particular kind of worseness."

The girl's undershot jaw dropped. This was too deep for her.

"Are you talking English, or am I crazy?"

"He's talking Welsh," the pianist went on . . . "You haven't told me your name. I'll bet it's Evans or Jones."

"No, Davis, Peggy. You can call me Peggy, as we're old friends."

"Help! I'm married already."

"*You* married?" she cried. "Well, you do look sort of married, come to think of it."

"Oh, I say!"

"Don't you think so? He has that look—you know, sort of meek." She gave a hoot behind her handkerchief, gleaming at him askance. "I'll bet he washes the dishes." She hooted again.

The pianist flushed, grinning. "What about you? Are you married, too? I'll bet you're married to a dozen!"

"No, I'm a widow. My husband died last month, in Providence—that's where we lived."

"A widow! . . . You're a widow?" The pianist was unembarrassed.

"Yes. I had a good job too, but my brother thought I'd better come back."

"A brother in Wales?"

"Mm! A miner. Oo, such a fine, big boy. He's going to meet me at Liverpool."

. . . Abstracting himself from the persistent dialogue, Demarest tried to read. A phrase—a sentence—but the dull dialogue which kept intruding, mingled with shouts and laughter blowing through the open porthole, and the softened *sh sh* of the sea, prevented him from much concentration. Malvolio, the bar steward, smirking, made a pretense of wiping the table and chairs; opened another port, smirked again at the girl; rearranged the brass spittoons, pushing them with his foot; then came and leaned his long black-haired hands (the wrists bony) on the table, the dusting cloth under one palm. He addressed Demarest ingratiatingly.

"Your friend was looking for you."

"My friend?"

"The old man," said Malvolio confidentially. "The one you played drafts with. He said he had something particular to say to you."

"Oh, did he!"

"Yes. Something about those two young ladies, I think he said it was."

Demarest felt himself blushing. Malvolio, still leaning his long wrists on the table, turned slow, greedy eyes toward Peggy Davis, who returned the look haughtily.

"Those two young ladies, eh!" pursued the pianist. "Seems to be a lot of young ladies on this ship!"

The bar steward smiled, gave one formal wipe at the table, and withdrew lightly.

"Why all the mystery?" inquired Peggy.

"No mystery. They sit opposite me at meals. Amusing kids—nothing but kids."

"Oh, yes—these kids! Traveling alone, I'll bet—under the chief steward's protection! Ha ha!" Peggy hooted unctuously—dabbed her mouth— gleamed lasciviously.

"You seem to know all about it," said the pianist.

"Ho! That'll do for you. You don't have to do it yourself to know about it."

"No?"

"No . . . Say, aren't you impertinent! . . ."

Looking at his opened book, Demarest wondered about the old man and the two girls. What was up? Smith had been frank about his interest in them—franker than he himself had been. He found the thought vaguely exciting. Had Smith made advances, taking advantage of the proximity of his cabin to theirs? He hoped Pauline—no . . . How perfectly ridiculous . . . Here he was, setting out three thousand miles to see Cynthia, and almost immediately allowing himself to be attracted by the small, impudent, brazen baggage of a vaudeville queen—good God, how disgusting! He flushed, thinking of it. "Off to my love with a boxing glove ten thousand miles away." Disgusting? No. A pluralistic universe—as plural of morals as of worlds. The magnificent "thickness" of things . . . A bugle blew just outside the porthole. "Church!" cried Peggy, jumping up. "Don't go!" the pianist replied holding her hand. She slapped him playfully and departed . . . Men began coming into the smoking room, evidently from a desire not to be seen on deck during the services. He rose, intending to go out and taste the Sabbath stillness and desertion which he knew would possess the ship at this hour, but as he rose a voice shouted, "Who plays bridge?" and he found himself automatically replying, "I do!" "What's your name, Mr.——?" "Demarest." "Mr. Demarest"—the Jew waved a thick hand which hooked a cigar—"Meet Major Kendall, Mr. Hay-Lawrence and myself—Solomon Moses David Menelik Silberstein." There was a laugh, slightly uneasy, while Silberstein placidly and heavily but with dexterous hands shuffled the cards. "I'm not one of those Jews," he went on, "who thinks it's a disgrace to be a Jew. And I always think it a good plan to be explicit on that point—if you'll forgive my little idiosyncrasy, gentlemen— at the beginning of an acquaintance. It helps to avoid mistakes."

"Hear, hear," said Hay-Lawrence faintly, unfrowning his monocle, which fell on its black cord.

"I've got time for one rubber—or two fast ones . . . I'm glad I found this nice corner with you gentlemen,"—Silberstein pursued—"cut, please Major—because anything more like a mausoleum than the first cabin is, on this trip, I've never even considered possible. Thirteen passengers altogether, of whom half are octogenarians. One old man in a wheel chair sitting in the smoking room being uproariously rowdy all by himself, and half a dozen female century plants sitting as far from each other as they can in the drawing room. They look to me like Boston's best . . . I perceived that if I was to live for another twenty-four hours I would have to seek life down here with you fellows . . . My God, the meals up there! It's like a funeral . . . Your bid, Mr. Demarest . . . You come from New York?"

"Yes . . . One spade."

"One spade he says. My partner's going to say something—I can see it in his eye. It's all right so long as I don't see it in his hand . . . Sometimes the eye is quicker than the hand, on these boats. No reflections, gentlemen."

"Double one spade," said Hay-Lawrence, frowning his monocle into place.

"Now that's a new one on me," said the bald-headed Major, flushing. It was explained by Silberstein, and the game proceeded. The Major polished his pince-nez, endeavoring to look firm.

"Observe," murmured Silberstein placidly, "the game in the opposite corner. Particularly observe the gent sitting with his face toward us. You notice that his left eye is glass—a little too far to starboard—the man, I mean, who strikes you as skull-faced. He was on the same ship with me two months ago. A professional card player, addicted to poker. Notice also the rabbit-faced timid little gent who sits two places to his left. Partners, though they pretend not to know each other. They never meet on deck, you'll find, and they probably don't eat at the same table."

"Poker, what?" said Hay-Lawrence, grimacing as he peered over his shoulder. "I'd like to have a go at him. I've got a score to wipe out against poker. I had a little experience in my hotel the night before we sailed."

Silberstein lifted a slow finger, diamonded, thickly reprehensible.

"Never play poker with strangers . . . Or bridge either. Not for high stakes."

"Of course. I'm not a fool, man! In this case, I was bored and I took him on for pure love of adventure. I knew quite well he was some kind of sharper, but wanted to see how he would do it."

"Well, how *did* he do it?"

"That's the joke! *I* don't know. For the life of me I couldn't see anything wrong with it. He sauntered up to me while I was reading in the lounge, and asked if I'd like to play. I bought a pack of cards, and we went up to my room. Then we sat down and drew cold hands for a dollar a hand. In an hour and a half I'd lost a hundred dollars. Then I quit. He thanked me politely, put on his hat and departed . . . I watched him like a hawk—mind—and I couldn't see a *damned* thing that looked wrong."

"No. You never do. Those men are artists. They wouldn't do it if they weren't."

"Three men asked me to play bridge with them on the train from Buffalo," said the Major, blushing. "I refused at first, but then as they said they'd been unable to get a fourth anywhere, I joined them, stipulating that there should be no money in it. After three hands, they said there was no fun in it without a small stake—say fifty cents a hundred. 'Goodby, gentlemen!' I said and cleared out." The Major giggled, blushing; then frowned severly, looking at his cards. Silberstein, with green eyes far apart, glanced at him casually and massively. The Frog Prince.

"The Major takes no chances," he said. "Even in the Army, discretion is the better part of valor . . . How do you know, Major, that Mr. Demarest and I aren't conspiring together to defraud you? . . . Consider the circumstances. We three meet, and look for a fourth . . . I sing out here in this crowded smoking room in my unabashed Jewish way, and out of all those present, and endowed with bridge talent, *Mr. Demarest*, total stranger, steps forward . . . Think it over! Looks sort of bad, doesn't it?"

"You alarm me," breathed the Major.

"And me too," said Demarest. "What am I up against?"

"And as for the Duke of Clarence, my partner," Silberstein placidly pursued, while he arranged his cards and Buddhalike serenely surveyed them with slow slant eyes from end to end of the firmly held fan, "just take a good look at him, gentlemen. I ask you, was there ever a more perfect specimen of the gentleman villain? One look is enough. Monocle and all. Raffles isn't in it, nor Dracula, nor Heliogabalus. That bored Oxford manner, the *hauteur*—you know, those English go in for a *hauteur*—correct me, partner, if my French pronunciation isn't all it should be—and the skillfully introduced little story of the hundred dollars lost to a New York con man——Well, I say no more."

"Oh, dry up, Silberstein," said Hay-Lawrence, grinning uncomfortably.

"See the guilty look? . . . That's the only weakness of these English sharpers. They're too proud and sensitive. Make personal remarks about them, and they'll betray themselves every time . . . Now, Mr. *Demarest* here has the cold, unmoving New England face, the sacred cod; he conceals his feelings better even than the Englishman, simply because he hasn't got any, Am I right, Mr. Demarest?"

"Perfectly," Demarest laughed. "As for *you*——!"

"Well?"—calmly staring. "What about me?"

"The Sphinx, beside you, has as mobile a face as an ingénue!"

Silberstein played a card, reached his hand (cigar-holding) for the trick, then drew back as if stung.

"Ouch. He fooled me. He saved that up."

"Yes. I saved it up," said Demarest, tapping the trick on the edge.

"Now that we're so well acquainted, Mr. Demarest, I should like to ask you about that young lady—the term may be taken to have some latitude—to whom you were talking just now. I wouldn't call her a beauty, exactly—but I think it could be said with some justice that her appearance is very remarkable."

"The Welsh Rarebit?"

"Ha!" cried Silberstein, rolling his large head back and half closing his eyes appreciatively. "Ha! is that what you call her? Welsh Rarebit is good, is very, very good. Welsh Rarebit she is . . . And what about her, if I may ask without seeming to be too impertinent?"

"Peggy Davis. A widow of one month—so she says. Returning from Providence, where her husband died, to Wales. Her handsome brother—a miner—will meet her at the dock."

"Yes? . . . It sounds fairly circumstantial? . . . It convinces you?"

"The damndest face I ever saw," said Hay-Lawrence. "It makes me ill to look at her."

"You mean"—the Major lifted off his pince-nez and endeavored to look fiercely out of gentle brown eyes, under a brow beetling but more academic than military—"the queer-looking girl who sat over there talking with the musician? . . . She looked to me like hot stuff! . . . *He he.*" He put on his pince-nez, bridling and blushing, looking naughtily from one to the other of the bridge players.

"Go to it, Major," breathed Silberstein smokily. "We give you a free hand—go as far as you like. Only I feel it's my duty, as one hideously experienced, to warn you that she will probably see you coming . . . Ha!" He took a puff at his cigar, shut narrow eyes ecstatically, and then, while the others laughed, gave another "Ha!"

"I'm no chicken myself," said the Major. "I haven't spent two years in Constantinople for nothing."

"Have you got any photos of your harem?" asked Demarest.

The Major quivered with delight at so much attention. "No," he giggled, "not this year's."

"I suppose," said Silberstein, "you Orientals change the houris in your harems—(By Godfrey doesn't that run off nicely?—houris in your harems! Have you a little houri in your harem?)—as often as we poor stick-in-the-muds change the goldfish in our finger bowls. What's a houri more or less? And you must develop a very fine, a very subtle taste in those matters."

"Smubtle," suggested Demarest.

"Score two for Mr. Demarest. Yes, you Oriental potentates must be full of smubtleties. Thank you for that word, Mr. Demarest—a permanent addition to my vocabulary . . . A smubtle allusion! Good."

"The poker player is mad about something," said Hay-Lawrence, turning.

"Is it true that glass eyes sometimes explode?" Demarest leaned to look at the angry face. "I've heard somewhere that they do. Here's hoping."

"This is nothing to what will go on, on the last night, when they'll propose a no-limit game. That will be the time to get your money back, Duke."

"For God's sake, don't call me *Dook*."

Smith's cherub face appeared at a window, looking in. He waved his cigar, disappeared, and then came in through the door, soft-stepping and sedate.

"Playing bridge, I see," he said perching temporarily on a chair arm. "I've been looking for you."

"Where were you at breakfast?" said Demarest. "It looked bad."

"Seasick? Oh, no. I'm never seasick. Never . . . Oh, I see, I see what you mean! . . . Ha ha . . . No—but I'll tell you something later. Come out and walk when you've finished. Beautiful air this morning—beautiful." He rose absentmindedly, stared wistfully out through the window, which careened against the smooth blue sea, then softly departed. His cherub face passed the port window outside, in profile, evenly gliding.

"He was clever," murmured Silberstein. "He knew we were playing bridge."

"A nice old bird," said Demarest. "Spent his life—thirty years of it—selling sheet music and opera tickets in New Orleans. Knows every nigger song and jazz tune from the time of the flood. He'll make life miserable for the ship's orchestra."

"Made a large fortune at it, I don't doubt!"

"Enough to go back to England on. It's really rather pathetic . . . He's going back to see his childhood place, where he hasn't got a living relative and won't know a soul . . . Why does he do it?"

"Nostalgia," blew Silberstein. "He's looking for his mother. He wants to die, and doesn't know it."

"Good God," cried Hay-Lawrence. "I believe that's what's wrong with me."

"And me!" said Demarest.

The whistle blew, vibrating the table. "Twelve o'clock," said the Major and they all set their watches. Ten minutes later, the Third Officer came in, swiftly stepping over the brass door sill, a notice in his hand. He affixed this to the green baize bulletin board. The day's run. Three hundred and one miles, fine light WSW breeze, smooth sea . . . "One day gone, gentlemen," said Silberstein. "The game is adjourned till later . . . Some time this afternoon?" . . . Demarest, loitering a moment to look at the chart, saw the glass-eyed poker player slam down his cards, face upward. "*Jesus Christ!* I never saw such a lot of pikers! . . . What's the matter, you afraid to bet? *That's* what I've got—a pair of deuces!" He drew the piled chips toward him. "Come on, ante. And put some ginger into it." He turned dissociated eyes arrogantly about the room, seeking approval.

Released from church, the passengers were pacing the deck briskly, in couples, or composing themselves complicatedly in chairs, entangled with rugs, cushions, mufflers and gaudy magazines. Smith, at the forward end of the second-class deck, leaned on a stanchion, watching a sailor chalk on the polished deck the squares for shovelboard. Demarest, his back against the broad railing, hearing behind him and below him the laughter of steerage passengers and the whine of a concertina, watched the figure of Smith, small, immaculate and pathetic, cigar in hand, rising slowly against the wide arc of sea and sky, and again as slowly, with a slight swerve, descending. He stood there immovable, heroic and tragic, describing unconscious patterns against the infinite, watching the stooped sailor. Was it only the imminence of sea and sky, the immense solitude, that gave poor Smith a sort of grandeur? No. These factors did not so much confer as reveal it. Selling sheet music in New Orleans ("Cuddle up a Little Closer," or "Every Little Movement has a Meaning All Its Own") or speculating in opera tickets during the opera's annual visit, or swinging like a tiny pendulum here between water and space—Smith was equally portentous. He epitomized superbly the tragic helplessness of the human . . . Better than himself for example—or Hay-Lawrence, or Silberstein? Yes, somehow better—better perhaps because he was less conscious of hostile destiny than these, and therefore gave the effect of being more impotent. He had also the air, somehow, of being extraordinarily complete. There were no loose ends . . . An ant in the grass, crawling up a dry twig, waving stupid antennas at the void; descending patiently again; exploring an enormous pebble all the way to its barren top—descending once more; and so on, and so on, one vast obstacle after another patiently and stubbornly encountered; an oak tree climbed, right out into the infinite, suspended in the blue; a stone wall, vast labyrinth of monoliths, stoutheartedly and minutely overcome. *Smith!* . . . Who the devil was Smith? . . . Demarest watched him rising and falling there against the ultramarine abyss; unconscious and infinitesimal; smoking the "expensive" cigar which Mr. Charlton had given him. His whole career was poised there—hung in the blue—twinkled—and disappeared. There he was, to begin with, in the stationer's shop in Bideford, rosy-cheeked and amiable, handing down boxes of blue envelopes for a customer, checking off returned books of fiction in the Circulating Library (two hundred volumes) and reading them all himself, particularly the works of Thackeray; on Sunday afternoons, trudging in the rain over the red fields to Hartland Point. Then the scar on his upper lip—some sort of row—over a girl perhaps? Disgrace, discouragement, love of adventure? Adventure! Straight from the stationer's shop in Bideford, to a music shop in New Orleans, there piling and turning music for thirty years! The opera tickets. He got a corner in them once—and sold them for five dollars each. Even to angry old Mrs. Schneider! (whoever *she* was). That was adventure. And now his second great adventure—the return! No doubt Silberstein was right—it was an unconscious desire for death, for the mother . . . The sailor was pointing at the shovelboard pattern. Smith leaned, goggling, and suddenly took a couple of quick unpremeditated tripping steps, irresistibly suggested by the sea. Recovering, he pointed along the deck, nodding his head. Then gave the sailor a cigar . . . Yes, one saw the whole of Smith's career transacted there on the swaying deck in sunlight, poised between sea and sky. It was amusing to run it off, like a movie film, at terrific speed, so that the whole life story unfolded itself like one of those flowers which the movie permits one to see in the act of blooming: the calyx breaking, the pointed petals whitely springing apart and curling back, and then in a little while the rapid shriveling . . . The sailor climbed the companion way; and Smith, turning, stared exophthalmically at the sea.

"Ah, there you are! . . . I was just wondering, because I saw that slimy Jew go up the stairs . . . Jews! deliver me. I don't like them. What you want to play with him for?"

"Ah, he's harmless. As a matter of fact, he's an extremely interesting fellow."

"Maybe, maybe . . . Come down to my room. I'll show you something. Something that'll make your hair stand on end. Yes, siree! It'll make your hair stand on end." Smith revolved his cigar softly between thumb and finger, his brown eyes solemn and comic under the arched gray eyebrows.

"Lead on, father!"

"Don't call me father. *Brr.* Makes me shiver. I feel my coffin . . . Look! There she goes now!"

He nudged Demarest violently. Mrs. Faubion came running up the companionway from the steerage deck—sea-blown, wild-haired, impetuous, —and flashed saucily round the corner and out of sight. Daisy Dacey, grinning fatuously, and picking her pink muslin skirt up a little too high (consciously) came after her. She too disappeared.

"Come along," said Smith. He walked rapidly after the two girls, turned the corner, entered the main door aft, and descended the red plush stairs, Demarest following him a little embarrassed. No sign of them in the dining room. The rows of white tables were set for dinner. Stewards went to and fro with napkins, turned the revolving chairs into position, put down forks or linen-covered dishes of bread. Smith passed into the corridor beyond the kitchen, the same corridor off which Demarest lived; but went to the alley beyond. Down this he turned and proceeded to the end, his room being at the left. The door opposite his, which had been ajar, was shut sharply just before they reached it. Smith, beaming, tapped it with white knuckles. "Coo hoo!" he cried.

"Who is it?" The voice was Pauline Faubion's, stridently challenging.

"The dressmaker. Any orders for lunch?"

"No. Go away! Don't be silly!" A trilled giggle from Daisy Dacey.

"Oh, very well, very well." He winked at Demarest, opening his own door. "Look!" he said, dramatically waving his cigar at the back of the door, which he had shut. Half a dozen dresses hung on it, suspended on hangers—black, scarlet, white, green, and two flowered muslins.

"What's the idea?" said Demarest.

"Dresses." Smith goggled mournfully.

"So I see! I know a dress when I see it . . . I didn't know you were traveling in dresses, as the saying is!"

"I don't as a rule. But I'm always willing to oblige." He smiled mysteriously, cunningly.

"Well, what's the idea?"

"Ha! I wish I knew . . . She knocked at the door this morning when I was shaving. She had on one of those pink things that you can't quite see through. Good morning darling, says I!—Good morning grandpa, says she!—What can I do for you darling, says I?—Have you got room for some dresses, says she?—Sure, says I!—Well, here they are, says she!—And she give me an armful of them, and helped me to hang them up. Not hooks enough in their cabins, and they were afraid the dresses would get wrinkled staying in the trunk . . . What do you think of it?"

"Think of it!"

"Mm . . . Funny idea." The old man gleamed cherubically. "You've got to hand it to father. I guess I made a good impression. What do you think?"

"Looks like it. Or maybe they think they can trust you!"

"Ha! . . . Maybe—maybe! . . . Nice dresses anyway." He ran his fingers down a fold of scarlet satin. "Look at the beads on this . . . Cost a lot of money, that dress, I'll bet . . . A party dress—cut kind of low. Soft, eh? Feel it. And there are the little straps that go over the shoulders." He took the frock down on its hanger, and turned it slowly, appreciatively about. "Velvet, too. Must feel nice to have velvet next to the skin."

"I wonder if she's been on the stage," said Demarest. "They almost look like stage frocks."

"Don't think so. She got married to this chap when he was stationed in Dover during the war. After the war she went out West with him . . ." He hung the scarlet satin up again, then lifted a fold of flowered blue muslin against his face.

"Mm!" he bumbled. "Smells nice . . . Heliotrope . . . Smell it!"

Demarest, agitated and embarrassed, pleasantly shocked by the old man's candor, lifted the blue muslin.

"Heliotrope . . . Yes! . . . I congratulate you." He solemnly shook Smith's hand. Smith smiled, but with something mournful and questioning in his puzzled brown eyes.

"Seriously," he said, pausing to fling his chewed cigar through the open port, "what do you make of them?"

"Make of them? How do you mean?"

Meditative but twinkling, they looked deep into each other's eyes. Why was it that Demarest felt an obscure impulse to discourage the old man? . . . Jealousy? . . . Pauline was, of course, attractive to him: and he resented the fact that her frocks hung here in the old man's cabin. But this was superficial. Wasn't it, more profoundly, that he enormously liked old Smith, and wanted to keep him out of trouble? Wasn't it also that he resented, savagely resented, this evidence of the unwaning magic of sex? He pitied him. The old ox being led to the slaughter. Did he also, pitying poor old Smith, pity himself—foreseeing, with dreadful certainty, himself grown old to no greater wisdom? . . .

"I mean," said Smith, rocking gently backward with the ship, "do you think they're straight?"

"Straight! . . ." Demarest gave a short laugh. "God knows . . . My guess would be that they are. Faubion is, I should think anyway—I'm not so sure about Dacey . . . I saw her flirting with the Chief Steward last night."

"Oh! You think Faubion's straight? . . . I wonder! . . ." He ruminated sadly. He sat down on the edge of his bunk, drawing himself up like a jackknife so as not to bump his tweed hat, still ruminating. He tucked his plump hairless hands under his knees. "What makes you think so? Sit down. We've got a few minutes before dinner . . . Nice sound the sea makes through a porthole—wish they wouldn't clamp it shut at night."

"I wish I had a porthole at all . . . I don't know, she strikes me as straight—that's all. Straight but fidgety."

"Straight but fidgety! No siree, Bob. I'm an old fool, and never knew a woman, if that girl isn't——!" He lifted a twinkle, sidelong, toward Demarest. Demarest sat down on the red plush divan. A sour smell came up from it; and the clicking of the water bottle in its wooden socket, and then the loosely delayed return click, hollow and slack, made him slightly giddy. He lifted his nose toward the pure stream of air from the port. Porpoises. Flying fish. Icebergs. Cobalt and snow . . . A slice of porpoise, Mr. Smith? Thank you no, Mr. Demarest . . . Wing of Faubion, Mr. Smith? A little off the breast, please, Mr. Demarest . . . Faubion gazed at him, morose and somber, reserved but yielding, implacable but affectionate. Poising the bread knife, with waved edge damascene, he prepared to make Faubion an Amazon. One-breasted. Tell me when it hurts, Faubion. Does it hurt? . . . A-a-ah-mmm—you're hurting—*now!* . . . Still hurting? . . . *Phhh*—not so—much. . . . She turned her head far to one side, closing her eyes . . . This was the moment—this was always the moment; that delicious moment of utter anguished surrender: the flushed face turned extravagantly aside, eyelids shut, mouth relaxed with pleasure but curved with apprehension and rigid with pain . . . The dew on the forehead . . . Singular, that we should so desire this of all possible moments, a moment the essentially fleetingest of moments, that one must dedicate one's life to its pursuit. A half dozen such moments in a lifetime—moments which yield the full goblet, the nymph-cry in the blood, the whizzing off into space of the body . . . Helen Shafter, lying face downward on the beach, crying, while it began slowly to rain . . . Eunice, suddenly letting her arm fall over the frayed edge of the couch, nerveless and abandoned, while with her other hand she covered her eyes, murmuring . . . Mary, on the hill near Banstead, looking at him through her fingers, frightened, while a little way off they heard the mowing machine clattering and slaughtering among tall grass and poppies . . . What is man that thou art mindful of him? Melancholy. Men, in a smoking room, recounting their conquests to one another. Was it, as always assumed, a mere boastfulness, a mere rooster crow from the dunghill? No . . . It was the passionate desire to recreate, to live over again those inestimable instants of life, so tragically few, so irrecoverably lost. *"That reminds me of one time when I was staying——"* Yes, you can see the wretched man trying to summon them back, those few paltry episodes, and make of them, for his solace, a tiny immortal bouquet.

"She's damned attractive," he said.

"Attractive!" moaned Smith. "She's a ringtailed screecher. She's got me going—yes, sir, she's got me going. She can put her slippers——"

He broke off, pondering. Click, and then cluck, went the water bottle, while he ponderously pondered. The throb of the ship's engines was the throb of Smith, pondering the imponderable. One could see him in the act of evoking Faubion; an old wizard, toothless and long-bearded, putting one claw out of his coffin to make the last sign, then hooking his nail over the coffin's edge, batlike. What, to him, was Faubion? *"Faubion!"* cried the withered brain; and saw flames dancing scarflike in a jungle of lewd sounds and sights. Faubion, flame-bodied, wavered toward the coffin, bearing a slipper in each hand. Zebra-striped were the slippers, white and green, ophidian, with ruby eyes; and a fount of ostrich plumes jetted from each. She placed these adoringly beside the coffin, kneeling, and the bat claw was drawn in, drawing with it flames and plumes . . . Are you warm enough, Mr. Smith? . . . Quite warm enough, thank you, Mr. Demarest! . . . And what is the flavor of Faubion, Mr. Smith? . . . Flamingo, hibiscus, and guava, Mr. Demarest! . . . Take then—eat, drink, live! . . . And lo, Smith lived; the coffin glowed about him, an incadescent chrysalis, burning translucently, within which lay Smith, gleaming and waxing; the fiery chrysalis flaked away, in small dissolving flakes of flame; and Smith, luminously waxing, with fiery veins and godlike nimbus, sprang up rejoicing, naked and blazing, a leafy vine of gold rapidly growing all over his body and burning off as it grew. To right and left of him jetted the ostrich plumes, spouted higher, arched flashing, and crashed upon him foaming. Caligula. King Caligula and the immortal daughter. *King Caligula setting forth: after a seven days' meditation: marched huge armies a day to the north: and in the evening took his station: on a green hilltop: peaked and——*

"I wouldn't like to make a mistake though. No, sir. Not much . . . Barnes—that officer—is supposed to be looking after her. Suppose my foot slipped?—Mmmm. No."

"You'd be shot at sunrise. Walk the plank."

"All the same—with care. And the circumstances are favorable. These dresses—and their cabin being just opposite—don't you think——?"

"Take my advice and go slow."

Smith blinked brown eyes under his tweed hat.

"You know—it's bad when you get to my age. Bad."

"When *isn't* it bad?"

"You wait . . . Specially if you're sort of a timid fellow like me. I never was much good at love affairs. Guess they don't like the timid fellows. That's where I always made my mistake . . ."

"Well, I don't think there's any golden rule for success. I'm no Don Juan myself."

"No? You look like the sort they throw themselves at. I've only had one what you'd call "affair" in my life—yes, sir, just one. And *that* was my wife."

"Oh . . . Is your wife dead?" Demarest smoothed his voice—discreetly, hypocritically.

"I don't know, and I don't care much. She ran away from me after six months. Flew the coop. With a little shrimp of a one-lunged candy salesman—married man, too. Sixteen years ago—all but three weeks. She wrote me a couple of years afterward and wanted to come back . . . Not much! No siree, Bob. She had another 'think' coming."

"Was she young?"

"Young? Yes—too young. Twenty-one, and I was thirty-five. She came to work in the piano department; played the piano, too; good little pianist . . . Last I heard of her she was playing the piano in a movie in St. Louis . . . Good riddance, I guess . . . Of course I've had a little fling now and then—you know—but never what you'd call a nice girl . . . That's what I'd like, to settle down for good with a nice girl."

"Marry again?"

"Oh, well, I'm not so particular about marriage—besides, I've never got a divorce . . . But some nice young girl to wash the dishes, and look after me, and get my money when I die. I've got a tidy little sum saved up and nobody to leave it to."

> *. . . I'm tired of living alone.*
> *I'd like some young wife of my own.*
> *Some bow-legged Venus,*
> *To call me Silenus——*

Smith had bored his young Venus? Too attentive and exacting, too worshiping. Pawing her all the time, probably. "Now, darling! I don't want you tiring yourself out. You stay home and rest this afternoon, and I'll come home early . . ." Mrs. Smith sat down at the piano when she heard the front door shut. *The Holy City. Ho-sanna-i-in the high-est, ho-sann-a-a-for-evAH mooore* . . . Singing captivatingly, eyes on the ceiling, nevertheless she revolved on her stool now and then to see if anyone was coming. Nope!—not yet. *Flutter—flutter.—Waltz me around again Will-ee; a-round—around—around.* A footstep on the "stoop?" Mrs. Smith turned sharply her eager white chin and oystery blue eyes. There he was. He had a newspaper in one hand and a box of candy in the other. He tapped with the folded newspaper on the window. She rose and opened it. "Did you meet him?" "Yes, but he didn't notice me. I've got tickets to Nashville. Four o'clock." "I told you not to." "Hurry up and pack your things." "Don't stand *there!*—wait for me at the station. I haven't got a cent." "Here . . . if you leave a note for him, *don't* tell him where you've gone." "Darling! Do you think I'm such a fool? I may be *crazy*——!" She took the five-dollar bill and the box of chocolates. Huylers: with pistachio acorns. Smiling, she put her forefinger to her lip, transferred the kiss to the back of his right hand, drawing it softly the whole length of his yellow-haired little finger, then shut the window and ran to pack . . . *Waltz me around again Will-ee . . . around—around* . . . At four-twenty Smith came in, beaming. "Coo-hoo!" he fluted, and then again softly stepping toward the kitchen, "Coo-hoo!" . . . No answer. "Waltz Me Around Again Willie" on the piano, and still hanging in the air. An opened box of chocolates, with only the pistachio acorns gone. A note on the dining-room table. "*Frank—I've gone away. Try to forgive me. I couldn't have stood it. I don't love you and wouldn't have made you a good wife. Terribly sorry. Will write you sometime. Miss Dillingham will be glad to take the cat. Try not to think too badly of me. I'm not good enough for you, and that's a fact. Maydie . . .*" Poor old Smith. Incredulous, he cried "Coo-hoo" again; then again. All a joke. He flapped his wings, goggled, and turned into a cuckoo, flying from top to bottom of the house, dashing against walls, looking repeatedly and dementedly in the cellar, the kitchen, the bathroom, the attic. "Coo-hoo!" he cried, and even put his absurd head out of the cupola window and coo-hooed at the roof, thinking she might be there. No answer. Not a sound. He returned to the kitchen, where he met Nicodemus, the cat. "Ptrnyow!" said Nicodemus. His saucer was empty, and Smith filled it. Tears came into his eyes. "Poor old Nik," he said, "was a nice old Nickums . . ." Gone. Gone. Gone. Gone . . . He had a sense of having been excavated—a hollow, aching shell. He sat and thought. At eight o'clock, getting hungry, he opened the ice chest. And at the sight of the butter dish he burst into tears. Coo-hoo: boo-hoo. Tohu-bohu.

(III

Hay-Lawrence frowned his monocle into his left eye socket, stretching the left corner of his refined cruel mouth. A point of green handkerchief protruded from the checked breast pocket. The offensive plushy shoes—brown suède?—were neatly crossed under the table. Blue cuff edges showed, starched and sharp, at the sleeves, as he held out his brown lean hands.

"Which?" he said.

"Right," said Demarest, touching the right with light forefinger, refined and arch.

"Right is white," said Hay-Lawrence, replacing the white pawn and then the black. He turned the chessboard. Pawn to king four—Pawn to king four—Knight to king's bishop three—Knight to queen's bishop three. Bishop to knight five—Pawn to queen's rook three. Bishop to rook four . . .

"Ruy Lopez," murmured Hay-Lawrence haughtily.

"Ruy Lopez."

The Major, self-conscious, smiling, blushing, stepped over the sill with the Welsh Rarebit, one hand under her arm, his tweed cap and book in the other. The gray flat sea washed in with the opening door, was shut out hissing.

"There's a corner," he said, consciously a man of the world, conscious because he was from Murryville, Ohio.

"Where?" The Welsh Rarebit wiped her mouth. She peered cupidinously into the smoke.

"There." He lifted his book and cap. "Hello! The intelligentsia are exercising their brains."

"You flatter us," said Demarest. "Do you play?"

"Not often. I used to play a good deal in Constantinople—I knew an old Turk general who played a most awfully good game. He'd have been too good for me—if he hadn't constantly made howlers!" He twinkled, apologetic and vain.

"What is it?" said Peggy Davis, smiling with moist affection at Demarest and then with fleeting slyness at Hay-Lawrence. "Halma?"

"The Royal Game of Chess, Mrs. Davis! Shame on you. He he!" The Major giggled, wriggling.

"Royal crumbs!" croaked Peggy. "Let's sit down." They moved to the next corner, stiff-kneeing past the table edge, the Major putting his book down, then his cap on the book, then his pince-nez on his cap. Leaning his neat striped arms on the table he turned and inclined his flushed academic brow toward the Welsh Rarebit, pinkly and intimately. He began speaking in low tones. Malvolio smirked at them through the smoke, corkscrew in hand.

"God," swore Hay-Lawrence, "that woman gives me the pip . . . Did you ever see such a face in your life?"

Knight to bishop three he curved with lean fist.

"Is this the face that scuttled a thousand ships? Opened the sea cocks. It's that undershot wet lower lip that gets me," said Demarest, castling. "Can you imagine kissing it? Holy Smackerel! It glistens!"

"Good God! Don't suggest it: *cloaca maxima*. Accidental death by drowning would be the verdict at the inquest."

"No . . . suicide while of unsound mind."

Hay-Lawrence, smiling retrospectively, with slow-consuming satisfaction, lifted the king's bishop. To king two. A careful player, orthodox and gingerly. Rook to king square, Demarest moved delicately, conscious of Hay-Lawrence's sharp refinement and expensive dress. He must be, in England, well connected. Latent arrogance, and rudeness overlaid by good manners. Sloane Square—or a Sloane Square Mews? . . . Cheyne Walk? . . . Perhaps he had met Cynthia. There was something a little flashy about him, however. And the sort of refinement that invites coarseness in the beholder.

"She reminds me," Demarest refinedly grinned with one side of his mouth, "of the little song about the spittoon."

Out came the monocle.

"The spittoon? No! What is it?" The pawn in his paw went to queen's knight four. Back, bishop. Draw in your miter! To knight three.

"Say not spittoon . . . Nor cuspidor . . . Spit not too soon . . . Nor yet too far . . . Spit on the floor . . . Not on the wall . . . Or better yet . . . Spit not at all! . . ."

"Ha!" cried Hay-Lawrence. "Jolly good! Ha! Ha! Jolly good, that." He grinned the monocle back into his left eye. "Nor cuspidor!"

"It's very nice sung, but I can't sing . . . A doleful hymn tune."

The half-opened windows opposite, rising, scooped a rapid green evening sky; then slowly, forwardly, swooped again, scooping a nacreous cloud touched with flamingo. The evening would be cold and clear. Stars indistinguishable from mast lights. Seal up the shipboy's eyes. Imperious surge. One of the poker players began humming the tune of "My Little Gray Home in the West," then all began singing, furtively, fruitily sentimental. "Ante, boys," said the glass-eyed gambler evenly in the midst of it. The words dissolved, lowering, into an ululating hum, richly harmonized. *Ho-ome in the We-est.* Faubion. She came out of the West, flamingo-winged, with eyes far apart, somber and absorbent. "Hello, you!" she cried, provocatively brushing past him with saucily jerked shoulders. The opera cape, flamingo-lined, streamed after her, billowing. "*Faubion!*" sang all the evening stars together. "Oh, Faubion!" they sang, strumming their psalteries of gold and chrysolite. Faubion, coming out of the West, unperturbed, darkly walked eastward on the dark waters, Napoleonic, sardonic, ironic, Byronic. And what of Cynthia, sleeping in the east, deep sleep of the undefiled? "*Cynthia!*" trilled the morning stars with diamond voices . . . And Smith, little gray homunculus, came out of the sunset, paddling furiously in his coracle, dipping now to left and now to right, birdlike nodding his cuckoo head as he paddled in the infinite. "*Faubion!*" he caroled—"*Coo-hoo Faubion! O Faubion!*" The paddled foam burst into trident flames to right and left as he coracled from wave to wave of the abyss. Phosphorescent foam dripped chrysolite from the paddles, from his fingers, from his drooped mustache; phosphor glowed on his arched eyebrows, outlining fierily his seriocomic eyes. "*Coo-hoo Faubion!*" he sang in tiny tenor, while behind him the evening stars drew together, blue cloak to cloak, psaltery against psaltery, their mountain shoulders touching, their eyes earnest and fiery. "Deep Faubion!" they diapasoned. "*Faubion in the lowest!*" . . .

"Say not spittoon," murmured Hay-Lawrence, and pushed the queen's pawn to queen three with three tiny pushes of a clean finger nail. Again orthodox and safe. The queen's knight undefended—but mobile. Queen Faubion—the black queen; Queen Cynthia,—white as the moon; and King Caligula, corrupt and lecherous monarch, ripe Camembert of kings. "I would that all the Roman people had but one neck." Was that a castration complex? . . . Ah—that dream this afternoon during his nap. The asphyxiated baby in the railroad station. Horrible and strange; for as he worked over it (the Schafer method) pressing with merciful palms the small back to induce breathing, regarding the small blue neck and wondering at the parents who had so casually abandoned it on a railway platform, he suddenly noticed that the head was not a head but a—— A spasm of disgust . . . Sleepless Caligula, much troubled by dreams, dreamed nightly that a figure, —a form—a shape—vague and terrifying and representing the ocean— came to him speaking. This was why he had bidden his army to collect sea shells, as trophies of his victory over the sea. Pawn to queen bishop three was the move. His horse, Incitatus, he had intended to make consul. What form to represent the sea? Seaweed-bearded, arms of green water and fingers of foam; coral-branching; eyes wide, hollow, glaucous, where phosphor bubbled slow-winking, blue and lemon-yellow, vitreous, moon-mocking. And the voice? The dithering crack of two boulders smitten together under the sea? The short cruel resonance of submarine bells? The skirling lollop of a wave running vortical into a dripping cavern, weed-hung, wagging anguishedly like a tongue against the horny barnacled palate, and then out again, inarticulately noisy? "*Oo-wash-oo-wallop-are-you-awake-King Buskin?*" . . . "Attendants! What ho! Attendants— lights!" . . . Sweating, staring, Caligula started up. Two frightened attendants, with torches, ran in, kneeling. "Is Pyrallis the prostitute there? Sleeping? Wake her and bring her in! Wake also Valerius." . . . "My

lord?" said Pyrallis . . . "Ah, Pyrallis, such a nightmare I have had!—
you would not believe it. That wave again, with eyes, but no face. What
can it signify?" . . . "Wine for supper, my lord." . . . "Ah, Pyrallis—a
throat so lovely—to cut when I like! Shall I cut it, to discover the secret
of its loveliness? I have told Caesonia that I will vivisect her, so as to find
out why I love her" . . . Pyrallis cringed, frightened, at the look in the
goat's eyes. If she said, "Yes, vivisect her," might he not—cruel madman
and pervert—vivisect herself? . . . "Let me soothe you, my lord," said
Pyrallis . . . Black slaves hoisted a canopy of purple. And Valerius, running out to weep in the street—listen, good Romans and you shall hear of
the midnight ride of poor Valere!—that mysterious Catullus Valerius rag.

"The climate?" said the Major, in a pause during which the poker
players arranged and examined their cards. "Delightful. Hot in the middle
of the day, but you retire for a nap . . . There! those are the stone
stairs I told you about. Look at the size of them. Each step two feet
high. It's a humorous custom there to take ladies to see them. You let the
lady go first, and if you loiter a step or two below—*he he!* That's Mrs.
Grant, wife of one of the officials. A jolly good sport. *She* didn't give a
damn—and didn't wear any petticoat either! . . . I stayed behind, admiring the view . . ." He laughed at the Welsh Rarebit with scarlet forehead;
his face, flushed with invitation, moving jerkily upward and downward.
The Welsh Rarebit, holding the photograph in one hand, regarded the
invitation snakily; with an air of stupid appraisal. Then she squeezed his
wrist.

"Naughty man!" she crooned.

"Well, boys," sang the glass-eyed poker player. "I think I'll have a look
at this. There's fifty, and I'll raise it ten. It's a great life if you don't
weaken."

Hay-Lawrence brooded downward with cheeks sunk upon fists. Thought
was moving in his brain. Like a train in a dark subway. A red spark coming nearer through the darkness, gliding round curves. Other thoughts too,
going in other directions—he was listening to the voices in the room, listening to the half-excluded sound of sea, the thrum of the engines which
vibrated his English body. What else? A brass telescope at Cowes; three
pairs of white flannels; four pairs of white shoes; tea on the lawn with
Lady Daphne Twinkleplume (slightly literary) followed by a week on his
little shoot in Wales. At home, his neurotic wife, Gladys, sitting by the fire,
looking out of the darkening window on which long bright gashes of rain
began to glisten, looking into the gloom of a London dusk, then again sitting by the fire, shivering. Tea at five. Vivien had sailed from Cartagena.
He had sailed from Rio. He had sailed (a postcard said) from Panama.
He was sailing (a cable said) from New York. The maid was taking Ching
(the Pekingese) for a walk round Sloane Square and perhaps as far as
Harrods. She ought to have known it would rain. "Vivien, tell me, why is
it you go away so much? Why are you always going away to sea? leaving
me alone?" "Are we going to discuss that again?" "I can't stand it, Vivien
—I can't stand it . . . and all my friends saying——" "Let them talk. Tell
them it's doctor's orders. Always tell them that. It's doctor's orders that
I should go to sea, and go to sea alone. Would you like me to go mad?"

Knight to queen's rook four, the black horse taken firmly by the ears. "This is the part of the game where I always go wrong," said Hay-Lawrence.

Exchange the bishop for the knight? No. Concentrate on the center—then the queen's pawn forward. Bishop back, out of reach, to bishop two. "The part where I invariably go wrong," murmured Hay-Lawrence lifting his queen's bishop's pawn to bishop four. Pawn attack on the queen's side—not too difficult to dispose of. Hay-Lawrence was human, after all—began shrinking to commensurable proportions. Refinement without taste, intelligence without originality. From either vantage point, one could probably intimidate him; for he was intelligent enough to know his weaknesses and weak enough to be snobbish, to want to make a good impression. Silberstein, for all his vulgarity, had ruffled him and put him at a disadvantage. "Why shouldn't *I?*" thought Demarest, secretly smiling. "*The Duke of Clarence, my partner.*" Pawn to queen four. Moses Caligula Silberstein. Solomon Caligula. Did Jael: with a nail: pierce the *viscera:* of Sisera? No, his head! He is dead . . . Caligula in Italian sunset under a purple canopy, on which flashed the eagle: Veronese, crouching in the dark foreground, saw the scene. The wide eye of Veronese saw the royal canopy, saw the black hand that drew the curtain, watched the distance brightening among the hills. The cold, precise, lavish hand of Veronese took possession of these things; but it lacked madness . . . Again: *King Caligula, setting forth; after a seven days' meditation; marched his army a parasang north; and in the evening took his station: on a green hilltop peaked and gleaming: in the last slant of Alban sun. Black slaves hoisted a canopy of purple—to hue the vision of the godlike one* . . . The movement too jaunty altogether—but no matter. Let it go—let it come—let it blossom and die. Why did it blossom, though, out of the massive face, dead white brow, and cruel eyes of Silberstein? . . . *There, as he slept, he had his vision:* but what was the vision? Elysian, fountain, mountain—threadbare rhymes, but let them serve. *There as he slept he had his vision: candles burned by the sacred fountain; sadly he walked, through a twilight Elysian, and came to the wall of the laureate mountain.* (Why laureate?) *Bathe your heart in the lustral water* (a voice, this was—a voice on the air, out of a grotto, out of a tree) *until like silver it burns and shines* (pleonastic), *and lo from the sky comes heaven's tall daughter—down from a star—by a stair of vines. Seven ripe peaches, from the walls of heaven—* not six, not eight, but seven. The Pleiades. Mystical seven. The seven moles on Juno's back. The seven stages in the life of man. The dance of the seven veils. Come seven—come eleven; everything at sixes and sevens. Seven. The word was extraordinarily beautiful, had a balance analogous to the balanced rhythm of the number itself—seven digits, of which the second was the s and the sixth the n. Neves: Eno, owt, eerht, ruof, evif, xis, neves. A less emphatic series, but decidedly more interesting as sound, more varied. Queen to bishop two. Yes. He might have withdrawn the knight, however—to knight two. No—a pawn given up. The king's knight to queen two, then? That might have been better? . . .

"Oo, no—certn'y *not!*" cried the Welsh Rarebit with all-embracing archness, loudly and proudly.

"Why not?" The Major leaned forward over clasped fingers. His eyes, without the pince-nez, were beginning to look strained—but he liked his brown eyes to be seen. He had probably been told that their effect was fatal. They twinkled, small, dark and bright, shy yet challenging, attractive in spite of (perhaps partly because of) their boyish vanity.

Peggy lifted her black-and-white striped coat collar against the side of her face as if she were taking the veil. Over this she swerved green eyes at him, upward. Then lowered the long lashes and looked away. An expression of practiced fright—yet perhaps there was some faint survival of genuine feeling in it. The Major, still gazing at her, as she did not reply, gave the little crisp musical giggle (very appealing) with which he was accustomed to fill in awkward pauses; and cast a quick glance over the small room to see if he were being observed. When his eye met Demarest's, he looked sharply away, preened his mustache briskly with thumb and finger, then leaned, flagrantly confidential, toward the Welsh Rarebit and said something inaudible, gravely. Peggy ululated, lifting her throat. The crumpled handkerchief was pressed against her lamia mouth.

"She drinks blood, that trollop," said Demarest.

"Who? Oh . . . Can I look?"

"No. The Major has his eye on us . . . The Major's a fast worker, as the saying is."

As the saying is. He had added this phrase for fear Hay-Lawrence might suppose him to use slang unconsciously—a disgusting cowardice! "Yet I feel, somehow, that the Major will play safe, oh, very, very safe." Queen's knight to queen two. "With masks and buttons—a friendly bout, no injuries, and a sweet heartache, not too severe, at farewell."

"He's welcome," muttered Hay-Lawrence, not looking up; unexpectedly severe. Something unconquerable in him after all. He scowled at the chessboard. Knight to queen's bishop three—retreat, confound him—he must be beaten; beaten thoroughly, but with inexpressive modesty, not to say apathy.

"I wouldn't touch her with a tent pole," Hay-Lawrence added. Hay-Lawrence with a tent pole, walked sedately, haughtily. The Welsh Rarebit darted before him, twittering. Spare me, Clarence! . . . Damn silly . . . Pawn to queen five: Now—move your blasted knight again—move it, damn you! And hurry up.

"Damn it, why don't they open the bar?" Hay-Lawrence was angry. "Absurd to keep us waiting like this. Steward?" A commanding finger.

Malvolio, languidly smiling, took four steps; steadying himself en route against a chair back.

"Yes, sir."

"When does the bar open?"

"Seven o'clock. Not till seven on Sunday. Ten minutes yet, sir."

"What's yours, Demarest?"

"Mine? Oh—double Scotch."

"Bring up a double Scotch and a port flip, as soon as you open."

"Double Scotch and a port flip."

"Utterly absurd on a ship . . . Absurd enough on land." Scowling he lifted the knight, held it a moment in air, choosing a landing place, then

deposited it on the queen's knight's square. Home again. Black was beginning to be bottled up uncomfortably. Malvolio tapped at the bar window, which was opened an inch.

"A port flip, to come at seven."

"What's that to me? I can't do anything without the keys, can I?"

"The gentleman wants it as soon as you open . . ."

Seven again—the mystic number. S for seven and Silberstein—Silverstone. Good morning, Silverstone! . . . Now to break open that queen's
side—a Caesarean operation—Caesarean tactics. Very simple. Pawn to
queen's rook four—that was it—that would do it. Afterward the knight
could get through. That is, if Hay-Lawrence, as he expected, moved the
knight's pawn . . . Those fingers of his, so damnably refined, poised,
clustered, above the pawn—like Cynthia's. Not really like Cynthia's; but
they belonged, somehow, to the same constellation. Cynthia, pondering
over the chessboard, frowning, poising her fingers thus—stately, reserved,
leaning forward for a moment out of a world so remote from his own,
stepping down for a moment from her heavenly treasure house, with a star
on her finger, to move the king on the board and then reascend—yes,
*heaven's tall daughter . . . Seven ripe peaches from the walls of heaven,
she holds in her hands. Bright, in her hair, the Pleiades glow: the Fireflies
seven, shine above her eyes and her forehead is fair . . . Angels follow
her; gravely, slowly; with silver and vermilion and rainbow wings . . .
One, more luminous—lost in his own light—sits on a cherry tree bough,
and sings: Blest be the marriage betwixt earth and heaven!* Cynthia's
fingers moved the knight's pawn to knight five. Ah! Cynthia—not so
skillful as usual! You will be checkmated, Cynthia,—or else you'll resign
. . . That first game they had had on the *Silurian*—when he had fetched
the board from the smoking room. She had received it with delighted
surprise—with what a lighting up of her face! "Why, where did you get
this? Is it yours?" . . . And the book. He had been carrying the book
under his arm when Billington stopped him and introduced him to her.
"I've found a chess player for you!" he had cried fatuously. "Miss Battiloro,
may I introduce Mr. Demarest? Mr. Demarest has been looking everywhere
for a chess player . . ." Then Billington had disappeared . . . The astonishment, the incredulity, on finding himself thus introduced to *her,*
whom he had been avoiding for three days! He had been excited, frightfully excited. What was it, about her, that had so agitated him from the
outset, when he had seen her climb up the gangway, slowly, then turn
about on the deck—flinging the brown scarf end over her shoulder—to
wait for her companion? The obscure shock had gone through him at once,
as he watched her from the deck above—gone through him like a tidal wave
of the blood . . . She, then—he had said to himself—is the one I must
escape! I must keep away from her . . . This had not been difficult; for
the simple reason that she had, from the beginning, produced a peculiar
change in him: She had made him shy, she had stripped him of his defenses, she had taken ten years from his age and made him again a callow
and awkward youth of seventeen. The thought of talking with her simply
terrified him. And then, from the blue, the introduction! . . . And regarding the title of the book, when he had put it down on the deck beside

her, she had said—"That's *lovely*, isn't it! Don't you like it?" . . . The effect of this commonplace remark had been overwhelming. Its nature, the nature of the magic, was dual; for first it was the slender beauty of her voice, which everywhere broke through and into him; and then it was the swift revelation, no less intoxicating, that she had a "mind."—The two perceptions came upon him together, came like the opening of the sky for a bewilderingly beautiful confusion of music. He was done for; and he knew it instantly . . . Pawn to rook five . . . Hay-Lawrence castled, not pausing to think. Now, then—knight to bishop four! *This* would make him think . . . Six bells from the brass clock on the fluted wall—*tan-tan; tan-tan; tan-tan.* The bar window opened with a bang, the bartender withdrawing a white linen arm. Malvolio stepped nimbly, ingratiatingly, with the tray.

"Double Scotch and a port flip," he smirked.

"Oporto fleep," grimaced Hay-Lawrence.

"To fornication," said Demarest.

"To crime," said Hay-Lawrence.

"No, sir," nasally boomed the glass-eyed poker player. "This is on me. Waiter! One minute. Now, gentlemen, give it a name and let it rest. You, what'll it be? Bass? Guinness? Double Scotch? . . . Well, then, three Basses, two double Scotches, and a Guinness . . . God, I'm as thirsty as a camel . . . If you'd 'a' come in, my boy, with that pair of tens, you'd have been sunk so deep they'd never have found you . . . that's the time I *wasn't* bluffing."

"There's much to be said for strong drink," murmured Demarest, filling his glass. "Aha! The Major is giving a little party . . ."

"Two Martinis," Malvolio was saying, while he regarded the Welsh Rarebit with a loitering eye. He clearly felt that he had more right to her than the Major had—he knew her level. This made the Welsh Rarebit uneasy. She was uncertain whether to be friendly or rude. Consequently she was both, alternately. Queen's knight to queen two . . . Hm . . . not so bad. Better threaten the queen's rook pawn? Queen to king two . . . For goodness' sake don't hold the door open like that! Someone outside was holding it open, and the night air, cold and full of sea sound, galloped round the smoky room. Silberstein stepped over the brass, cigar in hand, and lazily, leisurely, serenely, greenly, surveyed the lighted roomful of people. Oh! Silberstein. Sorry, Silberstein, didn't know . . . Annoyed with me, are you, for keeping the door open? Run home and tell your mother. Tell her a boy bigger than you hit you. Bury your blubbering whelp's face in her apron and bawl. I know you, you damned little coward and sneak and tattletale . . . Silberstein saw them and came toward them slowly, with unchanging expression. Something flippant must be prepared for him. Something smubtle . . .

"Well, Dook, is he trimming you? I'll bet you two drinks New England will beat you."

"Don't call me *Dook!*"

"Oh, all right, all right, Clarence—keep your shirt on . . . Ha! This was a Ruy Lopez . . . And Black, as they say in the books, has a seriously compromised position."

"He's clever," murmured Demarest. "He knows we're playing chess."

"Chest," corrected Silberstein. "In the army they call it chest."

"What army?" Hay-Lawrence scowled.

"The Grand Army of the Republic."

"I'm surprised they ever heard of it," said Hay-Lawrence.

"That's all you know, is it . . ." Silberstein leaned backward against the settee back, half standing, half sitting. He expanded his chest, lazily, narrowing his eyes. "My boy, the best checker players in the world are in the American army. They know all the numbers."

"Checkers! What the devil is checkers?"

"Never heard of checkers? No?"

"The same as drafts," simpered Malvolio; "they often ask me for checkers . . . You wanted something, sir?"

"Yes, will you repeat, gentlemen?"

"Not I, thanks," said Hay-Lawrence.

"Two double Scotches, then . . . You don't mind if I watch, do you? Of course not. Everybody likes an audience."

Hay-Lawrence pondered, brown right forefinger lying on ruddy right cheek. With the other hand he revolved his *oporto fleep*. He was annoyed. Liberties were being taken with him by one who was not a gentleman. A frosty silence. A pity to have the game spoiled, nevertheless. If one could only keep separate the things one liked! Bawdy conversation with Silberstein—chess or literary conversation with Hay-Lawrence. Philately with the Major. With Smith—what with Smith? Poor old Smith. I wonder who's kissing him now? Where is our wandering Smith tonight? Pawing her dresses in his stateroom: like the fawn. M-m-m-heliotrope!

"Go away, man! How can I think with you sitting there, a mass of expert knowledge?"

"Go away? Not by a damn sight. I came here to drink."

Rook to knight square. So: Hay-Lawrence would fight for command of this file. Bishop to queen three. Attack the rook's pawn. Can he save it?

"How!" said Demarest.

"*Gesundheit*," said Silberstein. "While he's thinking how to save his little goy—Christians, that's what they call them on the East Side, where they used to play you for a nickel a game—I rise to remark that there's a clairvoyant on this ship . . . A full-fledged clairvoyant. I dug him out from under a palm tree in the second-class dining saloon, where he was deep in the *Occult Weekly* or the *Mystic Monthly*, or some such thing—horoscopes on every page and ectoplasms running all over the place. Clairvoyant *and* clairaudient,—he's a wizard! You've got to take your hat off to him. A most peculiar specimen. And full of bright little predictions. 'You,' he said to me, after one look at my hand, and a glance at my left eye—'are hoping to sell chewing gum in England.' How did he guess it?"

"Too easy," said Demarest. "Probably your bedroom steward."

"You may be right, you may be right; the usual method—find out in advance. And easy enough on a ship. He also observed, sadly, that there would be a death on this ship. Not so cheerful, that. Who's elected? A chance for a pool. The dead man wins."

"Well—does he say how he'll die?"

"Murder." Silberstein was placid, but stared a little.

"Murder? On this ship? He's off his head." Hay-Lawrence sipped his flip. A signet ring on the fourth finger

"This grows interesting," said Demarest. "Also of personal concern."

"It does . . . He felt something wrong with the ship when he got in—something wrong with the ship's aura."

"I noticed that myself. Especially in that corridor beside the kitchen!"

"Then last night he had a nightmare. He woke up thinking someone was in his room, turned on the light—no one. Looked out in the hall—not a soul. Everybody asleep. Then he remembered his dream. An old man with a hole in his head, walking toward him, stretching out his hands—in his pajamas, he was—as if asking for something.'

"An old man? That lets *me* out," said Demarest.

"And me," Hay-Lawrence sighed. Rook to king square . . . Bishop to queen two, Demarest moved smiling. All as anticipated.

"An interesting question. He says he's sure to recognize the victim—hasn't seen him yet. When he *does* see him, ought he to tell him? If so, what?"

"He's cuckoo," said Demarest. "No harm if he *did*."

"Would *you* like to be told?"

Silberstein stared with lazy penetration, his eyes cruel, at Demarest. A shiver went up Demarest's backbone and coldly, slowly, flowered phosphorescent in his skull. Singular! No, he wouldn't. Not by a damn sight. Another shiver, more fleeting, followed the first. He felt it also down the front of his arms. Death. Murdered at sea. Demarest dead, with a hole in his head. A murder at sea—why was the idea so peculiarly exciting and mysterious? *Blood—blood—blood*—throbbed the ship's engines. A pale steward creeping along the corridor. Two bells. The steward threw something white over the side. His white linen jacket—bloodstained. An inspection next day —"Tompkins, where's your jacket?" . . . "Burned, sir." "Burned? How was it burned?" "Well you see, sir, I was smoking, and . . ." The knife discovered; a cook's knife from the kitchen. Usually a belaying pin. Or one of those red axes hanging in the corridors *For Use in Case of Fire*.

"Gives me the creeps," said Demarest. "What else did Jeremiah say?"

"Jeremiah, as a matter of fact, is a fatalist—that's funny, isn't it? Says he never interferes, even when he knows, because it's sure to happen anyway, and the knowledge merely adds to the victim's misery. Nice, isn't it? . . . It occurred to me that it might be me. Why not? I'm not young. Maybe somebody has discovered that I've got a trunkful of chewing gum under my bed. Maybe it's Jeremiah himself who'll be the murderer."

"Nothing more probable," said Hay-Lawrence. "If you don't shut up and let me think, I'll murder you myself."

"Don't be snotty, Clarence. Remember the freedom of the seas."

He took the pawn. Demarest retaliated. Bishop to bishop square moved Hay-Lawrence—to free the rook.—Was Silberstein making up all this yarn of the clairvoyant? *Well? It convinces you? It sounds fairly circumstantial?* Yes—it was circumstantial.

"Who is this bird?" he said, lifting the king's rook to the knight square.

"Clark, Seward Trewlove Clark, from California. Unitarian minister, clairvoyant and clairaudient. Smokes a kind of herb tobacco which looks like confetti and smells like hell. Turns in his toes when he walks, and is only four feet high."

"You've made a careful study of him. Does he wear B.V.D.'s? Boston garters?"

"A hair shirt, probably . . . Are you castin' asparagus on my story? Are you—as they say—questioning my veracity, Mr. Demarest? Have a cigar."

"Not in the least . . . Thanks; I'll smoke it after dinner . . ."

"Oh, he's full of it. Astrology, mediums, trances, crystals, table rappings, and the cold and slimy ectoplasm. Who knows? It may be an ecoplastic murder . . . Hello! Is that our friend the Major? Getting his hand in already, is he? Fie."

"Easy money," murmured Hay-Lawrence.

Silberstein, turtle-faced, impassive, watched the Major with reptile eyes.

"Check!" said Hay-Lawrence, taking the rook.

"Check, says he." Demarest recaptured the queen's rook. How much of the game was Silberstein taking in? A good deal probably. He had seen that Hay-Lawrence was uncomfortably placed, and that his vanity was suffering. This "check" too—no doubt Silberstein saw it to be partly histrionic. Hay-Lawrence stared, flushed, at the pieces, fists on cheeks. Then, frowning, he moved the bishop to knight two. The conception of defeat. *Blood—blood —blood*—throbbed the engines, impersonating the furies. How delightful, this discovery of Caligula's about the clairvoyant! Just the sort of thing he *would* unearth. One could see him coldly and implacably questioning the little fool—taking off his very B.V.D.'s. "You believe in these things, do you, Mr. Clark?" "Yes." "Well, I don't: but I shall be interested to hear any evidence you have to offer. Speak up—don't be frightened—I'm listening!" . . . "We must go forward with caution, reverence and hope," replied the clairvoyant . . . Now, then, knight to knight six—and the crisis arises. My horse for a kingdom. Hay-Lawrence stared, immobile, an expression of stupor, or perhaps terror, in the fixed unseeing eyes: loss of psychic distance. One could almost hear the blood hammering at his temples—gush, clang, throb, thrum, pound, pulse, boom. *Blood—blood— blood*—sang the furies. Hay-Lawrence is doomed. Hay-Lawrence is being done to death. Demarest is murdering him, murdering him in little on a chessboard. There lies Hay-Lawrence, disguised as fourteen pieces (still living) and two pieces (dead) dispersed on a checkered board, fighting for his life. There Demarest, disguised as fourteen pieces, articulated like the adder, coils, hisses and straightly strikes. Death in miniature. Death in a cobweb. Was there a tear in Vivien's left eye? No—the reflection of a light in the rondure of the monocle. A tear falling in Vivien's heart, like the reflection of a moving light, tiny, down a lacquered edge—the cold secret tear of a nobleman, falling remotely and soundlessly. Miss Gadsby, of Andover. "Why do people come to me in their trouble? It is strange. They come—they come. There was the case of Henry Majoribanks, only last month. He telegraphed from Chicago—or was it St. Louis?—to say that he was coming. When he came he walked straight into the drawing room, where I was sitting, knelt before me without a word, and buried his face in

my lap. I put my hands on his head. 'What is it, Henry?' I said. He wept
—for five minutes he wept, shaken by sobs. Then, without a word, he rose
and went away—went back to Chicago, or St. Louis . . . Why? . . .
What is it in me that is so unconsciously beneficient, so comforting, so
healing? I am only an ordinary woman. Why should Henry—whom I have
never known very intimately—come all the way from Little Rock—to weep
in my lap? Tears from the depths of some divine despair! . . . Yet I am
grateful for this gift which God has given me, even though I cannot wholly
understand it . . . They come to me for solace . . ." Knight to knight
square, moved Hay-Lawrence, the murdered man.

"You're sunk," sighed Silberstein. "See you later, gentlemen. I now
struggle into a stiff shirt."

"Good riddance," said Hay-Lawrence. "He's an interesting chap but he
can be a damned nuisance."

"He has a strange effect on me," said Demarest, moving the bishop to
knight five. "What is it, in such a man, that disturbs one's balance so
extraordinarily?"

"Thick-skinnedness."

"Partly, perhaps. But something more. Is it his massive confidence, rock-
like integrity? I lose, in his presence, my own integrity entirely. I feel as if
I have no personality at all. Or rather, I feel that my own personality is only
a complement of his—and I catch myself actually trying to demonstrate
this to him—trying to be as like him as possible. Such occurrences make one
wonder whether one has any more personality than a chameleon . . . I
have, afterward, a weary and disgusted sensation—as of having wagged too
much an ingratiating tail."

Hay-Lawrence gleamed. He placed the king's bishop at king two.

"By Jove, that's perfectly true. I know people who affect me like that
. . . My father always did . . . So does my doctor."

"Well, boys, later on," sang the glass-eyed poker player. He pocketed
two packs of cards. They trooped out, whistling and singing. Cold air from
the sea door. Bishop takes knight? No—next time. Queen to knight two.

"It doesn't seem to make much difference," Hay-Lawrence resignedly
murmured. "Suppose I advance the rook's pawn." Pawn to rook three. Now
—bishop takes knight! Hay-Lawrence dies slowly. A caterpillar attacked by
ants. Then bishop takes bishop. A piece will be gained? Knight back to
bishop four—the bishop twice attacked. Ten to one he advances the rook
to king two—he does. Queen to knight six: the *coup de grâce* . . .

"Oh—well! I'll hide the bishop in the rook's corner . . . No—*that's* no
good . . . Suppose I exchange queens?"

"Queen takes queen and rook takes queen," said Demarest, suiting the
action to the word.

"Absolutely nothing I can do—I surrender."

"I'm afraid you've lost a piece—whatever you do . . ."

"Yes. Thanks very much. We'll have another some time . . . Has the
bugle blown?"

"I think so."

Why "think so"? He knew it had. They descended the red stairs to the
dining saloon. The orchestra was beginning the *Blue Danube*: and the

music rose to meet them, mixed with a confused sound of voices and dishes.
The palm trees trembled, swayed slowly trembling, in the bright light from
pearly ceiling lights. Pink curtains were drawn over all the portholes save
one, which yawned black, night-engulfing. A hundred faces feeding as one.
Stewards running soft-footed on the stinking carpets, dishes clattering,
dishes chirruping, trays clanging—all interwoven, pouring, with the *Blue
Danube*. The pale pianist, with frayed and spotted sleeves, smiled wearily at
the score, *tum-tum:* the girl-faced flute player hooked his lip, uncous lip,
over the flute, and eyed Demarest mournfully, *tootle-too. Blaue Donau.*
Should he tell Hay-Lawrence Wagner's remark? . . . "My God, what a
melody! . . . But—*Jesus Christ!* what orchestration . . ." No, too noisy,
not the right moment for it. Save it up. *Da, die, dee, dum:—die—dum:*
die dee . . . Anita. He always, when a kid, at dances, danced the *Blue
Danube* with Anita. Her odd, delicious laugh, which ended in an inbreathing bubble, like the bubbling of a starling! Darling starling. Darling,
hoydenish, long-legged Anita. *Down from a star by a stairway of vines.* That
Sunday in the rain by the pond. "But *William*, you don't seem to *think*
anything about *marriage!* Do you?" Then the streetcar in the rain, the
rain-soaked curtain blowing against their backs; flap, flap. Rejected. Was
he heartbroken? Surprised at being able to eat a good dinner at Memorial
Hall. "Where are my waffles, Sam Childers?" "On de fire, suh—waffles on
de fire."

"Good evening, Mr. Barnes—Good evening, Miss Dacey—Good evening, Mrs. Faubion—Good evening, father."

"All right for *you*, Mr. Demarest!" Mrs. Faubion, mournful and reproachful, mock angry.

"For me? What have *I* done?"

He dived, laughing into the somber eyes, which darkened maliciously
to receive him . . . Swimming. I swim, you swim, he or she swims. We
swim, you swim—the rich sardonic mouth tearing bread.

"Oh, I know what you've done. And *you* know *too*."

"Cross my heart and hope I die . . . Not guilty. I appeal."

She cut her meat savagely. Roast beef *au jus*, underdone, in watery
gules. Green and celluloid cabbage. Barnes was drinking black stout. Jingle,
went Daisy's bangle.

"The little girl's in a bad temper, tonight," said Smith, lowering his
voice. "I wouldn't let her have the dress she wanted . . ." Then louder—
"Who's your dressmaker, Madam?"

"*You* be *careful!*"

"Careful! Reckless is my middle name."

"Water, Miss Dacey?"

"Oo thank you, Mr. Barnes." Titter, titter.

"Walking right by me like that!"

"Never!"

"You did! On the deck this afternoon. And I was alone."

"You don't ask me to believe *that*, do you? Alone!"

"Where was Australia?" said Smith. "How come?"

"I'm not talking to *you*, Mr. Smith. I'm talking to your *son*."

"Oh! . . . God."

"Sixpenny fine, Mr. Smith. Swearing at meals." Mr. Barnes serenely peeped over the tilted stout.

Da dee die *dum*—die *dum:* die *dee.*—Anita looked over the silver-spangled white fan, long-leggedly, gracefully gliding, the green irises of her eyes irregularly flecked, gold-flecked, the pupils dark and—witty. "I thought you were *afraid* of dances! . . . I believe it's all a pretense!" . . . That lesson in the dining room. "You don't hold me *tightly* enough—that's the trouble!" And the peal of laughter, bubbling, inbreathing. Her *Empire* gown—high-waisted, white, like the Empress what's-her-name, standing at the top of the stairs—stairs of alabaster. Sorosis; Sesostris. "But she's *nervous*—very highly strung," Anita's mother had said. "Ever since her operation" . . . Well, what of it? Why did she eye him (knitting) so meaningfully? Ah—! she had meant to warn him off. Die *dum*—die *dee* . . . *Da* dee die *dum*—Faubion was looking at him rather hard—but as if she were not quite focusing her attention—no, she was beginning to smile, but obviously the sort of smile which is an answer to a smile—it must be for someone behind him. He turned his head—it was Australia, the Romantic Young Man, who was now in the act of passing the water bottle. A well-dressed, vapid young man with a high collar and a high color; he was a little too self-conscious, elaborately polite, a shade too much of the traveling salesman's genuflectory manner. "Swipey—I don't like this cat—he's too swipey." O God that word—how fond of it Aunt Maud had been, and how terribly her choice of it lighted that part of her vulgarity which he had always hated. There must be the same stratum buried somewhere in himself, of course—or his disgust would not have been so intemperate. Where had he got it? No—he was damned if he had it! It must have been a natural dislike—that element in Aunt Maud's sensibility (or lack of it) had done him a violence from the beginning. What could so have poisoned her? Her mind, her character, her outlook blackly poisoned:—a savage coprophily, a necessity for dwelling on the foulness of things. Well—he did this himself! but not surely in the same unclean way. Aunt Maud's perceptions were somehow septic. A septic sceptic. Himself, an aseptic sceptic. Tut tut . . . This was probably completely wrong. More likely it was simply Aunt Maud's lack of sensibility—a failure to perceive things clearly, to make fine distinctions? A bitter and unbridled woman.

"Penny for your thoughts," said Faubion.

"The fleshpots of Egypt," said Demarest swiftly. Why? Faubion = fleshpot.

"What! . . ."

Smith shook sadly his close-cropped gray head.

"Eating *this* dinner, he thinks of fleshpots! . . . No. Give me a Creole chicken dinner. Okra soup."

"Would to God we had died by the hand of the Lord in the land of Egypt, where we sat by the fleshpots . . . For we, alas, the Fleshpots love . . . Man cannot live by bread alone."

"Shame!" cried Fleshpot. A flaming shame.

"It's all the Bible I know."

"Did you go to church this morning?" A finger uplifted, schoolteacherly.

"Certainly not. I played bridge."

"Bridge! Oo aren't we swell," Daisy derisively caroled.

"He's got too much brains," said Smith. "He plays chess, too . . . But I beat him at drafts just the same, didn't I?"

"You did."

"Got to hand it to the old man! . . . Chess is an old lady's game. I don't like chess. Let the old ladies play it. But I'll beat you at checkers any time. Yes, sir, I'm all right at checkers."

"And what do *you* play, Mr. Barnes?" Daisy Dacey wriggled, jingled, slanted her long white face, and wide blue eyes, leaning against the table-cloth with phthisic breast. Mr. Barnes, tolerant, slow-smiling, with slow-burning eyes of amusement, looked down at the proffered head. Herod and Salome.

"Golf," he said.

Daisy was disconcerted. Golf! What the devil was golf? She smiled a weak smile, too elastic, and looked sadly forgetful—Ophelia straying by the stream. Let me Ophelia pulse! There's rosemary—that's for remembrance. Wan, and oh so wistful. Weak, and oh so helpless. But no pansies —ah no: for never a thought had she. Straying with little white feet among the lilies. Oh, pity me, a shopworn Ophelia! Come and find me where I wander at twilight, sadly singing, or perchance weeping, among the cowslips! Put your strong arm around me, and hold me, hold me! Don't let me remember—O God, don't let me remember! . . . When I was thirteen. It was dreadful! . . . and I trusted him . . . Have you read the Rosary? . . . Where the cowslips, there slip I.

". . . a clairvoyant," Faubion was soberly saying.

"You don't say," said Smith. "Where?"

"Under the middle window, at the end of the table." Window equals porthole.

A little mournful sallow face, dark-eyed and shy. A hurt and frightened little victim, eating stiffly.

"Yes," said Demarest. "Silberstein was telling me about him."

"What did he say? Is he a real one?"

"Don't ask me! He told Silberstein that he's going to England to sell chewing gum—which was correct. He's also a clairaudient."

"Clairaudient! What's that?" Her dark eyes are wide and serious. Melodiously fluting.

"He hears things—at a distance. Voices. Probably hears what we're saying about him."

"Don't be silly! . . . I think they're all fakes." She looked witheringly toward the meek little clairvoyant.

"You can't fool *her*," said Smith. "She's from Missouri."

"He predicts," said Demarest, "a murder, on this ship."

Daisy Dacey gave a little screech, pressing her hands together. A crumb of gorgonzola shot from her mouth into Mr. Barnes's tumbler. She slapped a hand against her mouth, too late.

"Oh!" she cried, blushing. "Mr. Barnes! I'm so sorry!"

"Quite natural, I'm sure," said Mr. Barnes. "Worse things might have happened, under the circumstances! A little upsetting to hear a murder predicted, what? . . ." He lowered his left lid at Demarest. Poor Pol.

"An old man came to him in a dream—an old man, pardon me—wearing pajamas; he had a hole in his head. He stretched out his hands to the clairvoyant, as if beseeching . . . The clairvoyant jumped out of his bunk—and probably bumped his head—thinking there was someone in the room. He turned on the light, and of course there was no one. But he says he'll recognize the man when he sees him . . . Father!"

"*Don't* call me father! . . . What."

". . . . Nothing . . . A goose walked over my grave. I think it must be *me* . . ."

Why conceal it? He had suddenly thought—and thought vividly, with absurd apprehension—that it was *Smith!* Ridiculous, both to entertain the thought and to suppress it . . . Nevertheless, he had seen Smith, with shattered forehead, blundering into the dark stateroom. Plenty other old men on the boat. Poor old Smith. What if it *were* true? There was nothing in such predictions, of course—if it proved true, it was simply a coincidence.

"I dream things myself," he said. "I once dreamed three times in succession that a certain ship—the *Polynesian*—had sunk. I was shortly going to sail on her. The dream was confused, and it seemed to me in each case that she sank somehow in the dock—collided with it, or something . . A few days after the third dream I was walking in London, and saw a headline (one of those posters the newsboys wear, like aprons) saying: *Atlantic Liner Sunk. I knew*, absolutely *knew*, it was my ship; and it was."

"You're making it up," said Faubion.

"You *never* take my word, Mrs. Faubion! Why?"

She relented, smiling; but smiled coolly.

"When you dream about *me*, I'll believe you," she said, rising.

"I'll have something for you at breakfast!"

She turned her dark head away. The cold shoulder. Humming, she walked slowly, with abstracted thought, lifting her cape to her round neck. A coarse lace blouse, slightly cheap, well filled, through which one saw bits of blue ribbon. Ah Faubion! Ah, Fleshpot! How attractive, how vulgar, how downright, and yet how mysterious you are! "O *Faubion*," sang the evening stars . . . "*deep, deep Faubion!*"

"Coming for a walk?" said Smith. "Beautiful air tonight—beautiful."

"I'll join you in fifteen minutes. In the smoking room?"

"All right. I'll wait for you" . . . Smith departed sedately, brown eyes among the palm trees.

. . . A curious remark, that of Faubion's—"When you dream about *me*——" Extraordinary, her instinctive directness; this observation of hers, and his reply (of which she had dictated the key) left their relationship changed and deepened. To sleep, perchance to dream—one dreamed only of those for whom one had profound feelings? "When I walk, I *walk* with Willy——" He had never dreamed of Anita—not once. But on several occasions he had dreamed, erotically, of women for whom he had never consciously felt any desire; and had found them, when next encountered, magically changed; they belonged thereafter to the race of salamanders, opalescent and fiery. But Faubion had now, in a sense, saved him the trouble of dreaming—the suggestion of the dream was sufficient. It was a

tremendous step toward intimacy—intimacy of that sort . . . But a step
(alas!) which perhaps meant, for her, little or nothing. She would say the
same thing to everybody—to any male who was reasonably attractive? Was
she, perhaps (as the Welsh Rarebit had suggested), under the "protection"
of Barnes, and being handed about from one member of the crew to another? Such things, of course, were common enough. A special technique
was always employed in such cases. The girl avoided the officers in the daytime—consorted only with the passengers; but after the lights were out—
the dark ship sleeping, sleep walking on the dark sea—then it was her footstep which one heard, furtive and soft and quick, passing one's door, or
treading nocturnally over one's head. Was Faubion leading this kind of
double life? Time enough to find out. Meanwhile—

Tin-tin: tin-tin: tin-tin: tin-tin: eight o'clock. The flute player folded
his tripod, the pianist closed the yellow-toothed piano. The *Blue Danube*,
miles behind, sank into the Atlantic, was caught by mewing gulls.

"Good night, Mr. Demarest . . . Are you comfortable in your stateroom?"

"Quite, thanks."

"That's good . . . Good night."

"Good night . . ."

"G'night, sir," said the table steward, flicking crumbs.

. . . Smith's alley: but Smith was not there, and neither of the girls
. . . The long red carpet abruptly declined before him. The wind had
freshened. The sea was getting rougher. 142-156. Home. A light in the room
beyond his own—the Irish girl moved about, there, with door half opened.
Snap, went a suitcase lock. A tumbler clinked. The bed curtains were
harshly slid along, brass rings on brass rod—Zring . . . An electric bell
buzzed remotely, twice: a voice, remote, called "Mrs. Atherton! . . . *Mrs.
Atherton!* . . . One sixty-eight . . ." "Coming!" cried Mrs. Atherton . . .
Mrs. Atherton could be heard pelting down the corridor, a whirlwind, and
laughing, then a male voice, laughing, and Mrs. Atherton gave a squeal,
and "Don't!" she cried. "Get out of my way!" she cried, then both laughs
sliding down the scale, diminuendo . . . A madhouse. I am in a madhouse, thought Demarest . . . Figures given for the year 1920 show a
considerable increase in the number of cases admitted to institutions in
the United Kingdom. Of these 56 per cent were female, 44 per cent male
. . . It is noted with interest that few insane people die of cancer . . .
General paralysis of the insane . . . Certified as insane . . . All is insanity
. . . Who so among you that is without insanity, let him think the first
think . . . Shall we read, tonight? A nuisance carrying a book . . . The
amusements provided for the insane show a gratifying variety . . . Croquet, phonographs, picture puzzles in great numbers . . . We are happy
to report that the Society for the Encouragement of Vocal Therapy has
co-operated with us now for six months with . . . Music and hot baths
. . . Therapeutic value of jazz . . . Even staid old country preachers are
engaging tango teachers . . . You can't get away from it—can't get away
from it—you can't get away from it at all . . . If one could only establish
a direct mode of communion with another being, instead of undergoing
this pitiful struggle of conversation? Extraordinary, the way conversation,

even the most intimate (not at present *apropos*) concealed or *refracted* the two personalities engaged. Impossible to present, all at once, in a phrase, a sentence, a careful paragraph—even in a book, copious and disheveled—all that one meant or all that one was. To speak is to simplify, to simplify is to change, to change is to falsify. And not only this—there were also the special demons who inhabit language; and again, the demons who make a perpetual comedy, or tragedy, of all human intercourse, the comedies and tragedies of the misunderstood. These were the same thing— or aspects of the same thing? The experience of an individual is coextensive with the world and therefore infinite?—he is, in epitome, the history of the world, a history still being lived. But this "language"—by which one such epitome seeks to make himself understood or felt by another (felt, rather than understood!)—this meager affair of signs and sounds, this tiny boxful of shabby, worn trinkets, few in number, dim in color and crude of shape —how much, of one's infinitude, could one express by an earnest stringing together of these? Little or nothing. And these demons of language—they invited one, how tiresomely often, to disregard the reference of the trinkets, and to play a *game* with them, to toss and catch them, to match their colors and shapes, to demonstrate one's *skill*: turning human intercourse into a game of anagrams. Ah, the disgusting way in which one is always trying to "make an impression!" and the even stranger way in which casual groups of people actually co-operate to make a *collective* impression, a mutual deception of smartness, gaiety, good humor, good breeding, vulgarity, or wit! Their dinner table, for example—all of them unnatural. Bridge with Silberstein and the others—unnatural. Chess with Hay-Lawrence—un- natural . . . Smith? Ah—this seemed closer to the real . . . Faubion? Relations with her, too, would be real or nothing. And what a profoundly interesting experience! A marriage with earth . . . With reversed mean- ings:—*Blest be the marriage betwixt earth and heaven! Now, in the round blue noon of space* (round blue noon was delicious) *the mortal son, and the daughter immortal* (immoral!) *make of the world their resting place* . . . Not so bad: the colors a little aniline, perhaps, as in a flower piece by Hiroshige Third . . . Curious that Silberstein—Caligula (who seemed so almost identically one person!) should have started this train of feeling and precipitated a poem involving (so transparently!) Cynthia and himself. But, of course, the Caligula strain in himself was familiar enough—from the age of ten (that vacant lot, with ruined cellar walls, grass-grown, secret) all through the horrible furtive years of adolescence. Little Caligula ran on the sidewalk, pulling after him a toy fire engine, from which poured the thick smoke of burning excelsior. Little Caligula invited Gladys Dyson to come to the vacant lot. Little Caligula was kissed unexpectedly in the tailor's shop by the Italian tailor's black-eyed daughter. Walking through a slum alley, little Caligula heard voices, peeped in through the wet green shutters, saw a Negro and Negress embracing, heard the Negress moan. He had wanted to remain and watch, but hadn't dared. The vocabulary of little Caligula—the profane vocabulary—increased rapidly. The cook made startling contributions to it, screeching with laughter as she did so. Then there was that Swedish sailor, caught in the same doorway during a shower, who on seeing the two dogs had cried *"Jesus!"* Why Jesus? What connection? Little Caligula looked from dogs to Axel, from Axel to dogs, and sought a clue. Jesus, then, was not merely a god who had suffered crucifixion, but could be mentioned, laughingly, on such occasions as this? . . . There were also the singular totems carved out of wood by the "gang" to which he had once or twice been admitted. And there, too, strange words had been pronounced, which had rendered him more than ever a little Caligula—a Caligula with strange festered recesses in his mind, with wounds in his body. Love (he had been taught) was sensuality, sensuality was evil, evil was prohibited but delicious: the catechism of the vacant lot. But how, then, had beauty come in? How had it so managed to complicate itself with evil and sensuality and the danks and darks of sex?—It had come in with the trumpet vine. It had come in with the seven-year locust and the chinaberry tree. It had come in with the stenciled shadows, on a tropic moonlight night—shadows, on the walls and floors, which suddenly galloped. It had come in with the song of the Negress who walked in the sun with the basket swaying on her head and sang "Ay-y-y-y prawns—ay-y-y-y-y prawns . . ." No—the tissue was too complex;—it was impossible to say where beauty had come from, or even to predicate that there had ever been a beginning; to be born, to become conscious, was to be, and at the same time to face, pain and beauty . . . "All this, Faubion, is what I am trying to say to you when I make a vulgar joke and laugh at you! . . . It is Caligula, who nevertheless has the rainbow wings of a seraph; Caligula, corrupt and yet devout, who beseeches you to be kind to him. And yet it is not entirely Caligula—it is something less than Caligula, and also something more; it is a life small and innocent, inconceivably naïve and at every instant new, a life infantine and guileless; but unhappily this ethereal waif harbors in his heaven-born mind a little black seed, the gift of Tellus. This little black seed is the yearning to be Caligula. I MUST be Caligula. And is it not you who provide me with the opportunity to achieve my destiny—you and your sisters? It is in your presence that the black seed begins to grow. Eunice warmed it, smiling upon it. Helen Shafter wept upon it, watering its terrible roots. Mary gave her body to be devoured by the terrible roots. Anita, fleeing, tempted it to grow like a vine . . . And here are you, Faubion—vigorous synthesis of all these; the familiar theme repeated, but repeated more emphatically than ever . . ." O God, if he could only escape! But did he really desire to? . . . The Irish girl in the next room again moved the bed curtains, brass rings on brass rod—ZRING. The light, which had shone through the reticulated grill at the top of the wall, above the upper berth, suddenly went out. She was going forth—he could meet her. It was time to meet Smith. And the five minutes of solitude, of morose reflection, had been (as he had foreseen) just what was needed to restore him to himself. His periodic need of escape. To re-establish his boundaries —to re-establish his awareness of his own periphery. Now he could go forth calmly—to face the Irish girl calmly, to face Smith calmly, to face the sea with joy.

To have collided with the Irish girl would have been simple and agreeable; but in the very act of willing it he also inhibited the length of his stride over the brass sill.

"Oh!" she said, smiling.

"I'm so sorry!" said Demarest, drawing back. He regarded her with
friendly inquisition.

Lowering her soft flushed face, she passed him, close against the white
wooden paneling, the smile gently dying. Innocent gray eyes: not without
humor and boldness. My wild Oirish Rose. When I look into your eyes—
Then I think of Irish skies . . . Anita's favorite song—he used to sing it
in the shower bath. Sure as you're born, top of the morn . . . ! "Come—
come—come—" said her slippers on the red carpet, as she turned away to
the right. "No—too—shy,—" his own feet whispered, stammering and in-
articulate, as he turned away to the left.

The cloud of smoke in the smoking room was dense and turbulent. The
poker game had been resumed, bottles and glasses assisting. The glass-eyed
gambler sang loudly: "*Some* girls live in the country:—and *some* girls live
in town:—but MY girl can't keep her reputation up, 'cause she *can't* keep
her petticoat down:—By! God! she! is!—a lulu:—yes, b'God, a lulu:—a
lulu is that little girrrrrrl of mine . . ." All the players broke loudly into
the chorus, "By! God! she! IS—a lulu," to the grave delight of Malvolio.

"There you are," said Smith. "Come on. I've got an idea."

"What?"

"Wait, I'll tell you outside." The brown eyes were solemnly mischievous. "Somebody might hear us."

The night had become cloudly, and a cold wind came in damp gusts
from the northwest. A drop or two of rain—or was it spray? No—it was
rain. The deck was nearly deserted. Patches of white light fell over the
polished planks and tarred seams. A feeling of storm. At the forward end
of the covered deck, beyond the first-class barrier, two sailors were moving
to and fro under a ceiling light, stretching a canvas screen.

"Well," said Demarest, "what's this brainwave?"

"Why shouldn't we sneak up to the first-class deck—the upper one—
and have a good walk? Eh? I don't know about *you*, but I'd like some exercise . . . Down here you can't get started before you have to turn around."

"No sooner said than done."

"The question is—how do we go? Straight up the companionway?
with the light shining on it? Sort of public . . . The only other way is to
go through the barrier, and then up a companion way further forward . . .
It has the advantage of being darker."

"With so few people aboard, I don't believe they'll give a damn anyway. Let's go straight up . . . They can't do any more than kick us out.
We'll do a dignified retreat, with profuse apologies . . . When I was on
the *Empress of Ireland*, in the steerage, I used to go up and drink beef tea
with the first-class passengers every morning: and tea every afternoon."

"It's easy if the ship's crowded."

"Come on! there's nobody looking."

Smith climbed the iron stairs warily and softly, and swung the iron
gate at the top. It squeaked and clanked.

"Nobody in sight," he said, *sotto voce:* "not a soul . . . This is something like! A crime not to allow us up here—yes, sir, it's a crime. Absolutely
wasted."

The long white deck, exquisitely sloping and curved, stretched away

through alternating light and shadow. High as a cliff. Yes! This was something like. One felt at once like a first-class passenger, and subtly changed
one's bearing. If they met Purington—well, so much the better. They would
be under his protection. Purington meeting Smith—ha, ha! One could
see his discomfort—one look at Smith's tweed hat (absurdly big for him)
would be enough, and all of Purington's heavy snobbishness would begin
creakily operating. It would be rather a joke. They turned the forward
corner, walking through a crescendo of wind. Sparks blew from Smith's
cigar. *Ooo—wash—oo—wallop*, went the waves against the unseen bow;
the ship lifted slightly, he careened against Smith's arm,—and then drew
back in the deep shadow at the corner to let three women pass. Confound.
It wouldn't be so comfortable, this being inspected twice on each circuit
of the deck.

"Yes, sir—this is something like. This is what you come to sea for . . .
Now, if we only had those little girls—but no. No. They'd give the show
away. Nothing first-class about them! Ha, ha!"

"I suppose you'd let me walk with Faubion?"

"Not much, I wouldn't! She's the little girl for me . . . I dropped a
hint to her tonight. Sort of risky, I guess, but I got the feeling that I
couldn't help it . . . Hm."

"What . . . For the love of mud don't ruin yourself, Father!"

Smith meditated, his cigar in his mouth, his cheeks pursed a little, right
forefinger curved round cigar. He stared along the long deck.

"Oh, it wasn't very much—nothing at all, . . . It was when she came
to get a dress before dinner—I said, 'You know that song, don't you?' 'No,
what song?' says she. 'What's the use of all these things without the girl
inside?' I said. 'You naughty old thing!' she said—that's what she said.
'You naughty old thing!' . . . She looked sort of mad, but then she always does, half the time, anyway, so you can't tell . . . What do you
think?"

"That's harmless enough—but I'd go slow if I were you."

"Damn it, life's too short—*my* life is! Time I had a little fun."

"Do we walk right round at the back, where the second-class can see us?"

"Sure, they won't recognize us—too dark."

Turning the corner, they again met the three women. Tall women, easily
striding, keeping step. Demarest averted his eyes again, shy and conscious.
"No," one of them was saying—"I don't think——" A cultured voice, and
English. The rest of her sentence was blown overboard. Getting back to
England and Cynthia. Would he ever see Cynthia again? Would he dare to
go and see her? She had never answered his two letters—not a word, not a
sign. She had never acknowledged the book. She had thus rebuked him, of
course—he had not asked permission to write; and to do so, and particularly
to send the book, had been after so slight (!) an acquaintance a callow
presumption. A warm wave of shame and misery came over him. That had
been exactly characteristic of the state of mind she had induced in him—
clumsy adolescence, shyness, awkwardness, misplaced audacities, occasional
funks (as when he had allowed her to pay his fare on the bus!) and a
mixture of abruptness and preciousness in talk . . . As for the two letters
—again that wave of shame and misery came hotly over him. The letters

had been in his very worst vein—the sort of disingenuous, hinting thing, self-conscious and literary, which he always achieved (how revolting) when the occasion was emotionally important. Was it impossible to fall in love without loss of balance? No loss of balance with Eunice or with Mary —but both were of humble birth. Helen Shafter? Well, perhaps, a trace. Yes. But no more than that. That first night in the house by the bay. Helen's aunt's house, when Helen's aunt had been called away, and they had been left alone—had there been, then, a loss of balance such as he had experienced with Cynthia?

"You never can tell, in these cases," he said. "Never . . . Once I was spending the weekend with a respectable middle-aged lady and her niece. I'd known them all my life. There was no thought of anything between me and the niece—well, nothing to speak of: a mild intermittent interest, perhaps a little more physical than intellectual. The aunt got a telegram and went away for two nights, leaving us alone. Well, it was extraordinary the way a kind of tension grew between us! We couldn't talk naturally, we began to look at each other, our voices seemed to change in key—we finally said good night to each other in a panic. That was the first night. The second night was worse. We were seized with a terror lest the conversation should come to an end—we talked frantically, incessantly, and as impersonally as we could. Absolutely nothing personal was said: and yet the personal tension was every second becoming more unbearable. I was aware, of course, that she agitated me—but I couldn't make out whether *she* was agitated; and I was determined to avoid a false step, which for various reasons would have been fatal. What really happened was that we were both in that state, but neither wanted to take the responsibility of declaring it: the ghost of respectability, perhaps, but also the fear of rebuff and of making fools of ourselves. So we just sat and talked, and it got later and later, and first one lamp went out, and then the other, and then the fire began to die and the room to get cold. Should I put coal on the fire? It would seem to suggest too coarsely that I took it for granted we were going to continue sitting there in the dark, talking inanely, at one-thirty in the morning. So I didn't. We sat, finally, for ten minutes in silence, at the end of which she suddenly said, 'Oh! I feel as if the top of my head would blow off!' . . . That seemed, in a way, clear enough! and yet, could I be sure? I thought for a minute, and then I said, 'Why?' to which, after a long and desperate pause, she replied, 'You ought to know, I think.' So it was she, really, who took the final step . . . As soon as she had said that, we rose from our chairs as if hypnotized, and moved together . . . Unfortunately in the dark, I got one foot into the coal scuttle, and our first embrace looked more like a wrestling match—we staggered and fell."

"You fell," said Smith.

"We fell."

"I wish things like that would happen to me. Yes, siree. But they don't. And never did."

"It's luck simply. A friend of mine in a train, once——"

They again faced the three tall women, drawing modestly aside to let them pass. They had the light at their backs, and their faces were in darkness. The outermost girl was wearing a knitted jersey—remarkably like—

he turned to look, his heart beating in his throat.—But the gloom had swallowed them up. Impossible! Impossible! Impossible!

"—was practically proposed to by a young woman who sat beside him . . . Total stranger . . . She gave him, as the saying is, the glad knee. He was getting off at Philadelphia—she was going to—I forget where—Atlanta. She implored him to come along with her—absolutely implored him. Offered to pay his fare and all his expenses for a week's trip . . ."

He felt out of breath—excitement. Dyspnea. His voice had shaken absurdly (and a little high) on the second "absolutely." He cleared his throat. He must time the approach, so as to meet them under a light.

"Good God," said Smith. "And did he?"

"No. He was on his way to visit his fiancée . . . Poor devil!"

"Oh, don't spoil the story! My God . . . He just let her go like that? What sort of woman was she?"

"Beautiful, he said—about twenty-six. A buyer for one of the big stores —Gimbels or Wanamaker's."

Smith groaned. He took half a dozen quick puffs at his short cigar, holding it between thumb and finger, then flung it over the railing. The red spark described a swift parabola in the dark, and Demarest imagined —in the midst of all that thresh and welter—its infinitesimal hiss. Suppose they shouldn't come round again? . . .

"To think," said Smith, "of losing a chance like that! . . . Oh, *boy!*"

"She gave him her name and address—and he lost it."

"I don't believe it."

"Yes—and all he remembered about her name was that it was Mabel Tupper something . . ."

"He ought to be shot at sunrise," said Smith. "Yes, sir, he ought to be shot down like a dog. And she made love to him, did she?"

Smith turned an eager round eye under the tweed rim. An eye like a well.

"*Did* she! He said he was embarrassed to death—and afraid somebody he knew might see him. She simply wrapped herself round him—stem to stern. He put his overcoat across his lap so that the confusion of legs wouldn't be too obvious."

There they came, around the corner. He paused, feeling his pockets.

"Damn," he said. "I forgot my pipe . . . No matter." He continued feeling his pockets.

The jersey—yes. Tall, too. Being on the outside, her face was in shadow. No. Too slender, too girlish. Something queer!

"Don't tell me any more stories like that," said Smith. "Makes me too sad."

She came swiftly, gracefully—touched a palm on the rail, turning her face down toward the black water. Light fell on her lifting face—it was she. She looked, for some reason, slighter and younger—his recollection of her had not been exact . . . She had not seen him yet—they came nearer. Her mother—the one in the middle. She looked at him, but unrecognizing— no—yes . . . Suddenly her eyes took fire and she smiled, stopping. He moved toward her, slowly, putting out his hand, his awkward hand. The two other women, turning their heads, walked on. Smith drifted gloomily toward the companionway.

"How simply extraordinary!" said Demarest. He was aware that the speech was resonant with too much feeling, too many references.

"Isn't it? . . . I've been in America again!" The exquisite light voice was breaking through him: oddly childish, subtly simple.

They drifted slowly, and leaned against the railing, under a light; as they had leaned the year before; as it seemed natural for them to lean.

"In New York?" said Demarest.

"Yes . . . And Philadelphia!"

"For long?"

"Three months . . . I'm glad to go back."

She had been in New York and Philadelphia—without letting him know! Good God. At any time during the last three months he might have—— She hadn't let him know.

"I'm going to be married!" she then gaily added. She laughed delightedly, girlishly, leaning backward on the rail with lifted elbows—the striped and diamonded jersey of richly mingled Hindu colors.

"*Really!*" he cried. "How *delightful!* . . . May I ask——"

"And have *you* made up your mind," she interrupted, "where to live?"

"It's been made up *for* me, for the moment . . . I'm having—possibly —a show in London. So I shall stay a year or two—perhaps settle." He frowned, confused. Things were confused, distressing, ecstatic.

"Oh! . . . My mother always says it's a mistake for Americans to expatriate themselves."

"Yes . . . I remember she said so to *me*, last year . . . I'm not so sure! . . . It's an awful problem! Simply awful. If, when one's young enough, one develops a taste for Europe—I'm afraid it's incurable."

"I think I'd stay in New York if I were you—you have there such a priceless sense of freedom——"

She turned, somber, and looked down at the black and white of water. She had used that phrase in a letter.

"I hate it," Demarest said with surprising bitterness.

"Do you?"

Cynthia smiled at him amusedly. He must, somehow, mention that he was not in the first cabin—that he was a sneaking interloper; just what he had always been *afraid* of seeming! It was a perfect nemesis; caught redhanded. How surprisingly tall she was: how transparently young and beautiful. He remembered Wetherall's remark, "too innocent." Also Wetherall's comment on the ugly way her skirt hung, creased, at the back: that brown tweed skirt, with a small rip in the hem at one side. Blue woolen stockings. The rip stretching against her knee as she sat opposite him—sitting on the deck itself—playing chess, one hand supporting her (the long arched fingers crossing a tarred seam), the other touching her cheek. Sea gulls. And now, everything so complicated and difficult—her mother with her (who had disliked him)—and someone else.

"Yes, I really like London much better."

"It is lovely, isn't it! I can hardly *wait* for London in the winter!"

As usual, when they talked, he had the sense of their partaking of a secret communion, exquisite and profound: a communion in which their idle talk, fragmentary and superficial, and even their physical identities, had the remoteness and smallness of the trivial and accidental. It seemed merely to be necessary that they should be together: that they should stand together for a moment, saying nothing, looking at the same falling wave or the same white sea gull; or talk a little, lightly; or loiter a little, with lazy bodies. This had been true from the beginning—it was still true. And yet— was it? There was this other man. The communion could hardly, therefore, be as perfect as he supposed. And indeed, had it *ever* been? Was it conceivable that already, when he had met her a year ago, she had been in love? Was it possible that her luminousness, her lightness of heart and body, her delightful, delighted swiftness in meeting him, had been simply the euphoria consequent upon that:—and might it not have been precisely her love (for this other man) that he had fallen in love with? . . . On the other hand, there had been something—well, just lightly destructive, the loosing of a gay arrow, explanatory but not apologetic, in the quick laughing announcement *"I'm going to be married!"* This seemed to refer to a marked consciousness of former communion: to refer to it and to end it. As if she said, "I liked you—but how much better I like *him!*"

"It is astounding that we should meet again like this!"

It was a mistake—but Cynthia met it lightly.

"Isn't it? It makes one feel——" She hesitated, and gave a little laugh in which there was no tension, but rather an assumption of security and distance, the perfection and inviolability of her personal view, which she need not, if she did not wish, bother to communicate to him.

"How small the world is?" laughed Demarest.

"Oh, that! if you like . . . I was thinking rather, that it made one feel like Buddhists, or some such thing—meeting, reincarnated, every thousand years or so; and always in the same way; and always inconsequentially; and always with tremendous surprise."

She smiled at him delightfully, again rocking back with Hindu-bright elbows, on the railing, which burned vivid and real against the darkness of the sea. The familiar shape of her arms, the familiar gesture and attitude, the colors, the youthful frankness, all these, together, suddenly released in him a torrent of remembered feelings.

"Pilgrims," he said—falling in with her image, in which she had so candidly delighted—"who meet once in every cycle for the exchange of a remark on the weather? If they *have* anything so mundane as weather in their purgatories and paradises!"

"*And* infernos."

"Yes!"

The two women approached, slowing their steps a little.

"Mother—you remember Mr. Demarest?"

"How do you do."

"How do you do."

To the pale girl, who stood under the light, waiting cynically, he was not introduced. Flight, prearranged, was in the air.

"I'll let you rejoin your friend," said Cynthia, moving off slowly. Smith! His friend Smith!

She smiled: Demarest smiled and nodded: and the three women walked swiftly away. Good God—Good God—said the blood beating in his brain. He moved blindly toward the companionway. He must rejoin his friend— by all means. Yes. And he must take his friend down to the other deck— he suddenly felt that he didn't want to face them again, particularly with old Smith by his side; Smith and his comic-opera tweed hat. Nothing first class about Smith! Ha ha. Nor about himself either. He hadn't had time, worse luck, for the necessary light touch on that point. How awful. She would look for him in the passenger list, and not find him, and laugh. How much it would explain to her! "Mother—how very funny. Mr. Demarest must be in the second cabin!" "Funny? It doesn't especially surprise me— I always felt there was something——" Et cetera. Then that pale girl, cyni- cal—she would laugh, too. They would all laugh merrily together, with heads thrown back. What the Spanish call *carcajada*—loud laughter, boisterous and derisive. Sexual laughter, the ringing scorn of the female for the defeated or cowardly male, the skulker . . . He rounded the corner, but there was no Smith. Instead, at the far end, he saw the three women coming toward him. Cynthia appeared to be talking, the others turning their heads toward her. He must escape. Irresolute, he began pretending (absurd) that he was looking for a lost friend. What—he isn't here? Then I'd better turn. He turned, went briskly around the corner again, then rattled down the companionway.

In the smoking room, as he paid for his glass of port, Smith reappeared.

"Well, who's your swell friend?" he said, composing himself in the corner.

"Ah, that's the great chimera I was telling you about."

"What! The one you were going to see? How come?"

"The chimera—more so than ever," murmured Demarest. "Have a game?"

"Sure, I don't mind."

⟮ IV

Zring, went the Irish girl's bed curtains again, and *tschunk* went the electric switch on the wall, leaving dark the reticulated grill over the upper berth; and then the bunk creaked, and creaked sea-sawingly; as the Irish girl got into it, and creaked as she corkscrewed her Irish body down the ship-folded bedclothes; and an elbow thumped the matchboard partition close to Demarest's ear, and then grazingly bruised it again, and then a padded round knee bumped, and the elbow again more softly knocked . . . Who's there, i' the name of the devil? . . . Is it you, strumpet? Knock again. Knock at the door, or come in without knocking. Is it you, darling? In the dark? where? Listen to the wind moaning, humming through the venti- lators. Listen to the sea, the vast sound of sea, pouring down into the in-

finite, cataract of the world. What are we? We are silences drowned in an
abyss of sound. The ship is sinking. The world is sinking. God is sinking.
What difference, therefore, does it make who you are? Don't pause to
knock, but approach swiftly through the night of sound and water, step
serenely from thrum to thrum of the ship's engines, from heartbeat to
heartbeat of the terraqueous god. Is it you, with the candle in your hand,
you in a nightgown? Ah Psyche with the regions which! You with a pocket
flashlight? In, in brief candle! We'll fear not for scandal. But diddle and
dandle. And fondle and fry. Seven bells; the ship, sleepwalking, tintin-
nabulates like a gipsy. The shipboy, hearing bells below him, looking down
at the dark ship, and dark decks, and dark sea, and the dark bow lowering
into a wide dim wash of white, and the dark waves coming white-maned
and flattening in white—the shipboy sleepily strikes once the small sea bell,
and the bird of sad sound flies on short quick wings into the infinite misery
. . . MISERY . . . Misery is consciousness. Misery is death. Misery is birth.
Misery is creation. Rain is falling in Portobello Road, the evening is winter,
the cobbled mud is inferno, and the cold rain slowly falls in large, fat
flakes, *larghe falde*, snowflakes falling into slime and grease. The man,
shuffling, undersized, leans pushing the barrow, on which lies the two-
year-old boy under rags of sacking, unmoving, turning only his large eyes
full of pain. The woman hobbles beside the barrow, weeping, pressing the
back of a blue hand against her cheek, turning her shrunken face to one
side and downward as she whines. The man is silent, pushing the barrow
rapidly; the woman trots. Rain falls into the boy's eyes. They are hurrying
home . . . The man is thinking, while the dirty water runs under his cap
and down his face, he is used to it, he doesn't mind the cold trickle among
his hair and down his neck—but this other thing he is not used to, he
wants to shout out something horrible about it, shaking his fist, except that
he is too tired and can't find the words. Let me dictate for you a course of
action which will satisfy this longing. Begin by shouting at your woman—
"For Christ's sake shut your jaw and stop your bloody whining. Stop it, or
I'll knock your damn teeth out." Continue by striking her once in the back
of the neck, so that she stumbles and falls into a puddle, moaning, and
kneels there, moaning, as if unable to move. Grab her arm, twist it, and
wrench the slattern to her feet. Hit her again, this time in the face, your
fingers open—the slap will warm your hand. Shout at her, so that all the
people in Portobello Road will hear. "What's the matter—are you drunk?
I'll black your eye for you if you don't get a move on you." Think again.
Think of nothing but misery, of Portobello Road endless and eternal, of
yourself and your slut and your paralyzed boy walking there in the winter
rain forever. Do you require speech? Would it do you good to abuse her,
to call her a draggle-tailed, snaggle-toothed, swaggle-bellied, broken-gaited
ronyon? Enumerate her physical defects. A wart over her left eye; a wart
on her right eyelid; a wart (with hairs on it) on the chin; a pendulous wart,
like a little pink cauliflower, coral-hued and corrupt, between the lean
breasts; and a sore on the right thigh. Scars on the legs, bluish or coppery.
Puncture wounds on the inner surface of the left arm, below the joint: five,
and red. Five corresponding puncture wounds on your own left arm. Blest
be the marriage betwixt earth and heaven! Now,—in the open sore of space,

—the mortal son and the daughter immoral, make of the world their trysting place. Ten positives in succession, the hollow steel needle pricking and sliding under the taut skin, and into the swollen vein, the glass tube steadily filling with poisoned blood as the little steel piston withdraws. The blessed spirochete. Swarms. The blood boiling with hook-nosed spirochetes. MISERY. Horror, the maggot, hatches and quarries in the very pulse of love. Rain is falling in Portobello Road, hissing in the paraffin flares that light the barrows and crowds, illuminating the bestial faces and dirty hands. Barrows heaped with kippers. Rotten cabbages, rain-soaked. Collar buttons and woolen stockings. Terracotta Venuses. Winkles. Toy balloons. Detumescent pigs singing like cicadas on a hot night in New Jersey. The man, undersized, leans pushing the barrow on which the boy lies unmoving, turning an apathetic eye toward the smoky flares. The woman trots, moaning. Announce your grief. Stand at the corner where the crowd is densest, and shout it to them pitilessly—"You think you are miserable, do you! Well, look at me, look at us! Syphilis, that's what we got, syphilis!" . . . This was where Goya lived: in Portobello Road. The man pushing the barrow was Goya. The woman, trotting and whining, with averted eyes, was Goya. Goya was the paralyzed boy lying numb and cold under wet-glazed rags. Goya sold maggoty kippers from a torchlit barrow: he inflated the singing pig, over and over again. *Nga-a-a-a,* sang the pig, Goya holding it up by the spigot on its back before the circle of dirty-faced children . . . *Goya drew a pig on a wall . . . The five-year-old hairdresser's son . . . saw, graved on a silver tray . . . the lion: and sunsets were begun . . . Goya smelt the bull-fight blood: The pupil of the Carmelite . . . Gave his hands to a goldsmith, learned: to gild an aureole aright . . . Goya saw the Puzzel's eyes: . . . sang in the street: (with a guitar) and climbed the balcony; but Keats (under the halyards) wrote "Bright Star" . . . Goya saw the Great Slut pick The chirping human puppets up. And laugh, with pendulous mountain lip, And drown them in a coffee cup; Or squeeze their little juices out In arid hands, insensitive, To make them gibber . . . Goya went Among the catacombs to live . . . He saw gross Ronyans of the air, harelipped and goitered, raped in flight By hairless pimps, umbrella-winged: Tumult above Madrid at night . . . He* HEARD *the* SECONDS IN *his* CLOCK CRACK *like* SEEDS, DIVULGE *and* POUR *abysmal* FILTH *of* NOTHING-NESS BETWEEN *the* PENDULUM AND *the* FLOOR: *Torrents of dead veins, rotted cells, Tonsils decayed, and fingernails: Dead hair, dead fur, dead claws, dead skin. Nostrils and lids; and cauls and veils; And* EYES *that still, in death, remained (Unlidded and unlashed)* AWARE *of the foul* CORE, *and, fouler yet, The* REGION WORM *that* RAVINS *There . . .* STENCH *flowed out of the second's* TICK. *And Goya swam with it through* SPACE, *Sweating the fetor from his limbs. And stared upon the* UNFEATURED FACE *That did not see, and sheltered* NAUGHT, *but* WAS *and* IS. *The second gone, Goya returned, and drew the* FACE; *And scrawled beneath it, "This I have known" . . . And drew four slatterns, in an attic, Heavy, with heads on arms, asleep: And underscribed it. "Let them slumber! Who, if they woke, could only weep" . . .* MISERY. Say it savagely, biting the paltry and feeble words, and overaccenting the metronomic rhythm, the same flaccid-syllabled rhythm as that of King Caligula. Say it savagely, with eyes closed, lying rigid in the berth, the right foot crossed over the left, flexing and reflexing against the coarse sheet. Explore the first cabin in your pajamas, find the passenger list and the number of Cynthia's cabin, and putting your absurd chin (in which the bones are slowly being rotted by pyorrhea) over the window sill, recite in the darkness . . . not this, not this, but something exquisite, something young. *Awakening up he took her hollow lute, tumultous; and in chords that tenderest be He played an ancient ditty, long since mute, in Provence called "*LA BELLE DAME SANS MERCI.*"* The boy stood on the burning deck. Eating peanuts by the peck . . . Cynthia! are you awake? . . . Yes! Who is it? . . . Saint William of Yonkers. Listen! I will tell you all about my childhood—everything. You will see how pathetic it was. You will see what long, lonely, lugubrious life I have led. The Irish girl, separated from me by one inch of painted wood, is trying to attract my attention, knocking with her sweet little elbow against the wall. Last night I replied, tentatively. Tonight, so great in your heavenly influence upon me, so permeated is my gross body by your beauty, that I pay no attention. Are you listening? . . . Yes, darling . . . I am a man full of pity and gentleness! My face is the face of one grown gently wise with suffering—ah, with what years of untold suffering! I have been misunderstood—I have blundered—I have sinned—Oh, I have sinned; but I have paid the price. My father was cruel. When I was five, he burnt off my left hand because I had been striking matches . . . I begged in the streets, having no money to buy the necessary books; for even as a little child I had a passion for knowledge and beauty. A Chinaman gave me a quarter, and I bought . . . what was it I bought? *Nick Carter in Colorado. The Arabian Nights. Almost Fourteen.* Fiske's *Cosmic Philosophy.* Nietzsche's *Beyond Good and Evil.* Espronceda's *El Diablo Mundo.* The Icelandic *Voluspa. An Essay on the Trallian School.* A Variorum edition of *Twinkle Twinkle Little Star,* in eighteen volumes. A Variorum edition of *Thank You Kindly Sir She Said,* in two hundred volumes. Are you still listening, Cynthia? . . . Yes, beloved . . . I adore you, Cynthia. I have been a fool —I have lost you—but I adore you, and I will adore you forever. Your physical defects—do I not know them? A nostril just a suspicion too "painfle." A voice exquisite, light, Shelleyan—but lacking in those deep-throated qualities, voluptuous and resonant, with which I love a woman, now and again, to turn challengingly upon me. Breasts a little too low and large; a gait a shade too self-conscious; a bearing rather too much in the tradition of the "expensive slouch." But these are immaterial—forgive me for mentioning them. I adore them, I do not desire to touch them, nor to touch you. My feeling for you is wholly sublimated: I can trace in it no physical desire. I should fear and distrust any impulse to bring your tall body into contact with mine. I should like only to live with you in some strange, rarefied world—cold, clear, translunar and spacious; a world of which you know the secret, and I do not; a world of the subtle and the fragile, of the crepuscular and the vitreous, of suggestions dim but precise, of love inexpressive and thought unconcealed. An imparadised Amalfi, marble terraces of orange groves and camellias, rising out of the violet of the sea and ascending into the violet of the empyrean? No? Too much like marzipan? Let us, then, leave the world as it is; but make of it, by knowing

all its secrets, our terrestrial heaven . . . Are you listening, Cynthia? . . .
Listening, *smutsfink* . . . Tomorrow I will write out for you the history
of my childhood. All sorts of exquisite things will be in it—delicate perceptions, gentlenesses of feeling, of which you would not have supposed a
mere male to be capable. I have always been kind to birds, dogs, children,
cats and mice. Particularly mice. Once I found a swift, imprisoned in a
house. I saw it flapping against the window as I passed, flapping against
the curtains. The house was empty, deserted. I walked miles to get the key,
wondering how I would capture the poor thing when I returned. It wasn't
necessary—I opened the window and he flew out. He had fallen down the
chimney. . . . This, and many others . . . I would narrate them humorously, of course—but you would detect the gentleness and pity . . . A
kitten—I climbed a telegraph pole, when I was eight, to rescue a kitten,
which had got all the way to the top and was afraid to come down. I had
stationed my brother and another boy on the roof of the chicken coop—
they were to hold out a towel between them, into which I was to drop the
kitten. Unfortunately, Tom (he's a darling, Tom—you'd like him!) let
go of his end. Still, the kitten wasn't hurt . . . A dog, I saved once from
drowning at Keswick . . . Blind men I have led across the street . . . Old
women I have helped in and out of trains—several thousand . . . The
woman who fainted in the Grand Central Station—I helped to carry her
into the waiting room—how extraordinarily white she was. Beggars. Hurdy-
gurdy men. The tramp in the ditch, who said, "You might as well be cheerful, especially if you're miserable!"—and went on singing . . . Yes. All the
unhappy world—the overworked, the starving, the starved for love, the deserted and lonely—MISERY . . . Like the vampire I have been dead many
times, and learned the secrets of the grave; like the lobster, I do not bark,
and know the secrets of the sea. I am shy, I am sensitive, I am impression-
able. How many lovely things, how many horrible things, I remember! This
you would love in me if you loved nothing else: this treasure house, this
golden thesaurus, of my memory. If only I had succeeded in showing this
to you before you fell in love! You would have been astonished—perhaps
. . . Perhaps perhaps perhaps perhaps . . . On the other hand, you might
have thought me not sufficiently masculine? . . . A sentimental intro-
verted weakling, with that tendency to sudden cruelty which all the injured
manifest. But my trick of unexpected reticence, my impassivity of appearance, my proneness to fatigue and indifference, the rapidity with which I
tire of people—no matter whether they be angels or devils—these characteristics give an air of masculinity which might have deceived you? Are
you listening, Cynthia? . . . Listening, mud-puppy . . . My absurd chin
is on your window sill in the dark, but I am like Fama, and my feet are not
at all on this deck, as you might imagine, but way down upon the Sewanee
River, far, far away. I am like Daisy Dacey—England and the United States
rolled into one. To see all is to be all. But it is above all my childhood that
I should like to put into your lap—my romantic and beautiful childhood,
my suffering and pitiful childhood. I was disliked and distrusted. I was
cruelly beaten. I was humiliated. My pride and will were broken before I
had come to my seventh year. I was in a state of continual terror. I sneaked
in and out of the house, mouselike and secretive, my only purpose to attract

as little attention as possible. My favorite story—would you believe it?—
this is very touching—was the story of the ugly duckling. This held out a
ray of hope for me—I would revenge myself—someday—someday—by
turning into a swan. I read this story over and over, memorizing every
detail, and as I read it I searched in my soul for signs of the wonder that
was to come. How was this to be? What gifts had the good fairies given
me, that I might someday astonish and confound my cruel father, my
forgetful mother? It could not be strength, for I was weak, and I was
constantly ill. It could not be courage, for I hardly ever forgot what it was
to be afraid. It could not be beauty, for beauty was not a prerogative of
boys. Could it, perhaps, be wisdom? This was conceivable—it was only by
my teachers that I was ever given encouragement. I remember how I was
overcome, how I blushed, when one day Miss Baring said aloud in the
classroom (there was a drawing of Julius Caesar on the blackboard behind
her head), "William will some day be successful. He is intelligent, and he
works." Successful! What a blaze of glory, what a bursting of stars of light,
was in that word. Like sky rockets on Christmas Eve! Like Roman candles
vomiting their colored balls of fire and slow streams of fading sparks! So
perhaps it was in this way that I began to associate knowledge with success;
or mental skill of some kind. I began by copying the drawing of Julius
Caesar—I showed my drawing to Miss Baring, and this too she praised
. . . Eight bells . . . Changing the watch. With heavy boots, with oil-
skins, with a black oilskin hat, he climbs the ladder to the crow's nest. A
fine rain falling on his face and hands. All clear, Bill? . . . A light two
points off the port bow . . . Right. Getting a little sea up. Thickening a
bit, too . . . Smith is in bed at sea. Faubion, the Fleshpot, is in bed. The
Welsh Rarebit is in bed—whose? Vivien Hay-Lawrence is in bed. The
Major is in bed. Solomon Moses Caligula Silberstein is in bed. Cynthia is
in bed. Mrs. Battiloro is in bed. The pianist lies awake, thinking of his
wife and daughter in Blackpool. The Chief Steward is having a game of
bridge in his stateroom, whisky is on the table. All the others lie horizontal,
above and below the water line, like chrysalids, like corpses in coffins. The
clairvoyant? He, too; but his sleep is troubled by vatic dreams. He sees each
chrysalid being secretly attacked by ants, the larva destroyed, the psyche
released. Ah psyche from the regions which. MISERY. Last night as I lay
on my pillow—last night as I lay on my bed—last night as I lay on my
pillow—I dreamed that my bonnie was dead . . . You know the story of
Strindberg and the mouse? He was terrified by an electric influence, an evil
stream, which everywhere pursued and persecuted him. It came through
walls, aiming at his heart. He hid his head in the pillow, but the malevolent
stream came up through the bed. He ran out into the hall and lay down by
the banisters—but a mouse trotted up close to him and looked into his
face: and he fled screaming. I am Strindberg. I look at his photograph
and a feeling of self-love and self-pity, a profound narcissistic compassion
and tenderness, comes over me. Those harassed and noble temples, the
tortured deep-seeing eyes, the magnificent head, the small mouth, which
is the mouth of the child and of the adder! . . . I am wise, I am weak,
I am persecuted; I am unlucky, I am beautiful, I am strong. *Der Gekreu-
zigte*. I love my own body. When I was a youth, I used to stand naked

before a tall glass, or walk gracefully toward it, transported by the beauty
I saw, the exquisitely flexing muscles of abdomen and calf and thigh, the
suave Greek brow, the candid eyes. Ah, the profile of the body, with the
ribs arched, the lean hollow curve of the belly! The lightly hung and
powerful arms, the hands large, fair and strong as those of the David! This
is what is now rejected and despised. Therefore it is not beautiful. It is
obscene, gross, despicable. It is a whited sepulcher; a mass of secret corruption, of filthy juices and clots of half-destroyed food; an infirmary sicklied
o'er with the pale cast of consciousness. I have always been one in whose
consciousness illusion and disilluson flashed simultaneously. My hand remains still, because it releases even before it has grasped. Are you listening,
Moon? Are you listening, chaste Nymph? I am on the first-class deck beside you, wearing pearl-gray spats, carrying gloves and a silver-topped cane
of malacca, a gardenia in my buttonhole. There is no obstacle between us,
you are not in love with another man, you have all this time been secretly
in love with me. I am your social equal (indeed your superior) and my
stick is really the wand of Trismagistus. *How pleasant! Oh, how exquisite!*
Thy beauty framed for sweet delight! Thy stature like an upright palm!
Thy breasts like clusters dropping balm! . . . I my Belov'd first raisèd thee
From under the pomecitron tree; Thy careful mother in that shade With
anguish her fair belly laid . . . Queen and huntress, are you listening? . . .
Listening, but bored, wood louse . . . I was in a hurry—I hadn't time to
explain to you—I would like to explain to you—explain everything. I had
no right on the first-cabin deck, of course—I am in the second cabin.
Poverty. Poor but proud. I have often, for that matter, traveled in the
steerage. I believe in being democratic, don't you? I remember you said
your brother William . . . always got along well with people of humble
origin . . . Yes . . . So do I . . . I like them. Queer creatures, often,
aren't they? I really like them better than most people of my own class.
Why then, apologize for liking them—or why claim it as a virtue? *Tee hee*
—nervous giggle. I believe you are a snob, Cynthia. I remember my friend
Giles, who met you at a dance in Oyster Bay—Oyster Bay!—said "Battiloro? Oh yes. I remember. An awful snob—looked down her nose at everybody! . . . One of those damned English snobs." Ha ha! Apparently you
had been rather cool to poor good-natured Giles, Giles with his loud bark
and perpetually wagging tail, Giles who at college was known as "Susie."
Poor Giles, a failure at everything, but so disarming, so ingenuous, so eager
to please, so nice! How had you the heart to be cruel to him? Are you
cruel, Cynthia? Or was it that you thought *him* a snob? Well—perhaps
a little. He probably tried a little too hard to show you how much he
knew about England, and how many "fish heads" he knew there . . .
Lady Rustlebottom of the Mount, Torquay. Et cetera . . . He bought a
blazer especially for the purpose and spent a weekend there . . . I was in
a hurry—I hadn't time to explain—I must explain—all—everything—
Smith, for example. You probably noticed at once that Smith is not a
"gentleman"—in the accepted sense. The way he cocks that absurd great
tweed hat! His dingy clerical-looking clothes, and his shoes humped at the
toes! A mere ship's acquaintance, a rather interesting little character. You
wouldn't like him—he would bore you—but you would like to hear about

him, the salient features of his career brightly related by Demarest. Of course, you aren't a very good judge of character! You remember Wetherall? You said, "What a really charming face he has. I'm sure he's awfully nice!" Ah! The joke was on you. Wetherall was at the moment seducing a little trained nurse who was on board—he told me at every meal of his progress, and dear Billington was so shocked that he could hardly eat . . . One of their difficulties was that she had two roommates . . . But the weather, you remember, was warm, they stayed late on deck, and there was no moon. Also, they did not attend the ship's concert. Wetherall described it all to me—every detail, his kind brown eyes humorously bright, his Bradford accent at its very best. What a curious pleasure it gave me to share in that secret conquest, so passionate, so frankly carnal, so frankly obscene, and so laconically casual, while at the same moment I was conscious of falling in love with you, and falling in love in a sense so antithetical, so ethereal! While Wetherall was turning wine into blood, I was turning blood into wine. Yes. It was magnificent. A slow and beautiful counterpoint. Wetherall the bass and you the treble. You remember that afternoon when I encountered you at the foot of the companionway?—you were carrying a book—it was a book of Negro spirituals—and you smiled, and then immediately looked away, frowning, at the sea. You hesitated as if— you were perhaps really going somewhere, you had an errand, you didn't want me to suppose that . . . you in any way sought my company. I, too, hesitated—as if I knew that my company could not be of much interest to you, and yet—might we not pause together for a moment, touch our wings together in the air? And besides I—and perhaps you, too (we discussed this problem—so peculiar to ships—a few days later in the train to London, in the light of the queer implicit intimacy which by then had sprung up between us) feared that you might think me trying to avoid you—it is so difficult, on a ship, to avoid the appearance of persecution, or, on the other hand, of avoidance! . . . "Have you been reading?" I said, and you answered, "I've been trying to—but it's so extraordinarily difficult, on a ship, to *concentrate!* . . . I've had to give it up" . . . I too had found it difficult—even with *The Spoils of Poynton.* I told you of this, and we discussed Henry James, standing there, as we did so, a little uneasy with each other, or, as Mandeville (is it Mandeville?) puts it, in a mammering and at a stay. And then, taking my flimsy life in my hands, I said, "Shall we go up on the boat deck and concentrate *together?* It's rather nice forward of the bridge . . ." Singular and daring remark! You half smiled and turned, we ascended the companionway; and at the forward end of the deck, leaning our backs against the old plates of the *Silurian,* which we could feel buckling as the ship plunged, we talked deliciously for an hour, for two hours. And do you know what gave, for me, a special exquisiteness to that talk? It was my fresh sharp recollection of my conversation at lunch with Wetherall. Behind that forward lifeboat, on the starboard side—where later we played a game of chess, the young student of architecture watching us—behind that lifeboat, the evening before, Wetherall and Miss Kirkpatrick had lain together till one o'clock. They had been discovered and reprimanded. Of all this, naturally, you knew nothing; and still less could you conceive the nature of Wetherall's confidences to me. You would be

astounded—horrified! The grossness of the human being! And the vulgar
candor with which one man to another confesses it! Wetherall informed
me that Miss Kirkpatrick was, up till then, "inexperienced." But, setting out
for a two months' holiday in Scotland and Belfast, she had in advance made
up her mind that, should a sufficiently attractive man be available, she
would give herself to him. Wetherall—a married man, with a daughter of
eight—had been the lucky man. He had noticed from the outset that she
smiled at him a good deal, and somewhat intensely. On the second evening
he kissed her—and as he remarked, "Didn't she come up to it? . . . O
Boy! . . ." But I give you the impression—are you listening, Cynthia? . . .
Still listening, earthworm . . . I give you the impression—partly a wrong
impression—that this organ point, supplied for our intercourse by Wetherall, was unalloyedly pleasant. No no no no no. Good God. This is precisely
what I don't want you to think. It reminded me, certainly, of my own
obscenity; but it also served to show me already the immense altitude of my
—flight! Wetherall was precisely what I was proposing, with your support,
to leave behind. More precisely still, what I was leaving behind was Helen
Shafter: coarse, voluptuous, conscious, witty Helen, who had so ungovern-
able an appetite for the farcical, and who had so skillfully and swiftly and
horribly exposed the essential fleshliness of "love between the sexes!" Yes.
The experience was horrible. And how even more horrible was it to come
thus to you, before whom I so passionately longed to stand with something of Parsifal's mindless innocence, bearing on brow and palms the
stigmata of that crucifixion! . . . Misery . . . And what intricacy of fate
brings it about that again it is from a meeting with Helen that I come to
you, and that as I passed you twice on the deck this evening it was of our
so miserable affair—Helen's and mine—that I was foolishly boasting to
a total stranger? Is it possible that you overheard it? . . . Well, that is
what I am . . . Even supposing that we could have . . . even supposing
that you could have . . . loved me, it is impossible that I should always
have been able to deceive you—sooner or later I should have had to drop
the pretense (so skillful) of refinement and idealism and innocence; you
would have seen me for the Caligula that I am . . . Somebody out in
the corridor—a stewardess giggling. And a steward. Mrs. Antherton. "No—
NO!" and then a little appealing laugh, ending abruptly in "M-m-m," and
then the stifled laugh again. Tompkins is kissing Mrs. Atherton. Intervene,
Cynthia! This sort of thing shouldn't be permitted on shipboard. Now it
is Tompkins—I know his voice. "What did he say, eh? What did he
say? . . ." "None of your business . . ." "Well, I don't give a damn what
he said—he can stick it up—the flue" . . . "Sh!" What's the matter with
you? This ain't inspection time" . . . "No, but somebody might hear
you . . ." Murmur murmur murmur . . . For God's sake speak up! I'd
like to get to the bottom of this . . . "and said I wasn't going to have
anything to do with him any more . . ." ". . . drunk the first twenty-four
hours anyway—lying like a log in his bunk with a wet towel . . ." "It isn't
the first time either. Voyage before last they had to fetch him . . . Carter
and St. Clair it was . . . wife . . . she was standing outside there looking . . ." Murmur murmur murmur. Pause. Have they gone, or is he kissing her again? Have to do it like this, poor devils—on the q.t., late at night.

Snatches between watches under hatches . . . "Good night, then." "Good night, sweet dreams." "Cheerio." Gone: a rustle of starched calico, muffled footsteps, and gone. The Irish girl is breathing heavily and slowly—asleep. What is she dreaming of? Pittsburgh. She is in uncle William's house in Pittsburgh. Uncle William has grown a black beard, horrible, too long, obscenely alive. His mouth, seen through it, is unfamiliarly round and red, like a great red rose, but too opulent and fleshly, almost mucous. He sits and looks at her. Then he begins speaking harshly and says over and over again, "Thy belly is as an heap of wheat" . . . Yes. Everywhere this motif —everywhere. You too, Cynthia—who knows? What concupiscent pre-occupations, only fleetingly conscious and perhaps obscure, do you per-petually conceal? Eunice—until once I laughed—used to tell me her dreams. She dreamed one night that she was a nun, in a convent. A fire broke out. The nuns ran into the corridors, looking for the fire, but only finding dense clouds of smoke pouring up the stairs. They ran down the stairs, and coming at length to the celler, could see through the smoke every now and then a fitful glare of flame in what appeared to be a deep hole, or arched cave, at one side of the cellar, a sort of underground en-trance. The nuns dragged a garden hose down the stairs, thrust the brass nozzle into the cavern, and the fire began to go out . . . Darling Eunice . . . I wish she hadn't got married . . . disappeared. "Don't look at me like that!" she said—that was one night when we had dinner on the roof garden. We were falling in love. Blue taffeta. Those sleeves of a sort of gauze. That night she was suddenly sick in the street, and closing her eyes said, "*Oh*, I can't even love you a *little* bit . . . so . . . sorry!" . . . Then the time we were standing at midnight in the dark portico of the church —the church with the angels blowing trumpets from the tower . . . We thought we were concealed . . . but Eunice murmured too much when I put my hand . . . and the policeman . . . Good God what a fright he gave us . . . "Move on, now! haven't you got any better place than that? . . ." How delightful to remember it. I wonder if Eunice, married, lying beside her husband, thinks about me sometimes? She liked me, we were happy. But I couldn't see her often enough. "No—" she said, "this time you mustn't kiss me . . . I'm going to be married!" . . . MISERY. Absurd, if I could face Eunice's departure with so much equanimity, that this about Cynthia . . . Different . . . Not much intellectual or esthetic companionship with Eunice—well-matched emotionally and physically (and her sense of humor—delicious! and her courage!), but not otherwise. My longing to see her now is largely nostalgic. Still—I was frightfully fond of her . . . With Cynthia—so extraordinarily at one in all things—a kind of shorthand of understanding at the very beginning . . . *Tschunk.* The lights in the corridor are off. Dark. The engines throbbing; late, the night shift of stokers; sweating like a lot of firelit demons. The shaft, all the way through the ship, gleaming, revolving—ectoplasm. Somebody coming. Faubion? Light! Must be the watchman with a flashlight. At his priestlike task—of bold intrusion . . . Ship, I am on a ship. Cynthia is on board, but in the first cabin. Shall I transfer to the first cabin? Money enough; just barely. But nothing left for tips and drinks and the train to London. It would look too pointed. Cynthia is on board. Incredible! Anticlimax!

. . . How am I going to see her? Walk boldly into the first cabin looking for her? Besides, under the circumstances, do I want to see her? It would be useless. It would be "pleasant"? Good God . . . After all these dreams of ships, too! Always looking for Cynthia on ships . . . When I get to London, I won't dare to go and see her. No point in it. Spoiled. The whole thing spoiled. The world pulled down and wrecked. Better be like Smith and gather my rosebuds while I may . . . Poor old Smith! The cherub, in pink pajamas, sleeps surrounded by Faubion's heliotrope-smelling dresses, and dreams he is dancing with chorus girls. Lottie, Flo, Hyacintha, Vyolette, Dol, Maybelle, Parthenia. They all dance frou-frouishly around him, squealing, ring around a rosy, joining hands, and Cherub Smith stands in the middle, in the grass, with his finger in his mouth, looking coy. *Coo-hoo*, Parthenia! I see you, Maybelle! I know it was you who slapped me, Nottie Lottie! . . . There's a corporal in the grass . . . Smith, impersonating a satyr, runs with a resinous torch and thrusts it under a translucent chlamys, igniting it. Parthenia is burned. Goes off flaming. Ha ha! . . . Splendid old Smith . . . This is what it is to be *homo sapiens*, the laughing animal, the animal who remembers and foresees . . . Smith and the clairvoyant—the clairvoyant corporal springs out of the deep grass, skull-faced and hideous, and grimly pursues poor old Smith, who screams among the tombstones—Flottie, Hyacintha, Partha, Flow, Boybell, Dole, Violent. He is felled like an ox. To what green altar, oh mysterious priest? And all his crispy flanks in garlic dressed. The uses of assonance. Gloom and gleam. Birth and death. Love and live. Mingle and mangle. Fix and flux. Prick and puck. Pop and pap. Twit and tot. Point and punt. Dram and dream. So near and yet so far . . . What if it were at last possible to talk of *everything* with a woman? To keep no secrets, no dark recesses of the mind, no dolors and danks, which could not be shared with her? But then she would have ceased to be attractive. Is it simply because we have to *pose* before her . . . to pretend to be angels . . . the angel with the sword? . . . *Ah, the awful fixed curve of determinism!* MISERY . . . You overhear all these reflections, Cynthia? . . . All, maggot . . . Forgive me forgive me forgive me forgive me. I am horrible but I am penitent. I will crawl on my knees to the Bilbao Canal and drink of its filthy waters. I will bathe in slime. I will fill my belly with ashes. I will go naked, and show the corns on my feet, the mole on my right fess. I will work for ninety-nine years in a Chinese rice field, sleeping in the mud. I will pray to Kwannon to purify my heart. I will hop on one foot all the way from Sofia to Jerusalem, speaking to no one, and die at the foot of the cross: the weeping cross. You have seen, in Mount Auburn cemetery (beautiful isn't it), that tombstone of white marble . . . with a marble lamb . . . upon which, annually on a certain day, two drops of blood are found? Those drops of blood are mine. Expiation. On the twenty-eighth of February each year, in the evening, I go there and cut my left wrist, letting two drops fall on the stone. Twenty-eight is my fatal number. The moon is shining when I arrive. Snow is on the ground and on the graves. Snow covers the obscene vaults. Crows are asleep in pine trees. The snow plough moans along Mt. Auburn Street . . . And I, solitary, grieving, expiate the sin and horror of the world—its grossness, its cruelty, its ugliness; its triviality, its vileness, its deceit. Bowed with sorrow, I ascend the little snow-covered hill by the tower, pass over it westward, and come to the Lamb. Then I take from my wallet a razor blade (Gillette) and gash slightly the left wrist . . . In heaven, those two drops of blood fall like thunderclaps. The angels fly up like doves. God, asleep, has a dream. He dreams: "The infinite darkness is gashed redly with a sword, and from the gash pours a torrent of blood. I am no longer unconscious suffering—I become an awareness and a shape. I am the region worm —the undying and infinite and eternal caterpillar; and I am the host of red-eyed ants who attack him in every part and devour him forever. The infliction and reception of pain comes to me from every particle of the caterpillar world. And the particles become more conscious. The chorus of suffering swells unceasingly: it is the sound of the world—the sound of sorrow. Who will teach me how I may again return into the darkness of nescience? What Siegfried will ring his ram's horn and destroy both Fafnar and himself? What messianic atom among my wailing myriads will so crucify himself and die that his death will carry in its train ALL DEATH? . . . I writhe with all my length . . . Oh, man, save me! . . . But all I hear is the sound of gnawing and moaning, the sound as of the ten million silkworms which in China, at night, keep travelers awake with their champing of mulberry leaves . . . CLAP! CLAP! . . . What is that? Two drops of blood! Man begins to destroy himself: out of horror for his own nature, at the nature of Me. It is the beginning of the end! Ah! peace will return to me! I will return at last into the womb of nothing!" . . . *Tin-tin.* Two bells. One o'clock. I ought to be asleep. One three five seven nine eleven thirteen fifteen. Two four six eight ten twelve . . . One four seven ten thirteen sixteen nineteen twenty-two twenty-five . . . I'm on my belly with my palms crossed under my chest, right cheek on pillow. But the right nostril obstructs. On my back again, carefully, these damned ship-folded bedclothes come apart so easily. The cat's prayer. Give us this day our daily mouse. And forgive us our trespasses as we forgive those who trespuss against us . . . I really ought to give up this awful habit of punning. Just the same, I always regretted not saying, when her knitted sleeve caught in the log and stopped its ticking (reducing the day's run), "A miss is as good as a mile!" That was when we were discussing Brooke's poetry. And I quoted—"*And suddenly there's no meaning in our kiss . . . And your lit, upward face grows, where we lie, Lonelier and dreadfuller than sunlight is, and dumb and mad and eyeless, like the sky . . .*" I told her also of the Catholic poetess (so tiresomely self-conscious and exquisite) who remarked about his poem "*Heaven*"—"So stupid, don't you think? So very stupid!" Squamous, omnipotent, and kind. Mrs. Battiloro frightens and annoys me in the same way. What was her phrase about Moore, when I repeated his comment on Yeats? Something deliciously Victorian. Hm. Offensive . . . No. Noisome. No.—What the devil! Lie in wait for it. How exasperating, especially when sleepless. ODIOUS! Yes. An odious person! I laughed, and she was annoyed. She didn't invite me to come again—I said good-by to her in the dining room, where she was giving instructions to the maid for the dinner party. Who was coming to that dinner party? How I longed to know! Good-by, she said, and turned back to her silver and her refectory table (which I had been brought to see!). Refractory table. That's what

old man Tucker always called it—frosty-faced old fool. Table tipping.
Ectoplasm. That reminds me of old Duggan in his shirt sleeves behind
the counter, taking his false teeth out of the cigar box on the window sill.
I ought to have told Cynthia about him. When his wife died! "I miss her
terribly, the lovely little dear . . . I was looking at her grave . . . It looks
sort of bare. I ought to set out some flowers there. I thought maybe some
Christian anthems would look nice?" Chrysanthemums. When I took M.
there, hoping to get Duggan to repeat it (how heartless), it all went off
like clockwork, even to the furtive tear on his cheek. Poor old Duggan. His
wife was like the sheep knitter in *Alice*. Cancer of the liver. Dying in
that shabby little shop, selling tins of tobacco, ten cents' worth of stale pep-
permints, sardines, glue, shoe strings. Patient and kind. I was his only
friend—almost impossible to get away from him some evenings—he followed me to the door, talking, reluctant to have me go . . . Breaking out
violently about some of his neighbors—particularly the O'Briens, whom he
hated. Their hens getting into his yard, "smelling up" the place, waking his
wife in the morning. A God-damned nuisance. I've complained, and I'll
keep right on complaining. Yes, by God, I will: Think they own the place
by God . . . The shop shut, and cheap crepe hanging from the latch. The
curtains drawn. Afterward he had a fox-terrier pup to keep him company
—it was run over and killed. Then a timid little mongrel, sleeping in a box
by the stove. "Yes, you know, she keeps me company—and you'll be surprised how much she understands" . . . He got his own meals—bacon and
fried potatoes. Moonshine whisky—a fine plume he used to breathe out
sometimes in the evening! "These travelers you know—*they* know where
to get it" . . . The Greens were nice to him when his wife died—but
nobody else was. Not a soul. Poor old man. MISERY. Ashes to ashes and
dust to dust. Would you like to kiss your father? No. The others were lifted
up and kissed the dead face, surprised. Why did I refuse? Shyness and
horror. The people sitting there, after the service, staring and weeping.
The parson wearing a queer thing with white sleeves and the Bible with a
pale purple ribbon, and the parson's mouth getting moist at the corners
when he talked. Then we sat in the carriage . . . feeling that we oughtn't
to talk or look out . . . Trot trot. Clop clop. The palmettos swayed and
flashed. The moss was hanging in long gray streamers. The shell road glared
in the sunlight. Too hot to walk barefoot. What flower had that been that
smelled so sweet? . . . Tuberoses . . . The mortuary tuberose. Tomb-
smelling tuberose. Trot trot. The sidewalks lined with crowds of staring
niggers, niggers smelling blood and death. That murder I saw from the
front "stoop"—*bang bang bang bang bang*, and the man's felt hat falling
off, and his head sinking down on his breast, and the niggers flocking like
ravens, flocking and cawing, while the murderer (a fireman whom I knew,
who owned a pet monkey) stood there in his shirt sleeves, unmoving, as if
surprised at what he'd done . . . *Was* it he who walked past the porch, a
year later, in shirt sleeves, carrying an empty coal scuttle? Back from the
penitentiary, or the chain gang? . . . Disappointed at not seeing the mark
on his face. If I had kissed him—or perhaps it didn't show anyway. Somebody said—Harry it was—that one of his eyes had come out and rolled
across the floor. The bloodstained mattress had been put in the outhouse

—I and Harry went and looked at it, pretending that we were looking for the kittens. *Felo de se.* Being pushed forward, in the crowd at the cemetery, to the edge of the grave. Sandy soil. An arrangement of pulleys and bands of canvas. Ashes to ashes. A little dust taken in the same parson's clean fingers. And dust to dust. Then the shovels, more businesslike.—My father. My father which art in earth. It was just over there he took my picture once, on the bluff by the river. In the white duck sailor suit. Hollow be thy name. . . . Julian, who said that it was always in the presence of death, or in the thought of it, that life, and therefore love (reproductive) most astonishingly asserted itself. He meant the merely physical. Quite understandable. Ain't Nature horrible? Love and Death. In Latin almost the same—ditto Italian. Death sacred and love profane. Eunice telling me of her friend the trained nurse, Miss Paine. Miss Paine was fond of poetry, she read Keats and Shelley. Periodically, she developed a taste for lubricious fiction. Presbyterian. Strong self-control,—but also strong passions. On that case in East Orange, on the night when the father died, the son, aged eighteen, through whose room she had to pass, put out his hand to her. She said afterward she couldn't understand it—it had seemed so right. So absolutely right. The strain, the exhaustion, the grief, all breaking down into this other, this divine ecstasy, in which suffering has supremely its place. Her only experience of passion. Age: thirty. For a month afterward she did nothing but pray: the whole of Sunday spent at church. Forgive us, for we know not what we do. MISERY. A child crying somewhere. The most desolating of all sounds is the sound of a child crying. Harrowing—makes you feel helpless. Might as well run, but then you can't forget it. The echo rings in your ear. *Ahhhhhhhhhhhhh . . . oo-oo-oo . . . ah-h-h-h . . . oo-oo-oo-oo . . .* the first thing we do when born is cry. All language therefore must develop out of the sound of crying—it is probably most affecting when *plangent* for that reason. Make a note of that—and remember it. Spring it on somebody as if I'd always known it. There, there darling, don't cry. There, there, darling, don't cry. By baby bunting. When the bough breaks the cradle will fall. Lullaby. *Traumerei.* My father whistled the *Lorelei* to the cat—he had a theory that the *Lorelei*, whistled slowly, was infuriating to cats. But the cat seemed to be delighted. He would now be—let me see. He was thirty-seven. From nought is 8. Fifty-five. What would he think of me, I wonder. Would I be afraid of him still? I am taller than you are. I am more intelligent than you are. Freer from fetishes than you are . . . Look! You see that scar? You gave that to me, holding my hand in the gas jet . . . You see these plays? they come from the deep wound you inflicted on my soul . . . You see the unhappy restlessness with which I wander from continent to continent, this horrified and lack-luster restlessness which prevents me from loving one person or place for more than a season, driving me on, aimless and soulless? This is what you did to me by depriving me of my mother . . . Think of Silberstein saying that he wants to find his mother. He wants to die. O God— O God. To die—to die in the middle of a deep sleep, to sink deeper and deeper into the darkness . . . That's of course, what *he* wanted—that poem he left on the table—the darkness—"*closer, closer all about, Blotting all the light of living out.*" Intra-uterine reversion. Perhaps the fact that *he*

—will prevent *me*. Explode it. It was a sort of exhibitionism, leaving a
poem on the table like that—defeated ego. Vanity. See what a great spirit
has left you. Mighty, I spread my wings and left you . . . I suppose I liked
him when I was very small, before the other kids were born—before I can
remember. He must then have fascinated me and drawn me out powerfully
and skillfully. Yes, I can feel that he did. There was something angelic
about him—later it became diabolic. The angel that revolted. My God,
what basilisk eyes, eyes that shot through you, tearing out thoughts, blood,
and vertebrae. "Where is that other letter?" "There wasn't any other letter." "Look at me. Where is that other letter?" "But there wasn't any
other letter." "You brought back three letters. Do you deny that you gave
one of them to your mother?" "There were only two letters!" "Why did
you sneak in by the back door?" "It was because there were some boys I
didn't want to meet——" "Don't lie to me! . . . Why did you come in by
the back door?" "It was because I saw 'Butch' Gleason." . . . O God have
mercy upon us. Pity us and have mercy upon us. Shine down upon us,
star of the sea, and guide us gently to the haven of Heaven. Manumit us
from slavery to our passions; deliver us from the tyranny of all-too-human
reason. Take from us that part which makes us to suffer, and at whose
bidding we bring suffering to others. And lead us down into darkness forever. MISERY . . . *Can never change the swan's black legs to white.*
Curious I should have opened to that line when I tried the *sortes Shake-
speareanae*. The devilish *double entendre*. Swan—ugly duckling—play-
wright=compensation. Black legs=black leg=rotter=inferiority. My abid-
ing sense of sin. The feeling of being dishonest and filthy. This is probably
the cause of my curious failure in all human relationships. This is why I try
to write plays. This is why, when I feel a friendship failing, feel myself
failing to attract or hold by means of personal charm (a fake), I begin trying to *impress*—let my plays fight my personal battles for me. Take my new
play MS. to Cynthia tomorrow. Yes—the impulse is perfectly clear. *This* is
what I can do—*this* is the angelic sort of being I am! Read and admire!
Sound me and wonder! I sit near you with eyes modestly downcast while
you read. You wouldn't think, to look at me, that this rather harmless nice
creature harbored in his soul such a shattering power . . . How disgusting! . . . Never, never again will I show my work *personally* to a living
soul. Publish it, get it performed—yes, since that seems to be the mechanism by which I preserve my sanity. But employ it as a secondary sexual
characteristic—a bloodshot erect crest—a rainbow-eyed tail—a mating
call! . . . The Bulgarian weasel. That hideous tramp on the stage who
said he would now give an imitation of the cry of the young Bulgarian
weasel to its mother. "Mommer! . . ." in a quiet restrained voice. "Mommer!" . . . It was during the same performance that the Russian girl, playing the xylophone, looked at me so fixedly and invitingly. Did I go round
by the stage door? Can't remember. Probably not . . . Perhaps it's because
I fear my rainbow tail won't be liked, won't make a sufficient impression——? That would simply add, of course, to my ruling sense of inferiority . . . I wonder what it was about me that always made people
laugh. In streets . . . On street cars . . . How I hated to get into street
cars or trains, facing all the staring people! Probably only my self-conscious-

ness and sheepishness and furtiveness that attracted attention? Then I
would blush. Always blushing—with a sense of guilt, of having been found
out . . . Does your mother know you're out? That was when I had on that
gray Norfolk suit. It probably *did* make me look absurd—with my pale
little chinquapin of a face, and sorrowful baby eyes . . . I went home and
looked at myself in the glass, trying to discover what was wrong. As usual,
I looked admiringly, lovingly, into my deep deep violet orbs. The eyes
of a great man. All-seeing and all-knowing. All-suffering and all-saying . . .
She returned the fifth act without comment—except that she didn't understand it. "I'm like the servant girl," she said, "who remarked, when . . .
'I don't *presume* to understand' . . ." On board—Cynthia on board,
stretched out in a sea berth. Like a dead fish. "It's rather nice—" she was
saying to Billington as I approached—"to be seasick, and just lie there feeling like a dead fish!" . . . "But I don't *like* to feel like a dead fish!" I cried,
and she gave her exquisite swift laugh, gay and understanding. Ah Psyche
from the regions which. *And turn, and toss her brown delightful head.*
The conspiracy against poor Billington, to preserve her from his boring
attentions. "You owe me a vote of thanks . . . I sidetracked—took him
firmly by the arm just as he was starting toward you . . . and walked him
round the upper deck for over an hour . . ." She was grateful . . . She
rewarded me later by telling me of poor Billington's desperate efforts to
get himself invited to come and see her aunt in London—he tried in
various ways to find out where she lived. Cynthia, leaning over the Irish
sea, laughed lightly, slightly—in the act of gently deriding Billington, she
contrived to say, "You see—I take *you* for granted—that *you* should come
to see us is admitted! Isn't it?" Yes. And this paved the way. "Shall I encounter you in London, I wonder?" Off Holyhead; the pilot putting out;
his sail tossing in the white southwest sea. "Well—if you should go to
Battersea Bridge—and turn to the left—and see a shabby little house with
that number on it—and ring the bell——!" "I shall do all as instructed"
. . . That afternoon—I saw her sitting in her deck chair, wrapped in the
brown steamer rug, a book opened on her lap. Billington—hm—yes—was
kneeling on the deck beside her, talking, oh so very earnestly, with all of
his little academic intellect. What about?—poetry? He had been writing
a sonnet series, "*Sonnets to Beatrice.*" As he talked, wagging a finger, he
occasionally emphasized the point by touching, with that forefinger, her
rug-covered knee. A damned outrage. I was furious. Cynthia—how saturnine, how somberly and unutterably scornful and bored she looked. Twice,
when I passed, I saw him do it. Odd that it should have so sickened me. I
sat in the smoking room, absolutely trembling with rage and disgust. Partly
jealousy? I would have liked to be able to do it myself? . . . No no no no
no. Yes yes yes yes yes . . . It's true—forgive me . . . but only partly
true. I would have liked to be *able* to do it, but *not* to do it—to be sufficiently free from self-consciousness, that is. To touch Cynthia's knee! Good
God. Playing chess, I used to forget everything, as we sat cross-legged on
the stone-scrubbed deck, and watch her hands. How fearfully beautiful they
were, how intelligent, as they lay at rest or moved meditatively to king or
queen. The gentle frown—the dark absorption. Her Italian blood. Italian
nobility, I wonder? Italian+American=English. She introduced me to

her father there on the station platform at Euston. "Father, this is Mr.
Demarest—who played chess with me . . ." The delightful broken accent,
the kind and wise face, the greeting at once intimate—"And dances? You
had lots of dances on board?" "No—no dances!" "You see, there wasn't
any orchestra!" "Ah! Oh! What a pity!" . . . It was after that that I went
and sat all afternoon in Hyde Park, unhappy. By the waters of Serpentine I
sat down and wept. The separation: it was as if half of me had been
cut away. How soon could I decently go to see her? Not before a week
or two. No. She would be busy—busy seeing all the rich and rare people
whom she knew so much better than she knew me. Distinguished people,
people of social brilliance, wits, artists, men famous all over the world—
how indeed could she allow herself to be bothered by me? I would never
dare to go . . . But after her invitation—I couldn't dare not to go. I would
tremble on the doorstep—tremble and stammer. And what, I wondered
was the English formula—"Is Miss Battiloro at home?" "Is Miss Battiloro
in?" And suppose a lot of others were there, or a tea party! It would be
frightful—I would make an idiot of myself, I would be alternately dumb
and silly: just as when I used to call on Anita. The whole day beforehand
I was in anguish, wondering whether I would go, whether I would telephone. That time when Anita's mother answered, and I suddenly, from
acute shyness, hung up the receiver in the middle of a conversation! . . .
But of course I *must* go and see Cynthia—otherwise it would be—impossible to live. I gave her *The Nation* as I passed her compartment in the
train at Lime Street—"Why, where did you get this?" Delight and surprise.
Then later, an hour out of Liverpool, she brought it back—as a suggestion
that I might talk to her? "May I?" "Rather!" Her aunt, sleeping opposite,
with crumbs on her outspread silken lap, opening her eyes a moment, smiling, and sleepily proffering the folded chessboard, which we declined, looking at each other gaily. Then—no, it was before—we were standing in the
corridor, watching the English fields rush by—daisies, buttercups, campion.
The hedges in bloom. "I think," she said, "heaven will be that—a green
bank covered with buttercups!" . . . "Well—heaven might be *worse* than
that!" MISERY . . . And then I went after three days! That was my first
mistake . . . Or no . . . The first mistake was my going there the day
before, in the morning, *just to see her house!* Incredible mawkish folly!
Suppose she had seen me? Perhaps she did. Well—there it was. Which
window was hers? At the top? A young man coming out, and I crossed to
the other side with face averted. Brother, perhaps. Or someone she knew,
had known for years. A friend of her brother's. A cousin. A cousin from
Italy. That young artist she had talked about—Rooker . . . The child
crying again—A *a a a h h h . . . oo . . . oo . . . ooo . . . aaaahhhh*
—*oo*—*oo*—*oo*—*oo*. A child crying at sea, crying in the infinite, *noia im-
mortale*, cosmic grief. Grief is my predominant feeling—why, then, in talk,
am I so persistently frivolous? flippant? Probably for that very reason.
"Demarest has the 'crying face' "—it was Weng, the Chinese student, who
said that. The eyelids are a trifle weary. I wonder why it is. It had never
occurred to me before that—it shows how little one is able to see the character of one's own face. And that day when I said something, jokingly, to
M. about "my mild and innocent blue eye," he replied quite savagely and

unexpectedly, "Your eye is blue, but it is neither *mild* nor *innocent!*" Astounding! My eye was not the timid little thing I had always supposed? And good heavens—not innocent! I didn't know whether to be pleased or not. But it radically altered my conception of myself, and helped me in my painful effort to acquire assurance . . . *Aaaahhh . . . oo . . . oo . . . oo . . . oo . . .* Poor thing—everything horribly unfamiliar. It's probably crying because it misses one familiar trifle—the light in the wrong place, or the wrong color; the bed too dark; the smell; the humming in the ventilators; the throb, so menacingly regular, of the ship's engines. Or a shawl, which was perhaps left behind. Everything combining to produce a feeling of frightful homesickness and lostness. The way that kitten must have felt, when we told Martha to "get rid of it"—instead of having it killed she put it down in the street and left it. Poor little creature . . . It was used to us . . . Its funny long-legged way of walking, the hind legs still a little uncertain! It liked to catapult back and forth in the hall after dusk; or catching moths. And that night, when it rained and blew all night, shaking the house—where was it? Mewing somewhere to be let in. Lost. How much did it remember, I wonder—how much did it *consciously* remember? A lot, probably. A warm and happy place with kind people whom it trusted—irrecoverably lost. Paradise lost. *Where are they—where is that wonderful house?* Ask the policeman. Good God it was a cruel thing to do—to take it in for a few weeks and then put it out in the streets like that. How horrible the suffering of any young thing can be. Speechless suffering, suffering that does not understand—the child punished by the parent whose nerves are on edge. Struck for reasons which it cannot conceive—dogs and cats the same way. Man's inhumanity to dogs and cats. Cattle too, driven into the abattoir—no wonder there are complaints by the S.P.C.A. "Those who eat meat do not realize that it is not invariably at the first blow of the poleax——" etc. Falling down on their knees and bleeding, looking at man with surprise—that look ought to be enough to destroy the human race. *Lex talionis.* Cruelty is inevitable—all that one can possibly do is to minimize it. We could live on nuts and vegetables—but I go right on eating beefsteaks just the same . . . The consciousness, though, of a lost kitten—what an extraordinary thing it must be. I suppose it's exactly like ours, except that it can't be partly linguistic—probably almost wholly visual, a kaleidoscopic series of pictures. Memory? Hm. Not so easy. Perhaps in that case all it really felt was the terrifying unfamiliarity, strangeness, and of course the discomfort. It would be sentimental to ascribe any more than that—to think of it as being as aware as I was, thinking in bed about it, of the wildness of the night, the wind, the strange shutters banging on strange walls of strange houses, the torn puddles under lamplight, the deluge of driven rain rattling against windows, solid water sousing down from eaves. Yes, I remember how sharply and dreadfully I visualized it—seeing the black street blattering with water, a green shutter hanging from one hinge—and refusing (shutting my eyes) to visualize the kitten as somewhere *out in it*—damned cowardice, sentimental cowardice! . . . I remember getting out of bed early in the morning and tiptoeing down to the back door to let in the maltese. The time my father scolded me for it. "Don't ever do it again, understand! . . . I thought it was some-

one who had broken into the house—a thief—and I very nearly shot you
. . . Next time, I *will* shoot you!" . . . Perhaps *that's* the source—that
extraordinary cruelty both to the kitten and to me. I can't remember what
I felt about it at the time—but it must have been appalling. That's the
sort of thing, in one's childhood, that's "part of one's experience of the
world"—the discovery of the sort of nightmare into which we are born.
MISERY. A voice cried sleep no more. There's one did swear in his sleep, and
one cried Murder. Murder equals *redrum*. That's poetic justice. I waste a
lot of time in logolatry. I am a verbalist, Cynthia—a tinkling symbolist.
I am the founder and leader of the new school of literature—The Em-
blemists. I wear a wide black hat, a dirty shirt, boots with spurs, and shave
once a month. Traces of egg can be seen at the corners of my mouth.
I am hollow-cheeked, exophthalmic, prognathous: I express my views at
any and all times, savagely, and with a conscious minimum of tact. I glory
in my dirtiness—I am a Buddhist—I look at you with sleepy cynicism to
prove it—utterly indifferent to the needs of the body. Nevertheless, I eat
heartily, and I make no bones about the tiresome necessities of sex. I am,
into the bargain, slightly mad. I have persecution mania. They try to
ignore me—they slander me—they suppress mention of me—they whisper
about me and laugh. Insults are heaped upon me, but I stride on, magnificent, a genius manifest; the winds of my poems whirl them about and
make them whimper. Ha ha! That last phrase, Cynthia—would you believe it?—was actually used about me by a famous poet in an interview—
something I had said annoyed him. "The winds of my poems . . . make
him whimper,"—that's what he said. That reminds me of an article I saw
once—in the New York *Nation*, was it?—called "*Wind in Tennyson*."
Perfectly serious! Isn't it incredible, the singular things people will do . . .
I do them myself . . . Yes . . . From time to time . . . I am a poet of
the Greenwich Village school—slightly eccentric, but really quite commonplace. I make a point of never sleeping more than once with the same
woman. Hilda J—? Yes. Sophie S—? Yes. Irma R—? Yes. Madeline T—?
Yes. And Irma's sister, too. And her seven cousins from Utica. And every
actress in the Jack-in-the-box Theater. Typists, poetesses, dancers, reciters,
fiddlers, and organists. I have a particular passion for organists. You can see
me any noontime at that charming little café in Sixth Avenue—you know
the one. I look pale and bored. I carry yellow gloves and a stick, and my
utter indifference to everything around me convinces you that I am distinguished. I can tell you all the secrets of all these people. That girl in the
corner? Takes morphia. For ten years has been writing a novel, which nobody has seen. Smokes, drinks, swears, twice attempted suicide. M—, the
dancer, gave her an "an unmentionable disease" . . . That other little
girl, dark and pale, with one eye higher than the other? A hanger-on—
the hetaira type. A nice girl, nevertheless, and once or twice has really
fallen in love. No moral sense whatever—a rotten family in Flatbush. She
is hard up most of the time—on the one occasion when I slept with her
I found it necessary (or charitable) to give her a pair of my B.V.D.'s . . .
I am an unsuccessful artist, wandering from one city to another: New York,
Chicago, Boston. Everywhere I carry with me a portfolio of my sketches,
drawings, etchings, color washes, pastels. I show them to people on trains.

I show them to people in restaurants, or on park benches. I have a large pale head with shiny sleek yellow hair and the yellow stubble on my cheeks and chin glistens in the sunlight. Once I grew a beard—but although I adopt the pose of indifference to public opinion, I must admit that the jokes of small boys, and the more violent comments of roughs, finally led me to shave it off. "Look at the Bowery Jesus!" they cried: "Pipe the Christ!" . . . One critic referred to me as "that immoral and hypocritical *fin de siécle* Jesus" . . . In Chicago, I ran a private dance hall. In Boston, I conducted a tea shop and edited a little magazine. In New York, I have sold cigars, dictionaries, soap and fountain pens. In St. Louis, I nearly died of flu. When Hurwitz, the poet, came to see me I was lying under a sheet, like a corpse. "Why don't you take your shoes off?" he said, seeing my feet which protruded. "They *are* off," I said. It was only that I hadn't washed them for some time. I practice a saintly contempt for the physical . . . Yes . . . I am all these. A little flower of the slime . . . For a time, I was X, the novelist, the dabbler in black arts, alchemy, hashish, and all known perversions. How fearfully wicked I was! Women shuddered when I was pointed out to them: when I touched them, they fainted. I collected slippers—a hundred and sixty-three. The fifty-seven varieties were child's play to me, and the sixty-nine, and the one thousand. You know that poem of Whitman's—something about "bussing my body all over with soft balsamic busses"? That's me—the omnibus. In my rooms, with a few expensively dressed women who considered themselves New York's most refined, I celebrated The Black Mass. One of these women, I discovered, was a cynomaniac . . . Several women have supported me . . . While the stenographer was paying my bills, I was absorbed in a passion for an Italian *castrato* . . . You hear me, Cynthia? . . . Darling William! You do not deceive me for a minute—not for a minute. I see through all this absurd pretense of naughtiness!—I see the dear frightened, fugitive little saint you are!—Ah, Cynthia, I knew I could trust you to understand me! I knew it, I knew it!—Come, William, it is spring in New England, and we will wander through fields of Quaker Ladies. Don't you adore the pale-blue Quaker Ladies?—Yes, yes, Cynthia! Four petals they have, and sometimes they are blue, but sometimes ash color!—Come, darling William, and we will romp among them joyfully. We will climb birches. We will discover the purple-banded Jack-in-the-pulpit, hiding in the snaky swamp. We will tease the painted turtle, and give flies to the high-backed wood tortoise. —Yes yes yes. They sun themselves on stones. Plop, and they are gone into the water.—And the tree toads, William! Their ethereal jingling at twilight in the water meadows! Their exquisite little whisper bells!—Ah! the tintinnabulation of the toads! Poe wrote a poem about them.—How melancholy your New England is, William! One misses the hand of man. Deserted, forlorn, shapeless—but beautiful, wildly beautiful. I could cry when I see it. It fills me with nostalgia . . . A poor thing but mine own, Cynthia. These gray-lichened pasture rocks—I created them out of my tears. Out of my bitter heart grew these sumacs with blood-colored bloom. Out of my afflicted flesh came these white, white birches. Nothing of me but doth change into something rich and strange.—And those huge desolate frost-scarred mountains, the white and the green, lightning-riven,

scree-stripped, ravaged by hail and fire—ah, William, my dearest, what a
terrible weight upon the soul are they! . . . *My* burden, Cynthia—the
burden of my thought . . . *Aaaaahhh-oo-oo-oo* . . . *aaaahhh-oo-oo-oo-
oooo* . . . MISERY . . . Damn that child, why doesn't it go to sleep. Or
damn its mother, anyway. Women are so extraordinarily unperceptive. All
nonsense, this theory that the perceptions of women are acuter than men's
—or intuitions. No. I've never met one with perceptions as quick as mine—
I can skate rings around them. You hear me, vain, intellectual, snobbish
Cynthia?—To me, William, you would yield in this—to me alone. So
sensitive am I to impressions, that . . . that . . . that . . . that . . .
Quack . . . *quack* . . . And you beside me, quacking in the wood. For
God's sake, hold your tongue and let me love . . . The sagacious eye of
the duck—something of that in Helen. And how she loved to quack. And
how she loved to sprawl ungainly and kick her heels in the air and laugh
and fling her slippers about and make absurd, hideous faces! Too young—
it was merely the joy of release, rebellion, that she was experiencing—she
was, at the moment, incapable of love. Listen, chaste Cynthia! And I will
tell you . . . tell you . . . Speak fearlessly, William, as you always do—
I am looking at you with wide deep eyes of understanding. I see the pebbles
at the bottom of your soul.—Yes, Pyrrha's pebbles. Arranged in pairs. Rose
quartz, white quartz, gneiss. Rose quartz, white quartz, gneiss. And did
you see that little trout hiding among them? That was my very me. My
little trout soul . . . But I was going to tell you, Cynthia—tell you——
Wait, dearest—first let us find some quiet little backwater of the Cher.
There! the very thing. Under that low-hanging willow, to which we can
fasten our punt. Now we cannot be seen or heard. Oxford two miles away
—Lady Tirrell, my dear, dear friend, unsuspecting. Arrange the cushion
under my head. Is my dress pulled down properly? Put the bottles in the
shade to keep cool, or hang them in the water. I bought this dress especially for the occasion, so that none of my friends on the river would
recognize me. All the castles of England, Scotland, Ireland and Wales in
the pattern. Here is Dover. Here is Harlech. Bodiam there, and there, on
my left knee, Kenilworth. Why *will* these stupid people bring their
wretched phonographs? So vulgar, so very vulgar . . . *Aaaaahhhh-oo-oo-
oo-ooo* . . . I was going to tell you, Cynthia, of one night with Helen
Shafter. Would you like to hear it?—Is it something I *ought* to hear?—
Certainly. Why not? I believe in absolute frankness between the sexes—
don't you? Tooth brushes, sponges, cascara—everything. Our comings in
and our goings forth. Our sittings down and our standings up. One egg or
two. Linen changed once a week—twice a week—four times a week—
daily. The matutinal dose of salts. The nocturnal suppository. The applica-
tion of lip salves, clouds of powder, rouge, and deodorizers. The tweezers
forextracting superfluous eyebrows—henna and orange-sticks for the nails.
The stale sweetness of the clothes cupboard. All . . . Then, William, it is
my painful duty to inform the police that you are a *voyeur*. Need I remind you of certain episodes of this character in your childhood—adolescence—youth—and early manhood? There was that time in . . . But this,
Cynthia, has a kind of beauty!—Beauty, smutbird? Beauty? Beauty is that
lascivious life of yours? No—it's quite impossible. Quite.—But I assure you!

I go down on my knees! I swear to God! I kiss the Bible, the Koran, and the Wisdom of Lao Tzü. This experience, although sensual and sexual in origin and fundamentals, nevertheless had a certain beauty. I swear it had, Cynthia! Listen, and you will see! You will be moved by it, I'm sure!—Poor Little William—I recognize in you this imperative impulse to confess—it is not for nothing that I go to confession myself and tell the holy father of my little white sins. But are you sure I am the proper repository for this secret?—Cynthia! Orbèd maiden with white fire laden! Moondaughter, snow-cold and pure, but fiery at heart! It is from you alone that my absolution can come. I will tell you—But not so fast, William! This is Sunday, and I have tickets for the Zoo. Don't you adore the Zoo—simply adore it? The toucans. The pelicans. The ring-tailed tallula-bird. The whiffenpoof. The tigers, miaowing, and the lions reverberating, rimbombinando. The polar bear—trying to lift from the wintry water, with hooked claws, a pane of ice. The elephants, swaying from one rubber foot to the other, swinging their trunks, and lifting their teakettle spouts for peanuts. And the little baboons and monkeys, so ingeniously and ingenuously obscene!—te hee!—Oh yes yes yes, Cynthia! I saw a madonna and child, once, swinging in a little trapeze! The mother was searching intensely . . . *Aaaahhhh* . . . *oo-oo-oo-oo-oo* . . . This is really passing endurance. It shouldn't be allowed on a ship. Steward, take this child and throw it overboard. Push it head first through a porthole. Weight it with lead, or tie the anchor to it. Drape it with the star-spangled banner. Taps. The time the men in Company K, 4th Illinois, lent me a bugle and four bayonets—we paraded three times around the square. It was magnificent. The hot tropical sun on the asphalt. The trumpet flowers bugling on the graves, and Dr. Scott's terrapins scrambling in the tubs and bins. Then there was that terrifying green sea turtle with soft flat flappers flapping softly in a separate tub. The cook said they would have to build a fire behind it to make it put its head out for the ax. Turtle's eggs—soft, tough, puckered. They find them by thrusting a sharp stick into the hot sand—if it comes up stained, they dig . . . It must be the law of tetrahedral collapse that gives them that peculiar shape . . . Oh, that cartridge! I blush. I stole it—stole it from Private Davis's tent—after he had been so nice to me, too. Good God, how awful it was. It was Butch Gleason who suggested it—he said he always took money out of a cash register in his father's store. It must have been arranged. Sergeant Williams went out, and in a minute came back. I was leaning against the tent pole at the door. As he came in again, brushing against me, his large hand fell naturally (so I thought!) against my jacket, and he closed it on my pocket. Why, what's this? he said. O God, O God. Then they were all silent and ashamed—they wouldn't look at me. Why didn't you say you wanted one, Billy? That's no way to go about it, stealing from your best friends! . . . Here, take it! You can have it . . . I didn't want it, but I took it. I wanted to give it back to them—I wanted to explain everything—I wanted to cry, to wash the episode out of history with a vast torrent of tears. But I could say nothing. I crept home and put it on the mantelpiece in my room, above the toy battleship, and never touched it again . . . By George, how nice they were to me: that first day it was—I took them a big paper bag full of animal crackers, when they were just off the train, hungry. I believed them when they said they'd been living for months on nothing but tinned mule. Afterward I used to march into mess with them in the penitentiary yard—under a long wooden shed which had been built there, with long tables under it, tables of new pine. A tin cup, a tin plate, tin fork and spoon. *Soupy, soupy, soupy, without a single bean.* That heavenly melancholy nostalgic tune the bugler played when they marched along the shell road into the country—over and over . . . I was again given a bayonet and marched at the side, giving orders. Close up the ranks there! . . . Get me a coupla chinquapins, willya, Billy? . . . Then they were singing. *Good-by Dolly, I must leave you . . . Just tell her that I love her* . . . I wonder what place that was where they had their new camp. I got lost that time coming back from it—the conductor gave us transfers, but we didn't know what to do with them, when to transfer, and finally got off and walked. We walked miles through the Negro quarters in the dark. Mysterious lights. Noisy slatternly houses. Smells. That might be where the gang we were always fighting came from. Gang fights with stones. Sling shots. Pluffers, pluffing chinaberries. I cut down an elderbush in the park to make one . . . Sneaky Williams it was who saw me cutting down a young cedar to make a bow and arrow and took me home by my sleeve, my feet barely touching the ground . . . I thought I was being arrested . . . Ah, that delicious dense little grove of saplings with a hut in the middle! What was it that made it seem so wonderful? It was dark, gloomy, little leaf-mold paths wound here and there intersecting, twigs snapped. There was something Virgilian—I remember thinking about it four years later when I began reading Virgil. *Et vox in faucibus haesit.* It must have been the sacred terror. I can remember the time when I hadn't yet been into it. That day, when, after being ill for two months, I went out for the first time—my mother sat on the bench near it, and I made little houses out of dry twigs in the grass. The only moment at which I can *see* her—she sits there, absent-minded in the sun, smiling a little, not seeing the path and the cactus bed at which she appears to be looking. The penitentiary walls were behind us—the tall barred windows, behind one of which I saw a man looking down at us. He was moving his arms up along the bars high above his head. And the Sacred Grove was near us, and the red brick vaults, and the table tombs of white stone . . . Are you watching me, Cynthia? Surely I was harmless enough on that day? Surely you like my mother sitting there with her parasol? And isn't it nice of me to remember it all so clearly, after a quarter of a century? . . . O God, that swooning sensation, anguish that contracts the belly and travels slowly down the body . . . MISERY . . . This is what it is to be in love. Unmitigated suffering. The most all-poisoning of all illnesses. And nevertheless, it's the chief motive of all art—we return to our vomit. No, no, that's not fair. It has beauty! . . . Think of the extraordinary way in which it changes, suddenly, the whole coarse texture of the universe!—I remember, when I first fell in love, how I used to want to touch everything with my hands. Stone walls. Bark of trees. Bits of metal. Glass. Woolen clothes. All of them had suddenly become exquisite, all of them responded. And when I met you, Cynthia . . . But there's no concealing the suffering it has brought, that frightful and

inescapable and unwearying consciousness of the unattainable. The soul
aching every moment, every hour, with sharp brief paroxysms of intenser
pain: the eyes closing in vain, sleep vainly invited, dreams that concentrate
into their fantastic and feverish turmoil all the griefs of the whole life; and
the eyes opening again to the blindingly unforgotten sorrow—this is what
it is, this is what now returns to me in even greater virulence. The intolerable suffering entailed in trying to remember a half-recalled face! That
night at the Northwestern Hotel, when I had one nightmare after another
all night long, trying to find her . . . And then, when I went down to
breakfast in the morning, exhausted, and still in a kind of dream, all unsuspecting that she too had slept at the Northwestern, I found her, with
her aunt, alone in the breakfast room! What an extraordinary discovery that
was! She was lost, and she was found. The light, laughing "*Good morning!*"
The eggs being eaten in English eggcups! . . . And it still goes on. Her
face escapes me. Why should this be? It isn't really, of course, that it
escapes me any more than any other recollected sense impression. No.
Probably less. The trouble is precisely in the fact that one wants too
much of it—wants it too often, wears it out with staring, and not only that,
but one is also, in a way, trying to *revenge* one's self upon it. One seeks to
possess it—with a violence not thrust upon one's ordinary recollections—
simply because one has not been able to possess the reality. One evening it
is absurdly easy—I can't "turn it on" at any moment and luxuriate in it.
But the next morning it is gone; and no sleight of mind will give it back to
me. I try the chin, the mouth, the profile of the cheek, the eyes—all in
vain. The face is a complete blank. Perhaps one trace alone will be discoverable—I can see how, at that particular instant, when she found me
staring at her, she looked slowly down, lowering her eyelids, and with what
an extraordinary and baffling intensity of expression! There was pain in it,
there was annoyance, but there was also, from the dark of her unconsciousness—could I be wrong in thus analyzing it?—a frightful unhappiness
and desire, a relaxed and heartbroken desire, desire of the flesh, as old as
the world. This alone I can remember, often, when all other aspects of her
face have dislimned . . . Creek, creeky-creek, creeky . . . The Irish girl
moves from her left side to her right. Easy enough to remember *her* face—
because I don't feel any tension about it . . . Smith too. Or Silberstein—
that massive stone face! Bastile façade! Or Faubion. Ah! a pang. You see
that gleaming pang, Cynthia?—I see it, unfaithful one!—No, not unfaithful! Not unfaithful! I swear to God . . . Is fidelity an affair only of the
flesh? No—that's not what I meant to say. Not at all. It's very very complicated. It's absurd, this fetish of fidelity. Absurd and chimerical. It leads to
the worst hypocrisy in the world. It involves a lie about the nature of the
world, of God, of the human being; a misconception or falsification of the
mind and psyche. Ah, psyche from the regions which. I am not faithful—
and I am faithful. My feeling for Eunice will never change. Nor my feeling
for Helen. Nor my feeling for you. Nor my feeling for Fleshpot Faubion.
Why should it be considered an unfaithfulness, a betrayal, to love more
than one woman or more than one man? Nothing sillier could be conceived. It's preposterous. We love constantly, love everywhere. We love
in all sorts of degrees and ways. Can any one person or thing or place or

belief possess one's soul utterly? Impossible. It is true that when we "fall in love," experiencing that intense burning up of the entire being which now and then some unforeseen explosion of the unconscious brings to us, our one desire is to possess and be possessed by the one object. But this is largely, or to some extent, an illusion—it's an illusion, I mean, to suppose that this will completely satisfy. An illusion, Cynthia! Even had I been destined—had we been destined—had I succeeded—had I not too horribly blundered—had I not lost every brief and paralyzing opportunity and at every such turn shown myself to be a fool and a coward—even so, even had I possessed you as madly as in imagination I have possessed you—you would not wholly have absorbed me. No. There would have been tracts of my soul which would never have owned your sovereignty—Saharas and Gobis of rebellious waste; swarming Yucatans from whose poisonous rank depths derision would be screamed at you and fragrances poured at you in a profusion of insult, flagrant and drunken; Arctics of inenarrable ice; and the sea everywhere, the unvintagable sea, many-laughing. Do you listen, Moonwhite?—I hate you and despise you, lizard!—I am walking in Kensington Gardens, Moonwhite, telling you of these things. The man wades into the Round Pond with a net to catch his toy steam yacht. Nurse-maids pullulate. Would it shock you to know that I could love even a nursemaid? Is there anything strange or reprehensible in that? For that matter, I did, once, fall in love (mildly) with a lady's maid. Her name? Mary Kimberlin. Age? Twenty-four. Where did we meet? In Hyde Park, where she was taking the Pom for a walk . . . Afterwards she married. I liked her, and I still like her . . . Did Helen Shafter interfere with my fondness for Eunice? Not in the slightest!—You felt guilty about it, William! You felt guilty, you were furtive, you concealed it, and you were in constant terror that you would be discovered. You never met her with-out experiencing a sense of wrongdoing, you never returned from a meeting with her to your Eunice without a sense of sin, a sadness, a burden of duplicity, that you found intolerable and crippling. Isn't that true? . . . That is true, Cynthia. True. True. Oh, so frightfully true. And yet it ought not to be true . . . MISERY . . . I admit the sense of evil which permeates that sort of adventure, the sense of treason and infidelity; but I affirm again that it is a sin against the holy ghost to bring up humans in such a way that they will inevitably feel it. It's hideously wrong! It's criminal! It is *not* an infidelity for me to love Eunice and Helen at the same time! It is not! . . . No man can serve both God and Mammon, William.—The distinction is utterly false! If I find something precious in Helen to adore, and at the same moment find something equally precious in Eunice to love, and if both of them love me—then what academic puritanism or pedantic pietistic folly can that be which would pronounce it wrong? NO! It is *not* wrong. It is only that we are taught to believe it so that makes it appear so. It is true that I was furtive, that I concealed from Eunice my knowledge of Helen—but why? Only because I wanted to spare Eunice,— who perhaps believed (though I never tried to make her do so) that she possessed me wholly,—the pain of disillusionment, the pain of jealousy. Good God, how much I would have preferred to be frank! I hated the necessity for concealment . . . It is only the necessity for concealment which introduces ugliness; the thing itself is no less, and often more, beautiful than the rest of daily life. *Honi soit qui mal y pense* . . . No, William! You are not being honest with me. You admit that as things *are* constituted, as society *does* view it, these furtive and clandestine love affairs are ugly. What defense have you, then, for deliberately seeking the ugly? I can see to the bottom of your soul, William, I know everything in your past, and knowing that, I see everything that will be in your future. All. I can see the way, whenever you go out into the streets, or ride in buses or trains, or go to a concert,—in fact everywhere and at all times—you look greedily about you for a pretty woman, you devour them with your eyes, you move closer to them in order to touch them as if accidentally, you lean backward to touch them, you luxuriate in every curve of mouth and throat and shoulder, you step back (as if politely) to permit them to get into the bus first in order that you may see their legs as far as the knee or even a little farther. You note, as you walk behind them in a crowd, the way their shoulders move as they walk, the curved forward thrust of the thigh, the slight subtle oscillation of the hips, the strength of the gait, and the sweet straightness and resilence of the leg-stroke as observed from behind. You gauge, through their clothes, the proportion of torso to legs, the breadth of waist. You never tire of speculation as to the precise position and dimensions of the breasts; watching a woman's every slightest motion in the hope that by leaning this way or that, drawing closer her jacket against her body or relaxing it, she will betray to you the secrets of her body. Confess! Kiss the book and sign your name! You are indicted for erotomania! . . . Pity me, Cynthia! I will confess everything if only you will believe that never, *never*, NEVER, was this my attitude toward you. I would have given everything to have been able to wipe out my entire past. My recollections of Eunice, and Helen, and Mary gave me nothing but pain: —and all the countless minor episodes, of the sort you have been describing, constituted for me an inferno from which I seemed never destined to escape. Yes. Horrible. To come to the gateway in the rain of fire and looking through it to see the slopes of Purgatory; to guess, beyond, the Paradise; to see you as the gracious wisdom who might guide me thither; and then to know that LAW would not permit, and that in the Inferno must be my abode forever!—Do not think this is merely picturesque or eloquent, Cynthia. No. What I am approaching is a profound psychological truth. It is my own nature, my character as patiently wrought by my character, as the snail builds its house, from which I cannot move. *Why this is hell, nor am I out of it.* Do you remember what I wrote to you when you had gone to France? A silly letter, to be sure. Overeloquent, overliterary, sobbingly self-conscious. I told you that I had decided, finally, to go back to America. I had failed with you—to tell you that I adored you was out of the question. But my agile subconscious did the trick. "Do you think," I said, referring to your description of poppies in Brittany, "that I don't know a poppy when I see it!" Fatuous! Could anything have been in worse taste? Impossible. My double entendre, of course, is quite clear. The poppy is Europe, and also Cynthia. I was abandoning the poppy not because I failed to appreciate it, but because I recognized my own inferiority. It was my Sabachthani . . . *Tin-tin-tin.* Half past one. Good God. Try counting again, shutting my eyes more lightly, breathing through my nose. Hot in here. *Ten—ten —double ten—forty-five and fifteen. Um-ber-ella—Cinder-rella*—TWIST. What the devil could that have come from? A little girl bouncing a red ball as she said it. Lovely things little girls are—their extraordinary innocence, candor, transparency, charm. Grace. Something light and beautiful in women after all, in spite of their boringness and curious mental and emotional limitations. Toys. Nice to overhear them talking together and laughing in a garden. Nuns in a convent garden. Or singing. How beautiful they are when they sing! That girl, with scarlet-flushed cheeks, singing *Morgen*, waiting for the beautiful melody as given first by the piano to reach the downward curve, and then coming in so deeply and sorrowfully with the slow rich voice. O God, O God that strange mixture of the soaring melody, so perfect in its pure algebra, and the sad, persistent meditative voice— there were tears in her eyes when she finished, and she had to turn away. Then the piano melody, finishing delicately and ethereally by itself . . . O God, if I could only get that sort of effect in a play—not melodramatically, or with stained-glass windows and paper snow, but naturally and simply by that superb use of the counterpoint of feeling and thought . . . Extraordinary sorrow in that song. That queer feeling that comes over me when something moves me too much—a kind of ache that seems to begin in the upper part of the mouth and throat, and yet it isn't an ache so much as an unhappy consciousness which seems to be localized there, and then to spread downward through the whole aching body, a slowly flowering sort of echo in a hollow darkness, opening out with painful tentacles . . . MISERY . . . *Now the red rim of sight discovers* . . . No . . . *Where the red rim of life discovers* . . . no, sight, is better, suggesting . . . *Where the rid rim of sight discovers . . . The void that swarms with shapes of death . . . And the departing spirit hovers . . . Batlike above the failing breath* . . . Is it good or is it bad . . . Impossible to say. Nonsense. One more of the "*Where the . . . There the*" type of lyric. Give it up NOW . . . Dante would come into the next verse . . . How lovely she was, standing there under the dim lamp, elbows behind her, laughing, saying, "*I'm going to be married*"! . . . Lost. Lost forever. That afternoon at the concert, if I had only . . . It would have been so simple . . . Or walking back from those absurd dancers; over Waterloo Bridge . . . "You know, I simply adore you!" . . . But it was too soon—it really *was* too soon . . . It's never too soon . . . But I *thought* it was too soon . . . Is it really gone? that opportunity? Good heavens how often I re-enact all those scenes—impossible to persuade myself that they can be finished! The after-sense is so vivid. I was always expecting to meet her in the street— in the most unlikely places. Always looked at everybody in the street, or bus, or theater, expecting to see her. I even thought she might be on the ship again,—when I sailed back to America! And on Fifth Avenue, or at Aeolian Hall, or in the Museum—constantly feeling that I was on the point of encountering her, and that she was just round the corner, or behind the Rodin. She would be sure to be standing before the Manet parrot! . . . Why is it? . . . The frightfully vivid experience, with its appalling after-sense, destroys one's reason, one's belief in time and space. Over and over again putting myself into the middle of that concert—the

Bach concerto—sitting there in the Wigmore Hall. It was that morning just before lunch, while I was taking off one suit and putting on the other (which *reeked* of petrol, just back from the tailor) that the maid said, "Two ladies to see you, sir . . ." "Will you show them up?" . . . Who could it be? Americans? I was going to tea with Cynthia that afternoon—therefore it couldn't possibly be she . . . I hurried dressing . . . It was she, and that artist's daughter . . . "What a lovely room!" she cried, "and how extraordinary to find it in *this* street!" . . . The concert suggested . . . Delighted, but frightened—the complications . . . this other girl tall, grave, rather lovely. Ought I to ask them to lunch? No. Perhaps that had been their idea? Good heavens—I wonder! Anyway, I didn't . . . "Meet in the entrance at . . ." . . . then they were gone, and I discovered my awful hasty unkemptness—hair unbrushed, coat collar kinked up, buttons unbuttoned . . . and at the concert . . . smelling abominably of petrol, sitting beside divine Cynthia and listening to the pure rapture of that music! Cynthia so near me—her heart within eighteen inches of mine, her sleeve touching my sleeve—so that I could feel the rhythm of her breathing—her dress once or twice brushing my foot. O God o God o God o God o God . . . Squirming. Twisting and stretching my wrists. The crucified Christ by Perugino in that chapel in Florence—the wrists quivering, squirming like a spitted worm, worming like an earthworm on a hook, the worm that convulsively embraces the hook, the worm that squirms, the worm that turns . . . Kwannon, Goddess of mercy, serene and beneficent idol, Cathayan peace! Smile down upon me, reach thy golden hands to me with the golden fingers, touch my eyes that they may see not, touch my mind that it may remember not, touch my heart and make it holy. Take away from me my gross and mischievous and ailing body, let me lie down before thee and sleep forever. Let all be forgiven me, who forgive all; let all love me, and have compassion for me, who love all; let all sorrow cease when my sorrow ceases, suffering with my suffering, and life with my life. . . . One three five seven nine eleven thirteen fifteen seventeen nineteen twenty-one twenty-three twenty-five twenty-seven 1 3 5 7 9 11 13 15 17 19 21 23 25 27 29 31 33 35 37 39 41 43 47 49 51 53 55 57. One five nine thirteen seventeen twenty-one twenty-five. Too complicated —keeps me awake. *Child Roland to the dark tower came.* The dead sheep lying under the birch tree, in the wood, which the dead leaves swept away in a neat circle by the last struggle. The dead horse in the cellar of the burned stable. The cat with one red eye, blood-filled. The old woman lying against the wall, staring, indifferent, breathing slowly, while blood ran slowly from the corner of her mouth. Dying in the street, strangers walking around her in a ring, and she as inattentive as a dying animal. Her pocketbook, muddy, beside her on the sidewalk. B said afterward he had heard her "scream like a siren" when the accident occurred . . . *Dying, Egypt, dying* . . . Crowds walking past while she dies, cars and buses honking, taxis ticking, horses clop-clopping, children running and yelling, "Susie—wait for ME!" the policeman's whistle blowing, the church clock striking, the newsboys running with the EXTRY EXTREE and sliding with nailed boots on the asphalt, ferries hooting on the river, "she's dying, poor Thinggggg," "Dyinggggg." "Susie wait for meeeee." Suuuw-oo-or-nhoreeeeeee . . . Pax. Pox vobiscum. Dead. One hundred and thirty-two pounds. Five feet four and three-quarters. Torn flannel showing. The blood had run clear across the sidewalk in four separate rivulets . . . *When the red rim of sight discovers* . . . *The void that swarms with shapes of death . . . and the departing batsoul hovers . . . Above the fountain's falling breath* . . . Rotten. But there is, off in the void there, an idea, a sort of ghostly fountain, tossing up and dying down again . . . *Green light* . . . What goes on in the brain just before and just after death? Possible that the brain may live for a time. We may go on thinking, remembering, in a confused sort of way—a jumble of sensations. Or rarefied—a tiny gnat song of consciousness . . . Dr. Kiernan stated that when called in at 7.13 there was still a spark of life . . . she looked alive but extraordinarily still. Eyes shut. Mouth wide open, fixed in the act of screaming, but silent. Terror! . . . Perhaps she knew I was there, looking at her, and then walking softly, quickly, away . . . Strange, if that were true—but no stranger than anything else. "Yes, William, I am dead. But I know you are there. Do you want to know if an accident has occurred? Yes. A dreadful accident has occurred. I am quite all right, now. Run and wake Nanny. Shut the door into the nursery. Wind the clocks on Sunday morning. And say good-by to this house and world forever . . ." Misery . . . My bonnie has too-bur-kulosis . . . My bonnie has only one lung . . . My bonnie has too-bur-culosis . . . Hok Hoik! . . . My bonnie will surely die young . . . Be-ring ba-a-ack. Be-ring ba-a-ack. Oh, bring back my bonnie to me . . . I remembered how for a long time afterwards I couldn't hear a door squeak on its hinges without hearing her scream. Terror! I remember her face vividly. Very like mine, same forehead, same mouth. My bonnie lies over the ocean—she used to sing it to me, and what was that other one? that she said used to be sung in the Civil War . . . *Shine I shine I shine— shine like the evening star* . . . *Shoo fly, don't bother me* . . . *Shoo fly, don't bother me* . . . *for I belong to Company G* . . . I remember her singing and laughing and singing again: *If you don't wear a collar and a tie* . . . *then you won't go to heaven when you die* . . . *If you don't wear ruffles on your drawers* . . . *then you won't go to heaven when you die* . . . Negro spirituals. It was Krehbiel, wasn't it, that wrote that book? *Let mah—pee-pul—go* . . . And those stories the Negro nurses used to tell us in the mornings while they dressed us. The crane with the cork. What a story to tell children. It was Brer Rabbit who pulled out the cork. At the party, it was—and it created a scandal . . . Like Smith's story of the Starcroft Inn. Heavens, how superb—the real Chaucerian flavor. Pop-eyed Popper Smith watching eagerly from the door, with all the other men, while all the women fled from the ball room . . . She lying on her back there, laughing hysterically, drunk, with her skirt up, fallen down and unable to stand, screeching with laughter, and the jazz orchestra of niggers going suddenly cuckoo with excitement—drums banged, trombones yelling, saxophones bubbling the Himmelfahrt, the niggers themselves screaming and sobbing . . . Goodness gracious gawdness Agnes. Agnes Day equals Agnus Dei . . . "No-no!—too many ladies here," said Smith. Yes, there it is—that whole side of a man's life that must be concealed. So many things we conceal even from other men . . . We all have our little p-p-p-p-peculiarities which we don't mention; and which nevertheless are of great importance to us. Canyon yodling. Pearl diving. Muff barking. Palpation. The dance of the seven unveils. Arrangements of mirrors. That girl at the casino, when I was with Julian—there was a scuffle in the row ahead of us and the young man was taken out. "I didn't mind when he give me the leg, but when he give me the"—I wonder if he was arrested or what. . . . That time visiting with Julian for the weekend—at Plymouth it was—the young school-marm who was taking her Easter holiday alone at that little deserted hotel. She sat with her knees, oh, so carelessly crossed —black silk stockings. The misty wisty wistful yearning expression in Julian's eyes—he sat on the table edge and talked to her in a peculiar soft way, gentle, gently laughing, gently suggestive, gently agreeing and gently echoing: turtledoves, *Cooo—coooo*. A problem: both of us attracted to her, but neither of us admitted it or wanted to say to the other—"You go on to Plymouth—I'll stay here . . ." At breakfast in the morning I tried to touch her knee with mine under the table. But I wasn't bold enough. More wistful conversation, and then we motored away, both of us sulky for the rest of the day . . . Wonderful charm such incomplete adventures have . . . They take on gradually a special beauty . . . *Abbozzi* . . . Life is full of them . . . Familiarity breeds contempt. Sometimes they are too painful, though. C. I. E., on the train, for example. How frightfully unhappy that made me, and still, when I think about it, makes me . . . I got into the train and she was sitting opposite me, with her dress-suitcase on the seat beside her . . . C. I. E. were the initials on it— a fiber suitcase. In the rack above her was a violin. Small, she was, in a soft gray coat; with a mauve or lilac-colored hat—I could see white stitches in it. An artificial flower on her coat lapel. I couldn't decide at first whether I thought she was pretty or not—but I couldn't take my eyes off her. She was reading *Tilly of Bloomsbury*—I watched her blue eyes, small and of a sweet roundness, traveling along the lines. Now and then she smiled. Her mouth—it seemed to me extraordinary. I can't visualize it, but I thought it like a Michelangelo mouth—great richness and subtlety of modeling, voluptuous and yet suggestive of strength and curtness; the color rather peculiar, a pale coral. Freckled a little, with dark golden hair showing in circular plaits over her ears. Her eyebrows darker than her hair, and richly curved, softly curved, over shy eyes . . . She occasionally looked up obliquely at the woman who sat beside me—or looked at the woman's gay-striped stockings when she put her feet on the edge of the seat opposite. She avoided my eyes—if she found me looking at her, she slid her eyes rapidly across me and looked out at the fields, and the bare trees which had been etherealized by a beautiful frost, trees like white smoke. It was cold. The other window open. Had to keep my gloves on. Shy about taking off my gloves to unbutton my gray coat and fish out my handkerchief: she covertly watched me. Then I thought of that theater program in my pocket —so I read it to impress her with our similarity in tastes. Sorry I hadn't bought *The Nation* instead of *John o' London*. The cold wind whistling about our feet; she crossed her knees, and then drew them up under her, just touching the floor with the tip of the Cordova slipper, a slipper somewhat worn, but nice. Woolen gloves. Once—halfway, after an hour—she

looked at me—O God, what a look. Perplexed, shy, injured, reproachful.
"You shouldn't stare at me like that; I am a nice girl, intelligent and refined, sensitive. Nevertheless I perceive that we have something in common." Then she turned two pages at once. She read more rapidly, she
skipped. A station. Another station. Only an hour more. Clippity clop te
clap te clip te clap te cluckle, te WHEEEEEE. Tunnel! Shall I rise and shut
the other window? No: too shy. It might lead to a harmless and friendly
beginning to talk? No. In the dark (the dusty lamp burning dimly on the
ceiling) perhaps our feet would encounter? No. I uncrossed my knees and
crossed them the other way, away from the door and pointing toward her.
No . . . After she looked at me like that, in that desolated way, I turned
to the window, sorrowfully, apologetically, suffering, frowning. I'm sorry, I
wouldn't offend you for worlds. I too am gentle and refined . . . Then,
just that once, her foot slid scraping sharply forward and touched mine.
Should I look at her and appear conscious? No. Pay no attention. Out of
the corner of my eye observing, I saw that she showed no sign of confusion
or self-consciousness. She had withdrawn her foot instantly . . . We were
approaching London. She put *Tilly of Bloomsbury* into the suitcase—it
was neatly packed, full, covered with a transparent silk. No secrets disclosed. Would she get out at London Bridge? No—but the two old women
did. Now! What would happen? Her toe had touched twice, oh so faintly,
the cuff of my trouser-leg. Intentional? Probably not. Dare! . . . I dared
—I slid the right foot forward, resting a little more palpably in contact.
Not enough—it might appear accidental. Dare again! I dared again, as the
train started from Waterloo, with only five minutes to go. My right ankle
rested firmly and ecstatically against the side of the Cordova slipper. I
looked at her—devoured her—stared—but she kept her eyes averted, her
face suffused with—what? Unhappiness. Speak to her! But I was shy,
hungry, weak, cold, psychically out of joint. I had been desiring her too
long and too intensely, and though the words went round and round in
my head—Will you lunch with me?—I couldn't speak them. The Thames
covered with mist. We were sliding into the station, ankle and toe still pray-
ing to each other. Dare! The last chance! Dare! Say "May I help you with
your bags?" Hurry! A porter was at the door, with his red tie. I stood up,
trembling, to take my bag from the rack. I looked at her beseechingly, still
hoping for a miracle; but as I turned she leaned toward the opening door
and said in a low harassed voice, her dry lips barely moving, "Porter!" . . .
I got out and walked along the platform, walking slowly, so that she might
overtake me. How exquisite, small, graceful she was! The neat, precise,
energetic and charmingly girlish gait! She did not turn toward me—her
small chin was lowered humbly into the bright batik scarf. Gone. She was
gone forever. We were divorced, after a marriage—how divinely happy—
of two hours . . . MISERY . . . Why hadn't I said, "Will you have lunch
with me?" Why hadn't I said, "Need we separate like this?" Why hadn't
I said, "Do you like *Tilly?*" Or do you play? I'm passionately fond of
music myself. Do you know *Morgen?* by Strauss? or *Wiegenlied?* Do you
go to the Queen's Hall? Wigmore Hall? Have you heard Coates conduct?
Glorious, isn't he? Shall we lunch at Gatti's—or the Café Royal? . . .
Those side tables at Gatti's, with red plush sofas. The table legs so close

together that if two people sit on the sofa their knees must be contiguous. The music at the far end. That's where Mary and I went for supper when we came back from Banstead . . . It would have been so simple to say, "Won't you lunch with me? I should so much like it if you would!" We were so clearly "made" for each other. And especially now that Cynthia—it might have prevented that. Lost; gone into the jungle of London. I advertised three times in *The Times* Personal Column—there was no answer. I thought of employing a detective to try and trace her. Yes, I three times proposed in *The Times* that she should meet me at the platform gate, and each time waited for half an hour, wondering what we would say when we met . . . Where are you, C. I. E.? Are you in London? Am I destined someday to see you playing in a hotel orchestra, or in a cinema, playing with the spotlight on you, lighting your shyly downturned small and lovely face? . . . By that time you will have forgotten me. And as for me—Cynthia has intervened. I am on a ship in the Atlantic, passing the Grand Banks, with Cynthia. I am in love with Cynthia, miserably and humiliatingly in love. More intensely than I was with you? Who can say? Heaven knows I loved you with a blind intensity that made me unhappy for weeks after. But then, how much was my misery due to my feeling of having been so horribly and unforgivably inadequate? Inferiority complex . . . And so absurd, that I, who on a score of other occasions had . . . "picked up" . . . women here and there in two continents . . . should have sat in silence and allowed you to go out of my life—in spite of your so clearly and so desperately signaling to me. O God that with divine rightness . . . inestimable lightness . . . O God that with celestial brightness . . . merciful and benign Kuan Yin . . . O lamas riding on llamas and bearded ascetic Arhats hunched meditative on tigers. O Solomon, O Song of Songs and Singer of singers . . . I will never forgive myself, nor will she ever forgive me . . . She will say, over and over, "I met a man once, on a train from Folkestone" . . . C. I. E. The name—good Lord—might have been Cynthia . . . Do you hear me, Cynthia? . . . Hear you, tadpole . . . Forgive me! Absolve me! Let me bury my infant's face against you and weep! Like Father Smith, I am looking, looking everywhere, for my mother. Is it you, perhaps? I have thought often that it might be you. You remind me of her. Let me be your child, Cynthia! Take me to Kensington Gardens with you in the morning—carry my golliwog in your left hand, and let me clasp your right. Past the tea gardens. To the banks of the Serpentine, or the Ornamental Water . . . Who is it that has that theory of compulsory repetition. Freud, is it? . . . Orpheus. . . . Sequacious of the liar . . . I shall go mad someday. Yes. Etna will open, flaming and foisting, and I will be engulfed in my own volcano I can hear it, on still days, boiling and muttering. Mephitic vapors escape through cracks in rock. Red-hot lumps are flung up and fall back again—I have seen the livid light of them in my eyes.—And do you know, Cynthia, what form my dementia will take? . . . No—tell me, absurd one, poser! . . . I will weep. I will do nothing but weep. That is what I have always wanted to do —to weep. The sorrow of the world. I will sit and weep, day after day, remembering nothing save that the world was created in pain. The syphilitic family in the cobbled mud of Portobello Road. Goya. The lost kitten.

The crying child. The dog whose nose had been hurt, bleeding. The old
woman dying in the street, far, far from home. Lions weeping in cages and
dead men roaring in graves. Our father that weepest in heaven; and angels
with whimpering wings. Smith, walking among the stars looking for his
wife-mother. The Disciples waiting in vain for the miracle to happen. My
father, which art in earth. Billy, who was tied to the bedpost and beaten
across his naked back with eight thicknesses of rubber tubing because his
younger brother had told a lie about him. Μακάριοι οἱ πενθοῦντες ὅτι αὐτοὶ
παρακληθήσονται The dead sheep under the beech tree by the pond. The
numbed bee, crawling for the hundredth time up the windowpane, and
falling. The poet, who discovers, aged thirty-five, that he cannot write. The
woman who finds that her husband no longer loves her. The child who is
mocked at school for her stupidity. I will expiate the sin and sorrow of the
world for you, my brothers. You will be happy. I will give up all my selfish
ambitions and desires in order that I may help you. I am worthless—I am
nobody. Do not think of rewarding me. Anonymous, I will pass everywhere
like a spirit, freeing the imprisoned and assuaging the afflicted. The bee
I will catch in an empty matchbox and carry to Hymettus, releasing her
amid a paradise of heather and wild thyme. I will untie Billy from the
white iron bedpost and take him to see the circus. Elephants! Peanuts five
a bag! Speedy the high diver with a gunny sack over his head! The boxing
kangaroo! . . . For the syphilitic family, an immediate cure, money, and
a cottage in the country with a flower garden and a vegetable patch . . .
For the old woman who died in the street, believing in God and a future
life, the strangers walking around her in a ring will be cherubim and
seraphim, with rainbow wings, and angelic eyes of love. The throne of God
will be before her; and looking up she will see seated there—with Mary star
of the sea in a blue mantle at one side and Jesus in a fair robe of vermilion
at the other—not Jehovah the terrible, but her own father, with his watch
chain, his pipe, and his funny, flashing, spectacles! "Why, if this isn't my
little Blossom!" he will laugh . . . and she will cry for joy . . . I will find
the lost kitten and bring it back to a house even more glorious than that it
remembers. Saucers will gleam before every ruddy fireplace: there will be
fish tails; and there will be cream. Children will dart to and fro, pulling
after them deliciously enticing strings. Immortal mice of a divine odor will
play puss-in-the-corner, melodiously squeaking and scurrying. Moths undying will dance with her at dusk in the corners, and unhurt, sleep all night
in the cups of lilies . . . Smith, star-wandering, cigar in hand, will find his
mother. For the fly with torn wings, I will make new wings of an even
more Daedalian beauty. The clairvoyant I will deliver from his torment
of vatic dreams; and Goya, touched by my hands, will at last close his
eyes . . . The crying child will find his adored blue shawl . . . Hay-
Lawrence will recover the sight of his left eye, and his wife will no longer
sit alone by the fire reading letters three weeks old . . . From the whole
earth, as it rolls darkly through space around the sun, will come a sound
of singing . . . MISERY . . . And in order to accomplish this, Cynthia,
—how can I accomplish all this, you ask? Very simple. I will permit myself
to be crucified. My SELF. I will destroy my individuality. Like the destruction of the atom, this will carry in its train the explosion of all other selves.

I will show them the way. The Messiah. They will pursue me, mocking and jeering. They will crowd closer about me, stoning. And at this moment I will destroy my SELF out of love for all life—my personality will cease. I will become nothing but a consciousness of love, a consciousness without memory or foresight, without necessity or body, and without thought. I will show mankind the path by which they may return to God; and I will show God the path by which he may return to peace . . . Are you listening, Huntress? . . . Listening, madman! . . . Not mad, not mad—it is only the well-known doctrine of sublimation. Suicide of the unconscious. Nothing of it but doth change into something rich and strange. Recommended by all the best metaphysicians. Miss E. Z. Mark, of No. 8,765,432 Telepathy Alley, Chocorua, N.H., writes: "I suffered continually from ambitiousness, appetite, and reckless energy, until I tried sublimation . . . Now I do nothing but beam at the universe" . . . Used and praised by millions . . . Sublimation rules the nation . . . One three five seven nine eleven thirteen fifteen seventeen . . . Is it my heart or is it the engine? *Te thrum: te thrum.* Seems to me it's a little rougher. Creaking. Cynthia is asleep in the first cabin. I wonder what position she lies in and how she does her hair. Pigtails—one or two? Not pigtails? Clothes carefully arranged on a wicker chair. Pink-white-elastic. Mrs. Battiloro's middle-aged nightgowned body gently snoring and gulping. A crescendo, and then a strangling gasp, and the head turned, and silence, and the crescendo all over again. A Puritan. What is love to a Puritan? What does he make of the pleasures of the flesh? Shuts his eyes. A painful duty. Did you remember to wind the clock? . . . Oh, dear, I forgot to order the flour . . . The immaculate conception . . . Sublimation again . . . *Te thrum te thrum.* In my left ear my heart. Smoking too much. *Sua pipetta inseparabile.* Pressure on the eye makes a tree, one-sided, dark tamarack with downward claws, purpurate and murex. Tamurex. Tamarix. What was I thinking about, or was it a series of images simply, or a fragment of dream. Claws hanging from a tree. Claws paws clods pods. The purple locust claw. A green bright cataract of leaves. Tamaract! And a red fish leaps out and up! Gone. What a lovely thing. Now where did that come from I wonder. Ah Psyche from the regions whish. My little trout. Tree-trout, that swims and sings. Swings. Up from my cabin, my nightgown scarfed about me . . . fingered her placket. Coward Shakespeare. Her scarf blew away along the deck and I ran after it. The squall blew her skirt up as she went down the ladder. They laughed. In my left ear my heart *te thrum te thrum.* The Sea. Sea. Sea. Sea.

❴V

"It was Friday the thirteenth. I don't like Friday the thirteenth. We were all scared—every man on the ship. Waves coming right over the old tanker —they're low in the water you know—only about that high out of the water. You hear them going right over. Gosh, it's a terrible sound in the middle of the night when you're lying in your bunk. But no sleep that night. We were on our feet all night . . ."

"—is that so——"

"—is that so——"

"Friday the thirteenth. Who was it, Tom Lawson, wrote that book——"

"But the sound of the water on one of those iron tankers! Gee whiz, man, you think you're going down . . . It was a long trip, a long long trip—all the way from Tampico to New York, wallowing along in the old Gulf Stream day after day. Playing cards all day and half the night, new partners with every change of watch. Good God I got sick of the sight of a bloody card. And no smoking either—on the American tankers they let you, but not on the British, no sir."

". . . cockfighting—Havana . . ."

"Hello there, little Johnny Cagny! You looking for a fight, are you? You want to fight me, do you? Now don't you be climbing up on the back of that seat—you'll be getting a fall . . . There! Now you've been and gone and done it!"

"In Havana, sure. And all those places. Guatemala City, too, I've seen them."

"Long, you know, knives—little thin steel knives—fastened on to those what-you-call-'ems——"

"Spurs——"

"Yes, spurs . . . and one eye only he had, one little red burning eye."

"Yes, but the food's good on a tanker—better than this is, by God!"

". . . then she comes into the ring with a fine strapping black son-of-a-gun of a Tom cat. And he had a cock, of course, in his corner, holding it in his hands—and a beauty it was, too! And she says, 'I'll fight my puss against your cock,' she says, 'five dollars to the winner!' "

". . . ha ha ha ha . . ."

"What the hell's the matter with these hands?"

"It's the jinx."

"Ah, it's a great sight is a good cockfight. How they will fight! I saw one once in Mexico City. It was a fight to a finish in every sense of the word. Both of them covered with blood, getting groggier and groggier, falling down and staggering up again for more, finally one of them flopped over, dead. The other one stretched up his neck and gave a little rusty crack of a crow—and keeled over, dead too. That's the fighting spirit for you! You can't beat it . . ."

"I'll fight you! I'll fight you!"

"I tell your popper on you."

"No, you won't!"

"I will too! And the policeman, that fellow with the red face, will get you. He told me he was looking for you."

"Ah, he was not."

"They don't like little boys that come into smoking rooms. Those big fishes will get you—those fishes with great big mouths. They've had four little boys already this morning. They'd have been up again before this, only for the rain."

"Ah, they wouldn't."

"Here's the policeman now!"

"Sure—you look out for my badge!"

"No, he isn't either!"

"—a pair of sevens. Good little sevens! Come to mommer."

"Did you hear about that wild Irishman in the steerage?"

"No, what?"

"He came aboard blind to the world and put away whisky all the first night and all yesterday morning till he begun seein' things. I guess he was seein' every color of snake there is, from what they said. Then he beat up another feller so bad they had to put him in the ship hospital, at the back. Wild as a cockoo! Then a couple o' friends of this other chap beat *him* up so bad they had to put *him* in the hospital. And in the middle of the night he leap' out o' bed in a franzy and took all his clothes and tore 'em to smithereens and run out on deck and slung 'em all overboard. Well, now he's sobered up a little, and remembers that all the money he had, and his passport, and everything, was in the clothes he flung overboard . . . Too bad! He's got a wife and five kids in Brooklyn, and he had all his savin's with him to buy a farm in Ireland."

"—is that so!"

"Yeah. Will they let him in, I wonder. I hear they're passin' the hat fer 'im."

"For Gosh sake."

"Old Paddy over there is pretty near as bad. He's done nothing but souse since he come on. Whisky and a beer chaser. Them was the days, boys! Pawin' the rail with a blind foot! . . ."

"Was you speakin' to me?"

"No, sir."

"Yes you was too! . . . When you get through with that damn cigarette, come over here, and I'll fool you."

"What's that?"

"Come over here and I'll fool you! Write your name on this paper! I'm the immigration inspector."

"He's stewed to the eyeballs."

"You think I'm drunk? . . . I'll fool you . . . It's an awful thing to say—and I don't want to insult anyone that's present in this room—but what I'm telling you is facts and *figures!* There was an Irishman come to New York, and I knew him well. He went to stay with a Mrs. McCarty, who kept a boardin'-house. A widow, I think she was . . . And he was lookin' for a job. So we got him a job, over on Avenue A I think it was, where they was buildin' a buildin'. We got him a job screenin' sand . . . And when he come home at night, Mrs. McCarty says to him, 'Well Pat, what kind of a job you got?' and Pat says, 'Ah, I been foolin' the public all day! I been throwin' sand through a gate!'"

". . . ha ha ha ha . . ."

"Who drew number nine, please, in the sweepstakes? Did any gentleman here draw the NINE please in the sweepstakes? There was an error."

"Hell, I drew the eight."

"*I wonder—who's kissing—her now* . . . *I wonder—who's telling—her how——*"

"Did anyone see the sunrise this morning? It had a black mark on it like an arrow."

"If you saw any sunrise I'll eat my hat. Black mark on it like an arrow! Like a poached egg, you mean. Put up your ante."

"I *have* anted."

(How can there be any doubt about it? She looked right at me. "Do you know that lady?" I said to Purington. "That's Mrs. Battiloro, sister of A. B. Mandell, the novelist. She has just cut me. Walk around the deck with me again—I want to make sure that it was deliberate . . ." And it was. She came coolly toward me, talking with that tall fair girl—she looked at me coolly, still lightly talking—she shot me through with a blue eye. Why? It couldn't have been because of that business this morning, when I pretended not to see Cynthia and her friend? No. I'm sure they didn't guess that I saw them. My damned, absurd, diffidence. Of course it would have been awkward—I was so far away from them, there on the lower deck, and I would have had to shout, or wave a hand, or perform some other such horribly public action, and then go trotting, like a tractable little dog, to the foot of the companionway: to talk with them through the bars of my cage! No—it was a mistake; but I'm sure they didn't guess it. Why, then? Why? . . . I am blushing angrily and hotly at the recollection, while I keep a look-out through the open smoking-room window to see if she comes round by the sun parlor. Is it barely possible that her mother doesn't remember me, didn't get a good look at me last night on the dark deck? No. She cut me. It was a cool and conscious cut if there ever was one. She disapproves of me, and has always disapproved of me. Scheming for a "good" marriage! Cutting the throats of such outsiders as me! "*I know thee not, old man.*" Was there something I did or said last night? My overexcited greeting? And does it mean that Cynthia, too, will cut me? Of course. It's all been decided. It was talked over last night, and again this morning, with laughter—gay feminine laughter. My name looked for in vain on the passenger list—and the white-and-gold breakfast room scanned in vain. No Demarest to be seen. Where is Demarest, the laughing goldfish? He must be in the second cabin? But how odd! How funny! Now, Cynthia, take my advice, and *drop him at once.* He is not our sort. Those ridiculous letters he wrote to you last winter—and that awful book——)

"It isn't what you say, it's how you say it."

"Sure, when you say that, smile!"

"—a club. A little club, more or less. One little club."

"I don't believe I'll play, but I'll watch you, if you don't mind."

"What you doin', Susie? Where's Johnny Cagny?"

"I'm writing my name. This isn't as good as I *can* write . . . Say! Don't tear my paper!"

"You shouldn't be in the smoking room, Susie. It's too rough for you in here. And that little Johnny Cagny, he's too rough for you too."

"Jesus! Listen to that screw kicking out! R-*r-r-r-r-r-r!*"

"—and then I got to New York too late for the boat! Though if I hadn't stopped for a bath, and to go to the office for some money, I'd have been all right. But those damned agents told me four o'clock in the afternoon. Hell! And there's my wife, waiting for me all this time in Liverpool . . . Oh well, it's all in the day's work."

"That's right . . . I've missed plenty of trains, but never a——"

"—*perpendicular*——'

"—sick to death of them. Sixteen days on that damned tanker, and now *this* bloody thing——"

"—asleep. Are ye asleep, Paddy? Rocked in the bosom of the deep, deep, deep——"

"Ha ha ha."

"Half seas over. He'll *drink* his way to Ireland. It'll be a dry country by the time he gets there. *Oh Paddy dear and did ye hear the news that's goin' round*—Who's got anything better than a full house? Oh! Shandy-*gaff*."

"—told me about one trip he had, from Tampico to New Orleans, with some Mexican passengers. Indians, you know, those half-breeds. They had a *hell* of a time. Every time he turned his back, those damned Indians would light a fire on the decks! They're always making little fires, you know, —just for company, and to warm up a few old coffee grounds in a can. Well, on a tanker full of oil! Gee whiz, man! she'd go up so quick you'd never know what happened. All night they had to watch them——"

"—is that so——"

"—is that so——"

"Aztecs, I suppose those were. Those Aztecs were a wonderful people. Wonderful builders—all just as straight as a die, and according to the points of the compass, and carvings all over everything. They had a high state of civilization."

"That's all right, but they were heathen just the same. They sacrificed human beings to the sun."

"They thought Cortez was a reincarnated sun-god. That's how he got control over them with so small an army. Damned dirty shame, too. Still, the world has to be civilized."

"*Why* has it? . . . I don't believe we're a bit better than our so-called heathen ancestors."

"Ah-h-h-h what you talkin' about!"

"Well, look at Ireland, your own country, full of murders and burnings and treason and God knows what; and look at the Balkans; and look at the way we shoot down strikers, or burn niggers, or the whole bloody world going to war for nothing at all and all lying about it, every man jack of them, pretending there's something holy about it! Look at the way in England, when they launch a battleship, they have a red-faced Bishop there, or an Archbishop, to *consecrate* the bloody ship in the name of God for murder! *Civilized!* You make me sick. The world hasn't changed a hair for four thousand years."

"That's right, too!"

"Hear hear!"

"That's all very easy to say, but just the same there is some progress. Look at the toothbrush——"

"Ha ha—make the world safe for toothbrushes!"

"Porter! Bring me the car toothbrush please!"

"Yes sir, and when she come back there was a foot sticking out of every berth——"

"Ante, mister."

"—and when she whispered 'Sweetheart!' forty men answered with one voice. 'Come in, darling! here's your icky fing!' "

"Ha ha—that's a good old-timer."

"I—can sing—truly rural——"

"Then I was sent out scouting with a Dodge two-seater and a pocket full of cigars—throwing the bull, you know, you have to do it. Finding out what the other companies were up to. A sort of commercial spy, that's really what it is. I didn't know a thing about it, but I knew enough to bluff, and before they found me out I knew the game. Gee whiz, I had a stroke of luck once! I was up looking over some old wells—gone dry. They didn't say anything about it, but the first thing I noticed, right beside one of these wells, was a couple of dead birds—sparrows or something. Gas! That's what it was. Well, I kept mum, and drove over to a rival company about two miles off, pretending just to drop in for a friendly chat. The first thing I knew, I heard a chap complaining about a gas well on their place—'It's a funny thing,' he said, 'the way the pressure's dropped on that well.' That gave me an idea! I looked up the geological layout—and sure enough, their gas was leaking through our old *oil* well. And before they knew it, we had it tapped. A stroke of luck, that was! It gave me a lot of pull with the company."

"That was pretty good! There's luck in everything——"

"It's an awful thing to say; and I'm not insultin' anyone that's present here; but what I'm tellin' you is facts and *figures* . . . There was three Italians come to New York; and they didn't speak no English. They went to stay at a boardin'-house—I think it was kept by a Mrs. McCarty. The first night they was there, they woke up hearin' a great noise in the room beneath, and they was scared . . . So one of them went to a little knothole there was in the floor, and listened. Now there was three Irishmen playin' cards in the room beneath, but the Italian couldn't see nothin', and all he heard was a voice sayin'——"

"Major Kendall! Major Kendall! Is Major Kendall here?"

"Outside! Outside!"

"Two Scotch? Yes, sir."

"And a splash."

"Well, they was so scared they took their bundles and run out of the house; and after a while they come to the Harlem bridge; and when they was halfway across the bridge they come to a dead man lyin' on his back in the middle of the sidewalk with his throat cut and a knife in his hand——"

"I'll bet you've got an ace. Want to bet?"

"—kiddin'——"

"—and while they was standin' there lookin' at the corpse a policeman came up to them—*say! listen* to this! Are you listenin'?"

"Sure we're listening."

"—and says to them, 'Who done this?' 'I *drew!*' says the first one, 'I *cut!*' says the second one, 'I *had a hand*,' says the third: so he pinched all the three of them."

"Ha ha! Some story! Good boy, Paddy!"

"—at the Orpheum, in Boston, two weeks ago, dressed as a woman, with a great big brass padlock hanging down behind, and biting a little Japanese fan—saying he'd been followed right to the stage door by two sailors and a fireman——"

"Have you a little fairy in your home? Well, we had, but he joined the navy!"

"—and this guy went into a saloon in Chicago, leading a tiger on a leash! A big rattlesnake put his head out of his breast pocket, and he slapped it in again. When the tiger wouldn't lie down, he kicked it on the snout. 'Say!' says the bartender. 'The town you come from must be pretty tough!' . . . '*Tough!* You said a mouthful, bo. That town's so tough it kicked us fairies out.'"

"Ha ha ha . . . You know that one about the lonely fairy in Burlington, Vermont, and the alarm clock? . . . smothered it with kisses! I like that story."

> ("*My throte is cut unto the nekke bone,*"
> *Seyde this child; "and, as by way of kinde,*
> *I sholde have deyed, ye, longe tyme agoon . . ."* . . .

Of course it was deliberate. That cold blue light in her eye. She bore down on me like a frigate. Frigga, the goddess of fertility. Perhaps she and Cynthia had disagreed about it—and this was her way of forcing a crisis? She guesses that now I won't be inclined to approach Cynthia? Damned clever! *Damned* clever. I take off my hat to her. It was done so beautifully, too—like an aseptic operation—no feelings, no display, no waste of effort; a miracle of economy. The first time, I thought—actually!—that it might have been a mistake! I had made ready to bow to her—and I was so pleased, too, to be discovered walking there, in broad daylight, like one who "belongs," on the first cabin deck with Purington—so anxious, also, that I might be seen by Cynthia! I was positively wagging my tail, as I drew nearer—discreetly, of course, and to myself; the bow I had prepared was to be a very refined and quiet one. Alas! it will never be seen, that clearly preconceived bow on the deck of the *Nordic*, on the port side, at eleven o'clock in the morning, at latitude such-and-such and longitude so-and-so, with the sun x degrees above the horizon in a fleece of cirro-cumulus, and one sea gull perched on the foremast like a gilded finial! And now the question is—will Cynthia be told of that encounter? That depends on whether she is already a party to the plan. About even chances . . . No—more than that . . . After all, there was the copy of *Galatea* I sent her, and the two silly letters, which she never acknowledged or answered. She must, therefore, have been annoyed. In the circumstances, after so brief and casual and superficial and *unguaranteed* an acquaintance, I had no right to send them. Of course, I knew that. Just the same, if she had been as mature, as broad-minded, as *fine* as I thought——)

"No, you see, I miss boat in New York—got to take dis one, sure. I lose one week. Torino. I go Torino. How I go? Liverpool to Lond' is four hour,' tha's fi' dollar? Lond' to Dover is t'ree hour? . . . Naw, I don' care, I got plenty time, sure . . . Torino, I go Torino firs'. My fader liver in Ancona, ol' man, live alone. My moder, she die six, seven year ago. Look—she give me——"

"—pretty risky, yes. I saw a man killed on a derrick once. He was climbing up near the top, when he slipped. His shoes were worn down, and the broken sole of one of them—anyway, that's what we thought—caught on a girder . . . Another time I saw an oil derrick start to fall—eighty feet high—with two men on it, right at the top. They felt it beginning to go—and by gosh they *jumped*—first one and then the other,—eighty feet down to the slush vat—only a little thing ten feet square, you know—and both of them hit it, neither of them hurt! Gosh! The rest of us felt pretty sick. About five minutes after it, I began to shake so bad I had to sit down on a barrel. A thing like that makes you think . . ."

Lights of Library and Port Deck. Lights of Bar and Starboard Deck. Single Stroke. Trembling.

Sound Signals for Fog and So Forth.

In fog, mist, falling snow, or heavy rainstorms, whether by day or night, signals shall be given as follows:

A steam vessel under way, except when towing other vessels or being towed, shall sound at intervals of not more than one minute, on the whistle or siren, a prolonged blast.

"Well, Mr. Demarest, why so sad?"

"Sad, do I look sad?"

"You look as if you'd lost your last friend!"

"So I have—I've been crossed in love."

"No. You don't say so. You're old enough to know better. Were you on your way to the Library? Do you mind if I join you till dinnertime?"

"I should be delighted. I've been trying to read psychology in the smoking room. But the combination of disappointment in love with the noise there—was too much for me."

"Noise! My dear Mr. Demarest, you ought to be grateful. Up where I come from, if anyone is so careless as to drop a teaspoon, everybody else is upset for the rest of the day. I feel like screaming . . . What's the psychology?"

"Well, I'm a little hazy about it. Did you ever hear of the Bororos?"

"Bororos? Any relation to the Toreadors?"

"No—I believe they're a totemistic tribe in South America or Australia or is it Madagascar. Anyway, I know this much about them: their totem is a red caterpillar called the Arara. And they believe themselves to *be* red Araras. Van den Stein—of course you've heard of him—asked them if they meant that after death they would *become* Araras? But they were shocked and offended and replied, 'Oh no, we *are* Araras!' "

"Is this nonsense you're talking to me? It sounds like *Alice in Wonderland*."

"Said the Arara to the Bororo——"

"You aren't a psychologist yourself, by any chance, are you?"

"Nothing like that. I sometimes wish I were. Every man his own psychoanalyst?"

"What *do* you do, if you don't mind my asking so personal a question?"

"What *do* I do! That's what a good behaviorist would ask, and what I often ask myself . . . Accurately and dispassionately put, I'm an unsuccessful author."

"An author! . . . Well. You could knock me down with a toothpick. You don't *look* like an author."

"No?"

"No. Where's your long hair? your flowing tie? your—pardon me—maternity trousers?"

"Yes, I do lack the secondary sexual characteristics. That's probably why I'm unsuccessful. Or at any rate, the two things go together. If a man takes himself seriously enough to dress the part, and to look like a damned fool, he may perhaps be crazy enough to be some good!"

"Well now, *that's* an interesting point! . . . Wait for me five minutes, will you? I've left my old reekie behind."

"Sure."

"—well, that's all *right*. You have *your* opinion; and other people have theirs. Which kills the most—this last war—or tubercleosis? . . . So! . . . You would pronounce judgment on it without knowing the facts. That's what women *do* . . . Not all the people that's in the street is *bad*. And not all the people that's in the street is *good*. There's no grand rules by which you can lay down the law—if you're a good Christian. There's only special cases, that's all; and what you've got to do is to look into each case by itself, and judge it on its own merits . . . Everybody is aimin' for the same place, ain't they? That's the fact to be remembered, and not the fact that they go different ways to get there from what *you* choose. That's the way it is with religion. We all take different routes. But we're all aimin' to get to the same place. So what's the good of quarrelin' about the routes we take, or scorning one man because he goes this way, and another because he goes that . . . as long as they're honestly striving to get to the good place . . . But if there's a place on this earth that's a second Sodom, it's New York."

"How are you, Mrs. Simpson? Have you got hearts?"

"For fair!"

"Hearts are trumps."

"—the *dollar*, that's their god, the almighty dollar. You see what they mean by that, don't you?"

"Yes?"

"You remember the Jews in their journey through the desert. You remember how some of them, losing faith, backsliding, went whoring after false gods, and worshiped the golden calf. That is a *symbol*—the golden calf. And the golden calf is today the god of America. It's the Almighty Dollar; instead of Almighty God. Mark my words."

"Yes, that's true, that's a nice illustration for it. Everybody *does* worship gold——"

"I made a mistake!"

"That wasn't *fair!*"

"She *reneged!*"

"But what I say is, if they don't want to travel the same road with me, let them go their own way."

"That's what I say to my son, who joined the Christian Scientists. He's always after me——"

"—*Episcopalian*, they call it in America——"

"Well, that's the reason, you see, why I didn't want to *play* for anything."

"*Anything*, that'll keep you in touch with God, that's the great thing. But they all want to go their own way, nowadays. You can't prevent it—it's no use is it? trying to prevent it. But so long as they keep in touch with God, that's the great thing."

"—Christ, I mean."

"Well, I never played it much, I just started."

"They don't deny Him. But they say He's not the Son of God."

"—*beginning*——"

"They say that Christ was a good *man*. The only thing they deny is His *Kingship*. But what do we mean, I ask you, by Christ? Have you stopped to think about that? That's a point of very great importance. Is there any reason why we should reserve the title of Christ only for the one individual that was known as Jesus? There have been many Christs since Jesus of Nazareth. There was Saint Francis. There were some of the Popes, too, good and holy men. There was Moody and Sankey. There was Spurgeon. In what way was Spurgeon not deserving of the name of Christ? He gave his life to God—look at all those wonderful words and thoughts of his. And these are only a few. There have been many Christs—some of them lowly people that were never heard of in history. How many have been put on the rack for their faith in God? No man can say. There have been many Christs; and there will be Christs again."

"We couldn't have made a whole lot, could we?"

"The ace of diamonds was all I had."

"Nine of trumps——"

"You have to follow suit, you see."

"What'll you do?"

"One spade."

"One spade."

"Ha ha ha! You have to say something *different* from her! You don't follow suit in the *bidding!*"

"Well, if you've got one spade you'd better hold on to it!"

"They're playing euchre, is it?"

"Miss Kennedy? No. She wasn't a bigot. She might see things in a different light from what you do. But that isn't bigotry. Because you're Church—and she's Chapel—does that give *her* the right to call *you* a bigot? No. Miss Kennedy was a Unitarian, and a God-fearing woman. You might not agree with her, but that wouldn't make her a bigot."

"Well—I try to fathom all these things——"

"It's the way they've been brought up, that's it, isn't it, Mrs. Covey? They reverence God in their own way. And it seems good to them, just like your way seems good to you. It's all in the way you've been brought up when you're a child."

"Well—that's true, of course—and my husband is right where he says we should all strive to be tolerant—but just the same there's some things that's hard to understand or be tolerant of. I've had a good deal of religious experience, for after being brought up as a Churchwoman, when I married I became a Wesleyan. And then, singing as I did—I used to sing a lot—I

went about a good deal to different sects and societies, and saw a good
many different points of view. But some of the Catholic ideas, now, I cannot think they are good. And this although my best friend, a woman I've
known all my life, died a Catholic. To my idea, the way they use the crucifix is wrong, like a kind of idolatry. For them, their crucifix is just a kind
of talisman, to protect you. Just a talisman. And then the way they worship
the mother of Christ—that's another thing that seems to me uncalled for.
I used to ask Mrs. Jennings, 'Why is it you worship the mother of Christ
as if she was a god? She was only a mortal woman like you or me.' And
of course, that's just why it appeals to them. They have her there to represent all the mothers . . . Lots of my friends have been Catholics."

(I could see, watching them out of the corner of my eye, that Cynthia
and the fair-haired girl were turning, hesitating, there at the top of the
companionway, as if at a loss. Should they come down, approach me? Try
in some way to catch my eye? . . . They wavered, Cynthia was biting her
lip—they vacillated, waiting perhaps for some sign from me—and then,
receiving none, departed slowly forward and did not return. I believe that
Cynthia knew that I had seen her. Yes. She *knew*; knew from the stiff
unseeing way in which I stood and stared, staring meaninglessly, with awkward profile, at the wholly uninteresting sea. Good God. My folly and
weakness are abysmal. Why must I behave in this extraordinary fashion?
Ask dad, he knows! Ask Clara, the Negro nurse! Ask Mr. Greenbaum, the
Latin teacher, who watched me through the crack of the door to see if I
was cribbing! Ask that slattern under the arc light, in November, 1909, who
caroled at me "Does your mother know you're out?" Ask the burly Italian
in the Apennine train, who said, when I had dismally failed to shut that
infernal broken window (and the smoke was pouring in) *"Poco bravo!"*
Ask that detestable red-faced redheaded vulgar master (tuberculous, too)
who superintended when I was given the water cure, aged seventeen! And
the God-impersonating baseball coach who would never trust me with a
chance on the first nine! . . . Ask them all. And ask my dipsomaniac great-
grandfather, my charming imaginative fibbing mother, my sensual analytic
father, and the delirious wallpaper pattern on my nursery wall. *Behavior is
a function of environment.* Selah! I wash my hands of it. But I don't want
to behave like this? Or do I? Is it metaphysically—or physiologically—
possible to will the good and achieve the evil? to desire, and not to accomplish? and thus to *become* something which one had not willed? Cynthia's
conception of Demarest is not Demarest's conception———)

"Well!"

"Well!"

"Now I should like to ask you a whole lot of questions."

"Ask, and it shall be given unto you."

"May I inquire what it is you write?"

"Plays. Also an unfinished novel or two. And a few poems."

"Have any of them been produced?"

"Published, but not produced. That's the difficulty. Or rather———"

"I dare say you're too highbrow. Is that it?"

"No. The trouble is deeper than that. In fact, so deep that it's hard to
analyze. I've often made the attempt, never with much satisfaction. Not

that it matters very much. Ha ha! I always say that, at this point, and of course it's precisely *that* that matters . . . the fact that I say, and *do* often believe, that it doesn't matter, I mean."

"Not enough faith in yourself, perhaps."

"No, not exactly that—though that's a part of it. It's more general—a sneaking feeling that the whole thing is a snare and a delusion."

"I don't get you. You mean the world in general?"

"No—though I often suspect that too; but that's not just what I mean. No, the sneaking feeling I refer to is a feeling that the arts—and perhaps especially the literary arts—are a childish preoccupation which belongs properly to the infancy of the race, and which, although the race as a whole has not outgrown, the civilized *individual* ought to outgrow."

"Hm. I see. Or I *don't* see!"

"No reasonable person any longer believes in magic—but many of the ideas and words and fetishes, which we inherit from the age of magic, still survive in debased forms: mascots, lucky pennies, charms, lucky numbers, fortunetelling, and so on. Well, when we begin as children to use language, we use it as a form of magic power to produce results. We learn to say 'more' because when pronounced it will actually *get* us more. And, we never wholly lose this early conviction (though it becomes overlaid and unconscious) that some sort of virtue or power resides in language. When we like a passage in a poem or tale we refer to it as 'magical.' We thus indicate unconsciously the primitive origin and nature of the arts. Art is merely the least primitive form of magic . . . But all this relates chiefly to the *linguistic* side of the literary art. There is also the other side, that part of it which it has in common with the other arts—the psychological content, the affective and emotional necessity out of which it springs. You know Freud's theory that the ordinary dream is a disguised wish-fulfilment or nexus of them? Well, the work of art performs exactly the same function. Some of these esthetic critics say that *content*, so to speak, doesn't matter at all; they talk of the ideal work of art as one in which everything has become form, and of the ideal critic as one in whom there is no confusion of the emotions aroused in himself (by the work of art) with the work of art itself. That error seems to me perfectly extraordinary! And yet it is a very common one. For of course this pure form, and pure contemplation, are both chimeras; there ain't no sich animals. What is the pure form of a potato? The minute you leave out its potatoishness you leave out everything. Form is only an aspect of matter, and cannot be discussed apart from it. You can isolate the feelings and emotions which give rise to a play, but you cannot entirely isolate its form, for its form *responds* to these. Can you conceive of a play which would be entirely meaningless, one which was not only unintelligible, but which also aroused no feelings? Impossible. Language is reference. And its reference is dual: it refers to facts—as the word potato refers to a tuber—but also it refers to feelings; for every individual will have, as the result of his own particular experiences, his own particular *cluster of feelings* about the potato. Do I make myself clear?"

"Not at all. But go on, brother. I may catch up with you at the finish."

"I'm determined to make you suffer . . . Let's assume that I like a certain poem. Why do I like it? The esthetic critic would say that I like it because it's beautiful, because, in other words, it's a 'perfect expression of something'; the *something* you see, doesn't matter very much, so long as it has been 'esthetically' experienced! But this is based on the assumption that all 'somethings,' or experiences, are of like value. We know this isn't true. It would be impossible to make an Iliad out of the buttering of a potato, or a Hamlet out of the paring of one's nails. These experiences are universal—and could involve no confusion of reference; but they are not of very great interest, or significance, or desirability, *emotionally*. We are all, in a sense, frustrated—we are all of us, each in his particular way, starved for love, or praise, or power, and our entire characters are molded by these thwarted longings. I won't go into the details of that mechanism, for I don't know too much about it, probably no more than you do; the point I'm making for is this, that art's prime function is the gratification of these longings. We can see this, if we like, as a kind of cowardice. We don't like to grow up; we don't like to face the bare or ugly facts of life, its privations, its miseries, its failures, its uncertainty, its brevity; we don't like to see ourselves as mere automata, whose behavior is 'merely a function of environment'; we don't like to admit our ignorance as to our origin and destiny, or our impotence in the face of the laws that control us; and so we seek refuge and consolation in that form of daydream which we call art. Reading a novel, we become the hero, and assume his importance as the *center of the action*—if he succeeds, then we too succeed; if he fails, then we can be sure it is against overwhelming odds, against the backdrop of the colossal and unpitying infinite, so that in failure he seems to us a figure of grandeur; and we can see ourselves thus with a profound narcissistic compassion, ourselves godlike in stature and power, going down to a defeat which lends us an added glory . . . Art is therefore functionally exaggerative. When we find our response to things becoming jaded, when the bare bones of reality begin to show, then we clutch at the cobweb of the fairy tale. Think only of the world of love which literature opens to us! Solomon in all his glory of a thousand wives cannot rival us. We can range from Helen of Troy, or Lesbia, to Imogen with the cinque-spotted mole on her breast; from Isolde to tuberculous Milly Theale; from Cleopatra to Emma Bovary or Raskolnikov's Sonia; or even to the bawdy ballad of sister Mary, who was bilious!"

"Ah—*there* I begin to follow you!"

"Of course! . . . Well now, we jump from that to *another* psychological aspect of this process of wish-fulfillment. And that is this. A work of art is good if it is successful: that is, if it succeeds in giving the auditor or reader an *illusion*, however momentary; if it convinces him, and, in convincing him, adds something to his experience both in range and coherence, both in command of feeling and command of expression. And here we come to the idea which is terribly disquieting to the purely *esthetic* critic, who likes to believe that there are absolute standards of excellence in art. For if we take a functional view of art, as we must, then everything becomes relative; and the shilling shocker or smutty story, which captivates Bill the sailor, is giving him exactly the escape and aggrandizement, and therefore *beauty*, that Hamlet gives to you or me. The equation is the same. What right have you got, then, to assume that *Hamlet* is 'better' than *Deadeye Dick?* On absolute grounds, none whatever. They are intended for different audiences, and each succeeds. Of course, Hamlet is infinitely more complex than the other. And we can and should record that fact and study it carefully, seeing in art, as we see in our so-called civilization, an apparent evolution from simple to complex. Well, all this being true, why be an artist? Or for which audience? . . . That's the horrible problem."

"I can see you're in a bad fix. But if you feel that way about it, why *not* give it up? And do something really useless like me—selling chewing-gum or lace petticoats to people who don't want them? Why not?"

"Yes, *why* not? The answer is, that though I'm an unsuccessful artist —pleasing practically nobody but myself—and though, as a good psychologist, I scorn or at any rate *see through* the whole bloody business, nevertheless I have that particular sort of neurosis, verbal in its outward expression, which will probably keep me an artist till I die or go mad. . . . Suppose I'm a sort of forerunner, a new type. And what then?"

"A new type? Tell it to the marines! You don't look it. You're no more a new type than *I* am."

"Yes, sir! A type in which there is an artist's neurosis, but also a penetrating intelligence which will not permit, or permit only with contempt, the neurosis to work itself out! If you want a parallel which will make the predicament clear, conceive a Christ, for example, who *understood* the nature of his psychological affliction, foresaw its fatal consequences for himself, foresaw also that to yield to his neurosis would perhaps retard the development of mankind for four thousand years, and nevertheless *had to yield to it*. As a matter of fact, that illustration occurs to me because it is the theme of a play that I've had in mind for some time. *The Man Who Was Greater Than God*."

"It's a damned good title, I'll say that much for it! But if you ever got it on the stage, you'd be mobbed."

"Oh, it would be impossible at present. At any rate, it probably would be, if my hero was too palpably modeled on Christ. I could, however, and probably would, represent him as a modern man, an intelligent man, who nevertheless had religious delusions of grandeur. Perhaps an illegitimate child, who compensated for that flaw in his descent by believing himself to be the son of God . . . Or, I've also considered dropping the Messiah idea altogether, and having for my hero an artist, or a writer, or perhaps a social reformer. In that case, I betray *myself*—it's really myself I should be portraying in either character. The Strindberg and Nietzsche and von Kleist type, but with the addition of intellectual poise, or *insight!* However, what good would it do? What's the use of doing it? The predicament of the hero would be too exceptional to be widely interesting—no audience could possibly sympathize with him. The Messiah, on the other hand, would be a figure universally appealing . . . Yes, it would have to be the Messiah, much as I prefer the artist . . . But—why not *act* that play, in my own life, instead of thus taking flight from the problem in one more surrender to my neurosis?"

"Act it? I don't get you. How do you mean act it?"

"Well, in the play the hero would finally decide (perhaps he is pushed, somewhat, to this conclusion by his friend, a psychoanalyst) to abjure his art, entirely and forever. To anyone who is an artist, that scene would be positively *plangent* with invitations to narcissistic anguish—every artist, beholding, would weep for himself. Imagine it. A Shakespeare, for instance, deciding for the good of humanity, not to write plays! Seeing them all there—his Hamlet, his Othello, his Lear, his Cleopatra, his magnificent Coriolanus—and dismissing them unborn! Very touching. And to make it worse, he perhaps pays for this in a complete mental breakdown, or death . . . That's the *play*: in which, as you see, I have all the luxury of this suicidal decision, but also the luxury of having again, and thus intimately, *adored* myself. Now the question is—why not *do* it, instead of writing it? Why not give up, in advance, that play and all my other ambitions? I think very seriously of it; at the same time suspecting that my whole life would be deranged by it . . . It's a nice little problem. To write, or to commit suicide."

"Don't do either! but have a cocktail!"

"That's not a bad idea, either! a dry Martini would go nicely."

"Steward! Can we have two *dry* Martinis, please?"

"Two *dry* Martinis, yes, sir."

"Yes, it's very sad and complicated. If you look at the problem from a purely humanitarian point of view, and try to solve it solely in the interests of mankind—even then, it's not too simple. In the first place, there is always the possibility that the whole Freudian idea, as thus applied to art, is wrong. It may be that art will be a permanent necessity for man, a penalty that he pays for having become a social and civilized animal. How can we be sure? If I go on writing plays and novels, may I not at any rate give aid and comfort to a few verbalistic lunatics like myself, and help them to keep their spiritual balance in this melancholy world? And isn't that a good deed? . . . But no, I'm not sure. The intellectual side of me declines to believe in that—or balks at it. I have what my friend Tompkins, the psychoanalyst, calls a Samson complex."

"This gets deeper and darker. Have a drink. Here's to the Samson complex!"

"Your bloody good health!"

"Not bad at all."

"Shall we repeat?"

"We might!"

"Two more please, steward?"

"Two dry Martinis? Yes, sir."

"Well, now, Socrates, tell me about the Samson complex. I hope you don't mind if I just seem to listen, like a sponge."

"I don't mind, if *you* don't. But I don't want to bore you."

"Bore me! Great Godfry. I've been dying for something highbrow like this. But don't be surprised if I fall asleep."

"Well, the name for it was partly a joke, and refers to a dream I had two weeks ago, when I was visiting Tompkins. Tompkins has always been keen to have me drop all this literary folderol and become a psychologist, or at any rate a psychological critic of literature. When I was staying with

Tompkins, two weeks ago, he renewed his attack on me and once more
brought this schism painfully to the surface. Lately, I had been backsliding a little. After a year and a half of potboiling, which took the form of
book reviewing, I suddenly developed a tremendous *resistance* to criticism
—my destructive speculations, you see, were coming too close to a destruction of *myself*, not only by taking up all my time, but also by undermin-
ing my *amour propre* . . . How much, please?"

"Two shillings—or fifty cents. Thank you, sir. Thank you."

"Here's to your ectoplasm."

"And yours. May it never grow less. Don't forget the dream in your
excitement."

"I was just getting to it. It reflects, you see, this conflict in me between
the critic and the artist . . . The times, I should think, were those of
Euripides: though I'm not positive the place was Greece. I was a runner,
a messenger, and I had been running since daybreak, bearing some portentous message. What was this great message, this revelation? I don't know
—it was never clearly formulated in the dream. But at dusk I came to
a great stone-built temple, and entered it. I was exhausted: I could hardly
stand. The temple chamber, within, was immense, high-roofed, and ceil-
inged with blue and gold; and at the far end of it, before a grim stone
altar, a hieratic procession of tall priests was forming. It seemed, however,
that they were expecting me, and that whatever it was that they were about
to perform must wait till they had heard what it was that I had to say.
I approached them, spoke, and then, my message delivered, realized that
I was going to die, that the long run had killed me. Stumbling, therefore,
to a table-shaped tomb of stone, I stretched myself upon it like the effigy
of a crusader, my throbbing eyes turned upward toward the ceiling . . .
How high it was, how gorgeously azured and gilded, and how massive the
masonry of its arch! If it should fall—if it were only to fall—would it
not destroy—not only myself, already dying—but also these hateful priests
and their mysteries? the temple? And suddenly, then, with a last spastic
effort of body and soul, I cried out in terrific command to the ceiling
'FALL! FALL! . . .' And it fell."

"Is that all?"

"That's all."

"Good gracious Peter . . . I see, yes, where the Samson idea comes in
. . . I never dreamt anything like that in my life. All my dreams are in
pieces—I'm walking in one place, and then I'm in another. I look into a
room and see a *lovely* girl undressing, kiss her—oh boy! notice that she has
put too much rouge on her mouth, and looks consumptive—and the next
thing I know I'm watching a crazy play, with that girl, or another one
something like her, acting the heroine in *Why Girls Leave Home*. No good
at all. Do you always dream dreams like that?"

"Usually."

"No wonder you've got things to write about . . . Tell me—when you
write a novel, for instance, how do you go about it? Do you make up
a plot out of whole cloth—so to speak—or do you see something in life,
simply, and put it down?"

"I don't think it's either method, but a sort of combination. Personally, I find it hard to draw from life. I couldn't, for example, transfer you to a novel, or Hay-Lawrence, and make you real: you would only become real, for my purpose, if I had *invented* you" . . .

"Gosh! Now, suppose we were all of us just——"

"Characters in a novel? Yes! Every now and then one experiences that sense of a complete dissociation of personality, when one seems to evaporate under the glare of one's own eye. Exactly the way that when you've been lying in bed in one position too long you lose all sense of your body . . . You know, it's something like this, some analogous feeling of unreality and absurdity, a destructive sense of the profound *relativity* of my existence, that makes me a failure. It seems to me—I don't know whether this is idiotic, but thanks to the cocktails I don't hesitate to say it —it seems to me that I can *foresee* everything, exactly the feeling that one has in a hashish or mescal trance. Have you ever tried hashish?"

"No. Something like opium, isn't it?"

"Something . . . You lose the power to distinguish in time and place. For instance, you remember, as you sit there absorbed in sensory meditation, that you have forgotten to let in the dog. In the course of thinking this, you so sharply visualize the action of descending the stairs, passing the bust of Clytie in the wall niche, slipping back the cold brass bolt, feeling the injured screw under the doorknob, hearing the whimper of the hinge and the threefold scrape of the dog's nails on the worn door panel, and then (the door opened) seeing the mad swarm of stars above the Baptist church—you experience all this so profoundly, and the return upstairs, that you become convinced that you have actually *done* it . . . Am I losing my thread, or are these cocktails making me drunk?"

"I suspect you're drunk!"

"Yes, I have at all times, drunk or sober, a crippling sense of having foreseen every possible action or feeling or thought, not only of my own, but also of everyone else. All the alternatives, too. The whole blooming buzzing cosmic telephone exchange—every connection. This is so appallingly vivid that in its wake any *real* action performed by me, or any thought formulated, or any feeling observed in its progress from belly to thorax, and from thorax to—possibly—horripilation——"

"Pause there! That word again, please, if you don't mind, professor."

"Horripilation—when your hair walks backward on cold feet. Any such *reality* seems to me in consequence a rather stupid and meaningless repetition, not worth troubling about. Why write a book, which one can conceive so much more sublimely than anyone could possibly write? Why bother even to *conceive* a new unity in a chosen gamut of heterogeneity, when one also foresees disastrously the hour when that unity will have become merely one item in a larger heterogeneity, each new system absorbed by a larger system? Why bother to foresee that fatality of decay and change, of clicking and mechanical and inevitable death, when one remembers that even oneself, the foreseer, was foreseen *in the act of foreseeing,* and that even one's newness is old? . . . This is a poisonous sophistry from which I find it hard to escape. I only escape it when the attention of my senses has been sharply drawn. And even then the willingness to act or feel is only intermittent. As in love, for instance."

"Ah! Thank God! I was beginning to lose all hope for you. But if you can still fall in love, it's not so bad."

"But my God, think how terrible it is to be in love, and not to be able to believe in it or act on it!"

"Oh, come come, Mr. Demarest! Do you mean to ask me to believe that? No . . . No, no!"

"It's true, s'welp me Bob!"

"Well, if you weren't drunk, I'd think you were crazy."

"My dear Silberstein, I'm no crazier than you are."

"No, sir, you can't tar me with *that* brush. Believe me, when I'm in love—using that as a *very broad term*—there's plenty of action. I'm no Hamlet, by God! I either get 'em, or I don't. And if I don't, I don't cry about it. I look for another: the woods are full of them. It's as easy as tripping a cripple."

"Well, of course, I'm exaggerating slightly——"

"Ah! That's better. You were exaggerating slightly——"

"—but there's something in it. I don't mean so much as applied to—well, the more fleeting sort of sexual adventure. Though it's apt to be true even of those. But when one's really in love—it's a miserable business. All out of focus. No reasonable center to one's behavior. Or *my* behavior, anyway. I'm always a damned fool when I'm in love."

"If you're talking about Romeo and Juliet stuff, all I can say is that at your age you ought to know better. The female doesn't exist that can get me in love with her."

"But I wonder if there's any escaping one's temperament in that regard? Here I am, aged thirty-five, and more horribly in love than I ever was before—in love, mind you, in the most sublimated and sentimental sense imaginable. I actually don't feel the slightest *conscious* sensual attraction to the girl. Not the slightest. Oh, I don't mean that I don't think she's beautiful—I do. But her beauty affects me in a very peculiar way—it seems to me merely a clue to something else, some mental or spiritual quality (though I distrust the word spiritual) which is infinitely more exciting and more worth discovery. Of course, I admit frankly that I've had other affairs in which there was little or nothing of this. Usually, even when I'm mildly 'in love,' the desire for physical contact is at once uppermost—all my tentacles and palpacles begin to quiver. Why this difference? How can we be sure that one way is any better than the other? You simply take your choice. Both of them have something of value to offer. Perhaps it's the difference between poetry and prose. I always liked Donne's remark on that subject——"

"Donne? Never heard of him. But spring it, if you must."

> " 'For they are ours as fruits are ours.
> He that but tastes, he that devours,
> And he that leaves all, doth as well.' "

"Well, God deliver me from poetry. You can have it. Take all the lyrics you want, but leave me the legs."

"I'm afraid I've got to leave you. That was my dinner horn—quarter of an hour ago. I'm late."

"Was it! And I haven't changed yet . . . We'll resume this drunken discussion later . . . So long!"

"Yes, so long."

Lights of Library and Port Deck. Lights of Bar and Starboard Deck. Single Stroke. Trembling.

"Oh! Aren't you ashamed, Mr. Demarest!"

"Ashamed, Mrs. Faubion? What of?"

"Why being so late—we're almost finished! . . . Oh, we know all about *you*."

"Help, I'm discovered . . . No soup, thanks, steward—hors d'oeuvres, and then—let's see."

"Calf's head in torture is good—I had it. Very good. Good food on this boat."

"No—roast duckling à l'Anglaise, and vegetables. And ice cream and coffee . . . So you know all about me. Father's been telling on me."

"He *has*. He told us all about your swell friend in the first cabin. When are you going to announce the engagement?"

"Engagement! My God. The family jewels."

"Is it true, what Mr. Smith told Mrs. Faubion and me, that you first met her on another ship?"

"True as the gospel, Miss Dacey. Believe everything that father tells you and you won't go wrong. But didn't he tell you that we were secretly *married* this morning—at seven bells?"

"Ha ha! Wouldn't you like to, though! Merry laughter."

"Married, does he say. No, siree Bob. When Demarest marries they won't ring bells, they'll fire cannon and blow up the ship!"

"Why, what do you *mean*?"

"Does he look like a marrying man? Not him. Not much! He's one of these ice-bound bachelors."

"All right for you, Mr. Demarest—you can't pretend any more that you're a woman hater. *Now* we know the *real* reason why you avoid us all the time!"

"Avoid you! My dear Mrs. Faubion! What a scandalous and outrageous falsehood! Here I've been pursuing you from morning till night——"

"*Pursuing!*"

"—and I never can get any nearer to you than tenth in the waiting line. And you accuse me of avoiding you! Father, you can testify."

"Testify nothing! We'll never see *you* again on this ship. No, sir. You're a lost man. Sunk without a bubble."

"You hear that? And after Miss Dacey and I have been saying such nice things about you, too. Haven't we? Your ears ought to have been burning last night."

"Last night?"

"Last night after we went to bed."

"Do tell me! I'm dying to know what it was."

"Why, did you ever hear of such conceit? *Actually!*"

"That's right, darling, don't tell him a thing. Tantalize him. That's what gets 'em every time."

"Don't *darling* me! I'm not your darling, nor *anybody's* darling."

"She's getting mad again. All pink and mad . . . But didn't you say you had a husband? Ah ha! Look at her blushing!"

"I'm *not* blushing."

"Oh no, she's not blushing. Not blushing at all. I beg your pardon, Mrs. Faubion."

"Mr. Barnes! I wish you would teach your passengers better manners!"

"Is Mr. Smith behaving badly to you? I must caution you, Mr. Smith. You must remember that these young ladies are traveling under my protection."

"I think he's had a cocktail too many, Mr. Barnes."

"Cocktails! I like your nerve, Mr. Demarest! And you breathing brimstone all over the table. It's a wonder the flowers don't wilt."

"Where were you at the mock wedding, Mr. Demarest! didn't you see it? I thought you were going to be the wedding guest."

"So I was. But I forgot all about it till it was too late. How did the bride look, the pianist?"

"Oh, he was a scream."

"And you should have heard Mr. Ashcroft doing the marriage service! Oh! I thought I should die!"

"Oh, wasn't he a scream?"

"Yes, he certainly was a scream! What *was* it all about, all that about the man trying to catch the pigeon in the field, and getting it by the tail?"

"What, madam! didn't you understand that? That was the best part of it. Don't you try to let on you're as innocent as all that! *What was all that about the pigeon!* You were the one that was laughing the loudest."

"Careful, Mr. Smith! Careful!"

"Well, I ask you, Mr. Purser, as man to man——"

"That will do, father!"

"*Don't* call me *father*. A man is as young as he feels . . . Ha ha!"

"Well . . . what's funny in that?"

"Oh, nothing funny—it's damned serious. Yes indeedy."

"My little gray home in the west. Don't you *love* that song? I just couldn't *live* without that song. Are we ready to go, Pauline?"

"Yes, are we ready to go, Pauline?"

"*Pauline!* . . . Mr. Smith, your manners are simply *terrible*. Good night, Mr. Barnes—oh are you coming too? Good *night*, Mr. Demarest!"

"Good *night*, Mrs. Faubion!"

"Gosh, that girl gets my goat. Yes, siree, she sure gets my goat."

"She's damned attractive."

"Attractive! She's a dynamo."

"Dynamo—dynamas—I loved a lass——"

"Yes, siree. And you know, I've got a damned good idea."

"What is it?"

"Just between you and me and the bedpost——"

"I must caution you, Mr. Smith. You must remember that these young ladies——"

"No, sir, I'm not swallowing any bunk about those girls. If they aren't —I'll bet they've been in half the staterooms on this boat."

"I don't believe it. Not Faubion."

"Oh? You don't think so? Well, maybe not, maybe not. Just the same, I've got a damned good idea."

"Well?"

"It's simple, and I don't see how it can get me into any trouble . . . It's this. I've got a purse full of gold sovereigns—look! you don't see gold sovereigns every day! Not since the war you don't. They look pretty good, don't they?"

"Very nice."

"Yes, sir! They look pretty good. And I've got an idea that if I just take them out and kind of flash them at Mrs. Faubion—without saying anything, you know—anything that would give me away too much—what do you think?"

"Gosh, father! You're getting reckless."

"No! I don't see any harm in it. I'll bet these sovereigns would look pretty good to her. Don't you think so?"

"Suppose not?"

"Well, suppose not. Where's the danger? That's the beauty of it. If she's as innocent as *you* say she is, she won't know what I mean by it. Will she?"

"True."

"Well, I think I'll try it. If I can get up the nerve. That's where the trouble is! Guess I'll take a few Guinnesses first . . . And then do it the last thing before I turn in. I'll bet she'll know what I mean, all right! Yes, sir, if that girl doesn't know more than you and me put together, I miss my guess."

"Well, I'll put a flower on your grave. A syringa."

"You just wait! The old man'll show you something . . . The trouble is with you, you're too slow. How's your dollar princess?"

"She's dropped me."

"Dropped you! What do you mean?"

"Her mother cut me this morning. It's all over."

"You mean to say you're going to *let* them drop you?"

"Good God, man, you don't suppose I can run up into the first cabin forty times a day—where I don't belong, and where all the officers know me by sight—in pursuit of people who won't speak to me when I meet them? Nothing like that. I tried it twice this afternoon, but the only one I saw was her uncle, writing letters in the smoking room. And he doesn't know me."

"Well, why didn't you put it up to *him*?"

"Ask him why they were cutting me? Nothing doing!"

"Well, I guess the trouble is you don't care very much. Not like me! . . . Coming up? Take a turn on the deck?"

"As far as the smoking room. I think I'll get drunk tonight."

"Well, I may pop in later . . . What's the singing?"

Single Stroke. Trembling.
Sound Signals for Fog and So Forth.

> *"And the next time I met her, she was all dressed in pink.*
> *The next time I met her, she was all dressed in pink.*

All in pink—all in pink—what will her mother think?
Down in the alley where She followed Me . . ."

"That's a new one on me. Well, see you later. Gosh, look at the smoke in there!"
"—pure as the snow, but she drifted."
"She was pure as the snow, but she drifted."

"And the next time I met her, she was all dressed in gray.
The next time I met her, she was all dressed in gray.
All in gray—all in gray—what will her father say?
Down in the alley where She followed Me . . ."

"—two for a nickel poker player like you! Are you coming in or are you staying out?"
"*I'll* come in—I ain't no piker!"
"*He's* no poker piker!"

"And the next time I met her, she was all dressed in green.
The next time I met her, she was all dressed in green.
All in green—all in green—my, how she did scream, scream! . . .
Down in the alley where She followed Me . . ."

"The man said to the girl—'You know what your personality reminds me of? a handful of wet sawdust!' Flap, flap. And he shook his hand, as if he was shakin' sawdust off it. And the girl said—'Ah, your face would make a false tooth ache!" . . . 'Is *that* so,' the man said. 'Do you know what your face is like? It's like an exposed nerve.' And the girl said, 'Why, you're so narrow-minded you could button your ears at the back! Ha ha!' . . . And then the man took a long hard look at her and said, 'You want to know what you remind me of? . . . You remind me of a neglected grave . . . Where's your lily?' "
"Ha ha ha!"

"And the next time I met her, she was all dressed in red.
The next time I met her, she was all dressed in red.
All in red—all in red—I stole her maidenhead——
Down in the alley where She followed Me . . ."

"Yes, you hear some funny things there. Another time——"
"Ukulele, sure. I was lying right here, behind the back, and she didn't see me. She was inside the bar there with the door shut for half an hour. When she came out and saw me she turned red as a beet. She tried to laugh it off . . . Well, she's got a fine pair of shafts, by God!"
"Who can open it. Can *you* open it?"
"Who—? the guy with the long hair—? If he so much as puts a *finger* on me I'll knock his block off."

"And the last time I met her, she was all dressed in blue.
The last time I met her, she was all dressed in blue.
All in blue, baby blue—what will the poor kid do?—
Down in the alley where She followed Me . . ."

"Hooray! Here's old Paddy again."

"*One—more—drink!*"

"I didn't see you eatin' much, Paddy."

"Let me tell you somethin' . . . It's an awful thing to say—and I'm not insultin' anyone that's present here—but what I'm telling you is facts and *figures*. There was an Irishman once and his name, I think, was Mike. And he was living in N'York, at a boardin'-house that was kept by a Mrs. McCarty."

"She was pure as the snow, but she drifted."

"PURE as the snow, but she drifted."

"Prohibition—that's what drove me out of the country. As nice a little saloon as you could want! forty and one-tenth miles from New York. And everything as orderly and nice as it could be. And *now* look at it! *High-*school girls goin' out to dances, takin' their own old man's hooch with them, and gettin' so drunk they can't walk! *Paralyzed*, that's what they get. *High-*school girls!"

"—and the parrot she had—*ahip!*—he hated it, see? . . . And so one mornin' when he was shavin' he took his razor and cut the back of its neck, and dropped it into the——"

"ANTE, God damn you! You can't slip anything like that over on me!"

"You shut your face! You can't talk like that to me!"

"I can't eh? Well, tellin' me won't stop me!"

"Sure he anted. It was me that didn't ante."

"All right, all right, my mistake. No hard feelin's, pardner."

"—and the parrot said, 'By God, if she had that cut, and lived, there's hope for me!' "

"Ha ha ha!"

"I'll ask you a question you can't answer, Paddy . . . Who was it drove the Danes out of Ireland? Eh?"

"St. Patrick."

"Ah-h-h-h-h! G'wan with you. It was Brian Boru . . . And do you know who it was used to make wine out of the whorts? I'll bet you don't know that either."

"I don't know, and I don't *give* a damn . . . *Who* was it?"

"Ah, you don't know nothin'. It was the Danes."

(*"My throte is cut into the nekke bone!" seyde this child* . . . Bored Silberstein. Deliberately, in that particular way. Coming the highbrow. Why did I do it? Some sort of relief—catharsis. Too bad we had to stop when we did. A good thing we had to stop when we did. I'd have told him everything. I'd have told him about——Why did I lie to him about her physical attraction? But I only recognized the lie as I told it. So did he. She was pure as the snow, but she drifted. PURE as the snow, but she drifted. And the next time I met her she was all dressed in black. Back. Smack. Crack. Clack. Attack. Golden engine and silver track. The golden engine on the silver track. I am wounded with a deep wound. ὀτατοὶ ποποὶ δα. He prescribed whisky—hemostatic and astringent. Whisky; and a modest prayer.)

"—Mexico, if a girl is married, and her husban' find out she is not—

what you call? *verges?*—he take her back to her father and mother. And so, everybody know; and she have no more chances. No, sir."

"Is that so."

"Is that so."

> "*—plough mus' plough*
> *And the bull mus' bull . . .*"
> *The cow mus' cow,*
> *And the bull mus' bull . . .*"

"—and if I was to tell you the Soo Canal flows uphill—*ahip!*—you wouldn't believe it, would you, and you'd think you was smart! . . . but what I'm tellin' you is facts and figures . . . I was workin' there for three——"

"And he put his head out and yelled, '*Hey!* How do you expect me to find my ring when there's a guy in here lookin' for his motor bike!' "

"Ha ha ha ha!"

"Such is the life of the Queen of Spain."

"Three months of leisure, then——"

"A triple whisky, steward."

"*Triple?* yes, sir."

"—and the girl, she said, 'But, mama! how you can be sure this trick will work? How you can be sure it will fool my *fiancé?*' . . . And mama, she say, 'Well, I ought to know! It's the same way I fooled your old man!' Ha ha! And the old man, he was under the girl's bed all the time, listening! Ha ha! . . . That was a good one, eh?"

"Another jackpot. Who can open it?"

"Nobody can open it."

"Sweeten the pot, then, boys!"

"*Triple* whisky, sir. Thank you."

"Thank you."

"—and all the time she went on scrubbin' the floor, scrubbin' the floor. And then she said, without turnin' round her head to see who it was, 'Niggerman, Ah ain't seen yo' face—and Ah don' know yo' name; but lemme tell you, Ah's here every Friday afternoon——' "

"Hello! is that the foghorn?"

"Somebody said there was a——"

"Good evening, Major."

"Good evening, Mr. Demarest."

"You've been very inconspicuous all day? We're suspicious of you. How's the Welsh Rarebit?"

"I feared there might be suspicions! He he! That's the worst of attaching oneself to anything so flagrant. Everyone knows, unfortunately, that the attachment can only be——"

"Naturally!"

"Well, believe me, she's a hot one. And she's all there, too."

"You aren't suggesting that she's intelligent?"

"Dear me, no! She hasn't the intelligence of a—barn door. But she's all there physically."

"Oh, physically. So Ashcroft said."

"Ashcroft? What does *he* know about it?"

"She went up to his room last night. He told Hay-Lawrence about it."

"Did she! Well, I'll be damned. Went to his room!"

"Yes, twelve o'clock last night. He told her how to get there—up in the first cabin, you know—and she carried a book, so as to pretend she was just returning it, in case any question arose. But it all went off quite successfully. She's got plenty of nerve, all right."

"Well, I'll be—hoodooed! *That's* why she's been——"

"—what?"

"—stalling."

"She stalled with Ashcroft. He was mad as a wet hen. All she would do was fool about with him. He finally booted her out."

"Oh! . . . Well, that's just the conclusion *I* had come to—that she's a teaser. What they call a 'mugger.' "

"You ought to be thankful."

"Oh, anything to pass the time! . . . Did I tell you she wants me to take her out to Mespot with me? . . . Yes, she's begging me to take her, as a housekeeper. I can see the face of the General's wife if I turned up with Peggy Davis in tow! Great Heavens . . . She dropped a pretty broad hint that there would be more to it than housekeeping."

"I don't doubt there would."

"You know, there's something fascinating about a woman like that—I suppose there must be something wrong with her. Some sort of twist. I wish I could make out that husband business. She showed me pictures of him, all right—but the whole thing seems a little wanky. She reminds me of a girl that picked me up in a theater in Cincinnati."

"Oh?"

"Yes. The same type . . . It was a funny thing. I had an overcoat on my lap, and all of a sudden I felt something tickling me. At first I thought it was accidental. I waited a little and it began again. It was quite dark, you know—some scene with a spotlight on the stage, and the rest of the lights turned out. And this girl was, very timidly, exploring under my coat with her hand—trying to find *my* hand . . . *He he!* She approached and retreated several times before she succeeded, and when she did succeed she gave a jump, and withdrew her hand again. Only for a minute, though—back it came. First, just our little fingers kept foolishly tapping each other. It was ridiculous. Then she suddenly became bolder, and slid her hand right over on top of mine—and after that, things became really riotous. And then came the joke. Do you know what she was?"

"No—what?"

"A social service investigator!"

"What! No."

"Yes, sir, a social service investigator. She was connected with a college hospital out there. Someone told her there was lots of 'picking up' in the vaudeville theaters, so she thought she'd investigate. Anyway, that's what she said. So she investigated *me!* . . . It was quite apparent, however, that the investigation wasn't disinterested. She was out for adventure, in her half-scared little way."

"Well, I'll be hanged."

"Rum, what? as the English say . . . Well, it's early, but I'm off. Have a nightcap?"

"No, thanks, I'm half tight already. I guess I'll turn in myself. I was just on the point when you came in . . . Good night."

"Good night."

Single Stroke. Trembling.

Follow Red Arrow To Boat Station No. 2.

Gentlemen.

142–156.

Boddy-Finch Lifejacket.

—Is that you, Demarest?

—Yes, this is Demarest. Who is that speaking, please?

—This is Demarest Two-prime. How do you do.

—Same to you, and many of them.

—As doctor to patient, I would suggest—ahem—a little sublimation.

—Kindly take the first turn to the left and go straight on till you get to hell.

—Yes. A little sublimation. A nice little pair of wings, now? All God's chilluns' got wings? A pair of gospel shoes?

—Take them back to the pawnshop. No sublimation! *Inter feces et urinas nascimur.* So let me live until I die.

—You must be careful not to slip back. Onward and upward forever. To higher things, and more complex: the fatherhood of God, the brotherhood of man, the leadership of Jesus. This love of yours must be kept pure, precious, and uncontaminated. A guiding star. Dante and Beatrice. Art, too. *Ma tu, perchè ritorni a tanta noia? Perchè non sali il dilettoso monte Ch'è principio e cagion di titta gioia?* . . . Up, my lad! Up Helicon once more! Once more into the breach!

—Thank you kindly, sir, she said. It isn't sublimation I want, it's a bath of blood.

—Civilization is sublimation . . . Simple to complex. Animalcule to synapse. Synapse to holdover. Holdover to art. Selah.

—It isn't sublimation I want, it's drowning.

—That play, now—the very moment to begin it. There they are— you see them? On a darkened stage. The hero is lying in bed. He is unconscious, result of mental and spiritual exhaustion. Poor devil. And then, from the shadowy background, the Chorus comes forward! The tyrant father! The incestuous mother! Narcissus with a hand glass!

—It isn't sublimation I want, it's a bath of blood.

—Terror, with the dull brow of the idiot! and the Dark Self Who Wants To Die! You see them? And they have begun quarreling! They are quarreling for the possession of your poor body that lies on the bed! The Messiah! You!

—It's a bath of blood. Not evolution: revolution. Red riot. I'm tired. Tired of clutching the inviolable shade.

—Nonsense. This is momentary. Or else, enduring—leads you, by devious ways, through mists and poisons—you know it perfectly well . . . The very moment for the play. All this agony can be projected, and being projected will be healed. Fixed in immortal shape: turned to stars like Cassiopeia. Look! Look! How she shines already!

—Fleshpots!

—You deceive yourself. Granted the fleshly origin,—but it's too late to turn back. Know your fate, Demarest! You ARE complex! To return to the simple is for you impossible! Misery! You must follow out your neurosis!

—To its bloody roots. Enough, Two-prime! Pay attention to your collar button and leave this affair to me. Cursed are they thay enjoy their suffering: for they shall never be healed.

> —*You may bury his body in the Egyp' garden,*
> *You may bury his body in the Egyp' garden,*
> *You may bury his body in the Egyp' garden,*
>   *O his little soul's goin' to shine.*

❪ VI

The dew fell softly on the hurricane deck; stars swung over the heaven-ward-pointing mast, swung slightly to and fro, swarmed in an arc like swarming bees; and the large dew pattered from the wet shrouds, unevenly, now nearer and now farther off, on the moist deck and the hollow-sounding canvas-covered lifeboats. The forestay, black save for the little golden span under the yellow mastlight, slid under the Pole Star, and slid-ing dipped, as the prow in midnight followed the Great Circle, yielding with long leisurely pitch and scend to the persuasion of the sea. A fleece of cloud passed between Sirius and the shipboy. It flew to westward, fluent of shape, and from the starboard came another, coffin-shaped, and behind that, from the east, a low irregular cavalry of others, merging confusedly one with another, commingling softly and softly disengaging. With the freshening east wind the sea sound, from the darkness under the starboard bow, became louder. The wash of the short-breaking waves was nearer, more menacingly frequent. The stars, suddenly panic-stricken, rushed helter-skelter among the clouds. An eclipse. One bell: the sound veering dizzily down to the black water on the port side. A ship sighted? twelve-thirty? . . . Something cold touched Demarest's cheek, and was gone as soon as felt. A snowflake. Another caressed his lifted hand. There were no more—it was to be merely a hint, a suggestion: nature employing, for once, the economy of the artist. St. Elmo protect us! St. Erasmus, patron of the midland sea, guard your mariners! Castor and Pollux, bless this ship, and save this ghostly company! . . . The blue fires alighted softly then on the three mastheads; three corposants; and then two others, fainter, perched themselves at either end of the yardarm from which hung the wireless antennas. Was that a footstep? And were those voices? . . . Sounds almost imperceptible; perhaps only the whisperings of memory or foresight. It was perhaps the sound of Smith, giving himself a body in the darkness; or Faubion, coming up out of the unfathomable with a short sigh; or Silber-stein, muttering as he clove the cobweb of oblivion in which he found

himself enshrouded; or Cynthia, waking from granite into starlight. It was
perhaps only the little sound of the atom falling in his mind, the atom falling like a star from one constellation to another, molecular disaster, infinitesimal tick, which, in its passage, created, illuminated and then destroyed this night, this ship, the corposants; Smith, Cynthia, Faubion, and
Silberstein.

He moved a little aft, touching, as he did so, with his left hand, the
damp lashings of lifeboat No. 14. This was the motor lifeboat, the trial of
which (during boat drill) he had witnessed at noon. Fourteen is half of
twenty-eight. The Number of the house had been 228—228 Habersham
Street. But this too was only the silent falling of a mind atom. He moved
aft, turning his back on this fatal number, which held his life in its poisonous coils, turning his back also on that ghostly company—incorporeal
Smith, whose cigar tip dimmed and glowed; Faubion, on whose lifted
fingers little blue corposants danced; Silberstein, who muttered; and Cynthia, whose face was turned to the east. They were already beginning to
talk, standing far apart, so that their faces were only faintly discernible; but
for the moment he was terrified, and delayed at the after-end of the hurricane deck, looking into the black south west; hearing the sound of the
voices, but not wholly the purport. Smith, he knew, had begun by speaking
Italian; then demotic Greek; then Provençal French; then Macaronic
Latin. Passing then to ancient Greek, he had quoted Meleager, to which
Faubian had replied, soberly, with Plato's epitaph for the drowned sailor:
Πλωτῆρες σώζοισθε καὶ εἰν ἁλὶ καὶ κατὰ γαῖαν. Ah! Both by land and sea. Remember him. And remember him that lies by the Icarian Rocks, his soul
given to the Aegean; and him too that was lost under the setting of dark
Orion, borne helpless in ocean, eaten by fishes—Callaeschus, whom the
sudden squall overtook at night. And him also do not forget, Erasippus,
whose bones whiten in a place known only to the sea gulls. For everywhere
the sea is the sea . . . It was Silberstein who added this last phrase: Silberstein of Sidon, Antipater of Harlem. Yes! It was Silberstein, and Smith
repeated the Greek after him, taking his cigar from his mouth to do so:
πᾶσα θάλασσα θάλασσα. They were all four silent then for a moment, while
Demarest, turning, walked toward them, filling his pipe in the darkness
with trembling fingers. And as he took his place a little way off from them,
his back against lifeboat No. 14, Cynthia turned again and said:

"They are about us! They go with us where we go. They are our history;
and we are their immortality."

"Yes," Smith answered sadly. "It is ourselves whose bones lie unclaimed
in the deep water that washes the Icarian Rocks; or beside the Needles; or
at the 'whuling Cyclades.' The sea is the sea—this we know—but also
were not our prayers answered? for we had, after all, or we have, our 'safe
passage home.' "

"Yes, we belong to them, and they to us," said Faubion quietly.
Demarest could see that she had lifted her face, and was regarding the
blue corposants on the mastheads. "And they and we, together, belong to
the all-gathering memory of the future. Or is it possible that we shall be
forgotten? But that question, I can see, is already answered by all of you."

"Answered already by all of us," Demarest said.

"Answered already," laughed Silberstein, "in the negative-affirmative . . . But who will he be, the last one who remembers us? And where will he stand? In a world perhaps englobed in snow."

"The one who remembers last," said Cynthia, "will remember always. For He will be God . . . That, at any rate, is the affirmative. Of the negative, what can be said? We know it, but we cannot speak of it."

"But we see it there," said Smith, "we see it there! The cold cloud, into which we return, the dark cloud of nescience, the marvelous death of memory!"

All five faces looked in the darkness at one another, as if for the instant almost surprised. At once, however, they all began laughing together: lightly, with recognition. Of course, of course! They had forgotten that for the moment! All except Demarest had forgotten it—Demarest and Smith.

"Well!" Faubion answered bravely, "that is of course what we must see, and what we *do* see. Nevertheless, can we not remain individual in our *feeling* toward this? Choosing, for our *pleasure*, purely (since there can be no other virtue in the choice) the yes or the no? And I, for one, as you already see, will choose the yes! I will be remembered! We will all be remembered! And never, never forgotten. World without end. Amen."

"Amen!" echoed Silberstein. "But Smith and Demarest do not feel as you do. Smith is the dark self who wants to die! Smith represents clearly —doesn't he?—that little something hidden in all of us—in the heart, or the brain, or the liver, or where you will—which all our days is scheming for oblivion. It's the something that remembers birth, the horror of birth, and remembers not only that but also the antecedent death; it remembers that nothingness which is our real nature, and desires passionately to go back to it. And it *will* go back to it."

"Yes, Smith will die and be forgotten," murmured Cynthia. "He already knows himself dead and forgotten; and it is the death in Smith that gives his brown eyes so benign a beam. Isn't that so? It is the death in Smith that we love him for. We respond to it, smiling, with maternal solicitude. *Moriturum salutamus* . . . There, there!"

Smith tapped his foot on the deck and chuckled.

"No no! Don't be too hard on me. Is that all I can be liked for? I could be hurt by that thought! . . . But of course it's perfectly true."

"But of first and last things," sighed Faubion, "there is no beginning and no end."

The five people stood motionless and silent, their faces faintly lighted by the corposants. This is the prelude, thought Demarest. This is merely the announcement of that perfect communion of which I have often dreamed. They have lost their individualities, certainly—but was individuality necessary to them? Or is it possible that, having lost their personalities, they have lost that alone by which harmony or discord was perceptible? Or is it only that their individualities have been refined by self-awareness, so that the feelings no longer intrude, nor the passions tyrannize, bringing misery? . . .

"That is true," said Silberstein. "Here, at any rate, we are: poised for an instant, conscious and delighted, in the midst of the implacable Zero. We remember—well, what do we remember? We remember that our bones are under the Icarian Rocks. We remember, too, that we are *only* what we thus remember and foresee. We foresee our past, and remember our future. Or so, at all events to interpose a little ease! And that's saying a good deal."

"It means everything," said Cynthia. "It means not only the past and future we have in common, but the past and future that each of us has separately. And this, of course, is precisely what blesses us. It is this diversity in unity that makes the divine harmony. Think only of the joy of recognition, or discovery, when Smith tells us—what indeed we know already, do we not? but in a sense not so deliciously complete—of his life in Devon, his opera tickets in New Orleans, his forgotten yachting cap and his delightful passion for Faubion! To know what grass is, does not preclude surprise at the individual grass-blade."

"How nice of you to compare me to a grass-blade! It's exactly what I am. But you meant more than that. Forgive me for parenthesizing."

"Yes, I did mean more than that. What do I mean? You say it, please, Mr. Demarest."

"Consciousness being finite, it can only in *theory* comprehend, and feel with, all things. Theoretically, nothing is unknown to us, and nothing can surprise us or alienate us. But if imagination can go everywhere, it can only go to one place at a time. It is therefore that we *have* surprises in store for each other—we reveal to each other those aspects of the infinite which we had momentarily forgotten. Who has not known Smith or Faubion? Cynthia and Silberstein are as old and familiar as God. And this sad facetious Demarest, who when he laughs looks so astonishingly like a magnified goldfish, isn't he too as archaic as fire? Yet you had forgotten that one could be sad and facetious at the same time, and that in addition to this one might look like a goldfish seen through a sphere of water and glass; and the rediscovery of these qualities, which results when they are seen in a fresh combination, this is what delights you and delighting you leads to *my* delight. This is what Cynthia means, and in fact what we all mean . . . Yes, and this is what blesses us. For this—on the plane of human relationship—is infinite love, a love which is indistinguishable from wisdom or knowledge, from memory or foresight. We accept everything. We deny nothing. We are, in fact, imaginaton: not completely, for then we should be God; but almost completely. Perhaps, in time, our imagination *will* be complete."

"You could have put it in another way," said Silberstein. "Each of us is a little essay upon a particular corner of the world, an essay which differs in style and contents from any other; each with its own peculiar tints and stains transmitted from environment. A terrific magic is stored in these little essays! more than the essay itself can possibly feel—though it can *know*. Of the *power* of Smith or Faubion to give me a shock of delight or terror, can they themselves form a complete idea? No—not in the least. Not, at any rate, till they have felt the peculiar shock of seeing *me*! After which, of course, they can begin that most heavenly of all adventures, the exploration of that world of feelings and ideas which we then reciprocate in creating—seeing at once the warm great continents, jungles, seas, and snowy mountains, arctics and Saharas, that we can roam in common; but guessing also the ultraviolet Paradises which we shall never be able to enter, and the infrared Infernos which ourselves will never be able to communicate. How can I ever make plain to Faubion or Cynthia why it is that they cannot as powerfully organize my feelings as they organize those of Demarest? There lies the infrared. There perhaps, also, whirls the ultraviolet. Dive into my history, if you like. Look! This deck is no longer a deck. It is a narrow slum street, paved with muddy cobbles. Do you see it?"

"It is a narrow slum street paved with muddy cobbles. On the East Side, New York. There is a smell of damp straw."

"The sound of drays, too, and steel-ringing shovels."

"Cats, ash cans, slush, and falling snow!"

"You all see it perfectly. Or almost. You see it in the abstract—not in the concrete. What you do not entirely see is the basement which my father used as his tailor shop—dark, damp, steamy, and incredibly dirty—where, as he ran his sewing machine, or peered nearsightedly into cardboard boxes for the one button which he couldn't find, he taught me Yiddish, German, and English. He was always putting down lighted cigarettes—on the edges of the tables, on chairs, on boxes, on the ironing board; and then forgetting them. A smell of burning was always interrupting us, and we would jump up and search frantically for the cigarette. A good many yards of cloth must have been ruined, first and last—and once a customer's raincoat caught on fire and had to be replaced. There was a terrible scene about it when the man came in for it . . . We ate and slept, and did our cooking, in the basement room behind this, from which yellow brick steps went up to a yard. My mother was dead—I don't remember her. When I wasn't at the public schools, I did the errands—delivered trousers that had been pressed, collected bills, and so forth. Naturally, I learned to cook, sew, and use the gas iron to press clothes, myself. But I also, at the public schools, and in the course of my running of errands, learned a great deal else. I knew the crowds at every saloon in the district, and the cops, and the buskers, and the leaders of the several 'gangs.' I knew all the brothels, and all the unattached prostitutes. I knew—as in fact all the boys of my age knew—which of the girls in the district (the girls of our own generation, I mean) had already gone the way of Sara More—the girls who were willing to be enticed into dark basements or unlighted back yards. Beryl Platt, Crystelle Fisher, Millicent Pike, Tunis (so-called, according to romantic legend, because she had been born in Tunis, and had an Arab father) Tunstall—before I was eleven I knew that there was something special about these girls; and when Crystelle one day dared me to come to her back yard after dark, I knew what was expected, and went. After that it was first one and then another. I had no feelings of sin about it—none whatever. It was natural, delightful, exciting, adventurous—it gave color to life. But I never fell in love. I liked these girls—I particularly liked the dashing swaggering Crystelle, whose hair was magnificently curled, and whose blue long eyes had an Oolong tilt, and who knew every smutty word in the language—but if they transferred their affections to other boys I didn't mind, or if other boys forcibly ousted me I didn't resent it. What did it matter? Life, I knew, was not exclusively composed of carnal love, and there was sure to be all of it that one needed. Why bother about it? Billiards was interesting, too, and so was tailoring, and I admired my father. I enjoyed reading with him, playing chess with him, and going with him to Coney Island or the Museum. When I was fourteen he took me to the Yiddish theater to see *Pillars of Society*. It made a tremendous impression on me. Why do I tell you this? Not because it's especially interesting in itself; but because it's exactly the sort of item which you wouldn't *precisely* guess for yourselves—isn't that it? Yes. You extract the keenest of pleasures from hearing of that, and seeing me in the gallery of the theater with my father, eating buttered popcorn. Just as you enjoy, also, hearing of Crystelle Fisher. These details enable you to bring your love of me, and of humanity, and the world, to a momentary sharp focus. Can one love in the abstract? No. It is not man or nature that we love, but the torn primrose, and young Mrs. Faubion, who is being sued by her husband for divorce on grounds of infidelity; Demarest, whose fear of his father has frozen him in the habit of inaction and immobility, as the hare freezes to escape attention; and Silberstein, who was seduced by arc light under a white lilac in a Bowery back yard . . . However, it was my intention, when I began this monologue, to light for you, if I could, the reasons for the fact that I cannot, like Demarest, fall in love with Faubion and Cynthia. Is it now indicated? The only time I ever came near falling in love was after we had moved to the country, when Mabel Smith, the schoolteacher, took possession of me. Mabel was sentimental and maternal. She did her best, therefore (as she was also something of a hypocrite), to arouse some sort of sentiment in *me*. And she almost succeeded, by sheer dint of attributing it to me. She tried to make me believe that I believed she was my guiding star, and all that sort of thing. Pathetic delusion, the delusion that one needs to be thus deluded! But this holiness never became real to me. How could it? I had been a placid realist since birth, calm as a Buddha. One has emotions, certainly; but one is not deceived by them, nor does one allow them to guide one's course . . . How, then, can I respond to all the exquisite romantic Dresden china that Cynthia keeps—to pursue the figure —on her mental mantel? No no! It's not for me; or only, as you see, intellectually and imaginatively. It delights me to recognize this so totally different mechanism of behavior—and I love Cynthia, therefore, exactly as I love that hurried moon, the snowflakes, or the blue-feathered corposant who gives us his angelic blessing. But if it is a question of *erotic* response, I would sooner respond to Crystelle, who is now a prostitute, and with whom I've often, since growing to manhood, had dinner at Coney Island. Much sooner! . . . Much sooner! . . ."

New York. Spring. The five people walked in the darkness along Canal Street. In Fagan's Drug Store the red, green, and yellow jars were brilliantly and poisonously lighted. Sally Finkelman came out, carrying a bottle of Sloan's liniment, and a nickel in change. Red stains of a lollypop were round her mouth. She crossed the street obliquely, and paused beside Ugo's copper peanut stand to warm her knuckles in the little whistling plume of steam. Ugo, standing in the garish doorway, held a bag of peanuts, red and green striped, by its two ears, and twirled it, over-and-over, three times. An elevated train went south along the Bowery. The five people crossed the muddy cobbles of the Bowery under the roar of the elevated, and passing Kelly's saloon, and Sam's Shoe Shine Parlor beside it

on the sidewalk (where French Louise was having her white slippers
cleaned) went slowly toward Essex Place. In the window of Levin's Café
were two glass dishes which contained éclairs and Moscovitz; one charlotte
russe (dusty); and a sheet of Tanglefoot flypaper, on which heaved a
Gravelotte of flies. An electric fan whirled rainbow-colored paper ribbons
over the Moscovitz. Solomon Moses David Menelek Silberstein, aged
twelve, came slowly out of Essex Place, with a pair of checkered trousers
over his shoulder. At the corner, under the arc light, he stooped to pick up
a long black carbon, discarded from the light. Uccelli, in the alley, was
grinding slowly his old-fashioned carpet-covered one-legged organ. Bubble
and squeak. The monkey took off his red velvet cap. Crystelle Fisher had
given him a sticky penny, which he had put into his little green velvet
pocket. Winking, he took off his cap again. The organ's wooden leg had a
brass ferrule, worn down on the inner side: a leather strap, attached to the
two outer corners, passed round Uccelli's neck. Bubble bubble squeak and
bubble. *Ta-ra-ra-ra-boom-de-ayy.* Crystelle danced a cakewalk, knees flinging
her dimity high, a huge hole showing in the knee of her right stocking,
a coarse lace petticoat flouncing. She snapped her fingers, jerking backward
her shapely head of golden curls, her oolong eyes half shut. *Coon—coon—
coon—I wish that color was mine.* Beryl Platt put her head out of a fourth-
story window, between two black geraniums, and yodled. I can't come out,
she sang. I've got to wash the dishes. And mind the baby . . . At the
corner, overtaking Silberstein, Crystelle touched his trousered shoulder—
Would you like to know a secret, she said—I can turn a Catherine wheel—
would you like to see me. Ha ha! Pork chops and gravy—I wish I was a
baby . . . Are you coming round to the yard tonight? . . . Bubble bubble
whine and bubble. Yes, I'll be there, said Solomon, and sauntered toward
the Bowery. Twenty-six Mott Street. A warm smell of benzine rose from
the damp trousers. With the carbon he drew a black line along Kelly's
wall, just as French Louise was getting down from the high brass-studded
shoe-shine throne. She gave Sam a nickel, and said—Where is that mutt?
He said he'd only take five minutes . . . A train rattled north on the elevated; empty: a conductor reading a paper on the rear platform, his knees
crossed . . . The five people, drifting slowly in the evening light under
the few pale stars of New York, paused before a battered ash can on which
the name Fisher had been red-leaded. Passing then through a door, which
was ajar, they saw the white lilac in blossom under the arc light. Below it,
on the hard bare ground, lay the bright skeleton of a fish, picked clean by
the cat. There was also the sodden remains of a black stocking . . .
Crystelle came running up the yellow brick stairs from the basement, and
at the same moment Solomon reappeared at the door. Look! she said. She
turned a series of swift Catherine wheels, hands to the ground, feet in the
air, skirts falling about her head, her flushed face up again. Solomon, pulling a spike of lilac-whiteness toward his nose, surveyed her without expression. Pork chops and gravy, he said. You've got a big hole—in your stocking.
I have not, she answered. You have, too, he said. Where! she answered. O
Jesus, how the hell did I do that. Have you ever kissed Tunis? . . . Sure I
have . . . Where? . . . In her cellar . . . Was it dark? . . . No, not
very . . . Well, why don't you kiss *me?* . . .

"Πᾶσα θάλασσα θάλασσα," said Smith absent-mindedly. " 'Rich happiness, that such a son is drowned.' "

"Well!" cried Cynthia into the sea-darkness. "Why not? We must all, in that sense, drown someday. Is Silberstein's drowning at twelve any worse than ours at twenty?"

"I like it," said Faubion. "Isn't it really better, a good deal, than all the refined hypocrisy of the honeymoon? . . . Always supposing that the honeymoon is the first!"

"Was it—with you?" Smith's voice had a chuckle in it.

"Of course not! I didn't live in a village for nothing . . ."

Her voice trailed away like the dying sound of a wave. A sea gull, floating astern, and crying, with turning head, *Klio*. Where do the sea gulls go at night? The sea gulls in mid-Atlantic? Do they sit on the waters? . . . *Klio klio*. The five blue corposants preened their blue phosphor-feathers. Demarest, leaving lifeboat No. 14, walked aft again, sucking at his cold pipe. The five people moving eastward with the ship. Five corposants. Five sea gulls. *Klio, klio*. Interchangeable. If one thinks in terms of quality-complexes, then a very slight dislocation of affects will give one a world in which no identities are permanent. An alarm clock rises in the east. A sky swarming with stars, at two in the morning, is merely the sensation of *formication*—ants crawling, as when one's foot is asleep. Faubion, uttering a short word quickly, with averted head, is a sea gull going downwind, crying, with turning head, *klio* . . . The corposants are five celestial voices, singing in the tops of the trees. They ululate softly in chorus, while the treetops thresh in the wind, as the mad nymphs ululated when Dido and Aeneas fled into the cave from the thunder. *Angels follow her—gravely, slowly—with silver and vermilion and rainbow wings—One, more luminous: lost in his own light: sits on a cherry-tree bough, and sings—Blest be the marriage of earth and heaven! Now, in the round blue room of space, The mortal son and the daughter immortal . . . make of the world their resting-place* . . . The marriage hymn, prothalamium, for my wedding with Cynthia, the stained-glass widow. Stained-glass window.

"Poor Demarest!" Cynthia was laughing, in the darkness. "Poor darling Demarest!"

"Am I so much to be pitied?"

"Is he so much to be pitied?"

"Much to be pitied?"

"Pitied? Pitied?"

"Pitied?"

The bird voices echoed one another, *klio klio*, wheeling and screaming. The sea claws and sea beaks pitied him, and the waves, too, coming louder from the southeast, their surfy voices the voices of destroyed universes of bubbles, sea-froth, evanescent as human pity.

"Of course he is to be pitied. And loved, too, in his fashion—as Silberstein said we love the hurrying moon and the angelic corposant. Loved, therefore, and pitied, as we love and pity ourselves. Who is this William Demarest? this forked radish? this carrier of germs and digester of food? momentary host of the dying seed of man? . . . He came to me to play chess, a copy of *The Spoils of Poynton* under his shiny coat sleeve."

"Ha ha. Demarest, the goldfish chess player."

"Fool's mate. Watchman, what of the knight? The psychiatrist beat him in ten moves. The mandolin player gave him his queen, and then drew the game. Nevertheless, he considers himself a very talented chess player. Poor Demarest."

"Treasure him, nevertheless, for he is a mirror of the world."

"We cherish him as we cherish ourselves. Is he not an epitome of universal history? Here he stands, on the deck of a dark ship, which is moving eastward at fifteen knots an hour. The steersman shifts the wheel, his eyes on the bright binnacle. The stokers stoke. The second engineer carries a long-beaked oil can up a clammy iron ladder. The first engineer lies in his stuffy bunk, reading *His Wife's Secret*. Under the ship are two miles of sea, and under the sea the half-cold planet, which rushes through freezing space to destruction, carrying with it continents of worthless history, the sea, this ship, Demarest . . . Who is this little, this pathetic, this ridiculous Demarest? We laugh at him, and also we weep for him; for he is ourselves, he is humanity, he is God. He makes mistakes. He is an egoist. He is imperfect—physically, morally, and mentally. Coffee disagrees with him; angostura causes him anguish; borborigmi interrupts his sleep, causing in his dreams falls of cliffs and the all-dreaded thunderstone; his ears ache; his nostrils, edematous; frontal headaches . . . Nevertheless, like ourselves, whose disabilities differ from his only in details, he struggles—why? to avoid the making of mistakes, to escape the tyrant solipsism, and to know himself; like us, he endeavors to return to God. Let him cry out as he will, let him protest his skepticism ever so loudly, he is at heart, like every other, a believer in perfection! . . ."

Klio klio! Cynthia's was the harsh melancholy voice of the sea gulls. The five sea gulls wheeled and screamed over the brown mud flat, at the edge of the eelgrass, where the obscene fiddler crabs scuttled in and out of oozy holes. Brown viscous froth, left by the receding tide. Cape Cod. What is that dark object that attracts them? A dead man. The corpse of Charlie Riehl, the hardware man, the suicide. The bluefish have picked at his head and hands these six days, since he jumped from the bridge; and now the sea gulls flap over him, crying, and the fiddler crabs advance with buzzing fiddles, crepitant army of mandibles.

"A believer in perfection."

"A believer."

"Perfection."

"Rich happiness, that such a son is drowned."

The five people crossed the meadow, stepping carefully among the fishing nets which Mr. Riley had spread out to dry. The hot sun drew a salt smell out of them, marshy and rich, fish-scaly. Passing under the arrowy-leaved ailanthus tree, and then rounding the sand-banked corner opposite Mr. Black's forge (Mr. Black was shoeing a horse) they stepped upon the wooden bridge, tripartite, the first and third sections of which crossed the two branches of the forked river, the intermediate section being merely a built-up road-bed on the tongue of marsh. The telegraph wires were singing multitudinously in the wind, a threnody. A metal windmill clanked. They crossed the first section of bridge, looking into the deep and rapid water, and seeing the red sponges that wavered deep-down on the pediments of barnacled stone; and then paused on the squeaking path of trodden and splintered scallop shells, which was bordered with starry St. John's Wort, coarse sappy honeysweet goldenrod, and scarlet-blistered poison ivy. Leaning then on the red wooden railing, they watched the two Rileys and Mr. Ezra Pope, the town constable, rowing the dirty dory toward a point at the farther end of the marsh. Low water. Sea gulls rose in a screaming cloud as they approached. The younger Riley, in red rubber boots, jumped out and pulled the dory up into the eelgrass. The two others got out, and all three moved slowly into the marsh, lifting high their knees. They were stooping over. Then they rose again, carrying something. It was Charlie Riehl, who had drowned himself rather than appear as a witness at the trial. *Klio klio!* At five in the morning it was: there among those red sponges. Feet first; with his pockets full of lead. *Klio!*

"Those are holes that were his eyes," murmured Smith. "Nothing of him but hath fed——"

"Narcissus! He sees himself drowned, like this Charlie Riehl. And pities himself. Well, why not? *That's* normal enough . . ."

Faubion held up her hands, on which the blue corposants were beginning to fade.

"Scavengers!" she cried. "That's what we are. Devourers of the dead: devourers of ourselves. Prometheus and the vulture are one and the same. Well! I *will* not countenance it. Any more than Demarest does."

She gave a little laugh, and the others laughed also, lightly and bitterly. Something had gone wrong with the scene. Disruption. Dislocation of affects. Quarrel of ghosts. Fecal coloring of imagery. The night falling over like a basket, spilling miscellaneous filth. No! Only the atom in the brain! falling infinitesimally, but by accident wrecking some central constellation. The five ghosts quarreling on the deck with harsh voices were the five sea gulls in Trout River. Charlie Riehl was himself. Drowning was consummation. It was all very simple—you turned a screw, and everything at once changed its meaning. *Klio,* said Cynthia. *Klio, klio,* sang the mad nymphs for Dido, ululating; and the vulture, tearing with sadistic beak at the liver of Prometheus—*klio, klio!* it cried, turning the Semitic profile of Silberstein . . . But this was disturbing! One must pull oneself together—set the basket of stars on end again. What was it that had caused this trouble, this quick slipping brain slide, vertigo, that sent everything skirling and screaming raucously down the abyss? Whirlpool. Cloaca. Groping for trout in a peculiar river. Plaster of warm guts. Clyster. Death, with your eyes wide open. *Christ!* . . . He leaned hard on lifeboat No. 14 (the motor lifeboat —they took off the canvas cover to test the engine, and stepped a little wireless pole in the bow thwart) and shut his eyes. Think. Project. Sublimate. Everything depends on it. In the sweat of your brow, the ventricle contracted, the dew dripping——

"Is it not possible, then"—he cried—"this perfection of understanding and interchange? Cynthia?"

"Oh, as for that——" Cynthia's voice seemed to come from farther off, floatingly.

"As for that!" jeered Silberstein.

"That!" quacked Smith.

He opened his eyes. The four figures, in the now almost total darkness, were scarcely perceptible—mere clots in the night. The stars had been engulfed.

"He came to me with a shabby chessboard under his arm! And he had forgotten to button——"

"Please adjust your dress before leaving . . ."

"He permitted me to pay his fare in the bus! Yes, he did! You may not believe it, but he did!"

"Rear seat reserved for smokers . . . Lovers with umbrellas at the top——"

"And do you know what he said when I asked him if he would like to come one afternoon to hear my brother William play Bach on the piano? Do you know what he said, delicious provincial little Yankee that he is and always will be? . . . '*You bet!*' "

"Ho ho! Ha ha! He he!"

"Suppress that stage laughter, please. Silence! His impurial highness——"

"I beg you," said Faubion, "I beg you not to go on with this!"

"Silence! His impurial highness, greatest failure as a dramatist that the world has ever known, supreme self-devouring egotist, incomparable coward, sadist and froterer, voyeur and onamist, exploiter of women—William Demarest, late of New York, and heir of all the ages——"

"*Stop!*"

"What's the matter with Faubion? Is she in love with the idiot?"

"Perhaps she's right. We ought to be sorry for him. More to be pitied than blamed. After all, he's an idealist: a subjective idealist."

"Who said so? An automaton like the rest of us. Nigger, blow yo' nose on yo' sleeve, and let dis show pro-ceed!"

"You must remember that we are only figments of his——"

Klio! klio! klio!

The gulls, the waves, the corposants, all screamed at once. The wave in Caligula's dream. The sea ghost, seaweed-bearded, with arms of green water and dripping fingers of foam. *Oo—wash—oo—wallop*—are you awake—King Buskin? . . . And he never said a mumbalin' word. The blood came twinklin' down. And he never said a mumbalin' word . . . Tired, tortured, twisted; thirsty, abandoned, betrayed.

"—Silence! The transfiguration scene will now begin. Dress rehearsal. Special benefit performance for Mr. Demarest. At the first stroke of the bell, Miss Battiloro, arch snob and philanderer, several times engaged, virgin in fact but not in thought, she who stood on a June day perspiring and admiring, adoring and caloring, before the unfinished Titian, will take her place beneath the mainmast, on the port side, facing the stern. Her head will be bowed forward meekly, and in her hands she will clasp lightly, with exquisite Rossetti unlikelihood, a waxen lily. At the second stroke of the bell, the five angelic corposants will unite in the air above her, singing softly, as they tread the wind, the verses written by Mr. Demarest for the occasion—*King Caligula*. No weeping, by request. Listening to this heavenly music, with its message of healing for all mankind, Miss Battiloro will lift her eyes, in the attitude of one who sees, at long last, the light that never was on land or sea. While she is in this attitude, the third stroke of

the bell will be given by the shipboy; and on the instant Miss Battiloro
will be transformed, for all time, into a stained-glass widow. Beg pardon,
I mean window. Now is everything in readiness, please? Shipboy, are you
there? . . . He says he is there. Is Miss Battiloro ready to make this noble
and beautiful sacrifice?"

"Ay ay, sir."

"Miss Battiloro says she is ready to make this noble and beautiful sacrifice. And Mr. William Demarest—is Mr. William Demarest present? Mr.
Demarest, please?"

"Oh yes, *he's* here, all right!"

"Very well, then, we will proceed . . . Shipboy, the first bell, if you
will be so kind!"

It was painfully true, every word of it. The bell note fell down from
aloft, a golden ingot of sound, and Cynthia was standing under the tall tree
as announced; like a charade for purity and resignation; clad in white
samite; and clasping a tall lily with unimaginable delicacy. Wasn't it perhaps, however, more Burne-Jones than Rossetti? It was a little dark, and
therefore difficult to see; but Demarest thought so. Yes. And at the second
bell note—three minutes have elapsed, silent save for the hushing sound
of the waves—Cynthia lifted her meltingly beautiful eyes, and the five blue
seraphim, treading the night air above her, began softly, sighingly, to sing.
This was very affecting. In spite of the warning, it was difficult to refrain
from tears. Smith, in fact, gave an audible sob, like a hiccough. At the
words *"resting-place,"* the five seraphs disbanded, two deploying to starboard, two to port, and the fifth catapulting straight up toward the zenith.
At this moment, Demarest experienced acutely a remarkable temptation.
He desired to rush forward, kneel, bury his face passionately in the white
samite, and cry out—γύναι, ἴδε ὁ υἱός σου! Before he could do more than
visualize this action, however, the third stroke of the bell was given. The
whole night had become a Cathedral. And above Demarest, faintly luminous in the cold starlight that came from beyond, was a tall Gothic window,
where motionless, in frozen sentimentalites of pink, white, and blue,
Cynthia was turned to glass.

⟪ VII

*To his Lady, his Mother, his Wife, his Sister: her Servant, her Child, her
Lover, her Brother, and to express all that is humble, respectful, and loving,
to his Cynthia, W. D. writes this.*

ONE

You are not ill-educated, Cynthia—if for the first and last time you
will permit me so to address you—and you will therefore recognize this

clumsy paraphrase of the salutation with which Heloise began the first of her letters to Peter Abelard. It is not by accident that I choose this method of opening what will no doubt be the last letter I address to you. For what, under the peculiar circumstances—I refer to the fact that, for reasons into which I forbear to inquire, your mother and yourself have decided to drop me from your acquaintance—what could be more likely than this beautiful exordium to persuade your eye to read further? And that, for me, is all-important. The reasons for this you will readily understand. Suppose this letter is delivered to you by your stewardess. I shall be careful to address the envelope in a style which you will not recognize, so that you will at least not destroy it unopened; but having opened it, is there not a great likelihood that you will then tear it to pieces as soon as you see from whom it comes? Yes. And for that reason I have—let me confess at once my iniquity, calculated iniquity!—employed this striking method of greeting you. It will perhaps—that frail pontoon "perhaps," on which so many desperate armies have crossed—amuse you, perhaps even a little excite your curiosity. You might retort, derisively, that it is odd of me to model my salutation on that of Heloise rather than on that of Abelard? But unfortunately, Abelard is altogether too blunt for my purpose. He plunges in with a directness quite disconcertingly up-to-date; beginning with a mere "could I have known that a letter not addressed to you would fall into your hands." Would this be more likely to tempt you on, Cynthia? Or could I have the heart to begin, as Abelard began his fourth epistle, "Write no more to me, Heloise, write no more"? . . . This would be both melancholy and absurd.

And the impulse to write to you, by way of leave-taking, is imperious. It seems to me that I have an infinitude of things that I must say to you. You know how one feels on a dock, when one sees one's friend sail away, perhaps forever? the regret, almost the agony, with which one remembers a few of the things one has forgotten to say, or hadn't the courage to say? One never, after all, told him how much one loved him. Not even a hint. One never, after all, showed one's simple joy in the fact that one, at least partially, possessed him. One never so much as breathed the suggestion that one would feel his absence. And then, there is all the good advice that one has forgotten to give, all the solicitude for his future that one has somehow failed to express! You are going to a tropical climate? Do not forget your cork helmet and your parasol! Remember, when you get up in the morning, to empty the scorpions out of your boots! . . . You are going to the North Pole? Be sure, then, to take a thermos flask filled with hot rum and coffee, and plenty of almond chocolate, and your goloshes, and your heaviest woolens! . . . Nor do I mean this facetiously. The advice is usually just as stupid as this, just as useless. But it serves its purpose: no matter how clumsily administered, it serves to express the aching concern with which one sees the departure; and its expression is at once accepted as just that and nothing else. And so it is with me, Cynthia. I have never told you in so many words that I love you—partly because there was no time for it, our acquaintance being so brief and so scattered; and partly for psychological reasons: my profound sense of inferiority, my sense of filthiness, and my fear of all decisive action, all being partially responsible. And now it is too late, for I find you (again in mid-Atlantic!

surely one of the most remarkable coincidences that ever befell two human
creatures!) engaged to be married; and no sooner am I informed of this fact
than I am "dropped" by you—given, in fact, the "cut direct" by your
mother. Well! This has one saving grace, this magnificent disaster—for I
can now say, once and for all, that I love you.

Having said this much, however, I find myself oddly at a loss as to
how to continue. The truth is, my imagination has dealt with you so continuously, and so strenuously, and so richly, that I have no longer any
definite sense as to where, exactly, between us, the psychological boundary
lies. Two nights ago, for example, after our encounter on the deck (where,
of course, as I am in the second cabin, I had no right to be) I lay awake
all night, re-enacting every scrap of our little history, and improvising a
good deal besides. In this you were—as indeed you are in *all* my reflections
—"Cynthia"; and you were admitted to an intimacy with me (this may
surprise you!) which I have vouchsafed to no one else. As I look back on
that long orgy of self-communion, which had you as its chief but not as its
only theme, I find in it naïveté a good deal that amuses me. It is a curious
and instructive fact, for example, that in that moment of *Sturm und Drang*
I should have experienced so powerfully a desire to talk to you about my
childhood. I found myself constantly reverting to that—babbling to you
my absurd infantine confidences and secrets, as if you were—ah!—my
mother. Exactly! And isn't that the secret of your quite extraordinary influence upon me? For some reason which I cannot possibly analyze, you
strike to more numerous and deeper responses in me than any other woman
has done. It must be that you correspond, in ways that only my unconscious memory identifies, to my mother, who died when I was very small.
Can it be that? . . . Anyway, there it is; and as I sit here in my beloved
smoking room, waited on by Malvolio, (do you remember how, on the nice
old *Silurian*, you reproached me for sitting in the smoking room so much?
do you remember how, one evening, we listened, standing just outside the
door, on the dark deck, to the men singing there?)—well, as I sit here,
hearing the slap of rubber quoits on the deck above, it is again a desire to
talk to you of my childhood that comes uppermost. Strange! It really seems
to me that there is something exquisitely appropriate in this: it seems to
me that in this there might be some hope of really *touching* you. I do not
mean that I harbor any hope that you will break off your engagement and
engage yourself to me. (For one thing, I am not at all sure that I would
want to marry.) Nor do I mean anything quite so obvious as that you
should be touched *sentimentally*. No. What *do* I mean, then? Well, I
mean that this would be the most direct, simple, and really effective mode
of establishing the right communion between us. I don't think this is
merely a circumlocution or clumsy evasion. What I am trying to say, perhaps, is that to talk to you of my childhood—to tell you of some one particular episode—would be for us what the good advice regarding goloshes
was for the departing traveler: a profound symbol of intimacy. Even that
is not the whole story. For also—and here, I admit, I *do* plunge recklessly
into the treacherous underworld of effects—I feel with a divine confidence
that is tantamount to clairvoyance that to tell you of some such episode
would be to do you an *exquisite violence*. Why? Because I am perfectly

certain that whatever is true—I mean *idiosyncratically* true—of me, is also deeply true of you; and my confession would therefore be your—accusation! An impeachment which you would be the first (but with a delighted shock) to admit.

But no——— This *is* an evasion, an attempt to rationalize a mere feeling, *ex post facto*. The truth is, I am confused, and scarcely for the moment know what I *do* think or feel. Unhappy? Oh, yes! as the Negro spiritual says. What else could be expected? Yet I blame no one but myself for my unhappiness, and I hope I am too intelligent to suppose that my unhappiness is of any importance. Confused. My imagination darts in fifty directions, checked in each. I desire you—I hate you—I want to talk intimately with you—I want to say something horribly injurious to you . . . At one moment, it is of the purely trivial that I should like to talk to you. I should like to tell you of the amusing affair of old Smith (who was with me when I met you) and Mrs. Faubion, who sits opposite us at table; of how, last night, having made himself mildly tipsy with Guinness, he attempted to get into Mrs. Faubion's room, just as she and her roommate (an incredible young woman!) were going to bed; how he put his foot inside her stateroom door (and such funny shoes he wears! horned like the rhino!) and tried to engage her in banter, meanwhile displaying, as if guilelessly, a purse full of gold sovereigns! At dinner, last night, he had told me of this project, and I had tried to dissuade him from it. No use. He was convinced that Mrs. Faubion was *"that sort"* . . . And this morning at breakfast, when Mrs. Faubion and I were alone, it all came out, the whole wretched story. "What was the matter with Mr. Smith last night?" "Matter? Was something the matter?" "Yes! He came to our room, and got his foot inside the door, and *wouldn't* go away—all the time trying to show some gold money he had in a pocketbook! We had to shut the door in his face! . . . Actually! . . . And *then* he tried to come back again! I had to threaten to ring for the steward . . ." She looked at me, while she said this, with an air of profound wonder and mystification, perhaps just faintly tinged with suspicion. It puzzled her. What could have been the matter with the old man? And was I involved? . . . I suggested, of course, that he was just a little tipsy, and urged her to pay no attention to it. She remained, however, puzzled, and a little unconvinced . . . And Smith! When I walked round the deck with him later in the morning, did he say anything to me about this tragic—for him, I assure you, tragic—adventure? Not a word. Not a single word. But he was unhappy, and quiet—I could see the misery in him turning and turning round that dreadful and brief little disaster; while he revolved in his mouth one of the "expensive" cigars which his employer had given him as a parting present . . . Well, a horrible little episode, you will say, and why should I want to describe it to you? Again, because I am sure it will touch in you certain obscure chords which it touched in me, and set us to vibrating in subconscious harmony. Pity? Horror? Wonder? A sense of the disordered splendor and unexpectedness and tragedy of life? All these things, Cynthia; but chiefly the desire that we might again, as last year at the Bach concert, *listen together*.

And of course my childhood recollection is even better than that; for, narrated by me to you, it constitutes the playing upon us both of a chord unimaginably rich in stimuli. Consider some of these. The fact that I tell you this story—(as a "story" it is nothing—merely, say, the description of the sailing of a whaleship from New Bedford)—puts you in the position of the mother, and me in the position of the child; but it also makes our relation that of father and daughter. Again, it makes us both *children*—brother and sister, perhaps. Or, once more, it takes the color of a dual conspiracy, the delicious conspiracy of two adults to *become* children. Sentimental? No doubt. But the device, if anything so entirely spontaneous can be called a device, is universal. Baby talk! My baby doll! Icky fing! . . . Revolting when we detect others in this singular regression, but just the same the instinct is powerful in all of us, and given the right circumstances will betray itself without the least compunction . . . Very well, then—the right circumstances have arisen *chez moi*, and I must report to you this tiny episode taken from my childhood. Like the flowers that bloom in the spring, tra la, it seems to have no connection; but, tangential though its pertinence may be, its pertinence is none the less profound.

When my mother and father died, the children were distributed, for temporary shelter, among various relatives; and it was my good fortune to be sent for a winter to the house of my father's cousin, Stanley Bragg, in New Bedford, who had come forward with an offer to look after "one male child." Of course, I was at first bewildered by the abrupt change, the removal from tropics to New England, the separation from my brother and sister; but on the other hand I had always been fond of Cousin Stanley; and his house, which I had several times visited, had always seemed to me quite the most beautiful and romantic in the world. It stood well back from County Street, concealed by elms and huge horse chestnuts, on a high grassy terrace. On the lower lawn (and this had, to begin with, particularly fascinated me!) stood a life-sized figure of a stag, cast in dark metal. It looked very lifelike, especially when it had been wetted (as frequently in summer) by the garden sprinkler. The garden, behind the house, was divided formally into squares by high box hedges which were full of spiderwebs and superb spiders—the latter I used to tempt out of their deep funnels of silk by twitching a strand of web with a twig: and I had the feeling that they used positively to *growl* at me. Here there was an old-fashioned chain well, like a little latticed house, overgrown with honeysuckle, which worked with a crank; and which kept up a gentle clinking while from the revolving cups on the chain it gushed forth the most delicious water. There were also fruit trees, flower beds, a wilderness of nasturtiums round the pump, and at the end of all, before you got to the barn, grape arbors all across the back wall—so thickly grown that on a not *too* rainy day you could crawl in under the vines and eat grapes in shelter. In the stable, of which John was the benevolent king, were the two horses which Cousin Stanley kept; a solemn black closed coach; a light buggy, for country driving; and, in the cellar, a pig. On one wall, where the whips and harnesses were hung, was nailed a wood carving of a large heart-shaped leaf.

The house itself was a comfortable mansard-roofed affair, with a wide "piazza" (on which stood tubs of hydrangeas) and lofty rooms in which one got an impression of a good deal of white marble. Among its wonders, for me, were the wooden shutters, which slid magically out of the walls beside the windows, and a great number of small carved objects of jade and soapstone and ivory, brought from China and Japan by Cousin Stanley's father. Best of all, however, was the attic, and its cupola. Cupola! I remember how strange the word sounded when I first heard it pronounced by Miss Bendall, the housekeeper, who smelt of camphor. It struck me as "foreign"—a *Northern* word, surely!—and I hadn't the remotest idea in the world how one would go about spelling it. But from the moment when Cousin Stanley, stooping a little (as he was very tall) led us up the dark stairs to the warm wooden-smelling attic, and then, with triumph (this was several years before) showed us the cupola itself, I entertained no doubts as to its fascinations. Miserable child, who has no cupola for his rainy mornings! It was in itself a perfect little house, glassed on all sides, with a window-seat all around, so that one could sit on whatever side one liked and look out to the uttermost ends of the earth. Over the slate roofs of houses, one looked steeply downhill to the harbor, the bright masts, the blue water, the Fairhaven ferry, and Fairhaven itself beyond. Farther to the right one saw the long red brick buildings of the cotton mills (not so numerous as now) and then the Point, and the Bug lighthouse, and the old fort, and the wide blue of Buzzard's Bay. With a good glass, one might have made out the Islands; or observed the slow progress of a Lackawanna or Lehigh Valley tug and its string of black coal barges all the way from Fort Rodman to Cuttyhunk; or pick up the old *Gay Head* sidewheeling back from Wood's Hole, with its absurdly laborious walking beam.

You can imagine, Cynthia, how enthralled I was with all this, and how quickly, in my absorption in such wonders, I forgot the separation from my brother and sister, and the tragedy—now far off, tiny, and sound-less—which had brought it all about. It soon seemed as if I had always lived in New Bedford, with Miss Bendall and Cousin Stanley and old John (a perfect stage coachman!) and Mabel, the Irish cook, who churned the butter in the pantry. I knew every flower and spider in the garden, every branch of every tree, and whether it would hold my weight or not; and every picture in every one of the forty-odd bound volumes of Harpers which I used to take up with me to the cupola. The great black cistern, which concealed somewhere a sinister little tinkle of water, was my ocean, where I sailed a flotilla of small blue-painted boats provided by Cousin Stanley. In the evenings, there was often a game of cribbage with Cousin Stanley or Miss Bendall, or else Cousin Stanley would talk to me about ships and shipping—he was a shipowner—and the voyages he had made as a young man. Smoking a crackling great calabash pipe, he talked rapidly and vividly; so much so that I sometimes found it difficult, afterward, to get to sleep: my senses stimulated, my imagination full of sights and sounds. It was a result of these talks that I began, in the afternoons and on Saturdays, exploring the wharves for myself. With what a thrill I used to start down Union Street, seeing, at the bottom of the mile-long cobbled hill, the bright golden eagle of a pilothouse! Or how entrancing to discover in the morning, when I looked down from the cupola before breakfast, a new four-master coming up the harbor, with its dark sails just being dropped!

The magnificent climax to all this, however, came early one Saturday morning—when Cousin Stanley woke me and told me to get dressed quickly: he "had a surprise for me." The big bell in the Catholic steeple, a block away, by which I always went to bed and got up, was striking five, and it was just beginning to be light. What could the surprise be? I had no idea, but I knew better than to spoil Cousin Stanley's delight in it by asking. When I went down the stairs, he was waiting for me in the darkness by the door, holding one finger to his lips as a sign to me to be quiet. We stole out, tiptoed across the piazza, and down the flagged path to the gate, where John was waiting for us with the buggy. "To the Union Street Wharf, John!" said Cousin Stanley—and instantly I was lost in a chaos of intoxicating speculations. Were we going to sea? but how could we, without luggage, without even our coats or sweaters? . . . The sky was beginning to turn pink as we turned from North Street; the city was profoundly still; not a sound, except for Betsy's *clip-clop* on the asphalt and the twittering of sparrows and robins in the elms, where a deeper darkness seemed still to linger. But when we turned again, into the foot of Union Street, what a difference! For there before us, on the long confused wharf, was a scene of the most intense activity—a whale-ship was being made ready for the sea.

Dismounting, we plunged into the midst of this chaos. The ship, in which Cousin Stanley owned a share, was the *Sylvia Lee*: she was, he told me, pointing to her crossed spars, a brig, and one of the last sailing vessels in the whaling trade. Two gangways led aboard her; and along these shuffled a steady stream of men, carrying boxes, bundles, small kegs, and coils of rope. Cousin Stanley moved away to talk with someone he knew, leaving me beside a pile of fresh wooden boxes, the very boxes which were rapidly being shouldered aboard. Shouts, cries, commands, a fracas of voices—how did they manage to hear one another? A man with a brown megaphone was leaning over the bow rail of the brig (the white bowsprit pointed up Union Street) and shouting "Mr. Pierce! Mr. Pierce!" . . . Where was Mr. Pierce? and what was he wanted for? and who was the man with the megaphone? The tops of the masts were now struck by the sun, and became surprisingly brilliant, orange-colored, in contrast with the still-somber wharf and the dark hulk of the vessel herself. Sea gulls fluttered and swooped, quarreling, around the stern, where a man in a white jacket had emptied a pail of garbage. These too, when they rose aloft, entered the sunlight and became flamingo-colored. "Mr. Pierce! . . . Mr. Pierce! Is Mr. Pierce there?" I became anxious about Mr. Pierce. What if he should arrive too late? It might be something terribly important. "Jones! send one of your men up to the office, will you, and see if Mr. Pierce is there. If he is, tell him I haven't got my papers yet. At once!" Where was Jones? I heard no reply from him, but there must have been one, lost in the general hubbub, for the megaphone seemed to be appeased. Only for a moment, however: it reappeared immediately on the high deck of the stern, before the deckhouse. "Now then men, make it lively. I want those gangways cleared in five minutes . . . Mr. Jones, will you see that the slack in that cable is taken in." . . . A block began a rhythmic chirping in the bow— two men, leaning backward, pulled in short, hard pulls at a rope. The pile of boxes beside me was diminishing—a dozen, ten, eight, six—condensed soup.

"Well, Billy! Shall we go aboard?"

This was the moment of Cousin Stanley's delight, and in reply I could do nothing but grin. Was he serious? I didn't like to commit myself, one way or the other.

"Come along, then!" he added, and led the way to the bow gangway, which was now clear. It consisted merely of two great planks lashed together at the ends, and it swayed, when we reached the middle, with a shortening rhythm which seemed disquietingly to come up to meet one's foot in mid-air. In the dirty water between wharf and ship a lot of straw, bottles, and some lemon peels rose and fell, suckingly. I felt dizzy. I was glad to jump down from the broad black bulwark to the weatherworn deck. We walked aft, and climbed up the short companionway to the poop.

"Good morning, Captain! Just about ready, eh?"

"Mornin', Stanley. Yep—tug should be here now. . . . There she is, too. You haven't seen Pierce, have you?"

"Pierce? No. Why?"

"He hasn't brought my—"

The little tug *Wamsutta* (old friend of mine) floundered astern of us with ringing bells and a sudden up-boiling of foam over her reversed propellers. The pilot was leaning out of his little window, shouting, a corn cob in his fist. The *Sylvia Lee* began swaying a little, agitatedly, with creaking hawsers. The Captain turned his megaphone toward the *Wamsutta* and spoke quietly—

"I'll be ready in five minutes, Peter . . . Mr. Jones, get your men aboard. Has Mr. Pierce been found?"

"Yes, sir. He's just goin' aboard."

"All right. When he's off, throw out your gangways, and be ready to give Peter a hand. And have some men standing by to cast off."

"Yes sir."

The wharf had suddenly become perfectly silent. A dozen men stood motionless, in a group, watching us with an air of profound wonder, as if already we had passed out of their lives and become something remote, unexplained, transcendental. One of the last of the whale ships! But we were something more than that—we were a departing world, the moon taking its first flight from the earth. And I felt myself that I belonged to the *Sylvia Lee*, and was at last taking leave of everything familiar, setting forth at daybreak toward the unimaginable, the obscure, the unattainable. *Islands* somewhere! the Islands of the Blest! or wherever it was that old Ulysses went, beyond the Pillars of Hercules—those same islands that I still dream about periodically, lying in mid-Atlantic, two fair green isles divided by a deep strait, and inhabited by a tall race of surpassing beauty! Was it something like this I thought of? The *Wamsutta* had come puffing alongside, its bell ringing twice and then once and then three times; the hawsers were cast off and fell swashing into the dirty water; and the *Sylvia Lee*, trembling, began to glide stern-foremost into the breezy harbor. The men waved their caps and shouted farewells. "So long, Mike! Don't lose

your false teeth!" "Don't forget to tell Jim what I told you!" "So long, boys!
We'll be back for the next election!" "So long! So long!" . . . Phrases
were replaced by shouts, and then the shouts by wavings; and as the *Wamsutta* turned us handily about in midstream, and then strode ahead of us
with easier puffs and lengthening towrope, a pandemonium of bells and
whistles gave us a wild salute. Good-by, New Bedford! Good-by, Achushnet
River! We're rolling down to Rio, rolling down to the Horn, racing north
to the Pole, where the icebergs grind screaming together and the right
whale breaches through a sheet of ice and snow! . . . The lighthouse
keeper in the "Bug" ran out on his lowest circular balcony and blew his
little tin foghorn three times as we passed, and then, waving his arm,
shouted something unintelligible. He looked very small, and his dinghy,
bowing on the end of its painter under the balcony, seemed no bigger than
a peasecod. I felt that I was leaving this, too, forever; and the gaunt
scarred rocks of Fairhaven, which smelt so deliciously of kelp at low tide,
where I had so often explored the salt pools; and Fort Rodman, where the
tiny blue sentry crept back and forth by the barracks like a toy. Good-by,
good-by! William Demarest is going away on the *Sylvia Lee*; you will never
again see him driving on the Point Road, or gathering scallop shells on the
salt beach that looks westward toward Padanaram. Never again. Never
again.

Away on the *Sylvia Lee!* We had cleared the Point already, and now
we could glance up the deep inlet that led to Padanaram and Dartmouth.
Further off, on our starboard bow, lay the low green brightening shore of
Nonquitt, with its Elephant Rock, its Spindle, its rickety little wharf, its
mosquitoes, and its bog full of red lilies and orchids. I tried to make out
the Spindle, with its little keg on top of the iron pole, but it was too far
away. Farewell, Nonquitt! We are whalers sailing away to perils and
wonders in uncharted seas! . . . Cousin Stanley suddenly lifted me up so
that I could see into one of the whaleboats, with its rusty harpoons and
tub of coiled rope. Mr. Jones and the Captain were beside us; and Mr.
Pierce, who had not gone ashore after all.

"She doesn't look very smart, does she?" said the Captain. He rubbed
a harsh finger on the blistered gunwale. "But there'll be plenty of time for
paintin' and polishin' between here and Valparaiso . . . I think if you're
goin' to get some breakfast, Stanley——"

"Yes. I suppose we'd better have it. Like some breakfast, Billy?"

Breakfast! a deep qualm opened within me like a kind of marsh-
flower. I suddenly became conscious of the fact that I was on a *ship*. We
went down a steep stairway into the officers' saloon, gloomy and evil-
smelling, where a red and pink tablecloth covered a long table. At the
forward end, the table abutted on a slant mast-root which was beautifully
encased in varnished and inlaid wood, and around which ran a little
mahogany tumbler-rack, like a veranda. But the smell was appalling! The
smell of whale oil, perhaps, which, after years of whale voyaging, had
saturated the ship. My gorge rose, and I was terrified lest, on a calm day,
with no excuse whatever, I should disgrace myself by being sick. I sat down
gingerly. The idea of eating food became abhorrent to me; the bread looked
dusty and hard, the corned beef a thousand years old; the dishes, too, were

thick and grayish, somehow oppressive. And then, to have corned beef, and boiled potatoes, with their skins imperfectly removed, for breakfast! In a state of passive weakness, not daring to move or speak lest the paroxysm should seize me, I allowed Mr. Jones to give me corned beef and potatoes. Reluctantly, I raised my fork to begin, when the cook (the man in the white jacket whom I had seen emptying the pail of garbage!) put down before me a thick china bowl, full of *melted butter*. Into this he dropped a dull leaden spoon. "Help yourself, sonny!" he said. "Whale oil." Incontinently, I raised my hand to my mouth, and felt myself on the point of giving that horrible little crow which is the prelude to disaster. My mouth drew itself together—I felt my tongue cold against my cold palate—and then I rose and fled. Disgraced! The laughter that followed me up the steep stairway was kindly, however, and as I stood again by the bulwark in the fresh wind I forgot that momentary discomfort in the sheer romanticism of the voyage. Valpraiso! Was it really possible? These sails, which the men were now breaking out one by one, and which now gently filled with the following wind, and shifted a little with a settling creak of spars long unused, these sails would carry the *Sylvia Lee* all the way to Tierra del Fuego, and round the Horn to Valparaiso. What would Union Street seem like then, with its little green streetcars? Would the men remember Buttonwood Park, and the bears, and the motor-paced bicycle races at the bicycle track? Would they talk about these things, or long for them, these things which were now so commonplace and real? Would these things then seem as distant and incredible as Valparaiso seemed now? . . .

Well, Cynthia—I draw to the end of this simple narrative. I find myself losing heart or losing impetus. What if, after all, the impulse to tell of it should seem to you rather silly? . . . Yet, at the last minute, it had its thrill of terror, which perhaps more than anything else served to make it memorable. For when the sails had all been spread, and the towrope had been cast off, and the *Wamsutta* drew away to starboard and stopped, her nose pointing toward Cuttyhunk, it was then that the greatest moment came. One of the whaleboats was manned and lowered into the sea; into this we clambered, Mr. Pierce and Cousin Stanley and I; and the men pulled away toward the waiting tug. The *Sylvia Lee* hung enormous above us, her sails flapping, as we drew out from her shadow; but I now paid little attention to the beautiful tall ship, for I had discovered that the whaleboat was leaking, leaking fast! In a moment I had to draw up my feet. Before we had gone half the distance to the *Wamsutta* we had taken in about four inches of water. Were we sinking? Would we get there before we sank? What astonished me was the indifference of the men at the oars—they sat with their feet in the swashing water and hauled stolidly away as if nothing whatever were occurring. I felt, therefore, that it would be a breach of etiquette to comment, or show anxiety, and I scarcely knew *what* attitude to take toward Mr. Pierce's humorous observation that it looked "as if they were trying to drown us." It hardly seemed a subject for joking. I was measuring the water, measuring the gap between us and the *Wamsutta*; and seldom have I experienced such an acute sensation of relief as when we drew alongside and climbed aboard in a smell of oil and hot-breathing engines. More remarkable still, however, was the fact that the men in the whaleboat did not pause to bail out the water—which was now halfway up their legs—but at once turned the heavy boat about and started back again. How slowly, how laboriously, she seemed to creep! By the time they had come up once more with the *Sylvia Lee* her gunwales were only a foot out of water. They were safe, however—we saw them climb briskly aboard. And then we saw the boat being hauled up, while one man bailed with a pail, flinging great scoops of hollow silver over the side; and at once, majestically, with filling sails, the *Sylvia Lee* bore away. The men waved to us and shouted—the *Wamsutta* blew three vibrating blasts of her whistle—and while the ship moved statelily southward, we turned and chug-chugged back toward New Bedford. Good-by, *Sylvia Lee!* . . . Good-by indeed. For the *Sylvia Lee* was destined to be one of the tragedies of the sea. None of the men who sailed away with her ever returned. No one ever knew how she was wrecked. All that was found of her, two years later, west of the Horn, was the fragment of sternplate that bore her name.

(Not sent.)

TWO

My dear Miss Battiloro:

You will be surprised to learn that this is the second letter which I have written to you today—and that to the writing of the first (which I have decided not to send to you, and which I am not sure I *ever* intended to send) I devoted several hours. This behavior must seem to you very peculiar. Indeed, it seems peculiar to me, though I am (if anybody is!) in a position to understand it. Why should I be writing you letters at all? Why on earth? It is easy for me to put myself in your place (bad dramatist though I am) and I can therefore without the least difficulty imagine the mixture of bewilderment, curiosity, contempt, and annoyance, or even *shame*, shame for me, with which you will receive this last of my underbred antics. Why in God's name should this upstart young man (not so young either), this mere ship's acquaintance, this New Englander with intermittent manners, presume to write to *you*? you who so habitually and unquestioningly regard yourself as one of the world's chosen few? And how entirely characteristic of him that instead of coming to see you he should *write*—send you, merely from one end of a ship to another, a morbidly and mawkishly self-conscious letter! . . . All of which is perfectly just, as far as it goes; and I doubt whether I can find any very adequate defense. You have, of course, an entire right to drop me without advancing reasons. Who among us has not exercised that privilege of selection? If the manner in which you have administered the "cut" seems to me extraordinarily ill-bred and uncharitable, who am I that I should rebuke you for a want of courtesy? I have been rude myself. I have even, occasionally, to rid myself of a bore, been inexcusably cruel. One must, at times, defend oneself at all costs, and I recognize perfectly that this has seemed to you an occasion for the exercise of that right. Ah! (you will say) but if you admit all this, why talk about it? Why not take your medicine in silence, like a gentleman? . . . Well, I could reply that as I seem to have lost in your eyes the privileges of a gentleman, I have therefore lost also the gentleman's obligations; and as you have put me in the position of an outcast, I might as well make a virtue of necessity, and, as a final gesture of pride, haul up the Jolly Roger.

But no—that's not exactly what I mean. Why is it that I seem always, in trying to say the simplest things, to embroil myself in complications and side issues, in references and tangents, in qualifications and relativities? It is my weakness as an author (so the critics have always said) that I appear incapable of presenting a theme energetically and simply. I must always wrap it up in tissue upon tissue of proviso and aspect; see it from a hundred angles; turn laboriously each side to the light; producing in the end not so much a unitary work of art as a melancholy *cauchemar* of ghosts and voices, a phantasmagoric world of disordered colors and sounds; a world without design or purpose; and perceptible only in terms of the prolix and the fragmentary. The criticism is deserved, of course: but I have often wished that the critics would do me the justice to perceive that I have deliberately aimed at this effect, in the belief that the old unities and simplicities will no longer serve. No longer serve, I mean, if one is trying to translate, in any form of literary art, the consciousness of modern man. And this is what I *have* tried to do. I am no longer foolish enough to think that I have succeeded—I am in process of adjustment to the certainty that I am going to be a failure. I take what refuge I can in a strictly psychological scrutiny of my failure, and endeavor to make out how much this is due to (1) a simple lack of literary power, or genius, or the neurosis that we give that name, and how much to (2) a mistaken assumption as to the necessity for this new literary method. What if—for example—in choosing this literary method, this deliberate indulgence in the prolix and fragmentary, I merely show myself at the mercy of a personal weakness which is not universal, or ever likely to be, but highly idiosyncratic? That is perfectly possible; and it brings me back to my starting point. I *am* like that—I do think and feel in this confused and fluctuating way—I frequently suspect that I am nothing on earth but a case of *dementia praecox, manqué*, or arrested. Isn't all this passion for aspects and qualifications and relativities a clear enough symptom of schizophrenia? It is as a result of my uncertain and divided attitude toward you that you now finally wash your hands of me; the conflict in me between the declared and the undeclared produced that callow and caddish ambiguity of behavior which offended you. And now, in this letter, I continue the offense! I mumble and murmur and beat round the bush—and succeed in saying nothing. Why is it that I don't simply say that the whole trouble has been that, from the moment when I first saw you coming up the gangway to the *Silurian*, last year, I adored you and was terrified by you? Yes, you terrified me. But what use is there in analyzing this? None. The important thing is merely to say that I have loved you, that I love you, and that I must, now that you have dropped me, take any available way of telling you this, no matter how much the method may offend you.

Alas! all this is beside the point. Why is it that I cannot, in some perfectly simple and comprehensive manner, tell you exactly how I feel about you, and exactly what sort of creature I am? One wouldn't suppose that this would present inordinate difficulties. Yet, when I set myself the task this morning, do you know what form my unfinished letter was going to take? A long, sentimental reminiscence of my childhood! Yes, I actually believed for a moment that by some such circumferential snare as that I might trap you, bring you within my range, sting, and poison you with the subtle-sweet poison of a shared experience and consciousness. That again is highly characteristic of me. It is precisely the sort of thing I am always trying to do in my writing—to present my unhappy reader with a wide-ranged chaos —of actions and reactions, thoughts, memories and feelings—in the vain hope that at the end he will see that the whole thing represents only *one moment, one feeling, one person*. A raging, trumpeting jungle of associations, and then I announce at the end of it, with a gesture of despair, "This is I!" . . . Is it any wonder that I am considered half mad, a charlatan, or, worse still, one who has failed to perceive the most elementary truth about art, namely, that its first principle is selection? . . . And here I struggle in the same absurd roundabout way to give you some inkling of the springs of my behavior, in a vain hope that you will think better of my failure to—what? To attract you? But I did attract you. To capture you? To avoid disgusting you? Perhaps it is that. "Here I am" (I might say), "this queer psychopathic complicated creature: honeycombed with hypocrisies and subtleties, cowardices and valors, cupidities and disgusts; on the whole, harmless . . ."

But let me make a new start. Am I not, at bottom, simply trying to *impress* you? behaving exactly like the typical male in spring? And the behavior exasperated, in my case, by the fact that I must, if possible, overcome a judgment which has already declared itself to be adverse. However, I can see no possible escape from that predicament. *Any* behavior, if calculated (whether consciously or unconsciously) to attract, is in its origin sexual. Why, then, be ashamed of it? You, yourself—since we last encountered—have been embraced by the male of your species; the sexual instinct has finally flowered in you and taken possession of you. Is there anything repugnant in this surrender? . . . To tell the truth I think there is. Whether this is a mere outcropping of Puritanism, I cannot say. It may be. Anyway, I find something essentially horrible in this complete abandonment of oneself to an instinct. Mind you, I do not for one moment deny the appalling beauty and desirability of the experience. I have known it several times, and never without ecstasy. But there is something in me which insists that this ought not to be made the center or foundation of one's life; that it is a tyranny of the gross over the subtle; and that like every other attack on the liberty of one's spirit it ought to be met with all the forces at one's command. Must we be slaves to our passions? "For the poor benefit of a bewitching minute," must we give up our freedom forever? No —and it was with all these perplexities smoldering in my eyes and heart that I first approached you, Cynthia. And more than this, I approached you with a definite and peculiar hope in my mind. Will this hope seem to you a kind of madness? Perhaps it will. What I hoped was that at last I had found a love which somehow *transcended the flesh*. Yes—I actually persuaded myself that I had captured the chimera; and that in Cynthia and poor William the phoenix and the turtle were met anew. A beautiful, a divine illusion! One of those heavenly beliefs which, in intensity of being, makes the solidest of our realities seem insubstantial as a shade. I am not a believer in souls, nor in immortality; I have no sentimental conception of God, no religion from which to extract, for my daily needs, color and light; yet in encountering you I felt that I could only explain what was happening to me by assuming at least a *symbolic* meaning and rightness in the treacherous word "soul." For was I not at once treading a brighter star? And was I not—gross Caliban that I was—endeavoring, all of a sudden, to become an Ariel? And were we not, you and I, already partaking of a direct and profound communion from the moment that we looked at each other and spoke the first casual words of greeting? This communion was so perfect, so without barriers, and so independent of our bodies, our hands, our eyes, our speech even, that for the first time since I had become a man I found myself looking, startled, into the eyes of God—the God whom I knew as a child. Of course, the habit of criticism was too deeply engrained in me to permit any such illusion to go long unchallenged. I suppose, to tell the truth, that I never really wavered at all—unless my frequent visits to Westminster Cathedral (where, however, there was the additional motive that I hoped to encounter you) can be considered a wavering. Yet, if my mind was steadfast in its refusal to abdicate, it was also wise enough, or weak enough, to allow the soul a holiday. It observed, it recorded, it even despised, but it didn't feel called upon to interfere. And in the end—this is what astonishes me!—it has come very near to believing that in this extraordinary holiday of the affections it might discover some sublime first principle of things by which the whole melancholy world might be explained and justified. This miraculous communion between us, Cynthia— was this perhaps an earnest of what was to come? I do not mean simply for us, for you and me, but for all mankind! Was it possible to guess, from this beautiful experience, that ultimately man would know and love his brother; that the barriers of idiosyncrasy and solipsism, the dull walls of sense, would go down before the wand of Prospero? This possibility seemed to me not merely a thing to be desired, but a necessity! And what obstacles lay between us and this divine understanding? Only one—the Will. When we sufficiently *desired* this communion, when at last we realized the weakness and barrenness of the self, we could be sure that we would have sufficient wisdom to accomplish the great surrender.

To what pitch of intensity this illusion, this belief, this doctrine of sublimation, was brought in me by my loss of you—if truly it can be said that I have lost you!—may be suggested to you when I tell you of a very peculiar experience which I had last night. I do not deny that I had taken a drink or two. Whisky is a useful anodyne. And after a whole day of concentrated misery it became pressingly necessary to break the continuity of my thought. I had sat too long in one place in the smoking room, keeping a watch through the half-opened window for a glimpse of your striped and diamonded Hindu jersey—and what a pang I suffered when at last I saw it, worn by your friend! Was that an intentional twist of the knife? No, of course not—it was an accident. But I had sat thus too long, and for too long I had blown round and round in one fixed vortex of thoughts and feelings. The only relief I had known all day was a talk with Silberstein, a

Jew, and a fellow passenger of yours—a rather remarkable man: a seller of "chewing sweets" and a chess player. But, though I (to some extent consciously) sought release by talking of myself with reckless freedom to Silberstein, I had found no real comfort in it, nor had I found any more, at dinner, in the company of Smith and Mrs. Faubion. It is perfectly true—I may as well confess it—that Mrs. Faubion (vulgar little strumpet that she is) attracts me; and I discovered last night at dinner, with a gleam of delight which not even my prevailing misery could extinguish, that Mrs. Faubion is attracted by *me*. An extraordinary reflection on the deep pluralism of things, life's contrapuntal and insoluble richness! Here, in the very crisis of a passion, a passion which is as nearly all-absorbing as a passion can be, I pause for a moment's delicious flirtation with *another* woman! Nor is it so simple a thing as flirtation, either—it is darker and stronger than that, a deep current of mutual delight, which might easily, and might well, sweep us off our feet. We know this as we look at each other—we tacitly admit it. Between meals we always avoid each other, just as we always avoid any but the dullest banter, because we both know that to take any step whatever would be to be lost. Well! last night I was in no mood to be lost—lost in this sense. And when Mrs. Faubion—who *was* in a mood to be lost—touched my foot with hers under the table, I made no response, pretended that I thought it was an accident. Of course, it *may* have been an accident—but I sincerely doubt it. No, it was unmistakable . . . I rejected, then, this gay little overture from the pluralistic universe, not because it was in itself unattractive, but because—well, why, exactly? A psychologist might say that it was because my nervous system was at the moment too acutely in the state known as a "motor set"—a motor set which was directed to a woman named Cynthia. That is one way of putting it. My mandibles were poised, and pointed and ready to spring, but only in that one direction, and on receipt of that one stimulus. Mrs. Faubion, it is true, *might* have sprung the trap. I quite seriously entertained the thought. But I foresaw, or thought I foresaw, a more than usually swift disillusionment, followed by a horrible agony of self-reproach. She would satisfy, for the fleetingest of instants, the blind animal maw; but the mind, or soul, or whatever you like to call it, would be cheated, and being cheated would be even wretcheder than before. I do not pretend that I thought this out at the time as clearly as I think it out now for you. I merely felt the thing in an image or warm coalition of images, in a pang or an inkling of a pang, as I talked with Mrs. Faubion, withdrew my foot reluctantly, and met her somber eyes in a gaze a little too protracted. And I was saddened by it, and further and still more deeply saddened, when old father Smith confessed to me once more his amorous desire for her, and outlined for me the ugly little scheme by which he hoped to gain possession of her. A sinister and sorry little tangle! Demarest in hopeless pursuit of Cynthia, whose eyes were fixed on—whom? a captain in the Belgian army? while Smith desired Faubion, and Faubion (*pour mieux s'amuser*) rested her dark gaze on the absent-hearted Demarest. Why must things be like this? Why, Cynthia? I returned after a while to the smoking room, where men were singing smutty songs and telling smutty stories—where, in fact, as invariably occurs, the whole world was being reduced to its lowest common denominator—and drank whisky, meditating on these things. If only—I thought—we had some subtler medium than language, and if only we weren't, all of us, little walled fortresses self-centered and oversensitive and so perpetually on the defensive! If only we could more freely *give* ourselves, more generously, without shame or stint! . . . And it was out of these confused reflections, which were not so much reflections as feelings, that my peculiar experience developed, the peculiar little experience which I have approached in so roundabout a way, and of which in the end I shall have so absurdly little to tell you. For what did it amount to? Only this—that I had a kind of waking dream, one so vivid that it was almost a hallucination. A cynic would say of it that it was simply the result of whisky. But it was more than that, though I freely admit that whisky had broken down certain inhibitions and permitted to my unconscious a greater freedom. I was on the point of going to bed, when I decided to take a sniff of fresh air—up to the hurricane deck I went, therefore, disregarding once more the barriers; and there, as I stood in the marvelous darkness, alone in the world, alone with my ridiculous transitory little unhappiness, I indulged myself in a fantasy. I was then, suddenly, no longer alone. You were there, Cynthia, and so was Faubion, and so too were Smith and Silberstein. We were all there: but we were all *changed*. For when I first moved toward you, among the lifeboats, under the autumnal stars which seemed to gyrate slowly above us, I heard you—astonishing!—exchanging quotations from the Greek Anthology. Could it be true? It was true— all four of you had achieved a divine intimacy, a divine swiftness and beauty of mutual understanding and love, so that your four spirits swayed and chimed together in a unison, unhurried and calm, which made of the whole nocturnal universe a manifest wisdom and delight. I too participated in this gentle diapason, this tranquil sounding of the familiar notes, but my part was a timid one, less practiced, and I felt that I had not yet sufficiently passed out of myself to move as freely as you others among darknesses become luminous and uncertainties become certain. I still loved myself too much to love the world; too desperately struggled, still, to understand my own coils, and therefore, found the world obscure. But I did participate, a little, and I listened with joy. It was a miracle. These four utterly dissimilar beings, these four beings whose desires were in conflict, nevertheless understood each other perfectly, loved each other angelically, uttered one another's thoughts and faintest feelings as readily as their own, and laughed together, gently, over their own profoundest griefs! What could I do but worship that vision? For the vision was indeed so vivid that for an instant I wholly forgot that all this excellence had come out of my own heart, and I could joyfully give myself to a pure worship. Only for an instant, alas! for abruptly the fantasy began to go wrong. A jarring note was sounded, a note of jeering corruption and hatred, then the clashing of individual will with will. As sometimes in a dream one is aware that one is dreaming, so I began to feel my own ugly idiosyncrasies which underlay each of these four beings, and to see that they were only projections of myself; and though I could continue the fantasy, and indeed was compelled to do so, I could no longer direct it; darker powers in my heart had taken command of it. The beautiful harmony which love and wisdom had achieved, and of which it seemed to me that they were about to make something final and perfect, became a nightmare in which my own lusts and hatreds shaped events swiftly toward a nauseating climax. The scene was a parody of the Crucifixion—and of a good deal else. I find it impossible to analyze completely, for a great deal of its meaning, at the end, was in the insupportable ugliness of its *tone*. In this horrible scene, I beheld you transfigured, Cynthia—turned into a stained-glass widow! What can have been the significance of that? Does it represent simply an effort to sublimate my love of you? Or was it—as I suspect—intended to show that this attempt as a sentimental sublimation could only partially succeed? Certainly, it presented you, or my conception of you, in a very unattractive light. Perhaps that is tantamount to saying that it presented *me* in a very unattractive light. I was pillorying myself for hypocrisy. Perhaps I was—or certain darker forces in me, a profounder and truer animal honesty—perhaps these were taking their revenge by wrecking this pretty dream of a "perfect communion." Anyway, it is true that shortly before this waking dream I had been pondering the question of sublimation versus immersion. How can we possibly decide which is the better course to pursue? Shall we take the way of art, and lie, and try to make life as like the lie as we can—remold it nearer to the *child's* desire—or shall we take the way of nature, and *love*? Love, I mean, savagely with the body! . . . You can call that a quibble, if you like, replying that it is not really a question as between art and nature, but between two aspects of nature—the more primitive and the less primitive. But it makes no difference how you phrase it: the problem is there, and is insoluble. At one end savagery—at the other hypocrisy? Hypocrisy fine-branching and beautiful as coral, hypocrisy become an infinitely resourceful art? Either extreme is for us unreachable, or untenable if reached. We must struggle and fluctuate in the Limbo between—saving ourselves now and then from an art of life too fine-drawn by a bath of blood; or from an awareness and control too meager by a deliberate suppressing of our lusts, a canalization of those energies . . . And never, at any time, knowing exactly where we stand, what we believe in, or who we are.

It is to this awful dilemma that my failure with you has brought me. Of this schism in my nature, which has always been known to me, I have now become acutely and horribly and unintermittently conscious . . . What shall I do? Shall I go on, half-civilized liar that I am, and add a few more reefs of flowery coral to my already disgracefully massive production, and thus help deluded mankind to add delusion to delusion? Or shall I turn back, and do my best to destroy this terrible structure of hypocrisy? . . . I think, Cynthia, I will turn back. I think I must turn my back on you. I think I must decide, once and for all, that though you are beautiful, and though I have fixed my heart on you as on nothing and no one else, you are a sham, a fraud, an exquisite but baseless, or nearly baseless, work of art. A living lie. A beautiful betrayal of nature. A delicious fake . . . I remember that you refused to have tea with me, at a Lyons or A.B.C., because they were "such grubby little places" . . . But as for me, I like them; and the grubbier the better.

(*Not sent.*)

THREE

DEAR MISS BATTILORO:

To say that I am astonished by what has occurred is to put it mildly. What have I done which could so offend you that you must "cut" me? Heaven knows I have enough "inferiority complex" to enable me to supply my own explanations—as far as *that* is concerned, I could find sufficient excuse for it were the whole world to conspire against me. But that is not the same thing. I should prefer to know—if you could bring yourself to tell me—what it is that has moved *you* to this sudden action. Do I, in asking this, expect too much? Perhaps I do. I remember only too well—as I remember every episode of our brief acquaintance—how, as we left the Wigmore Hall, after the concert, you made me run with you, positively *run*, so that you could avoid someone by whom you didn't wish to be seen. This, at the time, rather disconcerted me. It brought pretty sharply before my eyes a feature in your character which alternately frightened, attracted, and repelled me, and which I had taken some care not to examine too closely. This was—is—your snobbishness. Well—now *I* am to be sacrificed on this exquisite altar, in this exquisite pre-Raphaelite boudoir-chapel of yours! Is that it? Perhaps you think I have been remiss in not coming to see you, or in failing to salute you yesterday morning? But I *have* tried, several times, to find you, in vain. I am in the second cabin, and therefore I cannot too freely wander about in your precincts. As for the other matter, I am simply too shy.

I mention these points in the very faint hope that the whole thing may have been an unfortunate misunderstanding. If that is the case, I am heartily sorry. But I know, at the bottom of my heart, that it is something more than that. It may even be—why in Heaven's name not?—that you have taken a dislike to me. But if you consider—no, there is no use in considering. I was on the point of advancing our delightful acquaintance of last summer as a kind of claim upon you, and suggesting that, these things being so, it would be only decent of you to give me some hint of an explanation. But, as I abruptly see, one does not, when one decides to cut a friend, hand him a nice little note of explanation. One just cuts him; with a hard eye. Exactly as you, and your estimable mother, have done to me. And if he presume to *ask* for an explanation—as I am doing—why that only makes it more apparent that the cut was required.

But it occurs to me, belatedly, that in such a situation as this I ought to show myself possessed of a certain amount of pride. And so I am. I am not lacking in *amour-propre*. I suffer from that form of egotism which vacillates between an excessive vanity and a humility equally excessive. And as a matter of fact, the injury you have done me is so deep that even should the whole affair now turn out to be a mistake, even were you to apologize, I could never forgive you and never again quite respect you. I may not cease to love you—why need I any longer conceal this, which may have been the point from which your action has sprung—but already a profound hatred has joined itself to my love. I shall hate you, loathe you, despise you,

as I have never hated before. Pride! If we encounter again, you will see that
I have plenty of it. It will be Satanic. And if any smallest opportunity ever
occurs, I will revenge myself upon you, "after no common action," with the
deftest psychological cruelty: for I am a master of that art, I am by nature
cruel. That I will still be in love with you will not in the least prevent this.
You have behaved like a charwoman. And if only once I may have the
chance to treat you as such, to cut you face to face, to turn my back on you,
it may be that I shall thus be able to rid myself of you forever, and recover
my lost self-esteem. It may be that I——

(Not finished).

FOUR

I am extremely sorry that things should have turned out like this. I am
sorry for any sins of omission, on my part, which may have brought it about;
though I am at a loss to know what they may be. I am sorriest, however,
that you should have felt it necessary to *cut* me, as if I were the most
ordinary of ill-bred nuisances. Good Heavens! That is a new and illuminating experience, and one from which I hope greatly to profit. You need not
have feared that I would ever become troublesome—I am sufficiently
sensitive to know when others want to be rid of me, and I usually know it
long before they know it themselves. To be misprized in *that* sense is an
extreme surprise to me. But not so surprising, perhaps, as the finding how
deeply I have misprized *you*.

(Not sent.)

FIVE

Sick transit!

(Not sent.)

SIX

. . . . . .

(Not written.)

❲ VIII

Demarest sat alone in the dim-lighted smoking room. A calf-bound octavo
lay on the green table before him, opened at page 544. On the black skylight, a heavy rain rattled: drumming dripping pattering whimpering. It
was not loud enough, however, to drown out the gusts of music that came
upstairs fitfully from below, where the masquerade ball was in progress. In
fact, he could hear Hay-Lawrence's voice—Hay-Lawrence was now a *chef*

—in shrill imitation of broken Gallic English, followed by a spate of expostulatory French. Demarest smiled. How admirable, to be able to throw oneself into a thing like that! With so little self-consciousness! He could see, in his mind's eye, the absurd actions with which Hay-Lawrence must be accompanying that fury of sound—the shrugged shoulders, the palms lifted and narrowed, the eyebrows extravagantly arched. *"Mais oui!"* Hay-Lawrence positively squealed the *oui;* and then was heard no more, lost in a combined outrage of rain and ragtime. Of course, he must be delighted at the chance to show off his excellent French . . . What was that tune. *An Old-Fashioned Garden.* Modern Bach. Drumming dripping pattering whimpering. Running whipping spattering scampering. "First, for the scene" (he read, "a *landtschap* consisting of small woods, and here and there a void place filled with huntings: which falling, an artificial sea was seen to shoot forth, as if it flowed to the land, raised with waves which seemed to move, and in some places the billows to break, as imitating the orderly disorder which is common in nature. In front of this sea were placed six tritons, in moving and sprightly actions, their upper parts human, save that their hairs were blue, as partaking of the sea colour: their desinent parts fish, mounted above their heads, and all varied in dispositions. From their backs were borne out certain light pieces of taffeta, as if carried by the wind, and their music made out of wreathed shells. Behind these, a pair of sea-maids, for song, were as conspicuously seated; between which, two great seahorses, as big as the life, put forth themselves; the one mounting aloft, and writhing his head from the other, which seemed to sink forward; so intended for variation, and that the figure behind might come off better: upon their backs, Oceanus and Niger were advanced." An admirable descriptive prose! And what impudence to assert that there was no prose before Dryden! Great sea horses as big as the life. And the orderly disorder which is common in nature . . .

Silberstein, in a dinner jacket, entered laconically; with a cigar, on which the red-and-gold band was intact. In a dinner jacket, with plump shirt, he looked more than ever batrachian. Brek-ek-ek-ek. He sauntered, he rolled, he twinkled, he trolled. Drumming dripping pattering whimpering. In an old-fashioned garden.

"I don't blame you," he said. "I never saw such a lousy collection in my life. Hay-Lawrence is pretty good, though."

"He looks the part to a T."

"I don't speak French myself, but I guess he slings it about as well as the froggies do?"

"It sounds all right to me. Have you been dancing?"

"No. I gave them the up-and-down—there's nobody there worth looking at, except that little Irish kid and Mrs. Faubion. And, of course, your friend the Welsh Rarebit. By Godfry, she's got up fit to kill!"

Drip drop drip drop. An old-fashioned garden in the rain.

"Have you seen her? . . . Hello—there she is. Mrs. Davis! *Mrs. Davis!*"

Mrs. Davis, a Hawaiian clad in swishing grass, with a white rose in her black hair and a purple Japanese lantern in each hand, leaned coyly through the doorway, one leg lifted behind her. Scarlet slippers. Then she was gone again.

The glass-eyed poker player came in, looking angrily about the room, and four others. Also Smith, soft-stepping in the rear, drawing back a little to avoid getting mixed with the game. He had been out in the rain—he had on his tweed hat and a rain-splashed raincoat. After him came a trampling troup of others, refugees from the dance. The thirsty hour was beginning to summon them.

"Didn't see you at the dance," said Smith, dropping off his coat.

"No, I'm not a dancing man."

"The little girl was asking me where you were—says she's mad at you."

"Mrs. Faubion?"

"Sure. Who'd you think? Looks nice, too. Got on one of those blue embroidered mandarin cloaks, and nice little white silk pantaloons."

"She's the best-looking thing there," said Silberstein, "which isn't saying much."

"She's all right! Yes, sir, she's all right. And she can dance, too. I wish I could dance—I'm too old to learn these newfangled things. But I'd sure like to dance with her."

"Well, gentlemen, I think I'll slide for home. I'll see you in the morning, if the rain doesn't sink us. Good night."

"Good night!"

"Good night."

Silberstein departed in a rattle of rain: the *Long, Long Trail* came mournfully up the stairs: a cork popped.

"Have a game?" said Smith. "He makes me tired, swelling in here with his dress suit."

"No, not tonight, thanks. I haven't got the energy. Lazy as a nigger."

"Lazy as a nigger! Ever seen niggers work in the gangs down South?"

"Yes, I have."

"They sure can work—when they want to."

"Oh, I have the greatest respect for the nigger. I'm all for him."

"He's all right in the fields and the servants' quarters. Yes, siree!"

"The Negro has genius—give him a chance and he'll prove it."

"Genius! I never noticed it. Give him a chance, and he gets too uppish."

"Oh, I don't agree with you. When he's uppish, it's only because he imitates the bad manners with which he's been treated."

Smith looked astonished.

"You don't know what you're talking about! You ought to live down South."

"I *have* lived down South."

"Well then, you ought to know better. Give him an inch and he'll take an ell."

"Why shouldn't he?"

"Why shouldn't he! . . . Do you think he's the equal of the white man?"

"Potentially, certainly! Good Lord, he's only had a generation or two of freedom, scarcely any schooling, and look what he's done already! His folk songs are the only American music, practically, that's worth a toot."

"Just plain savagery, that's what it is, and I'm surprised you fall for it.

You come down and live with them and look for their genius! Genius my hat! They're black, and don't you forget it."

"What difference does *that* make?"

"A whole lot! You can't let them mix. Got to keep them in their place."

"Nonsense. They're human beings, like any others. You can't condemn a whole race because of their color! Good Lord, I never heard anything so childish!"

"Childish! Would you sit down to dinner with a nigger?"

"Certainly! I not only would, but I *have*."

Smith stared.

"What! Well, no self-respecting man would. No sir."

"I suppose you're one of these people who feel the same way about the Chinese and Japanese."

"Sure. To hell with them. They're yellow—they're not white . . . Good God, sitting down to dinner with a nigger! Will you listen to that!"

Smith turned his head, showing a disposition to draw in, as witnesses, the men at the next table. His voice had become louder. Demarest felt himself flushing.

"Certainly. The Negro I sat down to dinner with was a human being, and as civilized and intellectual a man as you could find. And a man very widely known."

"Every man to his own taste, as the farmer said when he kissed the pig! I suppose next you'll say it was an honor to sit down with him!"

"So it was."

"You'll have to excuse me. That's hot air. You just fool yourself. Now look here. Suppose you had a sister——"

"I *have* a sister."

"All right—you have a sister. Suppose she wanted to marry a coon, would you let her? . . . You know you wouldn't."

"I admit I've got strong enough primitive racial feelings in me to make me feel that any crossing of species is a mistake. And I'd certainly do my best to make HER feel this, and to make her see the social consequences of such a marriage. But if she realized all that, I don't see that I would have any further business to interfere. No. She's an adult, and can manage her own life. I should regret the step, for various reasons, but among them would not be any feeling that the Negro is something subhuman. Not at all!"

"Oh, good Lord deliver me! Did you hear that, you people? This man says he wouldn't mind if his sister married a nigger!"

There was a mild, embarrassed laugh at the next table, and Demarest felt himself flushing under the scrutiny of amusedly hostile eyes. Loss of caste—this was what the smiling eyes said, but almost as if apologetically. He was made to feel, for a flash, the isolation with which a race punishes its individuals for excessive individualism, for disobeying totem and taboo. Outcast. Pariah . . . How idiotic of him, to discuss such a thing, with such a man, in such a place! Served him right. Drip drop. Drop drip. Better fill and light his pipe with ostentatious calm and care, and let them see his large new splendid tobacco pouch! the unhurrying fingers manipulating the sea-damp tobacco, with percipient care for every shred!

Smith, guessing that he had gone a little too far, watched, unseeing, the fingers working in the pouch. But the scene was now beyond mitigation. He rose, flushed, with angry evasive eyes.

"Funny ideas some people have," he said. He picked up his coat.

"*De gustibus*—as you remarked," said Demarest. His voice was cool, and he directed at Smith a glance which he intended to be penetrating.

"What? . . ." Smith wavered, hoping for a friendlier note on which to take his departure. "Well, I guess I'll take a look at the dance before it stops. Getting toward the end."

He moved off sadly, sedately, as if in padded slippers: quiet upholder of the conventions; modest efficient tool of society. *My Little Gray Home in the West*. And now he was on his way to watch Faubion—Faubion, who was wearing a blue mandarin cloak and nice little while silk pantaloons. Delicious! Smith watching hungrily, brown eye among the potted palm trees, wistfully, waiting. Misery. Misery is creation. Misery is love. Misery is——

He opened the fat octavo again. A book so massive, in a ship smoking room, smacked of affectation. Page 568. "The spurging of a dead man's eyes. And all since the evening star did rise . . . A storm of rain, another of hail. We all must home in the egg shell sail" . . . The cokwold's daunce would be more appropriate? *The cokwolds lokyd yche on other*—how did it go. Gone. *My Little Gray Home in the West*. His little gray head on her breast. Blue mandarin breast . . . "The mast is made of a great pin, the tackle of cobweb, the sail as thin——" Oh, I've got a pin and it must go in . . . "And if we go through, and not fall in——" Imitating Middleton and Shakespeare: but he did it supremely well. And then there were the mooncalves. Nymphs that smell of ambergris. And the Epicoenes, that laugh and lie down in moonshine. Where was that . . . Page 616 . . . "and stab with their poniards; you do not know the delights of the Epicoenes in moonshine."

Dripping dropping. Not raining so hard now. The ship, in a gentle rain, on a rain-dark sea. The dance had come to an end. Gooooood-night, Ladies—— A Bass, two Basses, and a John Collins . . . "And when they have tasted the springs of pleasure enough, and bill'd, and kist, and are ready to come away; the shees only lay certain eggs (for they are never with child there) and of these eggs are disclosed a race of creatures like men, but are indeed a sort of fowl, in part covered with feathers (they call them VOLATEES) that hop from island to island; you shall see a covey of them presently . . ." Happy Epicoenes! Too happy, happy Epicoenes! And what an exquisite solution of the problem! And what a light it let in upon the dark soreness of that soul! The same troubles then as now. The same troubles always, world without end, Amen. Horror becomes poetry. Horror becomes—he must go and say something friendly to old Smith. Yes. By this time he was probably in his room. Nothing about the quarrel, no reference, just a friendly remark. Ask him if he had anything to read? But no! Was it necessary? It was Smith who had transgressed. *Did you hear that, you people?*

They were still conscious of him, he could feel, as he passed them—they were noting the peculiar shape of his head, and the fat calf-bound octavo

awkward under his arm. Yahoos! Dabblers in filth! He would show them!
. . . But what would he show them? . . . Nothing. Nothing at all. They
were foolish people, simple people, helpless people, like himself; in an
analogous position, as one of a homogeneous group, he too would join in
the throwing of stones. "Have you read X's last book? . . . The man's gone
completely to pot. I *never* read such tripe!" . . . All of us murderers.
Single Stroke. Trembling. Forgot, in the excitement, to say good night to
Malvolio . . . The stewards in the dining saloon were dragging the long
tables back to their places and screwing them down. The pianist (pimply!)
was lunging away forward, with his sheaf of dirty music. Cigarette ends in
the palm-tree pots. The blade of a fan. A smell of face powder. After the
ball was over.

Smith, on the point of turning down his alley, waited for him, mournfully scratching his mustache.

"Well!" he said. "You turning in, too?"

"Yes, that damned poker gang makes too much of a row."

"They do, don't they. They saw the fellow with the glass eye is a
professional."

"So I've heard."

"Good man to keep away from, I guess. He looks like a tough customer
. . . Hello! *Here* she comes!"

Mrs. Faubion bore down upon them, threateningly, with a tooth brush
in her hand. In the blue mandarin cloak. The ship, the long red carpet,
pitched slowly downward toward the bow, and, laughing, she advanced
with a little exaggerated run, stopping short with her face impudently close
to Demarest's face, the tooth brush flourishing in her lifted hand.

"Well!" she cried. "Mr. Man! What would *you* like!"

He deliberated, diving delightedly into her delighted eyes.

"I'd like to bite you!" he said.

"Oh *would* you!" she said.

"Yes, and if you don't look out I will!"

She gave a little shriek of laughter, and darted down the alley that led
to her stateroom. With one hand on the doorknob, she paused, put the
toothbrush to her lips, and blew him a kiss, extravagant and mocking.

"The same to you!" he cried, suiting the action to the word. They
smiled at each other, for a moment, with fixed eyes. Then she vanished into
her room, the door shutting softly.

"Good Lord!" moaned Smith. "Why does she do that to *you*?"

"Yes, why?" laughed Demarest. "Good night!"

"Good *night*." His tone was brusque, and he turned on his heel almost
angrily. This was the death of Smith! A triumph! . . . Yes, why?
142–156.

Yes, why? and again, yes, why? How delightful she had looked, the
impudent little strumpet. Nothing epicene about Faubion. They call them
VOLATEES. A little rougher again tonight. Creaking woodwork. That charging run of hers—a skillful improvisation. And holding her charming savage
mouth so close, so startlingly close, to his! . . . He unhooked and lowered
the tin wash basin. A tepid trickle of water for the tooth brush. She had
been brushing her teeth: as now he brushed his, with lips quaintly arched

and an overflow of blood-streaked foam. Round, and round, and round, in front. Back and forth, back and forth, at the sides. Scooping downward at the nicotine-strained tartar on the backs of the lower front ones. Over the grinding-surfaces of the molars—*ouch*. That cursèd ice-cream tooth. Must be a little crack in the filling . . . Nymphs that smell of ambergris; and the wholesome dew called rosmarine. He looked once again, once again, once again, with a profound amused wonderment, with blank black pupils, into his mirrored eyes. What an extraordinary-looking object he was, with pink ears, animal hairs in his nose, and a blue mole on his cheek! And was this monstrous object making itself miserable for a—*female?* "But Socrates, you say these monsters are sometimes unhappy. Tell me, will you, what it is that you mean by unhappiness? For, if I can believe you, these creatures are endowed with reason; and as you will agree, a truly reasonable being cannot know unhappiness save as an attribute of the foolish . . ." *Te-thrum te-thrum: te-thrum te-thrum.* Delightful, this hour when the passengers were all gone to bed, and most of the crew, and the whole ship became quiet, absorbed, as if at last concentrated singly and solely on the business of crossing an ocean! One became aware of it—one heard the engines: the beating of its lonely heart. One felt the frame quiver, saw it change its shape even, became startlingly conscious of the fact that one was at sea; alone with the infinite; alone with God. These rows of white marshmallows on the ceiling—these little painted bolts that held the ship together—these were one's faith! But it all seemed ridiculous, unreal. What was a ship? . . . What were human beings? . . . What was a world? . . . Cynthia and himself were a world . . . Misery. The whole thing was somebody's dream. The whole thing was a tiny twinkle, a bursting bubble——

He turned out the electric light and crawled into the bunk, sighing. Not a sound from the Irish girl—she must be asleep. Cynthia—was she too asleep? *Te-thrum te-thrum: te-thrum te-thrum.* Yes, she was probably asleep. Or was she lying awake, anguished over the affair? Miserable over what she had done? really in love with him all the time? staring into the atomy darkness with eyes wide as the world? thinking of that time when—that time when—with a pongee dress—and a wide soft straw hat—with a floppy brim—English——

There was a soft footstep outside the door—it passed, then came back again—and then on the panel of the door something that sounded like a tiny knock, a knock as of one small knuckle. He lifted himself on straining elbows, the blood beating painfully in the side of his throat. Had he only imagined it—was it only the nocturnal creaking and knocking of the ship? *te-thrum te-thrum; te-thrum te-thrum.* He held his breath, concentrating all his attention, staring in the dark toward the suspected door, listening for the slightest sound. Suppose it was! Eagerly, softly, he withdrew himself from the pocket of ship-folded bedclothes. And as his foot touched the coarse carpet, the knock was repeated, the turning knob gave a little creak, and the door began softly to open. Faubion.

Great Circle

O frantick, fond, pathetique passion!
Is't possible such sensuall action
Should clip the wings of contemplation?
O can it be the spirit's function,
The soule, not subject to dimension,
Should be made slave to reprehension
Of crafty nature's paint? Fie! can our soule
Be underling to such a vile controule?

JOHN MARSTON: *The Scourge of Villanie*

⟦ I

Why be in such a hurry, old fool? What good is hurry going to do you? Wrap yourself in a thick gauze of delay and confusion, like the spider; hang there, like the spider, aware of time only as the rock is aware of time; let your days be as leisurely and profound as months, serene as the blue spaces of sky between clouds; your flies will come to you in due season. Must you always be running desperately from minute to minute? Have you such an appetite for action? Have you such a passion for decisions? Must you always be snatching your hat from its peg in Shepard Hall, Shepard Street, Cambridge, Mass., and rushing out to an encounter with some one, with any one, with every one? Must you forever be listening for the telephone to ring, or the doorbell; hoping that it will be Floyd, with news of a wild party; or Celia, who wants you to dance with her at the Brunswick; or Bert, drunk, with a new poem which he is frantic to read to you; or a total stranger with the keys to hell? By all means accept the invitation to hell, should it come. It will not take you far—from Cambridge to hell is only a step; or at most a hop, skip, and jump. But now you are evading—you are dodging the issue. You do not really desire to drink with Floyd at a wild party, nor to hear Bert's poem, nor to dance hieratically with Celia in the Egyptian room; you do not even desire to go to hell with a total stranger, for, after all, Cambridge is hell enough. What you really desire is the simple finality of action, or of decision; you have yet to learn the most elementary facts about life. And what, my dear Andrew Cather, are the elementary facts of life? . . . Why, you poor idiot, you know them perfectly well, or you ought to, at thirty-eight. Permit yourself to be sifted by time, slowly, —be passive—wait. Learn to rot gently, like the earth: it is only a natural rot that is creative. The least violence, the least hurry, the least eagerness for action or decision, the least forcing of the issue——!

Damn—blast—putrefaction.

The tendency of his thought becoming unbearable, he jumped up, snatched his ticket from the window sill beside the Pullman chair, and bolted toward the smoking car. A pale girl reading a magazine listlessly, her knees crossed under green satin: she looked up at him with wan evocation.

She was bored, she wanted to talk to some one, her reading of the magazine was only a pretense. Too bad, darling—but I'm afraid it can't be easily enough managed. The conductor, in a chair at the end of the car, counting tickets and making notes with a pencil. The green curtains over the men's room awry, and a fleeting vision of a sad salesman, cigar in hand, who stared uncomprehendingly at the sliding Rhode Island landscape. His suitcase, cracked at one seam, stood on the black-leather settee. Poor devil—on his way back to Boston, from Bridgeport, defeated; the other salesmen had been before him. He was cursing the trees, the hills, the wind, the infrequent drops of rain that grazed the windows, leaving chains of fine beads; he was cursing them without seeing them. . . . Then the corridor between cars, swaying violently, knocking and bumping, with the little iron stepping-stone which was always to be avoided by the wary foot: it creaked and sidled. He stepped over it, smiling, and entered the smoking car. The familiar smell of soot and tobacco smoke, of stuffy plush and foul spittoons —garboons!—arched his nostrils: he felt more masculine, and more at home, as he chose a chair in which was a newspaper.

The Premier of France was ill. The boxing commission of New York had disqualified Zylenski. Prices were lower on the big board, owing to the usual week-end profit-taking. The President had received a committee of boy scouts: photograph of a weary handshake. Miss Dolores Vargas, new star of the talkies, was said by her friends to be engaged to a prominent Chicago banker: photograph of Dolores waving a handkerchief from the rear platform of a train. The Maroons had beaten the Bruins in overtime. The boll-weevil was moving north, a drought in the east Sierras was causing serious alarm about the water-supply in Nevada, Oswald Morphy, well-known author, was dead, Klenkor would remove corns and bunions quickly and painlessly in two or three applications. . . . And the murderer of Jennie Despard, Providence schoolteacher, had not yet been apprehended. An automobile salesman was missing from his home in Putnam, and while the police authorities declined to state that they connected this in any way with the murder, they admitted that they were anxious to ascertain his whereabouts. Mark Friedman. A married man with two children: his wife was prostrated. Best of luck to you, Mark: you'll need it. And she probably deserved it, too—though was it entirely necessary to do it with a hammer? Still, there is no accounting for tastes. The poor man might have been in a hurry.

Hurry—hurry—hurry—everything was hurrying. The train was hurrying. The world was hurrying. The landscape was hurrying. The wheels rushed blindly over the rails, over the joints, over the switches: rat-te-tat-te-tattle-te-tat-te-tump-te-tattle-te-tee. The locomotive driver, or the fireman (it was probably the fireman), was obsessed with the panic of speed, and blew prolongedly and repeatedly on the whistle. Scarcely a minute was left un-punctuated by the moan of the whistle. Horses in twilight-brown pastures threw up their tails and galloped away for a moment, turning alarmed heads. Birds darted in clouds, zigzag, off wires, swooped, circled, glided to rest again. The whole world, it seemed, was to be made conscious of the important hurry of the train. For wasn't this train, this Knickerbocker Limited, like everything else a consummation of eons of evolution? Wasn't

it the categorical imperative? It was achieving its terrific destiny. Like the
daisy in the field, or the honeysuckle, or the hummingbird, or the fungus,
it was pushing its way blindly and terribly to its end. Nothing could stop
it. Nothing? . . . And here was himself also, Andrew Cather, hurrying
from point to point on the earth's surface, describing his swift little arc:
and all these things were a part of him, a symbol for him. Here was this
eternal rush, of which the external speed was merely an index, a portent, of
the internal panic. Panic! God forbid. Was it anything so bad as panic?
Must one always be taking things so seriously? Must this fever in his brain
be forever urging him to a passion for consummations?

Calm yourself, old fool. Survey this row of dead faces opposite you:
these hard business men, these watchers of ticker tape, these casters of
balances, these signers of important letters and foreclosers of mortgages.
Do they allow themselves to be rushed into decisions? Do they walk at
midnight, hatless, in a rain, plopping through puddles, because of a secret
anguish in the heart? When their offices are closed for the day, and the
stenographers are gone, and everything is quiet, do they stretch themselves
on the floor in paroxysms of weeping? Absurd. They have no hearts. Or if
they have, they have learned the secret of the granite: they are silent, they
wait, they fall instinctively into the slow rhythm of the stars, everything at
last comes to them. But you, you poor idiot, you simulacrum of a soul
—good God, what a fool you are. Here you go, outstripping with speed of
mind the speed of this train. You are already in Cambridge, you are already
noiselessly letting yourself into your flat in Shepard Street, you are already
standing, just inside the door, and listening to hear if your excellent wife
Bertha is at home. Not a sound—not a whisper—not the creak of a board.
You cast a furtive look at the chairs in the hall: what is it that you are
expecting, or even almost hoping, to see? A hat? A man's hat? No, you
avert your eyes from the thought. You had not really expected this. But
you are curious, just the same, and that is why you are here, three days
before she had expected you. It is like a melodrama. But that has nothing
to do with it. If life chooses to imitate a cheap melodrama, why then it is
obvious enough that you have to behave like a character in a melodrama—
a ridiculous hero with a permanent expression of long-suffering, or a villain
with violent mustaches. And so you are acting the part: you are stealthy,
you walk swiftly and softly on the balls of your feet, you half hold your
breath as you approach the sitting room, you crane your neck at an unnatural angle in your endeavor to reassure yourself that there is indeed
no one there. . . . But supposing there *should* be some one? Ah. This is
what you really want. You really want to find some one there. Do not deny
it—do not pretend. You are deliberately seeking a catastrophe—you are
yourself in the act of creating a disaster. You want to see your life violated,
broken in two, your precious secrecy exposed in a yellow light of pure horror. Could you not have avoided this? Could you not have ignored Fred's
letter? My dear Andy: it's none of my business, perhaps, and probably
you'll be the last to thank me; that's always what happens, but I wouldn't
be doing my duty to you as a friend if I didn't write to tell you— Oh,
Christ. Why read it again? Why remember it? Why act upon it? Why not
get off at Providence and return to New York, precisely as if it were a

return to sanity? It was growing dark, they were crossing a river, a row of
lights sped across rain-sodden ice, a lamp was lifted in a farmhouse window. *Whoooo—whooooo*—the demon fireman blew his whistle again,
prolongedly, nostalgically, into the gathering gloom, rain began pattering
again on the train roof and grazingly along the windows, came and went
in flaws of needles. My dear Andy, it's none of my business. My dear Andy,
it's none of my business. But whose business was it, then? Was it Tom's?
Was it Bertha's? Was it God's? Perhaps it was nothing at all. Perhaps they
were merely playing duets. Side by side on the long mahogany bench,
leaning together, leaning apart, Tom the bass and Bertha the treble, the
Haydn Surprise, the Drum-roll Symphony, his foot on the pedal, her hand
on the page. Shall we take that again? We'll start at G in the second bar.
Haydn duet, hide and do it. The clock was ticking, the curtains were
drawn. Shepard Street was outside in the rain, everything was cosy, everything was peaceful, New York was far away, merest of whispers in the southwest, and Andy—what was Andy? A ghost behind the music, a shadow
beside the hearth, an echo in the corridor. He was an old raincoat in the
cupboard, a towel in the bathroom, a napkin ring in the sideboard, a name
on the letter box. He was a handful of bills on the hall table, a catalogue of
second-hand books, a pair of rusty skates in an old trunk. And the cocktail
shaker on the Japanese tray, the shaker that leaked, Tom holding it muffled
in a handkerchief, shaking it over the hearth while he laughed—come on,
Andy, let's have another round—the night is young—let's get well oiled
and go and see Dynamite Gus—come on, Bertha; come on, Andy—I'll pay
for the taxi—we'll have some arak at the Greek's, and ringside seats at the
Garden. Have you read the *Childermass?* Let's experiment with the Kie-
seritzky gambit, or the fianchetto. The new record of the "Love of the
Three Oranges." Let's walk to Fresh Pond in the rain, visit the pumping-
station, or drop a tear on the tomb of Henry James. Plymouth for the
week end. Chocorua. A game of poker at the new bookshop. Come on,
Bertha, come on, Andy, I'm back from a faculty meeting and I want to
raise hell. Tea at 3.30. Meeting at 4. The committee appointed to prepare
a minute on the life and services of the late John Jacob Morrison, Professor
of English, *Emeritus,* will present the minutes to the faculty. Recommen-
dations from the administrative board for changes in the Regulations for
Students in Harvard College, of which the most important is that section
14 be amended as follows. Let's discuss methods of suicide. Potassium
cyanide. Tell Bertha you're spending the night with me, and we'll take
Louise and Molly to Concord. Treason! Treason! The treason spoke innocently through the Haydn, rose softly and guilelessly under the fingers
of Tom, under the onyx signet ring, under his long brown hands, the
wrists held high and arched, under the wedding ring on Bertha's fourth
finger, on whose inner surface was a fine incised inscription. Treason
chimed with the chiming clock, a present from Tom, wreathed itself in
a water color of nasturtiums, shone softly on the opened score from a
shaded lamp. Where is Andy? Andy's in New York, said the bass. Come
on, Bertha——

    This must stop, this turmoil must stop. The Maroons had beaten the
Bruins in overtime. The Prince of Wales had been thrown by his horse.

Beautiful Blonde Sues Millionaire Scion for Heart Balm. American Womanhood Purest in World, says Bishop. Tax Scandal Shocks Senate. Rain will be followed by snow. Unseasonable warmth soon to end. Blizzards in far West, Denver under three feet of snow, villages in Rockies cut off from the world. Krazy Kat Is On His Way. Says you? Says me. Utilities Lower on Curb. Love Baron Leaves Hollywood. Oh, yeah?

—You can't teach 'em a thing.

—You can teach 'em, but they won't learn.

—They don't *want* to learn.

—Believe me, I'm through.

—God! and those hotels.

—Never again for me, no sir.

—Say, porter, what about a cigar.

Pack of cards, informative bid, clubs, diamonds, pass. Amherst Quintet Invades Crimson Territory Tonight. Lapp Life Studied in Racial Investigation. The Lapps are a nervous class of people and would be termed neurasthenics . . . where a stick was whacked against the side of a tent, the inhabitants fainted from fright . . .

God's Providence is our inheritance. One hour to Boston. Once more the train gathered speed, fled through dwindling suburbs into the night, whistled for crossings, devoured immense spaces of darkness, clattered past interminable strings of freight cars on a siding, swooped over bridges, lurched, steadied, whistled again and again. Small stations whirled past, dimly lighted, their wooden platforms glistening with rain, their names telescoped with speed. Hurry—hurry—hurry—everything was hurrying, the world was hurrying, the night was hurrying. The bells for a crossing chattered madly ahead, rose to a higher note, fell away behind to a sad minor murmur, were lost. He closed his eyes. The back of his hand rested against the cold glass of the window, vibrating; smoke stung his nostrils; long lights flew beside him in bright parallels; this was Andrew Cather. Calm yourself, you idiot—pull yourself together—you must regain control. Think of New York, the stars in the Grand Central Station, the girl who dropped her ticket at the gate, blushing as she stooped to pick it up, looking over her shoulder. Think of the fern-fringed fountain in the lunchroom at the hotel, old Rodman scratching his beard with a pencil while he figured the cost of the textbook, the marble clock, the rows of brass keys behind the desk. Mr. Cather, please—Number 218—Mr. Cather, please. Fred's letter. My dear Andy, it's none of my business. It's none of my business. Think of the blocks of ice in the urinals, the disinfected sweetness of the telephone booths, the silent corridors of plush, the stealthy chambermaids with jingling key rings. Drive down Broadway at night, as if flying into the heart of a vast fiery opal. Take the express and change to a local at 14th Street. Climb the dirty stairs to the elevated, reading all the enameled advertisements, clacking through the heavy turnstile with a nickel.

—What I mean is——

—Oh, sure——

—. . . kind of a turbine principle——

—. . . on the level, yes——

Wah-wah-wah-wah—the voices all rose at once against the clamor of

the train through a deep cutting. It's none of my business—Oh, of course
not. But it was a mere disinterested love of music, that was all. Companionship. Years and years of it. Just like a brother. Come on, Andy—
come on, Bertha—we're going to Revere Beach, we'll have a drunken battle
with marshmallows on the boardwalk, we'll find the monkey in the cage,
we'll raise a little polite hell. He waved the gin bottle over his head, gave
a whoop, clutched Bertha, and began dancing along the hall. Bertha
screeched, slapped her hands against his chest, pulled his ears. A harmless
lark, they had so many tastes in common, like brother and sister. Why, for
years Tom and Bertha hadn't missed a night at the Sanders Theater concerts. No indeed. How they loved Haydn! How they adored Bach! What
about a little Brandenburg tonight? and a little ravioli to begin with? what
about the North End? what about the fortuneteller? Bertha's eyes were on
Tom while the dark lady studied her palm. What was the look in her eyes
which had so struck him at the time? Nothing. Sense of change, sense of
time, the flowing away of all things, cloud shadows on falling leaves. Who
was Bertha? Bertha, to begin with, then Bertha plus one, Bertha plus two,
Bertha plus three: never the same again. The sudden kiss in Craigie Street,
the laugh, the shock, the readjustment to terrific wonder, the wedding,
the honeymoon, and then the amazing flight of years and places, the dance
of rooms, the dance of apartments, the dance of houses, the chorus of
changing voices and faces. And now, after ten years, it was Bertha plus
four, Bertha with Tom, Bertha with music, her arms grown heavier at the
shoulders, her clothes more careless, fond of cocktail parties and dances,
golf at Belmont, lunch with the Sewing Circle. Well, by God, if it was
true—! Treason. Horror. He jumped to his feet, flung down the paper on
the seat, and hurried forward. Pocahontas. The passengers were beginning
to be restless, old ladies were waking up, the porter was gathering the bags
from their reluctant owners and carrying them to the vestibule. Swaying,
he touched the green velvet back of a chair, then another, then a third. A
long row of lights fled past the windows, illuminated houses rushed at them
and rushed away again, a cement wall converged on them perilously,
whipped a series of swift column shadows at them, and was gone. Corda-
ville? One of the Newtons? Auburndale? The houses closed in on them,
their path was narrowed, one deserted station succeeded another. He
sat down, put his feet on his suitcase, closed his eyes, and listened to the
delicate sound of the rain on the roof and windows, which could be heard
as a secret accompaniment to the train's violent storming of suburb after
suburb. The Harvard Club, first—cocktails and dinner at the Harvard
Club, a little leisure, a little peace, time to pull himself together, to muster
the phrases, the attitudes. What attitudes? A genial bursting in, gay home-
coming, followed by instant surprise? Bewilderment? An entrance quiet
and suspicious? Announced beforehand by the bell from below? Unan-
nounced? Suppose they were at the piano. Ah yes. Then the easy comradely
smile. But why are you home so soon? Why, indeed. But suppose, on the
other hand—! And the phrases. Hello, darling—are you there, darling? Or
perhaps it had better be in the plural. Idiot! What you need is a few
drinks at the club—that will put you right, don't worry, wait. Relax. Believe in God and the sanctity of marriage, not to mention the holiness of

friendship. Have faith in Massachusetts and the Pilgrim Fathers. How do you do, Tom; hello, Bertha—what a fortunate coincidence to find you together—did Gieseking play on Thursday? Is there any ice in the icebox? Wonderfully mild weather for the time of year, isn't it? But the papers say the rain will turn to snow before morning. Don't stop playing—do go on —shall I turn the pages for you—or the sheets? Have I come to the right place? Is this Shepard Hall, Shepard Street, Cambridge, Massachusetts? Or was it two other fellows? Excuse me for intruding. I must have made a mistake. Haven't we met before somewhere?—your face is very familiar— too damned familiar, if you ask me—and now let's all join hands and have a good laugh together. But on the other hand—? No, no, no, no, no. Not. Never. Couldn't. Not that! This is no place for old-fashioned melodrama, we don't do such things in Cambridge, no indeed. There are no beds in Cambridge—how could we be so vulgar? My dear Tom, it's none of my business, I'll be going, just dropped in to see how you two lovebirds were getting on; hope everything is going swimmingly, that's fine, O. K., see you in hell one of these days, good-by, good luck, God bless you, send in the bill. We aim to please. By the great love I bore you—Christ. Bores me, the sum.

With long thrusts, with smooth and powerful lunges of speed, they overtook another train, measured bright window against bright window, drew abreast of statuesque lethargic passenger after passenger, newspapers, hats, hands lifted or falling, swaying coats, listless inquiring eyes, men, women, girls, a final clack, and gone. The porter bent deprecatingly with his whisk, he rose and followed him, fishing in his pocket for a quarter, feeling for the right size, the milled edge.

—You all gettin' off Back Bay, boss?

—Yes, I'll take my bag myself.

—All right, boss.

The pale girl in green satin passed him, humming, holding her thin arms away from her thin swaying body for balance, the white hands a little lifted, self-conscious. Too bad, darling—where have you been all my life? If only you had introduced yourself more efficiently, perhaps at the ticket gate, or last night, or last year, things might have been very different. We'd now be like an old married couple. What secrets left? None. Do you perspire freely? Snore? Chew gum? Sing in your bath? Do you scratch the mole on your left clavicle every night till it bleeds? Cascara or castor oil? And exactly how good a liar are you? Liars need good memories. Yes, indeed. Don't forget how you were caught in that little fib about Mehitabel Mockingbird and the dead pansy, or that other one about Methuselah and his sponge bag. Ah ha! We know all about it. And my God, the quarrels, the late night wrangles, the three-day silences, the weepings in dark rooms face downward on disheveled beds, the blows struck in sudden fury, the livid eyes of hate over the morning grapefruit! And lying beside each other for sleepless hours at night, the hands clenched, the eyes wide open but unseeing, eyeless at Gaza, while the digestion of each in turn interrupts the dramatic silence with obscene squeals and snickers. Love? after all that? My dear woman, pull yourself together. Go your way, take your little smells and snoops to another station, send your laundry to the North Pole, order a sandalwood coffin at Woolworth's. . . . Marriage. In Cambridge there shall be neither giving nor taking in marriage, but all shall be as one sex, and that shall be without which is without, only the dead moon will dare to maculate the red macula. My dear Andy——

He put on his hat, his heart was beating, he felt a curious constriction in his throat, as if speaking would be difficult, his voice somehow misplaced. Think, you idiot! Think—don't feel. Be calm. Cast a sure and slow balance of the figures in the situation, weigh the years one with another, measure each room, each wall, against the last. Why, to be sure, the sitting-room in the Shepard Hall apartment was smaller, much smaller, than the lounge at the Harvard Club, and there was no bar beneath it, nor was there a bison's head above the fireplace, nor a pair of brass shells from the Somme. There were no palm trees in it, as in the lobby of the Touraine, not even a newsstand behind which one could take shelter: and as for the natatorium, why, the poor fool of an architect had left that out entirely. Just the same, they were getting on swimmingly. Come on, Andy, come on, Bertha, come on in, the water's fine. Let's walk down to the Square and get a cup of coffee; let's go down and skate on the Common; let's see what there is at the movies and make loud remarks about the hero. But it was all so innocent, so natural and boylike, so good-natured, so ringed about with brassy and wholesome laughter, how could one suspect anything wrong? . . . Patience. Run the eye slowly along the edge of the chair back, note the reflected lamp in the dark lustrousness of the windowpane, and another station passing; listen to the mournful rain-quenched cry of the whistle, cut off abruptly by a bridge, released again, silent. The train began shuddering and slowing, shuddering and slowing, lurched, glided, lurched again, and then quietly, evenly, with rhythmic soft hisses of steam which fogged the windows, no longer like a train, but like a ship on even keel in quiet waters, slid past slowing lights, and stopped with a last prolonged profound sigh.

—Back Bay . . . Back Bay.

—Back Bay.

—Back Bay.

Let Rome in Tiber melt, and the wide arch of the rang'd empire fall. Here is my—station. A taxi, please. And now the solid rain-drenched antipathy of Boston, the buildings in Copley Square all aloof and black, Trinity Church withdrawn and cowled in rain like a weeping nun, the Library staring down from an immense height with Florentine hauteur—what was this change, this difference, this withdrawal of friendliness? It was a new and hostile city. The people were foreigners, the wet streets were menacing, the bare trees brooded like skeletons over Commonwealth Avenue. We knew you, Andy. We know you not. We knew you, Andy. We know you not. Was this the guy that went to New York with bells on and now returns with horns? Give him a hand, boys, give the little fellow a great big hand. Drop a twig on him or a dead leaf, or maybe a brick. That's the guy—that little feller in the Armstrong taxi, with the text of a textbook on Spanish literature in his suitcase. *Tu pupila es azul. Y quando lloras*— What was that dirty crack? No more of that. Cold shoulder him, boys—it's nothing but *El Diablo Mundo*. The very spittin' image with number eight shoes, a Harvard Coop hat, and deformed toenails. Cut him dead. What he's got he deserves. He was askin' for it. Give him the snake's eye, Fairfield Street, Gloucester Street, Hereford Street, Massachusetts Avenue—! He's made his bed, let his friend lie in it. Wot's de flower bed between friends? Begonia. Look how nervous he is. He's sticking his finger down his collar for no good reason. Not a thought to his navel. Say, if he had to pay the taxi by the heartbeat! Call the taxicologist, and we'll have him stuffed. To the Peabody Museum with him, *quam celerrime*, we'll show him up. Give him a birthday present. Ha! For Christ and the Church.

Horror preceded him into the Harvard Club, but evaded him among these friendly walls and stained-plaster Corinthian columns. Even here the familiar, the warm, the assuring, eyed him aslant, sneered when he turned his back. My dear Andy, it's none of our business, but—! And what should stare him in the face but a row of telephone booths, five of them numbered, the sixth a pay station. A Greek Chorus. Stationary chorus. Call her up, Andy—give the poor girl a chance. Our ears are in Shepard Street. Warn her! Tell her you're coming home after dinner! Tell her to ask Tom in for a drink! Make it easy for her, leave it all in darkness, in subterfuge, in evasion, in the hell of the forever unknown. Hello, darling! Is that you, Chuck? This is Andy. Yes, Andy—your premature Andy, back from the bright lights, back from the unearthly paradise, wizened little Tithonus returned from false heaven. But we won't go into that, no, we'll talk of something else. I meant nothing by it. Just my foolish little joke, that was all. Make the bed up, hang clean towels in the bathroom, run to the corner fruit store for another can of grapefruit juice, and start the cocktails. . . . No, impossible. This must not be evaded—whatever the issue, the situation must first of all be faced. No warnings, no signal, not even an inquiry at Tom's apartment to find out if he were absent—in a melodrama one must above all be melodramatic. If later one prefers to turn it into a farce——

And who should be standing at the bar, eating little-neck clams as usual, but Jitter Peabody, that ruined scion of a noble race, half-shot too as always, leaning with supercilious languor against the bar, his long horse-face flushed with gin, his drooping mustache dripping clam juice on to his weak chin.

—Hello, One-eye!

—Mr. Peabody, I presume?

—You do presume.

—I suppose you wouldn't join me in a little mild elbow lifting? The better the deed, the better the day.

—No, I've sworn off till I finish these sea fruits.

—Tom, you might take this flask, and empty it, and make as much old-fashioned out of it as it'll make. And you might get me a dozen of these little pink little-necks. And two glasses.

—Good evening, Mr. Cather—yes, sir. That'll go quite a little ways.

—What've you been doing, Jitter?

—None of your damned business.

—That's the *second* time I've heard that today. Only the other fellow was politer.

—That must have been in New York—couldn't have been in Boston.

—How did you guess it?

—I was in the train with you.

—The hell you say! Why the hell didn't you tell me?

—I saw you, but I was asleep at the time. Only just waked up.

—Ah, I see. So you were in New York on business.

—Shhhhhh. Very private. I went down on the midnight and came back this afternoon.

—Alone?

—Legally speaking. I'd have stayed, but my fiancée expects me to dinner.

—Thanks, Tom. Come on, Jitter. I'm thirsty and heartbroken.

—What *you* need—! You damned walking textbook.

—We won't go into that.

—No, you wouldn't.

—Abstinence makes the heart grow fonder.

This turmoil must stop, and Jitter would help to stop it. Time out. Time out for a little peace, a little leisure, a little cool unhurried reflection, for a calm reshuffling of the pack of marked cards which is the mind. In the presence of a person so disorganized, it was easier oneself to become righteously or recognizably organized: one felt again vividly the numbered inches between the hat and the shoe. Think, you idiot! Think, don't feel! Your brain depends upon it, the brief roman candle's parabola of your sanity. Follow green arrow for shuttle train to Grand Central. Follow red arrow for trail to bottom of Grand Canyon. If one had been cornuted, was a chiropodist the thing? Or must one be chiropracted? Kindly remove the imaginary, but all too palpable, horns. A present from my best friend. Kind of him, but so inconvenient when one wears a hat, unless one is a horse. Let us order a striped calico bonnet, with holes for the ears.

—And so, Jitter, you've been spying on the Vincent Club again.

—Who told you?

—I won't have any soup—I'll begin with the fish.

—So will I.

—But just why you should have gone to all that trouble, to see Boston's Best Bosomless Beacon Street and Back Bay Beauties clad only in their canvas shifts, I can't imagine.

—My dear One-eye, that's only the half of it.

—What was the other half—the better, I hope.

—You're vulgar. You always were. . . .

A telephone was ringing. Bertha? University O!O!O! Put the salt neatly on the edge of your plate, my boy. Or fling it over your shoulder. An old Spanish custom, to avert the evil eye. The glass eye was the root of all evil. Green glass eyes on a plush tray—are you washed in the blood of the Lamb? *Tu pupila es azul.* And when you cry, you cry with two eye sockets, but one eye. How much had this affected Bertha? And that heartless nickname! Jesus. It was no wonder. She had probably heard of him as One-eye Cather long before she had met him. With sympathy? Pathos? Horror? Or more likely a mixture of pity and disgust. Poor fellow—he can't judge distances. Have you heard how he lost it? Such a shame.

—Drink up, Jitter—there's another round.

—Say, what's come over you? . . . anyway.

—Well, what do you mean by that?

Fool. You will now be accused of unnecessary sobriety.

—Aren't you drinking a little too much for one of your habits?

—Don't make me laugh.

Jitter pulled his mustaches mournfully, slouched back in his chair, narrowed his long low-lidded eyes.

—You always *were* a failure.

—Says you?

—Even your talk is a fake.

—One puts the fake in one's windows.

—Make it singular.

—Window.

—Well, to hell with you anyway.

—Keep the change.

But there was no clock in this room. Time, in this room, was not recognized, was excluded, relegated to the more conscious upper floors, where there was no bar. Singular foresight, for which perhaps one ought to be grateful. Where were they now? Dining at the Commander? At the Greek's? Oysters, followed by broiled live lobster, or chicken *pilaf,* or chicken livers *en brochette?* Sitting opposite each other, with their feet together on the table rung, or side by side in the leather seat in a booth? And where were his hands in that case? The little hard nodule of her garter clasp, felt through the skirt. Unprotesting. . . . Or in the kitchen at Shepard Hall, side by side beside the stove, a dishcloth hung over his arm, Tom the waiter and Bertha the cook—scrambled eggs or shrimp *soufflé.*

—What's wrong with you, anyway? Jitter was saying. I don't think I ever quite made you out. I don't think I ever really liked you, even at school. Something fishy about you. Too damned secretive. God knows you can talk the hair off a dog's back; you can talk all right, but Christ, what a life you lead. Now look at me, you think I'm a drunken rotter, and so I am, and I don't give a damn, I've done everything from digging ditches to laying rails or busting bronchos, I can't keep a job, every one thinks I'm just a good-for-nothing shite. That's all right, the point is I'm intelligent and I live my life the way I *want* to live it, family and conventions can go to hell. I'm honest. But you, One-eye, I think you're *yellow*—you're even afraid of a whore! Good God, I'll never forget that night when you spent the night at my place and sat there shivering in a blanket when I brought that bitch in at two in the morning to talk to you. Anybody'd have thought you were trying to talk to some God-damned duchess. And that wife of yours—where in the name of God did you ever pick *her* up! Just the sort of damned Brattle Street lemon you *would* pick out . . .

—Thanks for the battalion of compliments. No defense. I'm both yellow and secretive—that's the fate, my boy, of the self-conscious. Also manic depressive. Advance one day, retreat the next.

Jitter's drunken gaze, slit-eyed, roved about the room indifferently, as if delighting in nothing it saw, least of all in his vis-à-vis. His collar was dirty, his necktie was skewed to one side, his skeleton fingers were yellow with cigarette smoke. When he talked, it was as if to himself—his diction beautiful, clear, caressing, but the voice monotonous and whining, low-pitched, as if the effort, for one so picturesquely exhausted, were almost insupportable.

—Oh don't talk to me about psychology. I know all that stuff—I've lived it all—what do you know about it? You read books and think you know a lot, but I'd like to see you break a horse, or a woman, for that matter. I know you can sling words better than I can, but where the hell has it ever got you? Here you are writing rotten little textbooks and tutoring for a living and going to your damned little teas—what kind of a life is that.

But there was no clock in this room, this room which had once been the billiard room, this room where so many evenings had been spent in playing cowboy pool with Tom, and which now, decorated with Paris-green Audubon prints of precise birds in fantastic landscapes, had become grillroom and bar. There was no clock, the time seemed as vague as Jitter's wandering melancholy monologue, full of changes and pauses, ticking and then resting, but with this difference, that after every rest, every pause, it resumed its course more heavily, more menacingly, more swiftly, the tick becoming louder and more insistent, the bloodstream in the artery threatening with every beat of the pulse to breach its walls. It was as if, also, this stream more and more persistently and *meanly* were choosing and following an inimical direction, like a snake with its eyes on the heart, which nothing could deflect or dissuade. Pressingly and insinuatingly it encroached; forgotten or ignored for a moment, when next looked at it would be a little nearer, a little more vivid, a little brighter, a little more alert. To be in a hurry, but not to be able to hurry—the familiar nightmare sensation, of course, that appalling slow-motion, languid agony, with which one tries to escape the vague claw of the unknown. On the train it had been better, for there one had at least had the satisfaction of being immersed in speed, of rushing forward from one place to another; but even in the train he had felt at moments an almost overwhelming desire to get out and *run*, as if this more primitive effort might somehow be more effective. Hurry—hurry—hurry—the world was hurrying, the night was hurrying, and nevertheless here was this exasperating slow counterpoint of conversation, this idiotic talk, this exchange of profoundly uncandid candors, each lying laboriously and laconically to the other. And so odd to be perfectly indifferent to Jitter's drunken and intentionally injurious remarks! What would Jitter make of that? An added yellowness, no doubt. Yes, and then no, he said, no, and then yes, finding that Jitter had reached a point at which replies were immaterial to him. He was talking about the actress to whom he was engaged, describing her, reporting fragments of her vaudeville slang, what she had done in Paris, how they managed to sleep together on the steamer. My dear Andy, it's none of my business—but suppose it all turned out to be nothing, a delusion? No. It wasn't a delusion. There had been that look of Bertha's at the fortuneteller's, that strange deep, secret look, that appeal as to the person most intimately known and liked. And the episode at the breakfast table, when, breaking a lifelong habit of Cantabrigian modesty, not to say prudishness, Bertha had come to the table in her pajamas, very self-conscious and flushed and so obviously pleased by Tom's surprise. Was this the way all things ended? Was it inevitable? If not Tom, would it have been another? And precisely how much did it matter? Damn. Blast. Putrefaction. A deep wound opened in his heart. A gulf fell through him, dividing all things, he held hard to the edge of the oak table, trembling.

—She sounds very gay.

—What do I care what you think she sounds like?

—Oh, I don't give a damn about her.

—She wouldn't about you.

—That doesn't worry me, either. I've got enough cancers of my own. My dear Jitter, I'm lousy with them. I'm falling to pieces . . .

—And I'm supposed to be dining with her.

—Good beginning.

—It will probably end like the others. What the hell.

Smiling cynically, mysteriously, he rose without reply to this obviously quite true prediction, and walked rapidly past the bar, across the hall, and into the locker room which smelt of sour male sweat. This is what we smell like. Would a woman enjoy this quintessence? He took the jug and tin funnel from his locker, refilled his silver flask, and then stood for a moment with his forehead against the reticulated ironwork. Time. Nine o'clock. If a taxi to Harvard Square, driving slowly, and then on foot across the Common—the air would clear his head, prepare him for the scene—give him the necessary poise. But would it be late enough? Would they have—? Yes, at this stage, they would. Their time was still precious.

—Harvard Square, please—and make it slow.

—Slow, yes, sir, and which way would you like to go?

—Across the Harvard Bridge, and along Memorial Drive.

—Yes, sir.

A surprise: the bridge was jammed with cars: something must have happened. From curb to curb they were packed, their black tops glistening with rain. Newcomers, joining the slowly moving mass, honked, hooted, skirled their Klaxons, yipped and snarled; but farther on, halfway across the bridge, with its double row of lights, beautifully arched into the night, a string of brilliantly lit streetcars marooned among them, the mass of sedans and taxis seemed to be motionless and silent.

The driver slid back a glass panel.

—This looks like a long job. Will I go the other way?

—No, go ahead, plenty of time.

The motor humming, the clutch engaging and disengaging, they crept forward, weaving a slow passageway among the creeping vehicles. All faces were turned forward, intent, curious, artificially bright over dashboard lights, like illuminated death masks. A hand, holding a cigar, hung out of a window, was held sparkling for a moment in the beam of a searchlight, waved lazily, and withdrew. People sitting upright in back seats, hatted and cloaked, motionless as waxwork specimens, their hands on the window ledges or crossed on their knees. And as they advanced, as they crossed the drawbridge, passed the first of the streetcars, the silence deepened, grew ominous, began to speak a meaning into which all this procession was irresistibly drawn. They were moving into the orbit of something more powerful than themselves—their own purposes, aims, directions, ideas, were suffering a fascinated change—they could no longer go at what speed they liked, or where they liked, but moved, like the lemmings, to the dark sea of their unknown desire. Ahead, to the left, the lights of Riverbank Court, high up, lightly shrouded through the fine rain, appeared to be looking downward at something, as if the dark focus of all this attention were somewhere below them.

—Smash-up, looks like, said the driver.

—It does.

And why not, in the name of God? We specialize in smash-ups. If there's anything we dearly love, it's a nice little smash-up. We serve them hourly. And what more appropriate than this bridge, where Longfellow had once octosyllabically sentimentalized, and he himself, Andrew Cather, One-eye Cather, had won a bet of twenty-five cents by walking from Cambridge to Boston on the outside of the railing? X marks the spot. And here, too, the driver of the ice wagon, deep in thought on a summer's day, had suddenly been catapulted off his high perch, over this same railing, twenty feet down with his cigarette still in his mouth, and drowned. Perfect example of the inscrutability of fate. Because the driver of the car behind the ice wagon had got dust in his eye—! But now the stream of cars was moving a little more quickly—the string of bright street cars had drawn ahead and crossed Memorial Drive—the policeman in his little tower could be seen frantically waving a white-gloved hand—and as at last the taxi swung to the left he saw the dark police boat on the dark rain-stilled water, with a solitary lantern in the bow, and two dark figures leaning waterward over the stern. Ah! they were dragging. Somebody was down there, somebody who this morning had had an egg for breakfast, and a cup of coffee, was down there, aimlessly drifting, his mouth wide open and his hands clenched.

—Draw up where you can, and we'll have a look at this.

—Yes, sir.

On foot, they dodged through the creeping parade of cars and joined the silent crowd at the water's edge, three policemen stood on the float. The police boat, which had gone slowly upstream and turned, was now slowly coming back, and it could be seen that the two men in the stern held ropes.

—Who was it?

—An old man.

—They ain't sure.

—Somebody saw him step off the float at six o'clock. They been dragging three hours.

—Well, *he* don't have to worry about his income tax.

The crowd was hushed, all the faces stared downward at the water. The boat turned once more, moved out a little toward midstream, became invisible save for the lantern. The *put-put* of the exhaust came slowly and intermittently through the night.

—It'll take them all night. Let's get going.

—Hell of a job for a night like this.

In the taxi again, he lit a cigarette, and noticed that his hands were trembling. Good God, was this a symbol, a kind of warning? Cling to life, you poor bastard—have your eggs and coffee for breakfast—and be damned glad you're alive. Is it you down there, with your mouth open? Have you lost your felt hat? Has your watch stopped? Are you cold? What did you do with your money, and the incriminating letter in your pocket? Did you tell the Chinese laundry that they needn't bother to finish ironing your blue shirt? Did you write to Deirdre in Pawtucket and tell her you wouldn't be home for the week end? Did you did you did you did you? And if not, why not? And what did you want to die for anyway? Was it love or was it money? Speculation leads to peculation. The rain quickened on the taxi roof, he reached under his raincoat for the flask, unscrewed the silver stopper, and took a drink, a burning little gush of raw juniper-tasting gin, another, a third. No use trying to be sober. The scene would require reckless hilarity, a certain amount of blindness and denseness. Cheerfulness. No good being too sensitive. Let the imagination loose, let it run, let it fly. Give it a couple of alcoholic wings. What ho, Bertha, what ho, Tom, I'm home again with a boxing glove. I had a dozen little-necks with Jitter Peabody, and a flock of cocktails, and then, only pausing for three hours on the Harvard Bridge, I drowned myself, hat in hand. I am still there, lodged in the deep water against one of the piers, bowing, hat in hand, my mouth open in the act of saying Good evening, Madam. Do you see the water that drips from my shoes? The Charles River, my dears: I am newly come from the dead. This is my bright little *doppelgänger*, my alter ego, who stands before you and screeches with laughter at finding you thus together. Did you both brush your teeth before you went to bed, like good little children? Papa spank. Naughty naughty. You should never, *never* go to bed without first brushing the teeth. There's a new toothbrush with black bristles, I especially recommend it for smartness, particularly in cases of mourning. So tactful. Like that story of the young woman in the Paris drugstore—*Ah oui, Madame, quelle delicatesse!* Madame is a widow! You remember? Tom? Bertha? So run along now and do it and after that I'll tell you both a nice little bedtime story and you can go to bed again, with visions of sugarplums dancing in your little heads, and in the morning I'll be Santa Claus and bring you your breakfast in bed. Madam will have a nice little grapefruit? Or a pruin? A few wild oats and cream? My dear Andy——

And this was that street. Yes, that street. Where, a month ago, after the first rumor, after the first quarrel, the first quarrel about the first rumor, he had walked blindly in the snow, under that very arc lamp, along this path, past the power station, the power station where years and years ago there had been a little tank swarming with turtles and alligators and gold fish. Here was the agony in the garden, the public garden. Why must one do such things? Why must one be hurt? Why need one so helplessly surrender? Better have a drink, old fellow. A few minutes more and the taxi will have reached Harvard Square, and there'll be no chance, unless you prefer to tilt your flask in the rain-dark Common. He lifted and tipped the silver flask, the fiery trickle sluiced his tongue, ran down under his tongue against his teeth, burned the gums, burned the uvula, streaked the throat

with flame. A month ago—he had been dead, and then alive again, and
was now again dying. It was here that the first forsythia bushes would light
their little yellow lights a few weeks hence, here that the young couples
would lie on the scented grass in the early summer, the children playing at
the water's edge, where now were broken slabs of scabby ice. Crowds after
the football games. Crews practicing in the spring, the coxswains barking
through megaphones, the canoes, the motor-launches. And here once with
Bertha—under the birch trees beyond the Newell boat-house—at midnight,
looking across the velvet darkness of the river toward the lights—"No—"
she had said—"no—no—no." And "Yes—" he had answered, "yes—yes—
yes." The bells, the pleas of water, the slow sleepy seethe of new leaves, the
beginning of the world, the quiet beginning. Oh, God, that do'st with
toothpicks take the world apart and gladly break the mechanism of the
spring for schoolboy glee in such a thing!

   —Turn *right* here—up Plympton Street.

   —Yes, sir, I always *do* miss that turn.

He leaned forward, staring, watched the flight of buildings, wet poles
and trees, an empty yard with a forlorn and ruined car standing in gleaming mud, broken palings of a white fence, Mount Auburn Street, the
Lampoon building. Here with a snowshoe once. The polychrome marble
of the basement floor. The green lampshade full of Mib's homemade
punch. Dooley, with a roller towel around his neck, "pully-hauling down
the bay." And the midnight operas, with Tom at the piano, the screams
of bumwad, bumwad, Heeney's Palace of Pleasure, falling down the thickly
carpeted stairs, out of the shower bath, with a cake of soap in his hand——

   Bumwad, bumwad, bumwad, bumwad. The first step toward Haydn,
and a more refined appreciation of music. Oh, yes! Oh, yes, indeed.

   —All right—stop here.

   Enter, to grow in wisdom.

   A dollar, ten cents for the tip.

   And now to take the rain on the chin, and the world on the heart.
The solar knockout. Through the Yard? Through the Square? But Tao is
round and square by turns, and perfectly indifferent to its participant particles: what does it matter: salute the cheerful lights of the Square: walk
under them: bathe in the lamplit perpendiculars of the rain: count the
drugstores: the restaurants: the dealers in athletic goods: the skates in the
windows: the fur-lined gloves and neckties. In that lighted room up there,
as a freshman, I carved my initials on the window sill, meanwhile saying
over and over to myself, "*tu pupila es azul, y quando lloras—*" I who had
never wept, to whom tears were unknown, whose little griefs were the
merest trifling creak of growing wood. Christ. How things change. And
here, all of a sudden, it was almost half past nine, a hundred years later,
and gray hairs beginning to show above his ears, rain falling on a row of
yellow taxis beside the subway entrance, and now a deep swirling bell
striking the half hour, half past nine, half past God, and only a ten minutes' walk between him and a new destiny with a new dragon shape and
new dragon eyes. Be calm, old fellow. Look at it carefully and quizzically,
from a distance, measure it with a calculating eye, count the hackles and
spines on its back, offer it a tin of condensed milk. Perhaps it will be

friendly. Perhaps it will curl up before you like a pet cat, and go to sleep. Why worry? Will a mere disaster kill you? Is love so damned essential? Or pride?

But you should have called her up on the telephone. You should have called her up. It isn't fair. You aren't giving the poor girl a chance. Girl? Don't make us laugh. Yes, just the same, you know it's true, you should have called her up. Why not do it now. Here at the drugstore. What difference does it make? Even over the telephone, if she's guilty, she'll know you know she's guilty. Say you'll be home in five minutes: that wouldn't give her time to put things to rights. All the little telltale things: the caught breath, the changed voice, the ill-chosen word, the overdone welcome, and then the hairpins on the pillow.

He stood at the counter, put his wet hand on the edge of nickel, looked down at the rows of cigars in cedar boxes, the gaudy paper covers with lithochromes of Cuban beauties, flags, palm trees. The row of telephone-booths were just beyond, at the back, beside the little tables and chairs of twisted copper. He saw them with the corner of his right eye. Come on Andy, be a good guy and call her up. Give them a chance. But whose funeral *was* this? It wasn't Bertha that was going to suffer—it wasn't Tom —it was himself. This was nothing but cowardice, cowardice, cowardice masquerading as consideration. The thing must be cut off instantly, with a knife. Fsst: and done. Antiseptic. A pure and beautiful therapeutic murder, severance of connections now no longer real or useful, in order that each of them, released, might continue to grow. Of course. Why hadn't he thought of that before? Just the same——

—Yes, sir.

—A package of Camels.

Just the same——

His eyes were full of rain. Unreasonable. Church Street, where the lilacs used to be, and were no more, and the gray wooden steeple of the Unitarian Church, pointing upward toward the low bright illuminated clouds full of Cantabrigian and Bostonian rain. And the old gymnasium there, among the stables, and the huge book on physiology which they had all read in secret. Sex! Good jumping Jesus, to think of the nuisance, and nothing but nuisance, that sex had been. And after all this time, after a hundred years, at half past nine, or half past God, this final climax. This banal climax.

At the corner of the old graveyard, beside the milestone, he paused in the rain, hung hesitating, watched the brightly lighted Belmont bus splash through a wide sheet of water. Garden Street, or through the Common? Common or Garden? What on earth did it matter? Better take the shorter way, and get the thing over. Past the cannons, which he used to straddle. Past the baseball-field, where he used to strike out every time he came to bat. And the Civil War monument, about which the French architect had said, "*Ah! Il est sorti!*" This is your life here, here are all the days and nights, the sunlit afternoons, the school mornings, the bird-hunting expeditions to the Botanical Gardens or the Observatory, here was the dancing-school, misery of miseries, where later too, in freshman year, were the Coffee Parties, the Cheap and Hungries, all your past life here lies about you, *cauchemar* of echoes and whispers, here palpably still vibrating

in the rain and darkness. Take hold of them. Resume them. Immerse yourself in them. Pull yourself, as it were, together. You are only a football
field in the frost, the hard frozen turf, the raw knuckles, the mud on the
cleats, the baseball-glove rubbed with olive oil, the baseball with scarred
skin. You are only a drawing of a bowl of nasturtiums, the flowers drawn
faintly and delicately, with tenderest self-love, the leaves heavily and boldly
outlined, black-leaded, the veins deliberately varicosed. Here you are still
bringing across the dance floor a glass cup of lemon sherbet to your darling
Bertha, who waits for you in a varnished folding chair, with a white shawl
drawn across her young shoulders, the violets pinned to her waist, her eyes
still looking up at you shyly as you approach, as you continue forever approaching, like an eternal variable which never reaches its ultimate in God.
Shall we sit this one out? Shall we go down to the steps for a breath of
air? It's so hot in here. You know, I'm so afraid I bore you. Bore me! You
couldn't bore a hole in a wall. I saw you yesterday on Brattle Street.
Did you really—why didn't you come and speak to me? I saw you walking
with a girl by Fresh Pond. Oh, yes, we went to see the pumping station.
And the algae. The algae? The algae. You know, Miss Wentworth is so
interested in lichens and algae. Well, it seems a harmless taste, doesn't it?
Would you rather have had chocolate ice cream—I ought to have come
and asked you, but there was such a crowd packed round the table that I
thought I'd better get what I could. Tom wants the next dance—I think
I'd better let him have it. It would look better. Here he is, coming now,
laughing as usual, with that long athlete's lunge of a step, his beautiful
slippers turned inward in studious imitation of the Indian walk. Another
variable approaching another limit—and now—no no no no no no. But
it couldn't be. No. This is not that time, that year, this is later, another
world, another place, another pause between star-ruins, there is no connection, no logic. You are here alone in the cold rain, under the lighted
windows of the new apartment house, under those very windows where a
fortnight ago the man and girl were found shot in a suicide pact. Two
dead in Love Nest. You tear open the package of cigarettes, breaking the
blue stamp with your forefinger, pinch the edge of a cigarette between two
finger nails, draw it forth, light it on the corner of Concord Avenue and
Follen Street. This is you, Andrew Cather: you have changed: you are no
longer there, in that dance hall, nor there at Arlington Heights looking
for star flower and False Solomon's Seal and anemone, nor do you still
wait patiently for hours in the Botanical Gardens with a pair of opera
glasses, hoping to see the scarlet tanager or the grosbeak. These have
nothing to do with you. This is dead. You are dead. You are at most a
shadow of those events, they no longer concern you: cut yourself off from
them: give up forever that pale Narcissus who everywhere wants to walk
beside you: beat him down, away, break him as you would break a false
mirror, walk freely away from the shining fragments, which still would
whisper to you their intriguing lies. This is you, this being whose steps
stagger just slightly with alcohol, whose hands just now again trembled
as you again lit your cigarette, in whose hip pocket the flask of gin is beginning perceptibly to grow warm: taste it and see. Why this desperate and
eleventh-hour attempt to recapitulate? You are engaged in a victory, an

exodus, not a recapitulation. Cut them off with a word. Blow them out of the window, out of the world, out of bed, with a word. One ringing word like Roland's horn, winding among the wind-worn Pyrenees.

Bores me. The sum.

The immediate engulfed him once more, the fine rain saluted him, a gust of cold wind lifted the tail of his coat, and here was Montrose Hall. Tom. Enter, to grow in wisdom. He entered, slipped on the marble floor, the worn wet heel slipping metallically, and slid toward the row of brass letter boxes and the double row of bell pushes: Diana of the Ephesians. Thomas Lowell Crapo. To ring or not to ring. He leaned his forefinger against the button and pressed prolongedly, at the same time lifting down the receiver and listening: he could hear the faint buzz in Tom's apartment. Why must one hold one's breath? Was life as exciting as all that? He breathed quickly, held his breath again, again listened to the far-off cicada trill. Is there an adulterous human in that room, sitting perhaps by the window with a book on his knee, or maybe a married woman? Is Troilus at home? Taking a bath? No answer. The room is dark, the cockroaches are scuttling in the pantry, the melting ice drips in the ice chest, the little gold clock ticks patiently by itself on the yellow table. Tom is abroad. Tom has gone forth. He is probably at the Faculty Club, or gone to a burlesque show, or a prizefight. He has gone to the Square to see Greta Garbo. He is playing the grand piano at the Signet to an admiring audience of sophomores and a pederastic philologist. He is walking back from the Square with two doughnuts and a cup of coffee in his belly. He hums the waltz from the "Rosenkavalier," feeling the chords tensing his long fingers. He is dining with his aunt in Sparks Street. He is doing all these things simultaneously—Why? precisely to avoid doing anything else: safeguarding the world against a catastrophic suspicion: he runs from star to star protesting his innocence: he is a good fellow, a faithful friend. His pockets are full of spider wasps and colloids. He has tied a knot in his handkerchief to remind him of an innocent appointment. Come on, Bertha, come on, Andy, we'll drive down to Duxbury and have a lobster and some steamed clams. Clam broth. A drive out to the Long Beach, the Gurnett. Dead fish on the sand. The sea . . .

Christ, no.

He released the bell, turned, went out, was reimmersed in rain, walking rapidly and uncertainly, his eyes downward, watching the uncertain thrust of his mud-tipped shoes. Blood was in his face, his neck and throat felt swollen and vague, everything was dimmed and rushed and whirling. Garden Street. In this street once—you broke a watch-chain, wrote a valentine, threw snowballs at the feathered trees. In this street once. The red bricks glistened darkly, became near and important and highly organized, rich-patterned symbol of the complicated world. Speed must replace thought. Action must replace idea. You are now an automaton. Thank God, your revolver is at the bottom of the trunk; by the time you dug it out the impulse would have become ridiculous. Hurry—hurry—hurry—everything was hurrying. The world was hurrying. The rain was hurrying. The water in the gutter was hurrying. Be a child, why not, step into the gutter and walk along in the rushing water: it will conceal your spoor, you will leave no traces for the detectives to follow, and besides it will be such fun. Go on, I dare you. Wet feet? You have been drowned, and are wet all over. But these bricks, now, these dead leaves, now, these limpid braids of brown water, this elaborate pattern of the earth's floor, this curious wall of star surface on which you walk like a fly—admire it, Andrew, be bewildered by it, let it confuse you in such a way as will be cosmically useful to you in the coming scene. But what if there *were* no scene? It will be useful anyway. It is your insulation. It is holding you off from your agony. The unimportant has become important in order that the important may become unimportant. Found it marble and left it brick. Bumwad, bumwad, bumwad.

Shepard Street.

The turning point.

A letter box.

Arc light.

Dripping forsythia bushes.

Turn right along boardwalk for fifth act of "Uncle Tom's Cabin." Real blood hounds. See Eliza crossing the ice. See little Eva go to heaven.

He walked with dizzy carefulness, tried in vain to place his feet on the dark cracks of the boardwalk, gave it up, and began to smile. It was probably not Tom at all. Or maybe it would be a party. Bert with a new poem. Celia with a new frock. Floyd with a new dance record. Why, for goodness sake, if it isn't old Andy! But where are your things, Andy! Where's your bag! What's happened! Explain yourself! How come you're back so soon! Welcome home and have a drink. But what about your bag? What indeed. Left it at the Harvard Club by mistake, after too many cocktails— as you can see. Yes indeed. Telephone for it: they'll send it out in a taxi. All very simple.

Shepard Hall.

He stood, stared, the wind whipping his coat, held up his hand to shelter his eyes from the rain, regarded aslant and unseeing the large wet words of carved stone in the wild lamplight. In this house once. The little red table being taken up the stone stairs. The bedspring being juggled into the shaky old elevator. Old Mr. Macumber sitting on the steps in the summer evening to listen to the whirring of nighthawks. The bare floors, before the rugs had come. The bare walls, before the pictures had been hung. Old newspapers on the floor of the bathroom. The white enamel doors of the ice chest open, showing the lining of dull and stinking tin. Stale smells of former occupation: the history of the world. In this house once—but that was long ago. Prehistoric. Before the flood. Before Christ. Before Tom. Retreat, you idiot. Go back to the Harvard Club. Get your bag and hire a taxi and drive to Duxbury. Duxbury? Why Duxbury? Go to Concord. Go to Montreal. Anywhere. Let the rain and wind decide it for you: they are already shaking you to a decision: urging you towards Garden Street: obey them. This house has ghosts. Its walls are made of nasturtiums and Haydn, its ceilings are a gossamer of lost words and cries, forgotten embraces and tendernesses, rebukes, reproaches, and quick words of anger. Rain rain bubbling from right to left along the granite steps. This house has tears. This house has hates. It has arms, hands, and eyes, it listens to you with a conscious expression which is neither pity nor contempt: it knows you without remembering you. Bid it farewell.

He entered the rococo marble hall, ignored the elevator, feeling as he did so a sharp cessation of breath, and automatically thrust his hand into brass letter box number sixty-four. No letters. Of course not. Bertha would have removed them, as he perfectly well knew. Dishonest device to gain time. What for? Terror. Abject terror. His knees were trembling, blood was singing in the side of his neck, his wet hand still hung tremulously in the cold metal box. Remove it: bring it back to you, inform it that it is still yours. But the bell—what about the bell? Six rings, or seven, or the mystic nine? Something to alarm them and put them on their guard? He rang the bell twice, prolongedly, as at Tom's, smiled suddenly at his own instant decision not to listen at the receiver, unsteadily entered the elevator, and ascended. At the third-floor gate a woman was waiting, holding an umbrella. On the fourth floor a rubbish box of canvas. On the sixth floor— exit to grow in wisdom. He let himself out, trembling horribly, smiling, feeling like an idiot, paused insanely with one finger uplifted, took out his key, crossed the oilcloth floor on which were muddy footprints, and let himself in, closing the door with a bang. Good God—are you going to faint? Are you so weak? Lean your back against the door, and regard Tom's hat and stick on the chair, the fur-lined gloves, too, and the wet galoshes. Observe also that there is no light in the sitting room, but a dim light coming from the crack of the bathroom door. All very cosy. All very quiet. Christ. Rain flew across the Shepard Street window.

—Hello! . . . Hello, darlings! Lochinvar is home again.

He swept the gloves, hat, and stick onto the floor: the yellow stick clattered. In their place he flung down his own soaked hat and coat.

—View halloo! Tallyho!

The light in the corridor was switched on, and Bertha's hand and face were motionless, frozen, inclining forward from the bedroom door. The mouth was relaxed, the eyes concentrated, with fright.

—It's a melodrama, Berty. Will you come forward singly or in pairs?

—Andy!

—Andrew One-eye Cather himself!

The surprised face disappeared, taking with it the white plump hand. The bedroom door creaked very slightly.

—Take your time about dressing: I'll wriggle some cocktails. . . . Wriggle is the word.

He stumbled into the sitting room, turned on the light, stood in the center of the Kerman rug under the hideous brass chandelier, and stared out through the black window. Rain. All the way from Boston to New York. Rain devouring New England. Wonders of the Invisible World! And there were the Goddamned nasturtiums too—the nasturtium quid—and the damned little gilt clock, ticking subtly and complacently to itself, for all the world as if it were Tom's own pulse. Break it. Dash it to smithereens on the red-brick hearth. Step on it, kid—let time be out of joint. But where were they? What were they doing? What were they saying? He listened. Nothing. Not a sound. If they were saying anything, it was in a whisper—a frightened whisper—they were pulling themselves together—

wondering what line he would take—pulling on their stockings and shoes—perhaps not daring to look at each other. The room gave a streaming lurch, and to steady himself he put his hand on the corner of the yellow-grained mantelpiece. A Spanish grammar. He plucked the red book out of its place on the shelf, opened it at random, then flung it onto the couch. What about another little drink. Or the cocktails.

In the kitchen, unthinking, he assembled on the table a can of grape-fruit juice, a lemon, a small sharp knife, the sugar bowl, the cocktail shaker, and began chipping the ice in the ice box. A cockroach ran out and fell to the floor. Then Bertha's voice spoke oddly behind him.

—Andy.

He missed his stroke, his hand slipped along the smooth cold surface of ice, then he resumed his chipping, the chunks of ice clunking into the grooved pan.

—I'm sorry, Andy.

—Gosh, is that all. I said this was a melodrama, didn't I?

He flung the ice pick point forward so that it stuck, quivering, into the wooden drainboard of the sink. Then he began gathering up the broken ice between his two palms and dumping it in the shaker.

—I think we'd better talk reasonably about it.

—Sure. Go ahead. Step right up with a wagonload of reasons. This is going to be fun, by God. Go fetch Tom and tell him to have a drink.

—Look at me, Andy!

—Why the bloody hell should I? But I will, if it'll do you any good.

He put the cap on the shaker and started shaking, then turned and looked at her, smiling. She had on the Mandarin jacket, a band of black velvet was round her copper-colored hair, her eyes were deep, dark, tear-bright. She leaned against one side of the door.

—I see you, Berty! There you are—the known unknown at last.

—*That* ought to be something.

—Oh, it is, believe me. Hell, I forgot to put in the grapefruit juice. And the lemons.

He found the can opener, opened the can, breathing heavily, poured the contents into the shaker, sliced three slices of lemon, then shook black squirts of angostura over the floating ice. Five, six, seven, eight. He felt dizzy, and held an ice-cold palm against his forehead. Whoof. The world must be slipping sideways. Better grab on to something. Perhaps Bertha. The prop of your old age. Perhaps the rung of a sideways chair. A dish cloth.

—I don't see what good it's going to do you to get any drunker than you are already. For six months——

—For God's sake, don't talk to me about six months! Go on, get out of here, sit down and I'll bring the glasses. . . . Oh, *there* you are!

He tilted his head to one side, elaborately, and grinned at Tom.

—Hello, Andy.

—Nice little surprise you planned for me. Have a drink.

Bertha turned abruptly on her heel, went into the sitting room, and sank onto the couch. She sat upright with her hands beside her, staring at nothing. Tom followed her awkwardly. As if to avoid the appearance of approaching her, he went to the farther side of the room and stood for a moment by the black piano, frowning. Then he took a step or two back towards the kitchen.

—I don't think I'll *have* a drink, if you don't mind.

—Oh, sure, come on, might as well do it amiably, say the hard things amiably——

He put the shaker and glasses on the red table, and waved his arm over them.

—Go on—make yourself at home. Everything that's mine is yours. Don't try to smile, though, till you've got your face under better control.

—Look here, Andy, old man—I think I'd better go. You two had better talk it over first—don't you think so, Bertha.

—Yes.

—Nope. Nothing doing. This is now a *famille à trois*. Family conference. Every one to be represented. Though I must say you don't either of you seem to have much to say. Strikes me the scene is a little disappointing. Oughtn't you to say you were waiting for a streetcar? Or came back for your umbrella? Did you lose your motor bike? You know, something like that. But of course the thing isn't really a surprise to any of us, is it— we've all seen it coming for such a long time—months and months— Jesus, I've got to laugh.

He laughed, pushing his shoulders against the mantel, while Tom, his face white and strained, handed a cocktail to Bertha. She took it mechanically, without looking at it, and as mechanically drank it.

—Why did you come back tonight, she said.

—Why? Because a little bird told me.

—I don't think it was very sporting of you.

—Neither do I. But what can you do. I've never faced a situation quite like this, my dear, and you must forgive me if my technique is a little crude. As I remarked to begin with, it's a melodrama; and in a melodrama, you've got to behave like actors in a melodrama, haven't you? Suppose I'd telephoned from the club. Everything spoiled, postponed, all of us left in doubt and suspense and agony, nothing settled. What the hell was the use of that? I thought of it, believe me—looked at the telephones—but, no, I decided it must be cut off with a knife. Psst—and done. . . . Here's how.

Tom had perched himself on the arm of the big chair, and was tapping his glass with a finger-nail.

—You're perfectly right, he murmured—Perfectly right. Of course I don't need to say how sorry——

—Oh, no. We needn't go into that. We all know how sorry. One of those awkward complexes, *nicht wahr*, in which delight and sorrow are so painfully and inextricably mixed. I'll give you credit for the sorrow, which I know must be real. Of course. Naturally. You like me—I like you—we're old friends, aren't we—knew each other before we knew Bertha—grew up together—how couldn't you feel sorry? Same here. I feel sorry, too, though it may surprise you. Sorry for you and Bertha and myself in about equal portions. Yes. A sort of *weltschmerz*. Perhaps a little sorrier for myself than for either of you, which is selfish of me, but you'll forgive me. I suppose, as a matter of fact, I ought to kill you? I even thought of it. I thought of it at the corner of Garden and Shepard Street: had a vision of my revolver lying brightly at the bottom of my steamer trunk. But that would be ridiculous.

He walked over to Bertha, lifted her chin with his hand so that her eyes were raised toward his own, looked idly into them for an instant, saw that they were now hard and tearless, and turned toward Tom with a conscious brightening of expression.

—Besides, you've got on one of your most beautiful waistcoats, and the handsomest tweed suit in Cambridge, and I couldn't bear to spoil them. And if I missed—good God. You'd kill me with one hand. In self-defense. And I'd rather go mad than die. Oh, much. . . . Jesus.

—Thank you, said Tom—I appreciate your esthetic tact.

—Don't mention, old fellow—there's nothing I wouldn't do for you. Step right up and help yourself. . . . But as I was saying. What was I saying?

He frowned into his glass, then covered it with his hand. Tired. His wits were gone. He was saying things badly, saying the wrong things, off the track somehow. Something else must be found, some other direction, something deeper, more to the point, more plangent and poignant. Profound abstractions, self-sacrifice, nobility, a great constellation of bright and beautiful stars. A vast bouquet of planets in a purple sky.

—Why don't you say something, Berty? God knows you usually have enough——

—What is there to say. It's done.

—I suppose you didn't think of consulting me about it.

—Yes, I did. But it came too vaguely, and then too suddenly——

—He swept you off your feet.

—Oh, for the love of mud, Andy!

Tom stood up, very straight and angry.

—I wonder if you quite realize your own part in this situation, Andy. For six months you've left me practically alone. You've been drunk night after night. If Tom behaved decently to me, did a little something to make things happier for me—if I could get a little enjoyment out of life——

—I see. Yes, indeed. Tom as the good Samaritan. The neglected wife. But I suppose it hasn't occurred to you that it was partly just because I saw this business beginning that I withdrew myself?

—Oh, no! You can't get away with that. Oh, no. It had begun before that, and you know it.

Silence. This wasn't right at all. He stared at the carpet. He felt their eyes fixed upon him, and for the moment wasn't quite sure that he could look at them. A deep pain opened somewhere within him, a deep sadness, an enormous sense of lostness and futility. It was all no use. Impossible to explain. What on earth could one do with words? Memories? Ideas? A trifling little barter of facts? He walked to the table, refilled his glass, went to the window beside the couch and looked out, looked down into the rain-dark street, where the twin lights of Shepard Hall entrance illuminated the boardwalk, sodden with water. Perhaps it was himself, after all, who was wrong. Was it wholly impossible? Ten years. The dance of places, the dance of rooms, the dance of houses. Bertha plus one, Bertha plus two,

Bertha plus three, Bertha plus four. Bertha at the Coffee Party, at the skating rink, on the toboggan at Oakley, on the river at Concord, the Sudbury, the Assabet, walking in spring along the granite lip of the Frog Pond—and now Bertha here, Bertha belonging no longer only to himself, if indeed she belonged at all. Where was it all gone? Where was it now? It was nowhere. It was gone forever. Nothing could now ever be the same in the world, never again. This was no longer his Berty, that was not Tom—two new persons sat in the room with him, two strangers who looked at him with hostility and misunderstanding, whose minds and memories were now allied against his own. He was outnumbered, outmaneuvred, outwitted. What was the use. Better get completely drunk, and let it all go to hell. Speak out his bitterness and be damned to them. Yes. Be damned to them. Let them go to hell and stay there.

—All right, Tom, I suppose you're right—you'd better go home and leave this to Berty and me. Go on, get out. Put on your damned little galoshes and gloves and carry your pretty little malacca. But first I'd just like to call you, to your white face, a worm: a curious and very handsome worm. Don't you think so?

He lifted his glass in a toast and drank it off. He had come quite close to Tom, and they were looking with an extraordinary amiability into each other's eyes. Protractedly. Exchanging what? He felt his gaze move subtly from one to the other of Tom's two eyes, was for a moment conscious of Tom's ancient embarrassment at having to look at a glass eye, and felt it now as a peculiar but too fortuitous advantage. He was pleased at the thought.

—Good night, Bertha, Tom said.

—Wait a minute. There's one more thing. I suppose you'll want to marry her, and make an honest women of her? It'll be a divorce, of course?

—Andy! Is that quite necessary?

Bertha flung the words at him crookedly as she flung off the black velvet band from her hair, which she tossed angrily to the right.

—Perhaps not—perhaps not. . . . Go on, Tom—get out.

From the doorway, he watched Tom pulling on the galoshes, straining and flushing. This was fun. Awkward moment for Tom.

—Sorry your hat and stick are on the floor.

—It doesn't matter, old man.

—I suppose you'll be going to Sanders on Thursday?

—Probably.

—Well, sleep well!

—Good night, Andy. Come in and see me when you feel like talking about it.

—Yes, indeed!

He patted Tom delightfully on the shoulder of his raincoat, smiled, and softly shut the door. A beautifully managed exit. Couldn't have been better. And the idea of Tom's sleeping. Good God. Who would sleep after this? Who? Himself only, for only himself would have the sense to get thoroughly and completely and obliviously drunk. Yes. Drunk. He was drunk already. He was beginning to feel gay. Rubbed his hands on his forehead and then together and stepped quite nimbly into the sitting room, where Bertha, her back turned, was looking at the books on the mantelpiece.

—Well, darling, now we can discuss this quite amicably and privately. Isn't it nice? Now we can really go into it, without self-consciousness.

—I think you're behaving revoltingly.

—Revoltingly! What the hell do you mean. I'm behaving like a perfect gentleman.

—You know what I mean.

—I'm damned if I do. But I'll be delighted to hear. Have a drink?

—I think you might at least have kept sober, and not introduced, or tried to introduce, this element of disgusting farce.

—God, you make me laugh. Your usual total lack of perception. Blind as a bat. I suppose I ought to have sent some flowers first, in a taxi, with a little message? Congratulations and facilitations. The bridal chamber was decorated with roses and syringes. Typical of you not to see that the only way, the only way, of handling such a scene is humorously! Good jumping Jesus. It's that, among other things, that's always been wrong with us. Your heavy-handedness: this fatuous Brattle Street dignity: all these God-damned poetic hypocrisies. I suppose we ought to be tragic about it, and behave like people in a novel, or an Ibsen play. Ought I to have apologized for having come into my own flat and then cried about it? Tragic! Who's it tragic for, if not for me, supposing I wanted to give in to it? What the hell have I come back to? To a stinking void. To a part of myself that's dead. Well, all right. That's my funeral. Not yours, and not Tom's. If I want to make a joke of it, for the moment, so as to avoid cheap sentimental dramatics, the sort you act in at Brattle Hall, you might at least have the intelligence to see why I do it, and that it's my own business. I get drunk because I don't want to be wholly conscious. Because, I admit it, I'm partly a coward, and don't want to know, or to have you and Tom know, exactly how many volts of pain I'm carrying. Do you want me to cry? Do you want me to comfort you? Or do you expect just a calm rational discussion of the ethics and esthetics of sexual fidelity?

—There's no use discussing anything, if you're going to be merely abusive.

—There you go. If I state facts, I'm abusive.

—I think you might at least have tried to see my point of view. I've been starved——

—Yes, for Christ's sake drag *that* up again, starved for love! You don't know what love is. You're a thirteen-year-old romantic, a bleached little Cantabrigian Madame Bovary. I want *love*, she cries, and pulls on a pair of tarpaulin knickers.

—Shut up!

She turned suddenly and glared at him, her mouth dreadfully relaxed, the tears starting quickly from her eyes. He was looking at her quite coldly, with the familiar hatred, the familiar deep ferocity and need to injure. She was beginning to suffer. Pursue the advantage. Grind it in, beat her down. Give her the works. Analyze the whole marriage, drag it all up by the roots, reveal her to herself for once and all, all the piecemeal horrors laid out like entrails on a bloody platter. Bumwad, bumwad, bumwad, bumwad. The whole prolonged obscene and fecal grapple in steadily deepening darkness, year after year of it, the burden upon his consciousness becoming hourly more foul and more frightful. The history of a bathroom. Dirty water. Dirty clothes. Dirty habits. The upright soul indifferent to filth. Jesus, angel of grief, come down to me: give us a speech as pure as ocean. A tumbler of neat gin, fiery strangulation, a cough, tears on his marble eye which might be misinterpreted, a sudden impulse to make them real. The awful contraction of the belly which precedes weeping. A new red edge provided for anger.

—All right—I'll play the piano. . . . No, I won't, either.

He played two bars of a Bach gavotte, then stopped.

—Isn't it ridiculous. Why do we make such a fuss about it? Especially as we all flatter ourselves that we saw it coming. Or did we? I must confess though——

—What.

Bertha's face was averted, her voice flat.

—I hadn't really expected you to go through with it. I thought Brattle Street would be too much for you.

—I see. You thought as usual that I wasn't quite human.

—Not at all. Don't be in a hurry. I thought you were too damned moral. Or loyal.

—Loyal to what, exactly? I'd like to know.

—Oh, me, for instance.

—Yes! After you'd flaunted Molly——

—Don't be more of a fool than you have to be.

—Besides, if you admit withdrawing from me, what difference does it make. You know our marriage hasn't been a marriage for almost a year——

Of course. There was that. There was that, which he had forgotten. But how explain it to her? There was no explaining it. The problem of rhythm: the inevitable succession of approaches and retreats: love, indifference, hate—then over again, love, indifference, hate. Disgust, then renewed curiosity. Exploration, then renewed retreat. Soiled clothes, then sunlight, a concert, a few drinks, an evening of witty conversation, psychological discussion—and all of a sudden the divine recapitulation. Would this have occurred again? Had he really wanted it, or hoped for it, to occur again? Or had he at the bottom of his heart desired this precise consummation, this disaster? The sacrifice of everything. And in that case, why make a fuss about it: how could it hurt him? How, indeed. Step up, ladies and gents, and see the unwoundable pig.

—Oh, God, what's the use.

—I meant to tell you that I thought I was falling in love with him. And that he was in love with me. He meant to tell you too.

—How long have these discussions been going on?

—I meant to tell you before anything happened. But you see——

—I suppose you want me to believe that tonight is the first time?

—No.

Well, by God, *that* opens up a nice vista into the past, doesn't it.

To ask or not to ask. To pry or not to pry. He stared at the carpet, pushed a cigarette end with the toe of his muddy shoe, felt the blind agony beginning to contract his whole body. One night, or two. One week, or three. Before he left for New York, or after. In Tom's flat, or here. To think this was sickness, madness, disruption. Drunken and maudlin disruption. What was Bertha, then, that even now he should suffer? This pale oval of female face, with the speckled gray eyes and the always too-innocent mouth? A mere face. A mere idea. A mere history, now finished. Or *was* it finished?

He picked up his glass and crossed to the table. Bewilderment. The empty glass in his right hand meaningless.

—Yes, a *lovely* little vista into the past. The past suddenly becomes the present, doesn't it? And a damned pretty future.

—Well, you've always preached psychological freedom and honesty——

—Christ!

—Why not practice it?

—I can safely leave that to you!

—That's not fair!

—That's the coolest defense of whoredom——

A curious singing began in his right ear. He put down his glass very hard on the red table, which was unexpectedly near, then walked quickly, with Bertha's glare still fixed upon him, across the corridor to the bathroom. The door closed, he stared at his reflection in the greenish mirror. White as a sheet. First stage of drunkenness. Boy, you ain't seen the half of it. This is going to be a souse in a million. He watched himself swaying, rested his hands on the marble basin, and saw his face beginning to cry. The mouth curled itself grotesquely, like a child's, like the wound in a tragic mask, his eyes closed themselves to slits, the white face began absurdly jiggling up and down, in time with the rapid soundless convulsions of his chest. He turned on the two taps in the basin, to drown out the extraordinary noise Andrew Cather had begun to make. A sound like a swift departure of wings, pigeon's wings, whe-whe-whe-whe-whe-whe-whe-whe—then a shudder of breath quickly indrawn, and another hissing flight of wingbeats, and a long oooooooooooooo—subsiding to caught calm, as the tears fell into the steaming water. Grates me. Is this the face that launched a thousand quips? Is that you, One-eye Cather? Wash your bloody, driveling little map. If, the last time your mother spanked you, when you were seven, you refused to cry, why cry now? What is there to cry about? Is it manly to cry? Disgusting. Step up, ladies and gents, and see the weeping pig: the pig with wings, the pig with a glass eye. Look at the little red veins in his nose, heritage of six months' drunkenness, the whiteness of the white of his left eye, the redness of the white of the right. Wash your face with cold water, as you have often seen Bertha do after a midnight quarrel. Observe yourself from a great distance, as if you were an ant crawling over the toe of your shoe. Isn't he a funny little thing? Does he know where he's going? Has he a god? Does he distinguish right from wrong? Has he sexual appetites, loves, hates, despairs? Has he an ideal? A secret richness of soul, tenderness of heart, susceptibility to injury? Have you lost your wife, your friend, or is it only an egg? *Tu pupila es azul; y quando lloras*—the world is a lost egg. A mislaid egg. It will hatch, out of season, in a universe of intemperate weather, an absolute zero, and the god it contains will be born dead.

You are not angry: you don't want to be angry: you are hurt.

His face washed, the temples cold and transparent over the brain, he returned to the sitting-room. It was now Bertha's turn to cry. She lay huddled at one end of the couch, her back turned, her cheek on a green pillow, a handkerchief held over her eyes. One of her pianissimos, a soft whispering sound, persistent, uninterruptible, the kind that could go on for hours, for all night. She looked small and pathetic, but also absurd. He felt a profound detachment and irony towards her, watched the slight shaking of her body, the irregular lift and fall of the blue mandarin jacket on her left shoulder, the movement of the blue elbow, noted the heaviness of the upper arm: she was getting old.

—I'm not angry, Berty: I don't want to be angry: I'm hurt.

The rain answered him. Hurt? The word seemed singularly inadequate. But words in a scene were always inadequate: it was always like this: these midnight quarrels were always the same: ridiculous phrases followed by ridiculous silences, sudden shifts from fury to pathos, from the heroic to the absurd, and at last a bedside reconciliation dictated by sheer fatigue. But not tonight, not this time. No. Good God, no.

—Are you going to say anything?

No answer. His hands in his pockets, he walked into the kitchen, looked at the table, the empty tin, the tin opener, the half lemon, the sugar bowl, the spots of gin and water on the varnished wood. Still life. A cockroach signaled at him with alert antennae from the edge of the kitchen sink. The ice in the ice chest settled itself with a grating slump, metallic. Domestic interior: the persistent order that underlies all disorder, the useful tyranny of the inanimate. Say good-by to it, old fool—this is the beginning of the end. All is over. No more ice chests, shared cockroaches, fruit knives, gin rings to be mopped up with handkerchiefs. To hell with it. No more mosquitoes on the window screens in the summer evenings, to be squashed with one finger against rusty wire. The last day of the calendar, the calendar with the sacred cow. Out with it: this is the terminus. Let Rome in Tiber melt——

—Perhaps you're right. Yes, I believe you may be right. What's the use? How can we summarize everything in a few well-chosen words. Your life, and my life, our life together. *Non si puo.* . . . Just the same, I don't see what you're crying about—you've got what you want, haven't you?

He looked at her quizzically: she was quieter, but he could still see her left shoulder now and then spasmodically lifted, hear the sharp intake of breath. He picked up the red Spanish grammar from the other end of the couch, seated himself where the book had lain, being very careful not to touch the slippered feet which were so close to his knee.

—Impossible to find the right words, isn't it. Just as well read at random out of a book. For example. It is lightning, and I fear that it will rain. Is she unhappy? She appears to be so, but I cannot believe that she is so. He is sorry that he is ill, and I am sorry that he is ill. Use the subjunctive after expressions of doubting or fearing, joy or sorrow, or necessity. *Mientras dure la vida*—as long as life lasts. *Ella está enamorada: y si lo está, que mal hay en ello?* No harm at all.

The rain answered him. No harm at all.

—Or how about this. This seems to settle everything. It seems to me; it seems to you (fam. sing.); it seems to him; it seems to us; it seems to you (fam. pl.); it seems to them, I go to bed; you go to bed (fam. sing.); he goes to bed; we go to bed; you go to bed (fam. pl.); they go to bed. All life in a nutshell, by God. We hate each other; they (masc. and fem.) hate each other. We embrace and kiss each other. . . . Cardinals and ordinals. We shall reach the city of Waltham before night comes on. Let us take leave of the wounded man: he slept well yesterday, and he is not moaning tonight. This is a Spanish proverb: "Although the monkey dressed in silk, she remained a monkey!" It is snowing or raining all the time in this town: we hope that the weather is better in yours. . . .

No answer to his lifted eyebrow: he began to feel angry again.

—I like the "fam. sing.," don't you? He has a toothache, and is shedding a lot of tears. If you do not prefer to lend them the pens, do not lend them the pens.

The sound of Bertha's weeping became louder: she made a sudden convulsive gesture with her lifted elbow, turned her face farther away into the pillow, and said:

—Will you stop it, please?

—Certainly, if you like.

—I believe you have—I believe you have—no heart at all.

—Step right up, ladies and gents, and see the pig without a heart. . . . To drink is to live. An old Spanish proverb. Have a drink, Andy, old fellow. Yes, I will, thank you.

He sat still, staring, let the opened book slide to the floor, then rose and stood before her, jingling the silver in his pocket.

—Well, what do you suggest?

—Nothing. . . . Whatever you like.

—I see. You want me to make the decisions. Is that it?

No answer.

—By God, I could kill you when you take refuge in weeping and silence. It's a damned dirty way of evading your responsibilities, if you ask me! I'm going back to the club. I don't know where I'll go from there. Anywhere. I'll let you know——

He lurched into the hall, struggled into his wet coat, put his hat on, returned to the couch, where Bertha still lay motionless, squeezed her elbow once between finger and thumb, saying, "I'm off," and a moment later found himself running along the slippery boardwalk toward Garden Street. In this street once. He got into a yellow taxi, which started moving before he had quite seated himself: he found himself on his back, and for a few seconds lay inert, uncertain whether he wanted to laugh or cry. Lights. The expensive hum of a Packard. Bertha at the opera, in the borrowed car. Mrs. Skinner, the old buzzard, sat behind them. "They were just finding each other," she said. Just finding each other. Oh, yeah? And now they were just losing each other. One as easy as the other—now you see them and now you don't. Close the eyes. Let the chin come to rest, where it will, on mother's breast. Let us frolic on the hills at Arlington, under the shadow of the water tower. Wild barberry. Black-eyed Susan. Does some one see us. Is some one coming. Beams multiply in a scaffolding, the scantlings cant, the lashed ladder topples, falls, veers, descends dizzily down the booming well. She has bats in her belfry. Long sounds, long lines of sound, long lights on backs of sounds, rode like the *Valkyrie*, whooping through the tunnel. Let fall your chin on mother's breast. No, you mustn't here, this is too public, some one might see us, don't, Andy, you're too dreadful. The taxi ticking, Mr. Rodman said: I said: Mr. Rodman said: *tu pupila es azul*. Paid the bill. Saw the spittoons, garboons. The ice in the urinals, too, and the brass keys on the rack. Who's on the rack? Beams multiply in a scaffolding, the scantlings cant, cross levers, struts and stays, footholds and handholds, giant's jackstraws, you are lost among them, come down, oh, maid, from yonder height, get out from under before it all falls, it will fall, is falling, fam. sing. and all, go on and hoot your way into hell. Who was hooting? The dead man under the bridge, fumbling in darkness along slimy piles, bowing to the tide, felt hat in hand. Good evening, madam. Have they found me yet? Has my watch stopped ticking? What brick was it that spoke that about ticking? It was the train, over the joints, over the rails. In Rome too as the Romans too.

The silence——

—A dollar and a quarter. *And* ten.

—Thank you, sir.

—Don't mention.

That probably surprised him.

The club was empty and still, opened before him spaciously and with marble echoes, followed him downstairs with subdued lights and sounds, with portraits of philosophers and a bison's head, with shells from the Somme and a Chinese dragon on scarlet silk. The chessmen too. The Hoboken gambit? I'll pawn my queen. The bar closed for the night, but water would do. A Lily-cup of waxed paper, cold water on greased skin.

At the locker, he refilled the silver flask, took a long burning drink, filled again, then placed six Lily-cups in a white row on the table in the bomb-proof, two of them filled with water: supplies for the night. Within reach of his hand, as he lay on the red divan. Better have a night-cap. Jitter might have been here, often was. You know, Andy, I think there's something yellow about you. Close the eyes, to shut out swimming. Rest the chin on papa's hairy chest. Not very comfortable. Screwed his head from left to right against the hard leather. Sleep drunkenly, tomato juice in morning, cold clam juice, ice water, cold shower set you right. Wake up, Andy, it's time to get up: you have an appointment to tutor at eleven. That little Jew. Weisskopf. The long swift darkness swept over from left to right, here and there a streaked star, a dark pouring sound, the subdued roar of all blood. Bumwad, bumwad, bumwad, bumwad. Oh, bumwad. Now nausea plucking at the corners of the arid mouth, the twitch of sickness, the race between sickness and unconsciousness, the interstellar skid. The hands nerveless and placeless, now on the belly, now at the side, now hanging towards the floor, touching the cold leather, stubbornly conscious, waiting for something, afraid of sleep. Wake up, Andy, it's time to get up. That was a footstep, near, menacing.

—Mr. Cather, sir.

—Hello.

An attendant, deprecatory.

—Pardon me, sir, Mr. Cather, but would you like to be found here?

—Found and left.

—Yes, sir.

The long darkness swept superbly from left to right, the blood began its universal pouring over the small tossed body of the world, hurled it and whirled it, swung it obliquely through a screaming abyss, hoisted it again to a toppling pinnacle. Good evening, madam. This is my drowned hat that I am eating. We signed the contract. I am successful. When he saw the sparrow in the road, he got off his horse. It had a broken wing, the bones were sticking out. Of course, what did I tell you. More calmly now. More darkly now. Smoothly, on even keel, into the dark station, the tunnel, the banked lights stately and still on stone columns, birds of brightness, cold and light. I saw you before you saw me, yes, I did. Why didn't you tell me, and, besides. I was walking there.

In pure light came the remote flight, the little flight of a flock, coming nearer and larger and brighter, the flight of little winged bones, winging through heaven, little wrist-bones and delicate ankle-bones and even figulas and femurs and scapulas, and each with as neat a pair of wings as you'd see on a bleeding sparrow, and every one of them on its way to a star, far off; or was it God himself? He watched them with one eye, while he picked up the skeleton and began to eat it; first the feet, then working slowly up the legs; and dry going it was, what with no sauce, no mustard, no Worcestershire, and the bones getting bitterer as he crawled right up through the pelvis, devouring all, and crunched the ribs. The spine tasted like the Dead Sea, like ashes in the mouth, getting worse as he crawled nearer to the skull; and the skull itself was a black mouthful of charcoal, which he spat out. And in mid-space then he saw behemoth in the act of biting off the conning tower of an interstellar submarine, one of these ether-going craft with one eye, a little way off to the southwest of a pink star, which was wearing white drawers, like a woman. And in a canoe then, in a canoe, a birchbark canoe, up the marsh channel, above the red bridge, in amongst the hosts of seething reeds in the hot salt sunlight—the bright drops on the paddles, the bare arms freckled and wet—is this the way to the Gurnett?—Oh, no, that's the other way—you'll have to turn round—yes, it's the other way. The other way, to the Gurnett.

The other way, a long way.

And when he came, they gave him an oval reception.

⟪ II

⎧————particularly the smell of the pine-wood walls, soaked in sea fog,
but pine-smelling also in the strong sea sunlight, smooth to the touch,
golden-eyed with knotholes, and the wind singing through the rusty
wire screens, fine-meshed and dusty, or clogged brightly with drops of
⎩dew, or drops of rain, or drops of fog—the morning outlook seaward,
over the humped grass beyond the puddled tennis court, over the wild sea
grass windblown, beyond the new house of bright shingles, where the new
boy and girl lived, and then across the bay to Clark's Island, and the long
yellow outer beach, with its deserted and mysterious shacks of houses, and
then the Gurnett—the small white twin lighthouses of the Gurnett—I was
looking out of the window at this, at all of this, feeling the cool east wind
from Provincetown, but with no mirage to show precisely where Provincetown lay, and the voices came then over the low partition between the
bedrooms. I was dressing, and as I put on my khaki shirt I looked at the
fly-trap, which I had made out of fragments of window-screen wire, to see
if my flies were all still alive after the night. What would they be saying
now. The voices were low and secret, early morning voices, Uncle Tom and
Aunt Norah. I removed the screw in the wall beside the washstand and
peeped through into the maids' room, saw a pink chemise very close to me,
so close that I was frightened, and walked softly away, back to the window.
Did Molly know I was there, that I was watching her day after day? I had
seen them putting on their bathing suits. Afterward, when I met them on
the porch, they were embarrassed, tried to pull down the short skirts over
their knees, ran down the road giggling and looking back. Molly's skin was
very white, Margaret's was brown.

But why should he come like this, Tom? It isn't like him not to let
Doris, or anyone, know. Perhaps you'd better go to Boston and see him.
Do you think there's anything wrong.

—The whole thing is very queer. Do you think he suspects. Do you
think we ought to say something to Doris.

—I think you'd better go to town and see him. Before anything worse
happens. He ought not to come here, if that's what he's thinking of doing.
I'm sure he suspects. It would hurt him too much to see it. It would be
better if you talked to him.

—We'd better put off the picnic till next week. Too bad to disappoint
the kids again, but it can't be helped. It was queer to begin with that he
let Doris come here alone, with the children, when he could perfectly well
have come, too—his business was only an excuse. I think they had already
quarreled about it.

They were talking about Father and Mother, and I went close to the
partition, to listen, holding my breath; but the voices stopped, the door

opened, and I heard Uncle Tom going down the stairs, and Aunt Norah pouring water out of the pitcher into the washbowl. No picnic at the Gurnett this week—the third time it had been postponed. Porper would probably cry when I told him, but instead Susan and I could take him down to the front beach and build villages out of shells, and show him the dead seal. In that little cleared place between the banks of eelgrass, flat and sandy at low tide, where the horseshoe crabs were. The new boy and girl, too, Warren and Gay, except that Gay was always crying, as when we had taken her to the log cabin in the pine woods and tried to make her undress. Had she told her mother and father about that, the little sneak.

————particularly the morning walk to the village, along the Point Road, past all the houses and windmills, the wild cherry trees and crab apples, to get the morning mail. The wooden windmills were the best, with their wings of fine white-painted slats, and the great wooden tanks at the top, and the strong girders of white-painted wood, and of these I couldn't decide whether I preferred Daisy or Sunbeam. Of the metal ones, there were five Comets and three Aermotors, and our own Vulcan, the only three-legged one on the Point. They were all going busily in the east wind. The Tuppers had a special little shingled tower, with a red railing around the top, where Frank Tupper went with a telescope to watch the yacht races in the bay, but this I passed quickly, looking at the house and garden out of the tail of my eye, to see if Gwendolyn was there. Had she got the box of candy I had left on her porch for her, with the heart on it, and our initials. Would she laugh at me. Did I dare go in the afternoon to the drill of the Company at the Camp. Would she have told Frank about it, and would Frank say anything. When we were playing cross-tag I had caught her by her pigtail, and she had looked at me in a very queer way, half angry and half pleased, and then had refused to play any more. What was this about Father and Mother. Was it because she went sailing all the time with Uncle David, just like last year, and walks to the beach always at night after Porper and Susan had gone to bed. The stage passed me, coming from the morning train, the one named Priscilla, painted a bright yellow, with red wheels, and toothless Smiley driving the horses and saying "Giddup, giddup" out of the side of his mouth, spitting tobacco juice. I would be in plenty of time for the mail, in fact I would have time to go to the drugstore and have a chocolate milk shake at the marble fountain, which always smelled of vanilla. If it rained in the afternoon, we would play Gonko in the playhouse, and perhaps make some new racquets out of shingles. If it didn't rain, I would go for a row in the dory, through the long bridge and up into the marsh channel towards Brant Rock and Marshfield, for the tide would be low, and I could explore the channels. If I got stuck, I could pretend to be just clam-digging, the way Uncle Tom always said the yachtsmen pretended to do when they got stuck on the mud flats in the bay. They always took pails and shovels with them in case they got stuck, and then rolled up their trousers and went digging, as if that was what they had come for. Or perhaps Uncle David would invite us out in his cabin motorboat, late in the afternoon, with Mother, and Uncle Tom, and Aunt Norah, and that would be fun, except that I didn't like Uncle David. I heard Molly saying to Margaret in their room when they were

going to bed that he was always drunk. Did that mean falling down. I had
never seen him fall down. But I had seen bottles under the bunk in the
cabin of the motorboat several times and he had bottles in his room downstairs, on the table under the row of dried and mounted seaweeds, which
Uncle Tom and I had put there the year before.

————and beyond the golf links, where I always left the bicycle path,
paved with broken clamshells, to walk along the edge of the course, among
the bayberry bushes and cherry trees, hoping for lost golf balls, prodding in
the poison-ivy with a stick, beyond this the boarding house kept by old
Mrs. Soule, where we had stayed last year and the year before, with the
hen houses at the back, and the little sandy-rutted road which led down to
the cove and the stone dyke where beach plums grew. The floors were
painted gray, with white speckles, the whole house had a marine smell
like a ship, conch shells lined the path and stood against the doors, and on
the lawn, among the croquet wickets, I had found four-leaved clovers. Molly
Soule always sat alone in the swing, large-eyed, pallid, her thin little hands
around the ropes, looking sadly at us, because we never played with her.
Nobody ever played with her, because her name was the same as her
mother's, and she had no father. She was always hanging about and watching us from a little distance, and would run away and cry if we said anything to her, especially the Sanford boy, who asked her so many times what
her name was. This was where I played baseball with Father in the evening,
or ran races with him from one telephone pole to another. Was it true that
he was coming again this year. Why was it that this year we were staying
with Uncle Tom, and Aunt Norah, and Uncle David, instead of at the
Soules'. Though it was nice, particularly as Uncle Tom knew so much
about the wild flowers, and had that nice little tin cylinder to bring back
the flowers in, the one he had brought all the way from Switzerland a long
while ago. It hung over his shoulder on a strap, and we had found swamp
pink in the marsh near Pembroke woods, and arrowhead, and ghost-flower.
Jewelweed, on the way to the Standish Monument, pickerel weed, and
buttonbush. If only he could go more often—we already had more than
fifty kinds, pressed in the blank book, it would be easy to get a hundred
before the summer was over. Why was he so thin, and his knees so funny,
and he always wore that funny yachting cap with the green vizor, his ears
sticking out at the sides, walking in his bathing suit over the humped grass
to the Point with the rowlocks jingling in his hand. I said to him that I
thought I was getting fatter. He gave that nice little chuckle and said,
No danger, Andy. Why was it he and Uncle David had never learned to
swim properly——

————when we got to the oak woods we decided after all to go to the
pine woods instead, because the oak woods were smaller and closer together, there were no logs to build with, and no room anyway; so we took
Warren and Gay with us and we sat in the houses of logs while it rained,
and only a few drops of rain came through the roofs, which we had made
out of pine boughs. Susan was in one house with Warren, and Gay was in
the other with me. I asked if we should take our clothes off and go to bed,
pretending it was night, but she said no and began to cry. Warren and
Susan had taken off theirs. Warren didn't mind, but Gay said she wanted

to go home, and I was afraid she would tell her mother. So I told her about
the villages we made of shells on the beach, and the dead seal.

—It's swarming with maggots.

—What are maggots.

—Little white worms, millions of them, and it smells so bad that you
can smell it all the way up to the house when the wind is right.

—Do you go bathing every day, we go every day, and we have a sailboat at the Point.

—I have a dory of my own, and my uncle has a motorboat which he
takes us out in. It has a real cabin with doors that lock.

The smell was so bad that we couldn't get very near to the seal without
feeling sick, but I showed her the maggots. Then Mother came down the
hill walking very slowly, with Porper holding her hand. She was carrying a
red silk parasol over her head.

—Porper wants to see the village. Show him how you build houses,
Andy and Susan, I want to read my book. Are these your little friends?
What are your names, children? Oh, you're the little girl and boy who
have just moved in next door, aren't you.

We made houses out of rows of quartz pebbles in the sand, in between
the beds of eelgrass. First they all had to buy their land from me with shells
for money: scallop shells were five dollars, clam shells were one dollar, toenail shells were fifty cents. Mother had made a pile of dried eelgrass to lean
against, and was reading a book under her parasol. Warren sold quartz
pebbles to us for building material. Susan kept the bakery shop where we
bought bread and cakes, Gay was the grocer. I built a house for Porper, and
showed him how to go in and out of the imaginary door, and where the
bedroom was, and how to go along the streets without stepping into the
other houses by mistake. The tide was way out, all the mud flats in the bay
were showing, and a little way out two men with a dory were digging clams.

—Shall we dig some clams for supper, Mother?

—Not today, Andy.

—When are we going to the Long Beach for a clambake, and to see the
Gurnett. Tomorrow?

—Not till next week, I'm afraid. Now don't bother Mother, she's reading. And she may take a nap, she's very tired and sleepy, so don't disturb
her.

Susan took off Porper's sneakers so that he could go wading.

—There you are, lamb. Don't mind about the clambake, we'll have it
next week, and you'll see the ocean and all the dead fishes.

—What dead fishes.

—And here are some more scallop shells for you, and a horseshoe crab.

Warren and I walked along the beach toward the Point, and I showed
him the hunting box, all covered deep in dried seaweed. We got into it and
lay down for a while. It smelt very nice. There was an old beer bottle in
the corner, with sand and water in it, and we took it out and threw stones
at it until it was broken. Take that. And that. And that. And that for your
old man.

When we went back, Uncle David had come, and was standing in front
of Mother, with his hands in his duck trousers. He was looking down at her

and laughing. The parasol had fallen on the sand, she was lying back with her hands under her head.

—Say that again.

—Why not?

—Well, say it.

They laughed together, and then he turned his head toward us and said, Hi, there: what mischief have you fellows been up to?

—Andy, why don't you take your little friends down to the Point and show them your dory. I'm sure they'd like to see it. Wouldn't you?

————at the Company Camp, on the edge of the other oak woods, in the late afternoon, with the long yellow sunset light coming over the stunted trees, Frank Tupper drilled us in a row, Sanford and myself and Gwendolyn and the two Peters girls, Warren sitting on the grass and watching us, because he hadn't yet been elected. Present arms. Shoulder arms. Port arms. Ground arms. Parade rest. The wooden cannon was dragged out of the hut and loaded with a blank cartridge for the sunset salute. The Peters' windmill, a Sunbeam, was pumping, and water was spattering down from the overflow pipe to the cement base. Frank looked at his watch, looked importantly at the sky, at the oak woods, behind which the sun might or might not have set, then gave the order to fire. Bang. The sun had set, and the cloud of blue smoke floated quickly away. Gwendolyn hadn't said a word to me. What had she done with the box of candy. Had she shown it to any one. Was it she, or some one else, who had first found it there on the porch. Did she throw it away. Had she laughed. Was she angry. She stood next to me as we saluted the flag, which Frank was hauling down for the night, the folds winding themselves about his shoulders, but she was careful not to touch me. Did I dare to look at her. No. She was stronger than I, taller, but in the wrestling match I had got her down and held her down, with my hands hard on her shoulders. At the picnic in Pembroke woods, she and I had gone off by ourselves to look for firewood, and had gathered wood in a separate heap before taking it back to the others, but all the while we hadn't said a word. Why was that. Was she as shy as I was, or was she annoyed with me. What was their house like, inside. I had never been into it. They had a bathing hut of their own, in the Cove, and a long narrow pier which led out across the eelgrass to deep water, with a float at the end, where their green canoe was hauled up. It was near the place where Molly and Margaret went to bathe. Once I had followed them down the road, to watch them bathe there, but when I got to the beach I saw Frank and Gwendolyn there on the float, so I had slunk away.

—Moved and seconded that Warren Walker be made a private in this Company. All those in favor say aye.

—Aye.

————in the evening, after helping the cat, Juniper, to catch grasshoppers among the hummocks of wild grass, swishing his tail against my leg, and purring, Uncle Tom and Uncle David and Aunt Norah and Mother having all gone to a dance at the McGills', and Porper in bed, singing to himself in Mother's room upstairs, and Susan swinging in a hammock on the porch, with one leg out so that she could push herself to and fro, I walked across the tennis court and watched the moon rise over the Long Beach. The tennis court needed hoeing again. And it needed new lines of whitewash. There were lights in the Walker house, and Mr. Walker went from the house to the barn with a pail in his hand. Then we sat at the dining table under the swinging lamp and played jackstraws.

—I heard Uncle Tom and Aunt Norah talking about Father and Mother.

—You shouldn't have listened.

—I couldn't help it. They were talking while I was dressing.

—What did they say.

—What do you want to know for, if you think I shouldn't have listened.

—Oh, well, you don't have to tell me, do you.

—They said they had quarreled.

—Who had quarreled.

—Father and Mother.

—I don't believe it.

—You don't have to. And they said something about Father coming down to Duxbury.

—Andy! He's coming for the clambake! Is that it?

—How should I know. That's all I heard, nitwit.

—Well, I'll bet that's what it is.

—Anyway, the clambake's been put off again, hang it. We'll never get to that Gurnett. I think I'll go by myself. I'm sick and tired of waiting for them to get ready—first it's one fool thing and then another.

—Well, go ahead, why don't you. You could row there, couldn't you?

—Row there! Seven miles there and seven miles back? I guess not. What about the tides. Or what about a thunderstorm. How'd you like to get caught in a thunderstorm in a dory, twit! If I go, I'll walk.

—Well, you rowed to Clark's Island, didn't you?

————particularly also the sense of timelessness, the telescoping of day with day, of place with place, evening with evening, and morning with morning. The thunderstorms always coming from the southwest or west, the sky darkening first to cold gray, then to livid purple behind the Standish Monument, the wind rising to a scream across the black bay, the lightning stabbing unceasingly at the far, small figure of Miles Standish. Then the little house lashed wildly by the horizontal rain, the rush to shut the screens and doors and windows, the doors that would hardly shut against the wind, and the leaks everywhere, through walls and roof, pails and tins set out to receive the rapid pinging and clunking of drops, the struggle to get the hammocks in from the porch, take down the tennis net. Andy! Did you get the net in? The bows and arrows? Where are the rackets? Susan— Susan—where is Susan? Always the same thing. Or, at night, the splendid spectacle of the lightning across the bay, the storm advancing rapidly toward the open sea, and presently the lights of Plymouth far off across the water, like a long row of winking jewels, reappearing once more, and the lights of the Standish House, bright through the rain-washed evening air, as if nothing at all had happened.

Uncle David stared at them through the spyglass, from the wet porch.

—They must have turned the power off.

—Why do they turn the power off, Uncle David.

—Oh, I don't know—to prevent a short circuit, or something.

—But they don't turn them off in Boston.

—Well, Plymouth isn't Boston.

—There they come again.

—Yes, now they've turned them on. Take a look, Tom? Here, Doris, take a look.

They all looked in turns through the little telescope, the same one through which they regarded the moon-mountains, sweeping it along the row of distant twinkling lights and the beards of reflected light in the water, Susan and myself coming last. Nothing to see, why bother? It was always Uncle David who went out first to see whether the Plymouth lights had yet been turned on. Or what trees had been hit, or whether a haystack or barn had been set afire. Uncle David this, and Uncle David that. Was it because Uncle David was rich. Or because he had nothing to do. He was always there, he was always in everything, pushing about with his red mustache and blue eyes, as if the world belonged to him. It was Uncle David who made us hoe the tennis court, and mark the lines, and who beat everybody except Father at tennis. This year, he was forever playing Mother, sometimes before breakfast, when the rest of us weren't up yet, at seven o'clock. Several times I was waked up by hearing them, and got out of bed and went to the window to watch them, keeping back from the window so as not to be seen. Mother dressed in white, with her hair in a pigtail down her back, like a girl, and laughing a lot, and saying, David, how could you. Once she turned her ankle, running out into the field after a ball, and then Uncle David picked her up and carried her round the corner to the front of the house. It was because of those hummocks of wild grass, those hard tufts—it was easy to turn your ankle. But when I asked her about it at breakfast she looked surprised, and said it was nothing. Nothing at all.

—But, darling Andy, how did you happen to see? How did you happen to be up so early?

—I heard you playing, Mother.

—David, that was very naughty of us—we mustn't do it again—we woke them up.

—Oh, I think the little rascal was up on his own account—weren't you, Andy. He was probably catching flies for that cage of his.

—No I wasn't, either. I heard you playing, and then I got up to see who it was.

—It doesn't really matter, though I often think that on these summer mornings, when the light is so early, we might all get up earlier than we do. But, of course, Norah, we won't—I know your habits too well. And the children must get their full sleep.

————and the tiny little brown pond deep down in the cleft behind the Wardman house, only a stone's throw from our windmill, with the black alders around it, and the sumacs, and the frogs, and turtles, the turtles which sidled away into the dirty water when we came, and the high rock at one side. I went down to it in the morning and found a rose quartz Indian arrowhead in the sand at the edge of it, a perfect one, very small and sharp. It was a beauty. How Uncle Tom would be pleased when he saw it, for it was better than any we had found before, better even than the white quartz one we had found out at the end of the Point, better far than the flint ones. I sat there on the rock by the sumacs, and knew that it was Thursday, for on Thursday afternoons I had to go to the village and have my Latin lesson with Mr. Dearing, in the white house at the water's edge, with his knockabout moored a little way out, in which, perhaps, after the lesson, he would take me for a sail. His house was a nice one, with lots of books and pictures, it was quiet and small like himself, and smelt of lavender. He was like Uncle Tom. Uncle Tom, if Mr. Dearing asks me to go for a sail, can I go. Last time he let me take the tiller, and I learned how to come about. We followed the yacht race, and beat them, on the same course, too, but outside them at every buoy, which made it longer. The course with the first leg toward Clark's Island and the second toward the Point. You know the one, we've often watched them from the porch. Can I do that. Or can I go by myself to the woods on the other side of Standish Hill, to see if I can find some wild indigo, and press it, and see if it turns black in the book. Or would you like to come with me.

—No Porper, I can't take you to the Horse Monument this afternoon, because Uncle Tom and I are going to the woods to look for wild flowers.

—But I want to see the Horse Monument.

—But you've seen it dozens of times, Porper.

—I want to see it. I want to see where the horse was buried.

—Why don't you take him, Susan?

—Oh, Porper—why do you want to see it. You know what it's like—it's just like any other tombstone, only it's made of bricks, and it's because a horse was buried there, a man's favorite horse, and he put up a monument for it when it died. He was a nice man, wasn't he?

—I want to see the Horse Monument.

—Go on, Susan, and take him. It's your turn. I took him last time.

At Mr. Dearing's, the clock ticked on the white-painted wooden mantelpiece, between the model of a ship and a barometer, the clock ticked Latin, and Mr. Dearing's gentle voice asked me questions, went through my exercise, alternately chastened and sustained me, while through the open window, on the side of the house toward the bay, the soft sound of the waves came, lapping among reeds and eelgrass, and the knocking of a dory against the float. If I turned my head I could see Mr. Dearing's knockabout, with its boom, the mainsail neatly furled, propped up in its shears of wood. Now that declension again. You're a little shaky on that declension. Those ablatives seem to bother you, don't they? And those verbs. You must get them into your head. *Utor, fruor, potior, fungor,* and *vescor.* They have a nice sound, Andy, don't you think? *Utor, fruor, fungor, potior,* and *vescor.*

Uncle Tom had on his white yachting cap, with the green vizor, and the tin cylinder hung from his shoulder, and as we climbed the sandy road over Standish Hill, I asked him if he had heard the bell ring, the bell of the Unitarian Church. We were passing a clump of sumacs.

—These aren't poison sumacs, are they, Uncle Tom?

—No. But what about that bell?

—I rang it myself, at ten minutes past two.

And I told him how it had happened. The village barber was cutting my hair, and said that he was the church sexton, and that he had to go and wind the clock, and asked me if I'd like to see how he did it, it was just across the road. We unlocked the church and went in, and climbed up two flights of dark stairs in the tower, and then two ladders which went straight up through narrow trap doors until we got to a shaky landing beside the machinery of the clock, where there were lots of cobwebs and dust. The barber wound a crank, and we could hear the clock ticking very loud. Then he asked me if I would like to strike the bell, and gave me a short rope and told me to pull it: I gave it a pull, and the machinery began grinding to itself, a sort of growling, and then suddenly came the huge ring of sound, shaking the belfry, everything trembled with it, and I thought of the bell sound traveling all the way to Powder Point, and every one wondering what time it was.

Shad bush, wild sarsaparilla, St. John's Wort, sand spurrey, wild indigo, and checkerberry. The goldenrods belong to the composite family, there are forty kinds in New England; but this sort, *solidago sempervirens*, which grows in the salt marshes, or near them—the heaviest, the strongest, the most fragrant—the one that the bees love, and the flies——

——or again to remember the first arrival, the arrival at the end of June after school was over, that first and sweetest deliciousness of escape and renewal, the foresight of so much delight, the largeness and wideness and brightness, the sun everywhere, the sea everywhere, the special salt spaciousness, which one felt even at the little shabby railway station, three miles inland, at the bottom of the hill, where the road turned. Even the weatherboards of the wooden station seemed to be soaked in salt sea fog, the little cherry trees had about them a special air as of knowing the sea, and the old coach, the Priscilla or the Miles Standish, with Smiley driving it, or Bart Cahoun, waiting for us there with its lean horses, had on its wheels the sand of Powder Point. In the very act of getting down from the train we already participated in the rich seaside summer—our trunks, lying on the platform, on the hot rough pine planks, shared in the mystery, became something other than the humble boxes into which we had put our bathing suits and sneakers. The world became dangerously brilliant, ourselves somehow smaller, but more meaningful; in the deep summer stillness, the country stillness, it seemed almost as if already we could hear the sea. Our voices, against the little cherry trees which the coach was passing, their boughs whitely shrouded by tent caterpillars, and the gray shingled cottages covered with trumpet vine, and the stone walls and the apple orchards, were different from our Cambridge voices. Even Mother became different, was smaller and more vivid. Would it all be the same again. Would the tide be out or in. Would the golden weathervane still be there. Would the dam under the village bridge be opened or closed. Would it be as nice living at Uncle Tom's as at the Soules'. It was nearer to the end of the Point, nearer the long bridge, nearer the sea——

—Now you must remember, children, it's not quite like staying at the Soules', we are visitors, and Uncle Tom has built a nice play house for you, and you must try to play there as much as you can, so that the house can be quiet.

—Can Porper kneel up, Mother, he wants to look out.

—You can keep all your toys there, and on rainy days it will be very nice
for you. It's a nice little house, painted green, down at the foot of the hill,
near that rock——

—You mean Plymouth Rock Junior.

—Yes.

—What's Plymouth Rock Junior.

—Oh, Porper, you don't remember, but you'll see.

—Susan, will you keep hold of Porper's hand?

—Is that Plymouth Rock Junior.

—No, that's just a rock in front of the library. That's where Andy goes
on Wednesdays to get books, don't you, Andy.

—I'm going to read *Calumet K* again. And *Huckleberry Finn* again.
Would there be any new books. To carry home under my raincoat in
the rain, past the house that was always to let, and the bowling alleys, and
then along the lagoon to King Caesar's Road.

—Will Uncle David be there, Mother?

—Yes, I suppose so. He has a new motorboat.

—We must have a picnic on the outer beach soon, Mother, we must
have two of them this year, not one like last year.

—Will we have blueberries and cream, and blueberry muffins?

—Yes, yes, now don't bother Mother, Mother's thinking.

—Why are you thinking.

—Andy, for goodness sake take Porper's other hand. Sit still, Porper.
Look, do you see the weather vane? It's a rooster made out of gold.

——the particular breadth and suggestion of sea-wonder that began
always when the coach turned north at the fork of the road, under the
weather vane, and then rounded the lagoon toward King Caesar's Road,
and passing this, rattled along the rutted sand Point Road—we were getting
nearer the sea, there was now water on both sides of us, water and marshes,
we were going out into the Atlantic Ocean. We were getting nearer to the
outer beach, and the long red bridge that led to it, nearer to the Gurnett,
with its squat twin lighthouses. How soon would the picnic be. There
would be steamed clams, and sweet potatoes, and corn, hidden in the nests
of hot wet seaweed, on a bed of charred stones. We would gather shells.
We would find fragments of driftwood and take them home with us in the
little cart which Porper would sit in, with his legs spread out. We would
climb the dunes and slide down the slopes of hot loose sand. There would
be new breaches in the wall of dunes, where the sea had broken through
during the winter, wide flat beds of stones. Where I went wading last
year with Gwendolyn, and she held her dress up high, and I saw her garters,
the quick exciting flash of silver. We were looking for live horseshoe crabs.
I pretended to look for crabs, holding my head down, but was really
watching her knees, and she knew that I was watching her, and held her
dress higher. Andy, I've found three, and you haven't found one. And look,
here's the smallest one yet—! She held it up out of the water by its beak,
and it arched itself almost double, small and transparent. I took it in my
hand and we looked at it together, and holding up her dress she leaned
against me, and I heard her breathing.

——the night when Uncle Tom and Aunt Norah had gone to the
Yacht Club to see the fireworks, riding on their bicycles, with the little

lamps lighted, the red jewel at one side and the green at the other, and the smell of hot kerosene, we watched the little wobbling arcs of light moving away along the sand-ruts, and I pointed out to Susan the stars in Cassiopeia's Chair, standing on the tennis court. Mother and Uncle David were talking on the porch, each in a different hammock, slapping at mosquitoes and laughing, for they had decided to stay at home and watch the fireworks from the Point. We sat down on the edge of the porch and looked at the Plymouth lights and waited for the fireworks, but they didn't come. Perhaps they would be later. Mother was lying back in her hammock, with her hands under her head and her white elbows lifted and Uncle David was smoking a cigarette. When he drew in his breath, the end of the cigarette glowed and lit up his face, and he was always looking downward at the floor and frowning.

—Susan, darling, how did all that water get there on the floor.

—It was Porper, Mother, he was blowing soap bubbles before supper.

—Will one of you please clean it up. Andy, will you get a mop or a cloth from the kitchen and wipe it up. You're the porch cleaner, aren't you.

—Oh, Mother, I'll have to sweep it in the morning anyway——

—But it doesn't look nice. Run along. Perhaps afterward you and Susan would like to have a game of croquinole together.

—Could we go out for a row in the dory.

—If it's a very short one. You must have Susan back in time for her bedtime.

In the kitchen, I stood by the sink and looked out of the window at the back, and saw someone carrying a lighted lamp across one of the windows in the Wardman house. Molly and Margaret were talking to a man in the darkness on the back porch, probably the chauffeur from the Tuppers, who was always hanging around them. I didn't either. You did too. I didn't either. You did too. You're crazy to say such a thing you ought to know better than that I never said any such thing to him in my life, not me. I only said I saw them on the beach. I wouldn't say more than that. What were they talking about? I listened, but they must have known I was there, for they lowered their voices, and I couldn't make out anything else, especially as the windmill was pumping, and I could hear the groan of the rod and the regular gush of water into the cistern. I went out into the pantry to get the mop, went down the three wooden steps to the earthen floor, and stood there in the nice smell of potatoes and squashes and green corn and damp smell of earth, watching the indicator on the cistern, the little lead weight jiggling lower and lower against the pine boards as the water raised the float. Last year we had to pump all the water by hand. A hundred strokes without stopping. I rolled up my sleeves, and always felt my muscles when I had finished, to see how hard they were. Why was Mother always trying to get rid of us like this. With Father it was different, he always wanted to do things with us in the holidays. Like last year, when he gave me the camera and took me on walks and showed me how to take pictures, and I got the picture of the beach-plum dyke all crooked, so that it looked like a wave of cobblestones. And I took the Horse Monument, but it was out of focus, or light-struck, or something. But I had fifteen blueprints that were quite good.

When I got back to the porch Susan was alone.

—Where have they gone.

—Oh, down to the front beach or something.

—They make me sick always going off like that.

—Andy, you shouldn't talk like that.

—Well, they do. I bet they've gone out in the motorboat, that's what they've done, and without inviting us.

—They don't have to invite us every time they go, do they?

—No, but they might invite us sometimes. Come on, we'll go out in the dory, and I don't care if we never get back.

—But we won't see the fireworks, Andy.

—Who wants to see the fireworks, besides we could row around to this side of the Point, couldn't we? Don't be a twit.

We walked down across the humped grass to the Point, in the dark, the blades of the oars clacking together as I carried them over my shoulder, the rowlocks jingling in Susan's hand. It was warm and the crickets were chirping. Susan was ahead of me when we got to the bluff, I watched her white dress vanish down the sandy path to the beach, and then I looked out at the water and saw a light in the cabin of Uncle David's motorboat. It looked far out, because the tide was high, almost up to the foot of the bluff. Susan was already sitting in the stern of the dory, hanging her hands in the water, the ripples were slapping against the sides, and I pulled the anchor out of the bayberry bush and got in. Ought I to tell Susan what I was going to do, or not. If I didn't, she might talk, and spoil everything. If I did, she might not want to, and besides we might see something——

—I tell you what we'll do, we'll pretend we're spies, and row right around them. I'll row around them so close we could touch them, and they won't hear a sound.

—But, Andy——

—Shut up, will you?

I pushed the blade of the oar into the sand and shoved off with two shoves and then began rowing very softly, rowing backwards, so that I could face toward the motorboat. Why was I frightened. What was there to be frightened of. It was only like playing the Indian scouting game. It was only like the guerrilla war in the Pembroke Woods. How could they possibly hear us anyway, with the ripples washing against the Osprey, making that hollow coppery sound that you heard when you were down in the cabin. And they couldn't see us, because the little yellow curtains were drawn across the two cabin portholes. I backed out till we were past the white bow, which looked very high, and then shipped my oars and let the tide take us slowly alongside. We could hear them talking. The tender, which was tied with too short a painter, was bumping against the port side of the stern, and in the cabin there was a thump as if something had been dropped on the floor.

—Come on, Doris, let's have another.

—Oh, no, let's——

—Oh, come on, the night is young.

—I don't like it, David.

—What's wrong with it? Are you getting a conscience or something?

—Oh, no, but if they thought——

—Thought what.

—Oh, you know as well as I do.

—Let them think. Here, try this——

—Please, David——

I gave a push with my hand against the brass corner of the stern plate and we just barely cleared the gunwale of the tender, which was swinging across. They were drinking, Uncle David must be trying to make Mother drunk, that was it, perhaps the thump was a bottle falling on the floor of the cabin. I let the tide carry us a little way toward the bridge, where I could see the high wooden piers of the draw, and then I shipped my oars and began to row.

—We'll go through the draw, and then across to the outer beach. Then we'll walk along the beach to the dunes and watch the fireworks.

—Andy, what were they saying, what was Mother saying.

—I couldn't hear. Was the cabin door open or shut?

—It was shut.

I shot the dory through the draw, where the tide was swift, the deep eddies sucking and chuckling at the foot of the tall piles, and felt my face hot, and I wanted to do something, to go back there, to bank at the side of the Osprey, to shout. But what was the use.

——particularly always, too, the hour after lunch, the hot and peaceful hour, the sleepy hour, when Susan and Porper always had to have naps upstairs, and Mother and Aunt Norah stretched themselves out in hammocks on the porch, and Uncle David went into his room to read, and Uncle Tom wrote letters on the dining-room table, or painted screens on the grass in front of the house, the screens supported on wooden horses. What would we do later. Would we be sent to the playhouse for the whole afternoon, or would we go clam-digging, or take a walk to the cove, or would Sanford come to tell me that there was a baseball game at the Peters'. I went down to the playhouse by myself, it was very hot and smelt of new wood, greenhead flies were on the insides of the screens, and I thought it would be a good chance to see if I could take off the handle bars of Aunt Norah's new Columbia bicycle, so I stood on the table, the one we played Gonko on, and hauled myself up to the top of the wooden partition, and dropped over into the bicycle shed. This business of taking naps after lunch. This hammock business. Mother's hand lying over the edge of the yellow striped hammock, the fringe of long yellow strings rippling in the southwest wind, her book fallen to the veranda floor, the opened pages fluttering. Susan, pretending to take a nap in her room, but really reading. Uncle David pretending to take a nap, but really drinking out of one of those bottles, using the tumbler on the washstand, which always smelt like bay rum. I took the monkey wrench out of the little cylindrical tool kit under the saddle and got the handlebars off easily enough, but I was worried for fear I wouldn't get them back on again at the same height and angle, and sweated at the thought that Aunt Norah might notice it. It was a Columbia Chainless, and what I really wanted to do was to open the gearbox and look at the gears, but the nuts were too tight, and I was afraid. Besides, somebody might come—Uncle Tom might take it into his head to come down looking for me, maybe to ask me to go

on a wildflower hunt, and I wouldn't have time to get it together again.
I climbed back into the playhouse, and then I went outside and crawled
under the floor and got some more shingles, with crickets walking on them,
and took them into the playhouse to make some new Gonko rackets. We
would need some more Ping-pong balls. Porper was always losing them or
stepping on them. He kept throwing them into the bed of poison ivy at the
foot of the hill, by the stone wall. That was where all the golf balls used to
go when Uncle Tom and Father played golf. I looked at my shin to see
if the little blue map of the golf ball was still there, and it was almost gone.

I walked down the lane as far as the Horse Monument, went back into
the pine woods for a minute, near our houses, thinking about Gay, and
then about Gwendolyn, and wondered what she would think if she knew I
played house in the woods with my sister, like a little sissy. When I got
to the hotel I went first out on to the stone wharf, and watched a tug
towing a barge across the bay. Some of the maids from the hotel were in
bathing suits, sitting on the stone edge of the wharf, and when they saw
me they began laughing. I walked back to the hotel and went along the
edge of the golf course, toward the Point Road. There was nobody playing
golf, it was too early. Too hot. The sheep were all lying under a tree chewing their cuds. I threw acorns at them and made them get up, and then I
was ashamed and went up between the houses and through the small oak
woods to the Company Camp. The Peters were there, and Sanford, and
Warren, and Frank Tupper, but not Gwendolyn. They were lying in the
grass. What were we going to do. Should we go and play in the hayloft,
dive down through the chute, slide down the rope.

—Andy's got a sweetheart.

—Where's Gwendolyn, Andy?

—Shut up.

Frank Tupper looked at me and then got up and walked to the Company hut. He went in, and in a minute came out again holding up a baseball bat.

—Scrub one, he said.

—Scrub two.

—Three.

—Four.

—Five.

We played baseball till Gwendolyn came, and then we took turns
standing under the overflow of the windmill and letting the water splash
on our heads. I turned my face up, and let the water spout out of my
mouth.

—He thinks he's smart.

—Rats live on no evil star.

—What do you mean by that?

—Just what I say. Rats live on no evil star.

Frank Tupper spat in his baseball glove.

—That's an old one. A palindrome.

—A what?

—It spells the same thing backward.

Susan came running across the field and fell down and began to cry. I walked home with her, and we sat on Plymouth Rock Junior under the cherry tree, and she said that Mother and Aunt Norah were quarreling upstairs in Aunt Norah's room, and Uncle Tom and Uncle David had gone off for a walk not saying a word, and Porper was all alone with the maids, sitting in the soapbox sailboat—and Molly with an earache——

——lying awake, too, with the wind singing through the wire screens, and the soft muslin curtains sucking and fluttering against the screens, and the sea-moon shining through them on to the floor and across the foot of my bed, and the crickets chirping like mad, the mosquitoes, too, humming so loudly outside the window that they sounded as if they were in the room. What was that they had said at supper. When Aunt Norah was pouring the cocoa out of the jug. It should have been here this evening. Who was it that got the mail. It was Smiley that brought it. Why didn't Andy go. Well, anyway it didn't come. Mother was humming as she buttered more bread for Porper; Uncle Tom tapped with his fingers on the bare edge of the table as if he were playing a tune on a piano. What letter was it that hadn't come. Was it from Father. Were they expecting Father. What fun that would be. He would get out the cameras, and he would teach me how to pitch an out-drop. And now the two sets of voices downstairs— Molly and Margaret, at the back of the house, murmuring and giggling secretly, slyly, insinuatingly, and the others on the front porch, a little farther off, more intermittent, now and then more loudly, and Uncle David's deep laugh which always sounded a little angry. Andy's got a sweetheart. What did they mean by that. Had Gwendolyn told everybody about it, or was it perhaps Frank who had first found the box of candy. Perhaps he had found it and had never given it to Gwendolyn. Shame on Andy, shame on Andy. Let them say it. I would row right round Clark's Island, taking all day if necessary, and find my way at low tide through the channels, counting the seals on the mud flats. I would row to Plymouth. I would borrow Mr. Dearing's knockabout and sail right out past Plymouth Beach into Massachusetts Bay, and watch the Plymouth steamer going past on its way to Boston. I would swim across from the Point to the Long Beach. I would dive off the pier of the draw on the long bridge, twenty feet down into the swift current of the tide. I would strike out Frank Tupper every time he came to bat. And I wouldn't say a word to Gwendolyn, not another word all summer.

They were beginning to sing. It was always Uncle David who started them on that, he had a swelled head about his voice, and always sang when he was hoeing the tennis-court with us. Oh, you beautiful doll, you great big beautiful doll.

Margaret was talking to a man under my back window.

—Quit it.

—I will not.

—I said quit it, will you?

I got quickly out of bed and went to the window to see what they were doing, but I was too late, they had gone round the corner of the house into the shadow, to get out of the moonlight. I waited, listening, but they didn't come back. He must have been kissing her. I would keep awake until they came to bed. Watch them through the hole by the washstand.

It would be dark on my side of the wall, I would stand very still in bare feet, get back into bed without a sound, they would never suspect that I was watching them. Should I go to bed now or stay up. Better stay up, and watch the flies in the flytrap with the electric flashlight. I got the flashlight and looked at the flies. They were all asleep, standing upside down under the roof of screen wire, their white bellies turned towards the light. I ought to let them go, Uncle David was beginning to suspect why I kept them. Perhaps I had better give him one of my arrowheads. What mischief have you fellows been up to. Uncle David, I thought you might like to have one of my arrowheads, it's a quartz one.

I went to the side window, beside the tennis court, to hear them singing. They were singing the song that Uncle David had made up. When I slap on the kalsomine I think about those gals o' mine way down in old Kentucky where the moon is shining bright. When I slap on the Reckitts blue I think about the thickets through the mountains of Virginia where I walked with them at night. Walls and ceilings have their feelings the same as you and me. I'm only a paper hanger, but my heart is pure as mud. When they had finished it, they all laughed in the silly way they always did, the laughter rising and falling, mixing and unmixing, but I could make out Mother's and Uncle David's, particularly at the end, when Mother's went up and Uncle David's went down. The twits. The nitwits. But what about the letter, and why, come to think of it, hadn't I been sent for the evening mail, as usual. Instead, I had been sent to the playhouse with Porper, and when I brought him back, I had to sail him in the soapbox sailboat.

Footsteps were coming up the stairs, candlelight wavered on the rough, pine beams of the unfinished roof; it was Molly and Margaret coming up to bed, and I tiptoed with cold, naked feet on the bare floor and stood by the washstand, hardly breathing, and waited.

————the dust, too, as the stage coach rattled past me and turned up King Caesar's Road, to go to Powder Point Hall, skewing a little, the rear wheels slewing in the sandy ruts as Smiley touched up the old horses, the whole thing like Buffalo Bill. I looked through the packet of letters again, to make sure that there was none from Father. Harvard University. Jordan Marsh. Acme Cleaning Company. A small blue envelope, addressed in small handwriting, to Mother. Another, in the same handwriting, to Aunt Norah. Both postmarked Plymouth. Nothing that looked as if it might be from Father. By this time the train would be at Kingston. Or maybe at the Cordage. The people in the train would see the back of the Standish Monument, which I had seen only once, when we went to Plymouth to see the Plymouth Rock. We had lunch at that old house with four English elms in front of it, which Captain Something-or-Other had brought back from England in 1750.

I leaned against the wooden fence and looked at the two new knockabouts in the lagoon, exactly alike except that the *Bobkat* was brown, with a silver waterline, and the *Moujik II* was white with a gold waterline. The bowsprits were very short. Mr. McGill, who manufactured oil stoves, owned them both, and one or the other of them came in second in every race at the Yacht Club. Mr. McGill had that new house near Powder Point Hall, with the imitation windmill which had an electric pump inside. That was where the dance had been. Mother had brought back a Japanese lantern and Uncle David had brought home a clown's mask with red holes for the eyes. He put it on at breakfast. What was that thing he had said to Mother, when we were going round Clark's Island in the motorboat, something about drowning. To drown with thee. They were both holding the wheel, one on one side, and one on the other. Laughing, as I jumped down from the cabin roof into the cockpit. To drown with thee. It was that Quaker-talk that the old man had talked in Salem, putting his hand on my head. And Mother and Father had been talking it when I went to the top of the stairs that night after the card party in Cambridge. To drown with thee. What had they meant by that.

I played ducks and drakes, skipping one stone twelve times over the water towards the *Bobkat*, and then went through the bayberry jungle and the grove of wild cherry trees to the edge of the golf course. Should I try to kiss Gwendolyn or not. Did she expect me to. Was Sanford just trying to get me into trouble when he told me to. When she saw me diving off the end of the dory she laughed, turning her face back toward Dorothy Peters as if she were saying something about me. I swam out a long way into the channel, hoping they would row out toward me, but they didn't. They went along the shore, very slowly, not looking at me again. And disappeared round the end of the Point, still laughing.

There were no golf balls in the bayberry jungle, though I kicked the grass in the places where I had found them before, so I went along the west side of the golf course until I got to the bungalows, and then crossed to the road and walked along the sandy bicycle path. The telephone poles were humming in the southwest wind, a little boy was trying to fly a kite on the lawn of the mystery house, behind the trumpet vine arbor, but he couldn't run fast enough to get it off the ground. A pretty girl was leaning out of a tiny window in a dormer at the top of the house, watching him. I blushed when she looked at me, and walked on quickly, and was opposite the Soule House, where Molly was sitting in the swing, when Father—I was thinking about the box kite, meaning to ask Uncle Tom if we could hitch it to the cart and give Porper a ride over the tennis court——

He came out from the behind the lilac bushes and skimmed his panama hat at my head, twirling, so that it almost settled on my head, but fell on the path. He took the back of my neck in his hand and shook me, not saying anything. He was smoking a cigarette. Then he threw the cigarette away and sat down on the lawn where the four-leaf clovers were. His brown cigarette finger was tapping on his knee. He frowned and asked me how Porper and Susan were. I said they were very well, and asked him if he had come to the clambake. He wanted to know if Susan had learned to swim. I told him no. Had I played any baseball. Yes. Wild flowers. Yes. Done my Latin with Mr. Dearing. Yes. Was I a member of the Company this year. Yes.

He got up again, and we walked along the little road that led down to the cove and the dyke, past the henyard, where last year the trap used to be set at night for skunks. We had heard shots in the early morning and gone out to see the dead skunk. The road led through sweetgrass, the kind the

Indians made into baskets. Every year they came, selling baskets from door to door, old women and old men. We walked as far as the top of the little bluff, overlooking the cove, and stood by a crab apple tree, talking, and Father asked me how far out into the water I could throw an apple. I threw one, and he smiled, watching it splash at the edge of a mud flat, and then said, Watch me. He took a short stick out of the grass and stuck an apple on the end of it and then whipped it with a whistling sound over his head: the apple went clear across the cove and thudded into the soft mud at the foot of the eelgrass. I tried it several times and sent one apple half way across, into the middle of the channel.

—That was a good one.

—Where did you learn to do that, Father?

—Your grandfather taught me at Jackson Falls.

—That was where the wildcats were.

—And the moosewood.

He took out his packet of Sweet Caporals and lit another cigarette. We started walking back slowly towards the Soules'.

—Did you come down for the clambake, Father? Are we going to have it this week?

—No. I don't know.

He took off his spectacles and polished them with a blue silk handkerchief. He was frowning again.

—I don't know how long I'm staying: I'm staying at the Soules'. I don't want you to say anything about having seen me—understand? I may go back tonight, or I may stay for a week. But I don't want you to say anything about it. I suppose you go for the mail every morning, don't you.

—Yes, usually.

—Come here tomorrow morning to see if I'm still here. And now run along back.

He stood watching me, and I ran the whole length of the narrow bicycle path to show him that I could do it this year without slackening once. When I got to the end, by the crossroads, I turned round, but he had gone. I was out of breath, but it wasn't because of the running. Did he mean that I couldn't even tell Susan? Probably not, because, of course, the twit would get excited and say something without meaning to. What was it all about. Why was he staying at the Soules' instead of coming to Uncle Tom's. Why was he keeping it a secret. Did he want it to be a surprise, and did Mother know about it or not. Gwendolyn and Dorothy Peters coo-eed from the door of the Silliman barn, but I didn't stop. Let them coo-eee. I took the short cut past the Wardman house and the little brown pond, dropped a twig close to a frog so that he dived into the warm soupy water, and then ran up the slope past the windmill and round to the front porch. Mother was cutting Porper's hair, and laughing, and I didn't dare to look at her when I gave her the letters. Uncle David was mending the tennis net with a reel of white cord.

—Why not use a bowl. Clap it on the young feller's head and then cut round it.

———particularly also the food, the wonderful and perpetual sense of delicious and abundant food, the great jugs of rich cocoa, the great deep

dish of blue-misted blueberries, the piles of muffins with their warm
fragrance under the fresh napkins, the hot sweet corn wrapped in damp
linen, the mountain of steamed clams. Porper beating with his spoon and
saying second help, third help, fourth help, fifth help. The floating island
pudding with the little white islands of stiff-beaten white of egg, which
vanished on the tongue like sea fog, and the brown column of griddle
cakes, Molly laughing as she brought in a new batch. This is the grub that
makes the butterfly. Every time we had griddle cakes Uncle David said
that. And the procession of covered carts that brought the food every morning, standing at the kitchen door by the corner of the tennis court—Mr.
Crowell's shiny white one with all kinds of meat in it, hanging on hooks,
and the red board at the back where he cut it up, which he always scraped
with a knife when he had finished; and the little blue fishcart, and the
great truck of vegetables and fruit. Aunt Norah always standing with her
hands on her wide hips and chaffing with Mr. Crowell or Mr. Peterson.
You ought to grow vegetable marrows, they're as easy to grow as squash,
and have a much more delicate flavor. Why is it, Mr. Chase, that when we
come to live by the sea we never can get fish. Or have to pay through the
nose to get it. And those little mackerel—why they're not big enough for
the cat, let alone Porper here. Shall we buy Porper a whale?
—What whale.
—Juniper won't need any fish heads or fish tails today, he had a mouse
this morning.
—What mouse.
—But he never eats them, Aunt Norah.
Juniper followed me on to the tennis court, and I caught a grasshopper
for him, which spat tobacco juice in my hand. What's the use, what's the
use, chew tobacco and swallow the juice. I gave Juniper the grasshopper,
and he purred, crunching it, and swished his striped tail against my leg.
He ran after me, crying, when I went to the stone wall by the sumac, I
bent down the loose strand of barbed wire to stoop through to the other
side, and he stood on a lichen-covered stone as I walked away across the
field toward the front beach. The silly little cat, always expecting me to
take him with me, wherever I went. And now he would probably be sick on
the porch, leave a little waffle of grasshopper legs and wings for me to clean
up when I came back. Andy, the cat's been sick again. Andy, will you turn
on the windmill, the tank's low. Andy, will you get out the targets, we're
going to have some archery practice. Andy, will you mix some limewash for
the tennis court. Andy, you shouldn't feed him grasshoppers, you know it
always makes him sick. But he likes them, Mother. He likes them, Aunt
Norah. All right then, but you must expect to clean up after him when he
makes a mess.
The long grass combed and seething in the southwest wind, the dry
whistle of the sand in the wind, the sea grass hissing as it bowed in green
waves, and the short quick waves of green-and-white water rushing up
amongst the bared brown roots of the eelgrass. The fiddler crabs hurried
away, clicking, as I approached the edge of the mud flats, or farther off
stood and waved their little fiddles, dancing absurdly on their hind legs,
and when I trod beside the air holes in the mud, the clams squirted water

like little geysers. We hadn't had clams for a week. The clambake looked farther off than ever. This year I would help to build the fireplace of round stones, and fetch the driftwood myself, and lay the fire, and gather the wet seaweed, and put in the clams and sweet potatoes, the yams, the green corn. And we would take our bathing suits and bathe in the surf, the surf that came all the way from Provincetown. And after lunch, while the others dozed in the warm hollows among the sand dunes, Porper with his dolls and Susan with her collection of razor shells, and Uncle Tom reading Gray's Botany. I would walk all the way to the Gurnett, see the twin lighthouse at the end of the Long Beach, come back in triumph and tell them about it. Look, Susan, I found this shell at the Gurnett. Look, Aunt Norah, I found this new kind of seaweed, one that we never got before, at the Gurnett. Mother, do you think Father will like this, it's very fine, and a lovely red, do you think it will mount well, when it's spread out.

There was a mullein wagging in the wind above my head when I lay down in the grass at the top of the beach, it was in flower, a tall one, but not as tall as the one Susan had found in the field between the McGills' and the Horse Monument. Why did she always call them Grandfather Jacksons. And niggerhead grass, why was it called niggerhead grass, and who had invented the game of niggerheads. Uncle David always won, was it because he held them with a shorter stem, was it cheating, or did he pick out the good ones. Brothers looked very much alike, Uncle David looked like Father, but with red mustaches, like a Visigoth; he was taller too, and stronger, but his face was long and funny; I didn't like it, and he looked at you with narrow blue eyes as if he didn't like you. Why did he speak so much more quickly than Father, always making jokes. Why did he have so much money, and a motorboat, and an office in Boston that he never went to. And staying here all summer, making me help him hoe the tennis court.

I counted the flowers I could see from where I lay. Mullein. Marsh rosemary. Beach-plum. Vetch. Three kinds of goldenrod. Milkweed. Beach pea. Hawkweed. Button bush. Dandelion. Butter-and-eggs. And when we got back to Cambridge the chicory would be in bloom, with its large stars of pale blue, or deep blue, or sometimes pink——

——the quarreling hour after supper, the croquet hour, when we took down the soapbox sailboat, lowering the spritsail, which was made of gunny sack, and coiling the ropes, and putting the soapbox under the porch—and the wickets and posts put into their worn holes, among the crickets and grasshoppers, and our favorite mallets chosen. The black one was cracked, I always took it because it was cracked and no one else liked it, but it was heavy, and I liked it. The handle was too long for Porper, he bumped his chin and cried.

—Oh, Porper, how many times have I told you, why don't you hold it by the end, not the middle.

—How can he, twit, he couldn't get anywhere near the ball.

—He could, too.

—Here, Porper, like this.

—And don't try to hit the ball so hard.

The long sunset light lay glistening on the humped grass of the slope,

golden and ruddy, and clear amber through the gap in the oak woods. The
crickets chirped faster and faster. What were they doing now. What were
they talking about now. Why had we been sent out right after supper, like
that, and told to play croquet for half an hour. Why half an hour, exactly.
And why had they all stayed in the sitting room instead of coming out on
the porch as they usually did. Did they know that Father had come, or
think he was coming. The croquet balls went clop and clap and bounced
over the hummocks and went along the worn familiar grooves and path-
ways. Mosquitoes hung in a cloud round Porper's legs. I slapped them off
with my handkerchief.

—Andy, you cheated, you didn't keep your foot on the ball.

—I did too. It slipped. But I'll play it over if you like, and you'll see.
It was a split shot.

—Let's play poison.

—All right, let's play poison. Porper, you can be poison. Try to hit my
ball with yours. You can have two turns.

Molly and Margaret came out of the kitchen door, which slammed
behind them on its spring with a double clack. It was their night out, and
they were going to the village, dressed in dark blue. They looked over their
shoulders at us and went quickly round the corner. I pretended to make a
golfing stroke with my mallet, aiming toward the house, and let go of the
handle, so that my mallet flew up on to the porch and skidded along the
boards to the wall. When I went up to get it, I looked in through the long
dining-room window. Mother was at the other end of the room, with her
back turned, standing at the seaward window as if she were staring at the
tennis court. Aunt Norah was rocking in the wicker rocking chair. Uncle
Tom and Uncle David were walking to and fro, in opposite directions,
along the long room, with their hands in their pockets. Nobody seemed
to be saying anything. The lamps hadn't been lighted. I dropped my mallet
to the grass, and slid down under the porch railing. The boards of the
porch were still warm under my hands.

—Oh, I'm sick of playing croquet. Let's go down to the playhouse.

—But it's Porper's bedtime.

—Porper doesn't want to go to bed, do you, Porper.

—No.

—But, Andy, you know perfectly well——

—Stop arguing, will you? They're busy in there.

We sat on the doorstep of the playhouse, and made cups and saucers
out of green acorns for Porper.

—Look, Porper, we're having tea, this is what Grandfather showed me
how to do.

—Where is Grandfather.

—Grandfather has gone away.

—Where.

—Oh, a long way, never mind. Drink your cambric tea.

—What's cambric tea.

—Oh, you know what it is, Porper. It's hot-water-sugar-spoon.

—What's hot-water-sugar-spoon.

—It's cambric tea. Andy, what were they doing.

—Do you always want to know everything.

—If you go spying you might at least tell me.

—I wasn't spying.

—You were, too. You did that on purpose.

—Did what.

—Threw your mallet up there on the porch.

—What if I did. They weren't doing anything, if that's what you want to know, they were just talking.

—What about.

—How do I know. Nobody was saying anything when I looked in. But they looked as if they were having a quarrel.

—Is it about Father do you suppose.

—Why should it be about Father.

—Because he isn't here. Because he hasn't come to Duxbury this summer.

—Why should they quarrel about that.

—But if it isn't Father, what is it.

—Look, I can squash my cups and saucers.

—Why so you can, Porper. Would you like some more? Give him a Ping-pong ball, Andy.

—There aren't any. He's lost or squashed them all. Look Porper, I'll show you how I climb up into the bicycle shed. Watch me.

—I want a Ping-pong ball.

—But there aren't any more Porper, they're all gone. We'll get some more tomorrow.

He began to cry, and Susan took his hand and led him out again.

—Would you like to sit on top of Plymouth Rock Junior. And see the frogs and turtles.

It was getting dark when the horn blew to call us back to the house, the long sad tin horn that Uncle Tom blew from the porch to call us in for meals. But it was Mother who had blown it.

—Why, Porper, you've been crying—my poor lamb—what have you children been doing to him——

—Nothing, Mother, he's tired.

—My poor tired Porper—did you hear Mother blow the tin horn?

—Let me blow it.

—We'll take the horn up to bed with us, shall we?

—Yes.

She lifted him up and kissed him, and gave him the horn, and kissed him again, ruffling his short hair with her hand, and put her face against his cheek while he tried to blow the horn. But he only spat into the horn, as he always did, and made a whiffling sound. She opened the screen door with one hand and her foot and took him into the house.

—Andy, Mother had been crying.

—How do you know.

—She had shiny streaks in the corners of her eyes. And her eyes were red. That's always the way you can tell.

Uncle David came out, humming, he had on his gray knickerbockers

and a blue shirt opened at the neck. He looked down at us with his eyes
almost shut.

—Well, kids, how does your symptoms seem to segashuate?

He laughed, and went to the corner of the porch and took down his
rowlocks from the hooks, and his oars, and walked off toward the Point.
In a minute Uncle Tom came out, and without saying anything went down
the hill toward the playhouse. We saw him disappear under the trees
by the door to the bicycle shed, and saw a match flare, and another, and
then he came back, with the bicycle lamp making a little yellow fan of
light on the grass, bobbing up and down.

I think, Andy and Susan, you'd both better go to bed. I know it's a
little early, but we might be going on a picnic tomorrow. And don't bother
your mother, she's very tired.

—Oh, Uncle Tom, do you really think——

—I don't promise—I just say we might.

—Where are you going, Uncle Tom?

—Down to the village. Now go along, and be as quiet as you can.

And it was after I was asleep, it was in a dream, that suddenly Susan
was standing by my bed. I woke up with her hand on my mouth, and she
was saying *shhhhh.*

—Andy, be quiet, listen.

—What.

—I think Father is downstairs.

—Are you sure.

—I think so. I thought I heard his voice.

I got out of bed, and we tiptoed to the head of the stairs. What time
was it. Was it midnight. Had Molly and Margaret come back from the
village, and were they in their room, listening. We stood outside their door,
and for a while there wasn't a sound, and then we heard Father's voice.
It sounded far away, as if he were standing by one of the outside doors, or
on the porch.

—I think Doris and I had better discuss this alone.

The screen door squeaked and clacked. We listened, but heard nothing
else. Susan was shivering in her nightgown.

—Andy, let me come in and sleep with you.

—No.

—Please, Andy.

—No.

—Oh, please, Andy.

————with *Calumet K* under my coat, to take back to the Library,
because it was raining, though not raining very much, only a drizzle, and
it might get wet. Should I say anything or not. Should I tell him I had
heard him or not. All the pretending. Pretending we hadn't heard anything,
or seen anything. Pretending we didn't know anything. Pretending, pretending, pretending. I was sick of pretending. First from Father, and then
from Mother, and then from Susan. What was the use. My sneakers were
wet with walking through the wet grass, they began to bubble. I felt the
cold bubbles under the naked soles of my feet and swished them through

the thick weeds and grass beside the path to fill them and refill them with cold water. They squelched and squnched as I walked. The spider webs in the long privet hedge were heavy and bright with rain. I shook them and the spiders came out. The telephone poles were wet, the sand in the ruts was dark, the cherry trees were dripping slowly, but the sky over the village was beginning to brighten, in a little while the sun would come out again. And I ought to get *Tanglewood Tales*, to read for school. And *Ivanhoe*. But I could wait another week. I could get *The Sign of the Four. The Hound of the Baskervilles. The Black Arrow. The White Company.*

When Father stepped out of the white-sanded gap in the road, I was surprised.

—And what has he got there under his jacket? *Calumet K* again?

—Yes. I like it.

—So do I. A good story. Have you tried *Old St. Paul's* this summer?

—Oh, no, I forgot.

—Try it. But they may not have it. If they haven't got it, I'll send it to you.

He had his white raincoat on, but no hat, and his hair was standing up straight, and drops of rain sparkled on it. His hands were in his pockets. He took one of them out with an envelope in it.

—I'm sorry there was no picnic today. But we'll have it soon, I'll come down again soon, tell Susan and Porper I'll be coming back. And when you go back from the Library, give this note to Mother.

—But Father, why can't you stay——

—And tell her that I'm going up on the noon train. Will you?

—Yes, and I'll give her the note.

—Be sure. It's important.

—When you come back will you stay with us at Aunt Norah's.

—I don't think so. I'm afraid not. Not enough beds to go round, old fellow. Now run along——

—Can we take some more pictures.

—You bet we will. And now I must go and get ready. So long.

—So long, Dad.

He grinned and gave my white duck hat a tug so that it came down over my eyes, and then turned and went quickly toward the latticed porch of the Soule house. I walked along the path and then remembered the envelope in my hand. On it was written in Father's small print: For Doris. Kindness of Andrew. It was a gray envelope, speckled, and I noticed that the flap was gummed only at the tip, it would be very easy to open. What was he writing to her like this, and why was he going back so quickly. Especially if, as Uncle Tom had said, he didn't really need to for business. And why, after telling me not to say anything about his coming, had he gone to the house himself late at night. And why hadn't Mother come to see him in the morning, or said anything about him.

The mail was already sorted when I got there, and there were no letters in Box 36, only the little slip of paper that said the box was ours for three months. I saw Smiley come out of the drugstore with a golden-brown cake of chewing tobacco in his hand, a little red tin label on it. He was cutting a piece off the corner with his knife. At the bridge I stopped to watch the tide go in through the opened sluice gates, carrying nests of green and brown eelgrass, powerful and slow and deep, eddying and clucking. Why was the letter important. What did it say—. At the Library I chose *The White Company* because it looked longer. I looked at *St. Nicholas'* to see who had won the prizes for drawings and then started home. It had stopped raining, a pale beam of sunlight flashed on the wet golden rooster at the top of the flagpole, the railings of white wood along the lagoon were beginning to sparkle. The letter was in my raincoat pocket, I kept my hand on it, and my finger went under the flap of the envelope. Before I knew it, it was open. I blushed and took it out to look at it. It would be easy enough to stick it down again. Suppose Father should pass me on the road, going to the station. I turned to the right, along King Caesar's Road, and walked faster. I passed the cottage with the rhododendrons, and Powder Point Hall, and when I got to the pine woods I went in to the left of the road and crawled into my pine-log cabin. It was gray inside and I sat on the pine needles. I must ask Gay if she would come down again. We might do it this afternoon, especially if it was raining. Perhaps she would come by herself, without Warren, which would be more exciting. Or with Susan. If I couldn't persuade her, Susan might.

I unfolded the letter and began to read it, and then blushed and folded it and put it back, and then took it out again. It was wrong to read it. But I wanted to know what was going on. What was going on. Why all this secrecy. If anything was hidden from us, like this, and a chance came, like this, why not take it. Why not. "Pussy dear." I had heard him call her that, and it had seemed silly. But typewritten, in a typewritten letter——

Drops of rain fell on the roof, dripped from the trees, each one a sound of threatened guilt. Who would come, no one could come, I was alone. I took out the letter again, listened, and began to read.

Pussy dear, am I mistaken in detecting a lurking trace of sympathy in thy note of apology when dealing with that evident leaning of D's towards what thee calls the racy side of life? Does thee, as thee says he does, partake in that wistful eager-yearning to snatch, before it is too late, something that perhaps solely because it is forbidden, possesses the fascination of a last untasted morsel, wanting to insure completeness in the rounding of our little life? . . . Remember, dear heart——

I got up so quickly that I bumped my head on the low roof of the cabin, then ducked and ran along the road until I was out of the belt of pine woods, and went into the field. The letter was in my pocket. It was not that I had heard any one coming. I broke a switch of wild cherry off a small tree in a broken-down stone wall, and with this began whisking the nests of tent caterpillars out of the trees along the lane, and whipping the leaves of bayberry bushes. Take that. And that. And that. And take that, you bastard. And don't come again until you are asked. I walked slowly up the deep lane, whipping left and right, and wondered what the letter meant, and what the rest of it was. But I already knew. It was Uncle David. Did the racy side of life mean his drinking, his getting drunk, all those empty bottles, and his trying to get Mother drunk in the motorboat. Was that it. Or was it more than that. Should I read the rest of it. Would I have time. I could stop in the playhouse and read it, or I could read it here, but here I might meet somebody, and besides I was walking. And kept on walking. It was more—of course it was—than his trying to get her drunk, and I knew what it was.

I passed the playhouse, walking fast up the slope of humped grass, kicking at the grasshoppers which skirred away from me on heavy-rattling wings, passed the grass-mat targets, which had been set up for archery practice, and let myself into the house through the screen door. It was silent, empty, and when I hallooed there was no answer. Had they all gone bathing. I went back to the porch and saw that the rowlocks had gone, and the oars, and the life preserver. And when I went in again, and looked at the stairs, my bathing-suit and towel had been put on the banisters. I took them up in my hand and felt the dry sand in them. But all the while I was thinking——

In my bedroom I began to undress, slowly, pulled my shirt over my head, drew the necktie out and hung it over the mirror, looked at the ugly, dishonest shape of my mouth in the mirror, pulled it down with two fingers and stuck out my tongue and said "yaa!" at myself, then began flexing and unflexing my right arm to watch the muscle. But this was a pretense. The letter was in my pocket on the chair. To avoid it further, I took the flytrap to the window, opened the screen, broke the trap by pressing the sides together, and let the flies go. They went slowly, as if they were dying. Would I have time to copy out the letter. Would I. Before they got back from bathing. I could say that the mail had been late. Mother, I was just coming, I had only just had time to change into my bathing suit. And here is a note for you.

. . . *Remember dear heart, all the wisdom of the generations coined into the many world-old legends and allegories hung about this very glitter and seductive charm—trite little maxims and proverbs sure enough, but not wearing the outward marks of the pain and wretchedness, shame and filth, with which their lessons were learned, over and over again by the forgotten ones who in their own day thrilled with the excitement of adventuring and daring, of proving for themselves and filling out their own little lives! Surely, plenty have already put out forever the steady flame of their purity to follow the scintillating sparkle of gilded sin. And if thee ever fails to realize those broader, common, human warnings—if they fail to appeal to thee as too remote and cold to be real, or to touch thy heart with their warning of terror, then thee must remember that this other half of thy very self has been sent already and at thine own bidding through all the sin needed by thee and me! Treasure thy portion of the blessed purity at all cost, dear! It has to light my way as well as thine—and thee can never know how priceless it is in my sight! Will thee not believe me, dear, when I tell thee this is not mere jealousy or selfish temper or proprietorship on my part, but a loving yearning to protect thy soul as thee would guard one of thy babies from some dreadful disease like diphtheria? What brings this to my mind is something in my talk with Tom last night, that suggested the possibility of thy winter's loneliness, whether we decide that it should be without me, or without thy children, breeding a restlessness that might in some moment of reckless desperation cause thee to grasp at that treacherous glitter as a possible object of momentary interest and self-*

forgetfulness. Forgive me for entertaining for a moment such an idea, Pussy—but I must recognize it just long enough to tell thee that deep as my concern is for the needful reorganization of our home life and home relations, for the salvation of the children, I must, nevertheless, tell thee that rather than that thee should be exposed to even the remotest possibility of such a risk, I will gladly give up every consideration of them— throw up the whole plan—and act only for thy moral security. For in my heart and life, thee comes before everything else: and that one thing thy crown of purity, is to me so precious that even the moral loss of the three children would be a small sacrifice! So that if thee needed the protection of motherly contact to keep wholesome thine own life, I would gladly turn the little ones all over to thee and give up my struggles in their behalf. Will thee promise me as thee loves thy babies to call on me to make good this statement before thee finds thy need of them too great to be safely borne? . . . This matter has had to do with depressing me, lying in my heart all day, so that tired as I am I cannot go to bed tonight until I have written it for thy reading. Again I ask thy forgiveness for assuming such a possibility, but that flaw in D's otherwise charming character, and thy persistent championing and apologizing for him, together with my rule of safety—to deem all things possible—forces it upon me. Could thee not send D away? Ask him to go? Need I ask thee to ask? It is because I so reverence thine own purity and so shrink into a veritable soul's death at thought of any least soil upon it that I must speak. Does thee understand, dear heart?

THY JOHN.

2. A.M.

I copied it out on the yellow paper that I used for Latin, and folded the copy, and hid it in the wildflower book. 2 A.M. What had they been talking about all that time. And what did this mean about the children. The salvation of the children. I looked out of the window and saw Mother and Porper coming slowly across the field by the Walker house, Porper holding her hand. I stood and watched them. Mother had on a raincoat over her bathing suit. She was walking slowly, looking down at the ground without saying anything, and Porper was skipping on one leg. I would meet them at the porch, or by the tennis court and give her the letter and then go on, running, towards the Point, as if to be in time to join Susan and Uncle Tom——

——the timelessness, the spacelessness, but also the wonderful and ever-renewed sense of the nearness and brightness and largeness, the vividness of small things, the extraordinary intenseness of grass-blades and cloverleaves and acorns, the warmth of sand in the hand, the sound of leaves tapping against the wooden walls of the playhouse—the queer new sense of brilliant exposure to all this, each year as we came back to it, as if one had forgotten what it was to see a cloud driven with unchanging shape from west to east across the blue sky, or to try to stare at the sun until one saw purple and green blots, to lie in the warm uneven grass as if one were a part of it, the grasshoppers and crickets crawling and tickling on one's bare legs or getting into one's clothes and making spots of tobacco juice—

to come back to this, to be once more surprised by this and reimmersed in this, as if one again became a part of the wind, the sun, the earth——

—Look, Susan, if you almost close your eyes, but not quite, like this, and look at the sun, you see—wait a minute, and I'll tell you what I see——

—Oh, anybody can do that, I've done that millions of times, you only do it because you saw Gwendolyn doing it that day at the Long Beach.

—I don't either. Don't be such a nitwit. What day do you mean.

—You know perfectly well what day I mean.

—You mean that time when we went across the long bridge to see how many new planks had been put in after the winter.

—Of course, you silly.

—Well, I didn't even know what she was doing. Now it looks like a thick great jungle of hairy trees. All crisscross and savage and with a bright light coming through them. Gosh, isn't it funny, how huge they look, and they're only your eyelashes.

—That's exactly what Gwendolyn said.

—Oh, shut up, will you. You try to spoil everything.

—It was the same day we went to look at the place where we had the clambake last year. You know as well as I do. And we met Gwendolyn on the beach, she was with Dorothy Peters, and Dorothy took off her clothes in the sand dunes and you said you'd seen her.

—I did not.

—Well, anyway, you said so.

—Have you tried looking through your fingers to see the red blood in them.

—And Gwendolyn was lying against the side of a dune with her eyes squeezed up, just like that, telling us what she saw. She said it was like a kaleidoscope.

—Kaleidoscope.

—Isn't that what I said.

—I said *kaleidoscope*.

—So did I.

—You think so. That's all you know.

—And you stood there looking down at Gwendolyn with that silly expression on your face——

—Will you shut up? Unless you can learn to talk a little sense once in a while.

—What else am I talking, I'd like to know.

—You're talking nonsense, of course.

—But why you can get so excited about that stuck-up prig of a Gwendolyn, I'm sure I don't know.

—Who said I was excited about her.

—Why any *idiot* could see it.

—Oh, could they.

—If you could have *seen* yourself——

—*Shut* up.

—Oh, I don't care.

—Well, then, shut *up*.

—Nice manners older brothers seem to have.

—*Will* you shut up?

I closed my eyes, and felt the sun hot on my eyelids, and thought how queer it was that the redness I could see was nothing but my own blood. Susan knew too much. She was beginning to be a nuisance. What she said about my imitating Gwendolyn was perfectly true, the nitwit. But what did it matter. I was going to keep away from Gwendolyn for all the rest of the summer, and that would make everybody think there was nothing in it. Just the same, when I thought of the box of candy——

—Well if Uncle David thinks I'll hang round here all afternoon for the pleasure of getting my feet dirty hoeing the tennis court, he's got another guess coming. I'm going down to see if I can find Sanford. And if I find him I'll take him out for a row in the dory. You can tell Uncle David to put *that* in his pipe and smoke it.

—Good-by, and good riddance.

—Keep the change.

Would Father really be coming back to Duxbury, and what did he mean about Mother's being alone. Was she going away somewhere. And would we stay with Father in Cambridge, unless they bought the new house in Milton. And here it was August already, and no signs of a picnic! I climbed half way up the windmill, and then came down again. The leg nearest the house was getting looser, and ought to be fixed. Uncle Tom said it would have to be bedded in concrete—they would dig a hole and pour concrete in it. In a strong wind, when the windmill was pumping, you could see the whole leg lift up a little, sometimes almost a half an inch.

—Uncle Tom, I thought I'd ask Sanford to come out for a row with me, Uncle David doesn't seem to be coming back to do the tennis court, and I thought maybe I'd take a bucket along and get some clams for supper. Do you think it would be a good idea.

—Well, I'm afraid as a matter of fact, Andy, your Aunt Norah has already ordered some, from Gerald Soule. Still, if you want to get a few more——

—You bet I will.

—Not too many, mind you.

—Are you fixing the box kite so we can take Porper for a ride in his cart with it. Do you remember the time when it carried him right across the tennis court, and into the field, and upset him?

—Yes, I thought we'd get it out and fix it. All it needs is this one cross strut—and I *believe* there are some left-over battens down in the bicycle house——

He was pulling his chin and staring at the box kite on the grass, and humming to himself in that queer mournful way without any tune in it, the red cloth of the box kite flickering stiffly in the wind, and I ran then down the hill past the playhouse, and jumped with a long jump over the wall covered with poison ivy and walked through the blackberry jungle, feeling the thorns catch hold of my sneakers and try to rip them.

When I got to the Soules', Molly was swinging in the swing by herself, as usual, and said Sanford had gone to Plymouth in a motorboat with

his mother. He wouldn't be back till supper time. And not then, if they
got stuck in the mud.

—Whose boat is it.

—Mr. Pigeon's.

—Pigeons for ducks.

—My mother was invited to go, but she couldn't.

—Didn't they invite you, Molly?

—No, Sanford doesn't like me. Would you like to try my swing?

—No, thanks, I've got to go. I've got to dig some clams.

—Could I come with you?

—Sure, if you like. If we have time, I might take you out in my dory.

We went across the golf links, keeping an eye out for balls, but there
weren't any, and then walked down the drive past Powder Point Hall.
Molly kept wanting to hold my hand and then letting it go again. She said
that her mother worked in the afternoons at Powder Point Hall, washing
dishes, and wanted to stop and look in the windows to see if she could see
her, but a lot of ladies were coming down the side steps and I walked
quickly ahead, so that she came running after me and took hold of my
hand again. We went past the Horse Monument and through the woods,
where I showed her our houses, and she would have liked to stay there,
but I took her down to the beach near the hunting box and told her to
wait there without moving till I fetched the bucket and spade. I told her
I was responsible for her, because she was small, and made her promise. If
she would promise I might take her back to the houses afterwards.

When I got back, with the spade and bucket, she was crying. She was
wiping her eyes with her thin dress, and I could see her white drawers. They
weren't very clean.

—What are you crying about. Do you want to go home.

—No.

—Well, then, what are you crying for.

—I won't tell you.

—All right, then you can go home. I don't want any crybabies with me.

—It was your mother.

—What do you mean.

—Your mother, she scolded me. She came out of that little house, and
she was angry with me when she saw me. She said I ought not to be here
alone, and I said you were coming back, and then she went away——

I put down the spade and bucket on the sand and went to the back
of the hunting box, up above it, on the bluff, and looked down at it.
Should I go and look into it, to see if there were any bottles there. No, it
was like spying, or sneaking. The little door at the back was half open, and
there wasn't any sound, probably there was no one inside, but I didn't
like to go and look. Suppose Uncle David should be there, reading a book.
Or drinking out of a bottle. And pretending that he didn't know Molly
and I were right there on the beach.

I gave Molly the bucket to carry, and I took the spade, and we went
down through the beds of eelgrass to the mud flats, and began walking
to and fro, pressing the mud with our feet, to see where the clams squirted.
I began digging, and got some clams, but we put back all the small ones.

—Which way did my mother go.

—She went straight across to the pine woods.
—And there wasn't anybody with her, Molly.
—No.
—And you're sure she came out of the hunting-box?
—Yes.
—You saw her come out of it?
—Yes.

————and it wasn't that I hadn't tried to do my Latin lesson, either, because I had sat in my room all evening, with the kerosene lamp on the table beside the wildflower book, turning the flame down to stop it from smoking, and the mosquitoes humming on the hot window screens as loudly as if they were in the room, and Susan thrashing about in her bed in the room across the hall, and talking in her sleep, or groaning—how could I remember. Susan, will you keep still, please. Well, how can I get to sleep with this light on my ceiling. You've done it before, you can do it again, it isn't my fault if they didn't build the partitions up to the ceiling, is it? Well, anyway. Well, anyway! And how can I study Latin if you make all that noise. Who asked you to, I don't care about your Latin, I want to go to sleep. Well, for goodness sake, go to sleep and let me learn this verb.

—I'm afraid you've got to do better than this, Andy. You've got only two weeks now till I have to examine you, you know. I think you'd better begin reviewing. And I think we'd better not do any more sailing.

He told me to tell Uncle Tom, and to ask Uncle Tom to hear me recite the verbs and nouns. I had a chocolate milk shake at the drugstore, and ate the thick brown froth off the top with a spoon. On the way home, I watched the tide spilling out over the dam, and afterwards went into the long bowling alley, at the edge of the marsh, to watch the livery stable men bowling. Smiley let me throw one of his balls, but I missed, and it went along the groove at the side. I didn't want to go back to Powder Point at all. I wanted to go to Boston. I walked slowly along the Point Road until I got to the Soules', and went down to the dyke, where Father had shown me how to whip-throw with apples. Then I walked all the way along the beach until I got to the Tupper landing stage, with the canoe on it. It was wet, and the paddles beside it were wet, somebody had been out in it. Perhaps Gwendolyn. I had never been out in a canoe. Why did they never ask me to go. Was it because I had been so foolish about Gwendolyn. I took up one of the paddles, and found it was much lighter than my oars. That must be because a canoe was so much lighter than a dory. I put it down again and looked quickly up towards the Tupper lawn to see if any one was there, but there was nobody, and I climbed up the grass slope past the imitation windmill and pushed through the oak bushes on the other side of the road and went down to the little pond below the Wardman house. Had the Tuppers been up into the marshes towards Brant Rock, along my favorite channel. And at low tide, too. Where Uncle David was always taking Mother. In that deep, steep channel, with the sides of stiff, red mud and the marsh reeds growing out of it. Where the tide was so swift that you could hardly row against it. Was that where they had been. Did they go up all the way, and find that last hidden turning, the narrow one that led almost up to the Long Beach. Perhaps a canoe could go even farther up, at high tide, than a dory. And much farther than a motorboat, of course.

I sat down under the cherry tree by Plymouth Rock Junior, and felt tired. I wanted to lie down. I wanted to stretch out as if I were in bed. I put the Latin grammar on the grass, and ground my forehead against it, as if it were a pillow, pressing my feet against the base of the rock. I wanted to be asleep. I wanted to be dead. I wanted to cry, but I couldn't. I closed my eyes and counted to five hundred by fives, and then said first the worst—second the same—third the best of all the game—the rhyme Mother always said for Porper when she blew out the light. One—two— three! Out. Goes. She. But I couldn't get to sleep, so I opened my eyes, and watched the cherry leaves moving against the sky, and the clusters of wild cherries, which would soon be ripe. And I remembered the time when Susan and I had eaten too many, and Father made us drink a cup of mustard and water and we were both sick.

———the day of the storm, when the thunder went and came all day, moving in a great circle round the shore of the bay, crossing darkly over Kingston and Plymouth, from behind the Standish Monument, but never getting as far as South Duxbury, and then moving out to sea over the black hills at Manomet, the lightning stabbing down vividly from the belly of black cloud into the mass of white rain that hung over Plymouth and the sea, the thunder almost continuous. Before lunch, the wind rose to a steady scream, but on Powder Point the sun still shone brightly, and we tried to have archery practice. The wind blew the arrows every which way, blew our words back into our mouths, and Porper was always being flung down on the grass, and saying that he couldn't breathe.

—Porper, you silly, stand here behind the corner of the porch, it's nice and quiet here, you can watch the lightning just as well from here.

—What lightning.

—You see, the lightning over there, over Plymouth. And just listen to the thunder it sounds like lions.

—Where are the lions.

—At the zoo, don't you remember?

—I want to see the lions.

Uncle David went in and got the box kite with the two enormous reels of twine, and Uncle Tom said we ought not to try it, the wind was too strong, and it might break away, but Uncle David laughed and said no, it was all right, he would hang on to it, and hitch it to the cart and give Porper a ride across the tennis court, or even down to the end of the Point. The wind almost blew it out of his hands when he took it out to the tennis court, and then he lifted it up over his head, staggering, and let go of it, while Uncle Tom ran past the porch with the cord, and the red kite gave a swoop to one side and then began to go up so fast that Uncle Tom just let the cord whizz through his glove, while the reel danced up and down on the ground at his feet.

—Andy. Susan. Go and get the cart. Where is the cart.

I pulled the cart from under the porch, but as soon as we tied the cord to the handle and tried to let it go the kite dragged it over on its side and yanked it in leaps and bounds over the tennis court, so that we had to sit on it and stop it. Uncle Tom and Uncle David both had hold of the cord, but it kept on pulling them step by step towards the Walker house, while Mother untied the cart again. It was hard to hear what people were saying in the wind.

—We'll never be able to get it down.

—Of course we can.

—Everybody take hold, come on Doris, and you, Andy, and we'll see if we can pull it back and make it fast to the porch.

We all pulled, but we couldn't budge it. We stood there, holding it and watching it. It was high up, and seemed almost halfway to the end of the Point.

—Can we send up some messengers, Uncle Tom.

—No, I don't think we'd better—we've got our hands full as it is——

—Susan could cut them out.

—We might manage to make it fast to the Walkers' barn——

Susan was just running in to cut out the paper messengers, the little rings of paper to send up the cord, when suddenly there was a twang, the cord had snapped, and we all took a step backward, so that Uncle Tom almost had to sit down.

—It's gone. As I thought.

We stood there, all of us, in the wind, and watched it go. It got smaller and smaller and in a few minutes we couldn't see it at all. It was going straight out towards Provincetown, across Massachusetts Bay.

In the afternoon the wind dropped almost as suddenly as it had begun, but the clouds were gathering again behind the Standish Monument, getting blacker and blacker. Everything became silent. The trees and bushes were as still as if they were listening. We played bean bag in the sitting room with Porper, until Porper got silly and wanted to throw the pine-needle cushion at the board instead of the bean bag, so then we played the battleship card game, but Porper always wanted to have the *Amphitrite* and the *Vesuvius*, so he and Susan played croquinole, while I went down to the playhouse to study Latin. When I went out, Mother and Uncle David were standing on the porch, looking across the bay with the telescope.

—Are you going to the playhouse, Andy?

—Yes.

—Ten to one you'll get wet on the way back.

—I don't care.

In the playhouse it was almost too dark to read, so I left the door open; and I could watch the lightning behind the monument, and see the oak leaves beginning to stir again in an icy-cold draught of air that seemed to come very low over the ground. This was going to be a humdinger, and no mistake. What Aunt Norah always called a shingle-ripper, because it sounded as if the shingles were being ripped off the roof when the lightning and thunder came so close. *Utor, fruor, fungor, potior,* and *vescor.* The ablative absolute. Who wanted to know about ablatives. And what silly names they had for them, anyway. I went through the fourth declension three times, reciting it aloud while I bounced a cracked Ping-pong ball against the partition of the bicycle shed. That. And that. And that. And that. And then suddenly the wind came, and whirled half the pages in the book, and the window screen whistled, and when I went to the door I saw that the water in front of the Standish Hotel had gone completely white. I was afraid, but excited. Perhaps I'd better go back to the house, and be with the others. Before the storm actually got to us across the bay.

I closed the window and door and ran up the slope. By the time I got to the house the wind was so strong that it almost took me off my feet. I saw Uncle Tom standing at the base of the windmill, looking first upward at the top of it, with his eyes shaded by his hand, and then down at the foot. When I joined him he pointed to the leg of the windmill near-est to the house and then put his mouth close to my cheek and shouted.

—I'm afraid it will go over. We'll have to lash it. Do you think you could climb—I'll get the clothes line.

He went into the kitchen, while I stood and watched the windmill. The slender steel leg was heaving out of the ground and then settling again, four inches at a time. The mill was shut off, but spinning just the same, and pumping slowly; the wind was so irregular that whenever it caught the wheel broadside on, it whirled it and at the same time pushed it so violently that the whole frame of steel seemed to tug out of the ground. The diagonal struts were singing like telephone wires. I stood on the lowest strut and the leg lifted me right up with it.

Uncle Tom came back with the coil of clothes line.

Do you think you could climb up. You're nimbler than I am. Are you afraid.

—No.

—All right, then, take this, and climb up to the third crosspiece and make it fast to this leg, above and below the crosspiece, and then carry the rope round the next leg, that one and then back again round this one. Do you see what I mean?

I took the coil of rope and climbed up the little galvanized iron steps, one at a time, with my khaki trousers flattened against my legs like boards, hardly able to breathe, and stepped out on the crosspiece. The whole wind-mill was rocking like the mast of a boat. I lowered myself to straddle the gray crosspiece and dropped the coil over the corner of it and brought it up, twice, and made three square knots, the way Mr. Dearing had showed me, and then slid along to the other leg and looped the rope twice over and under the crosspiece there.

—Now the same thing with the first one again.

I slid back and did it.

—Now drop me the rope. And come down. Before you get blown down.

He yelled this up at me, grinning, and I dropped the coil to him, and he went towards the kitchen porch with it. When I got there he had taken half a dozen turns round a post with it and was knotting it.

—That ought to hold. What do you think.

—If the post will hold, Uncle Tom.

—Oh, the post will hold all right. I'm not so sure about the rope.

We went back to the windmill and watched it. The leg was still lifting, but not so much, the rope was holding it down. The first rain was begin-ning, coming in large fierce drops, almost horizontally, separate and sting-

ing, and smacking against the side of the house as loudly as hailstones. Aunt
Norah came round the corner to the edge of the porch and shouted something.

—What did you say?

She put her hands to her mouth.

—If it's all right——

—Yes, it's all right.

—You'd better come in—Doris and David——

—What?

—Come in.

—All right, we're coming.

It got dark very suddenly, and as we ran along the side porch I saw a
lightning-flash crawl quite slowly down behind the statue of Miles Standish,
a pale lilac color, very bright, and almost as slow as if it were being drawn
down with a pen. I remembered what Father said about counting the
seconds between the flash and the thunder, a second to a mile, and started
to count, but the crash came between the first count and the second, a
terrific shingle-ripper, and so low and close that it seemed to go right over
my hair. As I dived round the corner to the sheltered part of the porch
at the front the rain made me shut my eyes, but I could still see the little
black figure of Miles Standish with the sword stroke of light behind him.
What was this about Doris and David. Uncle Tom was holding the screen
door for me, but it got away from him just as I went in, and clapped back
against the wall. Then he pulled it shut by main force, against the wind,
which sang through it, and closed the inside door, and we were in the
dining-room-and-sitting-room, where everything seemed quiet by contrast,
and the lamps were lit, one of them hanging on chains over the dining-
table, the other over the table at the other end of the room, with a bowl
of bayberry leaves. I could hear Porper shouting to Susan upstairs. Aunt
Norah was holding her spectacles in her hand and wiping the rain off her
cheek.

—They've gone out to the boat——

—What do you mean.

—Doris and David. I tried to stop them——

—You mean in the *Osprey*——?

—It was David's idea, he thought it would be nice to go out in a storm
—do you think you could stop them. It isn't safe. It's crazy.

—When did they go.

—Five minutes ago. If you ran straight down to the Point——

—Can I go, Uncle Tom, I can run fast——

—No, Andy, you stay here.

—I'll go down and see.

He took his raincoat from the cupboard under the stairs and went out.
I wondered if he would be struck by lightning. And whether the *Osprey*
would be struck, because of the little mast at the front. What a silly thing
to do, it was just like Uncle David, he was probably drunk. I went upstairs to Susan's room, where Susan and Porper were building a fortress
in the middle of the floor with blocks and books and tin soldiers and the
rockinghorse and the elephant, and the wastebasket for a tower, and helped

them with it, now and then going to the front window to watch the storm, which got worse and worse. Every time the lightning came Porper shut his eyes, but he didn't cry. The whole bay was dancing with lightning, and now and then we could see all of it, every single detail, even the white houses on Clark's Island, in a green flash, but we couldn't see any boats, only the water, which seemed to be nothing but whitecaps. Uncle Tom must be down at the Point now, but what could he do. How could they see him or hear him, even if they were still there. But where would they go.

It was after supper, Susan was putting Porper to bed, when he came back, soaked to the skin, and tired, and said he hadn't been able to find them. They had gone off in the *Osprey*, and taken the tender with them, he could make out the mooring, but that was all. He had walked out on the long bridge as far as the draw without seeing anything, there were no lights in either direction. If they had gone out into the bay, and got caught, they might be safe enough by this time if they had got into the lagoon, by the village. Or they might have gone up through the bridge into the cove, and perhaps anchored there in the lee of the bluffs, or perhaps even beached the *Osprey*. In any case, he didn't think anything more could be done. They were probably all right. What could you do, in this rain that came in sheets, and this wind like a hurricane. Though he thought the thunderstorm itself was about over, was moving out to sea.

—Do you think we ought to telephone the police.

—What could the police do. And probably they've cut off the telephone service.

—If they aren't back by ten I think we ought to tell them.

—You mean send out a search party. But what could a search party do. Nobody would go out in a boat, not if he could help it. You can't see as far as your hand.

It was after I had been sent up to bed that I heard the telephone ringing. The thunder had stopped, and the wind had gone down, but it was still raining hard. And a little later I heard voices downstairs, and the doors opening and shutting, and when I got out of bed and went to the window I saw Uncle Tom and two other men going off towards the Point with lanterns, the three lanterns noddling up and down over the drenched grass, and showing the bright yellow edges of sou'-westers. I got back into bed and listened to the hard rain on the roof, but I couldn't go to sleep. It seemed to me that I was awake all night.

————and in the playhouse that afternoon, alone, it was hot and steamy there, and quiet, and Uncle Tom came in, and looked at me, tapping on the Gonko table with his fingers, and I could see that he was wondering if I had been crying. But I hadn't been crying. And then he said that Sergeant Homer was at the house and wanted to ask me a few questions. Just a few questions. About how I had found them. About how I had found the *Osprey* in the marsh channel that morning.

—Don't be worried, Andy. It's just official. Just tell him what he wants to know, it won't be long. It's all right.

The Sergeant was sitting at the dining-room table, with his hat upside down on the floor beside him. Aunt Norah was standing by the window, she had just said something when we came in, and the Sergeant was writing it down with a pencil. She was blowing her nose.

—And your name, young man, is Andrew Cather, isn't it?

—Yes, sir.

—You went out in your dory this morning at about five o'clock, that's right isn't it, and rowed up the marsh channel toward Brant Rock?

—Yes, sir.

—And you saw the tender of your uncle's boat there, in the channel, and that led to your discovery that the *Osprey* had been sunk there. How much under water was the *Osprey* when you saw it, would you say.

—I should think about two feet.

—So that you could see everything quite clearly?

—Yes, sir.

—Was she on her side?

—A little on her port side.

—You could see quite clearly into the cockpit, you could even have got into it—but you didn't get into it, did you, Andrew, or interfere with it in any way?

—No, sir.

—Was the door to the cabin open or shut.

—It was shut.

—You are sure of that. Did you notice whether the boat had been anchored?

—Yes, sir, the anchor had been dropped.

—Could you see anything through the portholes?

—I could see some brown cloth quite close to one of the portholes, and I knew it was my mother's dress, the one she had on yesterday.

—You didn't touch the doors of the cabin, did you?

—No, sir.

—Thank you, Andrew—that will be all.

I went out by myself to the tennis court, and met Juniper there, and he swished his tail against my bare leg and made the sound that Porper always called *puttenyarruk*, which meant that he wanted grasshoppers. I caught him a flying one, and he ate it. The tennis court was almost dry again, but the rain had made deltas in it, it would need rolling, and the lines were completely gone. It was August the 11th. I wished they hadn't put Mother and Uncle David in the same room. And would Father come down to Duxbury now——

《 III

—Perhaps, after all, I'd better go. I'm afraid you were busy, old man. And I think it's stopped snowing.

—No—I don't think it has. What about a drink.

—Well—well——

—It'll do you good. Release the inhibitions, et cetera. Remove your consciousness from one plane to another, you know.

—Oh, yes?

—Yes. . . . Here. . . . Say when. . . .

—When. Thanks. . . . Thanks. . . .

—And come to think of it, why don't you spend the night. You might talk it all out, between drinks. Plenty of whisky here—some Rhine wine, if you prefer—quiet as the tomb—you can sleep on the couch if you get sleepy—What do you say.

—Well, maybe—if you don't mind—after all—good God, I feel like crying.

—Why not sit down.

—No, thanks, I'd rather stand—walk—touch things and hold on to things—do you mind if I put my hand flat on that picture of Michelangelo and feel the glass——

—Why should I?

—He, too. I wonder if he ever went as deep. Did he ever talk to a psychoanalyst and weep? Did he ever pace about a room, at midnight, with a glass in his hand, a glass that might have been his heart, and drink his own bitter blood? Christ, what am I chattering about.

—Don't we all do it, sooner or later?

—Before I came here, half an hour ago, do you know what I was doing? I was walking in the snow, hardly knowing what I was doing. Oh, yes, I did know, too, for God's sake let's be honest. I was crying as I walked, and I enjoyed crying—I felt the tears at the corners of my mouth, tears mixed with melting snow, and I deliberately opened my coat and shirt, so that I could feel the snowflakes on my chest and throat. My feet were getting wet, and I didn't care, I stepped into the puddles and slush, thinking what a good thing it would be if I got pneumonia. Isn't it amazing how even at such a moment, when one is absolutely broken, dissolved, a mere whirlwind of unhappiness, when one walks without knowing or caring where one is going, nevertheless one still has to dramatize oneself, one sees oneself as a pitiful figure under an arc light in the snow, one lifts a deliberately tormented face to the storm, and despite the profound actuality of one's grief, there is also something false in it too. Suddenly the snow is paper snow, one almost expects to hear an accompaniment of sob music on nicely ordered violins, or the whole world breaking into applause! Good God. Let's laugh.

—Ha, ha. I'm laughing.

—Where is honesty then? I don't believe we've got an honest fiber in our souls. We're all colossal fakes—the more power we have, the more ingeniously and powerfully we fake. Michelangelo—what the hell. Did he ever tell the truth? Or Shakespeare? No, by God, they went lying into their graves, nothing said, their dirty little mouths twisted with deceit, their damned hearts packed full of filthy lies and blasphemies. Their whole lives wasted. One long fake, a pitiful and shameful glozing and glazing of the truth, slime upon slime and prettification on prettification, each new resolve to tell the truth coming to nothing, somehow turning to a neatly turned verse, a fine purple flight of rhetoric, a bloody little tune, an effective action, or a figure of which the very secret of power is artifact. Christ, Christ, what an agony—poor devils, they knew it too, and still they went on surrendering to the lies inherent in language and marble. Why? And why, even when I want to kill myself, do I have to cast myself as little orphan Annie with a rag doll clutched to her shawled bosom? I'm ashamed. No, I'm not either. Yes, I am too. I went into the Waldorf and cried into a cup of pale coffee. I could hardly swallow. I wanted to be dead. That damned dado of college banners made me sick. Old Turgenev, the cashier, was having trouble with a couple of drunks, they started to fight, and I got up with my coffee cup in my hand and went to talk to them—I persuaded them to go out to the sidewalk, and I went with them, holding my coffee cup. One of them, a tough guy from town, got the other down, the other was a mere kid, and when he got up his eye was cut open. I stopped the fight, with plausible words, feeling like a damned little pewter Galahad— Come on, now, I said, that's enough, the kid's had enough, leave him alone, what's the idea, and I smiled a God-damned sickly smile at them both as if I were a paltry little Messiah, and they quit. I think it was the sight of the coffee cup out there in my hand in the snow that did it. One of them went down Holyoke Street and the other into the Yard, and I went back into the Waldorf feeling important and sat down with my coffee cup, and began to remember that I had wanted to cry, to die, to lie down on the mosaic floor with my coffee cup, just to stretch out like a dead Jesus on the dirty floor of this dirty and stinking world. But of course I didn't do it. I merely thought about it, luxuriated disgustingly in the idea, imagined myself lying there among dead matches and wet sawdust, poor pitiful little Andrew Cather, him that was betrayed by the everlasting Judas tree. What is unhappiness, Bill?

—Defeated pride. A highball without ice. Ignorance.

—Ignorance be damned, and damn your eyes anyway. You and your amateur psychology. What the hell do you know about it, anyway? You sit there and goggle at the world as if you knew something—what the hell do you know? Oh, yes, I know, something hurt you irremediably when you were muscling your infant way into this cold, cold world, and you've never recovered, but you've fought your way back by superhuman intelligence to that drastic cold bath of a moment—isn't that it? So now you're wise and resigned, and smile Shakespearean wisdom on all the maimed host of mankind. You sit there and smile benignly at me, and wish to God I'd go home and leave you alone to sleep, you think I'm a fool, and you despise me because I've been betrayed and because I make such a fuss about it. What's the use. Tea dance today. Novelty dance tonight. There will be charming favors, and saxophones will syncopate your livers. How long is it since you've cried, Bill?

—Oh, not since I was five or six, I guess.

—Why don't you try it. It's great. I've got the habit. I cry all the time. I wake up in the middle of the night crying—I dream I'm crying, and wake up crying. Yesterday morning I cried while I was shaving—it was the funniest thing I ever saw, the tears running down into the lather. I laughed at myself and then cried again. I think I'll go insane. Deliberately—just think myself into madness. Why not?

—You're insane now. Manic.

—Manic, hell.

—You're heading a hell of a good time.

—Yes, indeed. Step up, ladies and gents, and see the trained lunatic, the miching mallecho Michelangelo, the pig with wings. Here lies the winged pig, feared and befriended by many, loved and betrayed by one. Why do I always dream about pigs? Last night I hit one in the snout with a walking stick—I thought he was attacking me, but it turned out I was mistaken. He merely wanted to attract my attention; but by that time I had fallen down in the mud, and my stick was dirty.

—It would be. Ha, ha.

—Don't make me laugh.

—Anal erotic, what.

—Scatological too. Step up and see the scatological hebephrene, watch him weep pig's tears into his snout.

—He eats them all.

—The pig with wings was a much smaller pig—a tiny pig, and such a little darling, as clean as clean could be. His wings were transparent and opalescent, lovely, and oh so tender—they were just unfurled, and scarcely dry, and imagine it, Bill, a dirty little bastard of a mongrel dog chose just that moment to attack him, biting at the wings! When I threw stones at him, he turned and attacked me.

—That dog was your best friend.

—My best friend—Christ. I mean Judas.

—You mean yourself.

—My polysyllabic soul, yes, of course I am guilty, I go about projecting my guilt like a magic lantern.

—Do you mind if I open the window a little, and let the smoke out?

—Oh, no, knock out the wall if you like. Einstein is waiting just outside with the fourth dimension on his forehead.

—I'll ask him in.

—Do.

—Meanwhile, have you called up Bertha today.

—No, I went to see the Dingbats. The Dingbat sisters. I met them in the elevator, and one of them was carrying a bottle of gin, and I was already tight and so were they a little, and what with one thing and another, though I'd never spoken to them before, we smiled at each other and they invited me to come in and have a drink. So I did. The mystery women of Shepard Hall. They're always getting telephone calls from the Navy Yard, and it amuses me to hear them at the public phone trying to answer indiscreet proposals in discreet words of one syllable. The older one took me into her bedroom to show me photographs of her two kids in Montreal. I hadn't known she was married, and that put me off a little—I understood then why her breasts were so—ahem—mature and maternal. She leaned one of them against me, Bill, but I didn't budge or feel a tremor. Not a tremor. Then they gave me six cocktails in rapid succession, in the dining room, a horrible room with red walls and fumed-oak furniture with an umbrella stand in one corner and such jolly colored prints of John Peel singing at the hunt breakfast. Why had I never been to see them, they

said. They were always glad to see the people they liked, and if I just rang
their bell six times, any time of the day or night, they would know it was
me, and get out of bed even, if necessary. Very obliging. I asked them if
they ever cried, and they were amused. I told them that I had a peculiar
passion for crying, and would be glad to come in from time to time and
have a good noisy cry with them while punishing the gin bottle. They
laughed their heads off, and thought I was a hell of a wag. Then I said I
must be going. The younger one, who is not so pretty, but who has no
children, she is tall and has a gentler face, not quite so tough, you know,
perhaps a trace of what you fellows call the anima type, she pleaded softly
and cajolingly with me at the dining-room door, standing so close to me
that I couldn't get past her without embracing her, and she followed me
to the front door and there, what do you think, just round the corner
from Alice, we had a ten-minute nonstop kiss, you know the kind. Alice
after a few minutes of the silence, said, Hey, there, what are you kids doing
out there, and laughed, and then I went back for another cocktail. Oh, it
was great fun, you have no idea. And when I finally came away I kissed
her again at the door, a long, long kiss, not forgetting the tongue, and so
went to the University Theater, where I suddenly and inexplicably felt very
drunk. An undergraduate in front of me said, I smell booooooooze, and
looked round. I smiled at him, very amiably.

—Well, and what was it all about? Do you understand it?

—Don't be simple-minded. Of course I do.

—And what about Bertha.

—That's what it was about, you idiot. That's what I'm talking about
all the time.

—So I see.

—Well, then, don't interrupt. This was my little attempt at a counter-
blast.

—Not the first, either.

—What do you know about it?

—Oh, I've been here and there myself, and in and out, and up and
down, and heard a thing or two, some from your own lips, before this.

—Too true, too true. I've always been your best case, Bill, your richest
specimen. What on earth would you have done without me. I'm one of
those talented fellows who combine all the madnesses in one—paranoia,
dementia praecox, manic depressive, hysteria—name another. And so I
watched faces on the screen—large weeping faces, eight feet high and five
feet wide, with tears the size of cannon balls on the common and teeth like
gravestones in the snow. Eyes—! You never saw such eyes. Like glassless
windows in a ruined church. I think bats were coming and going out of
them and into them. And the hair was like high-tension wires, and I saw
a louse the size of a sparrow being electrocuted. It was great. Did I ever tell
you of the time I stole a girl's hat in the University Theater?

—No.

—Then I won't. Now don't tell me what Freud thinks a hat means.

—What do you think a hat means.

—If I were a Martian, strayed to earth, long after the death of the last
man, I could reconstruct the whole of human civilization from one female

hat. Preferably one of those early specimens with a lot of ostrich plumes. But this is a hypothetical question and I won't go into it. The truth is, I want to cry.

—Go ahead and cry.

—No, I can't. You've become my alter ego for the moment, the skeptical and analytic part of myself, and you disapprove of crying. So do I. Did you every cry at a prize fight? No? Why, Bill, I'm surprised at you. I don't think you can have been to any prize fights. Everybody cries at a prize fight. The tears of Christ. You can buy them at the soda fountain, if you can get near enough to buy *anything*, which you seldom can, between bouts. And on Vesuvius once—but that was long ago, far away, and besides it was in the spring.

—You're a riot. I wish to God I could take this down. But I don't doubt *you'll* remember it.

—Why should I. It's my business to forget.

—So you think.

—So it is.

—The ostrich puts its head in the sand.

—I'm an ostrich, one of the best. An Arabian sparrow. Hiding my head in the desert of memory.

—I don't think you'd better drink any more. You're pretty well advanced.

—Not at all. How easily whisky comes out of a bottle—did you ever notice? Just like that. I think I'll sit down. I think I'll lie down. I think I'll put this nice cold silk cushion on my face. Oh, that's grand. Mmmmmmmm-mmmmmmmm. And so I came back from New York, in response to a note from Fred (nice fellow, Fred) and found a hat, a man's hat, a dirty felt hat, just as he predicted, on the chair in the front hall. What a melodrama. I had foreseen, in the train, every detail—that's my way, Bill, I always foresee. So the hat wasn't really a surprise at all. I was so sure it was there that I let myself in very quietly, like a cat, and banged the door behind me, and went up to the hat. It occurred to me to address the hat in Elizabethan style. O thou, most treasonable shape o' the human head, cornuting horror . . . but there were gloves also, and a stick—and what do you think of this —this is the dirtiest touch of all—a pair of humble muddy galoshes. Side by side, so meek and subservient, waiting for their exhausted master.

—For God's sake, Andy.

—Yes, for God's sake. You shrink from the horror, the plain physical horror, just as much as I did. Isn't it wonderful? What a symbol, what a symbol. The hat, the stick, the gloves, the galoshes—a little constellation in the front hall, of which the meaning was plain even to me, who am no astronomer. I saw the whole life which they signified: Thomas Crapo, idealist, scientist, professor of biology, my friend, excellent tennis player, frequenter of wrestling matches, lover of Beethoven, but also the lover of my wife. And the apartment was so quiet, Bill! I could have heard a pin drop—and perhaps I did. A hairpin. Ting! And then silence.

—I'll shut the window. It's getting cold.

—I hear a snowplow.

—It's one o'clock.

—Where?

—Here. One hour past midnight in the human soul.

—Then we're getting on. If I were a dead leaf I would swallow myself.

—Why wait to be a dead leaf.

—Ah, I see, you're bored, and quite rightly, with this harangue. Poor fellow, that's the unfortunate duty of analysts, isn't it? They only sit. I forget my Milton. But, seriously, have you ever found Christ's hat in your front hall? And his gloves and stick and galoshes? You wonder what to do. You feel—as you should—like an intruder. How can you most tactfully announce your inconsiderate arrival. It would be tactless to go to the bedroom door—don't you think—and say, Are you there, darling? Or perhaps darlings. It might be better simply to go to the bathroom and pull the chain, which would give them a cheerful warning that father was come home again. But there is this murderous impulse, too—have you ever killed a fly, or thrown a baby out of a window? I have, from time to time. Oh, my God. Look—I see my pulse on the radial side of my wrist, at the joint. I'm a doomed man, thank heaven. This is that blood that brought me where I am. You can throw the hat out of the window, of course—and perhaps that's the best solution, though not the easiest. Hat equals *schadenfreude*. Bilingual pun, Bill, which does you credit. But why not open the bedroom door dramatically, and stand there frozen for a moment, eyeless in Gaza at the mill with slaves? I don't like the smell of this cushion—I believe you've been entertaining young women here, Bill, and I think I recognize—do I recognize—yes, I've certainly come across that before. Now where was it?

—It doesn't matter—go ahead.

—Yes, go ahead. Forward into the untrodden—but that's an unfortunate suggestion. Do angels fear to tread? Not by a damned sight. And he was such an angel, such a white man, so gentle, so good, so shy—his little mustache is so neatly clipped with his nail scissors, on Tuesdays and Fridays always, and he always blows his nose before going to bed, and every penny he spends he puts down meticulously in his little notebook. Cup of coffee at Liggett's—five cents. Carfare to Boston and back—twenty cents. *Boston Evening Transcript*—three cents. But I'm forgetting about Michelangelo. Do you suppose Michelangelo ever saw the sea?

—The sea?

—Yes, the sea. You know, the ocean, the bounding main. That thing that has waves, and bears ships, and laughs unarithmetically at the moon. Did he ever see it? I wonder. I wonder if he wanted to get back to it. What do you think. Don't sit there and grin at me!

—Go on, let's get back to it. A little free association, please! While I have a drink and try to catch up with you.

—Oh, my God, I'm a fool, a bloody, bloody fool. Why am I always in such a damned panic, in such a hurry to make decisions, why do I run round in mad circles like a beheaded hen?

—You know pretty well why.

—For six months I've been doing it—I've done no work—I've drunk like a fish and gone from one wild party to another. An unreasoning terror, a terror that had no particular shape—nightmares one after another too, I'd wake up sweating, my heart beating like hell—dreams of falling, dreams of climbing and falling, desperate efforts to carry monstrous loads up broken and rotten ladders, fantastic scaffoldings which fell away beneath me as I climbed—night after night.

—You saw it all coming. You were already aware of the insecurity of your position—perhaps you even wanted all this to happen. Perhaps you were precipitating it. God knows your way of living can't have made Bertha like you any better, can it. I'm surprised she hasn't rebelled or broken out before.

—Now be fair about this, Bill, be fair. I admit it wasn't too good. But I think you go a little too far when you suggest that I wanted this to happen. Does a man deliberately want to cut himself in two? Jesus. Does he deliberately seek to be abandoned? Jesus. Does he carve out his own heart and throw it to the dogs? Jesus. No, I decline the gambit, thank you. Just because I vaguely foresaw and feared the thing doesn't mean I wanted it. I know I've been a damned fool. Why did I get into that rotten affair with Molly? God knows. But even that might not have done any harm if it hadn't been for the party in Prescott Street, when we all got drunk and took our clothes off and did a Russian ballet, and so on and so on, and that damned fool little Mary Thurston running all over town telling about it, just because some idiot of a Ph.D. student, a philosopher, thought he was a satyr and tore her shirt off. Those are the damned trifles that ruin our lives. Precarious, precarious. But nothing to the precariousness of the mind. I still believe I shall go insane. All of a sudden, my mind stops—goes blank—I can't either think or feel. I forget the simplest things, names, events—things I've known all my life. I carry my laundry into the Western Union telegraph office. Wild fits of shyness come over me, the kind I used to have when I was a kid, and I stand foolish and speechless, leering like an idiot, forgetting where I am and what I'm there for. The other day at the bank I found I couldn't write—my hand began to shake—God knows why —and I couldn't even sign my own name. The cashier looked at me in astonishment. I really thought I'd gone mad. I looked out of the window, trying to think of something, saw the sunlight, saw the window of my old room in Gray's Hall, with my initials still carved on the window sill after all these fifteen years, and the pen shook in my hand, and then I tried again, pretending for the cashier's benefit that I'd merely been doing a little calculation. Calculation! Good God, I was calculating for my very life. Then I managed by making a series of separate feverish little tremulous strokes to get a few quivering marks on to the paper, which bore no resemblance to my signature at all. Mr. Howe looked at it in surprise, but made no comment. I suspect he thought I was trying deliberately to disguise my handwriting so that the check wouldn't be charged to my own account. Now what the hell was that all about. I walked out shaking like the well-known aspen leaf, or a stricken doe, or something, and went straight to Molly's apartment, without even knowing what I was doing. Her door was unlocked and I walked in. She was taking a bath, and yelled at me in alarm from the tub, not knowing who it was. I opened the door and looked at her. She threw a sponge at me. Then I went back to the sitting room and stared at the cactus on the window sill, which had just given

birth to a purple blossom. It was very beautiful. She came in and said she
was surprised at me. She was obviously rather pleased. We sat down on
the couch, she in her kimono, and she expected me to make love to her.
Instead, I cried, and she was the most astonished woman you ever saw in
your life. When that was over, she gave me a gin and ginger ale, and I told
her my dream about the sea. I'm always dreaming about the sea. We all
know what that means, don't we? I'm going to be born again one of these
days. Oh, yes, we rise again. Back to the womb, and forth once more we
swim, like the mighty hero of the *Kalevala*, after nine months in submarine
caves. We all crowded to the railing on the port side, where the captain
was pointing to the masthead of a sunken ship, a masthead from which a
pennant still fluttered. It was a sunken galleon. I knew that, even before
the tide went out and revealed it to us all—the tide.went out in no time,
and there, behold, was a little island, submerged at all but low tide, and on
its shore was the little galleon. We got out of the ship and walked up the
shingle beach to the galleon, and I climbed up on to its deck and it was
very strange, it was a little museum of seashells and pearls and precious
stones, the decks were lined with glass cases, and all of them filled with
beautiful—indescribably beautiful—cowry shells and razor shells and wen-
tletraps and corals and ambergris and black pearls and God knows what.
I was enthralled. And to think—I reflected—that these poor fellows, four
hundred years ago, after collecting these rare and lovely things from parts
of the world and all the oceans, should at last have been overtaken by fate
and their marvelous collection buried here with them and forgotten. I
examined great scarlet shells like butterflies, and blue shells like dragon-
flies, and red sponges, and flying fishes with wings of opal and gold. Never
have I seen such concentrated beauty. It was all my childhood dream of
treasure-trove come true. All those dreams of finding nests of buried gold
coins, marbles made of moonstone, jackstones of silver—you know what I
mean. I climbed down again to the beach and walked round to the stern
of the ship—and there, what do you think? was a skeleton standing with
his hands folded on a rusted musket, standing upright as if to guard the
ship with its treasure, and staring with empty sockets at the name of the
ship, which I saw, when I looked up, was *Everest*. Ever rest. Now what
do you make of that, Watson. But I had no time to loiter—the tide was
rising swiftly again, the captain called us, and back we went to our own
ship, and no sooner were we on the decks once more than the tide had
risen, the little galleon, with its melancholy guard, was engulfed, and all
that remained was the fluttering pennant. And so we sailed away. I told
this dream to Molly—oh, yes, I know what it means, I daresay the old
fellow is my father—and before she could comment on it I told her we
were going to the Greek's for lunch, and so I helped her to dress, handing
her odds and ends of clothing, and I picked the damned little cactus flower,
which made her really furious—she stamped her foot and I thought she
was going to have a cry herself—but she recovered and we went to town
in a yellow taxi. And that was that. And, oh, yes, we went afterwards to a
hockey game at the Garden, and she was bored to death, though I gave her
a hot dog and a bag of peanuts to keep her happy. I think she thought I'd
gone crazy.

—You wanted her to think so.

—Of course I did. But also I didn't. Now just how do we dissect *that* out. But I'd prefer to have a drink. I'll have a drink. This is to Michelangelo, Shakespeare, and Melville, bisexual wonders of the transient world, magicians of the epicene, bastards of heaven and hell. Here's to you, Mike, old boy. May your shadow never grow less, nor your fifth leg shorter. And so they went to hell all three to learn the fraud of Calvary. Good old Mike —I know all about him. His best friend was a homosexual, a minor artist who is now forgotten, and none of whose works survive, one of the lesser Florentines, a small man with a beard, a courageous coward, an exquisite, with a taste for scarlet in dress and a passion for perfumes and silks. A gentle fellow, he carried himself well, square-shouldered and erect, and his sword he managed with a grace, though he never put it to use. He had red lips and green eyes and a thick Florentine cad's curl swept away from the fine feminine forehead, and his nose was proud and and of good breeding, and his accent in the reading aloud of poetry was of the very subtlest and finest. He was older than Michelangelo and richer, and his purse was open to his friend, for he could be, though a miser by nature, generous with those he loved. But this fellow betrayed him. Yes, he betrayed him. He left his hat in the hall, and his sword too, and his scarlet-lined cloak. So Michelangelo studied Plato, and modeled the titubant Bacchus, which is commonly considered his most ignoble work. And why was all this? Ah, Bill, you may well ask. Unable to draw Michelangelo to himself as he wanted to do, he took the next best course—viz., to wit, i.e., he took Michelangelo's mistress. Surely you understand that? And so we have a rare kind of incest, we have—and a sort most painful to the heart. Now if you had a brother, Bill, and you had also a sweetheart, and this brother, behind your back, slept with your sweetheart—would you be unhappy? But I'm tired.

—I'm not surprised. Why don't you lie down again.

—What about you, Bill? I feel damned guilty about you. Have you got lots to do tomorrow.

—Nothing that counts. This is much better. I've got a patient at twelve and nothing before that. So don't worry.

—Why do I talk such tripe.

—I think there's method in your madness.

—Madness in my method. It's all the same. You must forgive me. I'd do the same for you, Bill. I've got to talk, and talk frantically. This is what I've been unconsciously looking for for a week. Something is broken. What is it. I don't know. Suddenly I'm becoming, or trying to become, a child again. Now why is that—do I see it? I half see it. But, my God, Bill, how sick it makes me to mix so much that's fraudulent with all this—at one moment what I say to you is genuine, at the next it's almost deliberately a fake. I daresay you see through the fake with your fierce analytic eye, and so it's all the same. A calculated fantasy or lie is as good as a dream, for your purpose.

—Just about. Your fantasies are pretty transparent. Which I perceive you're quite aware of.

—Oh, am I, b'gosh.

—Anyway, you fit them in pretty well.

—In the pattern, you mean, the preconceived pattern.

—The preconceived role.

—Oh, Christ, yes. Isn't it disgusting.

—Not at all. I sympathize with you. You're all right, Andy. Why not get really drunk, and let yourself go. It won't do you any harm.

—I've been drunk too much, and it does me no good.

—It's all the path to regression. Healthy enough, too. There's nothing wrong with regression, so long as you don't stick in it. It's really, in such a case as yours, a sign of creative growth. You'll eventually come out of it with something new.

—To be sure. You mean I'll get rid of that damned little winged pig, that revolting little symbol of disguised sensuality, that little pretence of idealism, that sweet little romance as to the facts of life.

—I didn't say that. You said it.

—You might just as well have said it. Don't be so niggardly. What the hell is it, Bill, that gives you such a sedentary kind of composure? I believe at bottom you're afraid of life, and your calm is the calm of the ab-negationist.

—Perhaps.

—Now you choose to be Buddhistic.

—You choose to think me so.

—I believe you're a coward.

—Thou sayest.

—Now you're playing at Christ.

—Well, spit on me, and become the wandering Jew.

—I hate you extraordinarily, Bill. You're simply revolting, when you put on this superior manner, this know-it-all air, as if you were God. You think you can look right through me, don't you. Oh, yes, you see every little shred of dirt and rot in my festering soul. And you have an unfair advantage in having known me for fifteen years or so. And in having known Bertha, too.

—Why didn't you call up Bertha today.

—Very simple—I didn't want to.

—Why not.

—Why the hell should I.

—But why not.

—Oh, for God's sake, Bill—what do you think I am.

—I don't know what you are—I merely want to know why you didn't call up Bertha.

—I didn't want to hear her voice.

—Oh, yes, you did.

—Well, all right, I did.

—So that's that.

—Very clever of you. The professor is right every time. He wanted to hear his little wife's voice, he did, but he didn't want to either, and so he didn't call her up. He knew she was there at the other end of any telephone, just waiting, just dying to be called up by her little husband, not daring to leave the apartment for fear he would call up in her absence, and call once only. But it suited him not to call her up. So he didn't. He enjoyed thinking of her there, pacing restlessly from the bedroom to the hall, from the hall to the stinking, cockroach-ridden kitchenette, crying, with a wet crumpled handkerchief on the chest of drawers, another in her left hand, a third on the mantelpiece by the lacquered candlestick, a fourth on the top of the ice chest, a fifth on the edge of the gas stove, a sixth——

—Go on and be really funny, why don't you.

—I will. Go on and be really nasty, why don't you.

—You ought to be spanked.

—Oh, no, papa, please.

—In some respects, you're behaving like a child—and a damned cruel spoiled one at that. I thought you knew better than to give in blindly and stupidly to a mere primitive possessiveness. It doesn't seem to occur to you that Bertha is going through a tragic experience too—does it.

—Oh, doesn't it, Professor. I may be a child, but I wasn't born yesterday. What does that mean, yesterday? It means tomorrow. I shall be born tomorrow, and this time it's going to be an immaculate contraception, by God.

—You said a mouthful when you spoke of dramatizing yourself. You're deliberately trying to frighten Bertha with the idea that you're going to kill yourself. She's been ringing up every one in town to find out where you are and what you're doing.

—Don't I know it?

—Of course you know it. Why don't you do something about it. Don't be so damned selfish. Just because your pride is hurt you haven't got to be criminally selfish and mean.

—Straight from the shoulder. . . . Why don't I do something about it. For God's sake, Andy, do something about it. Take your heart out and tie it up with baby ribbon and send it to poor little Bertha as a Berthaday present. Pretty hot, that one. . . . Oh, Christ, Bill. I know you're right. You know I know all that. But it isn't so damned easy, and it can't be done offhand like that—you ought to see that. It isn't only that I'm dramatizing, either. Some of it, maybe—but much more is a need for time. I want time. Good God, it would be easy enough to rush back there and cry on her perjured breast—where else do I want to go, in God's name? To Molly? Not by a damned sight. To the Dingbat sisters, or old Mary's? Well, as a matter of fact, I've been to all of them, and last night I slept with old Mary and all her lousy little pomeranians, not because I really wanted to indulge in the flesh, but simply to avoid going to Shepard Hall. Just as the three previous nights I slept in the bombproof at the Harvard Club. . . . Give me time. Let me suffer in my own way. I've got to eat the ashes and bones in my own way. If I want to die, let me want to die. I want to die.

—That's all right—sure. Go ahead. But in the meantime it isn't going to hurt you to say a word or two to Bertha.

—What sort of word or two would I say to Bertha.

—Anything to calm her a little. If you propose to go on staying away from her, just tell her everything is O. K., but that you just want a little time by yourself to think things over. Why not.

—I did call at Tom's last night.

—The hell you did.

—He was out.

—Well, thank God for that.

—Oh, I don't know.

—What did you want to do.

—I wasn't going to kill him, or even beat him up. I couldn't if I wanted to; he'd knock hell out of me. Bertha always did have an eye for athletes—the hairy-ape stuff. Now she's got her refined caveman, let her keep him. Now she's made my bed for him, let him lie in it. All I want to do is tell him what I think he is—a merd. That's all. And I shall smile as I say it to him. Hello, Tom. I just came to tell you that you're a merd.

—You still believe in magic, don't you.

—I still believe in the right of the individual to do what suits him, so long as he doesn't break the God-damned laws of this idiot society. If Bertha chooses to do what she's done, I choose to absent myself without a word. And Christ knows we had words enough—I've got to laugh.

—Laugh.

—I'm laughing. I can't think of it without laughing. Ha, ha, ha.

—That's the funniest sounding laugh I ever heard, if you'll excuse my saying so.

—Step up, ladies and gents, and listen to the laughing embryo. He laughs through his primordial gills, like a lizard. He applauds himself with tiny dorsal fins, and his eyes, now shut with tears, are when opened much too large and all-seeing. He sees bang to the end of the world. The grave has no secrets from him, the tomb no horrors; when he is born tomorrow he will have a bone in his mouth, and this he will present on his birthday to his loving mother, who is none other than our old friend the worm. All his days he will walk attended by an orchestra of Elizabethan worms. The death-watch beetle will precede him in his march to the frontiers of consciousness; and arrived there on the final morning, it is he himself who, by thumbing his nose at God, will give the signal for the trump of doom. Which, in the circumstances, will be a great disappointment.

—You bet it will.

—Old Mary is a brick. You never met old Mary, did you. You ought to meet her—a grand old dame. Getting too fat, you know, and past middle age, too, but she's a good sport. And it's a liberal education to spend a night with her. What she doesn't know about this town you could write on a two-cent stamp. She knows the college inside out—you'd be surprised, Bill, you'd be really surprised. More than one member of the faculty has wept on Mary's ample scented bosom, and told her the secrets of Cambridge. Good God, did you ever go to Sanders Theater, to a Thursday night symphony, and see the wives of the professors? Of course you have. It's a joke. If it weren't for Mary and a few others, those poor fellows would be dead, that's what. Why, they aren't female at all. They're a kind of lichen. Have you ever talked with one at a dinner party, or a Brattle Street tea? Of course you have. Oh, God, they're so refined and intelligent—what a lot they think they know—and their estimable husbands have to sneak off to old Mary just to be reminded that they're alive. What a joke, what a joke. Mary knows the names of their children, and how old they are, and where

they go to school, and when they have measles, and when they die, or are
born, and what Professor X's bank balance is, and the fact that poor old Y
is going to be fobbed off with an associate professorship instead of a full
professorship—why she knows as much as old Terry used to know, and
that's saying a lot. And straight as a die, too. She never lets you down. I
told her all about Bertha.

—What did she say.

—Just what you say, only better.

—For example.

—Forget it, she said—forget it, kid. You aren't exactly an angel yourself, are you, to be expecting miracles of yuman nature. She always call it
yuman nature. She always calls me kid, too—I suppose because she remembers me when I was twenty-one or two.

—What else did she say.

—Is this the inquisition? Or judgment day? And are you God?

—I am God the Father.

—Then Mary is the Virgin Queen. She said—what did she say. She
told me not to be a fool. She gave me some damned good whisky, and
massaged my head, and showed me photographs of her one and only love,
some time in the last century, and told me not to be a fool. We discussed
the ethics of suicide, lying in bed with a pomeranian. She complained of
the streetcars in Massachusetts Avenue—they kept her awake at night. She
wished she still had her apartment in Day Street—she got fired out of that
because one of her visiting girls got drunk too often and was noisy. She was
sentimental about the apartment in Day Street, for she had lived there
twelve years. Old Foxy Smith—do you remember Foxy Smith, the gentle
old dodo who used to teach us history—was one of her regular visitors for
years. He used to come there straight from a faculty meeting, wearing
rubbers. Can you imagine it, Bill. What an old saint and prig we used to
think he was. And Mary was very fond of him, took care of him, sewed on
his buttons, darned his socks, gave him advice about his health, knew
he was dying of cancer long before any one else did: he told her about it
more than a year before he died. When he died, she went to the service in
Appleton Chapel, and saw his wife for the first time. Strange, isn't it? She
knew him better than his own wife did. She sent some flowers anonymously,
too. My God. Foxy used to talk about suicide with her. He thought of
killing himself before his cancer got too bad. She persuaded him not to.
When I asked her why, she said, well, she thought we ought to live out our
lives as God intended. If death by cancer was indicated, we must die of
cancer. To my suggestion that death by suicide might be indicated, she
replied with a stubborn no, no, no, no—slapping my hand each time. She
appealed to the pomeranian for support, his name is Yale, but Yale was
discreetly silent. Now that's a queer and beautiful business, Bill—I'm
having another drink, and one of these crackers. She gave the old fellow
what little joy he had. Just the same, his wife wouldn't have been very
grateful, would she, although I don't doubt she thought she loved him—
perhaps she did love him.

—You amuse me. That shoe seems to fit you.

—Not at all.

—Sure it does. Look at it.

—I'm looking. But I never did think the sexes were reversible in this regard. A woman can share a man, but a man can't share a woman. And that's all there is to it.

—Oh, for the love of mud.

—Thank you, I'm not very fond of mud.

—Anyway, I'm glad to see you're calming down.

—Don't fool yourself.

—Oh, yes, you are.

—Are you trying to annoy me? Don't bully me. When I want to be calm, I'll be calm. I'm not calm. I'm quiet, but I'm not calm. I'm so full of hate you could poison New York with me. Is it hate? No, it isn't hate. Yes, it is, too. I wouldn't at all mind killing Bertha and Tom. If mere feelings could kill them, they'd be dead. The damned incestuous——

—That's the keynote, all right.

—What is.

—Incest. Don't you see what you're doing?

—Your conversational manners are very insinuating.

—Don't you?

—Well, tell me, don't badger me, tell me.

—In every one of your love affairs, you've tried to make your sweetheart your mother. That's why they've all been unsuccessful. Why do you want to do it?—that's the question. It won't work. That's why sooner or later you reject or abandon them all, or they abandon you—they have to. You force them to. Bertha is no exception.

—You make me sick. Do you mean to say I've abandoned Bertha? Don't be a fool. Or don't *try* to be a fool.

—I don't mean you left in the sense of moving from Cambridge to Reno—that's immaterial. Abandonment needn't be geographical.

—God, that's funny. Abandonment needn't be geographical! You'll be the death of me. Was Casanova geographically abandoned?

—You may not have left her board—but you left her bed. Or so you told me.

—You're damned unpleasant. Let's talk about something else.

—You mean the subject is unpleasant. I thought you wanted to talk it out.

—What a hell of a lot of books you have, Bill. How did you ever pick them all up. Aren't the Japanese a wonderful little people? And the ants too. I once thought what a good satire on man could be written with the ant as the subject. You see? Everything would reduce itself to terms of ant. In short, one would reduce everything to the anthropocentric—pretty good, that. Naturally, from the ant's point of view, all the characteristics of the ant would be considered virtues. The highest praise of an ant would be that he was, as you would expect, antly. Statues, of heroic size, would be erected to the great ant heroes—warriors, builders, or what not—inscribed with phrases like, "He was the antliest ant of all time." . . . And of course there would be an anthropomorphic god.

—Resistance.

—What the hell do you mean.

—All this is just your evasion of what is for you a painful subject—
something you don't dare look in the eye. Yourself.

—Yes, indeed. There are many things I don't look in the eye, my dear
Bill. Why should I. Most, if not all, aspects of existence are disagreeable.
The art of living is the art of the exclusion or mitigation of the disagreeable. Why go about deliberately rubbing one's snout in the mud? Not by a
damned sight. What the hell is whisky for? What the hell is music for, or
painting, or poetry, or psychoanalysis? All of them escapes. Don't tell me
analysis is an abstract pure science—good God no. It's an anodyne, both
for the analyst and the patient, and they both enjoy it thoroughly. It's a
debauch at one remove. You can't fool me. No. There you are, in your
God-damned Morris chair—I hate that chair—goggling at me and leering
and having a hell of a good time ferreting out my secrets—why? Disinterested service to mankind? Not by a hell of a way. You're a paltry little
voyeur. Afraid to live yourself, you take it out by digging into other peoples'
little filths and disasters. Yes, by God. That's what it is. Vicarious sexperi-
ence! What a dirty little thrill you get in reminding me that I stopped
sleeping with Bertha! And in suspecting all sort of dirty little reasons for it!
I drink to you, Bill, old boy—you have a swell time, don't you. You wrap
yourself in all the dirty sheets of the world. The world is your soiled-clothes
basket. What's them spots on the sheet, Miranda? Oh, them's the
maculate conception, them is.

—Ha, ha. There's a hell of a lot in what you say.

—Of course there is. Have a drink.

—Why do you hate this chair.

—Oh, pitiful little Bill.

—You're fond of the word *little*, and the word *dirty*, aren't you.

—Dirty little.

—Equals fecal infantine.

—Look at the snow, Bill—it must be six inches deep.

—No, I think it's seven.

—We are seven. Against Thebes. Did you ever read the Anabasis? Do
you remember the Arabian sparrows?

—You mentioned them before. Why do you mention them again.

—Damned if I know. Rather funny.

—Why don't you sit down, instead of pacing around the room. That's
the second time you've knocked over that ash stand. Give it a rest.

—Perhaps I'd better. Whoooof.

—Do you feel sick.

—No. I'm all right. A little bewildered all of a sudden, that's all.

—Eat some crackers.

—No, I'm all right. I'm all right. But what a whirl. I thought I was
unhappy. What a whirl, what a joke. You know the feeling. Delirious,
delicious. Clutching the inevitable. The postage-stamp going for a ride on
the back of the ant. What did I say to her? *Ma non è vero. Voi credete che
si muove—ma non è vero.* And she laughed like hell. . . . Christ, what a
breeze.

—Yes, indeed. I suppose you see it.

—Why shouldn't I—pigs see the wind, and it's pink. But, my God, how

I hurt her feelings. *Ma non è vero.* She said she saw me in the Piazza, drinking a cup of *café nero* at one of those iron tables, and that I was thinking. I denied it. I never think. And she laughed like hell.

—What the hell are you talking about.

—From Venice as far as Belmont.

—Why don't you try to take a nap.

—Good God, man, what am I? Don't be insulting. Take a nap yourself if you feel like it. Go on, you take it. Take the couch. Wrap your feet in snow, it's pure. Puzzle record number two is now ready, on sale at the nearest dealer. Contains two tunes. Can you find them. I think I'll be an advertising man. There's no money in private tutoring. None. Never. But puzzle record number two is now ready, that's the think to remember. That ought to interest any analyst. Analist. How do you pronounce the anal? Christ, what a breeze.

—I'm laughing.

—That's good of you. Presently I'll laugh too, I'll join you. Take a seat, madam, and I'll join you presently.

—What's this about Venice.

—As far as Belmont. Shakespeare said that. He was always saying things like that. He said everything, the damned bastard, except the truth. But, my God, how I hurt her. I think she was in love with me. She was teaching me Italian at the Berlitz—excuse me—school. And I ran away from her. I paid off and left without even saying good-by to her. She saw me. She came out into the hall just as I was paying the bill, and saw me. And even then, I didn't say anything to her. I just smiled. What kind of a smile, Bill? There are many kinds of a smile. You know. This was a guilty smile, a Judas smile, a cut-throat smile, a tombstone smile. *E divieto il nuoto. Il nuoto è vietato.* As if anybody would want to swim in their foul canals anyway. Did you ever see them? Jesus. It's a lot of liquid garbage. But at the Lido, those German fräuleins, with their one-piece bathing suits and their delirious, upstanding breasts—Christ, what a breeze. And strawberries, too, *con panna.* She admired Tiepolo. One afternoon we took a gondola and saw them all. Putty cupids. Wings everywhere. Angels ascending and descending and all diaphanous—such pinks and blues, Bill, such pallors of pink and blue. But that was far away. And then there was—hell, I can't even remember her name. At Interlaken. I ran all the way from Venice to Interlaken, and the hotel was only just opened for the season, and I was the only person there, and the maid who waited on the table—I've forgotten her name. Elsa! When I paid my bill after a week, the manageress looked hard at me and said, "Elsa will be sorry you go. She will miss you." I went back into the dining room and gave Elsa a good tip, I don't remember how much it was. She was crying. I told her the number of my room, but she never came. I told her I would take her for a walk, on her afternoon off, but I never did. I said she ought to marry and have six children, all of them with blue eyes and golden hair, and she laughed, she giggled, she simpered, she went to the other side of the room and stood up on a chair, pretending to rearrange dishes on a shelf, so that I could have a good look at her legs. My God, I was excited about her. But when I saw she was excited too, I got frightened. I ran away again, this time to Paris.

What I really wanted was to get back to the Atlantic Ocean, to salt water, freedom. Something I knew. I wanted to leave behind me my wife, Elsa, and my six blue-eyed golden-haired children, by gum. Elsa, with her lovely teeth, false every one of them. That's what Alan said. I met him later in London, and told him about her, and he said he would go there, in Interlaken, and give her my love. He did, and she cried again. And he said, on a postcard, I love her false teeth, every one of them. Just the same, she was damned pretty, damned nice. I'm sorry about it. At this very minute I might be living in a Swiss châlet with Elsa and the six children and the cow. And an Alp-horn, Bill!

—What the hell.

—Where else, Cambridge, Mass. Harvard Central Kendal Park, through the subway in the dark. But this was later, much later. And now Alan is dead, and all the others are dead, everybody I loved is dead, whenever I pick up a newspaper somebody is dead. Anyway, Elsa's skull will have detachable teeth. What a rush there must be on the escalator to hell. Among the lost people. *Per me si va nella città dolente.* Have your tickets ready, with your passport, please—have your tickets ready, with your passport, please. Brattle Street is, as you might say, one of the main arteries of hell. Cambridge is a flourishing suburb. What swarms of hypocrites there be mounting the slopes of Calvary.

—Why Calvary again.

—Ah, but my dear chap, I've changed it this time. That's my cunning. You thought you'd caught me, didn't you. Why, here's some Rhine wine, some *echt* love-lady milk, as I live and breathe.

—I wouldn't begin mixing drinks, if I were you.

—But you aren't me, Bill. *Quod erat demonstrandum.* Why not hang yourself on the wall like a bat beside that rusty harpoon. Upside down, like Dracula on the turret. Jesus! What a turn that gave me, in Paris, on Christmas Eve! It was snowing, too, just like tonight. Snowbroth. . . . Oh, sorry, damn that ash stand anyway. Why do you have it. It's ugly.

—Why don't you sit down.

—I will. There's nothing I like better. Whoooof. My God, that went fast. But I saw it going, just the same.

—What.

—I think it was the *nasturtium quid.*

—What did it look like.

—Excuse me. I'm not really drunk, Bill. I'm not as much of a fool as you think. I can see pretty straight. I am thinking clearly, too. Very clearly. I see you distinctly, there, you with your three eyes, and an extra one in your ear. Oh, I know what you have them for, it's all right, I understand it perfectly, every man to his taste, as the farmer said when he kissed the pig. There's the pig again. But this death business. This dying business. These coffins. These funeral parlors. These greasy undertakers, and the ribbons on doors. Do you know what, Bill? We're dying piecemeal. Every time some one you know dies, you die too, a little piece of you. Now a fingernail, now an eyelash. A hair today, a corpuscle tomorrow. Slowly, slowly. The liver, then the lights. And the worst of it is that what's dead isn't buried: it rots in you. There's Alan, dead in my side. Elsa, dead in my prostate gland. Uncle David, dead in my right hand. My father, dead in my memory of geometry, turned to a putrid phosphorescent rhomboid. I'm a walking graveyard, a meditative dance of death. So are you. A bone orchard. Why if I were to investigate you, Bill—good God, how I widen my eyes at the mere thought! I'd probably know why you're an amateur analyst. I'd know why you're afraid to speak out. Why you sit there and wait for your poor fool of a patient to do the speaking for you. Who died on you, Bill? Who lies dead on your heart? Oh, Jesus. I feel sick. But that eye in your ear. What's that, synesthesia? Dislocation? *Per auram wollen sie? Und das hat mit ihrem singen. Per auram.* I suppose it was your little sister, who died when you were twelve. I'm sorry—I shouldn't have said that. Perhaps it was only a cat. But this death business—aren't you really dead, Bill? And if not, why not? I'm dead. Any further death for me would be merely, as it were, a publication. No essential addition. Just take the bones out, Felix, and spread them on the grass. Burn them, and spread them on the grass. I feel sick.

—I don't wonder. Why don't you try the Roman feather.

—Don't be simple-minded, you idiot. I don't feel sick in any sense so God-damned easy.

—No?

—No.

—Then where's your mother.

—Ah, ha! The cloven hoof. I knew I'd get you down to that at last.

—Down to what.

—The mother.

—Speak for yourself, Andy. I'm only trying to help you.

—Yes yes yes yes. So you are. Good old Bill. Top hole. But this death business. This dying, this piecemeal dying. This death that creeps in from the extremities, slowly, slowly—and up from the unconscious, too, darkly —these dreams of death, corruption, rot—it's all been said, I know, I'm tiresome. But it's real, just the same. To lie in massed corruption, and to stink. To walk through cold corruption, and to speak. To think through foul abstractions, and to live. You know what I mean. I hate you, but I'll tell you. Shall I tell you? Yes, I'll tell you. You don't deserve it. You understand nothing, you have no perceptions, you're a fool, a well-meaning fool, a failure, but I'll tell you. What is it gives you such a power over the subtle, Bill? Your pseudonymous calm? No doubt. Your rare combination of muscle and breadth of brow. Brawn and brains. But the brains, not so hot. Not so hot. Why, with your stupidity and my brains, Bill, we'd rock the world. Let me see—I was going to tell you something. What was it. Oh, yes, it was my dream last night. This will be easy for you, and I make you a present of it, gratis. How did it begin? I was asleep with Bertha, that was it—and she woke me. She said we must go upstairs. So I got up and followed her upstairs, taking my pillow with me. It seemed to be a strange house, and yet somehow familiar. At the top of the stairs we went into a dark bedroom, and there, in a wide double bed, with a single bed beyond, were my mother and father. My father was in the single bed, and Bertha walked around to it. Meanwhile, I myself—tee-hee—crept softly into the wide bed with my mother, who was asleep. Isn't this a beauty? Could consciousness go further in deliberate self-torture? I lay on my side, facing my sleeping mother, drew up my knees, and by accident touched her flank with one of my hands. I felt very small, my head and hands were small, my hair was close-cropped and thick (you see how young I was)—and also, suddenly, I was filled with horror. I got up hastily, and spoke to Bertha, who was somewhere in the dark. Told her I was going. She answered from the dark: "Do you call this a MARRIAGE?" I ran out into the hall, and darted down the stairs, which were dark, and there I discovered a strange thing—the stairs were strewn with the family silver—forks and knives and spoons were scattered all up and down, some of them still sliding slowly and heavily, as if only just launched downard by the burglar, who, I assumed, must be still in the house—a nameless ghost-like horror came over me, and I woke up. I woke up. Sweating.

—Jupiter and Semele.

—I don't get you, but we needn't go into it. Every man to his own interpretation, all of them correct. Oedipus complex, castration complex, anything you like.

—What about that silver.

—My family silver, that's all.

—You recognized it.

—You bet. Acanthus pattern and everything.

—I suppose you have it?

—Of course I have it. It came down to me from my mother! . . . Hot dog.

—Pretty good. I don't seem to know much about your mother. You've never spoken much about her, have you.

—Why should I.

—How did she die.

—She was drowned.

—How old were you.

—Twelve. Anything else? I'd got all my second teeth. I knew how to read and write. My favorite book was *Jackanapes*. After that, *Twenty Thousand Leagues Under the Sea*. As you might expect.

—You said it, Andy! You're helpless. None so blind as those who see and doubt it. You know all this, but you won't let it do you any good. Isn't that it? Think it over.

—Oh, for God's sake, Bill.

—Anything you like. That's a swell dream.

—Isn't it, though? By God, yes. I knew you'd like it. But wait till I tell you the one about the bones.

—Why not go into this one a little more, first.

—Oh, no, what's the use. It's all as plain as a codpiece.

—It is to me. I'm not so sure it is to you.

—Take my word for it. I know what you mean—don't be stupid! Sure, I'll have a cracker and a drink. Why, hello, Michel, old fellow! Are you still there? My God, if I could only sculp—is that the word?—I'd twist the whole damned college yard into a single group of agonized gods that would send the northstar west. What a chance, what a chance. I'd squeeze Appleton Chapel with one squeeze into such a shape of hypocrisy and cold slow sweat as even Cambridge would recognize. . . . Take it from *me*, kid, take it from me.

—So you're resisting again, eh.

—Why not. I believe in resistance. Why acquiesce.

—There's a lot to be said for acquiescence, Andy—and you know it. Don't you.

—Oh, have it your own way. You want every one to be a yes-man. A pitiful dirty little yea-sayer. No ironies, no doubts. Everything for the best. God is good, the snail's on the heart. And all that kind of honeycomb tripe. If you feel sick, why, yes, that's good, that is, and all the swarm of sick lights in the brain that go with it, now to port and now to starboard. I see them now. Maggots. What the hell. Put your head down. No, I'll open the window. . . . Thanks. . . . That's better. . . . How they drift, Bill, how they drift, did you ever notice? In little slow streams, and then hot swarms, and then little slow streams again and then all swooping upward like a lost meal. Woops, my dear. I'll put my lunch out into Massachusetts Avenue, shall I? A nice warm waffle for some nocturnal policeman to study. If he were really intelligent, he'd know what I'd been thinking, wouldn't he.

—Go on, try the feather.

—Get the hell out of here.

—Just as you like.

—Of course it is. This is just what I like. A cold band of air on my pituitary body. That intersteller current of the soul. Birdwings, too, and the albatross, and the arctic sponge of nescience. . . . This is free association.

—So I see.

—See something else for a change. Go fry yourself.

—Go kill yourself. Jump out, why don't you.

—I would for a nickel.

—Here's the nickel.

—Let me see it. Why it's actually a nickel.

—Why not cut out the melodrama for a change and settle down to a little hard thinking?

—You mean hard drinking, Bill. I've thought too much.

—You've behaved like a spanked child.

—Well, why not, that's what I am.

—You needn't be. And you needn't think only of yourself.

—So you're going to preach again.

—I'm just telling you the truth.

—Keep the truth for yourself. What I want is darkness. I want to sleep. I want the sea and the moon. Above all, the sea. Did you ever think of it. Did it ever really terrify you and delight you. You know, at midnight, under a brown wild moon, with a warm south wind, and a surf running. So that the surf is all of sinister curled bronze, and the sound fills the whole damned night, and the beach looks like a parchment on which nothing has been written. Nothing. Wide silver. Smooth. I know just where it is, too. North of the Gurnett. Not far from Clark's Island. The seals are on it, and I rowed there in the dark. I had a tin can to bail with. Did you ever row a dory, Bill. I had one, it was named Doris, and a little four-pronged anchor, which I buried in the beach. I love the feeling of a sea-soaked rope, a salt-water painter. And the slow sluggish slushy grind of the flat bottom as it slides up the sand and pebbles and swings to one side. . . . What was I saying.

—You were talking about your childhood.

—So I was.

—It made me homesick.

—You don't mean to say you had a childhood, Bill.

—You'd be astonished.

—Why have you never mentioned it.

—Why should I.

—Well, anyway, it's still snowing, isn't it.

—I note the interrogative touch, and congratulate you.

—Yes. . . . Mum's the word. . . . This snow on the wrist feels good. Try it.

—Do you remember——

—What.

—No.

—Christ. I see disasters, and I bring them back. The whole world fills with fecal madness. I am a—I am here, in Cambridge, Mass. You offered me a nickel to jump out of the window. I didn't jump, because you showed me up. So I'm quite properly ashamed. Evidently I don't want to die, which is what you wanted to prove, isn't it? If I want to live; what do I want to live for. What. Rhetorical question. For hot dogs and western sandwiches. The feel of walking, which is a matter of always keeping the left foot going. The sound of the clock. Step up, ladies and gents, and see the fellow who lives with his left eye on the almighty clock. It's all a matter of keeping the hand going. Har har.

—The right hand.

—*Voi credete che si muove, ma non è vero.*

—From Venice as far as Belmont.

—Farther, if you like. I'll ask no questions, and I'll tell no lies.

—For God's sake, Andy, settle down. This gets us nowhere.

—Don't I know it?

—Well, it's late.

—Where? Lateness is relative.

—For one thing, it's late in Shepard Hall. I mean, to be brutally frank, it's late for Bertha.

—Too damned late, if you ask me! But I'm sorry, Bill. You know how it is. How can I say it. I can't. There's all this—there's all that. The heres, the theres, the unders, the overs. The pasts, the futures. The dirty stockings, and the dirty sinks. Peeled potatoes. Beds, here and there. One after another. The clipped fingernails on the floor. Coffee grounds, Brattle Hall dances, lemon peels, the Dramatic Club, muddy galoshes in the front hall, and bills from the cleaner. Just ordinary human dirt and effluvia, you know. One night after another. Sweat under the arms, gouts of pink toothpaste clotted on the toothbrush that hangs on the wall. The little crinkled hairs left in the bathtub, too—so telltale. Intimacy! Why the hell do we want it? . . . Don't tell me.

—That's the question to begin with, perhaps.

—Or end with. . . . I'll close the window. The snow seems to be coming in.

—Thanks.

—That's the question to begin with. It can't be done. Not permanently. Everything against it. So beautiful, too, so beautiful, so bloody beautiful—but is it possible? No, I don't think it is.

—Not for you, perhaps. Why not.

—Why not. . . . The exquisite beginning, in mystery always—the subtleties of the approach—the sunrise wonder—Alpenglow on the Jungfrau—joke, Bill, joke. But when you've spent a night on the Jungfrau, that's another matter, by God. A different kettle of fish, a nightmare of another color. Now don't open your mouth with that supercilious arch—I know what you're going to say—you're going to quote Stekel about Don Juan and Casanova, or something like that. Oh, yes, indeed. Step up, ladies and gents, and see the juvenile don Giovanni. Why, the poor fellow's lost his mother, he has, and that's why he smokes and drinks. But old Mary's as good a mother as you could want. You ought to see her in her bath. Marvelous, the aplomb with which she sponges that enormous pink and white area, and the candor of it, the absence of shame—she's a good child of nature, and clean as a sea-cloud. Yes. Yale always barks beside the tub, and Mary scatters water at him and laughs. And the equipment of that bathroom, Bill! . . . What the hell am I talking about.

—Intimacy, I believe!

—So I was. . . . Intimacy. . . . That's where marriages break down. That's just where they break down. That's why Shakespeare left home, and Michelangelo never had one, or Beethoven either. That's why Melville tried to wring his wife's neck. Good jumping Jehosaphat, isn't it plain as day? Do I need to say another word? Why don't you go to bed.

—I'm wide awake. I may close my eyes, to rest them, but I'll be awake, you can go on talking. . . . So you've got the horrors.

—The horrors, yes. And don't misunderstand me. But what the hell do I mean, I wonder. What horrors. Why the horrors. What's wrong with it. Why can't it last. There are the obsessions, as when one is gardening. You kill aphids, millions of them, day after day—squashing them against the rose stalks between your thumb and finger, green juices, green pulp, tiny clots, one rosebud after another, and finally you get an obsession—at all times of the day or night you see the swarms of little green insects, feel them thickly under your fingers, you even begin dreaming about them, a foul clotting of them occurs in your dreams, you have them under your fingernails, they fall in solid green coagulations from behind your ears, they are in your hair—that's the way it is. That's the way it is with sex, I mean. I must have a small drink. Do you see what I mean. It's the endless repetition of what should very seldom be repeated. Is that it? I don't know. I've thought about this a lot. It's very baffling. By god, no matter how much you love a woman, the time comes when you don't want to sleep with her. For a while, anyway. Or at any rate one wants holidays. But how are you going to manage it. You can't say to your wife, Darling, I'm fed up with you—I know your body too well—the toes, the knees, the flanks, the moles, the hollows under the clavicles, the median line, the asymmetrical arrange-

ment of your breasts, the pelvis, the pink patch of eczema on your side,
your perfumes and undergarments and brushes and combs, your toilet
habits, every one, the faint bubble of caught breath with which you fall
asleep—but just the same I love you, will always love you. If only you'll be
tactful and not too exacting about this. Don't ask questions, darling, whatever you do. Don't say a word. Sing cheerfully as you go about the house,
greet me with the happiness of the lark when I come home, be busy, have
lots of things to do, put no pressure upon me, don't betray by so much as
the flicker of an eyelash that you're aware of the fact that I've abandoned
you (but not geographically)—and who knows, one fine night, or one night
when it's raining cats and dogs, or snowing like this, or we're both a little
tight after a party—who knows, who knows? Everything might suddenly
become beautiful and strange once more. You would be a stranger to me,
and I to you; we would commit a joyful infidelity with each other; each
of us would be new. Hell's delight, that's only the beginning of it. The
fringe.

—You've said it.

—What do you know about it, you're not married.

—I don't need to be.

—How many times have you told me that if you hadn't been analyzed,
you couldn't know anything about analysis. Woops, my dear. I've been
hit with a hammer. My head's ringing.

—Go on with this idea—this might be helpful.

—Ask me an easier one, old chap. Would you like to see my spleen?
It's a nice little spleen, never yet broken, either. Bertha never understood
that. No. Nor cleanliness either. The strange things she did. I read a short
story once about this. Yes. Very good. A husband who had left his wife
and his best friend fell in love with her. You see. They were quite amiable
about it, they were still good friends, and the other fellow decided to
marry her. You see. But he was damned inquisitive about the husband's
reasons, and one night when they'd dined together, he asked him, point
blank, why it was. The husband merely said that it was something absolutely unmentionable, that it would be a terrible injustice to his wife to
speak of it. Result—can you guess it? The friend went off by himself to
Bermuda, and the wife was left high and dry. . . . Zingoids! I've got rings
like Saturn. Can you see them.

—Not from here.

—Oh, yes, that lovely story of the idiot. What, from here? Ha, ha, ha.

—But those things can always be managed with a little understanding
and patience. No need to get excited about them. And what about the pot
and the kettle? Are you so damned immaculate yourself? I'll bet dollars
to doughnuts you sometimes don't change your socks often enough, or let
your toenails grow too long, or forget to shave, or smell of good honest
male sweat. What about it. And Bertha probably never said a word of it,
did she.

—Of course not. Why the hell should she. Women don't feel the
same way about the physical aspect of a man as he does about the woman.
No. No. You know that, what's the use arguing about it.

—The hell she doesn't.

—The hell she does. She even likes a little uncouthness—a rough chin, a careless shirt or tie—dirty fingernails—you know damned well she does, Bill, so there's no use trying to kid me. But Bertha is careless. She is unfeminine. Good Lord, you ought to see some of the underclothes she wears. They look as if they were made of cardboard, or sheet iron or something. Or cut out of circus tents. What the hell. Doesn't a woman know any better than that?

—I suspect this is just a cover.

—Cover! . . . What next. You make me laugh. I don't say there aren't other things, too, but that isn't saying that this business didn't hit me pretty hard. It would have hit anyone. You wait! Tom will get it. I'll bet he's got a surprise already. . . . Jesus. Jesus! I see disasters and I bring them back. Fecal madness. I didn't want to think of it. I didn't want to think of it. It's like a sword, a red hot sword. When I think of it I go mad —I see it in every detail. What time did he get there. Did they have dinner together. When was the first time. Where. In what order did they go to the bedroom. She first? Both together? Oh, God, Bill. Isn't it funny how, when a thought is too painful, you give way to definite physical impulses—find yourself actually averting your face, looking out of a window, making a gesture of erasure with your hand, as if at a child's blackboard—making speeches too to yourself, words that have no sense in them, just to divert the current of your madness. The moon, Andrew, what price the raucous moon. Third alive, third rail alive. Why did you speak to me like that you pimply pimpernel. Or you address a picture on the wall, or a candlestick on the mantel, you pace up and down and fling words at it over your shoulder, madder and madder words, you swear at it, you call it a merd, a pimp, a slut, a whore, you take the candlestick and wring its neck, shouting, then smash it on the floor—and then you turn away from it ashamed, as if it were watching you, for you know that if you don't turn away you're going to cry abominably, you already feel the contraction in the throat, a rigidity in your eyes, a stare of blindness that begets tears. No. I won't look at it. I won't remember it. I won't think of their going along the hall together, or to the bathroom. O God, O God, O God. Why did she do it. Why did she do it. Why the hell did she do it, Bill, how *could* she do it. If she'd come to me and confessed that she was falling in love with him, that would have been bad enough, would almost have killed me, but to wait like this till I was in New York——

—How do you know she did? What makes you think there was anything planned or deliberate in it? My impression, as a matter of fact, is that the whole thing was accident, an impulse.

—Don't fool yourself. Fred says he's suspected it for a week, and that Tom's been going there every night during that time.

—That's got nothing to do with it. I think it came by accident.

—I don't believe you.

—You wouldn't.

—Resistance, I suppose. Oh, damn you amateur analysts and all your pitiful dirty abstract jargon. Why can't you say what you mean. Why can't you call a spade a spade. What the hell's the difference between the soul and the subconscious and the unconscious and the will. Or between castra-

tion complex and inferiority complex and Oedipus complex. Words.
Evasions. Vanities, on the part of the respective respectable analysts. *Nicht
wahr*. For the love of mud, define any one of them for me, so that I'll know
absolutely what they mean. Or tell me where they reside in the brain.
Have you ever looked at a map of the brain? It's like those imaginary
maps of Mars. Full of Arabia Desertas. Canals, seas, mountains, glaciers,
extinct volcanoes, or ulcers. The pock-marked moonface of the mind. And
all that strange congregation of scars, that record of wounds and fissures,
is what speaks and acts. I speak with it, you listen with it. What the hell.
What have I got to do with it? Nothing. Something hurts me, and I act.
Something else hurts me, and I speak. If I could act, I wouldn't speak.
Voilà. All your bloody psychology in a nutshell. For which reason, Bill,
Cambridge, Mass., is the city of free speech. The women talk freely, the
men sometimes act, but more often die. Isn't it funny? The colossal hum-
bug of it. But it's changing, just the same, it's changing. And that's funnier
still. All the gentle dodos going down Brattle Street in their rubbers to
lecture on Grimm's law or the finals in syphilis or the abrogation of the
electron, and their fiendish hatchetfaced wives going to mothers' meetings, where they discuss the psychology of the child, without knowing to
begin with what the devil a human animal is, and meanwhile their adolescent sons and daughters are dancing naked on Belmont Hill or going on
moonlit bathing parties *au naturel* at Gloucester, or simply getting quietly
and lubriciously drunk together in Prescott Street or where have you. And
the secret little affairs that go on. Good God! How the old dodos would
faint if they knew about it. Just cast your eye over the list of our acquaintances. How many happy married couples? Eh? You could count them on
your nostrils. X flirting openly with the wife of Y, while his wife, talking
about it frankly everywhere, sets her cap at Z, and tells you at tea about the
roses he sent her. If he does it, she said to me, why shouldn't I? Where do
the children come in. Then look at Ann. Did I tell you about my little
flurry with Ann. No. It didn't amount to much, but it was significant. Is
that the word. . . . I feel funny. Rarefied. Is there any oxygen in here.

—Help yourself.

—I thought you'd gone.

—Oh, no. I'm waiting for Ann. Who is Ann. I never heard of her.

—Ah, Ann. Neither had I. That's part of the joke. A total stranger, but
not teetotal.

—Yes, yes.

—Yes. It was when I went once, a month ago, to call on Tom, you
know, in Montrose Hall. I was a little tight, as usual. Just a little. Vague.
You know, I have a key to Tom's apartment—I used to use it to work in, or
play the piano. Oh, yes, many's the time I've played the "Liebestod" there.
But that's not the point. What's the point . . . I feel floooey.

—Ann.

—Ann. Yes. Was I talking about Ann? But I never told you about Ann,
did I. No.

—No. Go ahead.

—Well, it was funny about Ann. . . . Hell, I feel drunk. Wait a minute. I'll eat some crackers again. Perhaps if I stand up. Can I put some water on the fire. It's much too hot in here. Much too hot. Can I.

—Sure, go ahead.

—Look at the steam.

—This amuses me.

—What's this mean. A symbol. Symbolical Bill the sailor.

—All right, it's out. Don't pour any more in, it will make a mess.

—Ha, ha, you're afraid of messes, aren't you? Why is that?

—Why are you afraid of fires. I've seen you do this before.

—The hell you have. You know too much. Anybody'd think you spent your time shadowing me. Good God, Bill, a fire in a steamheated apartment is an affectation anyway. But to go back to the key——

—Yes, the key. You've been stalling long enough.

—Oh, go crawl up a gum tree. The key—yes, the key. Let me see. Just how did it happen. I can't seem to remember. Oh, yes, oh, yes. Now I remember. You see, I was a little tight, just a little vague, you know, and I got out of the elevator at the wrong floor. The floor above. And they all look just alike. And so I went to the door of Tom's flat and opened it and walked in: and what do you think. It wasn't Tom's flat at all. No. It was a different one, or else everything in it had been changed. Very puzzling. I stood there and stared at it, there was a picture of a clipper ship right opposite the door, where it had never been before, and a banjo clock beside it and an umbrella stand with a red umbrella in it. You can imagine my surprise. I stood and goggled at them. Funny—I thought—what the hell has Tom been doing. Then I walked into the sitting room, and the piano was gone, everything else was changed, and where the table ought to be was a terrible green plush sofa, under the window, and on the green plush sofa was Ann. And I stood there with the key in my hand—you see, the key had fitted the lock—and stared at Ann, and Ann stared at me. You can imagine my surprise. And Ann said, "Well, who let *you* in." And I said, "My little key let me in. Isn't it funny? What floor *is* this, anyway?" And Ann said, the sixth, and began to laugh at me. So I laughed too, just to be agreeable, and we laughed together, and then she said that as I was already in, I might as well stay, so I stayed. In no time at all we were talking about God and life and death and love and marriage and babies and birth control and the morals of the new generation and the difference between the East and the West and the difference between the sexes and whether pure friendship is possible between them and what a young girl should do in a big city if she's a stranger there and what drinks we liked and whether it was better to marry or not and at what age and if one didn't marry whether one should remain a virgin (you see, she meant herself) and if you didn't remain a virgin whether you should tell your husband when you *did* marry. Just like that. Bang, bang, bang. Everything opened with a zipper. We had some drinks, and then we made some coffee, and she played the phonograph, a lot of jazz, and we had some more drinks, and we told the stories of our lives, every damned detail, and she cried and said she was terribly lonely in Cambridge, where she didn't know a soul, and she was bored with the art school and hated everybody there, they were all so cold and superior and so unlike the Westerners and she couldn't make friends of them. It was terribly sad, terribly. You have no idea. I was overcome. I told her I would give her a good time, take her to dances, dinners, shows, prize fights, introduce her to lots of people, and she cried some more and kissed me very, very nicely. About three o'clock, when I suggested that we go to bed, why not, she looked archly at me and said, "Be yourself!" That was her favorite remark: be yourself. She must have learned it from Socrates. So we talked some more, and kissed some more. Now and then she would draw back very coyly and bat her long golden eyelashes at me and tidy her beyootiful curls and say, "Too much kissing spoils a friendship!" Isn't that wonderful? By gosh, Bill, isn't it wonderful? Too much kissing spoils a friendship. A whole new philosophy of life, presumably from the Middle West. What a light it sheds. What a light. I gather that in the Middle West, where the heart beats warmer and there aren't all these God-damned Eastern superiorities and conventions, everybody kisses everybody. I could hear Ann saying it to countless men, old and young, in back seats, at movies, at dances, in canoes, on beaches, at Sunday-school picnics and bean suppers and burgoos and corn-huskings—No, too much kissing spoils a friendship. Be yourself! . . . I learned a lot.

—Well, and what was the upshot.

—The voice of the scoptophile. Aren't you ashamed? You want to know whether I slept with her.

—Of course I do! Don't be an idiot.

—Well, I did. Innocently.

—Says you?

—Says me. At five o'clock we went to bed, worn out, and slept side by side with our clothes on, like babes in the wood. Pretty as a picture. When I came to, I didn't know where the hell I was. There was Ann's little white face, close beside me, one hand under her cheek, with the damp golden curls beside the temple, and her little poached knees drawn up and protruding charmingly from under her dress. The most innocent-looking thing you ever saw in your life. Yes. . . . But why did I start to tell you this.

—I believe it was supposed to be significant of changing morals.

—Oh, was it? Well, I guess it is.

—Have you seen her since?

—Oh, sure, several times. I like her. She's a nice kid. Lots of fun. Absolutely direct and honest—no hesitations or ridiculous modesties—if she decided to make an affair of it—which she hasn't yet done—she'd say so. Very generous, very simple. Absolutely lost here. Why don't you go and see her. She'd do you good. She has a nice skin, too. When you put your hand under her dress, she smiles and says, "Why, no! That's my naked skin!" and giggles, and waits for you to take the hand away, which you do. . . . Was that a pistol shot?

—Backfire.

—Backfire. In this street once, I ran up behind a taxi and put my chin over the back of it, it was an open one, and screamed. The two old ladies in it nearly died. It was after my initiation—Good God.

—What.

—How can you bear to sit there, Bill, and watch my entrails being wound out of me on a winch.

—Oh, it's lots of fun.

—It *would* be. Damn all you intellectuals anyway, you cold fellows who—who——

—Who what.

—Live in your brains. I'm sick of it. I want to die.

—Need for punishment.

—Oh, sure. Nirvana principle and everything. I'm all for it. Step up, ladies and gents——

—Why not try a different formula, in dramatizing yourself, for a change.

—Are you trying to be nasty?

—I am nasty.

—So you are. And may you fry in hell for it. A lot of help you are! Why don't you go to bed.

—I'm seriously thinking of it. You seem to have come to a kind of stop. Unless you really want to get down to something——

—Of course I do, dammit! I'm trying to. I want to. I stand here, perfectly still, don't I, except that I rock a little—I stand here before you perfectly still—but inside I'm rushing from one end of the world to the other. Speed. I'm everywhere at once. There and back. Torrents of things rushing with me. All the dead men. All the living women. What stopping place is there—where can I rest for a moment and pick up one bright single detail and begin? I'm afraid, precisely because I can't stop, because there's no one thing that I want to hold on to more than anything else. Can I hold on to you? No. The truth is, there's not a damned thing or person or idea in the world you can trust, not one. You're alone. You run about falling in love with people, with things, with flowers, with surfaces, with weather, with *ids* and *quods* and *quids*, and what the blazes do you get in return? Nothing: or only a fleeting reflection of your own putrid little face flung back at you crookedly from a broken mirror. Isn't that it? Have I lost my self-love? Has it been devoured by the totem-animal? I think I'll be a pansexualist, and become a child again.

—You *are* one now.

—Of course. To be sure. I'm clinging to my mother's skirts again. I'm crying at the encroachment of the dark. I hear my father going to bed with my mother, hear them talking together tenderly, and in the horror of night I become once more a crawling little inspectionist. I creep to and fro, whimpering. What are they doing. What are they saying. Why have they hidden. Have I a right to know what they are doing or saying? Is it a real need or an imaginary one? But why do I want to know at all? Is it worth knowing? Or would knowing be any less painful than imagining? How can you decide not to know, or not to imagine? It can't be done. If you don't know, you imagine; and once you've imagined, you want to know. One of the penalties of consciousness.

—Now you're getting pretty close to home, aren't you.

—Oh, am I. You think so. I'm discussing general principles, Bill, general principles. Nothing homelike about it. To be aware is to suffer. One of the cornerstones of existence, you can't dodge it, you know you can't. It's all very well to say to the child, crawling there in the dark, listening and spying, don't whimper, don't listen, don't spy—it's all very well to say to him you don't need your mother any longer, she doesn't belong only to you, nothing belongs only to you—or to say the same thing to him when he's grown up—but the fact remains he can never get over that suffering. Never. All he can do is translate it into other terms, pretend it's something else, give it a lot of fool names, or comfort himself with the discovery that every one else is suffering in the same way. The right to suffer in our own way—that's what we demand, by God. And we won't be deprived of it. No.

—Who the hell is stopping you?

—Not you, anyway, you damned fool!

—Of course. You're projecting. You set me up in order to knock me down. I grant you your little necessity to suffer—you're not unique in that. Go ahead and suffer. Howl your head off. And if it will do you any good, abuse me for appearing to stand in your way. It's all part of the same picture, isn't it?

—Yes. You're right. I'm sorry. I seem to have missed my step somewhere. Tell me what to do, Bill. Hit me with an ax and sober me.

—You'll sober yourself when you're ready. Meanwhile go on howling. I'll lie down if you don't mind.

—You're tired.

—Kind of. But it doesn't matter—go ahead—I'm listening.

—Now you make me feel ashamed, selfish.

—Oh, for God's sake don't worry about that. You'd do the same for me, wouldn't you? Or I hope so.

—Of course I would, Bill. Of course I would. We're interchangeable. But where was I.

—You were suffering, I believe.

—So I was. I was demanding the right to suffer in my own way. In my own terms. And not to have some one come along in a purple airplane, a kind of bloody little *deus ex machina* of psychology, and tell me that my little suffering—which we'll call x—wasn't really x at all but y—as if to call it by another name made it any the less suffering. That's what makes me sore with you fellows—you seem to think that merely by driving us back from one set of phrases to another, by a series of historical substitutions, you've settled everything. Childish, by God. Childish. I say sweetheart to you, and you reply, brightly, mother. I say drawers, and you say diapers. I say whisky, and you say breast. All wrong. All completely wrong. Mere jugglery. Granted that the child's suffering is the exact equivalent of the man's—for the sake of argument—you're left just where you started. You've still got on your hands the initial quantum of suffering, unanalyzable, the burden which we pick up in the act of birth and carry until we damned well die. Perhaps you'll argue that my suffering in the present case, my loss of balance, is excessive, and that to force me to revalue it in terms of my childhood experiences will bring me back to my senses. But will it? I wonder.

—Try it and see, why not. Isn't it at least useful to observe that it's all relative? And that it's all determined? If you'll take the trouble to know a little about the aetiology of behavior, and of emotions and feelings, then you can't take yourself so damned seriously. You can laugh at yourself.

—I don't want to laugh at myself—not yet. I want to indulge in a good primitive yell. Good God, Bill, do you mean to say we aren't to be allowed to know pain? What's the good of being conscious, then? Of being a man? Hell's delight, it's something, isn't it, to know what crucifixion is, in a complicated modern form, and to make an outcry about it! If we find ourselves here, on the surface of this little planet, and feel like shaking our fists at God, and cursing Him for giving us the thing we call life, is some paltry little society for the prevention of unkindness to gods going to rush up and say No, no, you can't do that, you aren't really suffering at all, and even if you were you have no right to say so, you only misunderstand things, everything is for the best, come along now and see the sunrise? I like to think that this existence here is hell. That's what, *hell*. We ourselves are the doomed, and our pitiful little ideals and hopes are precisely our torment.

—Very ingenious. Our little pewter Christ is now ready for the great betrayal.

—Gosh, yes. It's all arranged. Did I arrange it? Months ago? Did I will it? Zingoids. What depths there are in the hell of human nature. What a theme for a play that would be—think of it, Bill. Myself willing my own betrayal: myself my own Galeoto: sowing the seeds of my own dishonor. Did I do it? How can I prove I didn't. I see them coming together—watch them approaching each other—encourage them subtly to see more and more of each other—to go to concerts, dances, parties—I stay away myself, get drunk night after night, confess my delinquencies with Molly—seize every occasion to discuss the necessity for complete freedom in such matters, so as to accustom them to the idea—and then when the situation is ripe I go away to New York and leave the coast clear for them, thus providing the final temptation. Clear as a nutshell. It isn't their fault at all, is it? No. Step up, ladies and gents, and see the man who cuckolded himself. See the man who grew his own horn in a window box, watering it with his tears. But if I did it, why did I do it? What does it mean. Could I prove, psychologically, that I didn't want to do it? Doubtful. You're asleep. You aren't listening. Why should you.

—Saint Pandarus.

—Yes, fry, lechery, fry. Isn't it wonderful. Along the banks of the Styx on the obscenic railway. In that room once, in that bed once. But it's impossible that I should have willed it, Bill, impossible. Why should I want to do such a thing? Or half want to do it. Am I in love with Bertha? The angels are coming to tell me what love is. I can hear them: they are galloping along Massachusetts Avenue in a fleet of—. What. They are giving tongue. The snowflakes are their voices: innumerable: I hear them calling me. I shall attend the convention of angels in the ballroom of the Statler Hotel, and make an inaugural address on the nature of love. Love is cruelty. Love is hate. Love is a desire to revenge yourself. It's a bloody great butcher's cleaver, that's what it is. It has eyes of a ferocity known only to comets, its hands are red, its feet are claws, its wings are scythes of jealousy. Its will is destruction: it tears out the heart of the beloved, in order that its own heart may break. Love is murder. It's a suicide pact, and all for what? All for death.

—The little boy has been reading Latin poetry again. *Odi et amo*. Ah, yes, the cruel ambivalence of life, poor Andy. Where have I heard all this before. Who bit you.

—I bit myself, in the cradle, when I first puked my mother's milk.

—I thought so. Little Andrew Suck-a-Thumb.

—So this is love: we reach a new conception of love, Bill, and one that does us credit. I see it exactly—exactly. It's nothing on earth but a domestication of death. Our little domestic death. It's a ballet. See them go to bed together—listen to them murmuring adoration—hear them whisper and kiss—O God, all that silken sinuosity and hypocrisy and ecstasy—the beautiful painful dance—which twinkles starlike, moves so swift and fine— and all of it a thin masque to cover the raw red tomb-face of primordial hatred. Skull purring at skull, death's-head kissing death's-head, the caress a strangle, consummation a swordthrust. It's killed me: I'm dead. I've eaten my father's skeleton and I'm dead. I shall never love again, any more than I'll ever be able to stop loving. Christ, what a fix we're in. Helpless. Burn off our hands. Drink ourselves into permanent unconsciousness. Love— don't make us laugh. It's automatic—no virtue in it—might as well praise the grassblade for being a grassblade—the weather vane for turning in the wind—the blood for pouring from a wound. In the spring the young libido lightly turns to thoughts of lust. Pressure of the seminal vesicles, and Tom falls in love with my wife. And meanwhile what am I doing? What indeed: the answer is nothing. I stand still like a whirlwind that hangs in one spot, uncertain where to go. Enormous concentration of energy, aimless, like an undischarged lightning flash. What in the name of God shall I do—where shall I go—tell me.

—Go back to Bertha. And hurry up about it. Try to be civilized. Or pretend to be, if you can't. Give the poor girl a break, why don't you. She probably hasn't slept a wink for a week.

—Doesn't deserve to, either. No. Plenty of time for sleeping later on. Let her lie awake for a while and think: she's put it off too long. She ought to have done her thinking beforehand. Now it's a battle of wits. And do you know what I think I'll do? Gosh, I've got an idea. Yes, I see it all of a sudden, and it's going to be good. This bottle's empty. I'll have to go back to whisky.

—Well, what's the bright idea.

—I'm going to surround them.

—What do you mean.

—Just exactly that. I'm going to surround them. That's my one great advantage, don't you see? I know more about it than they do. I know more about Berty than Tom does, and more about Tom than Berty does. And there I am, and there by God I'll stay, like a third consciousness, present at every damned thing they think or do. I'll haunt them like a ghost. I'll go to bed with them and get up with them. I'll make them so self-conscious that they'll go crazy. I'll be everywhere—they'll find me in the bathtub, at the piano, on the pillow, in the kitchen sink. My whole history constantly before them. How can they empty their memories of Andrew One-eye Cather, overnight? Can't be did. All the habits they've shared with me for hundreds of years—the jokes, the odds and ends of intimacy each of them has in common with me—how can they escape? They can't. And here's the point—they love me. Don't they? Well, that makes it all the worse. If I just stand aside with meditative irony now—if I just watch them cynically from across the street, as it were—saunter by from time to time—send them a picture postcard from Montreal or Timbuctoo —reappear before them at a Sander's Theater concert, disguised as one of the bats that circle above the orchestra—speak to them from the forsythia bushes in the spring—eat hot dogs with them at John's—laugh at them from the comic strips at breakfast—Christ, Bill, it's going to be good. Don't you see. I'll surround them like a cloud. When Bertha kisses Tom, she'll think—this isn't Andy. This is Tom. He doesn't kiss in quite the same way. He doesn't place his arms in quite the same way. And what's the result—she's kissing two people at once. Now I ask you, Bill, can she be happy, doing that? For long? No. Nor Tom either. He'll be thinking—she has kissed Andy like this. Ten years. Night after night. He has seen her in this hat, this dress, this nightgown, these tarpaulin knickers. He is here now. And is she thinking about him when I slip my arm under her left shoulder—is she wishing, at the bottom of her heart, that it were he. Will they discuss that, I wonder. And what good would it do if they did. None. They would at once begin to tremble on the brink of the unspeakable, the unformulable, the realm of doubts and suspicions, where passionate reassurances drop dead like birds into a volcano. Isn't it wonderful? Hrrrp. Excuse me.

—You're insane. I never heard anything so disgusting and cruel in my life. You ought to be ashamed.

—Not at all. All's fair. Love and war. I think I'll do it. But come to think of it, I don't have to do it. It will do itself. I can't even help it, if I wanted to. Automatic. Guilt. Suppose I decide to be a trumpeting little angel about it, take it all with good grace and magnanimity, tell them to go ahead and make a bright little affair of it for as long as they like, Andy standing meekly and beautifully aside—all right, you fool, suppose I do. What then. It will be all the worse for them. I was just exaggerating, you see. I really have nothing to do with it. Just one of those assumptions of imaginary power. The truth is, I can't help it. Two rapid falcons in a single snare condemned to do the flittings of the bat.

—Nice. A wonderful vision. But there is something else——

—You're asleep.

—No. But there is something else——

—Well, all right, all right, go ahead, spit it out. Don't goggle at the ceiling like a pekingese.

—It's my business to goggle, you poor prune. The Freudian technique of the colorless and dispassionate auditor.

—Dispassionate hell.

—But just the same, I'll give you an idea.

—Oh, very kind of you, darling little Bill. How much will I owe you.

—Your life, very likely.

—Keep the change. Do you think we'll have an early spring? Will the
Bruins win the Stanley Cup? Or what have you.

—If you'll shut up and stand still for a minute, instead of running up
and down the room like a——

—Pterodactyl.

—I'll tell you. That is, if I can get hold of it. Wait. This idea of the
surrounding consciousness—there's something in it. Yes, something in it.
But not as you foresee, quite—no—because you want to use it as an in-
strument of revenge. That wouldn't do any good—in fact, it would ultimately punish yourself most of all. But suppose you do it with real kindness—I mean, real love—for both of them. You admit you love them.
Presumably, therefore, you want their happiness. Don't you?

—Well, for the love of mud.

—Don't you?

—I don't like this turn. You're disgusting.

—You know you do. That's why it hurts you so much, of course: that's
simple enough.

—As simple as murder.

—If you love them, then you want to keep them. And you must choose
that course of action which is most likely to keep them. And this is where
magnanimity of consciousness comes in. Go ahead and be conscious—let
them feel that you are constantly there with them—but let them feel that
you are there in the role of the person who most loves them. Why not. If
anything could be calculated to bring things to a happy issue, that's it. In
this way, you will absorb or digest the whole situation—embrace both
Bertha and Tom—and as a result of it, you will grow: you will become the
wisest of the three: and the strongest. If there are latent wrongnesses in
their position, this will bring it to the surface. If they are weak, or guilty,
or not profoundly set on this thing—as I suspect—then this will sooner or
later make them horribly aware. . . . That's all.

—Well, for the—if somebody was to—and so saying he knocked me
down with a fountain pen. Just like that. He drove up in his chariot and
blew me over with a whisper, that's what he did. With bright little words
of love and kindness, too, and adjurations to Christlike mercy. You make
me sick. You'd better go to sleep, if that's the best you can do, that's all
I can say. Your complete lack of comprehension simply staggers me—if I
weren't already staggering. Yes yes yes yes yes. I ought to do everything
for them. I love them dearly. They're so kind to me, day and night, aren't
they. So considerate of me. They put me first every time, don't they. Tom,
that God-damned snob—what did he ever do for me. What. Oh yes, he
got me into the Institute of 1770 as an honorary. I forgot that. And tried
to get me into the Gas House. Helped me get the football managership.
Long ago and far away. Wonderfully kind, he was—I'll never forget it
as long as I live. I owe him everything. So now that he presents his bill, of
course I'll pay on the nail. Yes. I'll help him in every way. I'll give him
five dollars for the Sacco-Vanzetti fund, and make speeches for his parlor
Reds at Ford Hall. I'll run his errands for him. I'll mix his prussic acid for
him. I'll give him my rum, my Hogarth prints, my first editions of Henry

James, and my collection of pressed flowers. From Duxbury, too. Why not. And all as a preliminary to the greatest gift of all, which you foresee already. Little Bertha, the Brattle Street Bovary. Let him have all he can get of her, and all he can keep. With both hands, with auricle and ventricle, with liver and lights, I give her up. And she too. The immaculate. Whom I had to teach, whom I taught, whom I made what she is today. What is she today? She is Andrew Cather, that's who she is. Saturated solution of A. One-eye Cather. What would her hair have been without me? Her hats? Her music? Her mind? Her body? A few timid Vincent Club jokes, a conversation about maids at the Sewing Circle lunch, a hundred visiting cards left in silver dishes in Brattle Street and Marlborough Street and Scott Street and Highland Avenue. I made her over in my image. Is that why I don't know whether to hate her or love her? I made her over, gave her one eye in exchange for two—ah, but what an eye, what an eye—myopic but precise—the eye of imagination—taught her the animal pleasures and with them gave her the great gift of horror—and now that she is a Cather, now that she is Andy, Tom wants her. Oh yes. He is moving in on me, closing in on me. It's the Michelangelo thing. Hello, Mike old boy—are you still there? Keep one eye on me—we're going on to bigger and better things. Dawn of the artist's consciousness, which is consciousness awaking with the last beat of the dying heart. The eye that opens in the coffin. Monsieur Valdemar—the mind that blossoms to terrific thought with the energy thrown off by the final catalysis of corruption. Christ, I must get away from here. Not geographically, but on the wings of Father Imago. Did you ever hear of him? My best friend. Myself. The one who was left—who was left—what was I about to say. I'm going too fast. Left high and dry. I must maneuver back to the sea, that's it. I knew that all along, too, and wanted it before. Yes, I told you about it. The long, blond beach in moonlight, the bronze waves in moonlight, the dory whose name was Doris, named of course after my mother, the dry curled waves of seaweed, the blackened stones left from clambake fires, the Indian arrowheads of white quartz—there it all is, spread out, miles long, worldlong, on the way to the Gurnett. I shall go to the Gurnett. Along that frightful beach. At midnight, in mournful moonlight, alone, or with a whore.

—Take Bertha with you.

—That's rather witty of you, my boy. I might do worse. I could point out the exact spot where we always had the picnic, the annual picnic, the clambake. On clear days, the mirage of Provincetown, and the smoke of the Provincetown steamer streaked along the horizon. Yes. And the Plymouth boat too, closer in, white and glittering. And all the dead fish on the sand, stinking in the sun. Shall we take off our clothes and bathe? Have we brought our bathing suits? Shall we divellicate? You're snoring, Bill. Go to bed.

—Sorry. Go ahead. I'll just put this paper over my eyes.

—It's funny—I get soberer and soberer, the more I drink. What's that—tolerance? Clear as a bell. And all the agonies in rows, as separate and distinct as sea shells in a glass case. Were we talking about that before somewhere? Seems to me we were. Where was it. Let me think. Those wet ashes remind me of something—there's a puddle on the hearth, too—what

is it they remind me of. Not Bertha, no. Not that camp in Maine, no.
Not Jaffrey, or Jackson Falls, no. But what. Was it the Madison Hut at
sunrise—no. But it was Bertha somewhere, yes it was Bertha, much
younger, before she'd got such a belly, and begun to shave her legs with
pumice. Yes. Did she shave—did you know she shaved her legs with
pumice so that the hairs wouldn't come sparkling through her stockings,
Bill. Did you know that. Must be painful, I wonder. Before the bath or in
the bath. Did you know there was a barber in Washington Street where
women used to go and get shaved all over, or depiled, or whatever the
word is. Can't be *depiled*, can it. Did you know that. You don't know
anything. You're snoring again. But this has been a wonderful nonstop
talk, hasn't it, you didn't know I had it in me, did you. And now as you
see, I'm all at peace with myself—like hell I am—with all the little separate agonies in rows like sea shells, the ones I was telling you about.
      —Oh, sure.
      —Yes. Did you know that.
      —Oh, sure.
      —If you can't say anything but Oh, sure, go to sleep. You're no use to
me.
      —I think I will if you don't mind. Here. And when you get tired of
addressing yourself you can have my bed.
      —Greater love hath no man than this. But I would feel guilty. But
you're already snoring again. But I'm alone again, alone as always, alone
as you are in your subterranean world of sleep, you with your middle-aged
and far too fat hands crossed on your breathing and automatic belly. Good
god what a thing it is—and the snow too—all night a night of snow—
covering the college yard so innocently, so that all the sad traces are obliterated—even the President's footsteps gone, and the little privet bushes
mantled, and the neat little vomit by Appleton Chapel covered over, and
the little trefoil bird tracks filled in, and the dog-stale and cat-stale gone.
How many times have we crossed it? How many times our footsteps lie
there, Bill, immortal but invisible, on the way from Heeney's Palace of
Pleasure to Seaver, from the Union to University 4, from the Bursar's
Office to the Coop, from *x* to *y*. Do you see them all, sleeping Bill. That
network. Do you see them all, Mike old boy. You with your Homeric curls.
Shall I tell you a dream while I walk up and down with this drink in my
hand. Shall I. Yes I will, thank you. I will start with the simple premise of
the actual and delicious dream, that one, the one of the crucified pig, my
old friend the bleeding pig, Andrew Pigsnout Cather, the winged pig,
whose wings were bitten off in childhood. It was like this, or like that, but
you won't mind if I just change it a little as I go along, will you, and touch
it up like a photographer; you know, just to make it brighter. Shall I do
that. Oh, Christ. I don't care. It comes out like a ribbon and lies flat on
the brush. Listen Bill, listen you prostrate and sleeping guts—it was like
this. I was in the Swiss Navy at the time. I was in Gibraltar, with my
Spanish grammar in my hand. I was on my way to my castle in Spain, the
ideal, the everlasting, the infinite, the beautiful. Do you hear—all those
lovely words, all the evanescent ones, the pale plasma of sublimation. Alloplastic, autoplastic. Have you ever ridden in an autoplastic? Bores me.

And it was in the spring, it was when birds fly north, and I too was flying north, and I sent Tom a wire to say that I would meet him and the two other fellows at that little place in the mountains, way off there, at that high altitude, in that remote village, and in that familiar and dearly-beloved little inn, where we knew all the people, and had gone so many times—you know the place. I wired him, and took a train and rode all night. Who were the other fellows. I didn't know, but one of them was a Spaniard. I rode all night in the train, and got to the mountain village before sunrise. And walked in the twilight up the muddy road, for it had been raining in the night, and I knew my way perfectly to the little inn, with its yellow plaster walls and the purple clematis growing on the trellis, and I went in and turned to the left, into the little breakfast room where I knew they would all be sitting and having their morning tea, and sure enough there they were—Tom, burly and athletic, damn his athletic eyes, in his rough tweed jacket with shapeless pockets full of books and his English pipe stinking the room out, already in possession, and the Spanish fellow, and the other fellow, whose name I never knew—there they all were, their breakfast finished, the tea cold, the dishes dirty, the early gray light coming in on to the soiled red tablecloth, and as soon as I had come in they all got up and said they must be going. Yes, they must be going. They must be in time to see the waterfall, the famous waterfall, which was the show piece of the village, by sunrise: for that, ladies and gentlemen, was the Thing to Do. Oh, yes. You always had to go and see the water-fall in the glen by sunrise. And would they wait for Andrew? No, indeed. Out they went, taking alpenstocks with them, just like God-damned moun-taineers, and Tom rang the bell to tell the landlady that Mr. Cather would now have his tea, and they would go ahead, and Mr. Cather having had his tea would follow them to the waterfall. Do you hear me in your sleep, Bill. Do I influence your dreams. Do you hear the waterfall, is it rushing down in a shapeless pour past your subconscious ear. Do you feel in your pancreas the sunrise light that never was on land or sea. Do you feel the cold peaks of the Cantabrigian mountains, the sunrise clouds, towering above you there on your putrid sleep-ridden couch, you with your hands on your belly, which is full of Liebfraumilch. Do I draw you forth into that realm. Are you climbing goatlike among those wet crags of slate and gravel. Are you stumbling or slipping there, your feet wet and cold. Oh, Christ. So I had my tea and followed them, but they were already out of sight, they had gone down into the glen. And as I went down the muddy road to the village I knew that I didn't quite remember where the path was, the little field path, that led from the road across the fields to the glen. And I stood there by a stone wall and wondered, and a peasant with a bicycle stopped and pointed out the path to me, but said that it was al-most impassable with mud, as I could see. We leaned over the wall, and I saw that what he said was true. The mud was knee-deep. It was like soup. But he added that if I walked further down the road to the next farm I would come to a barn, and if I went into the barn, and through it, and out at the back, I would find another and better path which would lead me safely down to the glen, from which I would easily enough find my way to the waterfall. So I did it. I went to the barn, which was on the right hand side of the road. But this was the appalling thing, Bill, you must dream vividly about this. I'm telling you about it. This was the appalling thing, for as I entered the gloom of the barn, in the morning twilight, I heard, from somewhere near me, the most dreadful and heart-rending screams, animal screams, animal agony, and I stopped, terrified, and looked about me to see where the screams came from. And in a dark corner, then, under some cobwebbed stairs, in a sort of pen, so dark that at first I could hardly make it out——

Christ, Bill, it was the pig, the crucified pig. You won't believe it when I tell you about it. Nor you, Mike, you won't believe it. It was the huge naked pig—supported upright, with arms outspread, as on a cross, by a devilish machine, an affair of slowly revolving wheels and pullies, with an endless belt which was attached by steel claws to the flesh of the pig. But my God there was practically no flesh left on the pig; none, except on the breast over the heart; the belt had torn the rest away, and as I went a little closer, appalled by the screams of the pig—whose head was flung back in a final ecstasy of anguish, turned to one side, the mouth wide open—as I went a little closer, and watched the endless belt slowly moving down the red breast of the carcass, between the ribs of which I could see the entrails, the steel claws fetched away the last strip of flesh, the pig was automatically released, and with a final scream of pain rushed out of the pen. It was nothing but a skeleton full of guts, but it was alive and sentient. Sentient. It whirled madly about the floor of the barn, driven by such a demon of suffering as compelled it to translate the consciousness of pain into the wildest energy—and this was only last night, are you listening, Bill—and I was frightened of what it might do, and ran out into the street again and climbed with incredible speed up a waterpipe on the wall of the house opposite, and managed to hang there, out of reach. And sure enough the pig came rushing out, as if it were going to destroy the whole world. But at this very minute the miracle happened, Bill. I saw in the road a little scaffold hung with gay cloths, like the ones mountebanks use at country fairs, and on this a monk, in a gray gown, with a rope tied round his middle, stood and rang a brass bell. And he began announcing, as the pig galloped up the stairs and stood upright beside him—Ladies and gentlemen, you will now witness the farewell performance of the dying pig. The pig will first give you an example of his acrobatic prowess, on the parallel bars, the trapeze, and also without the use of any implements whatever.

Before he had finished speaking, the pig began performing at lightning speed—standing somersaults, running and double somersaults. Catherine wheels, handsprings, chinned himself rapidly innumerable times on the trapeze, whirled to and fro over the parallel bars, and finished with a series of giant swings so swift that I could hardly follow them. Ladies and gentlemen, ladies and gentlemen, ladies and gentlemen, the dying pig will now play the Chinese whole-tone scale on an arrangement of coins, with his hoof. And instantly on a table, where the monk had flung down a haphazard handful of gold and silver coins, the pig tapped out rapidly with his hoof the Chinese whole-tone scale. I could see that the pig was dying. But the monk rang the bell again and said—ladies and gentlemen, the dying pig will now give you a demonstration of the fact that the death-agony can be transmuted into pure genius of consciousness. Without previous knowledge of Sanskrit, Hebrew, or Greek he will translate passages from those languages as I read them aloud. He will first translate a passage from the Sanskrit Upanishads, which, as you know, represent the earliest attempt of the Hindu mind to understand the nature and reality of existence. The monk read aloud, and the pig translated. The bell clanged again, the pig translated a passage from the Hebrew version of the Book of Genesis, at the end of which the monk said that the pig had corrected several inaccuracies in the King James Version. The bell rang again, the pig was about to translate from the Greek, but suddenly——

Are you dreaming about this, Bill. Am I making you suffer. Are you and Michelangelo listening to this. As you should by God. But at this minute I couldn't stand it any longer. I didn't want to see the pig die—perhaps not unnaturally, for I know as well as you do—damn you—that the pig was myself. Oh, yes indeed. Step up, ladies and gents—so I slid down from my waterpipe and went hurrying up the road again toward the path that led to the waterfall, leaving that scene behind me to finish itself as it would. I went toward the path, and I thought—Tom is here by this time, he and the others, they have seen the beautiful waterfall in the sunrise. Christ yes—they've seen the ideal, which I have missed. While they have been looking at the ideal, I've been seeing the real. Shall I go and join them—is it too late—will I be in time to see the ideal. Do I want to see the ideal. Or is it—tell me Bill—is it enough to have seen the real. Is it enough? Can you tell me that, you with your outer eyes shut. You with your two eyes. Can you tell me that. Does it tell you everything or doesn't it. And don't feel that you must wake up like Lazarus and explain it to me. Oh, no. You go on sleeping, you go on rotting there in that deep mulch of the underworld, where good and evil meet. While I drink and walk up and down here on this dirty carpet and spit into your dirty fireplace. Yes, you go on. While I unwarrantably despise you merely because I'm more conscious than you are. Or am I. And put my hand on your arm to see if you react. And you don't do a thing or say a thing, you're to all intents dead. Christ, what a dream. Did he die, will he die. Performing. Turning his very death into an entertainment. Turning his pain into perception. Christ, what a dream. And where do we go from here. Is this the turning point, do we turn back from the underworld, do we move to the bloody little sunrise now—the little Christmas card sunrise—is that where we've got to go. Do we go back to the sea from here, Michelangelo, as we said before—is it there—is what we want there—shall we burrow back to the sea, while Bill sleeps with his hand over his eyes to keep out the light—instinct again—do we feel sorry for Bill—have we been mean to Bill—must we give Bill a present to make it up to him—what shall we give him. A dozen bottles of Liebfraumilch. An Australian wimpus. A fountainpen filler. An old shoe. Shall we cry on the floor beside him, lie down and cry, so quietly that he won't wake. Shall we walk out into the storm with the glass in our hand, walk all the way to Fresh Pond, meet the ghost of Bertha, salute her among the algae, how-do-you-do, madam, and have you slept well. Or else. What. What else. Fatigue again, the feet are slow and uncertain. The feet are reluctant. They do not miss the legs of chairs or stems of ash trays. No. The feet and hands are detached. But shall we continue to say all this aloud or merely think it. It is becoming—a little— false. Unconvincing. Parepractical. Without a listener, why does one become dramatic. Or so much more dramatic. Alloplastic and autoplastic. And all these books here, these masses of words—must we swallow them only to spit them out. Bill, there is a fly walking on the back of your hand, and you don't know it. You don't even hear me tell you about it. He doesn't know that I am thinking about the Gurnett again, walking along the beach again. Brant Rock. He doesn't know how heavy the sand is, how it pulls at your feet, as if you were falling asleep. How it seems, as you drag slow footsteps, even to come up over your eyes, over your brain. He doesn't know that. He doesn't hear the nymphae singing as we slowly divellicate the waves of sluggish foam. How could he know that. Have we translated the book of nosogenesis, or done our dream work. Can we unravel the perception material on our feet, walking slowly, walking slowly, from one bipolarity to another. Have we devoured the id, or seen the dead ids lying on the beach and stinking in the east wind. Am I going toward the bedroom or first to the bathroom. Bedroom. Put the glass down you fool. Are we inclining toward, swooping toward, the streaming horizontal. Christ, to sleep—to sleep now—and without a single dream— not even those lumps, those clots, those whirls—not even those sickly lights —that fringe of lanterns under the eyelid, that fringe of slatterns—nor the mounting of lattices—textures of bedspread under the hand—the threads, the thralls, the threshes—must the leaning of the chin lead us into the southwest inevitably—into the dull darkness of whiteness with the room in the other light still on—forgot it—or this edge under the cheek— this cold edge of sheet—must we go downward there, leaning downward, and all for a last long slow deluding and terrible curve O God—is it there we go with a last little spinal effort——

⟨ IV

——*one thing and then another one thing and then another the fresh wind the thickness the fine webs tender about the extended fingertips the dust sifting on the point of the shoe the cart track the car track the long glong trail into the sunset west of mountains purple gashes and the sun gone gloom and walking there walking westward with the solitary ghost above my head is this the bad sort is this the good sort where are you going and what do you mean why do you float there flow there just above my head to the right of my face avoiding the edge of my felt hat what is your precise shape old fellow and are you harmful I will turn away down this little muddy path look those trees there I will go down there swiftly I will run am running but the solitary ghost is still there this must be a bad* one a ghost a ghost one of the white kind the cold kind the penetrating kind the thin and snowy kind o god shall I wake up in time will he enfold me chill me kill me SCREAM

one thing slower and then another thing slower it is a bulge a block a bulkhead a buttress of rock a wall there is a light there above it and a tree hanging over the light there was a face there but it is gone and I knew that face it was that girl no it was Susan no it was Doris no it was a Negress with gold hair no it was gold teeth grinning in the lamplight it is gone the wind comes evenly warmly slowly caressingly hums under the edge of my felt hat burns my left cheek and I am climbing among the sun-warmed rocks my hand is no warmer than these rocks is there a volcano under them will steam come out of the fissures will it all crumble and sink in it is crumbling and sinking crumbling and sinking and shaking my foot goes in my other foot I sink to my knees among warm disrupted rocks they are all falling apart and inward downward SCREAM

first second third fifth first second third fifth it is the fifth of forth the forth the forth and in the bed on the wall in the bed on the edge of the wall beside the lilac hedge beside the path between the two strange houses in this strange place and evening too or is it early morning in the bed ill or half awake I am lying here at a loss I should not be here and look there are people coming out of the other house three people three women no a mother and her two daughters and the path brings them close to my exposed bed shall I pretend to be asleep

But we don't know the way to the beach
Shall we ask someone mother
But there is no one to ask
We might inquire at that strange house
Yes at that strange house what a queer house
Did you ever see such a house it's a ruin
It has no wall on this side
And how dirty it is
Do you see how dirty it is

out of my bed then and running across the lawn and then slowing down so as to pass them not running and veering off from them toward the porch while they approach the side door they have not seen me I am safe I can get in without being seen I can get into this strange house where Bertha lives and all our children and all our relatives and the stove and the ice box and then they will come in and ask the way to the beach which is the way to the beach can you direct us to the beach

You must go through the village the little wooden village of a winding two-storied road and flagpoles and shingles and the white church I know the way well I have often been there it has a flat and washed look slightly crazy the houses are flimsy the beach is small the sea is cold

Can you tell us the way to the beach
Yes you follow this road to the beach

they didn't see me in my bed on the wall beside the hedge although they came so close to me no they didn't but here is sand on the floor filth and mud on the sitting-room floor and under the dining-room table the blood comes into my hands and face I am angry hit something it is all one

room but there too is a door to the pantry and there is Magma standing
  This room is dirty you must sweep it out Magma
  Sweep it out yourself
  Give me a broom
piles of sand under the table under the chairs along the walls on the sills
heaped against the screen doors shavings too blocks dolls paper soldiers
with wooden props toy cannons rags dirty clothes
  This room is filthy you must clean it at once Magma
  Clean it out
with the broom I am in the pantry and rush towards Magma the freckle-
faced sister where is Bertha and where are the children but now we are
in the corner of the sitting room again blood is in my hands and face and
neck I am angry
  I will not be made a Christian slave by the Berthas
  What did you say
with the broom hitting the saucepan on her head crash have I killed her
but she is moving away and the brothers and cousins lean silently closer
to me press closer and lean closer on all sides five six seven evil faces hard
faces American army faces tough mouths menacing
  What was that you said
  I will not be made a slave to the Berthas
  Squads right
  Give him the bootsit
  Is it
  Squads left
  Out with him
  It's the wibbots what
this is that ghost again under the rim of my hat this is a dream is it the
bad kind or the good kind shall I wake or not what will it be this squads
right and bootsit tar and feathers hanging a beating and merciless men shall
I keep still fight now or later SCREAM
  peace on the left ear left hand peace
  one shape and then another the little turmoils lead to big turmoils
turmoils turmoils who said turmoils what is a turmoils this is the way to
the this is the way and it is a clear landscape a clear cold landscape such
as you saw in ice but far off cold and small the tiny splinters come out of it
against my face there are splinters of ice stars fragments glass bright
landscape against my face against my eye and now the glare must be a fire
and in the mirror I see the reflection the little red bead from the unseeing
eye it was those glass eyes on the little plush carpet all looking in different
directions watchful and quiet how often do you wash them how often do
you take them out can I do it myself must I use a lotion an eyewash and
I am walking along the beach alone the little lonely beach is it Nantucket
is it Plymouth is it Nantasket no it is somewhere else it is Melville it is
Shakespeare it is the edge-beach the wild beach the beach where I shall see
the octopus it is the end and far Bohemian seacoast
  Go ahead and wait for me
  I will go ahead and wait for you

I have something
Is it the what is it where
It is crying
alone I see it I step over the long black thick tentacles of a quivering
celluloid jelly I am among them what if they should move seize me but
it is really dead here on the sand it is quite dead I am sure it is dead o the
poor thing it is dead shall I touch the tentacles with my stick shall I turn
back and look at the body the corpse the crystal globe the bell-shaped body
motionless on the wet hard sand with the tide going out it was left here
by the tide and is dying look it is still alive look the eyes are watching me
and what is that it is but don't SCREAM it is a it is a quite the largest
octopus I ever heard of vast enormous the enemy of Moby Dick WHITE
too but look

Go ahead and wait for me
I will
o christ it has a man's head inside the transparent jelly a man's face a
fine man's head a magnificent face a face in aspic a head in aspic it is
Michelangelo's head in aspic and o god it is still alive the life is ebbing
backward along the long lucid tentacles the tentacles which are drying
on the sand and this face is watching them dry watching them die feeling
them die watching the tide go out and see the agony on that face the lips
contorted in hatred and scorn the eyes that watch you with malevolent
godhead that watch the receding waves wtih horror and hatred it is conscious it sees you and despises you even in its death it does not want your
pity or your help how can you help it what can you do it hates you anyway
if you saved it even if you could save it even if you could cast it back in the
sea it would want to kill you for it is more intelligent than you and knows
it but what is it thinking now that it is dying what terrific thought is it
thinking for the face is wonderful it is intelligence meeting death with a
vast thought

and walking away walking away
now the man with mustaches is showing us the new house the peculiar
house with glass walls we follow him up the stairs all four of us follow him
the three others ahead of me I am last going up the glass stairs the glass
curtains too and the cupboards of glass it is all very bright and clear and
artificial it is an artifact where have the others gone I hear their voices but
I do not see them they have gone round the corner or into another room
and here is a w. c. and I am determined yes I will have time will I have
time yes there is plenty of time but the voices suddenly come nearer they
are all looking in what a nice bathroom too O isn't it a nice bathroom but
the stairs we go down are narrower and darker than before and who are
these people these three people and the man who has gone ahead somewhere with mustaches into the street and along toward the factory alone
the waterfall is pouring out of the side of the factory across the sidewalk
how can I get past is it safe shall I cross to the other side of the street no
I will stay on this side but it is poisonous water it is acid it is yellow I can
feel the spray burning my cheek and hands it spouts out in innumerable
jets and splashes upward from the sidewalk yellow and acid

Is that you Andy is that you Bertha Andy and Bertha
and this medical student whom I knew at Harvard too walking beside
me and looking at me in a peculiar way over the tip of his mustache
No I don't live there any more do you live there still
I am married
I am now a gynecologist
I will walk with you as far as that little Catholic church
We played tennis once on Soldiers' Field the ball hit you in the face is
that why you are blind or was it because you were looking through a peep-
hole I can see that you don't like me
he grins at me as if he knew that I am afraid of him he is tall and takes a
longer step wears tweeds brown shoes and an A.D. hat band or is it the
Gas House we separate in silence before the church and I am going in be-
side an old woman it smells of incense and is full of images chasubles
crucibles chrysms chrysoprases columns and columns and columns of white
plaster the cheap painted stations of the cross gaunt yellow jaundiced
marble crucifix and all the old women kneeling among the images I stand
behind them and look at all the bright brasses and silvers and hanging
lamps the rows of little candles and the priest is coming down the aisle
toward me as I go out again his crooked mouth
My dear friends I would like to tell you that although this is the house
of god you need not only think of it as a house of images it is not only a
collection of images and objects and simulacra it is a place of friendship
here you can speak to a friend of that which is nearest and dearest to your
heart lay down your burdens before embodied kindness I am your friend
the voice dies down behind me dies away here are the fields and the trees
there with sunlight on their bark and leaves and the stone wall beside the
road here under the tree I am sitting in the grass on a little knoll and
looking into a green wood and in the secret grass what is this a thimble a
crushed thimble Bertha's thimble and also the rouge compact but I open
it and there is no rouge in it no powder only three old corroded pennies
and I walk with them to the corner of the park opposite the tall apartment
house where the Negress is standing watching me by the door it is Clara
the cook does she know what I am coming for yes she knows and is watch-
ing me Bertha has told her to watch me
Good morning Mister Cather
I am not coming in I am going down there where the children are
playing in the meadow beside the marsh picking flowers the little boy and
the little girl picking flowers spring flowers too wild columbine and
crowfoot violet look children there is another flower over there do you
see it in the marsh how is it you have forgotten to get that one too it is an
orchid you can see it is some kind of green-and-white speckled tall orchid
perhaps it wasn't there a moment ago but now it is there you can see it
but can you reach it or is there too much water in the marsh yes it is very
wet but wait by the wall don't go back to the city yet and it is I who will
nobly go to the edge of the marsh stepping now on the spongy moss the
water bubbles my hand out body stooping can I reach it yes the rare
orchid for the two strange children
the shape of my left foot made of hollows built like a crystal a bone of

slow dark crystals off there too curving downward as if a pain of accretions items but this is a walk I am walking this is Harvard Street Arrow Street Bow Street the College Yard and there is Fred walking ahead of me turns his head a package under his arm looks away from me the buildings have changed moved away where is Gore Hall the path strange too yellow sand no trees but a wideness

Widener

Are you going to the poolroom

pays no attention goes to the left walks ahead of me looking back is on wheels in a little car cart an old Ford is it Rodman saying the Spanish Grammar has been read and is a deep sleep yes a deep sleep I am rolling a large hoop ribbons tied round the rim he watches me it leans always to one side the wind blowing the ribbons it careens why

Why don't you hit it on the other side keep it straight and here is the Fair will you go round or through it if you go through it you may lose your hoop and once we played Ping-pong in Concord Avenue or was it Shepard and the Fair here

Good-by I am going in I will get through diagonally the narrow crowded path of children drums horns the squealing merry-go-round calliope steam spouting an inclosure of wire a long alley for Ping-pong the Japanese hits the ball to the other end of the wire enclosure look it explodes when the other hits it it opens becomes a go-cart rolling quickly back to us on wheels with a child in it no a doll a puppet nodding and another ball hit another explosion flash bang a little balloon going up diagonally then I am turning to the right and cross the street something my foot lifting the two feet together hopping see I am walking slowly queerly like an animal what animal is it a penguin can I get across doing it without being hit by that car yes it is all right and Shepard Hall there but changed redder brighter smaller and a restaurant in the hall no letter boxes what has happened but I was living here where is the janitor where is Mister O'Connor where is Jack a strange janitor with a mop on the wet marble floor this is now a dormitory for students

Can you tell me Jack's address

No he is gone perhaps I could find it

Send it to Widener

Yes

obras obras obras that book is out Mister Cather for another week but here is the key with the large wooden handle and on the handle is Jack's address Waxage Street somewhere in Somerville carved on the handle and his name too carved the last thing he did before he went away Uncle David is of course dead Uncle Tom has gone off for the day not back in time the house he lives in now too far away take a Belmont bus walk through Craigie Street and find the house with open walls go upstairs Aunt Norah is very old and small bending down to the floor her white head wants to go downstairs you will have to carry her how small light white she is as I go down the carpeted stairs her arm is round my neck

I am your child now

the saucy face impish smiles detachedly looks at me indifferently wide-eyed like an infant at the breast but on my shoulder the small head I have been

kind am being kind will give her a conch shell a house by the sea in that
village leave her here and call Bertha
    Bertha Berty
lifting from the dark the open suitcase the nightgown holding it up laugh-
ing but it is spotted dirty a large spot he is laughing can't be helped you
don't mind do you what can I say nothing say nothing but turn away sadly
in the hotel room no it's all right perfectly all right but sad I am going up
the hill on the grass behind juniper trees birches the road dusty she is
coming up the other side yes there she is look it is who is it not Berty no
Molly no a girl with red hair comes through the oak trees beautiful loves
me puts out her hand kisses me we are kissing become one face floating in
air with wings one fused face with wings Turner sunset and this and this
and this and this and this WINGbeat and WINGbeat where whirled
and well where whirled and well where whirled and well——

To come upward from the dark world, through the mild shafts of light, as
a swimmer in long and curved periphery from a dive; from the whirled and
atomic or the swift and sparkling through the slower and more sleekly
globed; effortless, but with a drag at the heels of consciousness—to float
upward, not perpendicularly, but at an angle, arms at sides, turning slightly
on one's axis, like a Blake angel, through the long pale transverse of light—
with the sounds, too, the bell-sounds, the widening rings of impalpable but
deep meaning, as if someone far off with spheral mouth said, Time—and
the goldfish mouth released its bubble, and closed, and then again opened
to say, Time—to come upward thus slowly revolving, thus slowly twisting,
the eye scarcely opened and almost indifferent to light, but opening more
widely as the light with obscure and delicate changes teased at the eyelid,
teased at the sleepy curiosity—and the textures too, the warm or soft, the
wrinkled or knotted, those that caressed whitely and obliquely, and those
also that withdrew, or focussed slowly in a single sharp point and pressed
—to float upward like this, from plane to plane, sound to sound, meaning
to meaning—the attitudes changing one into another as the hands shifted,
the feet shifted, the breathing altered or the hearing cleared—from turbulent to troubled, from troubled to serene—but with the bell-sound nearer
and nearer, as if the head were emerging into a glistening ring, and as if
over the edges of this ring came the words like bubbles, at first meaningless,
and then with half-meanings, and at last—not with meanings precisely but
with gleams, as of fins that turned away in a flash and vanished——
    To move upward like this, surrounded by one's own speech, and con-
tinuously more closely surrounded by one's own body, the hand heavy on
the heart, the heart beating insistently in the ear, that which a moment
ago was the chime of a dream become the rhythm of the pulse, the
distorted faces and filaments of the dream becoming only the fluttering
defense of the eyelashes against the square of light from the window—all
the somatic disturbances, as of cramped elbow and bent knee and cold
hand and stifled nostril, which were a moment since so marvelously translated into wastes of snow or ugly corners of rock or difficult escapes from
social awkwardness, now again assuming the simple physical reality, against
which the dream had fought, as it were, a rear-guard action—to say again,

after all this obscure welter of images and spaces, this kaleidoscope of times, "here," "now," "time," "I"—I that was there, twisted, twisted into that strange shape, am here again, but with a queer difference——

The confusion fell slowly away, in ebbing rings of sound, he looked more firmly at the window, putting one hand up to touch the brass knob at the head of the bed above him, he looked and listened, and knew that the sound was the bell of Memorial Hall. How many strokes he had missed, or heard only in his sleep, he couldn't know, but he counted four. Four. Not in the morning, it was almost that when he had fallen asleep. It must be five or six in the afternoon. The light from the square of window at the foot of the bed was that of winter twilight, and lamplight, mixed—cold natural gray tinged with artificial orange: and something in it, too, suggested the pale reflections of snow. Thursday. Another day gone, soundlessly gone, an agony got through without pain, as if he had been anaesthetized. What a good thing. And to wake up, or come to, comparatively refreshed, comparatively calm! But *how* refreshed? He explored dry lips with his tongue, tasted the salt, opened and shut his mouth experimentally, and found himself thirsty. Turning his head from side to side on the pillow, he felt no headache, or only a very slight one, at the base of the skull. He looked at his watch. Seven o'clock.

But it was difficult to get up, if one didn't know what one got up for. Or at such an hour, so dislocated, in such a place, after such a series of nights, with so much of oneself gone, so much of one's secret gone. Idiot! You have confessed: your virtue is lost. Only the reticent man retains his virtue. But was virtue precisely the word? Or if not, what was it? He tried to remember the details: Michelangelo, the sea, Melville, the Gurnett, the secret of intimacy—intimate secrets. Sleep was better, or perhaps laughter.

He laughed lightly, almost gaily, but as if without meaning, and turned his head toward the door that led to Bill's study; then cut the laugh short and said "Bill." There was no answer. He heard the study clock ticking. He said it again, and listened again, and still getting no answer clasped his hands under his head. So it all came to this. After all the agony, all the confusion, all the death, one came to this. One awoke on a strange bed, at twilight, and found that suddenly everything was—peace. No longer a need to run, to hurry, to evade, to escape. No problems to solve. No people to avoid. No single person to hate. Except perhaps oneself. And why bother to hate oneself? Why bother? This curious amiable little collocation of wishes and repugnances—but more amiable than hateful—decidedly more amiable—with his hands clasped under his head and a fixed small smile—and the sounds of the Memorial Hall bell agreeably in his ear—why hate him? Or had it been the Unitarian Church. No, it was Memorial Hall. But was it still snowing?

He groaned, and heaved himself off the bed, and went to the window, which was six inches open at the bottom—that must have been done by Bill. A soft current of rainwashed air flowed in coolly over the sill, it was raining a little, and when he looked down at the street lamps and the College Yard he saw that most of the snow was gone. The slope of the hill towards the Union was white, but a white soddened and darkened; the street was cleared; only at the sides were the piled and hardened drifts.

And the sound of the snow shovels, scraping the rain-loosened snow—the raucous scraping and chopping, the ringing of steel on stone——

The face that looked back at him, from the lamplit bathroom mirror, was pale, the cheeks pale and a little sunken, but it faced him steadily and calmly, and the eye was not as bloodshot as he might have expected. Nor did the hands, which supported him on the cold marble, tremble, though he felt weak. You, Andrew Cather—old One-eye Cather. You in the flesh again, redivivus; you emaciated and with a hangover; but with that soft-clear sort of hangover which a fried egg and a stiff whisky would put right. Clear-headed, amused, detached—and with a queer deep historical sense. Wash your face in cold water. Dip your face in the cold green basin of water. Your hair too. The time-worn temples. And the three-days' growth of brown stubble, so long as to be getting soft. And shave, with Bill's dirty little brush and rusty safety razor. The little ridged clots of soaped hair, floating testimonially in the water, the dirt-streaked water. And a borrowed collar from Bill's bureau.

But where was it all gone, where was all the tumult gone? Into what remote sunset sound, what slow and distant and delicious thunder of crumbling, as of a world lost in entire peacefulness?

He switched on the light in the silent study, and found that the chaos had been once more reduced to order; the empty bottles had been removed; a new fire of white birch logs had been laid neatly in the brown brick fire-place; the cigarette ends were gone from the ashes and the ash stand. A fresh bottle of whisky stood on the brass tray, and on the table was a folded note, over which lay a small key and a pink ticket. Sanders Theater. Of course, the symphony concert tonight. From Bill. And the small bright key. "Andy. Going to Portland for a few days. Use the ticket if you like. Also my car, at the Church Street garage. Why not go off and think it over quietly, if you can—first telling Bertha, please! Not a bad idea. I suggest Duxbury. Were you saying something about a pig when I fell asleep. Bill."

The crucified pig, of course! He touched his smoothed chin and smiled, recollecting; feeling again the drunken glass in his hand, the precise torrent of eloquence in his mouth, the spate of ideas and images. Had it been absurd. Had it been as logical as it had seemed. Had he been as wonderfully in control of it as he had thought. He went to the window and looked across at the lights in the Widener Library and Boylston Hall, watched the dark figures going and coming through the gate to the Yard, figures in raincoats, figures hurrying in the soft rain. All the Smiths and Joneses of the world, accumulating knowledge, the ransackers of others' words, the compilers and digesters. Those who knew nothing, and those who knew a little, and those to whom life would painfully teach more. Were they jealous. Did they betray, or had they been betrayed. Were they sex-ridden, was sex a monster for them, a nightmare, was all this busy come-and-go a mere flight, a disguise, a pretense, a raincoat surface which concealed——

Concealed what.

The slow pang, recapitulative, rose in the darkness of his thought, lazily, languidly, as with the perishing last little energy of an exploding rocket, undecided at the last whether it should be propelled further or fall in a broken and slow dishevelment of fire-streaked pain. Bertha. Bertha and Tom. Yes. This deep violation, which was now past, this blood which was now shed and lost. This wound which was now beginning to be a scar. The inevitable, and God-to-be-thanked-for, cicatrix; the acceptance—but was it cowardly or was it merely wisdom—the acceptance of all of life as a scar. The pig, not crucified, perhaps, after all, but merely cicatrized. Circumscribed. But we mustn't be misunderstood—! Like that unfortunate fellow in the hospital; who said—*"circumcised—that's* what I meant!"

He poured himself a whisky, smiling, measuring the quantity idly by the deepening of the color in the green glass, held it, looking at the picture of Michelangelo, and walked to and fro slowly, before the hearth, as if for the pleasure of repeating, or re-enacting, a lost attitude. Here's to you, Mike, old boy. The insufferable vanity of the human being, who identifies himself with everything that's greater than himself! I identified myself with Michelangelo. With Shakespeare. With Melville. I was their grandchild. And why not, after all. I inherit them. They produced me, I couldn't escape them. They taught me how to suffer. They taught me how to know, how to realize, gave me the words by which I could speak my pain. They gave me the pain by giving me the words. Gave my pain its precise shape, as they gave me their consciousness. As I shall give my pain, my consciousness, to others. Did I say this to Bill.

He drank the whisky at a gulp, shuddered, set down the glass. The warmth in his belly crawled slowly about, like a crimson rambler and he smiled, putting a cool hand against his forehead. It had been a good show, it had been funny; and it was strange, it was disconcerting, to think that an agony could take such a shape—it made one distrust the nature of agony—was it possible, as this suggested, that all sincerities, even the sincerity of agony, were only sincerities of the moment? Only true in the instant? Relative? And for the rest insincere and unreal? Had it all been a fake? And had Bill seen through it? Absurd. In that case, the present calm was just as unreal, just as insincere, just as much an affair of the precise point in the sequence of cause and effect. How do you know your calmness is real, old crab. Do you really dare to think back, to feel back, into the yesterday which has now made itself into today? Are you really calm, or is it a mask which you have put on in your sleep. Have you changed—have you, have you, have you. Shall we look at the face in the mirror again, to see if it is calm. Look at the hand, to see if it shakes. Take the Binet test, to see if you are intelligent. Could you cry, now, although you think you feel like laughing. And how much part in all this has been played by alcohol. At what point in your spirited dramatization of yourself did the drama become drama for the sake of drama, and cease to be even so justifiable as a dramatic "projection" can be? Ah—ah—and is it true—can it *possibly* be true —that sudden and terrible idea——

He returned to the window, to gaze downward at the dark wetness of Massachusetts Avenue; emphasized, by the arc lights, between the piled snow; and found himself staring at the idea. Could it be true—and if it was, what a relief! what an escape!—that consciousness itself was a kind of dishonesty? A false simplification of animal existence? A voluntary-involuntary distortion, precisely analogous to the falsification that occurs when consciousness, in turn, tries to express itself in speech? As the ani-

mate, then, must be a natural distortion of the inanimate. Each step a new
kind of dishonesty; a dishonesty inherent in evolution. Each translation
involving a shedding, a partial shedding or abandonment, and an invention
of a something new which was only disguisedly true to its origins, only
obviously true to itself. But in that case, what was truth. Was truth the
suffering, or the calm that succeeds the suffering. Or the comprehensive
awareness of both, the embracing concept. Was suffering, as it were, merely
an unsuccessful attempt at translation, in this progress from one state to
another? An inability to feel what one is, to say what one feels, to do
what one wills? A failure, simply, to know? A failure of the historical sense?

He lost himself in the succession of half-thoughts, a genial dissipation
of ideas, of which he troubled only to feel the weights and vague directions;
feeling that he could, had he wished, have followed each divergent and
vanishing fin gleam or tail gleam to its psychological or physiological or
metaphysical covert; but that to do so would add nothing to what already
he deeply and animally and usefully knew. Bores me, the sum. If it was a
fake, all that dramatized and projected agony, it was a genuine fake:
suffering, even if it is only a transition, is genuine. Speech, even if it must
be only incompletely loyal to its subject, incapable of saying all, is genuine.
The fluidity of life, as long as it is life, can never have the immobile integrity of the rock from which it came. It will only be honest rock again
when it is dead. And in the meantime, if it suffers, if it is aware that it
suffers, if it says that it is aware that it suffers, and if it is aware that it
cannot say completely *why* it suffers, or in severance from what, that's all
you can ask of it. In sum—idiot!—it is only unhappy because it is no
longer, for the moment, rock.

He put his hand out of the window to feel the soft rain, as if in
demonstration of the smaller uses of feeling; the minor advantages of the
temporary emancipation from rock; the pleasures of dishonesty, or treason,
to which evolution has led us. Item: rock suffering rain. Rock enduring
infidelity. Rock conceiving a philosophical synthesis which explains, if it
does not actually diminish, the pain involved in being not-rock. And as-
sures the not-rock that it has, in a sense, a kind of reality. Andrew Cather
has really suffered, but his suffering has no importance, except to himself,
and only to himself insofar as he fails to realize—what? That rock, sundered
from rock, does not cry.

The clock on the mantel struck the half hour, with a single surprising
stroke, and he was interested to notice that the clock itself went on ticking,
as if in no astonishment at that sudden comment on division of time. Half
past seven! The clock was fast. The concert would be at eight. If a little
walk, to the river and back, perhaps along Memorial Drive, and then a
newspaper and quick supper at the Waldorf, the stock market and sports
column surveyed over the fried eggs—if this interval, in which to accept
more rationally what in fact he had already accepted, the idea of meeting
Bertha at the concert—and perhaps Tom as well—the idea which had been
fully formed as soon as he had seen the pink ticket on the table, and so
exactly as Bill had foreseen——

And the little key. Duxbury. Had Bill foreseen that too.

When he emerged into the street, and drew a long breath of rain-soft air, abruptly throwing back his shoulders in the gesture he had learned from Tom, he stared at the dull piles of snow and said aloud—Duxbury. Of course. What could be simpler. All that wild magnificent farrago of nonsense had been leading back to Duxbury—or had it been Bill who had been leading back to it. And all the drunken fantasies and fandangos—it was too absurd. It was too obvious. All this mother-fixation business, as if everything in the soul could be charted like a sea! No, Andy, no. Be honest, on this rainy night in February. Walk honestly down Linden Street. Cross Mount Auburn Street honestly; and proceed as honestly toward the Charles River as you would proceed to death. It is not Bill who has given you this idea—not Bill, not Tom, not Bertha, nor any combination of these, nor any disaster to you, any accident; it is yourself; it is your own little worm-curve; the twist that is your own life; the small spiral of light that answers to the name of Andrew Cather; the little rock-pain which chooses this particular fashion of saying that it is tired of being not-rock and would like again to be rock. Touch your hand against the wet wall beside you, the dripping icicle on the wall, which breaks away so softly and falls soundlessly into the snow—feel the wet coldness, the moist surface which will again soon be glazed with ice—know these things, as you know the wet and slippery bricks beneath your feet—the river toward which you walk—they are not more real, more solid, more permanent, than the past Andrew Cather, who has now suddenly and painfully told the present Andrew that there is also a future Andrew. Murder him, if you like, but he is yours.

Would Tom be there; or would Bertha be alone.

He ran quickly across the lamp-reflecting river of Memorial Drive, dodged the twin headlamps of an approaching car, which funneled bright swarms of raindrops out of the night, and on arrival at the other side, suddenly slipped and sat down hard on the half-frozen gravel path, striking his left knee. The pain sickened him, he hugged the lifted knee derisively, sat still for a moment, laughing silently, then rose and limped forward, looking over his shoulder to see if he had been observed. And what sort of pain was this, was this not-rock too. Was it real or unreal. Less real, or more, than the pain of separation. Ridiculous! Tuberculosis, intervening, will arrest the progress of dementia praecox. Good God. If everything was as relative as this—if a sudden physical pain could thus completely shut off a psychological pain, and make the return to it seem forced and deliberate and false—a mere self-indulgence——

Boylston Street, a lighted garage, another garage, the bookshop sign swinging and dripping in the narrow dark street, Erasmus, the lights in the gymnasium. Rodman had said that he must have the completed text in two weeks; and here a week was almost gone—twenty more translation exercises to be compiled and written out—but that would be easy. That Ronda poem. That absurd guidebook. Correct the errors in the following. And at least two of the exercises devoted to the *corrida*—a novel idea to introduce the bullfight into Spanish grammar. With perhaps a spirited photo or two. *Sol y sombra*. And what about a quotation from the Spanish translation of "The Waste Land," *Tierra Baldia*, by Angel Flores. *Abril es el mes màs cruel; engendra—Lilas de la tierra muerta, mezcla*—And the guidebook, *Guia de Ronda*. "Ronda is an intricated old Moorish town.

Being highly salubrious the longevity of the place is proverbial." And the "polite youngs." Translate these passages into what you think might have been the Spanish original. Or something from *Toreros y Toros*.

At the bright door to the Waldorf, beside the subway entrance, three cents for *The Boston Evening Transcript*; and then the ticket, accepted from the ticket machine, with a slow clink; and the fried eggs, fresh country eggs, and bacon. Old Turgenev at the desk, with his beautiful white tobacco-stained beard. Eddie, the Negro taxi-driver, sprawling in his usual chair beside the door, reading a paper, his taxi drawn up at the curb outside, in readiness for undergraduates bent on pleasure. And the marble clock with black hands.

Was suffering one's nearest approach to an acute realization of life? Of existence? And therefore desirable?

—All I can say is, he's a stinker. It ought to have been a D.

—Why don't you go and see him.

—The squash courts——

—Sure. Five o'clock.

—And a side order of bacon. Three to come. Blue plate.

—Oh, gosh, it was good. It was the cat's pyjamas. It was the bee's knees.

—No, it was Crab that seconded him. Not me.

Complete Wall Street And Boston Stocks Closing Prices Heiress Fights to Keep Her Baby Child Flogged Boy Is Black and Blue Boston Stage Star Dead Famous Singer Began Career With Medicine Show at Age of Ten Years.

But where was it all gone, where was all the tumult gone, into what remote and dwindling sunset sound? And as Bill had said, Bertha must be suffering too. Walking to and fro with a soaked handkerchief in her hand. Unable to sit down, to rest, to think. Unable to sleep. Telephoning to all her friends. What had she said. Had she told them that he had left her. Or what. How had she explained it. Had she told them that she and Tom——

He crumbled the paper napkin, as if to crush once again the recapitulative pang, pushed back his chair. What dress would she be wearing—as if it mattered, by God. The blue velvet opera cloak. And all their friends, all the wives of faculty members, to see them when they met. Look, there is Andrew Cather, he's talking with Bertha, do you see them, in the back row, you know what they say about them don't you, they say—and do you suppose Tom Crapo is here tonight—can you imagine——

In Bill's room again, without turning on the light, he poured himself a whisky, drank it straight, resumed the automatic buzz of phrases. Was there no way to stop it. Was it wise to go to the concert at all. Should he go to see Molly, invite her to come to Duxbury with him, simply to have some one to talk to. The light from Massachusetts Avenue filled the room with imitation moonlight, sharply angled, ghostly; Michelangelo gazed down somberly through a diagonal shadow. Telephone to Molly now, or later perhaps. Go to Shepard Hall while Bertha was still at the concert, to have a look around, get the mail, put on a clean shirt. And telephone to Molly from there. Hello Molly, this is your old friend Andy, I wondered if you would like—I wondered if we might—what do you say to a little elopement —expedition—would you like to drive me down to Duxbury tonight—all expenses paid—what ho, Molly, how about a little spree to Montreal. Dance at the Lido first if you like. Or stay in your flat and drive down early in the morning. It's all over but the laughing.

He chose a book at random from the shelf by the fireplace, turned on the light and began to read, standing with his back to the hearth.

"Man is pre-eminently distinguished from the lower animals by the enormous development of his libido . . . he loves a great deal more than is necessary."

He loves a great deal more than is necessary. Christ!

The impulse to fling the book down violently was translated quietly into a precise reinsertion of it in its place on the shelf. These psychologists. These fellows who become psychologists because they understand neither themselves nor any one else. These phrase-makers—man with his enormous libido, man with his persistent libido, man pre-eminently distinguished from the lower animals because his love is not confined to the rutting season! Pre-eminently distinguished from the birds by his lack of wings. Look at the poor devil, staggering through the world under his enormous burden of libido. I forgive you, Bertha, for now I realize that the burden of libido which you carry everywhere with you is far too much for you. Yes. Let us share it with you. Hand it about to the audience at Sanders Theater—God knows *they* could stand a little more. And if they and Tom don't want it all—if there is something left over—a quantum, a surd, one tiny flame-plume—one eyelash-flicker of a loving look——

But no. Not that. My dear Bertha—Bertha my dear—need I explain to you the so very simple fact that after what has happened it will be impossible for us to resume—I mean, impossible for us to live—we must wave away the notion of a shared bedroom. You understand that. Old-fashioned of me, I daresay, but honest. Honest Andrew. What arrangement shall we make. Can we discuss it now quite calmly and sensibly. Shall I take a separate apartment next door. Shall we separate, or is it possible that now —now that this action has freed us—we can come together more usefully on another and perhaps more realistic plane. But not exactly—need I say— the planes of Abraham. No. And strange too that it is still with such a pang, though partly retrospective, and therefore sentimental——

And why was it with excitement, with quickened heartbeat, with unseeing eye, the familiar sensation of the face lowered so as to avoid the impalpable psychological problem, precisely as if it were a thing physically visible, that he approached Memorial Hall in the rain, slowing his steps as he passed Appleton Chapel, and even tempted, as long ago, to make a deliberate circuit of a block or two, for the mere gaining of time? Dismay? fear? doubt? animal distrust of the unknown? Pull yourself together. Enter. Climb the stairs. Ten minutes to eight. Take your seat and look about you.

The brown program in his hand, he climbed the steps to the balcony, found the seat near the parapet, which overlooked the absurd brightly lighted little auditorium of wooden Gothic, which Tom called late Visigothic or early Swiss Chalet, and watched the musicians filing on to the stage. The concert-master, Burgin, came last, and tucked his feet backward under the rung of his chair, as if for leverage when drawing the bow. Like the bird who tightens his claws on the twig, in order to release a particularly fine burst of song. And the squeakings and squawkings and runs and trills began, the grunts of the cellos, the tappings and listenings of the kettle drummer, all the delicious miscellany of tuning—while the audience of dodos and baldheads and wonderfully-bedizened frumps settled, and preened, and cooed at one another, or studied programs through telescopes. But was Bertha here. Was Tom here. Dared he lean over the edge and look. Would he be seen looking.

He looked, and she was not there. Nor Tom. The two seats, in the last row, were empty. But there were still people coming in—along the back— he watched them—and not finding her there, he looked down the aisle into the audience on the floor, where here and there little groups of women stood talking. Who was it who had made a standing bet with some one that if he could find more than three men in any one row of seats—and look at them tonight. Solid phalanxes of females. Aged females. As you progressed forward, toward the stage, solid rows of white hair, with now and then one solitary gleaming baldheaded octogenarian of a professor. Music to hear, why hear'st thou music sadly? Echo answers why. What did these creatures care about music, what did it mean to them? O God, O Cambridge.

"*Overture to 'The Magic Flute.'* . . . *Wolfgang Amadeus Mozart. Born at Salzburg, January 27, 1756; died at Vienna, December 5, 1791. Thirty-six years old.*"

Koussevitzky came quickly on to the stage, stepped with mathematical precision to his little dais, ascended, took up his baton, and as the applause drew him, pivoted with choreographic neatness. At precisely that moment, Bertha entered from the door at the far side and walked with quick, short steps, almost running, along the back, her hand clutching the blue velvet cloak against her breast. Alone. And as she dropped into her seat, he leaned over the edge of the parapet and felt that he drew forcibly upwards the surprised gaze that she lifted to him. She started visibly, controlled an impulse to rise again, and while still she looked at him he lifted his program, pointed to it, raised one finger in the air, and then with the waved program indicated the door. She nodded, and the overture began.

The Masonic chords drew themselves out, melancholy, profound, and the sad slow air followed them, the theme that later would be given to the delicious little hurdy-gurdy tune—"*Emanuel Johann Schikaneder, the author of the libretto of 'The Magic Flute,' was a wandering theater director . . . poet . . . improvident, shrewd, a bore. . . .*"

She was very white, she had on the blue velvet opera cloak, and under it the black satin. The white coral necklace. She sat stiffly, as if unseeing, but also as if aware embarrassedly that she was being looked at.

"*He asked Mozart to write the music for it. Mozart, pleased with the scenario, accepted the offer and said——*"

Why was the overture considered gay, happy—for an undercurrent of sadness ran all through it. Papageno. Papagenesis. The birdcatcher. She was turning her face a little away from him, with a sort of frozen precision, self-conscious and a little evasive, but firm.

"*Mozart said—'I have never written magic music. . . .' . . . Goethe once wrote of the text . . . Hegel praised the libretto highly . . . symbolical meanings.*"

And now the break, the cessation, the almost imperceptible pause, and
then the rapid chatter of the fugue, the sudden sawed-off bursts of fiddle
sound, the harsh quick downward scrapes of simultaneous bows, the brave
sforzandi followed immediately by the swift twinkle, the delicate pattern,
of the fugue, the mouse-dance, of light quick sound——

*"Schikaneder knew the ease with which Mozart wrote . . . knew that
it was necessary to keep watch over him . . . put Mozart in a little pavilion
which was in the midst of a garden near his theater . . . inspired by the
beautiful eyes of the singing woman, Gerl. . . ."*

She looked ill. Her face was thinner, her eyes looked larger, were
sombered, she was somehow nicer than he had thought her to be, she had
been hurt. She was watching Koussevitzky intently, but the way in which
her elbows were drawn in at her sides meant that she was conscious of the
people who sat at left and right: who, nevertheless, were paying no attention to her.

*"Velvet of itself is a natural response to the new quest of lovely ladies
for a fabric, luxurious unto the demands of this exacting mode. . . ."*
*"Schikaneder's name was in large type on the bill: Mozart's name was in
small type underneath the cast. . . . Schenk gave Beethoven lessons. . . .
At the end of the Overture, he went to Mozart and kissed his hand. Mozart
stroked his admirer's cheek. Mozart went behind the scenes and saw
Schikaneder in his costume of a bird. . . ."*

And now—ah, yes, how lovely—the absurd but magnificent dialogue
between god and the little hurdy-gurdy—the majestic chords, the great
sweeps of sound, the laws and the prophets, the thunder from the mountain, and then the delicious and ridiculous and so humble bubble and
squeak of the clarinets and oboes and bassoons, the birds singing in the rain
—and then god again—and again the undaunted little tumbling tune—so
childish——

*". . . Mozart died shortly after the production of 'The Magic Flute' in
deep distress . . . this opera was in his mind until the final delirium . . .
he would take his watch from under his pillow and follow the performance
in imagination. . . . 'Now comes the grand aria'. . . ."*

Her fists doubled under her chin, she leaned forward, as if with an air of
saying, look, you see I am even smiling a little, I am amused by all this, you
needn't think I am afraid, or that I'm not an independent person. Nor that
I won't face you bravely.

*"The day before he died, he sang with his weak voice the opening
measures of 'Der Vogelfanger bin ich ja' and endeavored to beat the time
with his hands. . . . Schikaneder, 'sensualist, parasite, spendthrift' . . .
built the Theater an der Wien . . . on the roof he put his own statue,
clothed in the feather costume of Papageno. His luck was not constant; in
1812 he died in poverty."*

The Masonic chords again, ascending, altered, but with the same deep
sadness; as of trains crying to each other across a wilderness at night;
the prolonged and lost nostalgia, the sound of pain abruptly introduced
into a scene of festivity, of candles, of minuets, as if coming in on a wind
that blew out lights;—and then again the lovely quick fugue, the elf dance,
rising and rising to broader and bolder sweeps of sound, the intricate and

algebraic pattern—this gesture coming in again, and then that other, the delicious bustle as of lights being relighted, servants hurrying with tapers, the music striking up, the dancers reforming——

The blue velvet cloak had slipped from her left shoulder, she sat with her two hands flat on her knees, still leaning forward, but now as if at last the music alone had become real for her, had taken her away; as if she had forgotten the things which had darkened her eyes, and given the new pallor to her cheeks. She was absorbed, she was by herself, she looked young.

"*Here the master, wishing, so to speak, to glance back and to give a final model of the old Italian and German overtures with a counterpointed theme, which had served, and still served, as preface to many operas, pleased himself by exhibiting the melodic theme that he had chosen, in all its forms, adorned with the riches of harmony and instrumentation. The result of this marvellous work of the carver is one of the most perfect instrumental compositions ever produced by human genius.*" Oh, yes indeed.

And now again god was speaking to the hurdy-gurdy—but this time a kindlier god, less remote; the god stooping from the mountain, gentler and nearer; and the hurdy-gurdy, changed and translated, but still essentially the same, speaking in a bolder and firmer voice—and then god again—as if the two voices greeted each other—and now the beginning of the end, the slow, falling rhythm of the melancholy gaiety—the last downward sweep of Koussevitzky's arms, of the bows, the held chord, another, the upward flick of the baton, the silence—and then the applause, mounting, mounting, like a storm of rain on gusts of wind——

She had risen from her seat, was looking upward at him for confirmation; he signaled with his program, and turned to move toward the swinging door. The applause dimmed behind him as he descended the stairs and began to cross the lofty marble-paved hall to the other entrance. She emerged, and came toward him, a little self-conscious, her head tilted a little to one side, the rich copper hair gleaming, the silver buckles of her slippers alternately thrust forward, the sharp heels striking clearly on the marble. She stopped, and waited for him, holding the cloak together with her hands. He had thought she was smiling. But when he came close to her, and she made no movement to disengage her hands, he saw that her lips were pressed tight, and that in the widened and darkened pupils of her gray eyes was a curious mingling of defiance and defeat. She was as frightened as himself. He put his hand against her elbow and said——

—Let's walk up and down here.

—Do you think this was a very tactful way——

—I'm sorry. But what else——

—Everybody in Cambridge saw it——

—Good God, Berty, surely there are more important things——

—It's typical.

—Not at all. On these occasions one simply obeys one's instinct, that's all.

—Is that an excuse for bad manners, or lack of consideration?

—It seemed to me the most *neutral* way of managing it.

—Perhaps you're right. But I should have thought——

They walked to the end of the hall in silence, embarrassed, past the rows of sepulchral memorial tablets, the interminable lists of dead soldiers. Antietam. The Battle of the Wilderness. Gettysburg. Bull Run. Born, and died of wounds. Killed in action. Died in a Confederate Prison. Died in Libby Prison, of a fever. Born and Died.

—Is Tom coming.

—No.

They turned, and started slowly back. From Sanders Theater came the sudden sound of renewed music, the beginning of the second number, a fanfare of bright trumpets and a thumping of drums. Muted by distance and the valves of doors.

—Tell me. Did Bill call you up.

—Yes.

—Did he tell you that he was giving me his ticket.

—Yes.

—I see. Just as I thought. He arranged it. You expected me. And you told Tom he'd better not come.

—I told Tom that I thought it would not be advisable.

—For *both* our sakes, I suppose!

—For *all* our sakes. I think the sarcasm is uncalled for.

—Sorry. I was only thinking aloud.

Lifting her hand from her cloak, she touched a quick finger to the corners of her eyes.

—I think you might have let me know before, what you were doing, or where you were——

—I wanted to be alone. Surely you understand *that*.

—Of course I understand it, but just the same I think you might have let me know.

For the first time she turned and looked at him, hesitating, half inhibiting her step, as if she were going to stop, or even going to touch him, as if for the first time she were meeting him. But she averted her face again.

—Andy, you don't look well.

—Neither do you, Berty, for that matter!

—Isn't it silly——

—What.

She made a downward gesture with her hand.

—Life. The way we make each other suffer.

—That's the most sensible thing you ever said.

He found himself holding her elbow quite tightly, and at the same time frowning, as if to control an excess of feeling—but what sort of feeling he could not possibly have said. Not anger, not self-pity.

—There's a lot of mail for you at the apartment.

—Yes, I thought I'd go round there now—that is, if you're staying for the concert—and get it. And a few clean shirts. I thought I'd leave before the intermission.

—What are you going to do.

—Do you mean now—or do you mean in general.

—Well—both.

He gazed downward, at the worn and dirty marble of the floor, trodden down by the hungry generations of undergraduates, among whom had been himself, and watched the parallel thrust, preposterous, of Bertha's slippers and his own mud-splashed shoes.

—I'm damned if I know yet, Berty—doesn't it really depend on *you*.

—Not necessarily.

—What I really came for was to say that I thought *time*—that I thought we ought to take plenty of *time*——

—Do you think we need any more?

—It sounds weak of me, but I don't know.

—Do you mean——

—What do *you* mean!

He stopped, and turned her toward him with his hand, and looked hard at her eyes. The look of defiance had gone, the look of defeat remained. She withdrew her arm from his hand, gently, and resumed the walk, and for a moment they listened in silence to the queer muffled and abortive sounds of the music, walking slowly, both their faces downcast.

—You ought to know. But do you want me to say it first.

—No, Berty. No. No.

—Well, then——

—I think I'll go away for a few days, if you don't mind—just to think it over quietly—by myself—I don't mean anything invidious by it——

—Where are you going.

—To Duxbury. It's absurd, but I've got a queer desire to go there. Not so queer either. It's all plain enough—I just want to go there.

—Andy——

—What.

—Take me with you. Let me come with you.

—No, Berty, I think it would be better not.

—Please.

—No, really, Berty, if you don't mind——

—Please.

—No.

There was a strained pause, they faced each other, she had tried to smile.

—And now I think I'll go—I think it's better if we don't talk about it too much yet—will it be all right if I leave you here—I suppose you can't get into the theater again, until the intermission. But if I'm going to drive down, I ought to be starting——

——Of course, Andy. Run along. I'll sit on the top steps and listen to it through the door.

—All right. If you're sure you don't mind. . . . Good night.

—Good night.

He turned as he went out, and caught a last glimpse of her climbing the stairs, lifting her frock at the knees. Poor Berty—or was it poor Andy? It had stopped raining. He skirted the edge of the College Yard, crossed Massachusetts Avenue, and in the Church Street garage asked for Bill's car, producing Bill's note and the key.

—I'm a friend of his.

—Yes, sir. I guess it's all right. Can you say what kind of a car it is.

—Dodge coupé.

—O. K. I'll bring her down for you.

So it was all coming out like this—all queerly ending like this—with a humble little anticlimax like this. And what would happen now! Impossible to say. It must be thought of, felt of. And with Tom still there, but now a little farther off——

—Thank you. How is she for oil and gas.

—All set.

—Thanks.

He drove slowly up Church Street, and into Brattle, as if to go to Shepard Hall; but then, suddenly he decided against it. Why go there at all? Why not start at once; merely stopping at the Club for his bag? Yes. . . .

Turning, he swung the car through Brattle Square, down to the river and across the little arched bridge, and then accelerated as he entered the wide new boulevard. So it was all like this. Bertha was like that. He himself was like—what? A queer confusion, a queer relief, a queer delight. In two hours he would be in Duxbury, would pass the dark rain-soaked railway station, the library, the flagpole. Find a hotel. And in the morning, at sunrise—how absurd it was—he would drive down to the Point, and cross the long bridge, over the rattling boards, and, see the beach again—or even walk to the Gurnett—unless, as was more than likely, he decided to sleep.

For already, to all intents, he had revisited that scene, in this week of so much revisiting—he knew it, every coarse or delicate detail of it—the matted waves of dried seaweed which were wet underneath, the caked salt on the pebbles, the shells, the bleached bones of fishes—the little piles of charred stones, too, on which were written the histories of clambakes—what more, now, could these things say to him? Or say usefully? But it would be good to touch earth. It would be good to touch, for the last time, that agony, and to exorcise it—to drown in it derisively, savagely, or even, at last, indifferently. No, not indifferently—at last with acceptance; as one accepts such simple things as daybreak. Such simple and shattering things as daybreak. The strange and exciting mixture of astonishment and suffering with which—at a moment of discovery—one loses oneself in order to create oneself! The end that is still conscious of its beginnings. Birth that remembers death.

He watched the swarms of raindrops coming toward the headlamps, arriving and mysteriously vanishing, the continuous vanishing swarm, and suddenly, with a sense of power, he pressed his foot on the accelerator, and laughed. Life was good—life was going to be good. Unexplored, unfathomable, marvelous and terrible. Filthy, and incalculable. Cruel, and inexhaustible. Like this unceasing swarm of bright raindrops, like the waves breaking on the beach at the Gurnett, innumerable as the atoms in the brain. The wonderful nightmare, the wonderful and acceptable nightmare! When I slap on the kalsomine I think about those gals o' mine. I'm only a Spanish grammar, but my heart is pure as mud.

King Coffin

"I think you are wise, and I shall mar my philosophy with no more murders. If, indeed, I have killed him; for I assure you that beyond administering the poison to his wretched body I have done nothing. Perhaps he is not dead. Can you hear his heart beating?"

"I can hear the spoons of my children beating on their empty platters!"

"Is it like that with you? Poor devil! Oh, poor, poor devil! Philosophers should have no wives, no children, no homes, and no hearts."

—RICHARD MIDDLETON

Contents

〖 I   The Particular Occasion

In the prime assurance of his youth, in the fresh arrogance of his wisdom, and power in wisdom, with a sense of his extreme handsomeness, if not indeed beauty (for Gerta had said more than once that he was beautiful, and his own mirror had pleasantly corroborated this) Jasper Ammen leaned from the sixth floor window and projected his own image upon the world. In particular, he projected it against the sunset: a more melancholy, and therefore more pleasant, form of this occupation, and one in which he frequently indulged. The sunset lay long and level and bright-banded above the hills of Belmont and Mount Auburn. Against a streak of white light, horizontal and cold, the black tower of the cemetery marked the presence, or the absence, of Henry James; to the right of it, slowly darkening, as the evening deepened to mystery, ran the irregular line of trees toward Belmont. And as he leaned his cheek on his left hand he felt once again how all this scene, this width and depth of air and light, was becoming himself. This was all Jasper Ammen, a singular magnification or distillation of his own essence, it was himself gone abroad for the greater exercise of his subtlety and power. The tower was his strength, the trees were his strength, the evolving and changing of the light were merely, as it were, the play of his thought over an earth everywhere his own; and the clear abyss of twilit sky, the lucid profundity into which he now figured himself as looking not upward but directly and amazingly downward, was simply his own mind. Below him, across the little street, the horse chestnut tree was uncurling its first soft-russet fingers of leaf: in another three weeks, it would blossom, and this too he felt as a precise and surer emanation of himself. The gesture would be as simple as his now taking out his pipe: as his remembering the sight of the folded newspaper protruding from his letter box in the hall downstairs: or the letter from Sandbach which just perceptibly stiffened his side pocket. Sandbach, like the chestnut blossom, could wait: one could curl a handsome lip at Sandbach, one could defer or dismiss him as an inferior part of oneself, keep him at a distance, measure him from afar with an omnipotent and all-understanding eye. It was exactly like viewing and appraising one's own past: or even despising it; for the past should always be cut ruthlessly away, allowed to fall from one, remembered not for its leaves but for its seeds. . . .

In this sense he despised the gradual sentimental dislimning of the spring sunset: without any sense of loss, he watched it go, gave it to the evening, allowed it to drown slowly in his own receptive darkness. He felt his face assuming its habitual expression of proud contempt, the feeling as of looking down at something very small and unimportant from a Himalayan summit. He became increasingly conscious of his high cheekbones, his narrowed green eyes, the sleepy superciliousness of his fixed gaze, the curtness of his mouth: but then he relaxed, and permitted himself to play another, and equally habitual, part, one which he often used (and to effect) in social gatherings: the part of the poet,—detached, remote, inscrutable: the Zarathustrian prophet. Ridiculous, to consider how few people knew enough of themselves to be able to use, for such social effect, their own presence, their own bodies! An elementary mistake, a fault of adolescence, if not of childhood. To know one's moroseness, and to use it, one's meanness and to use it, one's hatred, and to project it vigorously and without mercy—this was, after all, only the beginning, only the beginning. One should know with scientific minuteness one's *exact* appearance from every angle—the back, the sides, the look of the shoulders as they turn away, the value of one's six-feet-two, the rhythm of one's gait. There must be no accidents! But above all, one must value one's capacity for hate, and use it with the finest justice. And one's deliberate rudenesses must be carefully relished.

Bringing back his gaze from the deployed subtleties and cold venoms of the faded sunset, he turned it shortly downward toward the two flat roofs which were immediately below him. On the nearer, beyond the cement runway of the garage, a young man was sitting in a deck chair: one of *The Crimson* editors. His head was thrown back, his arms were lifted behind his head, a book was open on his knees. Examined, he was at once understood. A faithful and earnest joiner and belonger: a member of society. To see through him, disemboweling all his little clipped ambitions with a single penetrating eye, was as easy as it would be, from this window, to shoot him; and to consider the justice of the metaphor was only to weigh, pleasurably, one's sense of power in a situation as superior in altitude as it was in consciousness. The young fool was comprehended, or killed, without knowing it. He had stopped reading not because it was as yet too dark, but in a twilight mood of narcissism: something had passed into him from the opened pages of that book, and he was now weakly luxuriating in that something: he was as helpless as a schoolgirl. To demonstrate this helplessness and also to prove to himself that he was not afraid of a direct action, Jasper whistled. The head turned round a little, then turned up, the eyes were surprised, the mouth was slightly opened—in short, the whole expression was foolish. The young man stared upward for a moment, but finding that his gaze was met without sign and without discomposure, turned away again, embarrassed. He was blushing. He then closed his book, rose, and walked very self-consciously to the steps which led down into the building on the far side. The dignity of his disappearance was terrific.

The flat roof beyond was a narrower and longer one, covered with tar paper and gravel; and to look at it was to observe, of course, that the cast-iron chimney pipe, at the back, had been restored to its upright position. An excellent minor example of the value of habitual observation: and it had given him pleasure to recognize in the street the woman who owned the house (merely by the way she walked) and to inform her (she not knowing him from Adam) that her chimney had fallen on the roof in the snow and might prove a source of danger. She had looked at him as if he were mad. So *that* was why her kitchen fire hadn't been drawing properly! She was still saying this, from beneath her umbrella, and staring, when he bowed and walked away. . . .

Quarter to seven.

He took Sandbach's letter from his pocket, the blue envelope, tapped it against his long thumb, and walked along the linoleumed corridor toward his room. He walked quickly, with a slight self-conscious scuffing of the heels, pleased with the total effect (which he had often studied in street mirrors and shop windows) of graceful casualness, and also with the echoed sound of the light iambics: his shoes were expensive. Arrived at his door, he hesitated. Sandbach might be inside, or Gerta, or both—not that it much mattered. Ostensibly, they would have come to take him to the meeting at Tremont Temple, they would chatter about that, nervously no doubt, and of course Sandbach would as usual, in that oblique sniffing way of his, be hinting about money for the sacred cause of anarchism or the strikers at Haverhill. But beneath all that would be the real sense of *crisis* —the sense of the personal and psychological crisis which he himself had so carefully constructed; and he was not quite sure whether, supposing Gerta and Sandbach had now decided to make common cause, he wanted to see them together or separately. They had spent the entire day looking for him, they had left notes, they had repeatedly telephoned, Sandbach had finally sent his special delivery letter; it had all gone off just as he had willed it and planned it; and he himself had remained hidden in the University Theater all afternoon, enjoying, in that seclusion, the muffled sense of their frightened activity, while he analyzed the social function of Popeye the Sailor Man. The universal Oedipus complex, no doubt? But it would perhaps be better not to see them until immediately before the anarchist meeting, when it would of course be impossible for them to be personal, to be anything but professional—to meet them lightly and coldly there, and to make it clear at once that he did not intend to have any disgusting emotional dealings with them, none whatever. Not that he wasn't, of course, profoundly curious about their little mutual fever, their co-operative eagerness, and their desire to turn toward him a joint expression of bright and sympathetic explanation—not at all! But that pleasure he was already, and deliciously, tasting. What they must learn was that *he* could intrude, but not they. . . . Hearing no sound from the room, he entered.

One candle had been lighted on the white mantel, beneath the mask of Nietzsche, and against it was propped a note from Gerta. Jasper my dear— I have waited here all afternoon in your hushed little chamber, hoping to have a private word with you before you see Sandbach. I have the feeling, as no doubt you intend, that you are avoiding me: of course I understand that, for if you'll forgive me for saying so I do know you pretty well. But don't you think you could overdo it? There are features which might better be discussed without Sandbach—I mean, you and me. I make no preposterous claims: you ought to realize that I respect your privacy and individualism and don't want to infringe. But my dear, human nature is not as easy as that, there *are* obligations—well, of a *shadowy* sort; you could find a better word. It's quite all right, of course, and as it should be, you needn't be so afraid, but what I suggest is that what is private for us—you and me—might be a little bruised if Sandbach is allowed to participate *at the outset.* Do you see what I mean—or would you regard *this* as a claim? I am not going to the meeting. But I shall be in my room all evening, and I wish you would come there when the fireworks are over. I gather you are going to resign, from what S says, and he is hurt, and of course is divided between that and anger, and also tries to comfort himself by saying that you were never really sincere anyway. He thinks you are just an esthete, and that anarchism is no more important for you than the taste you exercised in the decorating of this very chaste and epicene room. It *is* chaste and epicene—good lord, yes! Gerta.

Good lord, yes! Gerta.

So that was what Sandbach thought—or said.

With his hat still on, he sat down at the little red table, on which was a blue and orange square of Chinese embroidery, and looked across the room at the window. The curtain ring, hanging motionless, made a sharp little oval against the pale sky, beyond which, on the roof of the A. D. Club, was a rapidly spinning chimney pot. Chaste and epicene? It was exactly what Julius Toppan was always saying downstairs, Gerta had probably been discussing it with him, and come to think of it that identical remark had appeared in Julius's diary. That was a week ago. There must, by this time, be several more entries in Julius's diary, entries about himself—it was time he went in and read them. Perhaps by now Julius had definitely reached the conclusion—to which he already tended—that he was crazy: he would certainly think so if he knew that his diary was one of Jasper's chief sources of entertainment. An abuse of hospitality? of trust? But Julius knew his views about these things, knew that he proposed to live beyond ordinary morals, so it hardly mattered. If one's brains could be picked by others, let them be picked.

Yes, Gerta had been discussing his taste with Julius, she had been to Toppan's room, perhaps several times, perhaps today—that was worth knowing and noting, it was a significant little light, and of course the import of it was clear enough—she too was trying, in her little way, to surround him, to triangulate him into view, and that was admirable enough too, although bound to be futile. It was all a sort of conspiracy of fright, with which also a little designingness and greed was mixed: Sandbach looking for his money, Julius for his "influence," the secret of his power, Gerta for his love. The fright was perhaps genuine as far as Gerta was concerned, she genuinely and unselfishly—questionable, though—liked him; anyway, she was concerned, a little foolishly so, about his sanity, and of course had to run to and fro discussing him with her friends and acquaintances: little realizing that on a lower and simpler plane of morals this would have been very reprehensible. In fact, it *was* reprehensible on *her* plane, but not on *his*. The dear little fool, playing desperately at a losing game! And so earnest about it, too.

He opened Sandbach's letter.

Gosh, you certainly are an elusive cuss, I've been pussyfooting all over town after you to tell you that a Chicago member will be there tonight and that as the attendance will be very small I hoped you would come and also that you would perhaps refrain from throwing any bombs of a private nature, they could be postponed for a better occasion—unless you have really decided to clear out. From what Gottlieb said at the C Bookshop the other day on the Hill, I gather you have finally decided to take an individualist turn and go the whole metaphysical or Hegelian Hog and coddle your ego in the footsteps of Max Stirner. Maybe you were only kidding, but in the light of some of our talks I can see it might be logical for you, though you can't expect me to applaud. I have always hoped you would become one of our most active and useful members, would really help us, as you are in a position to do, not that you haven't already helped us a lot. But what I mean is, please don't choose tonight for any bust-up, it would be a little impolite to Breault (Chicago), if you don't mind. I also wanted to see you about Gerta, you know how things stand there, and I just wanted to assure you that there isn't and hasn't been and won't be any treachery. S.

Treachery by Sandbach? A contradiction in terms, for one could only be betrayed by an equal, never by an inferior. A treachery foreseen and understood, or even to some extent fomented, was not a treachery, it was simply one's own action: and to explain this to Sandbach would be his natural punishment, or rather, humiliation. And Gerta's too, though Gerta perhaps *did* understand it, and *was* (at any rate partially) an equal? . . .

Just the same, he quite recognized his own quick anger, as he tore one strip and then another from the edge of Sandbach's ill-written letter and laid the strips along the table before him: it was necessary to be angry with Sandbach's "belongingness," his politicalness, his Jewish mixture of guile and affection and effrontery: his parasitism. It was necessary to be angry, but to be only privately angry. Publicly, only a gentle contempt, only the natural expression of a natural superiority: the mere exercise of personal presence. And this was easy enough. One simply looked down at little Sandbach, one smiled, one wore one's clothes, one lighted one's pipe, one entered or left a room, and Sandbach knew what one meant. Sandbach knew that one knew all about his dirty little sycophantic hand-rubbing soul, quite as clearly as one knew that he seldom changed his underclothes and socks. He would resent this, and would scheme an answer to it, he was always wanting to make, as it were, an injurious little place for himself in the souls of his superiors, just as now he was no doubt enormously pleased with himself for his conquest—permitted, and partial—of Gerta. His ascent to Gerta was seen by himself as a climb over dangerous scaffolding towards Jasper? And now the moment had come, perhaps, to kick him down, to kick him in the face, but precisely by not *bothering* to kick him. Beyond that, he had no importance, and it was absurd to be angry at all: except as one was consciously aware of one's anger with oneself.

But Gerta was more difficult, Gerta was deeper. Gerta had a real virtue of her own, or a partial one, she had in her the power to challenge. She was challenging him now.

He dropped the strips of Sandbach's letter into the metal wastebasket, forgetfully, and with his hat pushed back on his head went to the mantel-piece and examined the mask of Nietzsche; and it was exactly as if he were examining Gerta's challenge. Lighted thus from below by the little calm candle flame, the mad face looked madder than ever, demonic, voracious: it was the face of a revenger, the eaten one who wanted to eat. "Oh, my brethren, am I then cruel? . . . Everything of today—it falleth, it de-cayeth; who would preserve it! But I—I wish also to push it!" Yes, one must separate oneself. And Gerta's challenge was just there—it was the last line of her defense of "belongingness" that thus she would invoke this thing she wanted to call "love." It was her only obvious weakness? For otherwise——

The sense of her came immediately into this room, too immediately, as if she were herself entering and taking possession, her face was between his and the mask, somber and sibyline, but mischievous as well, and as he turned away, toward the window, it was difficult to suppose that she had not herself moved also, to stand there against the last of the sunset, as she was often in the habit of standing. She was decidedly more difficult, he was always thus projecting himself in her image and with a weakly disguised tenderness, it must stop. Take care lest a parasite ascend with you! But the parasite was actually, in such a case, simply oneself—one was oneself only the cage for the bird, the container; the cause of one's hatred was not without but within; it was not therefore a question of getting rid of Sandbach or Gerta, not at all, but of getting rid of one's *need*. If one could not dismiss them, one could perhaps replace them with symbols more innocent: with this mask of Nietzsche: with the brass Russian teapot on the window sill, dark against the pale sky, the little Woolworth cage of glass hung from its spout: the seashell: the blue-green ginger jar. Could one not successfully deploy oneself in these simpler images? and thus keep one's virtue harder and clearer, readier for the fine purity of hate? less *roiled?*

—Do you ever feel—he suddenly said aloud, thrusting his hands deep in his pockets—that the whole world is nothing but a kind of pale fantasm?

He stood still, a little surprised and perhaps embarrassed by the abrupt and vibrant sound of his voice, a little ashamed of the conscious dramati-zation, but then he smiled and saw how ridiculous it would be to do any-thing but surrender to an impulse which was obviously genuine and in any case very moving.

—And especially people. Especially people. With what person or per-sons, Jasper, do you ever manage to establish even for the tiniest fraction of a second anything like a reality of understanding? Good God, no. They are nothing but shadows.

At first he had kept his voice low, but now he allowed it to rise in volume and pitch. He walked across the room to the Chinese waterfall, looked at it, then returned to the window.

—That waterfall. And this seashell, if I touch it—it gives itself to me without asking anything in return. The truth is, you're alone, every one is against you, and that, even if you don't like it, is all for the best! Yes,

you've got to like it. They all want to kill you, they all want to kill the
spirit. Isn't that true?

He stopped in the middle of the room and stood still, staring out of
the window.

—Chaste and epicene! There it is, by God, there it is—that was Gerta's
little murder. And that's the way it always is. We go around trying just
like that to hurt people, to revenge ourselves, but always, like that, dis-
honestly and obliquely and crookedly and for private *reasons!* Good God,
how dirty it all is. And how dirty I am. But I'm damned if I'll be dirty. I'm
damned if I will. I must be *pure.*

The silence, when his voice stopped, seemed almost self-conscious. He
controlled an impulse to look quickly right and left, the motive of which
was quite apparent (namely, to see if any one had overheard him), and
examined with sharp despair, and then with amusement, the singular fact
that one could not thus even talk aloud to oneself without feeling unnatural about it. Or, what was worse, much worse, without being, or becoming, unnatural in the thing itself. One had to become eloquent even
in addressing remarks to oneself—that was it—and it was disgusting. And
if that was so, was it perhaps also so that even in one's thinking——

But the fantasm notion was true. It must be that every one felt that—
here could be nothing private or delusory about it—it was true that no
human being could ever achieve a *real* contact with anything or anyone.
And in a world of unrealities, how could there be rights or wrongs or obligations? or injuries or thefts? how either join or separate, when there could
be no question of *touch?* Suum cuique. His thought came round on itself,
he was puzzled, frowned, looked down into the wastebasket, at the scraps
of Sandbach's letter, saw the word "bomb," the word "expect." If it was
all as scattered and meaningless as that, as intangible, or almost intangible,
then the only course was to extend oneself violently outward, to thrust
everywhere, to occupy the world entirely with one's own entire length. . . .

He went into the little bedroom, turned on the electric light, and
looked at his face in the dressing-table mirror, turning it first to the right
and then to the left. It was an intelligent face, and the eyes looked back at
him steadily, but also with an unanswerable question. Yes, it was a noble
face, and fine, as Gerta had said—the conscious end of the conscious
world. The room was gray and pictureless, there was no ornament save a
small bronze Buddha on a scarlet shelf. This he could see behind him in
the mirror as he began passing the comb backward through the dark luxury
of his hair.

◖ II   The Idea Germinates

He looked in through the wide window of the Merle as he passed, and particularly at the chair by the table in the corner, behind the end of the
marble soda fountain; the impulse was the familiar one of recapitulation,

the desire to see himself sitting there, where he had sat half an hour before, eating his supper of sandwiches. Julius Toppan was now sitting at the same table, and was looking straight at him, and nodded, half raising his hand with a knife in it. The gesture, the situation, his eating there in such a position as to command a view of the pedestrians outside, was a flagrant imitation, of course, and deserved the rebuke of a "cut": accordingly he passed the window without any sign of recognition, nothing but a cool stare and the merest trace of an ironic smile. So much for flattery, so much for Toppan. He could return to his law books, he could make a new entry about that madman Jasper in his diary. Saw Ammen tonight and am more than ever convinced the man is a megalomaniac: he evidently thinks he is the only liberated and intelligent person alive. He is gradually closing himself in. . . .

The necessity for recapitulation—yes, this must be recognized, and tonight it seemed especially necessary—the well-known backward glance, the embracing gesture with which one must gather one's past, one's collection of identities, in order to take the next forceful step forward into the future. The Buddha, for example, was still there behind him, in the mirror, on its scarlet shelf, and with the Buddha, as he walked along Massachusetts Avenue past the lighted shopwindows, came the brief experiment with the hardening doctrine of yoga, the deep breathings, the concentration on the thought of drowning, the concept of the individual. But other things must be freely admitted as well—if one took a dime from one's pocket for the subway fare one must see it as a symbol of much sore history, behind it came the image of his father sitting at a mahogany desk in Saint Louis, his arms extended sideways on the desk, both fists tightly clenched, his gray face suddenly darkened with hatred and surrender. And not only surrender, but sundering—their hatred for each other had at last become outspoken, had been seen by both of them as positively a kind of psychological food without which they could no longer live. And his father's words, too, hung before him on the platform of the subway, amongst the cement columns and slot-machines, above the newsstand, against the lighted windows of the waiting train. Unfortunately, I told your mother, before she died, that I would give you an allowance, and make you independent: otherwise, take my word for it, I wouldn't give you a cent, not a cent. What you need, and what you've always needed, is discipline. The words effected the final silence between them, the silence which had in fact always been the inevitable outcome, the natural silence as of a profound chasm of misunderstanding between them. In the silence, he had come east, he had begun to build in it his new life, had been able to turn round on himself for the first time in order to discover, spherically, his own dimensions and reach, like a man learning to swim. It had given him room for his bitterness, he had been learning to hit and hurt: and that was good. The fact that his father still sat there, his fists pressed hard on the mahogany desk, didn't really matter. It was entirely natural, just as his mother's death had been natural, or the insanity, so progressive and orderly, of brother Kay. No less natural than his own detective curiosity about this progressive insanity, his secret collection of photographs of Kay at all the different stages, beginning at the age of three, the sharp-eyed sharp-faced child who gazed with such burning intelligence over the back of the gilt-

knobbed chair, ending with the fat and sleepy and stupid face of twenty-
seven, from which all awareness of reality had suddenly faded. A gross face,
of which the secret was a cunning defense of a private idea. The hands
curiously small and birdlike, and always *picking*.

The bell rang, the doors slid softly shut, recoiled from rubber flanges,
shut again more firmly, the motors began their ascending whine, and his
eye rose to the long line of advertisements above the porcelain handholds.
A salesgirl was saying—wash it with Ivory. When years steal away the gold,
restore the golden hair of girlhood. Golden Hair Wash. Priceless the life
of a child.

The detective impulse, the spying mania—it would be possible to evolve
the natural history and origin of that, one could develop it *ad lib.*, trace it
from childhood up, but what would be the use, it was all quite clear, it
could be seen very neatly and comprehensively in perspective: the reading
of forbidden books, the exploration of forbidden streets, the cultivation of
forbidden acquaintances, the special sharp delight in all duplicity, above
all the really exquisite pleasure in knowing more than one was supposed to
know. Reading, for instance, the doctor's letters about Kay, the reports of
the teachers and psychiatrists; watching the anxiety of father and mother;
observing the subtle deterioration of Kay. More recently, his new game
(and what a joke that it was Julius Toppan who had put the idea in his
head) of picking out a stranger in the street and following him—but again
it was sufficient simply to note this, and to see that the Jasper was the same
Jasper, the same superior consciousness, the same one whose perceptions
had the invisibility of extreme subtlety. It was the Jasper who loved to keep
secrets, and who prevented his friends from becoming intimate: who had
a kind of genius for dividing up his daily life into separate departments,
so that no one individual knew anything more of him than the one department to which he had been assigned. Very satisfactory, it gave one an
enormous advantage with people if one could thus play on their defeated
curiosity: it gave him the whip hand with Sandbach and Gerta, even now
they were beside themselves with frustration, though they didn't like to
admit it, and were clearly upset because they didn't know what he was
going to do. They felt something impending, they knew they were in the
midst of a crisis, they suspected danger, but what shape it would have
they couldn't guess. Nor whether perhaps the whole thing might not turn
out to be a joke.

—The post office buys the stamps?
—Yes.
—And they give the girls that space?
—Yes.
—She has three windows?
—Yes, she has to sell a hundred dollars' worth of stamps——
—Well, I don't know, I don't understand it.
—Why should the post office——
—and a rake-off on every stamp she sells——

He took out his pipe, looked to see if it was empty, put it to his mouth
and blew out the little bubble of caught moisture in the stem. Yes, he had
them on the run, and all by the simplest turn of the wrist—a postcard to

Gerta, saying dislocation number one, another to Sandbach, saying dislocation number two, and then the quick little insult to Gottlieb at the C
Bookshop, in the presence of Mrs. Taber, she standing there astounded,
her mouth open, the gaps in her teeth showing, the ragged little feather
duster in her hand. Amateurs, you are all sickening little amateurs, not one
of you has any guts, not one of you would have the guts to act alone, to
take any risk by yourselves. It's all play-acting, exactly like the tiresome
tepid little immoralities of Beacon Hill and Fayette Street. No brains, no
pride. Just rats. You go round together like rats.

—Say you are selling light wines——

—Well, now listen, how would it be if——

—That to me is outrageous, why should they pay that woman a rake-off,
it's the cheapest service——

Like all human situations, the thing was a composite, the elements in
it were on at least two different planes, if not more; above or below his
abandonment of federalist anarchism, his abandonment of the "cause" and
the Boston Group, was his sharp warning to them that there was to be a
personal change as well, that he had risen above them and was henceforth
consigning them to a lower circle. It was this which they found painful
and bewildering, their affections and pride were hurt, Gerta's affections,
Sandbach's pride, he was hurrying them into a defensive alliance which
they both found humiliating, and insofar as they had thought they *possessed* him they now felt exposed and defrauded. Certainly they were feeling rushed, they had been caught unaware by the sudden action, the unexpected psychic speed, it was as if he had forced them into an emotional
stammer; but the question was, whether he himself could now stand *outside* the results of his action, avoid being caught in his own whirl, get away
in time to a higher and safer ground. The question was also whether he
knew quite where the hurry was going to lead, and quite why it had happened, or happened so suddenly. The sense of hurry was at any rate acute,
he had felt it mounting day by day and hour by hour, as if there were
somewhere a destination (a little vague) to which he must go with the
utmost directness and despatch: the sense as of a map spread out before
him, and a watch ticking excitedly in his hand, and nearer every moment
the sound of a coming invasion. He was going to *do* something, he must
do something, there must be the final action by which he would have set
the seal on his complete freedom. To escape the company of rats, to express the profundity of his contempt—to *kill* a rat——!

His eyes rose slowly and heavily from the thought, he saw the knees
of the man before him, a loose thread, the edge of the soiled and worn coat,
he heard the man's voice saying post office, in the post office, observed the
little fold of shirt protruding between trousers and waistcoat, resented the
oppressive nearness of the strange human body, and got up from his seat
angrily and abruptly. He pushed contemptuously between the two men,
sundering them, was aware of their turning heads, looked back at them
with a little smile as he squared his shoulders through the crowd, and
pressed toward the opening door. A moment later, as he walked quickly
along the cement platform, he found himself laughing, and slapping his
hand against his side, he felt a little drunk, a little drugged, for if his

eyes had risen heavily from the thought he had himself risen as heavily, it was almost as if he had experienced a slight blow on the head, a concussion. Something had happened, something important had happened! It was always like that. It always came like that. There was just exactly that kind of accidental conjunction of idea and fact—the thought occurring precisely at a moment when the mere physical nearness of a stranger's human body was beginning to oppress and stifle him, making itself felt as an unwarrantable and disgusting intrusion. The feeling of hatred, intolerable hatred, had come like a flash and had revealed to him as never before the rightness and terribleness of the *deed*: as under lightning, the whole landscape leapt out of darkness in green and maplike and logical minuteness. The mere presence of the strange human body had shown him not only what he wanted but exactly why he wanted it. And not only that, but also how *right* had been the idea.

The discovery, as he ascended on the escalator and emerged under the red brick tower at Park Street, had an odd effect on him. He looked round him with a sharp sense of relief and detachment, he felt alone and tall and superior amongst the disorderly crowd of nocturnal pedestrians, and almost indeed as if he belonged to a different race or species; and as he stood still by the corner, observing first one face and then another, one hand jingling pennies in his pocket, the other holding his unlighted pipe, it occurred to him that a cat must feel something like this: a cat alone in a cellar, sitting perhaps on the top of a flour barrel, and watching the naïve and unconscious antics of mice. Close at hand, in an Independent taxi, the driver was reading *The Traveler*. Red Sox Win Slugfest with Senators. The solemn face was chewing gum. A woman stepped out into the street in front of the cab, paused, looked into her bag, checked her balance as if to come back, then quickly resumed her way. A voice behind him said, the clock says quarter to nine, my watch must be slow, and two young men, wearing identical brown felt hats, approached the taxi with obvious intent. The driver leaned forward to hear the address, Lenox Hotel, clinked the flag down, and in a moment the two felt hats, behind the door of the cab, described a pair of parallel curves round the corner into Tremont Street and were gone. It would be easy and amusing to follow them? And there was now, all of a sudden, plenty of time—for with the sense of relief had also come a curious alteration of his sense of hurry—as if the hurry need no longer be transacted externally, but could become, and without pressure, *concentric*, an affair of his own, a mere matter of revolving within or around himself. No, the time had now come, as he might have foreseen, for a careful weighing, a careful and cautious inspection; a period of leisure and close scrutiny; and if there was still an urgency, such as was now causing his heart to beat a little more rapidly, it was wholly private. Between his own world and the world outside, a peculiar division had now arrived, and if time still existed importantly for himself, it had no longer any important existence elsewhere: in his own kingdom, the kingdom of thought, he could move as rapidly as he liked, stay as long as he liked, the outside world would meanwhile stand still, and he could rejoin it whenever he wished, and exactly at the point at which he had left it. The situation, or series of situations, which he had created, would remain as if suspended until he chose to resolve them: Gerta would be waiting, Sandbach would be waiting, everything would hang motionless in a kind of timeless limbo. So clear, so beautiful, was this impression, this divination, that he paused to give it visual form. It was like the story of the sleeping beauty—a whole world suddenly frozen into stillness—or the tranced figures of the Grecian Urn. The anarchist meeting in Tremont Temple would still be there, when he got there after his voyage upon voyage round the world, Sandbach would still be holding the black and sticky stump of a cigar in yellow fingers, and saying yes I think maybe, yes I think maybe but do you agree with me, Toppan would still be taking a safety razor blade from his pocketbook to sharpen a smooth red pencil, Gerta would be standing at her window to look at the Charles River Basin, a book opened before her on the window sill, an apple in her hand. They would be listening, they would be waiting, and for what? To be destroyed. To be touched, and waked, and destroyed.

He crossed Tremont Street, entered the drug store, found an empty telephone booth by the front window, and began dialing with the stem of his pipe. In the next booth a voice was saying but I can't, but you see it would already be too late, I'm way in here at Park Street, a woman's voice, peevish and whining, softened and made more nasal by the wooden partition. He half turned to listen.

—Hello?

—Ammen speaking. I wanted to be clear——

—Oh, Jasper; did you get my note?

Gerta's voice was anxious, a trifle high-pitched. She was self-conscious.

—I wanted to be clear that there would be no one else there.

—Of course. If there's any one else I'll send them away. I thought that would be understood, my dear.

—All right. I'll be there in fifteen minutes or half an hour. I don't expect to loiter at the meeting, if I stay at all.

—Very well, if——

He cut off the phrase by hanging up the receiver. No doubt she was now saying Jasper, hello, Jasper, hello, hello, while already he clasped the brass handle of the door. He listened again to the voice in the adjacent booth—but I said I was in here at Park Street, yes, at Park Street—and then went out. Like all fragmentary or uncompleted remarks, as in fact like Gerta's unfinished phrase, it had an oddly ominous ring, a ring of fatality; and one's sense of power arose precisely from the fact that one could thus cut them off oneself. As one should.

And what now should be said to little Sandbach?

He walked rapidly with the beginnings of the sentences, touched them against his teeth lightly with the cool pipe stem, let them down with him from the curb in Bromfield Street to pick them up again on the other side, allowed them to be dispersed by the lurid placard of announcements in the lobby of the Temple and to fall behind him on the wide stairs. His shadow rose huge and high-shouldered on the bare wall of the second story, dislocated itself sideways, raised an immensely long arm, and vanished against the open door, from which came the sound of several voices in animated talk. His shadow had, in fact, gone in ahead of him, and he followed it into the room with the feeling of having an immense advantage.

There were half a dozen irregular little rows of folding chairs, and be-

yond these, by the little platform, Sandbach was talking with a few people,
only a handful, it was clear that the meeting was a complete failure. Mrs.
Taber was there, smiling her perpetual sweet smile under a pale purple
bonnet, that immortal bonnet, and her husband the shyster lawyer, and
Mrs. Hays the amateur psychoanalyst.

—Here he is now.

Sandbach crooked his elbow and pointed at him, pointed with his cigar,
the dozen faces turned and looked at him with silent appraisal. They all
seemed more than ever small and shabby, ridiculous, unreal, and as he
bore down on them with his six feet two, stooping slightly forward, he was
aware of playing Gulliver in Lilliput, his shadow was over them like a vast
wing.

Sandbach, as always when he was a little frightened, smiled too much
and looked cunning, his face seemed to be all width and no height, the
eyes and mouth made long insinuating horizontals. Difficult to say where
the Asiatic began and the Semitic left off, it was very fawning and subtle,
no doubt about that, one could see in him the uneasy fertility which
attracted Gerta.

—What do you think, Ammen, what do you say, the meeting is so
small, it is a pity, this is our comrade Breault, shake hands with him, we
thought as it was so small we wouldn't try to have any speeches, but just
have a little talk together, maybe. We could all go to my room in Allston
Street. If you could come along, we were waiting for you.

Mrs. Taber put her skinny little hand on his arm, and cooed.

—Now do come, Mr. Ammen, I'm sure we need a little of your fine
young cynicism!

He looked over their heads toward the windows, then round the bare
and sordid little room with its air of cheap varnish, he remembered the
excitement of his first meeting here, when it had seemed that something
real and vigorous was being done, something dangerous and profound.
It had suddenly shrunk to the size of his hand.

—No, Sandbach, I told you in my postcard that I was finished, I'm
sorry, I just dropped in to tender my formal resignation. I'm afraid I no
longer see any use in it.

—I see. He no longer sees any use in it. If he ever did!

—The sneer is gratuitous, but I had foreseen it.

—You had foreseen my sneer? I made no sneer, I think I merely stated
a fact.

Mr. Taber began laughing offensively, then turned his back and walked
away. Mrs. Hays, dressed in black, and as usual trying to look sibyline,
put her head on one side and smiled condescendingly. Beneath their anger
and hurt pride, of course, was their disgusting disappointment in losing his
money, it was his own money which had paid for Breault. It was as if they
were his employees, his servants, and he had dismissed them, their anger
and hatred was slavish and cringing, they were clinging together against
him.

—I didn't come here to argue with you, but simply to make a statement. Unfortunately I find that neither your ideas nor your feelings have
any reality or importance whatever. I'm afraid I was mistaken in you—or
mistaken in myself, which comes to the same thing.

—Aren't you carrying your subjective idealism pretty far? Now, Breault, you can see what happens when young men read too much Berkeley.

—I can assure Mr. Breault that your concern about my reading doesn't interest me in the slightest. I think you're all a little grotesque, it seems to me a little shameful that I ever thought I had anything in common with you.

—Very well, I don't think we need to say anything further.

—You aren't dismissing me—*I'm* dismissing *you*. I'll be grateful, but not excessively so, if you'll take my name off your mailing list, and send back my books. Good night.

He looked at Breault, who was embarrassed and blushing, and felt that he hadn't yet done full justice to the situation. He laughed and put on his hat, then turned to Sandbach again.

—If you only knew how funny you are!

—Is anything to be gained from bad manners or impudence?

—Manners are of the mob, Sandbach, put that in your pipe and smoke it.

He swung his back to them and walked toward the door, a woman's voice said why he thinks he's God Almighty, Sandbach and Breault had begun laughing very loudly, somebody whistled turkey-in-the-straw. From the door he half turned and waved his hand. For a moment all the faces were quite still, it was like a photograph, and his final impression of them was that they were all *hungry*.

❲ III   The Background

The evening had deepened, with the completion of this action, but again it was only as if the evening were a mere projection of himself, and its deepening, or his own deepening, was of course due to the very fact that the action had not been entirely satisfactory. It would have been better if he had made a formal address, a formal and drastic analysis: if he had dissected their pitifulness and futility before their very eyes, shamed them, horrified them. He could have quoted Martin—"I am sick of this oozing democracy. There must be something crystalline and insoluble left in democratic America. Somewhere there must be people with sharp edges that cut when they are pressed too hard, people who are still solid, who have impenetrable depths in them and hard facets which reflect the sunlight. They are the hope of democracy, these infusible ones." To hell with their crowd-mindedness, their weak and slavish dependence on each other! What had *their* little anarchism to do with this? It was a contradiction in terms, an absurdity, they were themselves absurdities, and their unfitness was as clear in their sheeplike instinct of banding themselves together as in their sheeplike faces. Yes, this would have been better, he ought to have done it, but as usual his own sense of hurry—was it that?—had impeded him, his anger had produced the usual short circuit. At such moments one's

mere animal disgust became paramount, it was impossible to do anything
but turn one's back, it was a choice between that and killing them.

To kill them, yes: what was necessary was a machine gun.

The beautiful terribleness of the deed!

He stood still in the dark canyon of Beacon Street, between the somber
stone walls of his own canyon, at the bottom of his own sky, at the center
of his own world, and aimed his pipe stem like a gun across the paving
stones toward a small crowd which stood before one of Houghton and
Dutton's windows. The fascinating impulse was already quivering in his
index finger. The stupid backs were cut in two by death's mechanical rattlesnake chatter, the plate glass window was drilled shrilly from side to side,
the falling glass made an irregular tinkling and chiming, and then everything was again silent. It was toward a group of dead men that he crossed
the street, it was a group of corpses that he joined before the window,
and looking over the heads he saw that the window had been turned into
a little zoo, it was a cage of monkeys. A dozen little gray monkeys, with
long ratlike tails, skipped, sat, or swung, stared sadly, peered out of kennels,
or made rapid circuits of the interior, scarcely seeming to touch floor, wall,
trapeze or platform in their soundless flight. Close to the window, in the
foreground, oblivious of the onlookers, one of them picked with fastidious
little black fingers at the posterior of another, and tasted what he found:
the crowd laughed obscenely, face turned grinning toward grinning face,
their animal blood thickened and darkened. It was Sandbach observing the
obscenity of Sandbach, the foulness was irremediable.

Sandbach, speaking of treachery!

He turned away, up the hill, in the deepened evening, the darkened
world, felt in every direction and dimension the swift growing and extension of new structure, new thrusts and explorations into the infinite, but
all of it a little crazy, perhaps, a little headlong and awry. Why was
this? The affair of the meeting had been, certainly, only a partial success,
it was in some measure because he had gone there with his plans unformu-
lated, with nothing but his anger and contempt, and therefore it had got
beyond his control: or at any rate, his control had not been quite perfect.
This remained tethered to him, as by threads or eyebeams, as if himself,
the puppetteer, had become subtly and dangerously entangled in the
threads of his own puppets, could not quite escape from them, found their
voices still at his ears, like gnats. The meeting was still there, in Tremont
Temple, Sandbach was still breathing thickly down his nose at Breault,
Mrs. Taber cooed her professional old-lady's sweetness, they stood in a
group round the varnished platform and chattered about manifestos and
propaganda and the founding of a paper or the revival of *The Voice of the
People*, in Saint Louis, or *The Anarchist*, in Boston, or whether the No
Hat Club might be re-established, or they should join the Socialists,
secretly, and operate "from within." Now perhaps they were rustling down
the stairs, they were saying his name, Ammen, and again Ammen, laughing angrily, they walked in twos and threes into Pemberton Square and
past the dark courthouse, under the dark windows made foul with the piled
nests of pigeons. They must be dismissed, they had been dismissed, their
path lay now at right angles with his. They had gone to Sandbach's bleak

room in Allston Street, to look adoringly at the portrait of Bakunin which
hung above the fireplace of smooth-carven white marble, relic of a capitalist
past.

Dismissed. His fumbling amateurish past dismissed, his slave-self stran-
gled and cast out. He would be an infusible one. He said aloud—egoism
is the essence of the noble soul, every star is a similar egoist, I revolve like
Nietzsche proudly amongst my proud equals. But then from the street and
the houses, the hill of houses around him, came the ugly shapes of his
amateurish past, the sordid ill-directed history of two years, the voices and
faces of Sandbach, Gottlieb, Toppan, Mrs. Taber, Gerta (but with excep-
tions), the frequenters of the esthetic little candlelit restaurants on the
hill, the shadowy denizens of the radical "parties," smelly young women
and unwashed young men. It had been a mistake, a miscalculation, but
need one be too concerned about it? It was all there, no doubt, it was a
part of him, this alien city was a part of him, was in a sense himself, it
could be accepted and dismissed. It had now become simply a background,
it had receded from him, like the evening itself with its pale stars, it would
henceforth serve merely as the rich backdrop for the action to come. And
for this purpose all that scene of the past would be useful: the meetings at
Tremont Temple, at the printing press in Hanover Street, in Gerta's room
or Sandbach's, the midnight conclaves at the C Bookshop: Gottlieb's
drinking parties, the literary young men and women, the lesbians and
pansies, the endless pseudo-intellectual talk, the indiscriminate alcoholic
amorousness: it now died away drowsily like the chorus fading off stage at
the opera, fading and dying before the coming of that profound and meaningful silence in which the action will suddenly deepen to tragedy.

The action to come.

He quickened his step at the thought of it, the shape of it urged him
forward, but at the same time he wanted to delay the meeting with Gerta,
and crossed Beacon Street into the Common. Had Gerta, in fact, also become unimportant, dropped into that background? The idea was just
faintly disagreeable. To cut oneself off, yes—but might Gerta still be useful? actively, or receptively, useful? Some one to talk to, but of course
only *partially*, not with complete confidence. One must be aware of her
duplicity henceforth, the doubleness supplied by Sandbach: Sandbach's
shadow would be always just over her shoulder. What one said to her
must be calculated therefore for a double purpose, the echo must be taken
into account, and this in itself would actually be amusing . . .

He sat down on the bench under the light below Walnut Street. Two
men came down the stone steps, talking, one of them paused to strike a
match.

—Well, I'm a great soup-eater. I'm very fond of soup. Now I'll eat
meat only once a day as a rule, but I'm very fond of soup . . .

They went down the curved brick path toward the pond, talking about
soup. This too to know! But Gerta was waiting there, leaning out of her
window with a bitten apple, Gerta was the question, and perhaps the
answer was in the affirmative. And perhaps especially, perhaps all the more
so, because now, with the intervention of Sandbach, something of the
purely *personal* pressure between them would have ceased: the relation

could be calm, sexless, cerebral: the other aspect or possibility would be once and for all removed. He could make her listen, make her the receptacle of his hate, compel her to be, as it were, the *praegustor* of his new poisons, observe her horror. She could be forced into a half unwilling alliance, and one of which she would of course intensely disapprove. And she wouldn't dare to interfere, she wouldn't dare to discuss it with Sandbach. Or would she? And if she did, would it so much matter? But *how much* should he tell her? She posed as a liberal, a radical, as emancipated —but how much would she *dare*? To test and press her, in this direction, would be delicious, would be an important part of the venture, the experiment—yes, she would be indispensable——

He ran up the steps, remembered how once he had found there, on just such an evening, a woman's handkerchief and ten dollars in neatly folded bills, touched the iron railing with his hand, and in another moment, admitted by the old Negress, Sally, was on his way up the carpeted stairs. Apollo stood listening in his plaster niche in the curved wall, as well he might: from the front room, that of the two gay girls from Haverhill, came the sound of the eternal radio, did you ever see a dream walking, well I did, did you ever hear a dream talking, well I did, he heard them laughing, and through the partly open door saw one of them, the younger one, in her knickers, her back turned, one foot on a stool to pull up a stocking.

On the floor above, a shaft of soft light across the stair rail told him that Gerta's door was also open, she was standing between the two candles by the fireplace, her elbows on the mantel behind her, wearing her blue painter's smock, she had let down her hair, which had fallen in dark ringlets on her shoulders. Her sleeves were rolled up, her arms were bare. The effect was calculated and she looked at him gravely. Keeping his hat on, he said:

—Don't you ever get tired of your esthetic candles?

—I think they're very restful. I notice you use them yourself.

—I have them, it's a concession, but I don't use them. I suppose you had a *reason* for lighting one of them?

—Simply to light up your lovely death mask.

—That's very apropos.

—What?

—Nothing.

—I'll put them out if you like.

—Don't bother.

He went to the window and looked out at the Charles River Basin, the rows of lights along the Esplanade reminded him once again of the Steinlen lithograph, *Ballade d'Hiver*, it was as if winter had returned, the snow was falling.

—Why have you been avoiding me, Jasper.

—Have I been avoiding you?

—Of course. But I don't think we need to be quite so dramatic with each other.

—I wasn't aware of any drama?

—Then what about your postcard. Postcards. Dislocation number one and number two.

He turned around, looked down at her somber face, white and calm be-

tween its dark parentheses of hair, and smiled. He had her in the palm of
his hand.

—I'm afraid I move too quickly for you, don't I?

—Why can't you be simpler? The whole thing is quite simple.

—I didn't say it wasn't. You merely mistake my insistence on *clearness*
for drama. That's why I say I move too quickly for you: you don't follow
me: neither you nor Sandbach. You and Sandbach.

She was in the act of seating herself, crossing her knees, she looked
upward at him with baffled affection, deliberate affection, and he returned
the gaze downward with a conscious narrowing of his eyes, but amiably.
She stroked her silk-stockinged knee with a fingertip, ruffling the smock's
edge to do so.

—Me and Sandbach: you put us together invidiously, don't you.

He took off his hat and bowed.

—Again too quick, but not drama. Perhaps in due course I'll tell you all
about it. My postcards were a mere statement. I didn't have to, but I
wanted to give you a signal.

—I don't say you owed me anything, but we've been good friends, we
might even have been better——

—You mean we might have been lovers.

—Well, yes, why not?

—Because I don't want it and never did. There's nothing invidious in
it.

—There's something really wrong with you, Jasper—what is it?

—Only this: I won't be contaminated any longer, by you or any one
else. That's something the exceptional man must learn sooner or later, and
I've learned it. Nietzsche speaks of it in *Beyond Good and Evil*. The
exceptional man is subject to one great temptation—a sort of desperateness
—a sudden weak-kneed longing for the society of the commonplace and
orderly, the good little parasites. He thinks he gets a kind of healing from
it. It's a flight from himself, from his loneliness. The same with sex.
Nietzsche speaks of the fear of the eternal misunderstanding, and of the
good genius that prevents people of opposite sexes from hasty and degrad-
ing attachments.

—Good Lord. So it's *that*, is it. You're afraid I'll contaminate you, so
you prefer to have me contaminate Sandbach, or to be contaminated by
him. You prefer to get your contamination at one remove, and to experiment with us as if we were guinea pigs!

—Why not?

—My dear, do sit down, you make me uneasy when you pace about
like that.

That was characteristic of Gerta, her levelness, her calm, it was what
he most liked in her, and he sat down, stretching his long legs before him.
In the silence, he could hear the dishes being washed in the Women's
Club next door. Sandbach had lectured there, it was there that Gerta had
met him, it was after that lecture, two years ago, that she had first told him
of Sandbach's curious oriental detachment and humor.

—You're pretty insufferable, you know. Not many women would stand
it!

—I don't ask them to.

—Neither do I make any claims. I simply wanted to help you: that's why I wanted to see you today, and to explain——

—Oh, don't bother! I know all about it——

——that it needn't make any difference. It will simply be quite separate. But I wish you could talk about it, aren't you being a little too tense, this dislocation business and all that. It seems to me you're getting too deeply into yourself, it might be dangerous.

—Oh, of course I need a job to take my mind off it! Christ.

—You *are* changing. Something is happening to you.

—My assumption of power? It's only the beginning.

—It's very attractive, but isn't it a little unbalanced?

—Not at all, and you know it. You agree with me. The strong individual makes his own laws, you make yours and I make mine, at this point we agree that you shall go to Sandbach so as to leave us free from this sex thing and free to co-operate in something *new*. Dislocation number three. These two dirty years have got to be wiped out. I gave Sandbach his *congée* at the meeting, dismissed them brutally. I now propose to exist outside society. And I'm beginning to have a very beautiful plan. But I don't know whether I can trust you. Will you really be able to remain separate in this regard from S?

She put her fingertips together and thought, turning her head sideways, he admired the soft candlelight on her smooth arms, her artist's hands, he liked the gentle and unhurried grace with which she just perceptibly swung her knee. The door creaked slightly open in a draft, he rose to shut it, shutting out the renewed sound of the radio from downstairs, and returned then to a suddenly sharpened sense of the fact that something really extraordinary was impending. The shape of it hung beautiful and ominous. A new relationship, a new dimension, the dreadful taste of eternity in a new horror, the sense of *sharing*, himself and this woman, in a deeper and darker world of which a pure terribleness would be the principle. He was seducing her—his genius was in the very act of seducing her—her entire attitude, at this moment, was precisely that of a woman to whom an adultery has been proposed. She was fascinated, she was frightened, her balance half lost she was half consciously debating with herself whether to lose the rest, she knew that if she looked at him she would be destroyed. What fascinated her was the dimly guessed *thing*, the new and astonishing pattern into which she would be drawn with him. Perhaps even now she was a little impure—perhaps she thought that their co-operation in the "thing" would lead inevitably, or possibly, to an "affair"—or perhaps it was this very violence to her instincts that enticed her forward. *Could* she share all the way, all the way to its logical culmination, his hatred and contempt for mankind? And could she, at the same time, deliver herself voluntarily to its evil, in the shape of little Sandbach, and at his own bidding, for the sake of the completeness? And could she see how important it was that they were *alone*, together, that they must be alone in the world, as now they were alone in this room? Or at any rate that she should revolve around *his* aloneness?

—It's very queer, isn't it.

She spoke very quietly, with the characteristic combination of frown and smile. Then, the smile fading, the frown continuing, she added:

—I suppose it simply means that you're asking me to share your insanity. You *are* insane, aren't you?

—No.

—It would be interesting. I think Sandbach could be managed—of course you know that I share your feeling that he is inferior, he would be a substitute, it wouldn't be necessary to feel that he was being betrayed.

—*He* talks of treachery to *me*.

—And there's no need to be sorry for him. He's quite competent!

—God, yes.

—But aren't we insane?

—You're thinking of Kay. But purity is not insanity. An action could have the purity of a work of art—it could be as abstract and absolute as a problem in algebra.

—What sort of action do you mean, Jasper?

He got up from his chair again, went behind her to the mantel, and blew out first one candle and then the other. She sat quite still below him as the room darkened, and he knew that in ordinary circumstances, or with another man, Sandbach for example, she would have interpreted this as the preliminary move toward a kiss. He wondered why he had wanted to do it. His thoughts went back, for no reason, to Julius Toppan, to her phrase about his chaste and epicene little room, that unconscious murder, to the fact that she had discussed him with Julius, and he felt a tightening of amused anger. But she was now helpless.

—I didn't say. I don't think I'll quite tell you, yet. As a matter of fact, it has only become clear to me this evening. There will be plenty of time for that, when I've worked it out, and made up my mind exactly how it should be done.

—You and your precious inviolacy, my dear!

—Incidentally, don't think any part of my hatred of S is jealousy. It's not. He's not the only one—I hate them all, the whole damned crowd. There isn't a soul in this city that I wouldn't willingly kill, they're all alike.

He felt his bitterness rising, it came up from within him as if he were a deep well of venom and blackness, he must be careful not to go too far. At such moments it was only too easy to surrender to the vision, to give it its headlong freedom. The vision grew like a tree, like a tree-shaped world —he walked quickly to the window, turning his back, and looked down into the dark yard, across which fell oblique shafts of light from the windows of the Women's Club. He added, without turning:

—There's nothing abnormal about it.

—I wonder whether you dislike S because he is older——

—No!

—My dear, you are certainly very difficult. Do you mind if I turn on the light?

—Go ahead. It might change our tempo.

She switched on the table lamp, by the door, then came and stood beside him at the window. They both stood still. He thought again of Steinlen, but this time of the black cat on the farmyard wall, in the moon-

light, the two peasants embracing under a dark tree. Something seemed
to suffocate him, perhaps it was her nearness, like the nearness of the postman in the train: he felt as if he must move, or say something: Gerta
might already have guessed too much. Certainly, there were elements in the
situation which seemed to be unaccountable, a little incalculable——

—I suppose you don't want to tell me, Jasper, why you suddenly have
to *quarrel* with every one like this—and make things so hard for yourself——

—No. We've got to learn to be hard.

She gave a little laugh, which sounded half angry, half distracted, and
walked away from him, putting her hands to the sides of her head: and
laughing bitterly she thus crossed and recrossed the room several times,
shaking her head, while he watched her. Then she sank down into her
chair, as if she were suddenly very tired.

—I suppose I must wait, she said.

—Did you think I meant to kill some one? But I'm not as transparent
as I sometimes look.

—Of course not!

—Not that it would matter much, would it. I'd *like* to play King Coffin!

She looked at him soberly, and he smiled. Her lips were parted, she
seemed bewildered, perhaps a little apprehensive, she slid the silver bracelet
up and down her arm.

—What on earth do you mean?

—I'll tell you about it sometime. It was a doctor's sign I saw somewhere—or thought I saw, or perhaps simply *dreamed* I saw—I could even
swear it was in Commonwealth Avenue, near Massachusetts, on the south
side. But it may have been in Saint Louis. Just the name King Coffin. It
seemed to me a very good, and very sinister, name for a doctor—it sounds
a little supernatural. It might not be a *man* at all, but a sort of death-
principle. It would be nice to be King Coffin, don't you think? I've often
thought about it, I've thought I might make a story out of it. *The Cabinet
of Doctor Caligari!* But you needn't be frightened. It's just one of my crazy
ideas, no crazier than anarchism, no crazier than absolute egoism, no
crazier than the fact that we are here, or that Sandbach doesn't know what
we have arranged for him——

—Jasper, I'm very tired——

—I'm afraid I bore you——

—No, but it's all rather a strain——

—I see.

—If we could talk about something else for a while——

—Oh, of course. Oh, of course. Of ships and shoes and sealingwax, and
cabbages and coffins. Sandbach's taste in shirts, for example.

She was silent, with lowered eyes.

—His socks, too. His one necktie, and his yellow shoes, his East Side
shoes, by God! And always that little piece of nostril ingredient protruding from the left nostril——

He watched her blush, wondering how much of it was shame and how
much was anger. He picked up his hat from the table and put it on.

—Well, I'll go and make my plans, and communicate with you later.

If I decide to communicate at all. You'll of course consider how to deal with Sandbach, and how much to say to him, if anything. But you needn't bother to report to me, for of course I shall know.

—You don't need to be angry.

—I'm not—thanks for the taste of the future—dislocation number four.

He walked past her quickly, as she started to rise, ran down the stairs, heard her say Jasper but paid no attention, and on emerging into Walnut Street stood still on the brick sidewalk, thinking. The *shape* had not been exactly as foreseen, but on the whole the direction was correct, the huge structure was rising all about him, and himself borne upward with it, the arc of bright steel was beginning to threaten the sky. He breathed hard, ran his eyes along the row of dark eaves opposite, felt that with a simple gesture he could remove the tin gutters, making one sweep of the hand. Park Street Church was striking ten, Toppan would not be in till a little before eleven, there was still time for a further formulation before the plunge into sleep.

❲ IV The Friends Who Might Be Murdered

He looked in through the wide window of the Merle as he passed, it was possible that Toppan would have returned there for his usual glass of orangeade and his perusal of the stock market reports and in the hope that he or Gottlieb might turn up; but the room was empty, the waitress was wiping a table, he saw the cocoanut on the shelf, it would soon be closing time. Toppan was probably at his law club in Church Street, after all there would be plenty of time, or even if he had returned it hardly mattered, the diary could be read another day. Better however if it could be done tonight, for Toppan himself could thus be considered: if only to be eliminated. And of course he would have to be eliminated, for in his case the dangers, even if one were going to accept the dangers, would be too immediate, and the actual result perhaps less rewarding. Might it not be better to employ Toppan as witness number two—a figure in the half background—as one who, for example, would know more than Sandbach but less than Gerta? The problem might be posed for him as if it existed entirely in the abstract, in the realm of pure supposition. Moreover, the mere technique of it, the detective aspect, would interest him. From this point of view, of course, it was fascinating to consider that Toppan might become a *necessity*, even of the act itself.

But no, the idea was at once perceived to be secondary, it was already past, and on the level of mere observation, like the window of the Merle or the row of queer dresses hanging in Keezer's: it was as still and lifeless as those dresses, which in the lamplight from the corner looked like a ghostly Madame Tussaud's, as if the waxworks had stepped out of them for the night. Toppan would definitely be a stage-hand, useful but unimportant. And if at any time he became suspicious or pressing, that would merely add to the excitement, the pressure. He would simply *be* there, looking over Gerta's shoulder, as in a photograph. . . .

He turned on the lights in his room, all three, the sitting room and bedroom and kitchenette, deposited his hat on top of the scarlet enamel Chinese cabinet, then went at once to the mirror. Jasper Ammen. With his long hands flat on the glass top of the dressing table, he surveyed himself with the usual and desirable calm and leisure: after an action, or series of actions, and especially as now in the presence of a *prospect* of an action, it was necessary to see oneself from outside. It was necessary to see and re-capitulate what Gerta had seen, to study what Gerta had studied, and to judge himself through Gerta's eyes. It was therefore Gerta's Jasper whom he saw, mysterious, tall, a little languid perhaps, but with an obvious re-serve of tremendous subtlety and power, not to say of cruelty. The eyes were enigmatic and lynxlike, and with that profound and inscrutable im-personality which looks out of eyes which themselves see too clearly for any counteranalysis: all they offered was an anonymity of depth and light. They were pure vision. The controlled mouth, and the Greek serenity of the fore-head, accentuated the effect of philosophic essentialness: the face, the body, the hands (one of them surrounded by the tiny hexagonal wrist watch) were all *one thing*, they were a pure ego of unimaginable intensity, and it was this, above all, that Gerta had seen. She had felt the extraor-dinary virtue of this, it was this that always held her motionless and as if incapable of any separate action. Even in the act of moving toward Sand-bach she was moving not to Sandbach but to himself.

He said aloud: But there are grades and heights where pity itself is re-garded by him as impurity, as filth. Thus spake Zoroaster. He watched the words form themselves on the lips, which only restrainedly and slightly moved, the eyelids were a little lowered, the beautiful face remained im-mobile and cold. It was as if the word death had been pronounced by a flower, or by a mask of silver: and now the flower, or the mask, had be-come death's symbol. He smiled superciliously in the silence which was his own, then pulled out the top drawer and took from it a photograph. It was of Gerta, he had suddenly thought of it in the train, Gerta at Walden two years ago, she looked much younger: with one bare arm raised she was shading her eyes and laughing, her eyes squinting a little in the bright sunlight. He looked closely at the dress, remembering it as one which had since been discarded, and considered with it the sense of deepened time. It had been himself of course that she was thus peering at from under her hand, thus laughing at, not yet had the obscurities and tangles between them been discovered by either of them, though they were already taking shape; it had been their age of innocence; the day at Walden had been relatively simple. Thoreau, and the notion of egoism, had hung there a little, but not much: Gerta had been pretty sure that they would end by marrying, or at any rate that they would have an affair. But was there, just perceptible in the sunlit frown, the shadow of a doubt, the shadow of Sand-bach? Perhaps this was why she had written jokingly on the back "Gerta-dämmerung. Passed by the Censor."

The twilight of Gerta.

He slid the photograph into his side pocket, not for the moment wishing to be separated from it, since it might give rise to further considera-
tions, then retraced his steps into the corridor, leaving the lights on, and
proceeded towards the back stairs which led down to Toppan's room. The
electric lights had been turned off for the night, and the gas jets turned on,
the copper cylinder of the fire extinguisher gleamed in its corner, and the
corridor was still, except for the low voices of the epileptic and his wife
from the room by the stairhead. He paused to listen.

—and walking very slowly like that with the paper in my hand——
—She probably didn't see you at all.
—watching me just the same, I could see——
—matter. I ordered a packing case from Sage's——
But was Gerta quite as asquiescent as she appeared to be?

He descended the two flights, deliberately lightening his footsteps,
glanced through the window at the dark pile of Beck Hall, and his thoughts
reverted to Gerta's question. But aren't we insane? Certainly there was a
hint of "outside" observation or criticism in this, but if the aroma of challenge arose from it, very faintly, it needn't perhaps be taken too seriously.
The tone of acquiescence was already there, it need only be followed up,
the challenge was not aimed at rebellion but simply at—yes, there could
be no doubt of it, and he smiled—at her need for further coercion, her
desire for further coercion. She wanted to be persuaded, she wanted to be
forced, her real depth of pleasure would lie precisely in the fact that she
was being compelled into a conspiracy which perhaps she considered
insane and horrible. But did she think this? She knew his logic to be flawless. After the first step beyond morals, beyond good and evil, one was in
chaos and must trust one's own wings. *Her* wings she might mistrust, but
his——

There was no answer to his perfunctory knock at Toppan's door, he
stood for a moment looking at the visiting card, Julius Shaw Toppan, into
which some one had inserted, with a carat, the pencilled name Diogenes: a
reference to Toppan's reputation for unmitigated honesty; then entered,
switching on the light. A tray was on the piano bench, a half-filled bottle
of gin, a bottle of ginger ale, two glasses. Toppan was expecting him. This
was annoying, but it could be permitted to pass. He sat down in the swivel
chair by the flat-topped mission desk, pulled out the middle drawer, and removed the loose-leaf diary. Beside it, in the drawer, lay five or six new
letters, one of them in an unfamiliar handwriting and postmarked Chicago,
these would be interesting, but they could wait. There was also a theater-
ticket envelope, which he found contained two tickets for the ballet. Was
he taking Gerta?

"April 22. April 23. April 24. Chaste and epicene.

"April 27. Am resolved in future to make this not so much a diary as
a journal; but when I pause to reflect why I should make this decision I
am not so sure whether in the future such a record would really be as interesting as a record of facts? More amusing to know, ten years from now,
that today I walked round the Pond with Gerta, on *her* suggestion, and
just as I imagined it was because she wanted to talk about the great Jasper.

Not very flattering. Any fool could see she is in love with him. But why pick on me? Because she knows he interests me, which he does. She thinks he is behaving more *queerly* of late, but good God Almighty how could he? The people in this apartment house are frightened to death of him, those who don't just hate his guts. And no wonder. Just the same, a part of his fascination for Gerta (and for me) is in the very fact that he knows he is fascinating and uses it so deliberately and conceitedly. You can't help admiring the perfection of his technique. Gerta seemed to think he was changing. Said he was more "morose." I confess I hadn't noticed it, but maybe there's something in it. I told her about his call the other night (Thursday) when he came in, walked once round the room, looking at each picture on the wall in turn, and then went out without a word. The trouble about that is, it's hard to say whether he *knows* his behavior is odd or not. I give him credit for knowing that it is: Gerta says she isn't so sure, and particularly just in the last month or two. I could see she was dying to ask me whether I thought he was insane or not, but I decided quite rightly to keep out of *that* mess and didn't give her any help. Personally, I don't think he is. I think it's all a belated sort of adolescent pose, the business of playing genius. Especially when you consider all the esthetic stuff as well, the vague hints thrown out now and then of his mysterious "writings" and so on, which no one has ever seen and never will. My diagnosis is spoiled child, but that's only half of it: more than any person I ever knew he *has* something like genius, but God knows what it is—the only way I can define it is to say that he is or has the appearance of being terribly *concentrated*. Not that that butters any parsnips. Or that it will help Gerta. I'd like to warn Gerta to clear out, but what business is it of mine? She's free, white and twenty-one and prides herself on her independence, you can't tell these Lucy Stoners anything.

"April 28. Law Society, Hempy talking for an hour on torts, sheer waste of time, I could have done it better myself——

"April 29. Queer mixup with Ammen about tea. He left a note in my box, asking me, I scribbled an answer on the back of it and put it into his, a little later I found it in my box again and thinking it a mistake put it back into his, and this happened *twice more*. I began to be a little mad about it. And when I went to his room at half past four he wasn't in. God deliver me from these geniuses. I feel sorry for them. Signet for lunch, and Peters brought——

"April 30. . . . what Gerta said. I can't make out Gerta. Of course I don't suppose she is quite what they call a lady, she's knocked around a little, she's not one of that Beacon Hill crowd for nothing. But you feel that what the others do because they're unprincipled, she does because of an *idea*. You can't help respecting her—and you can't help feeling sorry for her either, especially this attachment of hers for J—good God what a burden *that* must be. Bad luck that she should have attached herself to him, who so obviously cares only for himself. . . . Sandbach came in for a minute and said J was resigning from the little anarchist group and making an unnecessary amount of stink about it. Wanted to know if I knew what was behind it. I told him J hadn't discussed it with me and wasn't likely to. Sandbach says he is behaving very *queerly* about it. It's certainly damned funny how his peculiarities and oddities lend a curious

sort of importance to his actions—whatever the reason may be he keeps
every one interested, not to say angry. Maybe because you never know
which way he'll jump. Which of course is one of the difficulties of dealing
with a deliberate egoist. And he has brains."

And he has brains.

Ten-thirty-five.

He returned the diary to its drawer, had a look at the Chicago letter,
which turned out to be merely a business note with regard to the sale of a
stamp collection, with reference also to a mandolin (apparently a former
roommate at school in Connecticut), then went to the open window and
filled and lit his pipe. Toppan was intelligent, but not intelligent enough—
he could easily be kept at the right distance, he was also sufficiently good
company, and his own peculiarities were themselves sufficiently interesting.
That business of the safety-razor blades, for instance, and the episode of
the girl's hair at Mechanic's Hall after the relay race. It had been put
down as an aberration due to overwork and overtraining, but the fact remained that Toppan had always been fooling with knives and razor blades
and scissors, always carried them round with him and was obviously in
some abnormal way fascinated by them. It was a weak spot, one could
exert pressure upon it, the odd thing was that Toppan had weathered the
business without a further or deeper collapse of some sort.

The difficulties of dealing with a delicate egoist. Insane?

He was looking closely at the color print of the Chinese painting,
Lychees and Birds, which of course Toppan had bought in sedulous imitation of his own taste for Chinese art, when Toppan came in. As usual he
blushed: the signal of inferiority: as if he had been caught doing something he shouldn't. He said, putting a book down beside the tray:

—I hoped you would be here.

—Why do you always blush?

Toppan gave an uneasy laugh, the blush deepening into the roots of
his reddish hair, and it was also noticeable that his hand trembled as he
held a match for his cigarette, but in spite of this he looked back steadily
enough, the blue eyes timid but sharp behind rimless round glasses.

—Ah, that's my innocence. Have a drink?

—No, thanks. You've been talking to Gerta, haven't you.

—How did you know.

—I saw her tonight.

—Yes.

—That's all right, it's your own affair, but I want to say that I'm quite
satisfied with things as they are and don't want any complications of an
accidental or external nature. Do you see what I mean.

—Certainly.

—I've got a project of a very important and private sort which I don't
want jeopardized. I can't discuss it with you now, I may later.

—I see.

Toppan, standing sideways, said this into the glass as he poured himself
a drink: he was very self-conscious in his obvious attempt to make it apparent that he was intelligent, that he understood. He was perhaps a little
frightened.

—Gerta doesn't mean to be disloyal and it might not matter if she were, but her present situation is difficult, she may be tempted to ask questions, and I think it advisable that they shouldn't be answered. I'm not asking a favor—I'm merely putting a choice before you. You can do as you like.

He smiled a little, watching the shape of Toppan's decision, watching Toppan's desire for importance in Jasper Ammen's eyes rise delightedly to the surface. He was as easy to handle as Gerta, and as translucent, there was even something to be said for making *Toppan* the victim, for then it would be possible to watch the *record* of the "closing in" in the diary, an extra turn of the screw. But no, this would sacrifice the notion of *purity*——

—Also I want to put a supposititious case before you. It was suggested by your passion for pure detection, detection for the *sake* of detection——

—Oh, I wouldn't say it was a passion——

—what is valuable in such an experience is the unsuspected mastery of another person's life: you know all about him, while he doesn't even guess your existence, much less that you are following him. Suppose you pushed it to its logical extreme, and *took* his life. That's all right, it's quite understandable if you had a contempt, like the Orientals, for the value of human life, it might for people like you and me be actually an essential accomplishment on the way to becoming completely realized. I'm not discussing that, we can take it for granted, we both agree about it. Beyond values and so on.

He directed at Toppan a look of deliberate openness, and paused. He wanted to feel the edges of what he had just said, to feel quite sure of its shape and direction, its weight and its speed, and he wanted also to give Toppan plenty of time for a flurried conjecture that it was now precisely the secret "project" which was being discussed. It was to be dangled before him just like that, dangled but not defined or named or admitted. He would be allowed to draw his own breathless conclusions and then, in turn, to doubt them. Toppan took a sip of his drink and put down the glass very guardedly, his hand remained on the glass, with his forefinger he was tapping the rim reflectively, he had nothing to say; the situation had already become too precarious for him. He was simply waiting.

—All right. Now suppose it was you who decided to do this, suppose you picked out some one, me or Sandbach or Gottlieb or Taber, and began planning your murder.

He stood still, with his back to the open window, looking downward at Toppan. The quarter bells of Saint Paul's Church began their melodious and lazy cycle in the still air, then the hour was struck, and before it was quite finished Memorial Hall began striking on the same tone, but farther away. Eleven o'clock. He listened intently till the last note had sounded, waited for the neutral returning silence to lift them once more into isolation, then pointed with his pipestem for emphasis.

—Suppose you decide there is a sublime rightness in the idea, that it is true to yourself and to nature, a deep principle vested in you and nature, as natural as being born, or eating, or loving: you might even say it is a profound obligation if you are to become complete, and just as inevitable as exploitation—exploitation is the natural order of things. To injure or destroy is natural, it's life itself: to deny that is to deny life. Well, you know it's right, and I know it's right, but society won't agree with us, will it? Consequently what? Consequently what ought to be a public action, and done openly, has to be private or secret: unless you make up your mind to go the whole hog and *do* it openly and take the social consequences. That's the way it ought to be, to be perfect, it ought to take place in *sunlight*.

He narrowed his eyes as he stared at Toppan, and Toppan narrowed his own a little in answer, but made no reply beyond a slight nod. A mere reflex, a mere automatism, he was hardly listening, or at any rate not listening intelligently, he had simply become a fascinated mirror.

—All right, suppose for whatever reasons you decide that your action has to be secret, even though this takes away some of its virtue: you pick out your victim and you make your plans; but then it occurs to you that although you can't tell every one about it, and do it with nobility, you can at least *tell one or two trusted persons*. Can't you?

—I suppose you could.

—You suppose you could. Suppose then you decided to tell me. In that case do I become an accessory before the fact, and am I criminally liable if you are caught?

—Certainly. That is, if I gave you away. But if you kept your mouth shut——

—It would be to my interest to keep my mouth shut.

—Good God, yes. But why——

—That's all I wanted to know. I'm thinking of writing a story about it. I've even got the title for it—King Coffin.

—King Coffin. That's a swell title. Real up-to-the-hilt nihilism.

—Not at all.

—I don't get you, then.

—It's just life, it's just hatred. The essential thing in life is hate!

He put his pipe quickly into his pocket, walked to the door without looking again at Toppan, and as he let himself out said without turning——

—Bear in mind what I said about Gerta.

Toppan's uneasy "of course" was cut off by the closing door, and the sound of his chair being pushed back, he had been interrupted in the very middle of his unhappy vision, he would now have time to pace to and fro in his empty room and to allow, in the silence, the nocturnal conjecture to pile itself to heaven in all its true horror. It was already beginning, the smaller shadows were grouping themselves about his feet and in the corners, the crazy shape was hinting itself first here and then there, and horribly against his will it would curse his sleep.

So much for Toppan, the seed of the vision had been securely planted, but what about his *own* vision?

Noiselessly and swiftly, and with a queer kind of exultation, he took the stairs three steps at a time, the vision grew like a tree, the immense whirl was once more above him, the sense of speed and hurry returned, it was almost as if something threatened to stop his breathing. But he must take it calmly, the thing must be thought out with precision: the tempo must be slowed down. The vision was all right, but it must not become too possessive or emotional; calculated or uncalculated, there must be an interruption. At the bend of the corridor, in the shadow beside the professor's door, the professor's cat was sitting, it watched his approach without moving, looked up at him when he paused, rose and arched its back when he spoke to it.

—Little cat, you can be the interruption. Come in.

He opened his door and stood aside. The cat preceded him into the room, advanced into the center of the rug with cautious dignity, and sat down, looking towards the window. The spiked seashell on the window sill was white and sharp against the darkness outside, the little glass bird cage sparkled, in the stillness of the room he could hear the voices of two students from Plympton Street below.

— All right, start her up.

—Wait till I get this thing under the back here——

—Well, go ahead——

As the self-starter began its rhythmic skirling he sat by the red table and drew towards him a sheet of paper and a silver pencil. On the paper in a straight small column he wrote quickly the names Toppan, Gerta, Sandbach, Taber, Gottlieb. But no—no! At once he drew a precise line through each name in turn, crumpled the paper into a ball, and rolled it along the floor to the cat, who, with a neat hook of the paw, skittled it under the table.

The terribleness of the deed must be kept pure: the problem had become a problem in art-form.

❲ V   But Perhaps a Stranger

The Angelus was striking in the campanile of Saint Paul's as he turned off the shower, the three urgent bells, and three others after a pause, and three more, and then the rapid complexion of the nine, as if the bell ringer had triumphantly added his significant sum; eight o'clock; no doubt some pious sort of hugger mugger was going on there at this minute, fellows in white surplices—or was it chasubles—shaking mysterious cocktails over a kind of holy bar, or waving red lanterns up and down; and all for the benefit of a few housemaids and nursemaids. It might be a good thing to go there: to drop in on the way to breakfast, stand at the back for a moment, look over the little audience, or even observe more particularly, and for a particular purpose. He stepped out of the pools of water which his feet had left on the oilcloth floor, slid into the red slippers, then leaned from the little window. Clouds and a wind, the skylight was gray, he could hear the humming. Looking downward, he could see into the bathroom of the apartment on the floor below: the fair-haired girl, Mrs. Finden, was leaning against the wash-bowl, naked, her hands thrust forward into the water. Her husband came and stood beside her, rested for a moment one hand on her hip, squeezed it, then took some small object from the shelf and disappeared.

It was like that, of course; it ought to be just like that. The unknown eye from above, the God's eye view, the death ray directed downward when least suspected. Like *The Crimson* editor on the roof, Mrs. Finden was now dead without knowing it; the thing was completely pure, completely motiveless: the anonymous tree stump had been struck by anonymous lightning. He watched Mrs. Finden dry her hands and arms, she turned her head to say something over her shoulder while still manipulating the blue towel, the muscles of her small upper arms trembling slightly, then she picked up two rings from the marble slab, slid them on to the fourth finger of her left hand, and vanished. Finden was laughing at something, then after a moment the bath was turned on, a masculine arm reached up and closed the ground-glass window.

In his own room, the curtain still lowered, he ran it up and let go of the cord so that it flapped round and round. Clouds and a wind. The man at the window of the room in Fairfax, a block away, was there as usual, in his B.V.D.'s, as close to the window as he could get, holding a mirror in his hand to preen himself. He stooped slightly, turned the mirror this way and that to get a better light, then put something that looked like a nightcap over his hair and went away for a moment only to return and resume his peculiar occupation. This too. The same thing. A dead man.

Yes: but these were a little too close, too immediate, to put one's hand on them was too easy. What was wanted——

The little ball of paper was still lying under the table where the cat had left it, he remembered first his impulse to drop the cat out of the window, and the curious repugnance which had seemed to rise as if from his hands; then the relief with which he had driven the cat out into the corridor. Odd. But the list of names was there, crumpled but still there, and the question with them, the profound question. And it could only be answered by himself: about this, there could be no conferring, not even with Gerta. The decision must be pure. The question was, was it still in fact a question? or had it actually—and as he thought this he stood quite still and stared at the necktie which he was holding—been solved in his sleep? There had been a dream, a queer and deep dream: a series of crisscrossed shadows, shifting and ominous. Further than that, it was vague, but as he had waked from it he had felt a kind of lightness or ease, something spacious but as if lightly etched with lines—analogous—was that it?— to the small script hidden inside the crumpled ball of paper, the list of rejected names. Rejected, yes, but for what, in favor of what? Something more remote, but *how* remote? He carried the blue necktie to the mirror in the bedroom, tossed it over his head, began to draw it to and fro beneath the collar. The Buddha was behind him on its shelf, the bed was unmade in the silent room, it was his own silence once more beginning to deepen and widen, and as he leaned closer to the glass to look into his black pupils it seemed to him that the sense of limitless silence and peace came from his own eyes. The mystery lay there, the solution lay there, was already known there, it was as if he were looking into an immense depth, an immense distance, and trying to make out some far-off and tiny and incredible action. *Had* it already taken shape there? But remember, if thou gazest into the abyss, the abyss will also gaze into thee. The abyss will gaze into thee.

But it is your own abyss?

The photograph of Gerta was still in his pocket of course, he removed it, dropped it into the top drawer, speculated idly as to the suspended line of thought which it indicated, dismissed it. That was over. For all major intents and purposes, Gerta was over. Dislocation number five. He said it aloud—dislocation number five—walked quickly to the red table, took two postcards from the upright stand and put them in his breast pocket. Perhaps the Findens would be going down in the elevator at the same time. Or Toppan. If Toppan, he would cut him dead, turn his back, not reply if spoken to.

Clouds and a wind. In Massachusetts Avenue the dust whirled under the bright wheels of a streetcar, a dirty black hat was blowing across the street with a small man in pursuit, rolling on its rim, the noise of traffic came all along the street from the Square, windblown and clamorous. The Merle was empty, the bookshop was closed, three starched shirts lay mute in the window of the one-day laundry, and beside them a pair of patent-leather shoes. Liggett's drugstore, and the telephone booth immediately to the right of the door, and its directory with splayed leaves: he hesitated. The impulse was clear and sharp, it was an obvious enough association of ideas, he had telephoned similarly the night before. But why now? To get her out of bed, wake her, startle her, remind her of the singular bond which now lay heavy between them. Gerta? Yes. Jasper speaking. Yes? Just to remind you, that's all. . . . The booth was unoccupied, it would be easy, he enjoyed thinking of her surprise, her agitation, not to mention the mystification in which she would be left. And it would be as well to add: I'm still without a formula.

The effect of daylight on the situation was odd, a little unnatural, like the sudden opening of wide windows into a secret theater, the stage moonlight abruptly dissipated: a queer sort of falseness was introduced, but also an unlooked-for intenseness: as if the actors all had at once to look in a new direction and for something unknown and terrifying. In this light, the events of the night before all turned like weathercocks, the events and the people too, Gerta and Sandbach and Toppan, and the sad little group in the Temple, it was as if they were all present here in Massachusetts Avenue and all turning simultaneously in the wind. Something new, something strange, was lighting and blowing them, as it was lighting and blowing himself; as if the entire constellation had brightened and shifted slightly to the left. It was because he himself had moved forward into another light, another time: he had turned to the left, and they with him.

Yes: *their* danger had passed.

He saw this in the haberdashery window, which he always looked into as he passed, he saw the phrase as if written there among the shirts and socks and neck ties. New woven madras shirts. New crochet ties. Boston Brace Garters. Varsity Shorts. Bostonia Hats. Double toe and heel hose, three pairs one dollar. Their danger had passed. Hab Ihr Das.

Yes, *their* danger had passed; he resumed his quick walk in the wind, avoided the faces of the early pedestrians, dropped two cents in the cigar box and took a *Herald* from beneath the brick, turned down Dunster Street. He would be early enough to breakfast alone, in the far corner at the back, a table to himself on which to spread out the newspaper, he

could be undisturbed while he prepared the next step. Breakfast dishes. He
surveyed the morning list, tray in hand, the firm little packet of linen-
rolled silver under his thumb. Tomato Juice, Poached Egg on Corned
Beef Hash Browned, Buttered Toast. He could have these things, himself
as well as another, he remained strictly anonymous as he watched the
waitress dip the poached egg from the boiling water, but just the same it
gave him a sense of remarkable power to stand before her embodying a
principle which, had she been able to divine it or understand it, would
have made her scream. The composition was of a Bachlike perfection, it
was the ideal counterpoint of good and evil.

—Graham toast, please.

—Yes, sir.

But if these were safe, if after all it was not to be a friend, or even an
acquaintance——?

He dissected the egg as delicately as one might dissect a thought,
looked into the moving liquid, paused. At this point one must go slow.
One must be orderly. One must avoid all flurry, all agitation, all unnecessary confusion, work the thing out as neatly and precisely as one would a
three-mover in chess. If it was a problem in philosophy, or a problem in
esthetics, and as a matter of fact it was a little of both, there could be no
room for sentiment and no excuse for excitement. *Their* danger had passed
—Gerta's and Sandbach's and Toppan's, and all the others'—simply because, and it was of course at once extremely obvious, the choice of any one
of them would immediately introduce extraneous elements. The murder
would not be pure. No matter how slight, there would be some little fringe
of emotional complication—his disgust at Sandbach, his idle scorn of
Toppan, his contempt—if that was it—for Gerta; there would be this
minute chemical trace of *motive*; the anonymity would not have been strict.
But if not these——

An acquaintance?

He lowered the newspaper, rested his hands flat upon it, surveyed the
half empty room of glass-topped tables. The girl who gave out the checks
sat at his left, on a high stool, her back turned: she was in the act of
estimating the contents of a tray, hesitating, her hands poised over the keys
of her machine. The man who was holding the tray was Mather, in the
English department. Not very bright, said to be good to his mother, harmless, defensively amiable, weak. No. Neither of them. Nor any one else in
the room. Certainly, at any rate, not a woman. It must be a man, he had
really known that all along, but what was now also just as unmistakable was
that it must be a stranger. A complete stranger! Some one chosen at
random. . . . Absolutely at random.

Mather came towards him tray in hand, nodded ingratiatingly, said
good morning, with any encouragement would have sat down at the same
table, but he froze him by staring past him. The weak eyes lifted away, the
tray swerved in its anxious course, the cautious footsteps moved away forward in the long room, toward the window. The kind of despicable herd-
member who was always on the lookout for some one to sit beside, some
one to join and confide in. In a moment he would look round to make sure
whether Ammen had really recognized him, unwilling to believe that his

coldness could have been intentional. He would do this obliquely and with a little cough. And then lower his head tenderly over his hurt little breakfast.

No, certainly not an acquaintance, and certainly not Mather, but just the same to consider Mather was useful, for it served to make clearer the essential principles, moral or esthetic, on which the final decision must be made. To look at Mather was to pity him and despise him—or at any rate to *want* to pity or despise him—he was despicable and pitiful, or pitiable: to remain completely indifferent to him was impossible. And that, of course—and he slapped both hands on the table and laughed— was exactly the point. The stranger must be someone to whom one could be completely indifferent. He must be neither attractive nor unattractive, not to be loved or pitied, nor hated or feared, some one whose strangeness and anonymity (in the sense that one knew nothing about him and *felt* nothing) was pure. The face must be quite ordinary, just a face, the bearing and gait must be neither offensive nor enviable, the clothes of a sort of universal characterlessness. In short, it must be simply "a man." A mere lay figure, or drawing of a man, such as you saw in a newspaper advertisement of ready-made suits for sixteen dollars and fifty cents.

Yes, that was it, it was the discovery, it was as if suddenly an immense fortune had been left him, the whole population of the world had become his capital, the whole world lay before him or under him like an unconscious victim. He slapped the newspaper down in the chair, walked rapidly toward the cashier's wire cage, smiled over Mather's head, while he waited for his change to trickle out of the machine drew a postcard and pencil from his pocket, then against the weighing machine in the lobby addressed the card to Gerta and wrote quickly on the other side: Formula found, dislocation number six. . . . Superb. With each little accretion of definition the situation became tighter, drew them all more shrewdly and painfully into false and unwilling postures, they came along with him willy-nilly and without knowing where, and he could see exactly with what expression of dismay Gerta would read this latest bulletin: the heels of her hands pressed quiveringly to the sides of her head, then quickly dropped, then a few swift steps across the room and back, the somberly curved mouth a little opened, the witty eyes a little dulled. She would want to call him up on the telephone but wouldn't dare, she would want to come and see him, she would remain paralyzed until she had heard from him again, at most perhaps daring to write him a note of desperate question. Or would she decide to go away, go back to New York?

Clouds and a wind, the morning was profound, from his own tower of vision he looked down at the sordid little human maze far below him, into which his lightning could now strike freely where it willed, and once more, as he proceeded toward the post office, along Mount Auburn Street, the sense as of a deceptive serenity and leisure arose from his own deployed creation. Deceptive, for of course there was much still unsolved if not insoluble—no, not insoluble, but unsolved, waiting, the actual terminus not yet selected. This day, and the next, and the one after—this week, or the next—the question of time was undoubtedly there, the thing could not be timeless, but must have a time; and in this lay of course the necessity for a decision. Today? begin today? Begin with a definite volition? or allow his feet to take him where they wished? or simply stand in midstream, as it were, and allow the human current to divide itself unconsciously against him until the right "moment" came? Deceptive, yes, for to consider this was at once to be immersed again in the feeling of hurry. And there were also the subsidiary problems, the merely practical ones: the choice of a weapon, the choice of method and place, the actual planning of the deed itself, and whether at a long or short interval after the selection of the victim. Whether with contemplation or with suddenness. And whether or not with precautions against detection?

But no, that element need not enter. He himself would be, from the victim's viewpoint, a complete stranger: the crime would be completely without reason: all of a sudden the fellow would be dead, no one could possibly be suspected, and that would be the end of it. The management of it should be excessively, almost childishly simple. A brief study of the man's daily habits, his goings and comings, the discovery of his name, some ordinary ruse to get him to the appointed place at the appointed time— Belmont? Concord?—and there it was. A profound surprise.

But how to select him!

He dropped the postcard in the letter box, turned, recrossed Brattle Square; a small cyclone of dust whirled from the open end of the subway, the clock on the police station tower said a quarter to nine.

A telephone directory opened at random, with the eyes shut, a pencil in hand, the *sortes Virgilianae*? He smiled, the notion was not unattractive, the merely geographic possibilities were very rich and unpredictable. Even more delicious if, for example, he were to invite Gerta to do it? . . . But perhaps that would be premature. For the moment, what seemed most of all desirable was the maintenance of his own deep secrecy, his own inviolable privacy and mystery. Gerta and Toppan and Sandbach, and the shabby little haunters of the C Bookshop on the hill, all these people must be kept in the dark, they must be given a sense of some impending action, some continuous but enigmatic and unfathomable activity; like the leaves and twigs which the spider draws imperceptibly but imperatively together in his nocturnal spinning, each in turn bent together, they must feel but not see, only with daybreak would come—if indeed it were permitted to come to them at all—the revelation that they had been organized into an arbitrary pattern by the will of another and for a purpose unknown. They must be touched, used, made to quiver, but kept in ignorance. This would be their fright, this would be a useful part of his own satisfaction. The whole hated city, this alien city of contemptible ones, the vast nest of rats, would become his own property, his own web.

No Peddlers or Solicitors Allowed in This Building.

He followed the gray coat, the round-shouldered gray coat, with the collar turned up under a black velour hat, past the Personal Bookshop to the Square. A green bag depended from the right hand, full of books, the gait was slack and middle-aged, the knees not quite straightening, the spectacled profile, when it turned to inspect the oncoming traffic from the direction of the subway, was gray and dry and mustached. Standing close behind him, it was possible to observe that the under side of the turned-up collar was worn and unbrushed, that there was cigarette ash on the crown and rim of the hat, and that the hand which suddenly rose to steady it against the wind was veined with an unpleasant blue. A professor, with a nine-o'clock, on his way to Sever or the New Lecture Hall. He balanced in the wind, then decided, but with obvious indecision, to turn left across Brattle Street, at the last minute had to make an ungainly little run, when the traffic signal changed: the whistle shrilling, he scuttled, head down, hand on hat, toward the policeman's canvas box.

To stand and watch him, as he then veered around the box and darted across the tracks toward the subway entrance, his hand still held anxiously against his hat, the green bag bobbing awkwardly at his side, conspicuous among all the rush of morning pedestrians simply because singled out for observation, was to renew and refresh one's sense of power: it would be child's play to follow him, find out who he was: in point of fact, it would be too easy altogether: to send a smile after the retreating figure was in itself, for the moment, a sufficient murder. No, this was not the sort of thing, though it whetted the appetite. Much more interesting, and much more fruitful, was the multiplicity of the morning rush itself. In this, as he began to walk slowly toward the subway, conscious of his great height, and conscious of his consciousness, was the real and unspoiled secret: an immense sense of wealth, a multitude of treasure, into which one merely needed to thrust an exploring hand. On the lower platform, where the ramps converged from the Arlington and Mount Auburn cars, it would be at its best. Moreover, there would be telephone booths, and telephone directories.

Descending the stairs, he crossed the stream of hurrying people and pushed towards the row of illuminated boxes, which looked like the lighted cells of a hive. A good point of vantage. He leaned casually against the edge of a booth, took the book in his hand, opened it at random, and while he watched the crowd let his finger fall on the page. There was a name under his finger, but for a moment he didn't want to see what it was: instead, he quite calmly smiled at one face and then another and then a third of those that passed him. The last, an old man, bareheaded, turned surprised eyes over his shoulder. Then he looked down. Joseph Kazis, 241 D Street, South Boston. South Boston—! A little remote, perhaps, but just the same, by way of experiment——

He closed the door, dialed with his pipestem, listened to the far-off ringing, heard the click of the lifted receiver, and the slow Jewish drawl, a woman's voice.

—Who iss it?

—Is Mr. Kazis there?

—No, Mr. Kazis has gone to work now, who iss it please?

—Can you tell me where I can get him, it's most important.

—Well, of course, you could try the paint shop on Stuart Street, but they don't like for——

—Can you give me the name——?

—Why, it's the Vacuum Paint Shop and Upholstery——

He hung up the receiver, laughed, dropped in another nickel, waited.

—Hello?

—Ammen speaking.

—Why, Jasper——

—I've just had a vision. Dislocation number seven, or is it eight! And listen——

—Yes?

—Here's a funny name just to remember, and then forget: Joseph Kazis. Came over in the *Mayflower*.

—What? Hello, Jasper——?

—But we shall see! No, it will not be Kazis. It will be someone else. . . . Someone strange! . . .

⟨ VI   The Stranger

To say that he was unmistakable, when he came a few minutes later, was not quite the truth: it happened, when it happened, very quickly, very lightly, there was really nothing in the little man's appearance which particularly answered to any previous notion. In that respect, it might even be said that it was *not* the man; the face was certainly not the face which he had vaguely foreseen. No, the decision was made automatically, somatically, with a mere physical gesture: he had simply, and before he knew it, stepped away from the telephone booth, against which he was leaning, and begun to follow him. This was no Joseph Kazis, no abstraction, nothing so remote as a mere name in South Boston, and in that sense it was already possible to feel an acute disappointment, a definite derangement of the basic idea. But of course, the minute he thought about that, he saw that it was inevitable; and what the little man supplied was exactly what mathematically would have *had* to be supplied—a real and surprising *existence*. He was actual.

He had come up the sloping ramp of concrete from the Arlington side, walking rather slowly, with his head a little down; he seemed to be hesitating; and when he had arrived almost as far as the telephone booths, having passed the barrier, he stopped for a moment and stood still. He looked straight before him with a half-smiling fixity, his hands were in his overcoat pockets, his overcoat was unbuttoned and hung loose at the sides with an effect of habitual carelessness, the gray tweed hat was rather far back on his head. He was obviously wondering whether to turn around or not. Something had been forgotten; or some plan had been, or was about to be, altered. That much was clear, it was amusing to watch the whole affair transacted so shamelessly in the open, as on a trans-lux screen, but it was also plain enough, from the continuous little smile, a slightly stupid smile, that whatever the thing was it wasn't of very great importance. The moment of irresolution passed, he gave a little cough and turned briskly toward the platform. He walked with an odd jauntiness, his feet turned out, and his head on one side. There was something birdlike about him, and the shape of his coat, which was too long for him, and had a heavy collar of cheap fur, somehow accentuated this. Lowering one shoulder, he turned neatly into the door of the train.

Pausing just inside the door, he looked quickly left and right, evidently saw that the forward end was the less crowded of the two, began to edge his way through the double row of passengers: to watch him from outside, and the slight patronizing smile with which he ingratiated while he made his way, was also to be able, without appearing to follow or any risk of attracting attention, to join him by entering at the front of the car. Accordingly, Ammen walked parallel with his victim: saw the gray hat appear and disappear: saw the hand go up once to touch a handhold and drop again: once glimpsed the half-turned smiling face, noticed for the first time the little mustache. Entering, he found himself almost too close to the little man, who had found a seat and sat down. But by standing opposite, with his back turned, it was easy to pivot slightly in order to watch him. It was also possible, by stooping, to see his reflection in the dark luster of the window glass. He could not leave without being seen—that much was at any rate certain. And that was all of course that was necessary. The danger always arose there: it had happened several times. In the case of a hurried exit at a more or less crowded station, it was necessary to be close at hand.

Revolving a little now, with his two hands above him on the white enameled handhold, he discovered that he could look obliquely between two swaying shoulders, and over a lifted newspaper, directly at the man's face. This was perfectly safe, for the blue eyes behind their frameless spectacles were turned studiously downward: with complete absorption, the little man was making notes with a red pencil in a red notebook. The first impression of smallness and neatness was at once corroborated. The face was not young, it was obviously somewhat worn, showed unmistakable lines of care and age—he was perhaps thirty-five—there were sallow hollows under the eyes, which on calmer inspection looked tired, but in contrast to all this was a quite definite boyishness and delicacy in the small neatness of the head, the features, the short-clipped mustache. It was a boy grown old; a boy hardened prematurely, by whatever chemistry, into a man. The maturity, or the appearance of it, might be artificial or forced, but it was unmistakable, just the same: the calm laconic assurance which had been evident in his gait was again evident in the clear and detached precision, the obvious *efficiency*, with which he was giving his whole attention to the making of notes in a notebook. There was conceit in it too. He thought well of himself, he was pleased with his ability to abstract himself from his surroundings, just as he had been pleased with the sharp little foresight with which he had found himself an empty seat in a crowded train. The entire impression was that of a child-actor's trained, and somewhat callous, small competence. When he looked up, presently, closing and pocketing the notebook and pencil, and glanced idly and again half-smilingly right and left, but not upward towards the face that watched him, his self-satisfaction was immense. He knew what he was doing, and that what he was doing was important.

Important?

But the importance was perhaps false.

The importance was simply a shell, the carefully elaborated defense of a weakling: it had no reality. The frog and the ox, as in Aesop's fable! Nothing could be clearer than that the little man's life was bound in shallows, if not in miseries, at any rate in smallnesses, and that the bright little notebook, the sharp little pencil, the detached little air of foresight and wisdom, all that careful assumption of precision and weight, were nothing at all but the feeble compensations of a barren and limited experience, a small body, a restricted mind. Already it was possible to begin the process of surrounding him: and exactly as it was easy to look down at him in the hurrying train, to study his mouth, his eyes, his hands, the large mole at the outer corner of the right eyebrow, the brown feather in the hatband of the cheap tweed hat, so also it was becoming absurdly simple to see the background, the suburban shabbiness and pretentious meanness, of his life. That life began already to lie open: with a single powerful glance one found its essential tissue: two suits of clothes, two pairs of shoes, dull lithochromes on the walls, a dirty tooth brush and a clean one, the cracked mirror over the kitchen sink, a comb always carried in the breast pocket of the coat, an umbrella stand in the front hall, in the zinc base of which was an old pair of rubbers. Or perhaps two, perhaps he was married. Perhaps even— and Ammen smiled at the advertisement at which he found himself staring, Morning Mouth Never Bothersome—he had children.

When the train climbed into the sudden sound of wind, the flood of daylight, on the Cambridge Bridge, sun flashing on windblown and dancing water, the sound of the train itself diminishing, it became possible to see the sallowness as more marked, the hollows beneath the eyes as more pronounced. And also a something melancholy or disillusioned in the eyes gave the lie to the amused impudence of the mouth. The eyes were a good blue, very deep, but inward-looking: self-centered. The mouth, under its short fair mustache, had about it a small air of authority. A tyrant in his own Lilliputian world: a domineering ant. A little bully.

At Park Street, it was easy to follow him, for as before he walked slowly and reflectively, hands in pockets, he seemed to be in no hurry, and to be enjoying the crowded scene, the cross-rush of opposed currents of pedestrians, some towards the North-bound cars, some to the South, himself sauntering beside the train, and now and then glancing into it, as he moved toward the escalator. Arrived on this, he stood quite still, did not turn, allowed himself to be borne upward to the surface with complete immobility. There he stepped off and turned to the left.

The thing was going perfectly: it could not have been better. And if now, as appeared likely, he was going to walk to his destination, it would be extremely simple. This was the advantage of great height. It was easy to follow because it was easy to see. Lagging fifty feet behind, one could observe every movement of one's victim as from a tower. Unless he took a taxi—but he had already passed the Park Street stand—there could be no difficulty. Except for the matter of turning corners, following people in the street was simplicity itself: but when they turned a corner, one must be prepared to run. More than once, on such an occasion, he had found that in the interval between the disappearance of the stranger round the corner, and his own arrival there, the stranger had vanished: and into any one of so many possible doors that further pursuit was impossible. This time there must be no such mistake.

At the corner of Bromfield Street—and it amused Ammen to reflect on the literalness with which his own path of last night was being followed —the tweed hat hesitated, as if about to turn to the right, but then proceeded. It crossed Tremont Street to the graveyard, sauntered slowly along beside the railings, turned once to look in at the pigeons and squirrels, but without pausing, and presently had crossed Beacon Street. It was curious: the fellow positively seemed to have the air of knowing that he was followed. That turn of the head, the peculiar way he had hesitated at the corner of Bromfield Street, and moreover the almost studied insolence and self-consciousness of his back—! Was it possible? No, certainly not. Any watched person looks watched. A suspected person looks guilty. Just the same, it would be as well to be careful. He remained on the other side of the street, strolled slowly beside the gray churchyard of King's Chapel, his eyes fixed on the little bobbing hat, and suddenly found himself thinking of Breault. Breault! This little man was like Breault—why hadn't that occurred to him before? Absurdly like him. The same sort of little homunculus, the enforced dignity of the man small of stature, the pathetic truculence of the weak. The sort of ridiculous boldness which is quintessentially an invitation to death: the one-who-wants-to-be-killed. The one who wants to be killed!

And why not Breault?

There would indeed have been a special and beautiful irony in choosing an anarchist—and a Chicago anarchist to boot. As if one had managed to murder Louis Ling. Or Czolgosz.

And odd how that the pattern should thus be turning round on itself, himself now again passing Tremont Temple thirteen hours later, with the echoes of that scene still whispering on those stairs, in that absurd room, still ordering the separate behaviors of those ridiculous people! Mrs. Taber, with her feather duster, was at this minute probably talking about it in the C Bookshop to Miss Gerber, the lumber merchant's daughter. At half past ten the shabby little fake analyst would come in—Meyer—to pick up gossip or blab the dirty secrets of his patients, throwing out dark hints as to their social importance. He would be told about it, and snigger, and recount for the hundredth time his story of the dinner he had given at the "Athens," —that experimental dinner when he had provided a department-store salesgirl for each one of his highbrow guests, with instructions to try to seduce them, so that he could observe their behavior—and particularly the behavior of Ammen. "And Ammen never said a word. He just sat here and never said a word. Do you think he's human, Mrs. Taber?"

Suddenly he found himself running.

At the Beacon Theater the hat had stopped, pivoted, and then with accelerated pace proceeded once more in the direction from which it had come: seeing that a change of traffic signals at the foot of Beacon Street was imminent, the little man had himself begun to run. As it was safer to run behind him than parallel with him, Ammen zigzagged through the traffic of Tremont Street, was just in time to drop to a walk again at the corner entrance of Houghton and Dutton's and to cross ten feet in his rear:

a little too close for comfort. A narrow escape, and it turned out, immediately, to have been even narrower than he thought: for at once the hat swerved to the right and entered the door of S. S. Pierce. Another moment and he would have been too late: caught by the stream of traffic, he would perhaps have been unable to see in what direction his quarry had gone, or into which of a multitude of doors. As it was, there was no great danger in following him into the store, which was reasonably crowded; there was plenty of excuse for dawdling, as if for inspection, first at one counter and then at another. The hat preceded him, with a firmness of purpose obviously born of familiarity, to the wine and spirits department at the back. A small bottle—to judge from its size and color a pint of whisky—was there procured, paid for, and pocketed; and this done the little man once more advanced to Tremont Street, once more resumed his interrupted journey towards Scollay Square, this time pausing just perceptibly at the entrance of the Beacon Theater to glance at the posters of the movies. Two facts had thus been learned about him: perhaps not quite facts so much as the possibilities of facts: one, that he drank, but with some indication that it might be on a minor and *retail* scale: two, that he might be a movie fan. A third seemed to be that whatever his job was—always assuming that he had one—it must be somewhat flexible; it was well after nine o'clock, and he still appeared to be in no hurry, but to be sauntering, and looking about him, as if his purpose was at most a half-purpose, and the mere killing of time not unpleasant.

This became more evident when he arrived at Scollay Square.

He stopped at the corner opposite Epstein's, stood still for what might have been three or four minutes, his hands deep in his pockets, the tweed hat turning first right and then left, but clearly not with any regard to the question of crossing the traffic lines. No, it was obvious that he simply hadn't made up his mind where he was going: or perhaps at any rate that he wasn't anxious to get there. For a moment, he half turned towards the right, and seemed to be looking fixedly down Court Street: but then he reversed his direction and began to ascend the slight hill to the Court House. It was all very peculiar: but the oddity of it was in a sense its most interesting and exciting feature. That he should be unpredictable, as much in behavior as in appearance, was of course of the very essence of the stranger: but while it was to be expected in outline, or expected in its unexpectedness, the details must naturally, like this, be surprising. No less odd was again the curious recapitulation of the events of last night. To come again past the Temple, and now to proceed by exactly the path which must have been taken by Sandbach and Breault and Mrs. Taber, to be moving as if by conscious design towards the C Bookshop, toward Sandbach's room—all this fitted beautifully, it was his own thought made manifest, it was once more—and the vision sharpened almost painfully—as if his own awareness had been simply externalized like a life-size model of the city itself. It was like a repeated dream, but with a difference,—for it was under control, it was being directed. The whole thing was simply his own chess game, projected: it advanced or developed before him exactly as he wished, just as helplessly as the smoke which he now blew from the pipe which he paused to light, all the while watching the tweed hat above his sheltering hand. Let him go as far as he liked; let him even round the corner at the top of the Square, turn towards Ashburton Place: let him, in fact, go *where* he liked: he was now under control, he would never escape. He was now—and the feeling was positively physical in its sureness and power—fastened. What was even surer than that he would turn to the right or left was that whichever direction he chose he was walking deliberately towards death. He was in the act of finding his grave.

At the back entrance of Houghton and Dutton's, a truck was being unloaded. A heavy crate fell from the tailboard to the sidewalk with a sharp clap, a pistol shot of sound, and the sound was at once echoed by the simultaneous slapping of a hundred pigeon wings as the startled birds took whistling flight from the sooty window ledges of the Court House. Round the Square they circled, and vanished northward at the far end of the Court House, his eye following them out of sight; and in that instant the tweed hat had vanished also, turning to the left at the top of the hill. No need to worry—he would still be there—but he quickened his pace, glanced hurriedly over the crowded array of second-hand books in the window of the Rebuilt Bookshop, noting one title, *Erring Yet Noble*, and presently, keeping close to the window of the Waldorf, turned the corner and looked down toward Beacon Street. The little man had disappeared: he was not there.

Impossible!

But yes, of course, possible.

He must be either in the Waldorf, at his left elbow, or in the shoe-shine parlor beyond: the Waldorf, at this hour, seemed improbable, but to inspect the interior through the large windows was simplicity itself. And sure enough, the tweed hat was standing at the counter, was in the act of receiving a heavy china mug of coffee, came forward with it, stepping cautiously, sat down at a table without once having raised his eyes, dipped sugar from the sugar bowl and began stirring the cup with a spoon.

A retreat, and a wait, becoming necessary, Ammen bought an *American* from the newsboy at the corner, crossed the street, stood with lifted paper by the door of the Newsboy Foundation. PICKETERS HELD IN CONTEMPT. Holy Year O. K.'d by Pope. NAZI SPY GANG IS UNCOVERED. Bootleggers, dope peddlers, and other racketeers, driven into temporary retirement by repeal and other causes, are back of the Boston welfare swindle, it was charged today. Mother Faber, a tiny slip of a woman, today stood in humbled pride on the witness stand. . . . The question now is whether the state trial should have proceeded, with habeas corpus proceedings pending in federal court. Fliers Hop for Rome Tomorrow.

The wind whirled the pages, the paper flapped against his arm in its effort to escape, a tall spiral of dust went spinning past the City Club. For a moment the sun flashed downward, filled the dull streets, sparkled on the cars, then was again dimmed by heavy clouds. He looked upward, watched the clouds in swift procession, ragged and gray, but not rain clouds, it would not rain. From Park Street Church came, with clamorous loudness, immediate and strange, the eight bells of the half hour, windborne and irregular. Half past nine.

The whole thing was peculiar: he had started a good fox, and no mistake. Perhaps he had no job at all, was going nowhere. Either out of work, or of independent means. But surely not the latter?

Picketers and racketeers.

Or of course he might be an "outside man" for some firm or other, whose hours were more or less his own——

This time, when the little man reappeared, it was with a new air of purpose and a noticeable quickening of pace. In a few minutes he had reached Beacon Street, Ammen keeping fifty feet behind; and then suddenly the hat had turned left into a narrow doorway which appeared to lead into a barbershop. Hurrying forward, Ammen found that it was not in fact the barbershop, but the entrance to a flight of shabby marble stairs which led to the upper floors: business offices of the humbler sort. Listening, he could hear the footsteps climbing above, and at once, taking three steps at a time, and without making a sound, he followed. The hall on the second floor was vacant: ground glass doors of an insurance office, a dealer in real estate: the footsteps were again ascending, and as he reached the bottom of the second flight of stairs he saw the feet just arriving at the floor above. They disappeared, he could hear them slowing, then a jingle of keys, the turning of a lock, the opening of a door. The door must be the one immediately opposite the stairhead. He waited a moment, listened, heard the door close, and mounted swiftly. Behind the gray glass he could see the moving shadow of a man in the act of removing his coat, very close at hand. The stenciled letters on the door said: Acme Advertising Agency. K. N. Jones and T. Farrow.

Jones! If only it was Jones!

And why not?

He knocked his pipe softly against the yellow-plaster wall, dislodged the light crust of ash, began to laugh. That it should turn out to be a Jones would be almost too good to be true. The anonymous one, the abstract one, the mere Specimen Man—it would be perfect! But even if it turned out to be Farrow——

Walking forward to the front window, he looked down into School Street, ticked the black pipestem against his teeth, reflected with narrowed and unseeing eyes. The thing was beginning; he was in the presence of it; his shadow was already falling upon the tree, like an immense frost of peril; and even as he stood here, in the shabby hallway, unknown to the tweed hat which now hung on its peg, his powerful influence was beginning to expand and penetrate. He had entered the stranger's little world, he was here inside it, learning its shape and size, taking possession of it. This worn wooden floor, the scarred plaster of the walls, the ground glass of the old-fashioned doors, the gas bracket in the corner—this was the stranger's domain, known to his feet and hands and eyes, returned to day after day, dreamed about, hated, loved. The whole little life was beginning to lie open, like a familiar book.

Opening the window, he leaned out; and at once something caught his eye. The telegraph office. His long hands tightened on the edge of the sill,—the idea was sudden, and like a pair of claws. It was as simple as lightning. And it would be as effective.

Two minutes later, in the telegraph office, he wrote Gerta's telephone number on a yellow telegraph form, added "please call after 11," and sealed it in an envelope. On the envelope he printed with the pencil the name "K. N. Jones."

—I want a messenger, please, right away.

—Yes, sir, for how long——

—I want him to come with me and deliver this note at the foot of School Street, while I wait outside for an answer. It will take him five minutes.

—Yes, sir, that will be——

—Give me the change from this.

Outside the barbershop, he handed the yellow envelope to the boy and explained.

—Just take this in and deliver it to Mr. Jones—or if Mr. Jones isn't there, to Mr. Farrow. The third floor. I want you to notice what the man you give it to looks like. That's all. Then come down and tell me, and I'll give you a dollar. Have you got it?

—Yes, sir.

—All right, beat it. And make it quick.

Within a minute, the boy was back, grinning.

—I gave it to Mr. Jones, all right! And was he surprised! He asked me where it come from, but of course I didn't say a word.

—What did he look like?

—Oh, one of these little guys, with a kind of a Charlie Chaplin mustache, and sort of bald.

—Was there anybody else there?

—No, sir.

—All right—here's your dollar. And keep it under your hat.

—Sure thing. Thanks. Say, are you a detective?

—Yes. And by the way, what's your name?

—Costello, sir. Peter Costello.

—I might need you again sometime. Now beat it, and forget it—see?

—Sure.

Clouds and a wind, the wild heavens opened and closed with wild light, the morning had deepened immeasurably, was deepening with each breath he drew: what a surprise was in store for Gerta, what a surprise was in store for Jones, what a surprise was in store for God! With his hand clenched tight in his pocket he held an imaginary revolver, he was already climbing the hill among the cedars to his particular place, the little hollow among birches and junipers, he was already taking aim at the rock, and now, rapidly and repeatedly, he pulled the fatally compliant trigger. Mr. K. N. Jones, of the Acme Advertising Agency, was as good as dead.

When he reached the Parker House Hotel, he suddenly decided to go in—he wanted not only to wash his hands, very carefully and slowly, but also to admire in the mirror above the washbasin the fine forehead and the extraordinary eyes of the man who had now so clearly and calmly seen to the end of a human life: King Coffin.

❮ VII   The Seven Words of the Stranger

If for a moment the thing, in coming closer, seemed almost in the nature of an encroachment, as if his own shadow were somehow falling on himself, or his own image walking toward him out of a mirror, the sensation passed immediately, with a mere knitting of the brows, and what ensued was a natural and profound laughter, the golden laughter of the *gaia scienza*, the gay wisdom. The heavens and the houses laughed together, the whole sound of the hostile city was gay, not to say ribald, and it was as if he himself were mounting rapidly up a spiral of air or light. The impulses were many and confused—to call up Gerta, for example, to call up Sandbach, call up Toppan, even Mrs. Taber; to call them all up and tell them what had happened. Ammen speaking! Yes? And I wanted to say that I've found a man, a stranger, and I have him on the end of an invisible cord, a cord three miles long, and with this cord I shall slowly but surely kill him. I shall dangle him there like a puppet, like Punch or Judy, until I want him. I shall then summon him to the place of execution, wherever I choose, and it shall be done. . . . But against this was also the contrary impulse, and the more natural—to make this the beginning of a new and essentially secret life: to go underground, into darkness, and to remain there. No one should know what he was doing, where he was, what planning, what evolving: at most, now and then, he would give them the fleetingest of little signals, the showing of a single and ambiguous light, glimpsed for only a moment and gone again, or the utterance of a deceptive word or two in the most disguised and bland of voices. They would know nothing, until he had returned at last from the underworld, wearing a new terribleness of splendor. And even then though they would recognize the new power, the new terror, they would guess in vain at the reason, find him as mysterious in the light as in the dark.

But only for the time being.

This fact must not be lost sight of.

He lengthened and quickened his pace, he had thought little about his direction, found himself now proceeding from the foot of Mount Vernon Street to the Esplanade against gusts of wind, the Charles River Basin lay before him half clouded, half flashing under the changing sky, the nearer waves leaden, the farther bright. The raw new works for the new lagoons, islands, bridges, the stretches of bare earth where as yet no grass showed, the heavy masses of unplaced stone lying awry, the ungainly bastions projecting against the river, windswept and sinister,—all this accorded admirably with his own changing scene, his sense of disruption and tumult. The ruthlessness and purposiveness of architecture, of the architect—yes, there are times when one must be a Bucyrus-Erie steam shovel.

Only for the time being: the shadow lay heaviest in that phrase, in the notion of *time*. Once the weapon had been aimed, one could not delay indefinitely the pulling of the trigger; there must necessarily be a limit to the time during which one merely observed, from a distance, and for whatever satisfaction, one's quarry: the one-who-wants-to-be-killed must be killed! But need it be at once?

It was a nice question.

Actually, of course, there was no hurry. Mr. Jones could not escape—for how could he take flight from a danger of which he wasn't even aware? He would be there, he would wait, as long as it was necessary for him to wait. But this wasn't really the problem. The real problem was once more in the matter of *purity*, and about this it was imperative to think very clearly, without any vagueness or any self-deception. One must be certain that one was not delaying for the wrong reasons: for example, out of fear, or a distrust of one's mere competence. But that was dismissed as soon as considered. The thing would be, if not entirely simple, at all events quite practicable: it would need, when the right time came, when the circumstances had been sufficiently studied or arranged only the cool exercise of a little logic. Some small and quite uncomplicated structure of deception would serve, all the more obviously in view of the fact that the victim was completely unsuspecting. An invitation to something, somewhere—Belmont, Concord, Nantasket——

No, there was no cause for worry, there was no fringe of self-deception, he was not afraid; the thing was as good as done. He could safely leave the actual form of the murder to be determined by future events. The revolver, with which he was an expert marksman, brought all the way from Naples, canoe on the Concord River—these details need not yet be considered. Or a casual lurch in the subway? What was far more important now was the other question, which he had not quite clearly foreseen though he had vaguely felt it—the question as to how legitimate would be the mere pleasure in *observation*, in the daily watching and study of Mr. K. N. Jones. In the last half hour, the intense reality of this pleasure had become only too manifest. It must have been, from the very beginning, somewhere vaguely in his mind—it was certainly a part of the pleasure of the pure detective-impulse, as discussed by himself and Toppan. But admitting this, how safely and for how long could it be protracted? The line must be drawn somewhere—the stranger must in essence remain a stranger—and if it was perhaps legitimate to learn as much about the little man as possible, by careful study, one must be scrupulous in learning only what could be learned *from outside*. Yes, that was it; that would keep it pure: everything would be all right as long as the stranger did not know *him*. The stranger must not become an acquaintance? Even this was not wholly clear, however—for if knowing about his victim was a perfectly legitimate part of his pleasure, then surely it was difficult to set any limit? . . .

Advertising; he was an advertising agent; a publicity expert. Presumably not a very good or successful one. What did such fellows do? And how could that be found out?

Two girls, one of them with an Alsatian on a leash, walked for a moment parallel with him.

—And from where I was sitting in the front row of the balcony I could look right down on his little pink bald head——

—Was his wife there too?

—Yes, I suppose it was——

—With red hair? and she has very skinny arms, you can see them when she wears——

He turned to the left, entered the rutted and shabby alley behind Beacon Street, paused to let a car pass, looked in and saw an old lady with a black hat and veil—the fierce bird's-eyes peered at him and were gone. For some reason he stood still, gazed after the retreating car, watched it swing slowly, bumping over the uneven surface, up the left turn which took it to Beacon Street. A final glimpse of that white and hostile Boston profile and it had vanished. Something in it, as in this wind, the rapid shift of cold spring sunlight with gray shadow, brought him an eclipse: his hatred rose suddenly and sharply, the vision returned to him at last night at Gerta's, it grew like a tree, thrust darkly and venomously above him, spread violent and lethal boughs to right and left over the hated void. As he stood still in the dusty alley, with tightening arms and hands held hard against his sides, it was himself who thus grew and darkened and obscurely multiplied. He had taken possession of the world. Conscious of his powerful arrogance, his half-closed eyes, his out-going intelligence and limitless vision, he looked to right and left along the alley as far as he could, saw the few people in the distance, knew them, dismissed them. They had not noticed him, and even if they had, they were as unaware of his true reality, his malevolence, as the oak tree is of thunder. If they saw him at all, they saw him simply as a man standing still in a dusty alley, a man with dusty shoes, tall and thin, dressed in a dark suit, his dark hair blown in the wind. Perhaps they thought of him as odd and solitary, or even as absurd and self-conscious: as if to be standing there close to the high brick wall, motionless in the swirling dust, was a kind of awkward pose, something either meaningless or ridiculous. Or shabby and mean. . . .

Mean!

But how could it be that?

He looked quickly upward toward the sound of an opening window, saw a maid shake a dusting cloth with a downward gesture of the white arm, felt for a moment something inimical in the mere notion of height. To be enclosed thus anonymously between high walls, and as if purposeless, at a standstill—this was to be enacting the "unrecognized" Satan, the Satan in disguise. It was that moment when Satan, humbly clad, has not yet declared himself; skulks in the background; pulls the hood low over his marked bright forehead; has not yet pointed toward the victim his mesmeric forefinger. Certainly there might be a kind of meanness in this,—as there was in any mere solitude. To be alone, in an absolute sense, was also to be mean, as the acorn or the toad is mean. But also to be alone was to be magnificent. . . .

He gave his laugh again, turning, he had come back again to his starting point, the laughter of the gay wisdom, it was all as clear and beautiful and ominous as a black beetle in a golden blaze of light. The scarab! He was the scarab. And with precisely that kind of hard and precious immortality. And its touch, when K. N. Jones felt it, would be cold.

But the telephone call was imminent, he must get to Gerta's room, be waiting there, listen—for the first time—to the stranger's voice. Gerta would not be at home of course, she was at the Museum, working in the print-room—perhaps he would leave a note for her. Crossing Charles Street, he ascended Chestnut, stamped the dust from his shoes, heard the sentences of the dialogue forming, listened intently to the new voice which crept all the way over the hill from an office in School Street. Advertising. The Acme Advertising Agency. The Farrow might be mythical. A one-horse show. Bought out, perhaps. And who went to such a firm for advertising?

When Sally let him in, unsurprised by his request to use the telephone and to leave a note, it was ten minutes to eleven. The room was empty, silent, smelt faintly of turpentine. The blue smock hung over the back of an unpainted chair, the green bowl of apples stood on the sill, the notice of an art show was propped against one of the candles. On the corner table, tilted to the wall, was a new painting—a new Gerta—which obviously she must have concealed the night before. Like all of Gerta's recent work, it was queer, it surprised him—as if abruptly she had begun speaking in a foreign language. It might be the interior of a lunar volcano,—the inside, the wall,—but it was vascular with silver, encrusted as with heavy silver veins which seemed to have a cold and heavy life, and above this, in a light as dead and clear as terror, were two winged things, not birds, not moths, which appeared to be at dalliance. Above these, in turn, was a little hard pale wafer of a sun.

What did Gerta mean by it?

He took it to the window, held it to the light, saw how heavily crusted was the paint, all that veined interior as solid as a honeycomb, but also with a queer phosphorescent unreality. A strange world, as strange as his own, she was a match for him, it was what he had always liked in her: she had secret depths and heights, there must somewhere be a Kay in her family. She had said—aren't we both mad?

No.

He replaced the picture, then stood still in the middle of the floor. At this minute, perhaps Jones had his watch in his hand, was putting out his arm toward the telephone, pulling it toward him, waiting. Or perhaps he was walking to and fro in the room, in the little dingy office, unable to sit down, wondering what the mysterious note could mean: and whether it meant a job or not, and why it had come by messenger. Perhaps the bottle of whisky stood on the desk, with a tumbler beside it. And an ash tray littered with matches and cigarette ends. Or had he forgotten the message already? was busy, wouldn't call at all? It seemed unlikely. The very fact that it had come by Western Union messenger would make it appear all the more urgent. . . .

Urgent! He little knew.

A faint premonitory buzzing, and then the telephone, as if clearing away an obstruction, began its sharp and rhythmic ringing. For a moment he stood and listened to it, gazed down at it, smiled as he put his hand on it and lifted it, the receiver still unremoved. Beware lest, if thou gazest into the abyss, the abyss gaze also into thee!

—Hello?

—Hello? This is K. N. Jones speaking, of the Acme Advertising Agency. I received a note asking me to call this number——

—I beg your pardon?

—I say I received a note this morning asking me to call——

—Oh, I see; this is Mr. Jones.

—Yes. Who is this speaking, please?

—The Acme Advertising Agency, is that right?

—Yes! Yes?

The voice was a little anxious, a little eager, a little mystified: but low-pitched and quite pleasant. After a pause, getting no reply, it went on:

—What can I do for you? . . .

—Well, as a matter of fact, I'm not quite sure as yet. I merely wanted to make an inquiry.

—I see. Well, I'll be glad to give you any information I can——

—You undertake all sorts of advertising work, I assume?

—Oh, yes. Anything and everything. Perhaps you could give me an idea of what it is you want?

Carrying the telephone with him, he took three steps to the window, placed the felted base of the transmitter on the sill beside the bowl of apples, looked down over the roofs toward the Esplanade, the bright surface of the Charles River Basin, the far-off Harvard Bridge. The window was a few inches open, and he closed it by bearing softly down upon the sash with his elbow.

—As a matter of fact, I'm making the inquiry not on my own account, but for a friend of mine.

—I see.

—Well, do you?

—Well, I mean I'd be very glad——

—It would be rather a confidential matter.

—Well, I guess that would be all right—would you mind telling me who recommended us to you?

—I think that hardly matters. But if you want to know, my friend simply happened to be in your building—in School Street, I think he said —and saw your offices.

—I see.

—You feel you would have to have references?

—Why, no, certainly not, I didn't mean that, I just wondered how you knew——

—But of course, if there are going to be difficulties, we'd better not be wasting each other's time——

—Not at all, not at all! Please don't misunderstand me! I was only——

—My own part in it is simply to make inquiries. It's a matter of political advertising which requires absolute confidence. Do you understand?

The gentle voice seemed to hesitate, then said:

—Of course. What medium, may I ask, did you have in mind? . . .

—That hasn't been wholly decided. What I was going to suggest—will you hold the line a minute while I consult my partner?

—Yes——?

Resting the receiver on the sill beside the bowl of apples, the earpiece downward, he crossed the room to the mantelpiece, lifted the notice of the art show from beside the candle, read it carefully, then went to the Colonial mirror which hung on the rear wall. His back to the light, he peered at the shadowed and elongated face which he saw there, leaned closer to it, grinned at it with a conscious evilness of expression, his hands all the while in his pockets, then turned again toward the window and stood motionless. The thing was so easy as to be meaningless. If it was all going to be as simple as this—! And the poor little man was so eager, so keen to get the job! Waiting there, hardly daring to breathe. Perhaps it would be a good thing to *create* a danger. If the enemy didn't hit back——

Returning to the telephone, he lifted it quietly and said:

—Mr. Jones?

—Yes?

—My partner thinks that perhaps the best procedure would be for me to have a talk with you in person. Now as it happens, I'm usually not very free during the day, and I wondered whether it would be possible for me to come and see you this evening somewhere. Would it be convenient for me to call on you at your home, for instance? Or have you a telephone there?

—Why, yes, I guess so——

—I mean, do you live in Boston?

—No, I live in Cambridge. 85 Reservoir Street.

—Reservoir Street. Let's see, just where is that?

—If you take a Huron Avenue car, it's only a couple of minutes from the car. I'll be there all evening, and I'll be very glad to have a talk with you. I'm sure you'll find we can give you satisfactory service, and our prices are very reasonable.

—I might come in about nine. Or if not, I'll perhaps give you a ring in a day or two.

—The Cambridge number is in the book, if you should want to call me there—K. N. Jones.

—I see. K. N. Jones.

—And as I say, I hope we can be of service to you. We're not a large firm, but I think we know our business as well as most!

Allowing the little boast to hang unanswered and plaintive on the wire for a few seconds, as if for the full savor of its eagerness, and for the completion of the picture, Ammen merely said "Very well," and hung up the receiver without waiting for any further reply.

In the ensuing silence, it was curiously as if some one had left the room. He replaced the telephone on the table, then began once more to examine Gerta's odd picture—but as he gazed at that surface of honeycombed silver it was not a lunar volcano, nor Gerta, he was looking at, or looking into, so prolongedly and earnestly, but the identity of K. N. Jones: the little man with the clipped mustache, the tweed hat, the fur-collared coat; the little man with the suave and deliberately ingratiating voice. It was as if he were sitting there, the one who wanted to be killed, in the depths of a mirror, his hands relaxed on the edge of the desk, towards which his curious inward-looking eyes were directed downward. The expression, and the attitude, were those of despair.

What was it, exactly, that had created this impression—which, though faint, was so definite?

And was the situation in any way altered by this?

But why *should* it be?

Opening Gerta's little writing bureau, he sat down and looked through the recent letters in the pigeonhole at the right. One from her mother in New York, with details of an attack of sciatica and iodine treatment; a card signed Petra from Washington, with a photograph of the Adams Memorial by Saint Gaudens; his own postcard of two days ago inscribed "Dislocation Number One." But nothing from Sandbach. Perhaps in the wastebasket? No. And after all, there was no reason why he should have written—yet. Quite likely they had arranged a meeting for today by telephone: to discuss the latest phase of the Ammen situation. And when they did, Sandbach would get a surprise: he would find himself perched on the top of a towering scaffold which had, as it were, grown up under him during the night. A nightmare.

85 Reservoir Street. 85 Reservoir Street!

The day opened swiftly to left and right, like an immense stage from which the scenery was being slid into the wings, the prospect widened, and far off he saw the godlike arm and hand thrust violently downward from the hurrying clouds, the index finger pointing silently at a single house, then gone like a whirlwind. The arm and hand were his own, the house would soon be his, all that was in it would soon be known. A map of Cambridge bought at Amee's, a taxi from Harvard Square, and before nightfall a new and terrible circle would have been drawn. At the center of it, Jones was beginning to be immortal, beginning to be still.

⟨ VIII   The Daily Life of the Stranger

The insomnia was not real, was not actual, since there was no real desire to sleep; it was merely the removal, in one dark strip after another, of insulation; the progressive laying bare of the bright nerves of perception; the painless flaying of the dark integument of consciousness. With the turning over, with the listening, now to the murmur of nocturnal water in the pipes, again to the faint *tyang* of the grandfather clock in the professor's apartment next door, or again to the intermittent snicker of the little motor in the electric refrigerator; with the lifting of his hand from beneath his head on the pillow, or the sliding of his fingers along the edge of the half-cool sheet; with each separate action of the restlessness which divided, into marked and conscious sections, the time-chasm which would ordinarily have been void and unconscious, it was as if he stepped closer to his own true being and purpose. On the hours, which came softly on soft air from the dark campanile of Saint Paul's,—the twelve, the one, the two—came also an incandescent indifference to sleep. To these and other sounds he could be as inaccessible as he wished, as little touched as by the diagonal of cold lamp light, from Massachusetts Avenue, which made a pale remoteness of the ceiling and threw into humble relief the little Buddha on its shelf. These immediate things, his room, his window, his bed, the soft sucking sound made by the curtains in the study against the wire screens, the creaking of a ventilator on the roof of the A. D. Club across the street, were in fact as remote as they could be: they stood at an infinite distance; to cross time and space to them would be like crossing the Milky Way. Their remoteness, of course, lay in their comparative unreality. They belonged now to another and dimmer time-space, they seemed so distant and so silent, measured by the nearness and loudness of his own heart, as to be without meaning and without motion.

And not heart so much as vision.

The vision was this little man, who now so obsessed him: this little man, his house, his clothes, his name, his daily orbit. He was here, in this room: walked like a fly across the ceiling, as if the ceiling were the large white map—(now pinned to the wall over the table in the next room)—of Cambridge: on that map, with its concentric circles which marked the distance, in quarter miles, from the City Hall, a whole week of the life of Jones was now over and over again enacted. He opened his door in Reservoir Street, stooped to pick up *The Herald*, went in again. He opened the door later, and came out. From the little copper letter box—first unlocking it with a key—he extracted letters, glanced over them, selected some, replaced others. He walked to Huron Avenue, crossed it, and proceeded west to a block of one-story dingy shops between Fayerweather Street and Gurney Street; entered a grocer's and left an order; then came out to wait for a streetcar. At half past five in the afternoon, he reappeared, carrying an evening paper; looked again in the letter box; unlocked the green door. The upper part of the door was of glass, and from across the street he could be seen going up a flight of stairs which turned to the left. . . .

His life went by the clock. He came out, to go in again; he went in, to come out again. The streets in which he walked were always the same. Perhaps that was why he so seldom lifted his odd, amused eyes or bothered to look left or right. Tuesday, Wednesday, Thursday, Friday—on Friday he had left early, at a few minutes after eight, and come back at four. And at the other end of his life, the School Street end, his goings and comings were just as precise, just as methodical. Always the same route, the same apparently meaningless circuit round Pemberton Square, the pause for the reflective cup of coffee, then the accelerated descent of Beacon Street to the office. And at half past twelve, three-quarters of an hour for lunch, sometimes at a sandwich shop in Province Court, sometimes at the Waldorf in Bromfield Street.

He walked on the ceiling like a fly: it was easy to see him there: easy to meet him, at the bottom of those awful little streets: he came quite suddenly around the corner of Vassal Lane, for example, so suddenly that Ammen jumped, and laughed, for a moment forgetting that Jones did not know him by sight. To turn and saunter away, obliquely across the street, with averted face, and taking cover behind a coal truck, had been very simple. Vassal Lane. That had been an exception, too, in the routine, for Jones had gone there, to the house at the corner of Alpine Street, the first thing in the morning, directly after breakfast. Moreover, he had gone there as if with hesitation: to begin with he had passed it, merely pausing to look rather earnestly at the door; and he had then sauntered, rather slowly, all the way to Fresh Pond Avenue. There, standing across the street from the Pumping station, he had waited for fully five minutes, alternately staring at the pond and the row of half-fledged willows by the station. A dark day, with now and then a little spatter of rain. On the way back, he went into the house—a two-family house like his own—and stayed there about five minutes. It was the sudden meeting with him, at the corner of Vassal Lane and Reservoir Street—(he hadn't thought Jones would have had time to get so far)—that had first suggested the advisability of hiring a drive-yourself car. Sitting in the closed Buick, parked now at one place and now at another, but usually on the south side of Huron Avenue, it had been easy to see without being seen. For the observation of the area immediately round the house, it was in fact ideal: but of course no good for following. For *that*, it had been necessary either to board Jones's streetcar at Appleton Street, having seen him get on, or to lie in wait for him at the top of the ramp in Harvard Square. . . . Thanks to the little man's regularity, both had been quite simple.

The neighborhood was detestable—it ought to be burned down. With all its inhabitants. A typical suburban swarm of wooden two-family houses, all exactly alike, brown shingles, dirty white-railed porches and balconies, one or two with projecting flagpoles. Here and there an attempt had been made at a clipped privet hedge: but for the most part the little front yards were bare, except for a forsythia bush or two. At exact intervals, for miles, the cement walk branched in toward a porch, from which opened two doors, one for the lower part of the house, one for the upper. On the right of each house another narrower cement path led to the cellar doors, at the rear. It was along this—on Monday evening—that he had seen Jones, with bare pink hands, bareheaded and wearing an old black sweater, trying to roll a heavy ash can on its rim. It was too much for him—it kept sitting down, wrenching itself away from his fingers. But after a deep breath or two, the hands still resting on the rims, the head bowed, he managed to heave it up again and to roll it a little farther toward the street,—toward the grimy border of ringed earth at the curbstone where week after week it waited for the ash man. The entire street was marked in this fashion. In front of each shabby little house was the deep pair of rings, grooved in the earth, where ash can and garbage can rested. And the inevitable residue of onion-skin and eggshell and orange peel. . . . Sickening.

The clock in the professor's room sounded, through the thin walls, its *tyang*—half past two.

He thought of the map, with its concentric circles,—Reservoir Street, one and three-quarter miles from City Hall, at its south end, where it joined Highland Street; but where Jones lived, a little farther. By Yellow Taxi, a fifty-cent fare from the Square.

K. N. Jones. 85 Reservoir Street. . . .

It had turned out to be Karl—not Kenneth, as he had guessed.

But who was the woman who was seen now and then passing the windows, with a white cloth bound over her hair? It had been impossible to make out whether she was old or young, or what she looked like. Once she had come down the outside stairs at the back, to the cement path, but before he could get a good look at her she had rapped her dustpan twice, sharply, on the edge of the ash can, and gone in again. It might be either his wife or his mother. It might be his sister. It was even possible that there were *two* women, not one; for occasionally she had seemed *taller* than he expected. But of this it was difficult to judge. Whoever it was, or whoever they were, thus far they had never come out of the house while he was watching. Probably his wife.

The curious thing was the repugnance which the actual scene had aroused in him from the beginning—from the very beginning. There was something really loathsome in it. The paltry houses, the ill-paved street, the ash cans, the litter, the air of furtiveness and meanness and defeat which overhung the whole neighborhood—there had been something in this which seemed a little outside his calculations. Of course, the unexpected was to be expected. Jones, Karl Jones, was not the sort of fellow who would be found living in a huge and grand apartment house—far from it.

The cheap fur collar had not meant that.

Nor the tweed hat.

But to find just this kind of meanness and sordidness, the sight of Jones wheeling an ash can with bare hands, then dusting, with dusty hands, the ash from the knees of worn trousers——

And all with such an air of good cheer and confidence. The cock-sparrowlike sideways tilt of the head, the ridiculous little strut of accomplishment with which he returned along the cement path! This was something to tighten the muscles in one's arms, to contract the fingers, to narrow the eyes. But just the same——

No, the objection was not real, could not be real, all this was a natural part of the *strangeness*, it was inevitable; and in its way, also, it was a fine enough sharpening of the whole point that in its discovery it should bring with it a pullulating ant heap of new and all-too-human experience: to have blundered thus into such an unforeseeable quagmire of the deformed and spiritually unvirtuous—horrible though it might be—was of the very essence of the chosen adventure. To think, for instance, only of the names of those streets, as contrasted with their actual nature—Vassal Lane, Alpine Street, Fayerweather, Fresh Pond Avenue—Alpine, of all things, in a district as flat as a dried river bed, and as noisome! And all the shabby purlieus, moreover, of filled-in clay pits and mudholes, acres of festering tomato tins and sardine tins, rusted fragments of cars, old bedsprings, blown paper, greasy rags. When the wind came from the northwest, one smelt a sour and acrid smell of slow burning, the animal odor of smoldering human refuse, worse than the ghats of India: it drifted day-long from the reclaimed quarries by Fresh Pond, covering the entire forlorn suburb of wretched houses in its bitter miasma. To think, in the morning, of opening one's windows to that! In the evening, if one walked forth toward the pond, in search of the picturesque, perhaps a sunset over Belmont to lift one's eyes to, one saw also the shadowy and sinister figures which poked, like hobgoblins, at a score of sickly little flames in that waste land, prodding with sticks to see if here or there some object might be salvaged from the heaps of refuse. Only the trees, in that district, had any dignity, the willow-trees; —and especially the one, an old one, with a trunk as massive as an oak,

which stood at the junction of Vassal Lane and Reservoir Street. And this
had been useful. Its great girth gave excellent cover.

Of course Jones was poor—no one would live in a neighborhood like
that if he could help it. If the Acme Advertising Agency did any business at
all, it must be infinitesimal. No further proof of this was needed than that
he had himself, twice, spent part of a morning in the bare hall outside the
office—not a soul had come or gone in the whole time. And of course
Mister T. Farrow must be a thing of the past—if he existed, he had at any
rate never been seen. Perhaps Jones had just bought the name and good
will. Anyway, apparently, Jones just sat there—three hours in the morning
and three hours in the afternoon—without doing a thing. Once or twice,
the telephone had rung, but it had been impossible to overhear what Jones
was saying—it might even have been his wife.

What *did* he do there?

Perhaps that was where the whisky came in. Though he never showed
any signs of it.

Or perhaps most of his business was mail-order advertising, the preparation of sales-letters—which could be managed largely by correspondence. A
typewriter could be heard there intermittently, and used, moreover, with
quite respectable speed. But always, then, came the long silence. In fact, it
had soon become only too obvious that the fruitful end for observation was
not the business, but the domestic, end of Jones's little life-pattern—the
study of the house, although a great deal more difficult, would in time be
more rewarding. But how to manage this? To be seen hanging about there
day after day, or even sitting in a car, would ultimately attract attention—
it might not be Jones, it might be any one, but it would be dangerous.
There was the problem of the postman, for instance. . . .

Toppan! The very thing.

He sat up in bed, switched on the light in the corner, looked at the
hexagonal wrist watch—quarter to three.

Why not present the whole business to Toppan as a mere *exercise* in
detection—the latest and best specimen—a particularly attractive problem?
It would join on to the previous conversation perfectly: and his pleasure
in it, both their pleasures, would be deliciously enhanced by the fact that
Toppan wouldn't quite dare presume that it was a question of the *other*
thing, the pure murder, or in any case that it was for anything but the
novel. Why not? And why not now? To rouse Toppan from his sleep,
startle him, take him thus off his guard, with all his conscious defenses
down, still surrounded, as it were, by all the naïve transparency of sleep—
it would be like turning a harsh searchlight on a naked soul. An experience
in itself.

In the study, knotting the dressing gown, he paused to look at the map,
leaning close to it to familiarize himself once more with the tangle of small
streets between Huron and Concord Avenues, and also to observe the
column of dates which he had entered in pencil on the upper left-hand
margin: ten of them,—the latest this morning's. It looked formidable
enough. Ten days. Possibly a little slow: but certainly there had been no
delay? *Map of the City of Cambridge. C. Frank Hooker Acting Engineer.*
1932. . . .

From the table beneath it he picked up the small green book which lay open there, with the pages downward, and read again the passage which had caught his attention earlier in the evening. "But there is the dark eye which glances with a certain fire, and has no depth. There is a keen quick vision which watches, which beholds, but which never yields to the object outside: as a cat watching its prey. The dark glancing look which knows the *strangeness*, the danger of its object, the need to overcome the object. The eye which is not wide open to study, to *learn*, but which powerfully, proudly or cautiously glances, and knows the terror or the pure desirability of *strangeness* in the object it beholds." Extraordinary that Lawrence should have said just that—italicizing the word *"strangeness"*—but wasn't he completely mistaken in assuming that there was no desire—in the savage eye—to learn, to study? In any case, what *was* the savage eye? Who was to say? or who was to say that—finally speaking—it wasn't the only true eye in the world, the only one which saw virtuously?

The terror, or the desirability of strangeness.

The pure desirability!

That was odd, too. An odd, but perhaps natural, antithesis. Something a little uncomfortable in it, as well. But why? After all, if the prime need was to overcome the object, then the study of it was absolutely indispensable, was simply a means to an end. The cat, in short, *understands*—in the deepest sense—the mouse: observes it with that sort of pure virtue of love which is the prelude to conquest. It sees, and knows, the mouse—*and that is precisely its playing with it*. In the savage eye there is therefore not merely the desire to kill, there is also that look which just as coldly embraces a tree, a landscape, a star, an idea. It must purify what it sees, and see what it purifies: the only vision which is noble. There is no compromise with the object, no placid or reasoned acceptance of it. It is seen, understood, and destroyed. The vision is pure.

He said it aloud, as he descended the half-dark stairs—"the vision is pure"—remembered his pipe and tobacco and went back for them, descended again with the pipe in his hand. Toppan's door was unlocked, he stepped in, switched on the light, his forefinger automatically finding the ebony button in the dark, then for a moment he stood unmoving in the silent room. The bedroom door, in the far right-hand corner, was closed, the green window shade had been pulled down, except for three inches at the bottom, where the night-dark showed, a sheet of music had fallen from the piano and lay open on the bench, a brown felt hat dangled from one corner of the mantel. Taking three steps forward, to the middle of the gray carpet, he listened: he could hear the deep and regular breathing. Toppan had not waked: lay there at his mercy. To read the diary now, with Toppan in the next room——

And there it was, on top of the desk.

It had been closed on a pen, tonight's entry was still fresh.

He turned the pages.

"May 2. The great Jasper has certainly stirred them up, and no mistake. Saw all of them—Sandbach, Gerta, Mrs. Taber, her husband, and that analyst chap, also a little fellow from Chicago, at the C Bookshop this afternoon, and what they wouldn't do to him if they could! Sandbach and Mrs. T. in particular. They had a long discussion of the episode at Tremont Temple—I must say I couldn't help laughing, for Jasper seems to have done a first-rate theatrical job of it: apparently just walked in and *dismissed* them. Not so bad! Goodness knows there is something rather fine about it, even if one doesn't feel moved to emulation. Gerta, however, I noticed, didn't have anything to say: what does she know? I had an impulse to talk with her, but of course, in the circumstances—I decided it could wait, perhaps she *doesn't* know what I know, or guess, and there's plenty of time. Mrs. T. says what he needs is a good spanking, that he's spoiled. Sandbach rather surprised me by suggesting that he's definitely insane. The analyst just said 'Oh, no, perhaps a little paranoid,' wanted to know what his relations were with his father. Gerta could have told him, of course, and so could I, but neither of us said anything. As a matter of fact, I'm not sure that would account for much, though I daresay an analyst would do him a lot of good. I never knew any one so *cut off* as he is—but then, you've got to admit that he seems entirely and horribly self-sufficient. It seems impossible to get at him, much less to hurt him. Walked back with Gerta, and she asked me in, but I didn't go. . . . Squash with Hempel——

"May 3. Law Society——

"May 4, 5, 6, 7——

"May 8. . . . and had a curious encounter with Sandbach and Gerta outside the Fogg Museum. They looked as if they'd been quarreling, anyway something was up, they were walking along very slowly ahead of me, and just before I caught up with them they turned and came toward me. Their voices were raised a little, they had that fixed and angry look, didn't see me at first, and then were both embarrassed. Very self-conscious meeting. I thought Gerta looked extremely pale. I asked them to tea, and Gerta came up, S pretending (?) that he had to get back to town to go over a talk he is giving at the Burroughs Foundation. Sounded like an alibi. Gerta was unusually quiet, subdued, didn't say anything about J till after we had had tea, then asked me if I had seen much of him lately. I said quite truthfully that I hadn't. She said she hadn't either, and just wondered whether he was 'all right'—wanted then to know whether I had *seen him at all.* As a matter of fact it hadn't occurred to me before, but when I stopped to think of it, I had been pretty busy, and I don't believe I *have* seen him, even a glimpse of him, for over a week. She thought this was a little queer, and asked me if I didn't agree: as before, I could see she wanted to discuss the question of his sanity, in fact she got as far as saying she was worried about him, but I pooh-poohed it, reminded her that he had always been like that, going in for temporary disappearances and so forth. I don't think I convinced her, but then I didn't try very much, for I was uneasy about perhaps getting in too deep. She's frightfully in love with him. I have a feeling Sandbach is jealous, and that the row was connected with it: of course S has been hanging around her for a hell of a while. She was a little hurt with me, I could see, managed to suggest something like 'well, if you don't want to talk I can't make you' but just the same was very nice about it, as she always is. A damned fine person, I admire her reticence, why in God's name must she throw herself away on that incomparable egoist! It certainly *is* odd that neither of us has seen Jasper all week: I wonder if by any chance he's gone to work on that fantastic Coffin idea: and I wonder what the analyst would make of *that!* Lordy, but wouldn't he get his teeth into it.

"May 9.———Could it possibly be J I saw in a Buick on Concord Avenue? If he's bought a car, that would account for a great deal—it'll be a load off Gerta's mind, anyway. Asked Jack, the janitor, if he knew anything about Jasper's getting a car but he said d-d-d-didn't know, M-m-m-mister Ammen hadn't been around much. What next?"

What next?

Replacing the fountain pen in the loose-leaf diary, he went to the bedroom door, opened it quickly, looked around the edge of it and saw the dark shape on the bed in the corner, waited for it to stir. As it did not move, he said:

—Hi. Are you awake?

Kicking the door so that it swung open widely to the wall, the light falling across the brass bedrail, he returned and unlocked the inlaid tantalus by the piano. He took out the bottle of Haig, and while he was stooping to see if there were any glasses he heard Toppan's voice, a little curt, behind him.

—Oh, it's you.

Not turning, he said:

—Yes. I couldn't sleep.

—What time is it—isn't it a little late?

—Not three yet. Haven't you got any glasses?

—You want a drink?

—I want a drink and I want to talk to you.

Toppan's blue eyes seemed larger than usual, without his spectacles, his red hair stood up straight in a sort of point, he looked gnome-like. He was in pajamas.

—All right. Wait.

He got the glasses, and his dressing-gown, came back a little sheepishly, it was obvious that he was angry but wasn't going to say so. He put the glasses on the piano-bench, ran his hands through his hair.

—Help yourself, Ammen. I won't join you.

—You're angry, aren't you?

—Not at all.

—But it doesn't matter—I want your advice.

—Advice? about what.

—That story I was telling you about. The question is—how much can I trust you—how discreet are you?

Toppan, putting on his spectacles, with very carefully raised hands, sat down in the mission rocking chair and smiled uneasily, ingratiatingly. He looked slightly silly, his transparency was too obvious, he had that almost offensive emotional nakedness which often goes with red hair; but also he was intelligent, he must be watched and controlled. He said, looking up obliquely through his spectacles:

—Ask and it shall be given unto you.

———Don't be an ass. The point is this. For ten days I've been watching a man—I won't mention his name, or say where he lives—just as I planned, it's a complete stranger, the—as you might say—*corpus vile* of my experiment. For the sake of convenience, we'll call him Kazis.

—It's a good name.

—All right. I've learned a lot about him. I know where he lives, what he does, that he is probably married, somewhat hard up. I know a lot of his habits. Technically, too, as you would say yourself—I'm thinking, of course, of your observation of that osteopath in Brookline—it's been interesting. But now I've come to a sort of impasse, don't know quite what to do next: you can give me some advice.

—Oh, well, I don't pretend to be an expert—but if you'll give me an outline of how you've gone about it——

—Very simple. I saw him first in the subway, followed him to his office in town. Then perhaps I made a mistake. His office door had two names on it—Kazis and another. I wanted to find out which one was his, so I sent up a Western Union messenger with a message addressed to Kazis: the messenger boy came back and described him to me, and of course it was Kazis.

—I see. I don't see anything wrong with that. I assume Kazis hadn't seen you.

—Certainly not.

—And presumably the boy didn't say who he brought the message from?

—No. You miss the point. It isn't Kazis I'm thinking of, it's the messenger. Don't you see, in this novel, King Coffin, if ultimately my hero *kills* Kazis that messenger boy might remember the incident, remember the man who gave him the message—remember *me*. Of course, in the present instance it doesn't matter, as naturally I don't intend to commit any murder.

—Naturally!

—Naturally. But for the novel I want a foolproof method—do you understand? Unless you think this might be reasonably safe.

Toppan reflected, a little embarrassed, his eyes downcast.

—But I thought, in your novel, it didn't matter if the hero *was* found out—that a part of the virtue of your pure murder would be in the very fact that—

—No. What I said was that in the circumstances it would have to be secret—only *ideally* could it be done with complete indifference to risks. For the purpose of my story, I want the detection itself completely foolproof.

—I see. Actually, there needn't as a matter of fact be much risk in the way you did it. I suppose you didn't sign any name?

—What do you think I am?

—Well then, assuming for the sake of argument that you eventually *did* kill Kazis, but not, say, for a month or two, the chances of your being found through the messenger boy would be practically nil. He'll remember the episode of course, and tell about it, and give a fairly good description of you, especially as you happen to be of somewhat striking appearance, owing to your height, but that would hardly be enough to go on. You'd

be safe as a church, as long as he didn't happen to *see* you again—which
you could easily avoid—or unless, of course, some *other* person or persons
happened to have reasons to connect you with the crime: in which case
you'd be brought before the messenger for identification. Without that,
his mere description of the mysterious person as a tall man who wore a
black velours hat would hardly be enough, would it?

—You think not?

—No.

Holding the green glass in his hand, he smiled down at Toppan, who
smiled back. Toppan was on his guard: he must be on guard himself. The
question about King Coffin's *indifference* to discovery, for example, had not
been quite ingenuous—or had it? But if Toppan was fascinated by the
possibility, clearly he didn't really believe in it: he speculated, he was a
little frightened, but that was all.

You speak of other persons who might have reason to connect him—
what do you mean?

Toppan laughed, drawing the dressing gown over his crossed knees.

—Why nothing special—it all depends.

—Depends on what!

—Well, to be frank, in the present case, assuming for the moment that
you are King Coffin——

—You can *assume* as much as you like. It's your own assumption, isn't
it?

—Of course. I mean, there's myself. *I* know about it.

—Do you?

—Don't I?

—You mean you're an accessory before the fact?

—Oh, I could wriggle out of that!

—In other words, my hero had better not discuss it—even with those
who share his views.

—Perhaps not,—there's also Gerta.

—No—you can leave her out of it.

—Very well.

He crossed to the mantel, lifted the hat from the corner where it hung,
looked inside it to see the maker's mark, replaced it. Revolving his glass
on the varnished ledge, he examined the delicate white flowers in the color-
print, the cluster of rose-tinted lychee nuts, the blue-breasted birds. The
bird not quite sufficiently stylized. Leaning closer to this, his back still
turned to Toppan, he said:

—It's a useful suggestion. . . . You know, I actually talked with him
for ten minutes.

—Good Lord. How was that?

—Quite simple. In my message I asked him to ring me up—at a certain
number—giving no name of course—and talked with him, pretending I
wanted some work done. Discussed it with him, and told him I'd ring
him again.

—And did you?

—Yes. At his house.

There was a pause, and as Toppan said nothing in reply to this, he turned and looked at him. His hand was over his eyes, his head was bowed a little forward. Perhaps he was tired—perhaps he was playing 'possum. The right foot, slippered, the veined instep showing below the green pajama leg, jigged up and down, mechanically, slightly, with the beating of his heart. Otherwise he was motionless. Looking down on him like this, one could see the white scalp through the disordered red hair: the hand across the forehead, by contrast, looked very living, very vital. Toppan's consciousness was perhaps in his hand.

—But never mind that. Are you awake?

—Of course.

—What I want to know is, what can I do next.

While Toppan pondered this, kneading his forehead with his fingers, Ammen filled and lit his pipe: he watched Toppan over the flame, began to wonder whether the whole thing wasn't a mistake, a miscalculation. Toppan was being a little too wary, and, as his diary had made clear, he perhaps now suspected a shade too much for comfort. He had begun to step out of his role as mere satellite, wanted to enjoy detecting the detective. If he and Gerta should now, as seemed not impossible, put their heads together——

—I said, what can I do next.

—It depends on what you want. And of course on how much you've already got. I take it you've already observed all that can be superficially observed——

—Yes. I know his daily habits, as I've told you, his clothes, his shoes, the papers he reads, the day he puts out the ash can, and so on. I know what he's like. A thoroughly commonplace and somewhat conceited little person, a sort of unconvinced failure. Certainly nobody you'd want to waste five minutes with, otherwise. You ought to see the house, for instance—a dreary two-family thing, one of millions, you know without going into it exactly what it will be like—cheap carpets that look as if they'd been designed in vomit, bead curtains, a wallpaper in the bathroom meant to look like tiles, a mission clock, a gas log fire. But all this is general—I want now the specific. You understand? And of course without meeting him.

—Not so easy. But there might be ways——

—What.

—If you want to go into the house, you could pretend to be canvassing for something. There'd be a risk in it but not much—if you went in the daytime, which you would, you'd see only his wife, or whoever lives there, and even if——

—What.

—Even if in your supposed role as an eventual murderer you later kill her husband she would have, presumably, no special reason for connecting you with it, or even for recalling your visit.

—Not a bad idea. But for one thing, I'm beginning to be uneasy about appearing in that neighborhood too much—as you've probably noticed, there is always a postman about, or a policeman. What about that.

—Yes, I know. It's not too easy. Have you thought of using a car?

—A car?

—Yes, a car. It's of course one of the recognized devices—you sit in the car a little way off, it prevents your having to dodge about behind telephone poles day after day, and so on. I told you I used one that time in Brookline.

—I hadn't thought of it—it might be a good idea. You mean, hire one.
—Yes.
—I'll keep it in mind.
—Or if there happens to be an apartment vacant across the street——
—There isn't.
—How long do you propose going on with it, anyway? After all, there isn't much to gain after a certain point——
—My dear Toppan you're sometimes very stupid. In a pure *study* of this sort there can be no limit.
—Incidentally, that time you had him call you on the telephone—isn't there a weakness there?
—You mean he'd have a record of the number? No. The occupant of that apartment has been carefully instructed, if Kazis calls again, to say that the whole project is off, and without mentioning any names. It would be a dead end in any inquiry—completely.
—Do you think it's quite fair to use Gerta for that?
—Did I say it was Gerta?
—It's fairly obvious.
—You're quite mistaken. It isn't.
—In that case I'm relieved.
—Keep the change.

There was a pause—he walked to the piano, touched one note, felt a little defrauded, the thing was not going exactly as planned, the tone was wrong, as out of key—somehow—as this too-vibrant c-sharp. He said:

—I'm afraid you're not much help, but thanks just the same. There's one thing further—I must remind you that I expect you to treat all this in the strictest confidence. And since you mention Gerta, I'll repeat what I said to you before, I think perhaps you're forgetting it a little—I don't want any interference there. I won't go into details, but there is a very delicate and peculiar situation between Gerta and me, of great importance to both of us, and I don't want any meddling with it—is that clear?
—Perfectly.
—Then why do you blush?
—As I said once before, that's my innocence.
—All right. Keep it. And keep *out*.
—Just as you say, professor!
—If you don't, I shall know it—I shall make it my business to know it. And I don't think you'd enjoy the consequences.
—My dear fellow——
—Thanks for the smell of whisky. Good night.

Arrived on the top floor, he felt a little breathless, a little stifled, he suddenly discovered that he was holding his pipe too hard, and with a perspiring hand. The whole thing had been somehow *forced*—it had not come naturally, was not natural now; the effect was of a slight jangling. The map still hung there, with its marginal notes, the list of dates and scenes, it was all just as clear as before, just as orderly; but there was also a queer something which was changing. For one thing, he had not, as he now saw he had intended, *presented* Jones to Toppan, and this had seemed important. He had wanted—that was it—to make Toppan vividly aware of him—as vividly as he was aware himself. He had wanted to *photograph* him for Toppan—tweed hat, fur collar, ash can, and all: the mole, the perpetual smirk, the mustache, the jaunty little vulgarity of bearing. Curious he hadn't seen that—his purpose had not been so much to ask advice as simply to talk about Jones; and in talking about him—was that it?—*to take further possession of him.* But for some reason, this project had broken down; Jones seemed if anything farther off than before; the excitement had cooled.

It must be simply that he was tired.

From the window he looked obliquely down at the deserted and lamp-lit stillness of Massachusetts Avenue, then, as always, lifted his eyes to the one mysterious light which always burned nightlong in an upper room of Boylston Hall. What secret was in that room——?

And at once, as always, when he thought of it, the vision returned; dimension after dimension rolled off soundlessly to disclose depth above depth, height below height; where vapor had been, the tree of clouds began once again to thrust upward with swirling boughs.

This was good, he could laugh again, Jones was still there. Let the clocks go as madly as they liked, Jones would still be waiting for him, waiting calmly.

⟨ IX   The Stranger Is Gay

The little procession was monstrous, it was absurd, it was mad and meaningless, and as he watched it from the safe interior of the car, which was filled with tobacco smoke, with his black hat pulled down over his eyes, the pale afternoon sunlight seemed to emphasize and isolate each element in it as grotesquely as if it were merely an outlandish figure in a dream.

Karl Jones had suddenly become new—he was being seen for the first time.

Bareheaded, wearing again his old black sweater, grinning a little self-consciously, as if something in the occasion made him shy, and as if he were trying to carry it off with bravado, he came down the wooden steps of the Alpine Street house with a small striped mattress over his shoulder and a worn suitcase in his hand. The suitcase he dropped on the cement sidewalk, where already stood a white-painted chair, such as are seen in hospitals, a Gladstone bag, a porcelain slop bowl, and a brown wicker hamper. He flung the mattress into the back of the open model-T Ford which waited at the curb, balancing it carefully over the child's cot which reared its white legs and bright brass casters into the air. A middle-aged woman followed him down the steps, bringing a rope; with this they proceeded to knot the mattress into place, first throwing a patchwork quilt over the whole shapeless pile. Then the hamper was with some difficulty wedged into the front, beside the driver's seat: it was heavy, tied with cord, and what looked like bed linen protruded from the gaping lid. As the woman reascended the steps Jones called after her:

—Guess we'll have to carry the rest! Hope you don't mind!

What she said was inaudible, she waved a hand, entered the house, and in a moment reappeared accompanied by a man. The man climbed into the front seat, slammed the tin door, started the car and began turning it. Jones lifted the slop bowl by its handle, laughing, his head tilted to one side: the woman seated herself in the white chair on the sidewalk. She too was laughing, leaning forward and clapping her hands on her knees. When Jones said something to her, she got up, took the slop bowl from him, picked up the suitcase, and began walking away towards Reservoir Street. Jones swung the chair up against his shoulder, seized the handle of the Gladstone bag, and followed.

The whole thing was unreal: it had no existence.

The woman might be a trained nurse: she was wearing a dark cloak from beneath which, as she walked, flashed the white of what appeared to be a uniform.

And the child's cot—what about that? If there was a child, in the Reservoir Street house, why had he seen no sign of it in all this time? And if the child was ill—as the presence of the nurse seemed to suggest—then it was difficult to account for the queer *cheerfulness* of the scene. The logic was a little wrong. . . .

He sat still, watched them turn the far corner at last, vanish out of sight. They had not noticed him, it would be easy enough to drive slowly through Reservoir Street and observe the end of this peculiar ceremony, but for some obscure reason he felt apathetic, indifferent. It hardly mattered: he had already seen more than he expected anyway, he had not really intended to come here at all, had simply made a last-minute detour on his way to meet Gerta. The thing was a windfall, it was in a sense outside the routine, needn't be too much bothered about. Just the same, it was certainly odd, among other things, that Jones should be here, and not at his office—it was three o'clock.

And this indifference, this apathy——

It was a part of the time problem.

He tapped a fingernail on his watch, frowned, opened the window to knock the ashes out of his pipe. It had certainly become unexpectedly difficult, unexpectedly vague—the queer thing was the way in which, from the moment when he had actually found Jones, marked him down, begun to learn about him and know him, the element of hurry, of pressure, had begun subtly to dissolve. It was as if abruptly he had stepped out of time into timelessness: what need could there be, any longer, for hurry? Jones was not only *there*, he was *here*: Jones had joined him, had joined his life: it was almost, in fact, as if Jones had become a part of his own "*self.*" He had again that queer feeling of encroachment, as if his image were walking toward him out of a mirror, or his shadow somehow falling on his own body; the feeling was not unpleasant, brought with it a sense of power, a sense of agreeable duplicity; but also in it was something a little disconcerting, or even dangerous. It was all very well for Toppan to say, in his smug insinuating fashion, that there wasn't any point in going on with it after a certain time—how could Toppan know anything about it? The pure vision—this was (as in the beginning he had of course not been able to foresee) the period of pure vision! To sit back and watch, to wait here now, for instance, actually *foregoing* his power to watch, was a very nearly perfect thing. It was comparable to the artist's intuition of the completed work of art: Jones was in the process of becoming an artifact. He remembered saying to Gerta—"an action could have the purity of a work of art. It could be as abstract and absolute as a problem in algebra. . . ."

Wasn't that still true?

Of course: and more than ever necessary. What must be kept firmly in mind was the inherent *necessity*. If the world was logical at all, then it must be logical in every item. And if it was despicable, if humanity was despicable, and if one was to sound one's contempt for it to the bottom, separate oneself from it, then the final and inevitable action in the series would be simply an act of destruction: it would be the only natural purification. It was not, in this sense, dictated so much by hatred as by a need for purification. Was that it? Or not hate *only*, at all events. It was the need of the superior being to separate himself violently from the one-who-wants-to-be-killed, the inferior, the crowd. . . .

He smiled, recapitulating; the whole thing summed itself up neatly and decisively; the constellation of events became once more precise and orderly. Gerta, Sandbach, Toppan, Jones—they were arranged and fell into place, the clock moved them in its geometrical orbit, their voices and faces faded as they passed, became vivid as they approached, faded again. Toppan's suspicions were powerless to take any shape in action; Sandbach's guesswork was too far off to find any accuracy of aim, his emotions too confused for any singleness of purpose; Gerta's devotion would continue, until too late, to constitute for her an effective paralysis. They circled with the clock, they watched as they moved, but their fixed orbit, fixed by himself, would never bring them any nearer to him. They, as much as Jones, were his own creation, they were falling into their grooves, they no longer had any freedom of will. To all intents, they had become puppets.

Two children, a boy and a girl, ran past him bowling iron hoops, the wooden sticks ringing dully on the metal, clanking regularly, the shrill voices raised in a meaningless and unintelligible gabble. An immense pile of white clouds had come up from the southwest, the sun went out, the afternoon became gray.

He took Gerta's letter from his pocket, opened it on his knee.

Jasper my dear—I suppose you suggested the place in Belmont because you knew I'd be teaching there in the afternoon, but I wish you had taken the trouble to let me know a little sooner, it's not too convenient— and don't you take a good deal for granted? I don't quite know why you should assume—as you appear to—that your plans are of such importance to me. If you had wanted to see me, any time in the past fortnight, you could easily have done so: and why you should now want to be so spectacular—shall I say melodramatic?—about our meeting I confess I don't

see. Don't you think the whole thing is becoming a trifle absurd? Why
on earth should I want to watch you at revolver practice? Don't be ridiculous! However, I *am* a little concerned about you, for Julius says you look
ill and haven't been sleeping, and of course I won't pretend that I
wouldn't like to see you, so I'll be there as soon as I can get away from
Miss Bottrall's dreadful little life class. I'd be somewhat relieved if you'd
kindly forget to bring your revolver. It hardly seems necessary. Gerta.

They had been talking together again—and Toppan had told her that
he looked ill.

What was more interesting, however, was the note of withdrawal in
the letter, which was distinct. This too might be Toppan's doing, but more
likely it was Sandbach's. Sandbach was beginning to struggle. He was saying to her—that madman Ammen. You must cut yourself off from that
madman Ammen. The quarrel in front of the Fogg Museum might have
been that—Sandbach had been urging her to drop him, he was frightened
and angry, and he disapproved of Toppan's influence because Toppan
didn't agree with him. That was why he had refused Toppan's invitation
to tea. And also, of course, he probably suspected Toppan of knowing more
about the situation than he did himself. He suspected all three of them
of keeping him at a distance, keeping him in the dark, he was struggling in
a web of which the filaments were maddeningly invisible. . . . The whole
thing was working beautifully.

But what should he say to Gerta?

He became aware that he had been listening to the radio which sounded
from an open window, Frankie and Johnnie—"bring on your rubber-tired
hearses, bring on your rubber-tired hacks"—the melancholy irony died
behind him in a sardonic drawl as the car picked up speed, and in a moment he had passed the house in Reservoir Street and was heading for
Concord Avenue. The Ford had gone, no one was in sight, but the cot and
bags stood on the porch, and the door was wide open. It was tempting—
the opportunity was certainly unusual—but on the other hand to turn
back now might be a little risky: some prying neighbor, standing behind
curtains, might notice it and think it peculiar, might remember seeing the
Buick there before; or remember it later when he came again. Better not.
And the day's work was already good enough.

But what should he say to Gerta?

And need it be shaped in advance, or could it be allowed to shape itself,
or to be shaped by *her*?

As a matter of fact, the necessity wasn't so much for saying anything
as for appearing: the real need, for the moment, was that he should simply
be *seen*, so that the weight of his character and purpose—above all his
purpose—should again, and at this critical juncture, be deeply felt. The
time had come for a subtle counter-balancing of Sandbach, a sly disturb-
ance of the center of gravity. To do this, it would be sufficient, as it were,
simply to cross the stage, to look hard at her for a few seconds, and then
vanish. The bonds would be tightened, Sandbach's work would begin all
over again, the shadow on him would have deepened still further, and if
in addition Toppan had fed her natural anxiety, so that she was concerned
for him, or even had begun to feel sorry for him——

He laughed, sounded the claxon derisively, once, twice, three times. Sorry for him! And of course it was exactly what was happening. It had been apparent in his last interview with her, she had pressed the point about Kay, she had subsequently tried to discuss the subject with Toppan, and now it was more than ever apparent in her letter. He looked ill, he was not sleeping. There it was, plain as a pikestaff! Accordingly, she would take the initiative, she would be inquisitive, she would want to find out exactly where they stood, both with regard to each other and with regard to Sandbach, and this would render her—in the deepest sense—vulnerable. On this pattern, the scene could be allowed to shape itself. She would question—she would stand there questioning—and he would simply *be*. We ask and ask—thou smilest, and art still outtopping knowledge. The abyss will gaze into thee.

The details shaped themselves beneath his hands on the wheel, flew in parallels of bright speed, seethed with the wind through the cracks in the glass, rose before him in the grey shape of Belmont. If he got there first, he would leave the car at the edge of the road, in the usual place, would precede her to the familiar little hollow of rocks and grass and junipers, with its wall of cedars and birches, so that before she could see him she would hear him. But if she heard the shots, would she dare to approach?

That risk must be taken. If she heard him, and decided not to come——

There was no sign of her at the top of the hill, nor in the path that led to the abandoned racecourse, nor on the grass-grown racecourse itself, where he got out of the car. The gray stillness was profound, it was like the Sabbath, he took the revolver from the pouch in the car door, slipped it into his pocket, also the little red box of cartridges tied with string, then put two fingers to his teeth and gave a long whistle, whip-lashed at the end like a whip-poor-will. There was no answer, no echo from the coppice of white birches, he noticed the dandelions in the short grass at his feet, and it occurred to him that he could leave a note for her. He wrote on the back of Gerta's letter: Quite safe to approach: firing the other way. Leaving this on the runningboard, with a pebble to hold it in place, he descended the short path of rocks and sprawling juniper which led to the hollow, lifting one elbow before his face as a protection against swinging branches. As he watched the last of the young birch leaves, bright green, slide across his blue sleeve, he heard Gerta's voice before him, speaking levelly:

—I had an idea it would be safer to be here first.

—You needn't have worried. I left a note for you on the car.

—Why the car? is that part of the plot?

—Of course. I thought Toppan had told you. And as a matter of fact, hadn't he?

—As a matter of fact, he hadn't.

Seated on the rock, her hands beside her, her foot swinging, she looked up at him with an air of challenge and mischief, her dark eyes narrowed but bright, a look which in other circumstances might have been disconcerting. The familiar blue cape was open, save at the throat, she was wearing the white Russian blouse, she was bare-headed, the dark hair turned away in wings from the calm forehead.

—Then I've no doubt he will.

—My dear Jasper, would you mind just explaining a little of all this?

—Must I? I thought everything had been made quite clear at our last meeting.

—I see. You assumed it would all go *on*.

—Why not?

—As I said in my letter, you appear to take a great deal for granted. Merely because in the past we've been very good friends——

—Am I right in saying that we came to an agreement? an agreement to co-operate? But I suppose, as I predicted, S has begun to influence you, you're no longer to be trusted. You were unable to keep yourself separate from him!

She got up and walked away from him slowly, her hands holding tensely the dark edges of the cape. Over her shoulder she said, with an effect of measured lightness:

—I expected you to say that. I've been completely loyal. Sandbach is certainly distressed and angry about it, and of course very much mystified, nor can you blame him, he's not content to let things just stand as they are, he wants to know what is happening.

She turned back towards him, stood still in the grass, the cape folded across her breast, her arms akimbo beneath it. Across the little interval of bright grass and dandelions she continued:

—Co-operation! What am I supposed to do when you go away and stay away? It's all very well!

He took out the revolver, held it flat on the flat of his hand, weighed it appreciatively with downward gaze.

—You were supposed to wait, to be trusted. You know that.

—Jasper, I *was*——

—You've doubted, you've drawn away, your letter makes that clear! We'll discuss it later—in the meantime do you mind if I try this out? A couple of rounds, just to see if it's working. Two years ago at Capri——

—Capri?

—It was all right. I could hit a stone the size of a watch at fifty feet. . . . I'll use that rock over there.

He placed the box of cartridges on the grass before her, the revolver on top of it, then walked deliberately across the hollow toward the large rock at the farther end, where it rose against the overhanging hillock of other rocks and cedars. As he went, he stooped, picking dandelions, choosing the larger ones, and these he hung over the lichened crest of the gray rock, their golden heads toward Gerta. The sun came out, accentuating their brightness and the paleness of his hands. Turning back, he counted off the paces.

—Twenty-five.

—I suppose you'd like me to hold one in my teeth?

—This is probably the first time in the world that *dandelions* have been used. Now cover your ears.

He smiled at her: she smiled back. Then, raising the little black pistol over his head and slowly lowering it to the level of the rock, and without perceptible pause, the first golden disk sighted, he fired. The rock seemed to have jumped, the first of the dandelion heads had vanished, the swift sound fled wildly off among the woods, the little smoke died in sunlight. Before the ringing in his ears had ceased he fired again, and again the rock jumped, but this time it was a miss; then again, again, again, and again. Four of the flowers were gone, the woods were singing with compressed clamor, one clap of sound folding hollowly on another, a muffled swoon of tumult. He clicked the empty revolver, lifted his face to the smell of drifting gunpowder, laid his hand over the short barrel to feel the warmth. When he turned round, he saw that Gerta had gone very white.

—Feel it, he said.

—No thank you. I'm not enjoying this.

—I'm sorry. Do you mind if I continue?

—Not at all.

—If you listened carefully, it might give you a sense of power!

—A sense of *your* power?

—Just as you like.

She was frightened, she sat down again on her rock, her lips tightly pressed together, her face averted: she was swinging one foot, nervously; perhaps angrily. What she was about to say was in her eyes, in her lowered brows: he watched her decision while he extracted the magazine of blue metal and reloaded it.

—If you don't mind my saying so, it all seems to me extremely silly.

—Why should I mind what you say? It *is* silly. Like many necessary things. And like many things we've agreed on before. Sandbach, for instance!

He gave a laugh, she turned and looked at him with a sudden sharpening of expression, something very like hatred, then as quickly looked away again. As if deliberately to pay no attention to her meaning he clicked the magazine into the grip, drew back the barrel, raised the pistol once more, lowered it, and fired. Another dandelion leapt in air and vanished, the bullet, ricocheting, whined away to the left, the hum of it lost in the swift sound of tearing which screeched in a circle round the woods; and then the five other shots, which followed in quick succession, doubled and redoubled the confused clamor. Only one dandelion was left, the echoes repeated *ee yah, ee yah, ee yah*, diminuendo, wingbeat on remoter wingbeat, a sullen dying of applause, and everything was again silent. He looked down at the empty shells, scattered about his feet, and said:

—Sandbach, for instance. . . . Ten out of twelve, not so bad.

She had stooped forward, had picked a single grass blade, was examining it, turning it between her fingers.

—And now would you mind telling me what it's all about?

—I said Sandbach.

—Sandbach was understood, wasn't he?

—It's an accomplished fact, then?

—If you don't mind, Jasper, I'd prefer not to discuss that part of it. You see——

—I see. I *foresaw!* I even foresaw that with it would go this withdrawal. And of course that he would say to you that you must drop me. But it's too late. You can't. You're here.

—Yes, I'm here, but I think I must tell you——

—I think I'd better tell *you*.

—My dear Jasper, I wish you would! If it's not too late. I mean, if *that* part of it isn't too late. I can't go on with it—I won't any longer have any responsibility—much as I love you—can't you see that the whole thing was a sort of hallucination? Couldn't we still make something much better of it? S means nothing, not a thing——

She had put the grass blade between her lips, was looking downward, tears had brightened her eyes. But her voice had remained as admirably level as always.

—What is it exactly that you'd like to know?

—I want to know what it's all about.

—We had that out. I haven't changed.

—Could you tell me about it?

—My dear Gerta, you're like an open book!

He laughed again, looking down at her tightly clasped hands, and went on:

—Well, I'll say this much, that if he isn't perfect he's at any rate very good!

—Sandbach?

Her expression of bewilderment might or might not be ingenuous.

—No. We'll call him X, shall we? It's not Kazis. Would you like to know his real name?

—No.

—It's Jones. The ideal name, and almost the ideal person. Good God, I didn't know such people existed! A real and complete nonentity. Lives in a two-family house, takes out his own ashes, wears rubbers on rainy days, rides on a streetcar every day of his life.

—I see. And that's enough, is it?

—Of course. Not that it's enough to *know*. It's curious how interesting it has become to *know* about him, to learn about him—and I've learnt a lot. Would you like to hear some of it? He reads *The Herald*, uses toothpicks, wears brown shoes with a blue suit, drinks a pint of whisky every day at his office. I suppose he has nothing better to do. He's in the advertising business, has a business, so-called, of his own. Reads textbooks on advertising in the subway. Yesterday it was a *Manual of Typographical Standards* published by *The New York Times*. Mezzographs, Line Cuts, Half-Tones, and Ross Boards—I've been studying it myself. . . .

—You *are* insane.

—Are we?

—Do you know S wants to report you?

—Oh, he does, does he!

—Yes.

He picked up the red-covered box of cartridges from the grass, put it in his pocket, took out his pipe; and as he did so a cloud went softly over the sun, the scene darkened. Everything looked smaller and nearer, Gerta seemed shrunken, he suddenly had a strange feeling of loneliness. This had happened before—it had happened only this morning in Harvard Square, when the sight of so many people, all rushing towards the subway, had given him a queer and unmistakable sensation of panic, of which the essential was solitude. This had been quite recognizable, was recognizable now, but had it any real significance? Yes, they all wanted to kill him, everybody really wanted to kill every one else, to be immersed in a crowd was to be immersed in a world of enemies. To face another individual was to face an enemy, even to face Gerta, who, under his own guidance, was in the very act of escaping from beneath his control. The eyes with which she looked up at him were Sandbach's eyes, the words she used were now Sandbach's, Sandbach had possessed her, still possessed her, it was to Sandbach he was speaking.

—I see. It is really Sandbach I am now talking to.

—Jasper, my dear, won't you sit down and discuss it calmly?

—Yes. Let's talk about it, for the last time, calmly!

He stretched himself, lazily, full length, on the grass, his hands under his chin: at once she came and sat beside him, crossing her knees: it was her intention to encroach. Leaning forward, and looking at him earnestly, she said:

—Now tell me, my dear. Do you mean to go on with it?

Not meeting her gaze, though he was aware of it, he answered shortly:

—The novel? King Coffin? Certainly.

—You know I don't mean that.

—I'm afraid I have no idea what you're talking about. . . . By the way, I liked your new picture very much. What do you call it?

—Jasper!

—You have a really extraordinary imagination. It's good—though I'm bound to say I don't know what it means.

—I see. You won't discuss it. I ought to have expected it, I suppose! I do what you ask, I accept Sandbach at your dictation, and this is what I get for my pains! It's really funny!

She started to laugh, stopped abruptly, he watched her hands, in the grass, clutch savagely at the blades, and let them go again. He could hear her breathing rather quickly, turned his head sideways to look up at her with amused eyes, saw that she was staring sightlessly into the distance, the somber mouth relaxed, the whole expression desperate and unhappy.

—You can't say I didn't warn you. I warned you specifically. I pointed out precisely this danger—that you would shift your loyalty to Sandbach. Well, it's come. What we were going to share—that new thing which we then both saw so clearly, dislocation number X—has come to an end because you failed me. You weren't good enough!

As she said nothing, he added:

—Isn't that it?

—Of course. You were quite safe, weren't you, either way! Simply because you didn't care. You care for no one but yourself. And surely that must begin to disappoint you!

—Oh, I miscalculate, like every one else. But I still have my amusements!

—Jones, for instance?

—Of course. A very harmless and pure entertainment. Like this target practice.

—Your notion of purity!

—And it's beginning to be rather exciting! I've sent him some theater tickets—a whole box at the Orpheum—marked them complimentary, you know——

—Why?

—Oh, just for fun! I thought it would be nice to see him close-to for a whole evening—also to see what he brings *with* him—his wife, I suppose!

Lighting his pipe, the little yellow flame bright against young grass, he listened to the sound of a car climbing up a road in the distance, thrust the half-carbonized match into the soft earth, frowned. The scene was not quite what he had expected—it was curiously relaxed, random, directionless— and of course it was easy to see why, it was because Gerta wanted desperately to know exactly what he was going to do, but didn't quite dare to ask him point-blank. She was probing, but probing without courage. Even now, in the slight droop of her shoulder, in the half-averted profile of which the expression was a deep powerlessness, he felt her to be about to give the whole thing up. She was discouraged, she was divided, her physical and moral loyalty to Sandbach was trying to assert itself, she was in the very act of listening to Sandbach's voice. That madman Ammen. You must give up that madman Ammen. She was listening to this, but also she was feeling, and feeling profoundly, as if it were a kind of poison, the deep seal he had himself put upon her, that culminating moment of mystic communion between them when they had—as it were—tacitly agreed to share an insane secret. The voice of Kay! Sandbach was struggling violently in her against this ghost, the voice of Kay; she sat perfectly still; it was as if he were watching a stage from the opposite sides of which two choruses were trying to out-shout each other. Sandbach! It was in a sense Sandbach himself who ought to be destroyed, the loathsome and insinuating voice of reason, of common sense, the slimy voice of universal belongingness, of social safety, the shrill chorus of a world of parasites. His hatred rose suddenly and violently, the vision made him raise his head, the muscles in his arms tightened, his sense of time suddenly sharpened and became positively visual, as if the whole world were a swift and vast escalator moving rapidly upward towards the sun, towards the final flash of action. His own wisdom was omnipotent there, he had but to extend his hand, the right moment was near. He said:

—You'd better hurry back to the lower levels. You'd better listen to little Sandbach. It's not very safe up here.

—My dear, it's not myself I'm any longer concerned about, it's you. It's not very safe for you. I wish I could persuade you——

—Give it up. I'm beyond the pale.

—But of course I don't quite believe you. It's really nothing but a sort of fever, isn't it? Couldn't you go away for a time? Couldn't you come with me to New York?

—New York! Good God!

—You're *not* in a normal state.

—Is New York more normal?

This made her angry: she glared down at him Medusalike, with an admirable and delightful air of challenge, she looked somehow Hellenic.

—And what's more, if you don't come to your senses, I suppose we'll have to do something about it!

—*Who*, exactly?

—All of us.

—Is that a threat?

—Just as you like!

He laughed, jumping up, stood above her laughing.

—Go ahead! But would you mind telling me what evidence you've got? Or who you propose to go to, or what you propose to say? Don't be a fool. Nothing could be more harmless than my little attempt to make a scientific study of the habits of a stranger—and all with a view to writing a novel! Any time you want to look at my notes, my dear Gerta, you're quite welcome. And if you think King Coffin would be of burning interest to the police, send them around, I'd be delighted to see them. . . . Can I drive you to Cambridge?

—No, thanks. I'm going back to Miss Bottrall's. And I think I'll walk.

—All right then—I'm off. Dislocation number—fill it in yourself! And I'll see you in hell.

She looked up at him calmly, her hands on her knees, she seemed to be about to say something, but her lips remained closed, he noticed the little golden cord with which her blouse was knitted at the throat. With a wave of the hand he turned away, walked off whistling, was aware as he entered the path that she had not moved, still sat unmoving. Let her imitate Buddha as much as she liked, exert her pressures, sit there all afternoon, lie in the grass and cry, as she probably would—by all means! It would come to nothing. She would begin writing him letters again, telephoning to him at all hours, conferring with Sandbach and Julius, but the gesture would be helpless and fumbling and feminine, all three of them were helpless, as helpless as Jones himself; they could accomplish nothing. He broke a branch of birch, whipped it, as he walked, against other birches, until it was stripped of its leaves, dropped it before him in the green path and trod upon it. This was Sandbach. For a few seconds he stopped, stood still, closed his eyes—something had made him feel slightly sick, slightly giddy, the turmoil for a moment seemed unnatural—like the confused clamor of the echoed pistol shots, *eeyah, eeyah, eeyah*, a concentric and derisive chorus—but this passed, he opened his eyes again, and saw the sun just emerging with swimming rim, a pale lemon-yellow, from a bright edge of cloud. It was time caught in the act of moving, time in its dizzy descent to time.

❲ X The Pure Murder

That he should fall asleep during the daytime was unusual, that he should fall asleep in a chair was stranger still; from a ragged fragment of dream, a wail of unintelligible voices in a darkening scene of leafless trees, he woke with a start to find that night had fallen, he had slept for two hours,

it was after eight. The sea shell shone whitely on the window sill, there was
a dim light in the little attic room of the club across the street, above the
dark cowl of the ventilator on the roof were a few stars. The effect was odd,
as of a profoundly mysterious hiatus in time, a sense of loss, and he sat
still, listening to the delicate ticking of his watch, and trying to remember
what it was, in the dream, that Gerta had said. Miles of aching arches of
eyebrows—? was that it? It was something like that, but the words, even
as he looked at them, seemed to be changing in shape, he could not be
sure. And that he should have fallen asleep like this, in the midst of
making notes, with the book on his knee—which now, with the pencil, had
fallen to the carpet—this was subtly disturbing; and as he thought of it he
felt his heart suddenly begin beating more loudly and quickly. Was there
anything abnormal in it? It was true that he had not been sleeping well, as
Toppan of course had reported gleefully to Gerta, but this was not at all
because he was really worried, or because his nerves were in any way upset—
not at all, not in the least. It was simply and solely because of late his
conscious life had become so severely and energetically *concentrated:* the
preoccupation had become so intense and unremitting that to break it off,
for sleep, seemed a waste of time. No doubt, in the upshot, he had been
more fatigued than he had supposed. One couldn't go on working indefinitely without rest. And if in addition one was by nature more conscious
than other people, and occupied, moreover, with a special problem, so that
one's consciousness was hourly deepening and widening, with a progressive
increase in this peculiar *interiorness* of one's life—an increase in its essential
silence—why then it was natural enough that this should constitute not a
strain exactly but at any rate a fatigue. That was it, of course! The scene
with Gerta at Belmont, three days before, had somehow accentuated this;
in some unanalyzable way had had the effect of still further *emptying* his
world; and of leaving him there, for the future, alone with Jones. Henceforth, as he had seen almost at once, he was alone with Jones. They stood
there together, at the center, like a man and his shadow. . . .

He gave a little shiver, the night had turned cool, got up to switch on
the lights.

Jones!

Of course.

That was why his heart had begun beating—it was the theater night, it
was Tuesday, Jones would perhaps be at the Orpheum. But there was no
rush—: if Jones went there at all, he would be there all the evening. The
show itself would probably be dull, it wasn't really necessary to go till near
the end. And in some respects this would be better. For if in fact (as he had
half considered just before he fell asleep) an opportunity should occur
tonight; if in some unexpected way Jones should prove vulnerable, or the
circumstances propitious, for the thing itself—if for a moment, in the subway, Jones should detach himself from whoever might be with him, or on
leaving the theater, or on getting off the Huron Avenue car—not that any
of these things was likely or that in any case the scene itself would be the
most suitable—he would be prepared for it, the revolver was in his pocket;
and it would be safer, of course, if he had not been too long visible in the
theater. . . . Yes, that had been the idea, when he fell asleep; but now,

after dark, after waking in the dark to a subtle sense of change, of void, it all seemed oddly improbable, and as if not properly outlined: a little vague: a little unreal. What he needed was a wash, cold water on the eyes and wrists—what he needed was a drink. Then the thing could be looked at more calmly, more clearly. And after all, what was the hurry?

Moreover, was it quite certain that the revolver was the best way? Better, perhaps, to make an appointment with Jones to discuss the advertising project, drive him out to Concord, into the country, as if to meet the mythical "partner"—there would be no difficulties about that, it would be ridiculously easy—no one would know about it, not a soul, it could be done in daylight—and even if done with the revolver, there, in some wooded lane——

He turned his back on the vision, walked slowly across the room to the Chinese waterfall, stared at it, in the silence seemed almost to hear the headlong rush of the gray torrent: it was his own silence, his own world, it was himself who waited there in the little red pavilion among trees on the edge of the twisted crag, listening to that sound as of a pouring and terrible chaos. He leaned toward it, as if the better to hear it, the better to see it, but found that it wasn't in fact the waterfall he was looking at, or trying to hear, but the little man who had become his shadow, the little man who stood alone with him in the center of the world. Jones was beside him in the car, Jones with his absurd tweed hat, the brown feather at the side, the cheap fur collar, the little red notebook in his hand. Jones turned toward him and said—what was it that he said? Jones was smiling at him sidelong, under the clipped moustache, was looking ridiculously competent as always, nodded with a knowing air, seemed to be about to say that he knew a trick or two worth two of that. And all the while, Jones was confidingly, almost invitingly, opening his heart to a pistol shot. . . .

In the bathroom, he ran the cold water over his extended wrists, let it run till it freshened, smiled slightly at the tall image which stooped forward from the greenish mirror. He said aloud:

—Are you getting into a panic about this? Are you being quite straight with yourself about this? Is your voice a little unsteady?

The weakness which he felt in the lips that shaped these words did not show in the reflection, the mouth was calm and curt, a little derisive, the fine eyes regarded him narrowly and ironically; and then as he stood still the whole beautiful face (despite its undeniable pallor) smiled at him with an air of enigmatic affection and power. The lynx-eyes were astonishingly clear, laughed with a private light of their own, the voice said to him:

—What are you afraid of? Don't be a fool. The murder is now pure. It has now reached a perfection in idea. To be alone with Jones—is that so difficult or painful? Is it any deeper a corruption—or evil—than to be alone with yourself? alone with your own shadow? It is merely the sacrifice of a shadow.

He repeated softly the word shadow, to watch the movement of his lips, drew the tip of a finger across an eyebrow, as if merely for contact with the bold image which seemed so haughtily to keep its distance, considered for a moment the resemblance of the forehead to Kay's. The speech was peculiar, did not quite seem his own, came out of a subtly different level of consciousness, like that of a dream—like the words of Gerta in the dream, miles of aching arches of eyebrows, or whatever they had been. But it was a comfort to hear his own voice, to hear it speaking so calmly and effectively, and to see moreover that his bearing was as imperturbable as ever. Resting both hands flat on the marble he leaned forward and said:

—The face is that of a genius. You must expect to have misgivings, that is the penalty of the solitary spirit! The one who dwells in the abyss.

The vibrant murmur died in the little room, he paused, then went on, speaking slowly, watching the shape of his mouth, the eagerness of his eyes in his white face.

—Behind this forehead is the tree, the vision of the tree, it is an imagina tion which can do what it likes. You hear? Do what it likes . . . Jaspei Ammen.

Jasper Ammen.

He turned smiling away from the smiling image, and extinguished the light; in the silence of the other room he picked up the pencil and book from the floor. The book lay open, he put it on the table and read:

"Rule 2. No bizarre typographical arrangement of text in obvious violation of good taste is permitted. Type of heads and text must not be more than 12 points wide (1-6 inch) in its widest stroke. . . . All illustrations to be no darker than the equivalent of a number 8 Ben Day when laid on metal. Where accents are required ⅛ square inch of solid black may be used, *but not as mass shading.*"

But not as mass shading.

The voice of Jones, yes; but this was beginning to be a bore, it was tiresome, and of course it was now a little unnecessary. Of this aspect of Jones, enough was already known, the notes were ample; if any further conversation with him should become needed—for instance, in the drive to Concord to meet the mythical partner—the notes would serve. It was even a question—and as he reflected on this he found that he was about to sit down again, but decided not to—whether enough was not known *altogether*. In a sense, yes! In a sense. A great deal had certainly been learned. The picture was pretty complete, it was satisfactory as far as it went, but there was still room for something more *immediate*. The scene in Alpine Street, for example, had partially supplied this lack; but only to suggest the need for more. What was the trained nurse for—if that was what she was? And the child's cot? It was possible to argue, of course, that the significance of these things lay outside the real problem—but that in turn depended on how one saw the problem. They might not contribute anything to the ease or success of the final action—that was true enough—but they certainly contributed something else, something almost as good. The Alpine Street episode had been profoundly and beautifully natural, it was essentially the right sort of thing, he reminded himself that in the talk with Toppan he had said there could be no limit in the matter of pure knowledge; and if Jones appeared tonight at the Orpheum, that too would have the same delicious weight and immediacy. It was even (if one looked at it like this) a question whether in the *approach*—! But no.

And then there was yesterday's thing—the failure of Jones to appear from his house at the usual time; and instead, the arrival of a mud-spattered doctor's car, with its little green cross, and the doctor staying in the house for over an hour. Was the child ill? or the mother? Why had the child never been seen in all this time, or the mother either? Was the child perhaps a chronic invalid? This would of course explain the good-natured casualness of the Alpine Street scene—or partially. Or on the other hand was it possible—and the idea suddenly arrested him in his pacing of the floor, it was as startling as a blow—that all this business was simply the *preparation* for a child? Good God! That would explain everything. . . .

The discovery came as a shock, he stood very still, stared out at the dark roof of the Club, saw the light turned off in the little attic window, heard voices from the club yard below. It must be an initiation night, the doors of cars were banging, the voices were loud, a little drunken. One of them was saying:

—Say, wait for me, will you?

He says wait. Oh-h-h-h, he floats through the air with the *greatest* of ease——

—The *flying* young man on the *daring* trapeze——

—Where's Putnam? Hi, Putnam!

—Oh, come on, let's go.

The car started, the voices trailed away round the corner, there was a sound of some one running, the slamming of a door, a moment of silence, then a simultaneous outburst of shouting farther off.

The discovery came as a peculiar shock, the night had mysteriously and deeply opened, but in one direction only; a swift tunnel of half-light; and as if it were an immense telescope, he looked along it to the far little amphitheater of brightness where obscure small figures were bending to obscure small tasks. His heart had begun beating loudly again, there was a real danger here, something uncalculated, a departure into a new dimension, a hindrance, a definite threat. But also there was a renewal of challenge; with the new danger came a fresh and sharpened necessity for energy and decision. If this were so, then once again the time element had become pressing; to look squarely at the situation itself was in fact to regard the face of a clock; and all the more so because of Gerta's threat, and her report of Sandbach's threat—the absurd possibility that Sandbach, in a moment of spleen or jealousy, might actually try to report him! How likely was this?

Gerta had not telephoned, had merely sent him a note, one line, saying, "I really mean it. Gerta."

Sandbach had remained silent, invisible, had not attempted to communicate either with himself or—apparently—with Toppan. And Toppan's diary, when examined night before last, had not been written up. Which might mean anything or nothing. At any rate, it had been impossible to confirm his suspicion that Toppan—presumably on Gerta's suggestion?—was watching him. Had it actually been Toppan?

On Saturday night, when he had first noticed the shadowy figure under the arclight at the corner of Sparks Street he had not taken the idea seriously, had merely and fleetingly thought something in the gait familiar, and something also in the slope of the shoulders under the white raincoat. But last night, when he had abruptly come on the same figure at the same place, and half a block later had begun to wonder whether it mightn't be Toppan, and doubled back through Royal Avenue, only to find that the figure had vanished—the suspicion had deepened, especially in retrospect. The technique, too, was recognizable—to stand so directly under the arc-light that the hat rim cast the face and upperpart of the body into a dense penumbra of shadow. And hadn't there been a momentary flash of spectacles? Moreover, when he had gone to Toppan's room, on returning, Toppan was out. Which again might mean anything or nothing.

The thing had become a little suffocating; like a physical pressure on the breast; there was certainly a shadow of danger, it was a nuisance, and observable in the foreground was the fact that to some extent the situation threatened to get out of control. But in essentials, this was good, this was right; he turned away from the window and regarded the map on the wall with a deepening of his sense of power; the city was there below him, the lights glided along those streets, the feet, the faces, the minds, beneath all those roofs the lives lay open, his glance went down to them from above. And this hostile alliance, if now it had at last really come into being, as Gerta's attitude indicated, had of course not only been foreseen by him from the very outset but actually willed. There was nothing new in it, nothing strange, it was all his own creation, and if now there was a danger the danger was simply the shape of his own idea. Toppan and Sandbach and Gerta might indeed be plotting together, they might be whispering, call each other up by telephone, have their secret meetings, they might flatter themselves that they knew more than he did, could outguess him, anticipate him, by studious co-operation attempt to surround him, but his own advantage remained what it had always been: that none of them, not even Gerta, was quite sure of his intentions, and none of them—especially now—shared his entire confidence. At no point could they be quite sure that he was not simply making fools of them, that he would not suddenly turn on them and say that it had all been a joke, an elaborate joke, simply the theme for a fantastic novel, and themselves nothing whatever but the dupes of an experiment. They were aware of this. Between the assumption that he was mad or cruel, on the one hand, and the hope that it was a hoax, on the other, they must run to and fro, their eyes perpetually fixed on a moving shadow, their hands perpetually withheld from any overt action. They could guess, they could spy, but what could they do? They were still, as much as Jones, at his mercy. Just the same——

Suppose they were to warn Jones. Suppose they had discovered Jones, knew who he was, where he lived. This much they might safely do?

It came down, in short, to the question of time.

If they were, as he had himself planned, closing in on him, if his own plan was narrowing its scope, then the moment could not be far off when, instead of the luxuriation in knowledge—which was after all nothing but a preliminary—must come the pure terribleness of the deed. One day: two days: or three. Three at the most. If a telephone call tomorrow, an arrangement for the trip to Concord on Thursday——

A copy of *The Cambridge Sun* lay on the red table under the map, he had brought it up from the hallway downstairs with a view to reading the strange little social notes, under the caption Observatory Hill, which dealt weekly with the lives of those unhappy citizens who dwelt with Jones in the waste land beyond the Observatory and Saint Peter's Church. He bent over it, ran his eye down the column of absurd paragraphs. These people of importance! Mr. Patrick Ronan of Upland Road, well-known druggist, is in Massachusetts General Hospital with an infected foot. . . . Last rites for Mrs. Margaret (McDonald) Connelly of Harvard, Mass., who died Saturday were held Tuesday at the home of her daughter, Mrs. F. F. Dugan, Fayerweather Street. A requiem high mass was said at Saint Peter's Church at nine o'clock. . . . Mrs. Clarence Ricker, of 299 Concord Avenue, entertained her friends at a party held at her home Sunday evening. . . . Miss Giulia Abetabile is sojourning in South Carolina. . . . Funeral of Mr. Riley. . . . Surprise party for the talented young dancer, Peter Willwert: a banquet lunch served. . . . A baseball game at the Timothy Corcoran ground on Raymond Street. . . . Glamorous Spring Formal Plaza. . . . Last Saturday's meeting of Bob's Kiddie Klub at the Central Square Theater opened with the usual Hi-Bob from the audience and the singing of the theme-song. For the first number Bob presented another Bob, namely Bob Murphy, a Cambridge boy who started things going with a snappy toe dance. Next came an old friend of Bob's, Marie Phelan, who pleased the audience with a toe-tap with a jump-rope. This number is as difficult to do as it is to say. The show closed with a snappy military tap by the Personality Kid, Aimee Dolon. . . .

Glamorous Spring Formal Plaza. What in God's name was that!

And all this ridiculous ant-hill, the activities of these ridiculous ants— Jones among them——

He slammed the paper down into the metal wastebasket, seized his hat, banged the door behind him without turning out the lights, walked with a kind of drunken swiftness along the corridor, and as he waited for the elevator to come up, said aloud:

—"A different sense and grade of purity. . . . Such a tendency distinguishes—it is a noble tendency—it also separates. The pity of the saint is a pity for the filth of the human, all too human. And there are grades and heights where pity it regarded by him as impurity, as filth."

The front door was open, the evening was warm and windless, arrived at the Square he turned to the left and entered the noisy and crowded little bar, pushed through to the back, leaned over the man who sat on the corner stool and ordered a double Manhattan.

—A double?

—Yes, I said a double. And with two cherries.

—Yes, sir.

And pity must speak with a revolver.

He patted the hard shape in his side pocket, picked out the two red cherries with the toothpick, swallowed the sweet fire at a gulp, and in another minute was running down the metal treads of the stairs to the subway, aware that it was half past eight. Much would depend on getting a seat on the left-hand side of the theater, as near the front box where Jones —if he came—would sit. But this ought not to be difficult, for at the Orpheum people were always coming and going, he could change his seat for one farther forward whenever opportunity offered, gradually get within range. Not, of course, for anything so absurd as rifle-practice, simply for vision. But it was amusing, just the same, to recall that queer business at the Beach Theater, several years before, when night after night the unknown individual had flung down his missiles into the audience—doorknobs, lumps of coal, fragments of metal—for his solitary pleasure in random murder, and for so long undetected. He had been an usher, had flung them down from the top-most balcony, over the heads of the gallery gods, and without being able to see where they landed: though most of them, he must have known, had to fall fairly far forward, so that as a matter of fact the orchestra had lived in perpetual terror. The ambulance stood always at the stage door, a doctor was handy, but all the while the newspapers hadn't breathed a word about it—superb example of the venality of the press. Had he been insane? and if so, what sort? Perhaps not at all. And if it had really been as easy as all that, and if in some way tonight an opportunity *did* offer itself—for instance, in the dark little passage which led at the side, beneath heavy plush curtains, to the ground-floor boxes——

He lifted his eyes from the idea, frowned, saw the red headlines of a newspaper immediately before his eyes in the train, was aware of the row of station-lights passing, Central Square already, the long line of accelerating lights, tried to concentrate his attention on the advertisements above the windows. These were Jones again. He knew all about them. His life was written out here in this ridiculous shorthand. Hear ye, hear ye! Now try a real ale. Eat foods that make you chew, say doctors, dentists, beauty experts. The Slouch Softie in Stitched Crêpe of Vibrant Spring Colors. A girl in a felt hat for two dollars and ninety-five cents. . . . This was Jones, the little man spoke with all these voices, all these pictures, an ice-cream cone, drooling, sprinkled with yellow walnuts, a town crier waving a huge brass bell, his mouth wide open, a disembodied hand spreading an immortal steak with immortal mustard, pouring juice from a bottle into a green glass, a muslined girl, wind-blown, laughing with a million teeth in a field of daisies. There was no escaping him: he nodded complacently in all these nauseating pictures, smirked in all this too-convenient jargon. This was the little red notebook, the pencil, the tweed hat, the clipped moustache. It was the office in School Street, the house in Reservoir Street, the fur collar, the Karl, the Jones. It was speed inscribed with the vulgar news of a vulgar and destructible human life: a Fury, flying with a cheap message in its beak.

And it was curiously oppressive. As oppressive as any too acute awareness of self. Like seeing oneself unexpectedly in a bad mirror——

And he thought of this again when he saw himself, sidelong, in the Orpheum mirror, behind the parrot, the tall and somber figure somewhat inclined forward, a little stooped as if with urgency, the dark felt hat at an angle, one hand just rising to remove it. Ammen! Jasper Ammen. On his way to an appointment. In the echoing lobby, among the palms, the cages, the tanks of goldfish, in a sound of discreet music, a smell of cheap scent, the vulgar women waiting on gilded sofas for their escorts, their knees langorously crossed under silk. The music crept here, there was a roll of drums, it loudened as he entered, climbing the stiff slope of plush carpet, died before him as he faced the bright sunrise-light of the proscenium arch, the stage, the leader of the orchestra standing in poised silhouette.

—Down front, please.

It would be easy—the theater was half-empty.

The little arc of light flittingly notched the red path before his feet, he sank into a chair by the aisle, looked quickly up toward the box at his left, saw that it was empty.

Jones had not come.

And a quarter to nine already——

Two Negroes were on the stage, the fat one, wearing white socks, yodeled softly and rolled his eyes, scraping sinuous feet, while the other stared disapprovingly.

—Did you all hear whut I said?

—No, I didn't hear nuthin'.

—I heard some news about you. I hear you goin' to night school.

—Night school?

—Yeah, night school. What you takin' up, nigger?

—Space.

—What's your favorite study?

—Recess.

—Are you takin' up psychology, technocracy, algebra?

—Algebra's my favorite study.

—What are you talkin' about! Go ahead, speak some algebra!

—Sure I will. Sprechen sie deutsch?

There was mild laughter, the white socks slid and recovered, the white-gloved hands were lifted in air.

—That ain't algebra, nigger, that's geography. But tell me, how many sneezes are there in a box?

—How big is the box?

A sudden snarl of music marked the joke, the orchestra leader joined obviously in the laugh, but the fat Negro, continuing unruffled his lazy and soft-slippered convolutions, added:

—Now I'll axe *you* somethin'.

—Sure, axe me somethin', big boy.

—Where is the east hemisphere and where is the western, and what are they doin' there?

—Boy, you got me. But do you use narcotics?

—Yeah, trans-lux! Now tell this one. Where is the capital of the United States?

—That's easy—doggone—it's all over Europe. . . .

They cackled together, the fat one yodeled, slithering to and fro, the orchestra played half a bar of The Star-Spangled Banner discordantly, what the thin one was saying was drowned in the sudden applause. They began to dance, soft-stepping, languidly, idly, the slow rhythm delicately accented by the barely perceptible whisper of the soft soles, the white-gloved hands now widespread, now crossed or swinging, the knees loose, the shoulders sagging. Above the muted saxophone the thin one could be heard saying:

—With this dance, boy, I might give you a job making a moving picture.

—Well, tell it to me, big boy, what is the moving picture?

—*Tah-te-te-tya.* Green Apples. That's the small one. I also made a large one.

—What part did you play in the small one?

—*Tah-te-te-tya.* I doubled with cramps.

—What was the big picture called?

—Showboat.

—Showboat! How come I didn' see you in it?

—What day did you see it?

—Thursday.

—*Tay-te-te-tya.* Thursday? Oh, tha's too bad, I missed the boat that day.

The fat one began doing a cake-walk, head flung back, a few swift and soundless steps, but at this moment there was a movement in the box, the sound of curtains drawn on rings, a gash of light, and Jones, wearing a derby hat, in the act of taking off his kid gloves, stood in the aperture, talking earnestly to the usher. The usher nodded, listened attentively, nodded again, Jones was emphasizing what he said by tapping the forefinger of one hand on the palm of the other. As obviously as if he were audible, he was asking the usher if he understood, and the usher was reassuring him. The usher appeared to be holding a card, peered at it in the dim light, then examined it with his flashlight. He withdrew, closing the curtains behind him, and Jones, taking off his coat, sat down by the edge of the box. Meanwhile, with a jig and a yell, to a crescendo of drums, the two Negroes were taking their bow, slid on again, slid off, reappeared once more, and were gone with a final clamorous discord. The illuminated name-plates changed at either side of the stage, the curtain rose, the scene was of a hotel lobby, decadently tinted with mauve and orchid, sumptuous with satins. Floodlights above poured a harsh light on a group of palm-trees in one corner, on a gilt sofa, where with round mouths a man and a girl sat singing.

—*I'm just putty in the hands of a girl*——

Jones, the little cock-sparrow, with his head on one side, seemed to be listening to this detachedly, it was easy to see him, for he was barely ten feet away, but as obvious as his air of detachment was his slight self-consciousness, as if the occupation of a box was a new experience. He sat a little stiffly, very guardedly now and then turned to glance quickly at the rows of people below him; perhaps felt even too close to the performers on the stage. And was he—possibly—looking somewhat pale?

Why should he look pale?

And what had he been saying to the usher?

A bellhop crossed the stage rapidly, intoning——

—Telephone for Mr. Frederick—telephone for Mr. Frederick——

It might be that he had been inquiring about the origin of the tickets. It might be that he was suspicious. But why should he be suspicious? There was little reason. Complimentary tickets were sufficiently common. No, it must be something else. And the most likely explanation—of course!—was simply that the other members of the party were coming later: he was alone, he had come in advance, he was waiting, had given instructions, by name, for the admission of the others. Cautiously, he now rested an elbow on the box-edge—and with returning confidence he had relaxed, his head was held a little farther back, he passed his left hand slowly backward over his thin hair. But he looked pale, he looked older, or ill—unless, of course, it was simply the effect of the unusual light, and of seeing him, so close too, without a hat. The face looked smaller than ever, whiter, the hollows below the cheekbone more marked——

The man, rising, was saying to the girl:

—A couple of wees and a couple of woos, eh?

—Oui, oui!

Her hands held out straight before her, stiff as snake's heads, she shimmied, she oscillated, undulated the sharp hips from which hung the straight line of beads, appeared to be about to encircle her breasts with the bright scarlet fingernails, approached him, lifting the eager mouth, then retreated again.

He said:

—Well, if you have to go, you'll have to go, I suppose!

He stood still in the middle of the stage, puffy red face above neat white flannels, the malacca stick wandlike in pasty hands.

—But if you don't go soon, we'll *both* have to go! . . . Suppose you do the fan dance for me, we're all paid-up Elks!

The laughter of the audience began uneasily, ran lamely from group to group, a little furtive, died out and began again, some one in the top balcony applauded loudly, a single and clear series of hard handclaps, but before the ensuing silence could become embarrassing the *pas de deux* had begun, the bellhop was again crossing the stage, doing it nimbly in patter-dance, the heavy mother emerged beneath the palms.

—Ride 'em cowboy! The last round-up! *Whoopee!*

—You like it?

—Like it? I should say so. Say, I can see you had coffee and doughnuts for breakfast.

—Oh, you *can*-can you!

With the fingers of his right hand, Jones was twisting his little moustache, he was laughing, a small cry catarrhal and descending laugh, the same four downward notes repeated over and over, *huh-heh-ha-hah, huh-heh-ha-hah*, then abruptly silent, the head tilted backward for dignity. It was easy to watch him, he sat there unsuspicious, exposed, immobile, near enough to touch with a tentpole. His coat was on the chair beside him, his hat on the floor, his heart, beating on the far side, naïve and vulnerable. Lighted thus, from above, the mole by the eyebrow was particularly noticeable, the slight curve of the aquiline nose rather more refined than one had suspected, the whole expression perhaps more intelligent, if also weaker. It was a homunculus, there was no mistake about that, a weakling —it was the face of a defeated animal, the sort of defeated animal in which a sense of humor has come to the rescue and has acted as defense: Jones was undoubtedly one of those innumerable ones who make a virtue of laughing things off. He was a belonger, a currier of favor, a propitiator, always ready to meet life halfway, a soft and guileful bargainer: the teeth and claws held in reserve. What mercy for this? What mercy for this, even now? It was a life, but it was also a symbol: its very nearness, now leaning on the box-edge, was an invitation: the arm, the raised hand, the pale cheek, shaved this morning in a paltry bathroom, the lungs full of foul theater air, the small belly with its little burden of half-digested supper——

To witness all this was to close the eyes to all other visible things, to forget on the instant the raised baton of the orchestra leader, the first violin leaning his face to his fiddle, the two girls who had sidled on to the stage, twin sisters, one blonde, one hennaed; it was to feel again the power and the vision; the vision arose, the vision grew like a tree, softly and soundlessly the magnificent boughs thrust right and left over the helpless world, it was like hands, it was like fingers, an all-exploring touch and grasp, one's own body became immaterial. The knees pressed hard against the seat in front, the elbows pressed hard on the arm-rests, the revolver firm against the hip——

Blonde was saying to henna:

—Jane, why don't you behave yourself?

—I would, but what's in it!

—Where are you going to spend your honeymoon?

—In France. He said as soon as we were married he'd show me where he was wounded.

It all suddenly clicked firmly into place, it was perfect, and to be sitting here within ten feet of Jones, anonymous embodiment of death, as if they had come together here, in this queer place and in this company, for the performance of some profound ritual, was suddenly the rightest thing in the world. These subhumans, these chattering apes, were the witnesses, they bore unconscious testimony to the perfection and necessity of the idea and the action. Complete in itself, the whole scene had fallen swiftly out of time and space, was isolated as if it were itself a separate star, a final symbol: all of history had been preparing from the beginning for this absurd culmination. Jones there, in his box, sniggering at the stupid and laboriously obscene jokes, the fools clowning under an arranged light, the silly music, the rows of gaping idiots—all this was the *reductio ad absurdum*, the ultimate monstrosity of life; the awful perfection of the commonplace, the last negation of all values. And if Jones was the negative, he himself was the destructive positive, the anonymous lightning which was about to speak the creative Name. A ritual, yes—it was in fact a sort of marriage. And to realize this——

The blonde wiped her nose on the edge of her skirt, and said:

—He said to me, you're just the kind of a girl I want for my wife. And can you beat this one, I said to him, well, you tell your wife she can't have me. See? Just like that.

—to realize this——

It was of course—and this was really funny—to give Jones a kind of dignity, a kind of importance, he had become the other chief performer in the rite, the acquiescent one, the dedicated ram led garlanded to the pure altar. In this light, it was even possible to regard Jones with something oddly like affection; for as he sat there, with two neat fingers adjusting his spectacles, he was being subtly and dreadfully transmuted into something sacred. The bond between them had deepened immeasurably, he turned and looked at him steadily, smiling frankly, almost wishing that Jones would turn and see him, would meet the smile which meant so much to him without his knowing it; but at this very moment, like something planned, the curtains beyond Jones were swiftly drawn aside, the usher had entered, was stooping towards Jones and speaking agitatedly, Jones was rising, had risen, had snatched up his hat and coat, and gone. The curtains were swinging, the box was empty.

Something had happened: some message had come.

He jumped up, walked quickly up the steep aisle, heard behind him the phrase "show you a broken-down dance," dived down through the marble and plush tunnel which led to the foyer, emerged into the alley, and saw, a block away, the illuminated front of the Park Street Church, and halfway to this, his hat in one hand, his coat in the other, Jones, in the act of running.

⟨ XI   The Regret

Before Jones had reached the corner, he had himself begun running, laughing a little breathlessly as he did so: the speed was a delight, the action was a relief, in the whole unexpected event there was something comically satisfactory. That they should be running thus along a half-lighted alley, separated by fifty yards, the one ahead grotesquely unaware of the one behind—as if, in fact, they were somehow *connected*, were two parts of a single mechanism—this was both ridiculous and right; and that the whole great adventure should thus suddenly accelerate and take momentary shape in a species of action so elementary and humble was essentially *good*. He had time to think this as he sprinted towards the florist's at the corner, where Jones had already turned to the left, and he had time also to foresee for Jones a choice amongst three possible actions: he could go out to Reservoir Street by subway and streetcar—which seemed in the circumstances unlikely—; he could go by subway to Harvard Square, and there take a taxi; or, if a real panic had possessed him, he could go by taxi all the way from Boston, sacrificing actual speed for the illusion of speed which is always to be extracted from a feeling of uninterrupted activity. All this, of course, was based on the assumption that it *was* to Reservoir Street that he was going—was it just possible he was going somewhere else?

Arrived at the corner, he stopped, stood still, glanced quickly south towards the subway entrance, saw no sign of Jones, but then at once noticed that a taxi in the Park Street stand was just at that moment snarling into motion, swerving left as it did so. It was turning north to go along Tremont Street, shot past him accelerating rapidly, and in the back seat Jones was fleetingly visible—leaning forward to struggle into his coat, his derby hat perched at a queer angle on the back of his head, obviously stuck there in a hurry, the earnest little face wearing an expression which was quite clearly something new, something different.

If it wasn't fright, it was something very like it: Jones was frightened. For once, he had lost his smugness and complacency, his perpetual air of competence.

Something had gone wrong.

He watched the taxi out of sight, glanced at his wrist watch, glanced at his wrist watch, glanced up also at the clock of Park Street Church, found that he had forgotten the time as soon as he had noticed what it was, stood irresolute. Jones was still there, he had not in any sense escaped, his swift departure was merely a blind movement from one part of the closed circle to another, he was as easily reached there as anywhere else, and as easily seen. Standing here motionless by the florist's shop, it was nevertheless as if he were watching Jones from above: looked down through the taxi roof, saw Jones nervously take out a cigarette, strike several matches in an attempt to light it with shaking hands. But if this was true, and if Jones could not really escape, it was also true that this new development had subtly altered the situation, the equation had been multiplied by an un-known quantity, the simple was becoming complex. To make the necessary arrangements now, in the face of this, would perhaps not be quite so easy: the greater pressure would have to be met with greater guile, or even with greater violence. The trap would have to be a more powerful one, and more enticingly baited.

But suppose it turned out to be something really serious.

He frowned, crossed the street, opened the taxi door with automatic hand, and said:

—Cambridge. Over the Cambridge bridge. If you go fast enough, you'll overtake the Independent Taxi that just left here. Keep a little way behind it and follow it: I'll tell you when to stop.

—Yes, sir!

Yes, the action had become unexpectedly complicated, the action or his awareness of it, the thing was on several different planes all at once, and in the very act of deciding to take a taxi he had still been on the point—sur-prisingly—of going across the Common to see Gerta, or even, if she had happened to be out, of then proceeding to Sandbach's. To see Gerta at this juncture was reasonable enough: for a moment it had seemed in fact per-haps desirable. To put in an appearance, and above all a cheerful one, to laugh loudly about the whole thing, discuss her queer picture with her, make plans for an expedition to New York in the following week, disarm her completely—the shape of this action had risen sharply before him, he had seen it vividly as he glanced across the Common toward the Frog Pond, had begun in advance to enjoy the simplicity of the deception. The words of the conversation were clear, the tone was precise, Gerta's initial surprise gave way to relief, even to gayety. Come out and have a drink. And I'll tell you the greatest joke yet. Come down to the Union Oyster House and have some little-necks. Or shall we go to that little bar at the end of Charles Street? I've made a very peculiar discovery, I'd like to tell you about it. The last dislocation! . . . But if Gerta was out, if Sandbach were there, or if he went to Sandbach's room—this wasn't quite so clear. Why? Why Sandbach? The image was repellent, the reality of Sandbach in Sandbach's room was twisted and a little nauseating, the sound and shape of the interview was drawling and feverish, unnatural. No, the im-pulse was obscure and unpleasant, there was really no need to see Sand-bach again, Sandbach was out of it for good. Sandbach had been defeated, even if he didn't yet know it—and didn't he actually know it? The tall shadow of Jasper Ammen was behind Gerta, Sandbach was aware of this and was angry about it, he struggled helplessly with it, knew that it would be useless. But just the same to stand before Sandbach now, in his own room, to smile down on him and patronize him, look idly at his books, ask casually about Breault, make no reference whatever to Gerta——

He closed his eyes for a second as the taxi shot up the curve of the bridge, kept in mind for a moment the image of the lighted train which had rushed past them full of people, felt suddenly a little sick. As against all this, this jangle of Gerta and Sandbach and Toppan, the Jones situation was still comfortingly simple. It had the merit of a pure perfection, stood off by itself, was as clear and beautiful as a single flower. To hold this up for admiration was still the best possible of all realities, it kept its finality, and having admired it to destroy it——

But exactly why, in the midst of this action, had he wanted to deviate from it, to see Gerta? With the revolver in his pocket, and Jones so close at hand, with the scene already so developed and so rich in potentialities, so rewardingly immediate, why step aside from it? The night was still young, the possibilities were immense, anything at all might yet happen. To intercept Jones might not be convenient, but to call him up by telephone, make an appointment, even to *meet* him later in the evening—what could prevent this, except of course this new development, his mysterious flight to Cambridge?

He watched the swift dance of streetlights, counted them, one, two, three, four, was half-consciously aware presently that they had passed the Technology buildings, crossed Massachusetts Avenue, and that there was still no sign of the other taxi. Perhaps they had gone by Broadway; but it hardly mattered. It would be just as well to keep a discreet distance behind, there was no particular reason for remaining within sight: the odds against his going anywhere but Reservoir Street were tremendous. Moreover, to realize this was to realize also his motive for wishing, at this point, to deviate. It was based on a sense of complete confidence, the feeling that poor Jones was now completely in the bag. In effect, Jones was still as close to him as he had been in his box at the theater: just as near, just as unguarded, just as unsuspecting. The flight from the box, from the theater, the dash to the taxi-stand, and the ensuing swoop on Cambridge, all this was really nothing more than the circumscribed panic of the mouse: the dart from sofa-shadow to chair-shadow. The door was still closed, the mouse was still within the room.

The taxi driver slid back the glass panel and said, without turning his head:

—That'll be Connor now—yes, that's him all right. How near will I tail him?

—Just keep him in sight, that's all. If you lose him, never mind, take me to the corner of Sparks Street and Huron Avenue.

—Sparks Street and Huron Avenue, okay. . . . Boy, is he stepping on it! You'd think he was going to a fire.

A hundred yards behind, they followed dizzily the bobbing tail-light, lost it for a few minutes when they were held up by the signals at River

Street bridge, caught it again as it slowed with glowing brake-light to turn left into Mount Auburn Street. Everything was going like clockwork, there could no longer be any doubt that Jones was on his way to Reservoir Street in response to a telephone call. He had arranged it with the usher, had given his name, and then waited: but presumably he had not really expected to be called, or he would not have come. And all this being the case, what did it mean? Either of two things: either that the child was being born, if that supposition was correct; or, if there was already a child, and the child was ill, that it had taken a sudden turn for the worse. Or was there just a chance—also—that it might be a question of the wife, the mother?

In any case, it could have no bearing on the situation. What had been decided was decided.

The only regrettable feature was that it indicated new avenues for exploration, which, with this sudden increase of pressure—if indeed it *was* pressure—from Gerta and Sandbach and Toppan, would have to be neglected. If life itself, or destiny, was about to take a hand, and tighten the screws on Jones, it was unfortunate not to be able to take advantage of the enhanced entertainment, even if the enhancement was purely adventitious. To watch his antics in this new predicament, whatever it was, and to observe what changes it might bring about in his habits—this would be of the finest essence of the experience. It would add the last fillip to the thing-in-itself, the perfect chiaroscuro for the projected image, the right silence for the *hearing of the cry*. And perhaps even now there would be time, it might be managed—the notion of seeing Gerta was not, on second thought, so bad, or even of seeing Sandbach. If too abrupt a transition was avoided, so that they didn't suspect him of merely acting, of playing a part, they could even now be lulled into inaction and inertia, put off the track. The little ritual with Jones would be by so much deepened and prolonged, yield just so much more of its vital juice. And the further fact that their intervention was actually impending, that they stood there, in the background, ready to protect and save Jones, and only prevented from timely action by their stupidity, this too would add its deliciousness: it would be worth trying. A telephone call to Gerta, perhaps an invitation to S, and the first soundings could at least be taken. And if the signs were propitious, then the time problem would once more have become elastic. He and Jones could proceed with due leisure and affection to their profound little collaboration. . . .

And this was odd. He saw it against the swift palings of a white fence, the lighted windows of a house, the turning headlamps of a car—he saw it concretely, and with an almost horrible vividness—the form of his sick hatred for that ridiculous trio of people, the three of them plotting while they smiled, bowing while they whispered behind their hands. It was odd, it was loathsome, but it was true, and also it was funny; he began, in the swaying taxi, to laugh a little, then stopped, then laughed again. What it came down to was simply this—that he and Jones were now actually in alliance against Gerta and Sandbach and Toppan: had their private plan, their conspiracy, which those three, bowing among the elm-trees, were attempting to frustrate. He saw them this minute, separately and together;

Gerta in the lunchroom at the Museum, talking earnestly with red-haired Toppan; Gerta pausing before the Kwannon with S, Sandbach's fat little hand on her arm, the sharp tooth showing at the corner of his mouth; Gerta saying at Belmont "then we shall have to *do* something." The images came together, fused, lost their identity only to separate again, their nearness so oppressive, and so actual, that he put out his hand toward the taxi window as if to destroy them. But he and Jones together—he and Jones together would defeat them.

The brakes began squeaking rhythmically, *eek, eek, eek, eek*, they had stopped in the silent emptiness of Wyman Square, the driver was saying:

—Do you want to stop here, Mister? He's just turning the corner up there. There he goes now.

—Yes. This is all right.

—Baby, was that a ride! I didn't know old Connor had it in him.

In another moment the striped taxi was reversing sharply to go back to Boston, he listened to the retreating sound, stood with his pipestem against his teeth and stared alternately west and north along Huron Avenue. There was no one in sight. Leaning over a fence at his elbow, almost touching him, a lilac bush was in bloom, the blossoms smoke-blue and artificial in the cold lamplight. The heavy fragrance sickened him, he began walking quickly towards Vassal Lane, debouched from Huron Avenue, looked over his shoulder as he did so to make certain that he was not being followed, and in half a minute had passed the willow tree and was approaching Jones's house. The taxi, of course, had gone. Instead, the doctor's car stood before the entrance: just as he had expected. The street was otherwise deserted, everything was quiet, he walked calmly up to the car and touched the radiator-cap with the palm of his hand. It was quite cool. The doctor had been here for some time, perhaps an hour—must have arrived very soon after Jones had set off to Boston. Stepping back, then, to the middle of the street, he looked up at the house.

All the windows on the second floor were lighted, and also the two windows at the right-hand corner of the top floor. None of the curtains had been drawn.

The three bow windows on the second floor were obviously the sitting room. Three bell-shaped lamp shades of ground glass hung from the plain brass chandelier in the middle of the ceiling, all of them lighted. Against the wall at the left the top of a bookcase was visible, with nothing on it but a glass vase, which was empty. Above this on the yellow wallpaper hung an oak-framed color-print—it looked like a single large face with a background of red flowers. Nothing else was to be seen, the room seemed to be deserted, and its quiet, under the three bells of light, took on a queer sort of significance.

The room to the right of this was not so easy to examine, for the white railing of the porch roof cut off what would otherwise have been an excellent view, through the glass door (which opened on to the improvised veranda), and the window, which, unlike all the others, was wide open. Through the door it was possible to see a table, on which was the telephone. Beyond this was an open door, which presumably led into the hall. Probably the room—as he had in fact concluded before—was Jones's "den," his office. In this room, too, there seemed to be no sign of activity; any one present would have been visible.

Of the room at the top, nothing could be seen, of course, but the ceiling and a fragment of wall: but these were eloquent. It was obvious at once that the entire life of the little house was now concentrated here. As in the sitting room, there was a brass chandelier, with three lights, but there must also be another light as well, somewhere lower down, for across the ceiling, and the visible portion of wall, shadows went and came with astonishing variety and rapidity, and not one shadow, but several. There were at least two persons moving about in the room, perhaps three,—the shadows moved separately, diverged, enlarged, blended; now and then altogether disappeared. Once, it seemed to be the light itself which had moved; for all the shadows shifted concertedly, and as if concentrically. Perhaps some one had moved a table lamp—for instance—from the table towards the bed. There was then a moment when none of the shadows moved at all. Everything was motionless, everything was silent. If only the windows had been left open——

He noticed again, what he had noticed before, but only casually, the ash can which stood by the curb just behind the doctor's car. Of course, it was Tuesday, Jones would have put it out the night before, had not yet got round to taking it in again. It had been emptied this morning, was waiting, but Jones had been too busy or too anxious to remember it. And if Jones was too busy to attend to it, if they all, up there, were so occupied with whatever it was they were doing——

The idea was perfectly sound, he glanced rapidly north and south along the street to make quite sure that it was still deserted, then more carefully examined the houses behind him and those that adjoined number 85. There were lights in all of them, but in all of them, also, the shades had been drawn, there was no sign of any activity anywhere, no one was watching, or very likely to see him. There would be a certain amount of risk in it, certainly, but not much,—not more, at any rate, than could be easily bluffed out of. Accordingly, he pulled his hat down over his eyes, said softly to himself the words "briefly done," and walked with careful but quick nonchalance along the cement path which led beside a privet hedge to the back of the house. It was necessary to act as if the action were customary: he must look as if he belonged there, had every right there, and he turned boldly at the corner to survey what he had found. The revolving clothesline lifted bare arms in the half-light from the street beyond, like some queer sort of desert tree, spiny and sterile; and before this, leading down to an open door, were the red brick steps which gave entrance to Jones's cellar. There was no light below; and thinking to himself that he must show no sign of hesitation, and complementarily also no sign of undue haste, he ran lightly down the steps, feeling the slight grit of ashes beneath his feet, and stooped through the low doorway. Striking a match, he found a switch at the foot of a wooden stairway, turned on the light, saw that the cellar was divided into two sections by a wooden partition—one for each of the tenants—and that while one of these was padlocked the door to the Jones cellar was ajar, and the cellar itself in darkness. To find the swinging electric light bulb, with a help of another match, was quite simple: he turned it on, and discovered that he was standing immediately in front of a furnace. Above, the half-dozen asbestos-jacketed furnace pipes seemed, like an octopus, to be exploring the grimy and cobwebbed rafters of the ceiling: so low that he had to stoop to avoid hitting his head. The furnace itself, of course, was not lighted: the door was open, the interior was dark and cold, and at the edge of the ash door was a neat little pile of clinkers. One cigarette stub lay among them.

He stood still, listened; footsteps were crossing the floor overhead, in the apartment of the other tenants; they crossed the floor and returned again, slowly and without urgency, it was nothing to be alarmed about; some one traversing the room for a paper, or a box of matches. When the steps had ceased, there was no other sound—the silence was profound; and it occurred to him that not impossibly something—from the Jones apartment—might be audible through the pipes. But no. He listened and heard nothing, the upper rooms were of course too far away. What they were doing there remained a secret.

Revolving slowly on his heel where he stood, he looked to all corners of the little cellar, saw the divided coal bins at the front, the shovel leaning against the coal-blackened wall, the wooden soapbox half full of kindling with a short-handled ax laid across the corner, a newspaper on the cement floor, a wooden snow shovel, a pair of worn-out galoshes. Under the little cellar window at the side there was a hole in the cement floor, where the surface had for some reason cracked and crumbled, it had been scratched away and showed the earth beneath it: it occurred quickly to him that if anyone should come—if Jones himself should come—he could say that he was there on behalf of the landlord to examine the floor with a view to repairs. But all this was nothing. It was gratifying enough to step thus closer than ever to the small and secret life of Jones, to know his furnace and his shovels; but for any immediate or practical purpose it came to nothing. The newspaper, when he went nearer, turned out to be a week-old *American:* the headline simply said CARNEY ORDERS ERA "CHIS-ELER PROBE." The question was——

Considering it, and noticing also that his heart had begun beating rather rapidly, with the odd effect of giving him a sensation of suffocation in the left side of his throat, he walked slowly back to the door and regarded the wooden stairs which led up—presumably—to the Jones kitchen. The question was, if he should wait here, secret himself here, where all sounds would be muffled, or even *completely inaudible,* and whence escape would be so easy and so quick——

Why not? . . .

It would be the simplest thing in the world. No one would hear a thing. . . .

But how likely was Jones to come down? or to come down soon?

A curious pain was beating in each of his forearms, throbbing down into his hands, which felt swollen; the sudden intensity of his vision seemed in effect to glaze or dull his eyes; and it was only after a moment or two that he noticed the brown wicker wastebasket half way up the stairs. He reached over the railing for it, lifted it down, stooped and spread out the fragments of paper on the floor. Torn envelopes, one of them with the business ad-

dress of the Acme Advertising Agency in the upper left-hand corner, the
receipted bill of a news agent, the crumpled page for the month of April
torn from a calendar, a nest of dead matches, a tiny hairpin, a pasteboard
milk-bottle top slightly bent, a fluff of hair combings, a few torn fragments
of paper which looked like shopping lists. Vegetables, groceries, cheese-
cloth—the items written in a small backward-leaning hand—but suddenly,
from another list, written more boldly and coarsely, he noticed a single
item—*1 baby's folding tub*—and rose with it to go nearer the light. There
could no longer be any doubt of it. "*3 papers small safety pins. 3 papers
large safety pins. 2 large agate pails with covers. 1 large agate basin. 1 bath
thermometer. ¼ pound boric crystals. 4 oz. olive oil. 1 can baby powder.
1 kitchen scales with weights—avoid springs. 1 bathing apron.*"

So it was that! . . .

At this instant, the little Jones was being born upstairs,—with Jones in
attendance, and the doctor, and the nurse. The child's cot, the hamper, the
slop-bowl, the hospital chair—the whole thing was only too disgustingly
obvious. The nurse, of course, lived in that house at the corner of Alpine
Street, had loaned these objects, had been summoned, Jones had gone to
the Orpheum not expecting any such immediate development, it was all
happening prematurely. The drama of moving shadows on the ceiling in the
upstairs bedroom was simply the drama of childbirth, a drama in which
these items were the humble properties. He crumpled the paper in his hand,
flung it down bitterly amongst the litter besides the overturned basket, ran
quickly up the brick stairs to the back yard. That Jones should come down
now was clearly inconceivable: the scope of action had abruptly narrowed—
perhaps psychologically as much as physically?—and therefore something
else must be done, something else must be thought of, the time-problem
otherwise dealt with. But what, and how?

He stood for a moment beside the uplifted arms of the clothesline,
stared at it, then walked slowly along the path towards Reservoir Street.
There was an odd smell—faint, but unmistakable: it was ether, a slight
sweet thread of ether on the night air, he paused to make sure, and at the
same time heard a cry. It was not a child's cry—it was a woman's, a soft
downward quaver, something between a sob and a moan, distant and
muffled. It was not repeated, he stood listening for two minutes or perhaps
three with angrily averted face, his hands clenched in his pockets, again
feeling the curious pain in the side of his throat. His position, too, was tense
and unnatural. He became slowly aware of the strain in his half-flexed
right knee, the pressure of his elbows against his sides. Did he want to hear
that sound again, or didn't he?

This was becoming decidedly unpleasant. What was needed was a
longer view, a wider horizon, something farther off on which to rest one's
eyes, a voice at the other end of a telephone, the simple reassurance of
something known and familiar, even if hated. Gerta? Sandbach? Toppan?
A rapid walk to the Square, to Fresh Pond, perhaps the getting out of the
Buick and a drive into the counrty? The time-problem, in this fashion——

To think this was automatically to begin moving. Without any clear
reason for it, he walked quickly to the street, passed the doctor's car, then
turned up the next path, proceeding thus again to the grotesque shape of

the clothes-line in the back yard; and before he knew, had walked completely round the house without once looking at it. There was no sense in this; it was stupid and meaningless, it might even be dangerous; nothing was now to be gained from loitering here, despite his reluctance to go away in the very middle of what was so obviously a "scene." He could ring the doorbell, of course, making some pretense of an inquiry, participate thus more intimately, perhaps even converse with his victim face to face— but to look up once more at the lighted windows on the third floor, to observe that now everything there was still, no shadows in motion, was also to decide that this too would be meaningless. The smell of ether had sharpened, he turned and walked rapidly towards Huron Avenue, feeling oddly defrauded, oddly reckless. It was curiously as if Jones had deserted him; as if the alliance between them had been denounced; as if he were now, precisely, walking away from the very thing which most clearly symbolized his own reason for living. This was the center, and to walk away from it——

An empty streetcar clattered past the corner, on its way to Harvard Square, he cursed it and turned in the other direction, already finding the angry phrases to telephone to Gerta. *I really mean it. Gerta.* What exactly did she think she meant? That she had discussed the whole thing, finally, with that dirty Jew Sandbach, told him all about it, cried with her face on his greasy shoulder and his ridiculous short arms about her? That they were working with Toppan? That they had told the police? Toppan would be here again tonight, no doubt, sitting in a car somewhere to watch him. Damn them all, and to hell with them. If they thought for a minute they could match their wits against his genius, against his freedom from scruple—the idea was crazy, he could laugh at it, and as he closed himself into the telephone booth in the drugstore at Gurney Street he was already feeling amused.

—Hello?

—Your dear Jasper speaking. I just wanted to thank you for your card: very kind of you.

Gerta's voice was very cool, very detached; she said slowly——

—Now look here, Jasper——

—I'm looking with all my teeth.

—I don't think you are taking quite the right attitude, do *you?* I'd be a little more concerned—for *you* I mean—if I didn't know of course that the whole thing is a fake.

—Oh, so it's a fake, is it?

—Obviously, isn't it, my dear?

—Oh, obviously! I've just, for example, been in his house—in his cellar. I suppose *that's* a fake. You and your Sandbach make me laugh!

—Of course it's a fake! I don't believe a word of it.

—Believe what you like. I assume, of course, we're talking about King Coffin?

—You and your King Coffin!

—Yes, me and my King Coffin! Size five by two! Silk-lined and silver-handled; you'd be surprised! If you want to come out here, I'll prove it to you. Is it a bet?

—Thanks, my dear, I'm afraid I've got better things to do.

—Suit yourself.

—And incidentally, I thought you were going to the Orpheum tonight.

—Certainly. I did!

—I see. You combined theater and cellar.

—Exactly. It's been a great success! You'd find a full account of the evening very entertaining, I assure you.

—No, thank you. I'd rather not!

—I might have known you'd get cold feet——

—Call it what you like, my dear——

—I said *cold feet.*

—And when you come to your senses drop me a picture postcard, won't you? Good night!

—Gerta—listen——!

He heard the click, listened, she was gone; she had played his own trick on him; he gave a little annoyed laugh, hung the receiver softly on its hook. A fake! It was an ingenious line to take, it did her credit, Gerta was no fool. She had calculated it cunningly to drive him out into the open, force him to show his hand. And so cool about it too. But behind this were other things, other shapes—imponderable but perhaps for that no less definite. She had not yet said anything, or much, to Sandbach, perhaps very little to Toppan. She was still hoping to bluff him, still hoping that she could manage the thing by herself. This much loyalty could still be counted on, to this extent she was loyal in spite of herself, or in spite of Sandbach; and to this extent by implication she was keeping open for him, if he should want it (or as she put it, come to his senses), a line of retreat. She had suggested New York—a holiday in New York. New York! But that was far away, impossible, it was another shape and another design, it was not and could never be in this pattern at all: for better or worse the thing had now taken its own deep direction. Jones was not in that world, nor New York in this, he and Jones were here together, more than ever together—and if the pressure of their queer relationship was becoming hourly more obscure, and hourly more subtle in its underground ramifications, it was perhaps for that very reason all the more tyrannous and inevitable. There *could* now be no New York, or "other" thing: any more, for example, than there could be life after death.

Life after death!

Exactly. It was like making an engagement for a party, or to meet a friend, or to go to a show, at eight-thirty on the evening following one's death. Gerta, with her New York, her Sandbach, her painting, her print-room at the Museum, the bowl of apples on the window sill, the life-class at Belmont, the smile from under shaded eyes in the two-year-old photograph, Gerta with her Gertadämmerung and her Russian blouse—this was now already another world, whirled away diminishing into the past or the future, beyond all contact or reality. To think of it was simply to think of an amusing contrapuntal device in time, a synchronization of the impossible. It was an act of laconic leave-taking, a laconic farewell, the cry of a sea gull over the last whirl of froth that marked a sunken ship. The thing was gone.

He found that he was tapping with his fingers against the glass side of the telephone booth, looked down at his stilled hand as if suddenly it belonged to some one else, gave a little shiver. He noticed that he was again standing, as in the path of the Reservoir Street house, in a slightly unnatural way, and with an unnatural tenseness, like an animal that is frightened. The slight surge of the body which is being electrocuted! Relaxing deliberately and angrily, he opened the door, went out, pondering the other project, the idea of ringing up Jones. But this would be better when he got back, this would be better from Hampden. In the meantime——

The man in the white jacket behind the soda fountain was saying to a customer:

—fired for wearing a colored shirt and a wrong haircut.

—What? fired for what?

—For wearing a colored shirt and having the wrong kind of haircut. . . .

He went out, smelt the smoke from the burning-dump at Fresh Pond, the stars above the mean houses were like sparks borne on the cool north wind, a man and a girl were talking in low voices in a car which was parked at the corner. At the sight of this he stiffened, and turned quickly to the right, as if some sixth sense, some dark animal instinct, had given him warning. It was of course just the sight of people sitting in a parked car, that was all; but it reminded him just the same of Toppan, he had felt sure, he felt sure still, that Toppan was somewhere about, somewhere near. It had the simplicity of a conviction: it was just the right time for Toppan: he had in fact *arranged* for Toppan: and Toppan would be there. He might be in a car in the southern end of Reservoir Street, or in Huron Avenue itself; but more likely he would be on foot, and near Wyman Square. Or possibly he was even now in the act of walking up from Hampden, but had got quite close, was slowing down and moving cautiously as he drew near the neighborhood. This was excellent in its way, but it was also tedious, it was the little extra something of annoying and belated complication with which, for some reason, he felt reluctant to deal. One's own past witticisms and ingenuities, one's own history, in short, could become tiresome. To *see* Toppan, but to avoid him——

Keeping on the right side of the street, so as not to face the headlights of the oncoming traffic, and also keeping as close to the houses as possible and using the tree-line wherever he could, he walked swiftly, pointing before him the stem of his unlighted pipe. Very well, let Toppan come, by all means let him come, there would be plenty to say to him. Why, indeed, avoid him since there *was* obviously so much to say, and since besides it was always so easy to speak from the shadow—as it were, from the tomb—to those who walked in the sunlit innocence of their folly? The image of the party after death had recurred to him, it pleased him, it was a good idea, it would be nice to ask a group of ill-assorted people to come to a party, for instance, the night after one intended to commit suicide: send out the invitations, timing them very carefully, so that the guests would arrive and themselves make the charming discovery. The Findens, for example, Sandbach, Mrs. Taber, Gottlieb, Gerta, a sprinkling of mere acquaintances, of the socially climbing sort, like Mather, and a few ordinary University prigs——

A coffin party.

Mr. Jasper Ammen requests the pleasure of your company at a coffin party——

The door would be unlocked, someone would eventually try the door and walk in, and there he would be!

At Wyman Square, he was about to turn down Sparks Street when he saw the familiar white raincoat rounding the corner at Concord Avenue, hesitating and then coming quickly forward down the little hill, the whole figure very alert. This time, the bearing was unmistakable. He stood still in the shadow of an elm, completely invisible, and waited for Toppan to arrive at the opposite corner of the Square,—grinning, but as yet undecided what he would do. It was good. It was *very* good. It had all shaped itself quickly under his hand like magic, it was part of the whole beautiful scheme, it was growing miraculously and hugely, like a cathedral, with Toppan simply a gargoyle. As he approached the swerve of Huron Avenue Toppan slowed down, clung more closely to the hedge before the house at the corner, revolved his head, peering this way and that. Twice the round spectacles flashed under the arc light, but saw nothing, he even stepped cautiously out into the road so as to get a longer view round the curve; then, reassured, and once looking behind him, was about to go forward, when Ammen whistled.

The effect was comical.

Toppan not only stopped in his tracks, as if he'd been shot—he somehow managed to look extraordinarily silly. He just stood where he was, looking, but also pretending that he *wasn't* looking, in every direction. One could imagine the slightly foolish smile. Ammen stepped out of the shadow and said:

—I'm over here.

Toppan came towards him rather slowly, his head a little on one side, his hands in his raincoat pockets.

—Oh, it's you.

Yes: it's me. I whistled because I had an idea you might be looking for me.

—And *why* should I be looking for you?

—Because, my dear Toppan, you don't always mind your own business. And it was obvious to me that you needed a little help. Aren't you being clumsy?

—Am I?

—Even your imitation of *me* is clumsy.

—Isn't *anything* an imitation of you?

—But I'm sorry to have to outwit you. You can now pretend, if you like, to be taking a walk around the Pond, but can I tempt you to ride back to the Square with me in a taxi? Otherwise you'd be wasting your time.

—You think so?

—Don't be silly. Of course it is. Of course you are.

—Is, or are?

—And there's a question I want to ask you.

—My dear Jasper, go ahead!

—Oh, aren't we clever! Oh, aren't we smart! Don't we stand with our heads cocked at an angle and feeling very brilliant! Jesus *Christ!*

Toppan was silent, merely raised his hands in his pockets, shrugged, turned his profile.

—Yes—breathing softly—there's a question or two I'd like to ask you. If you don't mind! And before you've become too impudent with *other* people's affairs! You've been following me, and a lot of good may it do you. I've known all about it, and watched you at it, and it's been funny. It's made me feel a little ashamed. Do you understand *that?*

—So you thought I was following you!

—Thought!

—Could your question wait till tomorrow? I'm just on my way——

—My dear Julius, you were on *my* way, if you don't mind my saying so, but let it pass. My question, which was about razor blades, can wait.

—Razor blades!

—Yes, razor blades. I'll see you tomorrow.

He turned abruptly, with a slight gesture of the pipe in his hand, left Julius standing under the arc light, was off towards the yellow taxi which he saw at the top of the hill. He listened for the sound of Toppan's footsteps, heard none as long as he was within range, figured to himself that Toppan must be standing motionless there, standing there fixed and smiling, fixed and thinking, but did not turn to see. To open the taxi door was in itself a dismissal of Toppan and the world, conscious of his height he stooped to enter, sank back and closed his eyes.

This giddiness again—this dizziness—it was the third time. It was queer. The sensation of speed, flowing past him and round him, catching him up and twirling him, with its steady pour of sound, was like a world of bright lines drawn swiftly in parallels, a vast river of bright lines. Amongst and against these rays of arrowy light he was borne rapidly forward in a half-recumbent position, with his eyes closed and his hands tightly clenched; and just above the roof of his mouth, on each half-painful crest of his breathing, was a new and peculiar darkness of helplessness and horror. This too it might be possible to visualize—one could see the shape of it, with a little trouble—but in a sense it was controllable, it could wait. The first thing was to call up Jones, and this could be done with perfect security from Hampden. To summon Jones down from that third-floor bedroom, make an appointment with him——

He dismissed the taxi by the barbershop, went round the corner of Plymouth Street with the phrases shaping themselves on his tongue. At the entrance of Hampden, Jack, the janitor, was standing on the granite steps with a dustcloth in his hand, bareheaded, his white hair bright in the lamplight. He pointed with the cloth towards the hall and said:

—Oh, Mr. Ammen, th-th-there's a *sss*-pecial delivery for you in your b-box, you must have missed it.

—Thanks.

—You're welcome.

He fished out the letter, saw the postmark, Saint Louis, the long blue stamp, slightly sinister in its suggestion of hurry, and his father's printed name in the upper left-hand corner. This was ugly. It had a meaning, there could be no doubt of that, it was part of the narrowing circle of pressure, the unseen blockade. Damn him! And damn them all. The impulse to tear it in two ran sharply down his fingers, he had already visualized the gesture and felt the contempt in it, but instead he slipped the envelope into his side pocket and went to the telephone by the elevator. With one foot reaching back against the door behind him, he dropped in his nickel, gave the number, waited. Far off, he could hear the repeated double ring, the little rhythmic cricket-cry,—*zeeng-zeeng*,—*zeeng-zeeng*,—*zeeng-zeeng*, —*zeeng,-zeeng*,—it was as if he himself were there in the front room beside the oak table, on which the telephone stood, waiting for Jones to come downstairs. The ringing continued interminably, and then as if very close at hand the operator's voice said:

—They don't answer, shall I——

—Try them again, please, there should be someone there.

—I'll try them again.

The little lost bell went on crying in its widening wilderness; with each repetition of the doubled sound the universe seemed vaster and emptier; it was as if Jones's front room had become the seed of a world. To be the cause of this, to be sending into the void the small sharp signal from which should radiate such an expansion of significance, was both imposing and frightening. This act of creation-at-a-distance perhaps involved responsibilities: and the wider the expansion of the universe before one provoked an answer, the more freighted with consequences might eventually be the answer itself. Listening, with the receiver loosely held against his ear, he looked out through the small windows towards the garage at the back of Hampden Hall, noted the wrecking car which stood at the top of the concrete runway, and the strong curve of the steel crane, and then suddenly there was a cessation of the ringing, a faint sound as of clearance, and a voice.

—Hello? Karl Jones speaking.

The voice was flat, soft, tired, he smiled affectionately as he heard it, it was as if Jones had come into the room and were about to be greeted with the very warmest of reassurances.

—Ah, Mr. Jones. Perhaps you'll remember that I called you up a little while ago about some advertising, political advertising.

—Yes?

—Well, now, I've had time for a careful discussion with my partner, our plans are fairly definite, and before we go any farther I'd like very much to have a talk with you.

—Yes——

—Now, my partner lives out in the country just beyond Bedford, near Concord, and I wonder if you would care to let me drive you out there, say tomorrow afternoon or evening sometime, to discuss it!

—Not tomorrow, no, I'm sorry——

—No?

—No. You'll have to excuse me, I can't talk to you now——

—Oh——

—You see, everything is upset, we've had an accident, my wife has just had a stillborn baby—just this evening——

—Oh, I'm very sorry—I'm extremely——

—And tomorrow is impossible, as the funeral is in the morning at Mount Auburn——

—I see, of course——
—Yes, I'm sorry.
—I suppose not for a day or two then——
—No, I'm sorry.
—In that case of course I don't want to detain you, but would Friday perhaps be all right, do you think?
—Perhaps Friday. Yes, *Friday* would be all right.
—Suppose then I give you a ring at your office Friday morning, and we'll arrange a meeting.
—Yes, very well. You'll have to excuse me now——
—Certainly. I'm afraid I——
—Good night.
—Good night.

He hung up the receiver on its hook, in imagination he listened to the retreating footsteps of Jones, the footsteps hurrying quickly up the stairs to that bright and dreadful bedroom on the third floor, on the ceiling of which the shadows were perhaps now again in motion. The footsteps were running up the stairs, the conversation on the telephone was already forgotten, Jones was returning to that sordid and huddled little human scene. The woman lay on a bed in the corner, a raised hospital bed, perhaps raised on wooden blocks, she was naked, her lifted knees were apart, beside the bed was a white enameled pail, a table with an enamaled tray on which were bloody cloths, steel instruments, forceps. Jones was returning to that stupefying smell of ether, to that hurried and meaningful silence, to the dead child and the unconscious woman, the doctor and the nurse. Sometimes, in such cases, didn't they use artificial respiration? In another room, in one of the other rooms, one of the bedrooms at the back, the doctor was perhaps working over the small body of the child, blowing into its blue mouth, trying to warm it to life. Outside the door, Jones, as he passed, could hear him working, knew already that it was useless, went on to the front room to help the nurse. The woman lay on the bed in the corner, unconscious, she didn't yet know, later she would have to be told. In the meantime, the pail must be emptied, its contents must be burned in the furnace. While the nurse stayed with the woman, Jones took the pail and went down to the cellar. In the cellar, he noticed that some one had spilled the wastebasket on the concrete floor, had left it lying there amongst the litter. He paid no attention to it, went slowly towards the furnace. . . .

The front door of Hampden Hall creaked slightly, Jack was coming in with the dustcloth in his hand. The scene in Jones's house suddenly became as small and remote as the picture in the finder of a camera, tilted brightly off and vanished, like a drop of light sliding off a leaf. He passed Jack on the stairs, and without sensible lapse of time was reading his father's letter in the elevator. The glib phrases were sickening, were like a sickness. Wash my hands of you. Grateful if you'd be so considerate as to keep my name out of the courts. The writer of this anonymous letter says——

The lights in the apartment were turned on, he must have forgotten to switch them off, he dropped the envelope and the letter under the table on the floor and without thinking went straight to the whisky bottle in the kitchenette, poured half a wine glass full, and drank it straight. The writer of this anonymous letter. Who could this be but Sandbach, who but Sandbach—behind whom was Gerta no doubt, and perhaps Toppan as well. But perhaps not Gerta? No, not Gerta, Gerta would have given him a more specific warning, she would have said something tonight if she had known, after all Gerta was honorable. Honorable? He began to laugh, laughed louder and louder, putting both hands down flat on the butterfly-table; his head hung lower and lower over the table as he laughed, the spasms of laughter wheezed into silence, and he found himself studying carefully the grain of the table, on the waxed surface of which two tears had fallen. It was extremely funny.

But it was impossible to stay here.

He could perhaps go up on to the roof, look down from there at the traffic in Massachusetts Avenue.

Or down to the river and the stadium.

Instead, a few minutes later, he found himself walking into Harvard Square, bought a paper, went into Gustie's and had a quick drink, crossed the street to the delicatessen place and had another. He held the paper before him with both hands and gazed at it without reading it, listening half-consciously to the talk.

—well, I should worry, I told him if he didn't come by half past ten it would be gone, and it's gone.

—served him right.

—Sure. It's his own funeral. *Next* time——

—crazy as a bedbug.

—and two whisky sours, that's three to come!

—and besides I don't think he could really afford it. No, I don't.

—You don't think so.

—No, I don't think so.

—can't make out what his position *is* there, he's always coming in, every evening, and they give him a handout——

—I heard he was unfrocked for something.

—poor themselves, too; Ada, she's the oldest, working as a cigarette girl at the Palace——

—No. It's a *local* beer. Only *local*.

He turned away from the counter, rising, went out, proceeded along Boylston Street till he came to the river, stood on the bridge and looked down at the dark luster of the water. Two men were standing close together on the float of the boathouse, talking intermittently in low voices: one of them stooped, put his hand into the water, then stood up again and wiped it with a handkerchief. They went slowly up the gangway into the club, which was dark, he heard the door close behind them, and at that moment he felt a single drop of rain on the back of his wrist. The sky was covered with broken clouds, ragged and hurrying, it was like a disordered mind, like a flight of disordered thoughts: with his hands on the parapet of the bridge, he tilted his head back and watched them, so long and so intently that at last he felt it was not the clouds which were moving but himself. And when he turned away, it was with such an acute feeling of giddiness that for a second he thought he was going to fall.

❨ XII What It Is to Be a Stranger

If the whole apartment house had seemed hostile, on his return to it in the evening, and uglier and more prisonlike than ever after his telephone talk with Jones from the pay station in the hall (in the shadow of the elevator), it now seemed, in the soundless turmoil of time, nothing but an enormous and elaborate trap. Lying down for the twentieth time, fully dressed, on the dark bed in the dark room, he stared through the little square of window: not for any sight of the clouded and hurrying sky, but for a sharper vision of Hampden Hall. In mid-air, it was if he could reverse himself, return from halfway across the street (or from the roof of Widener Library) to see his own building from outside; as if in fact he were a bird, looking in through his own window, looking cynically downward at the dark figure on the bed which was himself. Seen thus, under the hurrying heavens, the building was simply nothing but a monster: it stood upright and unapologetic, in the midst of the mad universe, a queer hard brickwork organism with hot metal arteries and tingling nerves of copper, breathing the night air through huge vent holes on a flat roof of tar and gravel. Inside it were the human lice on which it nourished itself—it had gathered them together for the night. Among these of course was himself, lying there with his hands beneath his head; now staring out past the roof of the A.D. Club to meet the gaze of his projected spirit, which hung there like an angel in modern dress, now returning for a scrutiny of the little Buddha on its shelf. It was a prison, a trap; but it was more than that, worse than that—the whole building had seemed somehow sinister as he approached it; and after the telephone talk with Jones it had begun to seem definitely *evil*. The impulse to take flight had been sharp enough, he had wanted to hurry out again at once, to go anywhere, to drive a car madly into the country, even perhaps simply to go to town and get drunk. But disgust had inhibited this impulse, disgust and something else—a fear, a suspicion, an uneasy edge of self-doubt. Not fear, no—disgust, disgust, disgust, this queer new horror which, rising periodically in the back of his mind, almost on the back of his tongue, made him want to close his eyes lest he should see the world in the very act of changing its shape. And all this was not *because* of the telephone talk with little Jones, of course not, not at all—at most the telephone talk was a part of it, it had certainly not *changed* anything. No, what was sickening was the way in which all the details of his plans, his scheme, were now at every point working so well together but in a sense *not quite his own*: as if his own speech came back to him, from a mouthpiece, translated into an unfamiliar language. There was an ugly sort of distortion in it, everything was meanly and sneeringly caricatured, as by concave and convex mirrors; it was like the strange drawling and snarling sounds which quite ordinary and pleasant words or voices can become in a dream. With a desire to escape this he had thought of going to town, or even of simply taking a long walk, but at once to realize that the thing was inescapable. Much better had been the impulse to put it all down, to make the last entries in his journal of the adventure, add the last date to the column of dates on the map, and even to attempt to codify these impressions as if for the novel. Almost immediately, he had found himself trying to outline a queer sort of essay, a philosophic essay, but not quite philosophic either, perhaps psychological was what he meant, but of course without in the least being able to get *at* the thing: he had written intermittently for hours, now and again going out to walk from end to end of the long dimly lighted corridor, pausing at the one end to look down toward the river, and at the other to watch a late car or two speeding urgently along Massachusetts Avenue. All night, the world had seemed full of clocks—the grandfather clock in the professor's apartment sent its soft *tyang* through the walls, Memorial Hall and Saint Paul's dutifully and sadly echoed each other, the dreary wooden steeple of the Unitarian Church added its deeper note; but even with these to mark the passage of his feet along the corridor, the expensive shoes placed swiftly one in front of the other, the heels slightly scuffed and dragging, his eyes intent on the slight swerve with which the right foot as if carelessly placed itself, even with these the sense of time had not been so much marked as diffuse. He had got up only to sit down again, had flung himself on the bed only again to rise and begin walking, or had paced the crooked corridor only once more to sit down and try to write. It might be four o'clock, it might be five. Above Beck Hall, the sky had begun to brighten. There was a little patter of rain, a little grazing of rain, on the window. It was as if it had touched his skin, it stung him to a sudden but perhaps false alertness, he jumped up and went back to the table, looked sharply at the map, sat down.

His father's letter——

It lay on the floor between his feet, the phrases of it looked up at him like round eyes—he had flung it there to forget it, flung it down in anger and hatred, but now it watched him. The phrases had of course stuck in his mind, only because they had so sickened him with anger and disgust— the typewritten phrases of a typical businessman's smoothness and complacency. I do not presume to advise—as you are doubtless aware—far be it from me—I can only report that the writer of this anonymous letter says—tired of your irresponsible behavior—dragging my name into the police courts—not enough that you were a continual worry to your mother —and so on and so on.

Somebody had written to him, obviously—probably Sandbach. And Gerta must have given him the address.

And they were threatening police action?

He looked down at it, pushed it farther under the table with his toe. The hard, firm, coarse signature, written with large open letters and a heavy pen, lay there like some ugly relic of his own past, something hateful and obscene, something to be destroyed. The angry energy of hypocrisy——

To find this waiting for him in the letter box, with its menacing special delivery stamp, had undoubtedly made its contribution to his increasing sense of evil and ugliness, it had at once occurred to him—so right was his intuition—that it might be better to destroy it unread; but also it had occurred to him that it might actually contain something in the way of *news*. It was as if, even through the unopened envelope, he had been able to feel a threat, the encroachment of something: perhaps, however, only because the arrival of a letter from his father was in itself so unusual. He had waited, called up Jones first—keeping the letter in his pocket—and it was odd now to consider the intimate and by no means accidental *connection* between the two things. So intimate, in fact, that had he read the letter first he might not have telephoned to Jones at all. At any rate, it would have been necessary to consider it, to consider whether in the light of this threat the immediate project had not better be abandoned, the meeting with Jones postponed; perhaps even to consider the substitution of some one *else* for Jones, since it was now possible that Toppan knew who Jones was. The letter lay in his pocket speaking of this, while he himself spoke with Jones; just as later, in his room, the conversation with Jones spoke softly and disconcertingly through the curt phrases of the letter. It was peculiarly right that the two things should thus have coincided in time—but it was also peculiarly unpleasant.

He teased a cigarette from the opened packet on the red table, lit it, walked to the window. The smoke drifted backwards over his shoulder in a wide flat band of gray, undulated a little towards the floor, then softly dispersed in an upward vagueness towards the ceiling by the bathroom door. He watched it, saw the last pale thread of smoke lick neatly over the top of the door, and suddenly remembered that long ago he had meant to make a study of drafts in this fashion. "The flight of cigarette smoke is only a draft made manifest." He said this aloud, as he crossed the room to open the door to the corridor, he said it with amusement, and then added:

—There goes the professor's clock.

The clock had struck the half hour. Standing just outside the corridor door he blew upward a long soft plume of smoke, blew it towards the top of the doorjamb, but not forcibly: with the effect, therefore, of merely releasing, for observation, a trial balloon of smoke, a willing cloud. After a barely perceptible pause, the smoke billowed downward very slightly and then swooped in a long wide dispersed wave upward into the room. Keeping quite still, lest his own movement create any artificial current of air, he repeated the action: again the smoke swirled neatly, after a moment's hesitation, into the quiet room—obviously the air in the corridor was warmer than the air inside. This being the case, the current near the floor must, of course, flow the other way. Stooping close to the linoleum floor he exhaled a soft cloud before him. It wavered, broke, and came loosely backward across and round his face. Exactly as one would expect.

The same thing would probably be true of the doors to the bedroom and the kitchenette? . . .

The bedroom worked beautifully—the draft was sharper, more dramatic, the smoke was as if violently seized, hurled headlong down invisible rapids. But the kitchenette, presumably because its window was shut, or simply because it was out of the path of the main currents, was a disappointment: the movement of the smoke, whether at floor or ceiling, was scarcely perceptible, sluggish, equivocal. In fact, it would go exactly where propelled. He blew cloud after cloud into the little boxlike room, it hung swaying and gently convolving over the table, over the white enameled refrigerator, over the gas stove, almost motionless, passive. It was like a backwater of a river: it was stagnant; and looking at it he became abruptly aware of the profound nocturnal silence. It was that moment between night and morning when the traffic is stillest, the brief interval between the end of the night life and the beginning of the day—the hour when life is at its ebb. In hospitals, people were now in the act of dying. And in Reservoir Street, at this instant——

He turned quickly away, walked to the corridor and closed the door. Returning, he stared out at the palely brightening clouds, heard again that grazing patter of the drizzle on the pane, saw the little chain of fine bright beads which had been lightly etched there. But the rain could make no difference—it neither added to nor subtracted from the wide appearance and nature of things. The structure beneath it was exactly the same,—undiminished, loyal, unsentimental: what one had made, or what one was making, was still the same, kept its hard and clear identity. And the whole face of the world, if one now dared to see it thus, was one enormous growing "thing"—a vast and dreadful or beautiful flower: a flower which, if beautiful, was also terrible: as if the universe might be simply a single outrageous pond-lily whose roots were murderous. Yes, it was exactly that. The blood drawn up by that profound taproot made possible the thrust and loveliness of the blind enormous flower: the perfect synthesis of good and evil. And if this was so, if life was in essence really like this, why then was it possible to feel any compunctions? Unless, of course, one simply failed outright in one's attempt to *identify* oneself at all points with life: failed, at it were, to stretch oneself co-terminally with the four points of the cross, and to become, oneself, cruciform. . . .

The idea was not new, he had thought of it in fact at the very beginning, though not perhaps in quite such terms or so neatly. The structure of evil had been manifest and omnipresent, the evil in himself he had always quite recognized, or had at all events *wanted* to recognize: it needed no justification, was natural and right, and the whole action had in the end revolved quite properly around his decision to face the real shape of the world and to shape his own deed accordingly. But it seemed to him that he had never actually *seen* the vision, the tree-shaped vision, the lily-shaped vision, so clearly and perfectly as now. It was something of this that he had tried to put down in his rapid notes, the orderly sheets of which lay on the table beneath the map—but to look at them now was only to realize that vision is one thing, action or speech another. He said aloud, tearing the paper with deliberate hands:

—Many are the thyrsus-bearers, but few are the mystics. Few are the mystics! I must have a drink, and I must go slow.

But he made no move toward the kitchenette, where the whisky stood on the shelf, he stood still, aware that he was looking at nothing, he thought for a moment that perhaps the best thing would be to write, quite suddenly and quite *simply*—as if for the renewal of a lost contact with a swiftly sinking world—to Gerta. *My dear Gerta, if it is not now, not al-ready, too late—if now with the impediment in my speech removed——*

Impossible.

It was not the conversation on the telephone with Jones which had done this—how could it be? It was not even clear that the conversation with Jones had anything to do with it. The logic of that, the logic of the con-sequences of that, was flawless: there had been no mistake: the whole thing now stood, from beginning to end, as perfect as a theorem in algebra. Jones, Karl Jones, would meet him on Friday, they would drive together to Con-cord—to meet the mythical partner and discuss the mythical advertising campaign—Jones had assented to the plan almost with alacrity—and with this was concluded the final pure curve of the idea. The ultimate cutting-off had thus been accomplished, the separation from humanity; the individ-ual had asserted himself, stood alone in the full horror of a light which per-mitted no moral shadows: or none, at any rate, save those created by his own will and for his own purpose. The stranger had been identified—hadn't he?—as Jones, and as such could thus be destroyed: the *strangeness* in Jones had been recognized, with its terror and its pure desirability; it had been observed carefully and inimically as the thing-that-wants-to-be-killed; it could be killed. There is no compromise with the object, no placid or reasoned acceptance of it. It is seen, understood, and destroyed. The vision is pure.

Yes!

But suddenly he felt that he must close his eyes; and opening them again, he as suddenly felt, for no clear reason, that he must clap his hands sharply together before him, turn quickly, look at something else, some-thing *new*—do something, go somewhere. He clapped his hands together again, walked toward the waterfall without seeing it, revolved quickly away from it, and made as he did so a gesture with his hands such as he knew (and painfully) *he had never in his life made before:* a queer forward thrust of the hands, stiffly parallel, the fingers tensely apart, as if he were in fact *reaching* for something. It lasted only a moment, his arms fell limply to his sides, limply and a little self-consciously, almost perhaps ashamedly. This wouldn't do, this wasn't right at all! Once more he began to feel as if he were in some subtle way being indecently hurried; like a per-son who in stepping on to an escalator miscalculates its speed. It was as if one were rather cruelly and undignifiedly *yanked*, dislocated—and with that feeling of disgust with oneself which makes one disinclined for the time being to look at oneself in a mirror. To lose *control*——

He stepped into the dark bedroom, approached the dressing-table mirror and without turning on the light leaned on his hands towards the obscure image which he saw coming forward to meet him there. For a second, the face that looked out at him was not his own face, but the face of Jones. It looked at him merrily, impertinently—exactly as if it were going to wink. It was only a trick of the light—it was because the light was behind him—the sharp illusion was gone as soon as it had come—but the effect was nonetheless extraordinary. The face was his own, of course, he leaned again towards it on trembling hands, feeling weak and shaken, and as he examined his eyes, his mouth, his cheeks, the wide and pallid forehead, it seemed to him that his face had somehow *changed*. It seemed, in fact, in some subtle and dreadful way, to have lost its meaning. There was no character in it, no significance—it had become a more featureless area: a kind of mask: something seen from outside . . .

Had Jones done this? . . .

It was as if Jones, in that moment of vision, had said something, or been about to say something: as if, in thus interposing himself, he had somehow managed to make some preposterous sort of statement or claim. He had been about to say "I am no stranger than you are"; or perhaps "Aren't you really a stranger yourself? Have you thought of that?"; or else, simply, "Now you know what it is to be a stranger."

The words seemed actually to hang in the air; and it was with a feeling of automatically echoing them that he said aloud:

—Now you know what it is to be a stranger. Now you know! Jasper Ammen.

And certainly, now, he was looking at himself from an immense distance, and with a detachment which amounted really to cruelty and enmity. Or was it fear? Or was it amusement? One could say calmly, now, that the face was absurd, one could say that it was just an arrangement of lines and planes and colors, that it was obscene, that it was ugly. It was as surprising and as mean, as vital and objectionable, as definitely something to be suspected and distrusted and perhaps destroyed, as some queer marine creature which one might find on overturning a wet rock by the sea. It was conscious and watchful, its eyes looked out of the pool of the mirror with a hard animal defensive sharpness, clearly it was dangerous and alert. It might have to be killed. If one were to put out a hand or a stick and *touch* it——

But the thought was unbearable, he flung himself on the bed and said:

—I must try to sleep. I must try to get a few hours sleep.

He closed his eyes, and immediately the conversation with Jones on the telephone began to repeat itself. *Not tomorrow, no. I'm sorry. You'll have to excuse me. I can't talk to you now, you see everything is upset, we've had an accident, my wife has just had a stillborn baby, and tomorrow is impossible as the funeral is in the morning at Mount Auburn. Yes, I'm sorry. No, I'm sorry. . . . Perhaps Friday. Yes, Friday would be all right.* . . . The dreadful shameless gentleness of the voice, the soft accent of concern, in which nevertheless there was no self-pity: the naked raw glibness of the confession on the telephone, the awkward glibness—the ordinary humble unavoidableness of the calm voice having to say such things on the telephone—*You'll have to excuse me now*—as if he merely had an engagement for lunch, or had to go to the toilet. It had seemed so entirely simple, so almost meaningless, this series of tragic and placid statements, there in the corner of the marble-floored hall, beside the wrought-iron grill of the elevator; as if they might have been discussing the weather, or the prospects for the baseball season: except, of course, for the careful gentleness of Jones's voice, the rather unsophisticated and surprised gentleness, calculated for the occasion. Not quite calculated, either—for what had been really disconcerting was the *natural* sound of the sorrow in the voice, as if Jones, taken off guard, didn't know how to conceal his suffering. And thus, the whole scene had come to him over the telephone—the smell of ether in the garden, the revolving clotheshorse lifting its spiny arms in the lamplight, the empty ash can waiting at the curb, the doctor's car, the shabby cellar, the coal-bins, the swiftly moving shadows on the ceiling of the upper bedroom, and then that moment when the shadows had suddenly ceased to move, and finally the woman's cry, so queer, so quavering, so soft——

Christ!

He opened his eyes quickly and blindly, as if to do so would stop the whirl of impressions and phrases—it was if he were drunk, or sick, and sought any sight of the world, any fragmentary and lurching vision of a wall or ceiling, to check the wild swoop of his vertigo. And now the daybreak was square and bright in the little window, as sharp and immediate as the tiny jeweled picture in the finder of a camera, each moving cloud separate and round and distinct and with a color forever its own, never to be repeated, immortal. It was as good as a cinema, as comforting as the sight of moving water, he lay and watched the irregular regularity of the cloud-procession, listened to the faint intermittent claw-grazing of the little rain, tried to fix his attention there, to avert his attention by averting his face. And for a while it was in fact as if he had managed to fall asleep with his eyes wide open. He felt like a cat, with the cunning of a cat, allowed his mind to be lulled by the activity of his eyes, permitted all the motion of his consciousness to concentrate there on the surface, in those two points of sight. His hands were still, his body was still, his feet were softly pressed against the footboard of the bed, he breathed as lightly as possible. It was the process of becoming a cloud, or of becoming nothing but a *consciousness* of cloud: even the sounds came to him only indistinctly and tangentially: he refused to admit them: the bell-sounds, the car-sounds, the slamming of a door, the milkman hurrying along the hall, clinking his bottles, the first morning hum of the elevator, summoned down to the second floor by Jack, the janitor—aware of these, he also dismissed them, allowing himself to become simply a recipient of light. It was all like a world of glass, translucent, brittle, precarious, but infinitely precious. It was like having an enormous pain, which even to breathe was to invite: as long as one held one's breath, it vanished. When one breathed again, one tried it cautiously, round the edges and corners, one sent down to begin with the tiniest little tentacle of air, a silver thread of exploration——

But it was no use. It was all no use. As soon as one *did* try to breathe, that preposterous and incredible mountain of sensation was there again, the unbelievable shape once more had to be believed. As in a nightmare the figure of the old woman seen in the street reappears vaguely again in the distance at the quayside, or on the ship, perhaps altered and unrecognizable, and later is heard mounting the stairs behind one, with a sort of scrambling and sinister haste, coughing and sneezing as she comes, and to one's gaze over the banisters lifts at last the face of which the horror, hitherto not admitted or confessed, is freely and lethally given, so to his consciousness, through all its elaborate structure of dispersal, came the beginnings and misremembered fragments of that conversation with Jones. It could not have happened, and yet it *had* happened: that he should have leaned there at the public telephone in the hall by the elevator, with Jack standing at the front door to take his last nocturnal look at the weather, holding a dust-cloth in his hand, and that instead of an unruffled arrangement of the final plan should have occured this sudden plunge into the murkiest and ugliest and most painful of unsolicited intimacies——

But why *should* it be painful? Why *should* he want both to think of it and *not* think of it?

You'll have to excuse me, I can't talk to you now, you see everything is upset, we've had an accident——

An accident! The word looked a mile long, he was walking slowly from end to end of it, sparrows were chirping on the window ledge above Plympton Street, he must have slept. It was a quarter to eight, and still lightly raining. There was no time to lose, for Jones would probably go to Mount Auburn early—it wasn't the sort of thing one dawdled about. And to make the necessary inquiries, one would have to get there first.

❲ XIII   The Stranger Becomes Oneself

The impulse was absurd, but he obeyed it, obeyed it with a kind of angry arrogance, he turned away from the Merle, deciding not to have any breakfast at all, and walked quite deliberately in the wrong direction, his back to Mount Auburn. At this point, when the pattern of one's life was all speed and no detail, it was idle to ask oneself the reason for one's decisions: one simply followed one's feet. He followed his feet in the drizzle, the gray light, down Bow Street to Saint Paul's Church, looked up at the Siennese tower—or was it Verona?—to observe through a light cloud of rain that the clock was on the stroke of eight, and that he would be in time for the Angelus. And as he entered, and stood at the back of the ornate and hushed interior, watching the priest and the mass-servers begin the service for three or four women and himself, and hearing the bell strike its first faint triad of notes far up in the steeple, he became aware that he had really been intending to do this for a long time. It was only the other day, in fact, that he had almost done so——

—*Angelus Domini nuntiavit Mariae.*

—*Et concepit de Spiritu Sancto.*

—*Ave Maria, gratia plena, Dominus tecum; benedicta tu in mulieribus, et benedictus fructus ventris tui, Jesus. Sancta Maria, mater dei, ora pro nobis nunc et in hora mortis nostrae. Amen.*

Blessed Mary, God's mother, pray for us, now and in the hour of our death.

He tried to remember, while the priest and the mass-servers intoned the responses, and the soft bell again sounded its remote three overhead, just when this had been, and what had made him think of it. *Et verbum caro factum est. Et habitavit in nobis . . . Ave Maria.* The Latin phrases echoed with silver purity in the hollow church, as always the Catholic service seemed curiously hurried and casual, almost undignified, and yet from this very appearance of carelessness, even in the shambling movements of the surpliced priest and mass-servers, came all the more a sense of power and certainty: they themselves might cough or stumble, be graceless or inaudible, but the mystery sustained them. He watched them, frowning—half listened to the final sentences; suddenly the thing was unceremoniously finished; and it was then, as he turned again toward the door, that he remembered. It had been the very morning——

The thing shocked him, he walked quickly along the wet brick sidewalks of Mount Auburn Street.

It had been the very morning of his first discovery of Jones. And his purpose in the notion of going there, of course, had been simply to see if actually, in the church, he might not find his victim: some member of the congregation might turn out to be the supposititious Jones. He remembered it now quite clearly; he had thought of it while he was taking his shower, hearing the bells of the Angelus through the little window—the window from which he had then watched Mrs. Finden drying her hands and arms, putting on her rings. Yes. It seemed very remote, a long time ago, very remote, and oddly bright and innocent: it had been spring; and although it was *still* spring, somehow now it seemed as if he were looking back to it from another season, another year. The plan had then been formless, of course, and this had given it the charm and vagueness of all new things, new undertakings—the stranger had not yet been discovered or his strangeness identified—the whole problem still remained metaphysical—a mere formula—and it was now possible to recognize that at that stage there had been an unmistakable sense of *freedom* which had at once, with the actual selection of Jones, disappeared. But more curious still was the fact that today, of all days, he should *again* have the impulse to go there. This was very peculiar, it had about it the air as of a compulsory completion of some obscure sort, like a forced move in chess. The idea had occurred to him casually, no doubt, but could he be sure that it had occurred without some deep reason? Its queer appropriateness—the appropriateness of the whole thing, the scene, the service, the words themselves—suggested a kind of *rootedness* in the pattern which it would be painful to investigate.

But it hardly mattered.

With the fine rain cool against his face and hands, like an added sensitiveness, he walked quickly, his raincoat half unbuttoned, and at the corner of Boylston Street, by the Square, found that his car had already been brought out for him; the man was waiting in it with the door open, stepped out as soon as he saw him. For a moment after entering, he sat still, stared ahead through the delicately misted windshield, looking at nothing, thinking of nothing. He could drive straight to the cemetery. Or he could go first to the house in Reservoir Street, wait till Jones came out, and then precede him to Mount Auburn—which would of course be easy. But he felt indifferent; it was perhaps unnecessary to take so much trouble; there was little, after all, to be gained in seeing Jones emerge from the house to the undertaker's car, or in knowing whether it would be Jones or the undertaker who would carry the coffin. What did it matter? The thing was nearly finished. It would be enough to get a glimpse of Jones at the cemetery, a final glimpse—and if he went at once there would be plenty of time for the asking of questions and the taking up of a good position.

He drove slowly up Brattle Street against the traffic, switched off the windshield wiper when he noticed that the rain had almost stopped, and for the first time, listening to the loud irregular patter on the car roof, the large drops from trees, began to feel tired. His eyes were heavy and wanted to close, the whole length of his body felt relaxed and remote, his hands lay lightly and reluctantly on the wheel. The thing was dreamlike—everything had a dreamlike sharpness, the heavy immediateness and separateness of objects seen in a fever: the pale hands on the ebony wheel looked more *real* than his own; and the stopped sound of the windshield wiper was so palpable as to seem audible. The wet houses and fences, the dark rain-soaked trunks of elms, the blackened stems of bushes, went past him with an extraordinarily dense and meaningful solidity, each shape making a sound of its own—*whish-whish-whish-whish*; and from the total complex of noise made by the car itself each particular item was distinct: the faintly burred hum of the motor, the grazing clink of the key ring against the dash, the click-cluck of the clock, the delicate ticking of the watch on his wrist, the snicker of the wet tires on the slippery road. It was time made intensely audible, time made visible, time solidified in a concrete series of individual shapes—a slow-motion of time, almost in fact a "still." As if, at a given moment, one could take a cross section of the universe, or slow down life itself to the point at which it was only once removed from death. . . . Was it that?

He had already decided to leave the car on the opposite side of the street from the entrance, he got out and walked deliberately across the car tracks toward the massive Egyptian gates of gray granite. In the office which adjoined the squat little chapel he leaned against the counter and said:

—A friend of mine, Mr. Karl Jones, is coming here this morning. Could you tell me when he's expected?

—Mr. Karl Jones? Yes, I think I can tell you.

The man stooped over a table, ran his fingers slowly down a column of names.

—Also I should like to know in just what part of the cemetery——

—Certainly. . . . I see that we expect the interment to take place before nine. At nine or a little before. As for the other—if you'll just wait a minute——

Interment!

An open book of grave-certificates lay on the counter, he found he was leaning above it, and began reading the blue certificate which was uppermost, still attached to its stub. *Proprietors of the Cemetery of Mount Auburn. Vesper Lot 5000, Grave No. 591. This Certifies that* . . . . *. . . . of* . . . . *by the payment of twenty dollars, the receipt whereof is hereby acknowledged, has purchased the right of interment in Grave numbered 591 in the Vesper lot which is owned by the Corporation, and has paid in addition Twenty-five Dollars to be added to the Repair Fund, for perpetual care of the grass. For each interment after the* first, etc. *Not more than two interments shall be made in the same grave, and the later interment shall be at least three feet below the level of the ground. When any such grave shall have become vacant, etc.* Turning the leaf, he read on the back: *Received of* .... *five dollars for grading and sodding Grave No. 591.*

Grading and sodding. But how did a grave become vacant?

—Ah, yes, just as I thought; it's in the Vesper lot, and that's right at the western side; if you go straight along the front here and turn up Glen Avenue, by the railroad——

—Is it far?

—Oh, no, only a few minutes, it's just where Glen Avenue meets Vesper——

—Thanks.

A curious idea had occurred to him, he gave a little laugh as he went out and followed a workman with a wheelbarrow along the narrow tomb-lined road, it had occurred to him that it was a very neat and fitting opportunity for buying a grave—why not? And cheap at the price, with grading and sodding thrown in, and perpetual care of the grass. Across the wheelbarrow lay a rake and a hoe, and beside them, nodding in a square box, a dozen little potted plants: destined, no doubt, for somebody's border—somebody's counterpane. The workman was whistling softly, but stopped at once as he heard footsteps behind him, looked quickly sidelong as he was overtaken. The nod he gave was guarded, professionally friendly.

The city of the dead. That was what they always called it. And certainly, if one paused to visualize the skeletons underground, all the placid bones lying horizontal in boxes, or amongst tarnished remnants of silver and wood, it was a city of a considerable size, a metropolis. But the whole surface of the earth, if one paused to think of that too, was nothing but a mausoleum: all that living surface was nothing but a rich mulch of death. And this little collection, at Mount Auburn, of the refined dead, the rich dead, the distinguished dead, the pretentious dead, was, if one saw it in due proportion, a very paltry affair. This absurd business of putting them all in one place, collecting them, as if they were rare stamps, or coins, or first editions! As if there weren't time enough in which to duplicate them! Good God. The world would be the same forever. The same people would be arriving, and being important, and dying, forever. *In this vault are deposited the remains of. Here lieth the body of. This stone is erected to the memory of. Here lie the remains of. In memory of. Sacred to the memory of.* And they were all alike, in the long view they were all alike, all they ever managed to say was a feeble and stammering "I." They said this with an air of extraordinary importance and bewilderment, made what they considered to be a unique gesture, and were gone. And then after them came the hordes, the shapeless hordes, the innumerable and nameless hordes, of the others, world without end, who would feel the same importance and make the same unique and imperious gesture. Each in turn would believe that in some extraordinary way he had really produced himself, wrought his own intelligence and power, created his own individuality. Each would say "I have this *right*," "I have a *right* to happiness," "I have a *right* to love," "I must live my own life," "I have thought this

for myself," "It is *I* who first felt this, thought this, needed this." Each
would believe himself unique. . . . And after him again would come, until
the dying world was inherited briefly by grasshoppers and ants, the human
swarm of others who would say and believe identically the same thing. All
the Smiths, the Robinsons—the dead earth would become a tomb, sacred
to the memory of the Smiths and Robinsons. And beneath it, like those
who lay here now under inscribed stones, or broken columns, or slabs of
marble engraved with the hour glass or the serpent, would sleep the whole
human race.

He looked angrily at the stones, and then away,—the little white lambs
of marble with crossed forelegs, the doves, the cherubs, the angels, the
skulls—all silent, dripping in the fine rain; even the wet spring flowers, the
daffodils and tulips, had a mortuary look, seemed somehow morbid. He
walked along the grim avenue, taking long steps on the neat gravel, out-
distanced the workman with the wheelbarrow, came to the turning and
Glen Avenue. Beyond the wooden fence was the railway line,—the hard
note of the quotidian and temporary. In this corner of the cemetery, not yet
so crowded, the family lots were fewer: the graves humbler; many of them
were unmarked save by the little oval metal plaques which gave their numbers. Noting the succession of these he found easily enough the new ex-
cavation at the juncture of Glen and Vesper Avenues. Beneath a small tree
—a Judas tree?—which was covered with pink blossom, and some distance
back from the road, it appeared harmless and natural enough. He walked
across the sodden grass, looked into it, observed the carefully sheered sides
of wet loam, as glistening as if they had been cut with a knife, and the little
pile of soaked earth which had been neatly laid on canvas beside it, and
the curious cat's cradle of broad tape which lay across the aperture in
readiness for the coffin. The whole thing was indescribably ugly: it was
obscene: the falseness of it was profound. This note as of carefully prepared artifice, of concealment and mitigation—! Christ.

He turned, looked back over his shoulder toward the road, felt curiously
ashamed and guilty: he felt sick: it was impossible to avoid the contamination, the sense of complicity and betrayal: it was himself who had done this,
his own mind had conceived this dishonesty. And it was Jones who had
been betrayed. To be standing here—to be seen standing here now——

He must get away quickly, before they came.

He must walk off a little way, perhaps to the tower and back, or to one
of the ponds, and then, keeping always within view, return to the scene at
the last moment, as if casually. That would be enough—there was no need
for more—just to saunter by, have a last look, dismiss with a final gesture
the dying world.

He hurried back to the road, and found that it made a loop towards the
fence at this point, rejoining Vesper Avenue farther on,—it would be possible, therefore, by walking around this, examining methodically all the
inscriptions, the flowers, the trees, to fill in the time and reappear at the
right instant. He knocked the bowl of his pipe against the palm of his
hand, but decided not to smoke; took the right turning; found that he was
staring at the hideous stones and their monotonous inscriptions without
seeing them, listening to the passing of a train, beyond the fence, without

turning his head. *Who departed this life, to the sorrow of his wife and three children . . . In hopeful rest I here remain . . . My faith to heaven ensnare . . .* The phrases and sentences were all alike, so many precise wounds of the chisel in Vermont marble or granite; and if the rain had made them more vivid to the eye, they were too familiar to be meaningful to the mind. More actual than the death it symbolized was the cutting in the stone; it was as if only the stones were real, and the incised marks on them, half filled with water, more important than the thing they chronicled. In the gentle and windless drizzle, the scent of the flowers—the lilacs, the narcissus, the daffodils—was oppressive, stifling; it was like the smell of ether; weighed on the consciousness like a cloud; and with his pipe in his hand he was thinking this, and feeling as if he had been half anaesthetized, and walking amid the intermittent patter as if half asleep, when he heard behind him the sound of a car.

It could not have been better managed—he was at a safe distance, just far enough away to be unnoticeable—he stood still and watched the black limousine come slowly along the avenue and stop. There was a moment's pause, the black door swung open, the hand that had pushed it was visible for a second and then withdrawn, and Jones, stooping, stepped down to the grass-edge. He was wearing the derby hat, turned round toward the car buttoning a soiled raincoat, he appeared to be saying something, his head a little on one side, and as he did so a second figure stooped from the car, holding with gloved hands a small white box. From the other side of the road a workman had mysteriously appeared, as if from nowhere, and the three men began to walk slowly across the grass toward the little grave, their heads just slightly lowered. The man who held the box wore a black frock coat—presumably the undertaker. The box he held was hardly bigger than a shoe box, it was astonishingly small, it made the whole affair seem more than ever ridiculous and meaningless. That it should all have come to this—that all the elaborate structure should amount only to this—! This absurd little ritual in the rain.

He watched them group themselves before the grave, Jones standing a little in the rear, as if in a measure detaching himself from the queer proceedings, and then the undertaker placed the coffin on the cat's cradle and the workman began to lower it. Jones, with his hat still on, and his hands in his raincoat pockets, suddenly turned away and began to walk quickly toward the car: the undertaker, after a final look into the grave, while the workman drew up the bands, followed him. Apparently, not a word had been said. The whole business had been done in silence. No earth had been flung; only the soft rain fell into the grave.

It was unbelievable. And yet it was what he had expected? . . .

He found himself standing very tensely, as if he had been about to take a step but had inhibited it—his weight slightly forward; without conscious decision he began to walk toward the little scene, saw the two men get into the limousine, and had just reached the juncture of the two roads when the car passed him, driving slowly. Scarcely a yard away—their two orbits at last almost touching—Jones was sitting upright, his small chin raised as if proudly or challengingly, his blue eyes fixed straight ahead on the road beyond the driver. He was pale, it was obvious that he hadn't slept, and it was just as obvious that he hardly knew what he was doing or where he was. Possibly he had been drinking. Beyond him, the undertaker was looking out of the window on the far side with an air of professional embarrassment, touching his gloved fingers together. Neither of them was speaking. In another minute, the car took a sharp left turn, and moved off toward the Egyptian gates. He watched it flash slowly in and out among the columns and pyramids and vaults, saw it make a final swing to the right, and then disappear.

And as it did so, a strange thing happened to him. He felt that he had died.

He must have known that this would happen—for when the car had turned to the left, and for a brief interval crept along the road which paralleled the one on which he was himself standing, he had suddenly felt an almost overwhelming impulse to *run*, to shout at it, to keep abreast of it, shouting—like the people on a wharf who rush excitedly, desperately, along the dock's edge as the ship begins to move, trying to keep up with it, trying to hold it, crying to it, as if they were mere bodies whose souls it was taking away. He had felt this, but of course had done nothing. He had stood still. And it seemed to him now, as he stood motionless, watching the departure of that somber limousine, with Jones inside it, as if life itself were going away from him, moving farther and farther away, fading and dying like the melancholy last flare of sunset seen for a moment through lifting rain. The thing was finished.

Finished! . . . *Finis coronat opus.* King Coffin . . .

Before he knew it, he was in his car, was driving fiercely down Mount Auburn Street. He was angry, he half closed his eyes and said aloud, bitterly —it oughtn't to be like that; to think that it was like that; my God, that it should be like that! The rain had stopped again, the sky over Boston was brightening, a pale beam of sunlight glistened for a moment on a distant roof and was extinguished. To write to Gerta—to write now to Gerta. Yes. He decided not to take the car to the garage, but parked it immediately in front of the fire station in Eliot Square, and hurried on foot to Boylston Street before they could have time to notice it and protest. Let them protest! By all means. Let them look him up, and come hunting for him— the more the merrier. View halloo! In Boylston Street, he stepped into the Western Union office, sat down, drew the yellow form toward him on the glass-topped table, seized the chained pencil, and began to write.

My dear Gerta—the impediment in my speech removed——

He crossed it out, took a fresh sheet, closed his eyes for a second, and began again.

"My dear Gerta—the master builder builds better than he knows. Things have happened. I write too quickly to shape my thoughts, this *is*— so to speak—the *final* dislocation. Is it the shadow of Kay, and were you right after all? You were wise, anyway, you saw the queer shape of things more clearly than I, and I can now salute your narrow vision with respect if not with gratitude. To hell with gratitude! I don't know any longer what it all is, the show is too profound, *goes too fast*, it begins to escape me, if you know what I mean, or care to know, but with the impediment in my speech removed I can at least say that the thing will be perfect as it now stands, or only lacking in perfection as it lacked you, or a clear vision of you: but even this I can now look back to *with Kaylike detachment.* That isn't quite all of it either, there must be a *halfway point which would be good*—too difficult, however, for me to try to analyze for you now. No, it's all too despicable. . . . Ammen."

The large electric clock over the counter said nineteen past nine. He sealed the yellow envelope, and addressed it; then marked it, after a moment's thought, Not to be delivered till eleven o'clock. At the desk he said:

—This is important, do you understand? It might be a matter of life and death. I want this note delivered to this address at *precisely* eleven— not a moment before, and not a moment after. I'm willing to pay for it. Can that be done?

—Yes, sir—at eleven o'clock—we'll send the messenger and have him wait there till the correct time exactly. Walnut Street?

—Right.

His calculations might or might not be exact—it was difficult to tell— but it ought to make a very nice little gamble. It was Gerta's day at home, she wouldn't be going to the Museum, and the chances were, of course, that she wouldn't have gone out before eleven. If she *had*——?

The sun was coming out again, the rails in Massachusetts Avenue were brimming and sparkling. It was spring, it was more than spring, it was almost summer. There would be track meets at the Stadium, boat races, perhaps a revival of the straw hat. In another month Gerta would go to Ogunquit, Greenwich Village would move to Provincetown, everywhere the human being would be creeping out of his cellar or attic to lie naked on a beach and admire the beauty of his body, as if it were something of transcendental importance. Young ladies would be photographed on headlands doing ridiculous dances with wisps of scarf. In secret places in the Maine woods, in half darkened bedrooms of seaside boardinghouses, in the warm hollows of Cape Cod sand dunes, lovers would once more be renewing the flesh at the expense of the spirit, as certain that in this way they had discovered God as that a year hence they would be embracing the same partner. . . . The wrens go to it, and the small gilded fly.

He looked through the wide window of the Merle as he passed, saw the Findens sitting at the table at the front. He had always thought they might be lonely, had thought of asking them to come and see him, to come and have coffee or a drink. Opening the screen door, he leaned in and said:

—I've meant for a long time to ask whether you'd come in and have coffee with me some evening, or a drink—if you're not doing anything special tomorrow night would you care to drop in?

They were visibly surprised, Finden half got up from his chair holding a paper napkin, Mrs. Finden, over a glass of orange-juice, was looking at him very peculiarly, her mouth open, her gray eyes narrowed: as if she were looking at some one whom she thought very queer. Finden said:

—Why, we'd like to very much, I think!

—Thank you, Mr. Ammen, we'd like to!

It was not entirely satisfactory, but he hugged it, just the same, he thought of it with grim pleasure as he ascended in the creaking elevator and walked lightly along the corridor. The empty metal wastebaskets stood at the doors, Jack had already done his morning round, he entered his apartment and flung his hat violently on to the sofa, under the seashell on the window sill. The room seemed very quiet. Dropping his raincoat on the floor, he went into the kitchenette, looked down at the gas-stove, returned to the sitting room to make sure that the window was open, and to pick up the little green book from the table. Then he went back to the kitchenette, closed the door behind him, turned on all four taps of the stove, and sat down at the table with the book.

The gas behind him made a steady *sh-h-h-h-h-h*, *sh-h-h-h-h-h*, soft and insistent, and opening the book he started reading—(all the while conscious of the little watch ticking on his wrist, the tiny hand creeping slowly towards eleven)—the page at which he had left off.

"*This reaction is still subjective. When a child stiffens and draws away, when it screams with pure temper, it takes no note of that from which it recoils. It has no objective consciousness of that from which it reacts, the mother principally. It is like a swimmer endlessly kicking the water away behind him, with strong legs vividly active from the spinal ganglia. Like a man in a boat pushing off from the shore, it merely thrusts away, in order to ride free, ever more free. It is a purely subjective motion—*"

Like a man in a boat pushing off from the shore.

He raised his eyes, looked through the kitchen window, saw the immense Greek coping of the library, the huge words cut in granite, Harry Elkins Widener Library, then beyond it the slate roof of Boylston Hall, and farther still the gray wooden steeple of the Unitarian Church. There was a faint smell of coffee coming from the professor's apartment, it mixed oddly with the not unpleasant smell of the gas, he was aware that he was hungry.

But also he was sleepy, it would be very easy to fall asleep. By this time, Jones would have got back to the shabby little house in Reservoir Street—the grave at Mount Auburn would have been filled—the khaki-clad messenger was sitting in a subway train on his way to Beacon Hill. And Gerta—would she be there? would she come? was she standing there at her open window, with an apple in her hand, looking down over the roofs to the morning sunlight flashing on the Charles River Basin? wearing the white Russian blouse?

Half past nine. The professor's clock sent its soft *tyang* through the walls. He closed his eyes.

A Heart for the Gods of Mexico

⟪ I

"Ommernous, that's what it is, ommernous, every bit of it is ommernous."

Six o'clock. . . . The tall man with the Jewish nose, and lean as he was
tall, and with clothes that were too large for him, avoided looking at his
reflection in the glassy water of the Frog Pond—which he was circling for
the fourth time in Boston Common—but thought of it just the same, and,
as always, with cynical amusement. He enjoyed walking as close as possible
to the pond's edge, along the familiar granite curbing, and enjoyed the
notion of his image there, stalking angularly among budding boughs against
a twilight May sky. Blomberg the crane, he thought. Blomberg the derrick
—Blom the steam shovel.

"Ommernous," he muttered again (thinking at the same time how
characteristic it was of Key to be late); "need money, always need money,
and as soon as they need money I'm supposed to find it; what's the good of
being a Jew if you can't find money! And even to bargaining with a ticket
agent, by God, and him with the name of Albumblatt. . . ."

He smiled grimly, and looked up at the fading sky over the spire of the
Arlington Street Church, and the empty roof garden of the Ritz—bare
ruined choirs, where late the sweet birds sang—and the image of the snow,
but recently melted on the roof, and the awnings and box trees which would
soon replace it, came to him as one thing. Where are the snows of yester-
year? and if winter comes, can spring be far behind? He turned once more
towards the tall soldiers' monument, rounding the toe end of the little
granite-paved pond, and there before him was Key, coming towards him
cockily on his short legs, the derby hat set crookedly like a tiny peanut on
the tiny head, the dark glasses looking blind above the already smiling
mouth.

"So you want some money, and is *that* a surprise."

"It's not for me. Now look here, Key——"

"You're wasting your time. Why in hell don't you go to work? I mean,
at a job that *pays* you something. . . ."

They turned and walked slowly towards Charles Street, went off the

path on to the grass, moved slowly side by side down the slight slope in
the twilight. Blomberg smiled at the amusing and cynical little face which
leered up at him with affectionate hardness from under the hat's brim,
and took Key's arm. He quickened his pace.

"Now listen, Key. What I said on the phone is straight: it's not merely
an emergency, it's a matter of life and death."

"Where have I heard those words before?"

"Yeah. She wants to take him away on the one o'clock train tomorrow
—*tomorrow*—and me too. To Mexico. *Mexico*, of all places! It costs money.
What can I save out of my twenty-five bucks a week? I've got a little over
a hundred, laid up against the rainy day and the dentist. And Noni's got
maybe four hundred and fifty."

"And the boy friend, I suppose, won't put up a nickel!"

"Don't be nasty. I like Gil, I admire Gil, you've got to hand it to him,
he's an idealist, a real dyed-in-the-wool Puritan, self-sacrificing, honest,
everything. Jesus, that man makes me mad! He gives everything away, every
cent. Right now, God damn it, he's probably sitting up there in Joy Street
thinking up novel ways of giving away what little money he has left, as if it
wasn't enough that he gives all his *time* for nothing to the Legal Aid
Society! God. . . ."

They veered by tacit agreement to the left, towards the gravel expanse
of the baseball field in the Boylston Street corner of the Common, now
beginning to look gray in the vanishing light of evening. The sweet sound
of a batted ball, tingling and round and willowy, floated up to them, and
they turned their eyes towards the gray-flanneled figures which moved there
in the dusk. Even as they watched, one of the players, with arms raised as
in some ritual, and small white face lifted to the sky, performed an absurd
little crablike balance dance under the heaven-descending ball, until the
sharply lowered elbows, and the barely heard *clop*, showed that it had been
caught. Beyond the field, lights were beginning to come out in the Boylston
Street shops.

"Well, but why do you come to *me*? I don't even know them."

"I come to you, because you've got a heart of gold."

"No kidding?"

"No kidding."

"Heh, heh, it is to laugh!"

"No."

Blomberg frowned a little, looking down at their feet, their four feet
moving synchronously on the spring grass, and thought the beginning was
not too auspicious. But it was as well to avoid undue pressure at the outset,
even though his own sense of the shortness of time was becoming so stifling.
And especially with Key, who really enjoyed the preliminaries of maneuver-
ing: the trout playing the angler. He said, a shade too nervously, half
smiling:

"It really ought to interest you. It's absolutely the damndest situation
I ever heard of, much less got myself involved in! It's a wonder."

Key looked up at him speculatively, his face sobered, his guard for the
moment relaxed.

"You've known Noni for a long time—but what about this Gil? I never heard much about Gil before, did I?"

"She wants to marry him."

Blomberg pretended not to notice the sharp look which Key gave him on this. His face stiffened, impervious to scrutiny. Key said:

"I thought she was married already. But of course nowadays——"

"She is. That's the point. You see——"

"God, look at the traffic. Let's go down through the subway to the Little Building. And then, of course, we'll be in the alert position for a quick one at the Nip. Would you like a quick one?"

"Does a camel?"

Emerging from the Tremont Street entrance, by the post office branch, they paused a moment on the curb to survey the slowing traffic between themselves and the gay windows of the Nip, with its hospitably open door, then walked swiftly across, to an accompaniment of squealing and squawking brakes.

"Not too far back," said Key. "I don't like the odor of sanctity at the back! Dry martinis?"

"Two dry martinis."

Key swiveled towards him on the stool, his hands in his side pockets; looked up at him smiling, his head tilted to one side. His attitude was one of amused expectancy.

"Well, go on, tell me about the boy friend. Where does *he* come from at this late day? Kind of a dark horse, I'd call it!"

"Oh, no. Gil has always been around—he's the old faithful. They've known each other since the year one; I guess they played marbles together in the Public Gardens, while their nurses knitted, at the age of two. And then he wanted to marry her, but she wouldn't and married Giddings instead—"

"Giddings?"

"Here's mud in your eye. Yeah. Giddings. A first-class A-number-one bastard; full of charm, but without an honest bone in his body. He began as a society bond salesman, one of those pretty pink college boys that they have by the hundred at all the best brokerages, with the social register written all over them, and ended by being something damned like a crook. Ran a little private investment pool of his own, and got a lot of Noni's money into it, and a lot of other people's as well, and then slipped out from under when it went flooey. And of course it was all very nicely hushed up, and he just went gracefully out West, where, as far as anyone knows, he still is."

"Ah. One of those. And how long has *this* been?"

"Ten years."

"And being a nice Boston gal she didn't do anything about divorcing him, of course. Of course not! As you were saying."

"No. She didn't want to remarry—why should she? She was fond of Gil, but not enough—you see—"

"Christ, there's that goddamned tune, what is it, the Chapel in the Moonlight—I wish they'd lay off it."

They turned their heads towards the machine at the back, the little glass coffin full of records, listened to the gross throbbing of the music—like a bad heart, thought Blomberg, and winced—then turned back again to their drinks.

"But she was always sorry for him. You see, he had had a bad time of it. Made what Boston called a mismarriage."

"You mean to say he's got a wife?"

"No. No. She's dead. It really *was* a sad business, at that. He never would tell anyone about it, but from what one can gather she got some sort of hatred or dislike of him right after the marriage; maybe she fell in love with someone else—damned beautiful, too; I've seen photos of her. Which raised hell with him. Noni says he nearly went crazy. Nice to him in society, you know, when they went out together, but wouldn't have anything to do with him at home. And always going away, somewhere or other."

"Ahem. A marriage in name only. So what?"

"So of course he enlisted as a private when the war broke out, hoping to get himself honorably killed with a bullet in his eye or something; and then, by God, what do you think she did?"

"See if you can surprise me, Blom—and let's put this down and go an' get a clam. Or an oyster."

"Yeah, sure, Key, but listen! . . ."

They lifted their glasses simultaneously; Key was again smiling a little, but with obvious sympathy. It began to look hopeful. Just the same, you never could tell with Key, he could be as stubborn as a mule, and he hated to admit his feelings. Better soft-pedal the sobstuff, and take it easy.

They slid off their stools, and turned to the left as they went out. Key had a toothpick in his mouth, and the jaunty angle at which it wagged was amusingly in character—like, in fact, everything he did. As for instance, his habit of looking over the tops of his dark glasses, the blue eyes suddenly very bright and mischievous. Like minnows. And of course the very quaint hat. The neat small derby, on the neat small head, was perfect, like something out of a comic strip.

At the oyster house they were in luck: the two first seats at the bar were vacant.

"What a break!" said Key. "And, by God, there are Fairhavens, too."

"Baby! and big enough to go skating on. Two half dozens?"

"This place gets me. What with all them fee-rocious red lobsters about, and that bowl of tomalley, and old George here opening oysters as easy as winking—sometimes I just can't bear it."

"There's something about marine life, and the fruits of the sea—it must be an atavism. When you were a tadpole and I was a fish."

"Yeah. But now, go on and surprise me. With what Mrs. Gil did."

"Well, it seems that Mrs. Gil, when she saw Gil off for the front——"

"What was the old song? He left her to go to the front!"

"Never mind, Key. It seems she repented of what she had done, and how she had treated him; maybe she was tired of her lover, if in fact she had ever *had* one—my own theory about it was, she was just one of them queer psychological 'cases,' with a funny kink or squeam or something—and anyway, whatever it was, she told him before he went that if he got back alive she would reward him by having a child. See?"

"You could knock me down with a lily!"

"Yes. Isn't it nice? He *came* back; and she *kept* her word; and she *had* a child. And it killed her. And the child died too. . . . A very handsome little specimen of poetic injustice; one of those magnificently generous gestures of the oversoul or destiny or the universal time machine that make so much sense that you want to turn handsprings of joy. For six months Gil wouldn't even go outdoors: it was Noni that saved him."

"I take it this was some time ago."

"Oh, sure! Years."

"Okay. But it doesn't quite explain, does it, why she should up and want to marry him now. You can be sorry for someone, but dammit, Blom, you ain't got to marry them, have you? Oh, look what George has done! And shall we say, fair haven?"

He looked down at the noble dish of oysters, beaming.

"Fair haven! You know, that's funny—she used to go there, or near there, in the summer, when she was a kid. . . . Nonquitt. . . . I went there once myself, and you never saw such wild roses in your life. . . . Gosh, aren't these good!"

"Don't talk—eat!"

They ate the oysters in silence; sat still for a moment, as for the completion of a ritual; then Key paid at the desk (as usual) and they went out. Without a word they crossed Tremont Street, and proceeded slowly to the foot of the marble stairs, in the middle of the next block, before Blomberg said:

"I take it we are once again going up these stairs to the Greeks?"

"It kind of looks like it, doesn't it? Two minds with but a single thought. . . ."

In a front booth, from which they looked out at the fantastic lamplit rear walls—smooth and sinister as precipices—of the Metropolitan Theater —a view which unaccountably always made Blomberg think of Hamlet and Elsinore—they studied the pale blue mimeograph of the menu.

"I think while we're *thinking*, Henry, we'll have a couple of those nice big dry martinis. And then we can think even better."

"Yes, Mr. Key."

"Ha! I see lamb with okra, Blom. And I see stuffed vine leaves. And I see chicken livers en brochette! My God, it's awful! What are you going to have?"

"Lamb with okra, every time. That little hexagonal vegetable is what I don't like nothing else except."

"Lamb brochette for me; I like the taste of the hickory wood."

"Yes, the hickory wood."

"Hang your clothes on a hickory limb! But you see, what I don't get in all this, Blom, is why the rush to Mexico; why the hurry to marry a man she never wanted to marry before, and doesn't love anyway; and above all why all the *panic* about it, when there's so little cash that it's got to be borrowed. Don't think I'm being suspicious, because I am!"

He lit a cigarette, snapped the small silver lighter shut with a very

competent little thumb, blew smartly on the lighted cigarette tip to make
it glow, then removed the dark spectacles and placed them on the linen
tablecloth. The question, in the tired blue eyes, was candid but friendly.
. . . And this, Blomberg, thought, was the moment at which to go slow;
the necessity must now come almost as if reluctantly from the circumstances of the situation; it must be in a sense as if he himself were only
now making up his mind. And where to begin? At what obscure corner?
Northeast or southwest? And with Noni, or Gil, or himself? Not himself,
certainly, for it was apparent that Key was already sufficiently suspicious of
his own connections with the affair. He stared out of the window at the
mysterious blue-red lamplit brick of the walls of Elsinore, whistling softly
a little ghost tune while he did so as if to gain time. Then he said gravely,
and at once aware of the power of his dark face and conscious eyes on the
quick receptivity of Key's:

"She's got to die."

"What do you mean?"

"She's got to die. The doctors have given her six months—maybe a year
at most—and maybe much less."

"No! . . . You don't mean it."

"Yes. Heart. Something wrong about the heart. She won't tell me the
details—won't talk about it at all. Except for the main fact. She got the
final confirmation day before yesterday, and called me up, and I went
down to the Hull Street house—you know, she lives in a little wooden
house down there in the slum by Copp's Hill burying ground—and, my
God, Key, I can tell you I never want to go through such a night in my
life again."

He stopped abruptly, to regain control of his voice, which had begun
to sound a little queer—how odd, he thought, to find that one's voice *does*
tremble at such moments—and then resumed, speaking very slowly, very
solemnly.

"All night, mind you, watching a woman, an ineffably lovely woman,
and a wonderfully intelligent one, suddenly at battle with the idea of death.
And conquering it, by God, Key. She didn't rave—she didn't cry, though
I've seen her cry, many times—she just became an embodied question.
Embodied suffering. I'll never forget the expression of her face as long as
I live. It was as if she were looking *around* me all the time, looking past
me, trying to get through to something on the other side, or even *seeing*
something there. It was curiously childlike—a persistent, baffled, hurt, un-
comprehending, but perpetually *questioning* stare, as if I had become for
her the only living evidence of a world of evil, or mystery, which she
couldn't accept. Do you see what I mean?"

"Jesus!"

"Yes. The incarnated 'Why?' of all tragedy, all human misery. All night
she was that. And facing, of course, as *if in me*, that was the awful part of
it, the fact that there was no answer. *I* was the pitiless and unanswering
void; the whirlwind; the trap; the six-foot pine box; the gallows; the run-
over child. No arguing about it, mind you—not much talk; she would sit
perfectly still, and look at me for half an hour, then suddenly get up and
walk out into the little garden at the back and stand there, staring up at the

catalpa tree. We would just stand there for a while, looking up at the tree and the sky—my God it was extraordinary—I never *saw* the sky or a tree before—the sky was rushing away above us at a million miles a second, rushing away to annihilation; the tree was dying before our eyes, like one of those quick-motion movies when it all shrivels up like melting tinsel—and she was holding them there together, holding them to herself, by an effort of will which I could *feel* going out to them. Living out into the void with all her senses; that's what she was doing; and making me do it with her. . . ."

Key lifted his cocktail glass, turned it so that the olive stirred. He said quickly:

"Blom, have a drink. How!"

"How! That helps."

"And here's Henry. One lamb brochette, Henry, and one lamb with okras. And some beers. And I guess a little rice, just for *fun!*"

"Yes, Mister Key. The lamb is *very good* tonight."

"Fine! . . . Now go on, Blom."

Blomberg looked down at his half-emptied glass, saw nothing, resumed:

"Yeah. You can imagine what it was like. I'd never *seen* anyone dying before—and that's of course what she was doing. Dying! Dying with her eyes wide open, *looking* at death. It's changed my feeling about life, Key, believe it or not—God knows I've sneered often enough at the messy and muddled and horrible business that life for the most part seems to be—so much of it so dirty and ignoble—but here was Noni all by herself, and with no one to give her a cue, setting such an example of courage as I shall never forget. And so simply. No bravura about it, no melodramatics—just herself."

Key lifted his glasses from the table, held the bridge pinched between finger and thumb, his head a little on one side.

"You like her a lot, don't you?" he said. "I'm damned sorry."

"I've always liked her. Yes."

"I suppose there's no mistake, possibly?"

"Oh no. Not a chance."

"I see."

There was a pause; they finished their cocktails, and presently Henry brought the two glasses of beer. Blomberg stared out at the walls of Elsinore, his eyes fixed and unseeing. What he was seeing, once more, was the catalpa tree in starlight, the stars showing frostily through the bare branches, and Noni's white face uplifted beneath it, so intense, so still. He could see her there; he could see her leaning against the doorjamb, with her hands tightly clasped behind her; he could see her suddenly turning to go back into the little basement sitting room. And he could hear her saying quietly, as she learned slightly forward towards him from the low chair: "It seems so ridiculously *random*, Blom—it's *that* that's so puzzling!"—for all the world as if the problem were a purely metaphysical one, and herself the person in the world least involved. . . .

Key was saying:

"Well, I'm damned sorry. But I *still* don't see where Mexico comes in —it makes less sense than ever. You'd think, with a bad heart, and the chance of cashing in any second, the sensible thing was to stay where she is and take it easy. What's the idea?"

He gave a little half smile, slightly cocky, as if to say, "Let's keep it light, for God's sake, if we can!" and put on his glasses. The effect was in a sense as if he had disappeared.

"Ah," said Blomberg, slowly, "that's the most interesting part of it. Mind you, when I talked with her, she'd only known the full facts for a few hours—she saw the doctor at four; she saw me at eight. But in that time, in that small interval, when most people would have been simply blind with self-pity, or in a state of complete collapse, she had made her plans; discussed it with her lawyer; called up Gil to tell him about it, and had him to the house for half an hour; called up me; and several other people as well, who she hoped might help out with the money problem. She had decided at once, you see, that she owed it to Gil, after holding him off all these years, to get a divorce, and marry him—she wanted to make it up to him, all that lost life, she wanted to *give* him something—in fact the best thing she had: herself."

Key simply stared.

"But, good God, Blom, it's insane!"

"Yeah. I thought so too. I said so. I still think so and say so; and I've done every conceivable thing I could to prevent it. Not an atom of use, Key; she won't argue with me; she just stands there and tells me. You see, the idea is this. A Mexican divorce, for what it's worth, apparently is much quicker than any other, and cheaper. Twice as quick as Reno, and twice as cheap, and just as good. But the quickness is the main point. She's not only counting the days—she's counting the hours. She wants to give Gil as much time as she can. And so, God help us, off we go, the three of us, to Mexico City. . . ."

"Ah, here's the food."

"Good. Let's eat. The little hexagonal okras, by gum!"

"Somehow, I always feel like whinnying, when I see Henry bringing food—guess I must have been a horse in a previous incarnation. And this here beer, Henry, is very nice, only there ain't enough *of* it. Two more, please. . . ."

"Sure, certainly, Mr. Key!"

"It's crazy. And do you mean to sit there and tell me you'll *go?* And that Gil will go? My God, I'd have thought *Gil*, at any rate, if he's in love with her——"

Blomberg lifted a long finger, held it before him, glared.

"Yeah! But you don't know *this*, my dear Key: *Gil*, believe it or not, *will not know a thing about it*. Not a thing. She won't tell him, and she won't let *me* tell him. She puts it simply that for a year or more—and it's partly true—she's been planning to take a trip like this, somewhere to the south, and that now the doc's told her she needs a change—"

Key was dumbfounded.

"Gil won't know she's going to *marry* him?"

"Oh, sure, that—of course. The divorce and marriage. But the *reason* for it, just now, and in all this rush!"

"*I* see; she'll marry him and then drop dead on the wedding night!

That's my idea of a swell break for Mister Gil, if anyone was to ride upstairs on a policeman's horse and ask me! Yeah. Swell. Has she thought of that?"

"Don't be a fool—of course she has! And sure it's crazy—don't I know it? It might be *unspeakably* cruel to Gil—Christ, when you think of what happened to him in his *first* marriage, it's everything you can say about it. I wanted to yell it at her—I almost did. I even wanted to beat her. But she won't budge. She says she knows the risk, and will run it, and that Gil's damned well got to run it, too."

"That's nice."

"Yes. . . ."

They ate in silence. The little Italian newsboy came by as usual with his *Evening Records,* and Key bought one; the noisy party of undergraduates and girls at the long table got up, pushing back their chairs. They were all a little tight, and they looked cheap. Blomberg had noticed that the German girl at the end of the table, the one with the dog—its lead was fastened to her chair—and the young fellow who sat next to her, the only sensitive-looking face in the crowd, hadn't spoken more than two words to each other in all this time. Shy? Or a quarrel? He glanced away from them, and briefly out over Stuart Street, thinking idly, even in this fleeting connection, of the wonderful multiplicity of life, its inexhaustible richness. Then he said, looking hard at Key:

"So now you see. What I said, that it's an emergency. And the most extraordinary situation in which I ever got myself inadvertently involved. It's an emergency, Key, get *that* through your mulish head. And it's got to be gone through with. As soon as I realized that, I went to work. I've been to see everyone I know in Boston, that might be the slightest use, or telephoned to them, and I haven't found a red cent. Not a cent. Even if we go in day coaches—which Noni insists on, the idiot—we'll need another hundred bucks, at the very least. And Noni ought not to do it. She ought to go in a Pullman. Three and a half days—sitting up in those god-damned chairs—"

He shook his head.

"So I suppose you expect *me* to put up the hundred bucks."

"Yeah."

"Try and get it!"

"Once we get down there it won't be so bad. It seems Gil's got a friend, or friends, in Cuernavaca who will put us up."

"What I don't see," and Key put his head on one side, and half closed his eyes, "is why *you've* got to go. Or what the hell Gil thinks you're going for, if he doesn't know the situation. Kind of a fifth wheel, aren't you? Which will take a lot of explaining. Unless, of course, this Gil is the kind of guy who *likes* an extra man on his honeymoon!"

"Don't make me moan, Key! Noni's *like* that, that's all. And I know it, and Gil knows it. Though of course Gil——"

"—doesn't know a thing about it, the poor fish!"

"If only Noni hadn't made me swear, I'd tell him."

"I think you ought to. I don't think he ought to be allowed to go, if he isn't told. No, sir."

"No, Key, it can't be done."

"Well, then, how *are* you going to explain your presence, may I ask?"

Blomberg hesitated.

"That's up to Noni. She can say I'm a sort of chaperon—and there's something *in* that, too—or that she's suggested the trip a long time ago, and didn't want to break her promise—or simply that I helped to raise the cash. Or a little of all of it. It might get by. I think it will. Gil, damn his funny puritan little soul—my God, Key, my blood boils when I think of him, not lifting a finger, while Noni and I sweat blood to make the whole thing possible—Gil is queer. Sometimes I don't think he's got any feelings at all. One of those cold-roast dry-cleaned Bostonians you read about in the books, who may be a roaring volcano within, but certainly never shows it. I suppose he's been hurt so much that he waits a long time before he makes a move; so Noni says, anyway, and she may be right."

Key, leaning forward on the table with his elbows, sat with lowered eyes. What was he thinking? The small face was composed and unreadable. Certainly the quick reference to the hundred dollars had come in rather too soon, and not too happily—and Key's laconic "try and get it" hadn't sounded too promising. But that he was interested and curious, even if incredulous and disapproving, was perhaps evident; there were even traces of sympathy. But what train would he be taking for Concord from the North Station? And how much time was left? Better not raise the point, of course. He said, feeling a little false:

"Yeah. I'm the money-raiser. They always pick a Jew when they want money! As I was saying to myself just before I met you . . ."

"And incidentally, what happens to your job, while all this goes on! Not to mention Gil's. It seems to me your gal Noni expects quite a lot."

"Easy. I'm only on piecework now, and I can always pick it up, any time. And Gil doesn't get paid, anyway, not for his work with the Legal Aid; he volunteers. He's got a little income; I don't know how much. I could even take some reading *down* there with me—not that I'd get much done."

"What does she look like?"

"Noni?"

"Yeah."

"Noni. . . ."

He spoke the name as if in a sort of bemused, almost incredulous, evocation; then continued:

"Not pretty, Key—too irregular a face for that—cheekbones too high—but sometimes beautiful as all get-out. Medium height to smallish—slender; —very fair skin, *very* white hands. A *Norse* look about her; very blonde; eyes like the fringed gentian, if *that* means anything to you—bluest things you ever saw. But as a matter of fact you don't know quite *what* she looks like, somehow, because what you always notice in her face is the movement, the light. The naughtiness, and the courage. She laughs simply delightfully; and when she does, she always turns her face just a little, just a *little* away from you, but keeps her eyes towards you—very shy and very bright. She *is* shy. But the shyness gives her a lovely abruptness and boldness. You feel that she's *got* to see and tell the truth, or her feelings, or whatever—and

she does. My God, what honesty! I've often thought, you know, that she's
the *nakedest* soul I've ever met. . . ."

"Good Lord, Blom!"

"What do you mean!"

"I'm beginning to understand. I think I'm beginning to understand."

"I only wish you did, Key. She's the sort of woman you'd do *anything*
for. And I don't know—it's funny. That stuffy little house of hers has been
like a home to me—and I guess it's been that for a good many others. It's
alive. It glows. It's got a heart. Everything in her life has gone into it, onto
the walls—it's all Noni, all the way from tomboy and pigtails, and Nonquitt in the summer, and dances and orchids at the Somerset, and the
disaster with Giddings, down to the secretarial work, and the social service,
and the music, and now the broken heart. She plays the piano very badly,
but more movingly than anyone else I ever heard, bar none. Always Bach,
nothing but Bach. Gil can play rings around her—Gil could have been a
professional if he'd wanted to—but it doesn't mean a thing by comparison.
You ought to see her at a concert—her face opens like a flower—she clasps
her hands flatly together, and leans her face sideways on them, and goes a
million miles away. I just sit and look at her, it's as good as the music.
Better! How do some people do that—doesn't seem quite fair, Key, does it,
that some people have that astonishing integrity of living or loving, or
seeing and feeling—*really* love and feel—while the rest of us poor guys have
to wait and be *told* when to love. Not Noni. She goes to it like the bee
to the flower, absolutely as if she and it were the same thing. I've stood
outside the house in the dark, when she didn't know I was there, and listened to her playing, without lights—and I can honestly say that it was
about as near the pinnacle of happiness as I could get. . . . A pity you
never would come down there, Key—you and your notions."

"Yeah. Me and my notions. What about yours."

"What."

"It's all becoming blindingly clear, like a sunrise in a melodrama in the
best Woolworth style, complete with a noble sacrifice. You know, you
almost make me sick."

"Speak."

"So you're willing to do all this, at the drop of a hat, and on a shoe-
string—practically give up your job, spend all your savings, run yourself
ragged to raise money, work your head off and generally worry yourself to
death, and all to provide a goody-goody little husband for the gal you're in
love with!"

Off came the dark glasses: Key's blue eyes were laughing. Blomberg felt
his own smile expand and contract, forced into his staring eyes the expression he willed, a far and shrewd foresight, a contemplative wisdom superior
to the absurd antics of time. This could be turned to advantage. It was
nearly eight o'clock, Key would now move towards the North Station,
something must be done, or decided, soon. He must call up Gil, call up
Noni, get, or not get, the tickets from Mr. Albumblatt at the South Station
—he had promised the little man that he would be back before ten—and
after that, packing, or helping Noni to pack. Time with its hundred hands,
Time with its thousand mouths! The vision of a train came sharply, too, be-

fore him—all trains that he had ever seen or known; the melancholy, slow *ylang-ylang, ylang-ylang,* of the little switch engine in the frost-bound train-yard; the profound cries of freight trains climbing dark defiles of mountains at midnight; rows of phantom lights sweeping across a lonely station-front. And the transcontinental track, the curved parallel rails embracing the three-thousand-mile-long curve of the submissive and infinitely various earth, from night into day, into night again—this, too, he saw, deep in Key's eyes. And Noni, solitary as a bird, on the great circle to Mexico. . . . He said, as if he were only formulating these very things:

"Not in love with her, Key, no."

"Yes."

"Not in love with her, no. I love her, yes—I'm not *in* love with her, it's been for years. Do you love sunsets and sunrises? Or your own left hand?"

"You don't convince me."

"You don't listen."

"I'm listening."

Their voices had insensibly softened, and it was on a quieter note still that Blomberg went on.

"It's been for years, and always just like that; just like this—even, and calm, and leisurely, and serene, on both sides. There never was anything else, not a trace. I never wanted to make love to her, and she never made the slightest sign that she wanted to be made love to. In a way, it was really too good and too deep for that—don't smile, such things do happen. I love her, I think in a sense she loves me, just as I think she loves Gil. But she has very odd and individual, and perhaps old-fashioned, views about sex—she gave me a lecture once, when I was a little tight and tried to kiss her, and it was one of the most moving things I ever heard. I wish I could remember it. It was like being talked to by Emily Dickinson, or the sunny slope of a New England pasture in spring. Something about the soul's election, the soul's eligibility—said very quietly, but with intense convic-tion, said very shyly, too, as if it were something infinitely precious to her. As I'm sure it was."

"You interest me strangely."

"Yes. For the whole doctrine of sex as pleasure, and promiscuity as a kind of loving kindness to all—you know, the preachings of the shabby little bedroom philosophers of Greenwich Village and Beacon Hill, who under the guise of brotherly love turn all their womenfolk into prostitutes—she has nothing but contempt. Not even contempt. It just doesn't mean anything to her. It just seems to her a little dirty. But Noni *loves.* Everyone who knows her knows that, and everyone who knows her loves her. I'm damned if I know what it is, Key. I suppose sex must play a part in it, but if so it's so deep and anonymous as to become in effect spiritual. You don't have to believe me, but it's true."

"Okay, just for fun I'll believe you, Blom! And what about some coffee."

"Turkish coffee medium."

"Make it two, Henry. And bring me the bill."

"Yes, sir; certainly, Mr. Key."

"And to go back to what you said, about my being a fifth wheel, and raising the question of my going with them at all—and the effect on Gil—

well, that's the answer. Noni needs me. Noni loves us both, and knows that we both love her, in our very different ways, and what she *needs* right now is love. She wants to take all—I was going to say, all she loves—with her—for she's going off to die. What could be more natural? Do *pretend* to try to understand it, Key—it scares me and horrifies me, the whole thing, I can't tell you how much, but all the same I think it's wonderful, it's like the creation of a work of art, a piece of superb music. What can I do but say yes, and try to do everything I can to help her?"

"Work of art! . . . If it's a work of art, I'm a horse thief. And you're a sucker!"

"No, it's the most heroic thing I ever encountered. And the noblest. She's taking this pitiful little tag-end of her life, this handful of days with already a shadow across them, and making of them, and of us—herself and Gil and me—a farewell symphony; like that one of Haydn's, which you probably don't know——"

"—keep the bouquets——"

"—where, as the orchestration thins, towards the end, the different sections of the orchestra rise, as soon as they finish their parts, and go quietly out, and the lights in the hall are extinguished one by one, to the last note and the last light. Just like that. I'm being *used* like Gil, in the making of a piece of music; I'm being *used*; and if nothing else ever happens to me again in all my life, this will have been enough to justify it, and to give it dignity. . . . To change the subject, Key, I've got some first editions I could sell you."

"First editions! What would I do with them?"

"Or you could have them as security on a loan."

"No, Blom, I don't want no first editions; I want a train to Concord. What about taking the subway down, and stopping for a nightcap at the Manger."

"Yeah, sure. But I can warn you, Key, I'm going to curse your conscience like the very *devil!* You wait and see."

"Henry, you can keep the change out of that—if they'll give it to you. And good night."

"Good night, Mr. Key, and thank you, sir. Good night! Good night."

Key lit a cigarette as he rose, Blomberg took out his pipe and held the bowl of it in his hand, reflecting that he would not have time to light it until they got to the North Station. Eight-twenty. As they descended the marble stairs, the sound of time once more came around him, oppressive and rich and nostalgic, and again as if in the form of the train itself, the train to Mexico. They would be taking a train. This time tomorrow, where in God's name would they be? In a strange world, on their way to a strange world, on their way to the unknown. And Noni, above all——! He closed his eyes to that notion, the notion of *that* terminus, and watched Key precede him into the street and the mild May evening. Was it going to be all right? He smiled grimly, looking down at the funny little man, and wondered. "The odds are even," he muttered to himself, "the odds are even, the odds are about even." He might give twenty-five, he might give fifty— he might give nothing at all. But the fact that he had suggested the drink at the North Station—and something in the persistence of his *attention,* his

dwelling, even though it was in itself somewhat hostile, on the circumstances of the situation, was just possibly indicative of a latent sympathy
and desire to help. If he didn't—but the idea was unthinkable, it was to
plunge at once into chaos again, a swarm of irreconcilables and accidentals
and impossibles, exactly like the senseless hurry and confusion of Washington Street, which they were crossing towards the subway station. There
was no one left to turn to now; no one. Except possibly Edes at the office.
But no.

In the crowded subway train, they stood close to the door, Key reading
his paper, which he held before him with one hand, the other reaching up
for a handhold. His absorption was complete: it was as if he had already
forgotten the whole thing, wiped the slate clean. Nothing—not even life
and death—could be allowed to come between Key and the stock market.
For a moment, Blomberg felt himself becoming angry and bitter, it distressed and shamed him to be thus helpless and at the mercy of another,
and so appallingly dependent, moreover: particularly as in the very moment
of his self-indulgence he could so sharply visualize, in advance, his telephone call to Noni, and her terrible disappointment. "Hello, Noni—it's
no good." "Oh no, Blom; no, oh no!" "Yes, Noni, it's no good. It's absolutely no good; I can't raise a single solitary cent more. We'll have to put
it off. We'll have to wait. We've got to think of something else . . ." "But
Blom, we *can't* wait, we *can't*, you *know* we can't, we've got to go
now! . . ." And then the dreadful waiting silence, in which they would
both listen, as it were, for the sound of comfort, relief, or some impossible
reprieve, some sudden and wonderful Christmas tree of an idea which
would make everything as simple as daylight. But in vain. They would
know that it was in vain. Mexico, that fabulous land, that land of savage
ghosts and bloodstained altars, began to swirl and vanish like smoke, undulated once more away from them, foundered like a red cloud. And with
it, Noni's dream.

The train had climbed up out of the subway into the bright light of
Canal Street, swaying lightly, the noise died behind them, now they were
stopping. Key folded his paper, looked up with amused and primmed
mouth. He said:

"Where were you."

"I was in Mexico already. And enjoying every minute of it."

He said it bitterly, as they went out on to the elevated platform, and
until they had descended the wooden stairs and emerged into the street,
Key made no answer. They walked, side by side, toward the far corner of
the station front, past the drugstore, the florist, the shoe shop.

"I've got fifteen minutes," Key said, "just time for a nice little nightcap. Not that I won't have to have another when I get to Concord. Gosh,
when I think of Dooley and that car——"

He smirked, and chuckled, remembering; they turned sharp right and
entered the horseshoe-shaped bar. As they swung themselves on to the
stools, the little white-mustached bartender nodded smiling, and said:

"Whisky?"

"Two!"

The hand was already on the bottle; the glasses were already on the mahogany. Key sipped water through the sparkling cracked ice, then neatly tipped into it the bright jigger of liquor. He said:

"And when do you think you'll get back?"

"Don't know. That's one of the catches. Nobody here knows exactly how long it takes. Might be two weeks, might be a month or more. It's wonderful, Key, how little anyone knows here about Mexico. Even the railway tickets, they don't know about—apparently nobody ever *dreamed* of going down by day coach, without a Pullman, before—I've had three different quotations on the cost, and chosen the cheapest: Mr. Albumblatt, at the South Station. Bargaining for railway tickets is a new one! Jew against Jew."

"Well, I wish you luck. And send me a postcard of the doings."

"Thanks for nothing."

"Keep the change."

"Which reminds me. They don't even know how often we've got to change. Or where. You'd think we were going to the South Pole, or an uncharted jungle! All we know is we've got to change at St. Louis, one o'clock the next day, and wait there four hours. After that, we seem to be in a desert. We'll be like the babes in the wood—none of us ever went west of the Hudson before. . . ."

Something, in the way he had spoken the last two sentences, sounded a shade too despairing; he hastened to correct the impression, by giving a little laugh, adding:

"But I suppose it will be kind of fun. I've always wanted to see my own country first! . . . Hadn't you better be moving, Key?"

"Yeah. I'd better be moving."

Key looked up sidelong at the clock, finished his drink, then with every appearance of leisure took out his wallet, opened it with an air of faint surprise, his eyebrows slightly raised, and extracted from it what looked like a folded check. The perforated edge! He proffered it between two fingers, and smiled cynically.

"You don't deserve it, Kid, but there's your hundred. Buy yourself some candy on the train! And if you could get some sense into the head of that crazy woman——"

He was already in easy motion towards the door which led from the bar into the hotel lobby.

"Thanks, Key."

"Forget it."

"I can't tell you what this will mean to Noni."

They passed through the lounge bar, entered the vast sonorous hall of the station. A truck passed with chattering bell. Key turned, putting out his hand.

"Good luck, Blom. I'm going to run. But I wish to God it was *you* she was marrying!"

They shook hands silently, then Key began to lope towards his platform, with a final sidelong grin, and wave of the arm, which were somehow almost derisive. In a moment, the absurd little figure was out of sight; and in another Blomberg was standing in an illuminated telephone booth, still smiling to himself while he dialed. Mexico came round him like a cloud of strange voices and faces, swarmed into and over him, he felt himself trembling a little; it was all beginning, despite everything, and despite his own profound incredulity, to be true. It was true! Fantastic, but true. Noni's voice, very light and bright, very warm and near, came over the telephone:

"Hello?"

"Noni! Blom speaking. Now be *calm*. Do you understand? *Calm*. Be nothing but *calm*, for I've got good news."

"I'm already calm, Blom. I knew you had."

"Hell, you mustn't take the wind out of my sails like that, you confounded woman, you! What fun do I get out of life?"

"Well, I can't help it, can I, if I know? What have you got."

"I've got, to be exact, one hundred, *one hundred*, bucks. Count them."

"Key gave it? Bless his heart."

"Key gave it, bless his heart!"

"That's lovely."

"It is, and I'm now on my way to the South Station to get the tickets from my dear friend Mr. Albumblatt. Did you hear? *Albumblatt*. Sounds like a piece of music by Bach! The latest quotation was about sixty-four, so I'd better take it. Now do you want me to come and help you pack? Or shut up the house, or anything? Or do you want to *see* me. And will *you* tell Gil, or shall I."

"Gil's here now."

"Oh!"

"He's downstairs."

"Oh! Then I suggest we meet at the train, South Station, or rather at the platform *entrance*—the entrance, mind you—at twelve-thirty. O.K.?"

"O.K. And listen, Blom——"

"Listening, Noni."

"This is important, Blom, dear——"

"Shoot."

"I said it before, you remember, but I'll say it again——"

"Speak, my lamb."

"We must keep the whole thing just as cheerful, and *normal*, as we can. There mustn't be the slightest sign—on either your part or mine—to make Gil uneasy. I think we can do that, don't you? As a matter of fact, it's going to be rather a lark!"

"Of course, Noni. Word of honor, and cross my heart, and hope I die. . . ."

Die: he bit his tongue. Damnation! But the clear silver of the reply came without hesitation, and with a little laugh:

"*Faux pas* number one!"

"Yeah, kick me."

"I guess that's all, then. You've got the tourist cards——"

"I have, and I'll have the tickets, and I'll have my little bag, and I'll try to pick up a guidebook."

"Bless you, Blom dear—so we're off to Clixl Claxl—and a new world!"

"A new world."

"Good night!"

"Good night."

He heard the click with which she had hung up the receiver, the little sound of cessation itself, and suddenly a feeling of anguish possessed him; a powerful cramp of pain, shutting about his heart, his vitals, his whole body. It was with just so slight a gesture, at last, that she would finally have taken her leave of them, hung up her receiver on the world. The wire was dead, he listened in vain, then he hung up his own receiver and strode forth into the station again. He smiled grimly, and whistled a ghost of a Bach tune, and thought of the walls of Elsinore, and Key, and Gil; and once more the sound and swiftness of the journey came around him, palpable almost as a stream of light or water. The wheels, the bells, the whistles, the sliding and whirling land, the centripetal and tumultuous descent into the Inferno, the descent into Mexico—Oh God, how were they ever going to endure it? It was as cruel as forgetting, or like throwing flowers into the sea. Flowers into the sea.

(II

Boston and Albany—Boston and Albany—Boston and Albany——
Boston—Springfield—Westfield—Pittsfield——

Everything had dissolved in time and sound, everything was dissolving and in solution, the only remaining reality was the train. The earth was a dream, the past was a dream—that they had met, the three of them, on the platform of the South Station, Noni in blue, with a blue-winged Viking hat, and the shiny black hatbox, and gladstone bag, laughing, and Gil in a shabby brown tweed suit with a broken suitcase, looking a little solemn and strained through the thick spectacles, and Gil's flat-chested little sister bringing a book, and himself standing tall and a little embarrassed among them,—Blomberg the crane, Blom the steam shovel—all this was nothing but a kind of vision, a fragment of ether-dream, a little picture seen in a picture book, brightly colored but unreal. It was gone, and Boston was gone, and the Berkshire hills, with the spring buds barely showing, where only a few weeks before he had seen snow under the trees, ice in the ponds, on the Indian-haunted road to Deerfield, these, too, had fled soundlessly away into a past which had now neither meaning nor existence. Those people might still be there, the Berkshires might still be there, and the Puritans who had conquered the Indians, and the wilderness which had conquered the Puritans; but the train, hollowing a golden and evanescent tunnel through the darkness, fleeting and impermanent as a falling star, denied all things but itself. "Good-by, Gil; good-by, Noni," the flushed little face had cried, with open mouth, and Noni had stooped and kissed her, the black hatbox bumping against her knee, and the book had almost been forgotten, thrust at the last moment under Gil's arm, it had all been flurried and

confused, as with all partings; as if the reality, in its contrapuntal hurry
to take shape at all, had somehow not taken, or been able to take, its
proper shape, or had even fallen *short* of reality. "And good-by, Mr. Blomberg," she had murmured hurriedly, half-averting her face—ah, these
Jews, if they've got to *be* Jews, and have Jewish names, they might at
least *look* like Jews—and so on to the train and into motion, and out of
time, too, in the sense that they had now *become* time. All day, all night,
the landscape whirling and unfolding and again folding, rising and falling,
swooping and melting, opening and shutting, Blomberg gliding evenly
among the haunted birches and junipers of the Berkshires, a puritan among
puritans—and weren't the Jews, after all, the oldest puritans in the world?
—Blomberg defending the stockade at Deerfield in deep snow, Blomberg
bowling at ninepins with the Dutch trolls of the Catskills, Blomberg gazing down from the railway bridge at Hendrik Hudson's little ship, the
Half Moon, which vanished away down the broad river like a rose petal
into the sunset. And what was it the Negro porter had said, there on the
platform at Albany, while they waited to change trains—said to the fat
lady, who insisted that this was the train to Chicago? The train now gave
him the rhythm, embodied the burred voices, brought them back alive and
eerie out of the past—Okay, lady, you can take it, but if you do you got
to change, this ain't no through train, this train goin' to Cincinnati, yes,
ma'am!

The train to Cincinnati, the train to the west, the south, the train into
darkness and nothing—

Unreal, but also uncannily real, the business of settling into the empty
car, the car filled with smoke, the forward door open and swallowing smoke,
scooping smoke, like a hungry mouth, while they climbed swiftly, and then
less swiftly, and at last laboringly, and with delayed rhythms, into the
Berkshires, along ledges of rock, above brawling little mountain streams,
past deserted farms and stations, tilting slowly round an embanked curve
to stare intimately, for a lost moment, into an old apple orchard—settling
into this motion, this principle of placelessness, Gil flushing and smiling,
self-conscious and awkward, as he lifted Noni's black hatbox up to the rack,
and hung the raincoats. And all the idle chatter, in the empty car, with
only half a dozen salesmen for company, and a woman with a child, and
the Italian foreman, and the Mexican. "Air-conditioned!" Noni had cried.
"Air-conditioned—I like that! But it *is*, in a *way!*"—as a particularly thick
cloud of smoke whipped downward in a defile and swept over and past
them. She had put her handkerchief to her mouth, coughing; it was then
that he first thought she was already showing signs of fatigue, signs of
strain, signs of the struggle to keep up appearances. And all for Gil, the
bewildered but good-natured Gil, Gil peering a little anxiously at them
both, perhaps already suspecting a secret, some sort of league against him,
but too decent to ask questions, as yet. As yet! But the time would come.
The time was sure to come. It was all absurd, wild, mad, meaningless—
what good could it do—what good could it do anyone, Gil least of all!
What good can it do, Noni? What good can it do? He said it half aloud,
staring out into the shapeless speed of night, through the black lustered
window, for he had said it to her so often—on the swan boat, in Boston,

as they plied solemnly round and round the little pond in the Public
Garden: "No, Blom; you will see," was all she had said—and in the bar
of the Ritz, and in the upstairs cocktail room of the Lincolnshire, eating
potato chips and peanuts, "No, Blom, you will see"—and as they walked
across the Common towards the golden dome of the State House, showing bright through the fledgling leaves of the beech trees, the elms: "What
good can it do, Noni? What good can it possibly do?" And then the blue-
winged head turning towards him, almost merrily, with the patient, "No,
Blom, you will see!"

Christ, it couldn't be true, none of it was true! Only the train was true,
with its prolonged quadruple cry into the night, its banshee wail across the
darkened counties of Ohio, Indiana, Illinois—only this was true, and himself sitting with the guidebook on his knee, vibrant as himself—and the
blue coat swaying by the window, and the black bag above him in the
woven brass rack, the label dangling, too, and swaying, turning now the
leather side and now the celluloid. And his long hands, with the dark hairs
on the backs of the fingers, and the headache, and the strained eyes. . . .

But he turned abruptly, and looked back, and there they were: it was
true: Noni with her knees drawn up on the seat, lying on her side, her
head pillowed in a folded coat against the window sill, the small white
hand half-folded beneath her chin, the eyes closed but conscious: and opposite her, across the aisle, the top of Gil's head, tipped at an angle, the
thin tawny hair disarrayed in sleep, showing above the next chair back.
Noni was pale, and the eyes, behind the closed eyelids, were thinking. The
hand, too, was conscious. She knew the train, she knew the night, in its
half-sleep her whole body was aware of the violent magic of time and place
which was affronting them, and in its own subtle rhythmical oscillation,
half submissive and half reluctant, it made its awareness manifest. With
her eyes closed, she was *living* time, feeling it and taking it, this minute
and the next and the next, this hour, this transit, this speed, and all the
complications of texture with which they were woven. Her knees, under
Gil's raincoat, the green plush chair back, the two punched ticket vouchers
which the conductor had ingeniously wedged in the parallel thumbholds
of the window shade, the dimmed lights in a row along the bronze ceiling
of the hurrying car, the ever varying sound of the wheels, singing and
throbbing beneath them, the weight now thrown to one side now to the
other, sudden staccatos of rattles as they clattered over a crossing, and the
hard resonant rails now seeming to groove musically upwards almost into
one's body, then to withdraw again, until one felt effortless and ethereal,
swung in a circle on the lightest of cords, out into space itself—all this he
could see her knowing, even now, almost as if she were saying it aloud to
him. All this, and how much more! Noni on the great circle to Mexico,
taking her heart as an offering to the bloodstained altar of the plumed
serpent, alive now between Gil and himself, and looking with closed
face at both of them—her face, closed like a flower, but ready to open as
soon as the sun shone—and this, too, she knew and waited for, the sun
that was already pursuing them westward across the dark rondure of the
turning world. Presently the first ray would leap up over the curve of the
earth's surface, leap after and overtake them, shoot beyond them into the

waiting west. St. Louis, the unknown Mississippi River, magnificent red
aorta of a rank continent, the Bayous, Missouri, Texas. . . .

He turned away from the defenseless face, with the firm little mouth
and fringed eyes, and closed his own eyes only to open them again. Lucky
unconscious Gil, the poor lamb! But let him sleep. Let the poor devil
sleep. For him, even more perhaps than for himself and Noni, a bad time
was coming, all the misery of awakening that comes to the unconscious.
Suspicious he might be, just a little—surely, however, no more than that—
and everything had been so gay, so good—the reading of the absurd guidebook, with its atrocious style, which Gil had found so amusing, and the
names, and Noni's mad description of the floods in the Connecticut valley
—and then, suddenly, Albany and the long platform, and the attempt to
buy a drinking cup for the whisky. Of the whisky Gil had seemed a little
disapproving. A little stiff. Maybe just the idea of drinking it so un-
ashamedly in public, out of paper cups—handing the bottle over the chair
back—he had given Noni a quick and queer look when she first took
it out of the hatbox—but afterwards, in the diner, as they sped in the
gathering darkness along the Erie Canal—*Schenectady, Utica, Syracuse,
Rome*—how magical the time change had been, with its bizarre marriage
of present and past! Red and green lights of barges on the dark water, the
dim towpath, a woman hanging washing on the stern deck in the twilight,
a cat beside her, Noni telling about the cry of "Low Bridge!" with which
in the old days the helmsman warned his crew, and everywhere the wonderfully fertile country with its fantastic baroque suburban houses, huge
filigreed and porticoed façades, like the County Street houses of the Victorian period in New Bedford. He closed his eyes again, and all the voices
rose in a chorus, rose all at once—here's to the bride, here's to the groom—
here's to the best man—there's nothing like getting divorced and married
in the same place—when you do that, it *takes*—but who said we had to
change at Galion, there's nothing about it—well, we're off to Clixl Claxl,
Ixl Oxl, and Popocatepetl—that's where Hart Crane went, just before he
drowned himself in the Caribbean—they say it's a death country, a murder
country, and the buzzards—

He opened his eyes to see the tall conductor leaning over him, one
hand on the corner of the seat, looking for the voucher—it was the conductor for the new section, different, but generically the same. The dried
leather face, pallid and ascetic, tall and stooped.

"Change at Galion."

"How long do we have to wait there."

"The St. Louis train will be waiting for you. Through train to St.
Louis."

"Thanks. Will somebody let us know, or wake us——"

"You don't need to worry. The brakeman will put you off."

"Thank you."

Galion, at four-forty. A head had turned, a bland face, the figure was
rising, approaching.

"Did I hear you say you were going to Galion?"

"No—we change there, for St. Louis—"

"Because I used to be a citizen of Galion—"

"Is that so—no, we only change there——"

"In fact I was born there, but I haven't been there for a long time and I thought maybe I might have found a fellow citizen—"

"No, I'm sorry—"

"Well, not at all—"

The heavy figure lurched along the aisle to the ice-water tap, swayed as it bent to extract a cup, filled the cup and drank. A citizen of Galion. But what was Galion? Galion, Galion, Galion. The whistle cried mournfully into the night, cried again; far ahead on the long train, with all its Pullman cars full of sleeping people, the lost voice could be heard, as the engine sped blindly, cometlike, through the night. *Ohio, Indiana, Illinois* —even now the pioneers were crossing these in their covered wagons, building their homesteads, their snake fences against the snow, laying the broadax to the foot of the tree, felling the savage forests. But what home now was here, what home for Noni? A spiritual drought only, an unconquered and savage land, a bloodsucking land, which had slowly but surely taken the souls from the people who lived upon it. The wilderness was coming back, here as in the Berkshires the melancholy waste would return, the towns would be invaded by marching trees, grass would grow over the doorsill. There was no home here, could never be, it was as well that Noni would only pause here, in the dark, to change from one motion to another, touch the alien earth only in transit.

The book had slid from his knee to the floor, slid from darkness into light, and with it himself from sleep to waking. Rising with it, he turned and saw that Noni's eyes were open, that she was smiling. Smiling sleepily and peacefully. He got up, went to her softly, leaned over her. She put her fingers to her lips, motioning towards Gil.

"Asleep!" she whispered.

"Yes, and why aren't you!"

"How much time."

Her eyes fluttered, didn't quite focus on his own, the pupils were wide and dark, near but unseeing, she was barely conscious.

"Lots. Hours, Noni. The brakeman's going to call us."

"Oh."

"Do you want anything. A drink of water."

"No."

"All right, then; go to sleep!"

The blue eyes fluttered and closed, opened, then closed again. Perhaps now she would really sleep, really let go and be taken downward—he straightened up, giving the raincoat on her knee a pat, looked along the aisle of the deserted car, turned and saw Gil's open mouth, his hand crumpled against his cheek, the loose head nodding with the motion of the train, the spectacles folded on the window sill. Sleep, that knits up the raveled sleeve—but not this sleep, not this, by God, nor any such sleeve as this! For what was at work even now in Noni's golden head——?

He pressed his hands hard to his forehead as he sat down, leaned into the corner by the window, willed himself to sleep. Sleep, Blom; sleep. You *must* sleep. And what better than a train, a day coach, with that nostalgic whistle, far ahead, for a lullaby. And these square wheels, these octagonal wheels. And Noni lying there, looking so extraordinarily well, so young and pretty, as if nothing in the world was the matter!

Footsteps passing, and a change of light through the closed eyelids.

"Can't help it if she did."

"By no means."

Steps, voices, wheels, and in no time at all to an accompaniment of wind sound, a prolonged wind sound, he crossed the Texas desert on foot, up and down the sand hills, through ravines of rock and sage, and then more precipitately into Mexico, but repeatedly lost. No road, no path, no guide. But at last a single sign post, a finger of wood, woebegone in the wilderness, and on it in almost obliterated letters the one word Mexico. Southward, timelessly southward once more, through the wilderness of rock and sand, day after day and night after night; and over the bronze mountains, the eagle-haunted sierras, sawtoothed and jagged against the sky, and then at last the long descent into the fertile valley. Now before him, far down, he could see the city itself, the strange city; light flashed from the bright roofs and domes; light flashed too from something else— was it water? He could not be sure, but already now he was in a house of his own in the old city, he had been a citizen in this strange place for a long time, he knew it well. And nevertheless, it was with surprise—although also with familiarity—that he found the house to be built in water, for lifting a trap door in the floor he stared straight down through a water so marvelously pure and clear, and so deep, that it seemed to him he was looking into the very center of the earth. Like a crystal it was, and as he gazed into its wonderful depths, lucid and sunlit, and yet somehow also dark, he had the feeling that here below him was a profound meaning, something that he had come a long way to find. This was Mexico, this underworld sea, it was this he had come to live in, this was his soul's dwelling place, and Noni's too—he was holding a candle up now, and looking down in the less light, wondering what creatures inhabited this dark water, when abruptly the walls of the house began to shake, everything shook violently as if in an earthquake, the breath suddenly left his body——

Angry and dismayed, he saw the brakeman's hand just leaving his shoulder; the brakeman's hand had been shaking his shoulder; the brakeman was still standing before him, lantern in hand. He blinked at the white-gloved hand, felt as if he were still being shaken. And the brakeman was still saying—or saying again:

"Galion in five minutes; change for St. Louis."

"Galion——"

He jumped up, turned, saw Gil just rising also, with his spectacles in his hand. Noni, on the other side of the aisle, lay exactly as she had before, but now her eyes were open, she looked from one to the other of them with a sleepy half-smile.

"Five minutes, my lambs; we've got to hustle! We've got to get a move on! This is no less than Galion, believe it or not; *Galion:* and God help us if we don't find that train to St. Louis. Come on, shake a leg, Noni! Wake up!"

"I *am* awake!"

"Gil, you'd better spank the gal."

"Of all the unearthly hours to make poor long-suffering travelers change —it's peonage, that's what it is, Blom, to push the coach passengers off— you notice the *Pullmans* go right through!"

Gil reached up to the rack for his suitcase, Noni for her hat. The engine's quadruple cry, far ahead, came softly and unevenly back to them; all three looked out into the starless and lightless night, the unbroken dark. One after the other, the six salesmen, their coats neatly folded over their arms, their smart bags in their hands, passed them, going forward into the vestibule. A feeling of departure was in the air, a severance, a feeling of hurry—the future was reaching back to them with secret and powerful hands, they must bend their wills to it. Out into the unknown, bag in hand—but Gil, characteristically, had quite forgotten Noni's hatbox and gladstone, Noni was climbing up on to the seat——

"Stop that, Noni—you let *me* do that——"

Too late, Gil stepped forward, peering and smiling, apologetic; Noni half fell, half jumped, the train swaying suddenly, and flung her arms round him laughing, while Blomberg reached over their heads for the shiny hatbox.

"Can I have this dance, Noni?"

"I suppose we ought to make it a rhumba! or a *toltec,* or something. . . ."

The train sounds were changing, changing and slowing, the car lurched and shuddered, its speed resisting the brakes, it seemed to balloon and sway like a zeppelin. Blomberg said, looking down at Noni's blue wings, and below them the now sobered blue eyes:

"Now have you got everything? What *you* fellers need to learn is organization."

He smiled grimly and consciously straight into Noni's eyes, looked for a moment deep down into them—for all the world as he had looked into the mysterious water in his dream—and sought there an answer to the question which he dared not ask. Far and faint, too, the signal came—like a tiny light at the very horizon's edge, seen once, seen twice, then gone. It was both reassurance and reproach, a "yes, I'm all right," but also a "now you must stop looking at me like that, or Gil will guess." The eyes wavered aside then, shyly, the lips were half parted, as if she had thought to say something but had changed her mind. She turned quickly then to Gil, behind her, touched the tweed sleeve.

"My book," she said.

"Gosh, yes! Where is it?"

"Can you put it in your pocket. I forgot to pack it."

The sound of time grew louder, a bell rang with two-voiced melancholy across a roar of steam, the forward door was slammed open, and in it stood the brakeman with his lantern. Galion, he was singing; Galion! They had come to Galion; this point in chaos and eternal night was Galion. To get off. To go out into the night and look for another train, or wait for it, or miss it! To hurry! And with sleep still blinding one's eyes—

"Come on," he said.

He took Noni's gladstone, and his own bag; Gil had his broken suitcase

and an armload of coats; Noni had the hatbox. The train shuddered and
slowed, gave a final prolonged squeal, and stopped. In the unnatural
silence, they stepped down the steep lamplit stairs into the featureless black
of night, found themselves walking stiffly on gravel. The six salesmen had
vanished into the profound gloom, only their footsteps could be heard
dying away somewhere ahead. The brakeman was saying:

"Straight on, St. Louis train on the other side, you'll have to walk round
both trains, and cross the tracks up ahead—straight ahead——"

"Good heavens," Gil said, "there's nothing here——!"

Noni lifted her face to the starless sky—he could just see her.

"It's the Black Hole of Calcutta," she said.

They walked quickly into the night, past the lighted car which they had
just left, and another, and, reaching the end of the train, crossed the track
to the mysterious new train which stood beyond. Somber and unlit, save
for a faint glow from the vestibules, the interminable row of dark sleeping cars stretched ahead of them, apparently for miles. The salesmen had
disappeared entirely, not a sound was to be heard save their own quick
footsteps on the dry gravel. Suppose they took too long in getting round—
suppose the train started—how could anyone possibly tell whether all the
passengers had found their way from one train to the other? A feeling of
panic hurried his heart's beating, he thought he heard Noni give a little
gasp, peered sidelong toward her but could see nothing of her expression.
He said:

"I guess we'd better step on it. If those travelers get there without us,
they might just think——"

"Damndest thing I ever saw," said Gil. "Not even a light. And as for
porters——"

Another sleeper, and another, and another; the green curtains drawn,
the sleeping humans lying there in unconscious tiers under the sky, men,
women and children; while outside, unknown to them, Blomberg and Gil
and Noni walked anxiously past them on the gravel, staring ahead for a
glimpse of the engine. The express car, the mail car, and at last—the great
monster breathed softly above them, gleamed, vibrated. The cab seemed to
be empty. The driver would of course be at the other side. Suppose he got
the signal to start just as they were crossing——

Without a word they crossed, close to the hot headlight and the blunt
angry-looking cowcatcher, found themselves squeezed between a wooden
level-crossing guard arm and the engine, so close that they could touch
it, and began the long journey back to the day coach, which of course would
be at the very end of the train. Now there was a row of dim lights, each
showing a little arc of dirty wooden pillar; they hurried up the worn wooden
ramp to a low platform, and it was here that Noni suddenly stopped,
stood still, let the hatbox fall from her hand.

"Ohhhh," she wailed, "I *can't!* Someone *please*——"

She blew out a long breath, clapped her hands against her breast, looked
comically from one to the other of them. She seemed to be swaying slightly,
she was out of breath. Was it possible that her heart——

"Here, Gil," he said quickly, "throw those coats over my left arm and take Noni's hatbox. And *hurry*, my lad! And Noni, you take it easy, follow us, don't worry, we'll keep a piece of the train for you!"

"Thanks, Blom dear!"

She was still standing motionless, as they hurried off ahead, standing there with her hands lightly crossed on her breast, looking amusedly after them—he could see the smile on the half-averted and half-lamplit face—but then he heard her steps slowly begin, heard them follow more firmly, and he listened to them as he might have listened to the beating of his own heart. She was coming; she was all right. To Gil he said:

"I'm afraid she's tired. Couldn't sleep."

"Yes. Guess she'll be all right. She worries too much!"

The thick spectacles flashed, the mouth looked somewhat prim. Before them the conductor waited by the train, his hand on the handhold, the lantern on the splintered platform.

"Is this the coach for St. Louis?"

"Yes, sir; through car to St. Louis."

"Good. There's a lady coming, just behind us. . . . Guess we'd better get the bags aboard, Gil——"

"Okay."

Brown seats instead of green, and pale green metal walls, and an almost empty car, except for the six salesmen who were already composing themselves for what was left of the night. Time with a hundred hands, time with a thousand mouths! A man drinking water, a man in his shirt-sleeves, a man taking his shoes off. Poised for departure in the extraordinary stillness of the night, poised in a wilderness without shape or sound, placeless and nameless—(but no, Galion!)—they waited for Noni. And now Noni's light steps came up the echoing stairs, and along the littered aisle, and she walked towards them, taking off the blue-winged hat and brushing the fair hair back from her forehead with a white ringless hand. She came towards them gravely, said simply, "I'm *tired*"—and sank into the seat beneath the rack with the hatbox. Gil, his battered felt hat still on, took her hand in his, sat down beside her, said something to her; she was staring out of the window, her shoulder against his. What did she see there? And what was Gil saying? They sat very still together; and then, subtly, softly, the train had begun to move, the murmur of time had resumed its everlasting monotone.

Galion—Marion—Sidney—Muncie——:
Ohio—Indiana—Illinois——:

"Ommernous," he muttered; "it's all ommernous; every bit of it is ommernous! Waking and sleeping we lay waste our powers. . . ."

The cry of the whistle punctuated his sleep; and then the glaring ball of the sun above the low rich land, blazing straight into his eyes over the cindered window sill; the rich land reeling fanlike in ribs and volutes of green, a file of cattle, a dog, haystacks by a clump of trees, a house dark against the brightened east. Blades of yellow light, too, from beneath the lowered curtain, light and sound mixing confusedly as if positively they might interchange: the rails beating at his cheeks and eyes like light, the sun's rays assailing his ears in an overbearing intricacy of endless rhythm. And then the early morning passengers, the new arrivals, the intruders——

"—well, I always think——"

"—yes, isn't that strange——?"

"—rather annoyed at a reaction a child gave, several years ago——"

"—and so long, and then we flop——"

"—yes—and he met her *that night!*——"

"—worldly, mundane sort of a girl——"

"—place where you stay is *very* comfortable, single room with bath——"

"—association. No, I don't keep up——"

"—well, what I don't know about T.B.——"

"—expose the whole pleural cavity—right middle left lower lobe—lot of lymph——"

"—and use a cautery along that line——"

"—no, just a——"

"—capillary?"

"—just an ordinary——"

"—Christian Scientist, with a tumor of the lung—back five weeks afterward—yes, sir, five weeks——"

"—hope you'll give my regards to the good wife——"

"—I surely will——!"

"—and my regrets that she doesn't turn up at Atlantic City any more——"

Blah—blah—blah—blah.—Comfort. Safety. Scenic Interest. A great fleet of fast trains at convenient hours between the East and Midwest. Centrally located terminals. The ever beautiful and historic Hudson River and Mohawk Valley. Majestic and inspiring Niagara Falls. Electric automatic signals and automatic train stop. . . .

Swaying and cursing in the tiny lavatory he had shaved the sleep-blanched face, noting the hollows under the dark eyes, steadying himself with one hand on the metal basinrim, his legs braced apart. Blom the lighthouse, Blom looking not quite so well. The floor had been flooded by someone's indiscretion, he tried to keep his feet in the drier places. Paper towels only; he was glad they had thought of pinching towels out of the Pullman on their way back from the diner the night before—that had been Gil's idea. Clever. The night before? Already it seemed centuries ago. The clamor of the train was louder and more immediate in the lavatory, came up rounded and echoing, drafty, almost musical, through the w.c. A good thing to shave today and tomorrow, because after that, when they got into Mexico, God alone knew——

And then Gil was saying, as they waited for Noni, wiping his hands a little nervously with a handkerchief, just the tips of the fingers, then tucking it back in his breastpocket:

"Look here, Blom. I haven't wanted to ask you before, in fact there hasn't really been any chance, and I don't quite know how to say it, but don't you think all this is a little queer?"

"What do you mean, Gil?"

"Well, the suddenness of it. The abruptness."

Gil swayed his head and shoulders forward and back, very slightly, very quickly, a habit he had when he was nervous: the pointed lean face, ascetic and Bostonian, but kindly, and the gray eyes, peering through the thick glasses, were frankly puzzled.

"To be candid, Gil," and he tapped on the tablecloth with the prongs of his fork, "I hadn't really thought about it. I've been too damned busy just getting it arranged!"

"Just the same, doesn't it strike you as odd——?"

"I don't know—Noni's of course sometimes impulsive."

"Yeah, Blom, but not like this, it's not really *like* her, in a thing so important—she's usually, if anything, rather deliberate."

"Well, maybe you're right. What were you thinking about it."

"That's what I thought *you* might know."

"Me? No."

He shook his head slowly, smiling at the slightly swaying tweed figure, the earnest eyes. Gil looked back at him rather fixedly for a moment, then said:

"When was it exactly that Noni first talked to you about it?"

"Sunday afternoon. Just after she had called up *you*. And then I saw her later that evening of course."

"I thought maybe she might have told you earlier."

"No. That was the first I knew of it. She told me she'd already talked with you and the lawyer."

"Well, it's really very funny. It's not a *bit* like Noni—after all these years, so suddenly like this——"

He stared out at the sliding landscape—a farmhouse surrounded by tall trees, two red silos, a car speeding levelly along the flat road parallel with the train, a vast plowed field with the plow lines telescoping in swift perspective—then added:

"Not, of course, that I'm not frightfully glad. As you know."

"You bet. I think it's simply grand, Gil. My own only *real* regret is that you fellers haven't got together years ago."

"Yes. It's just a little bewildering. But I suppose she must have had her reasons. For the sudden decision, I mean."

"Possibly. Just possibly! But my guess is that she just up and did it on the spur of the moment. Because if she *had* any special reasons, it's not like Noni to conceal them. You know as well as I do, Gil, that the one thing Noni *cannot* do is keep a secret! . . ."

Smiling broadly for the exchange of this shared knowledge, he elicited deliberately an answering smile from Gil; Gil's face relaxed, lost the slight sadness which had clouded it; for the first time he seemed to feel a little at ease. With just a hint of some reservation, nevertheless? Gil had perceptions, Gil was no fool. In a way it was a dirty trick—the mere deception, quite apart from the *nature* of the deception—to keep anyone so lucid, so lucid by nature, thus helplessly in the dark. It wasn't fair; it wasn't fair even to himself. An accessory after the artifact! He smiled at the thought, whistling the little Bach tune. For a moment he felt almost gay; smoke sprawled in sinuous shapelessness past the window, the swift shadows forming and vanishing beneath it, the sun shone, the hurrying train drew him powerfully into its deep-rhythmed nostalgic hypnosis. Again and again the engine, far ahead, cried for the innumerable crossings of this dull rich flatland, its voice now half stifled, now clear, as the wind shifted. *Whooooo —whooooo—whoo-whoo*—a somber and deep-timbred voice, whose tone he likened, as he listened, to the color of bronze, the color of winter sunlight on black ice. Everything was so beautiful—everything—but then the cold metallic pang shut round his heart once more, for all this beauty was nothing at all but the backdrop, the décor, for Noni's dream, Noni's ballet, of which the end might so easily be tragic. The *reason* for all this beauty, this wonder—the train, the new and strange landscape, the incredible adventure, this hurrying breakfast table with Gil and himself sitting at it, and all the unshaped but already so powerfully creative future beginning even now to tower in vaguely predictable color and form above them—the *reason* for this was the possibility that Noni might die. It ran through the landscape, ran through the whole world, like a shadow. It grew in a dark corner of the picture like the deadly nightshade. It was the first note, offstage, tentative and tender, of the tragedian's song, the goat song. Goat song in Mexico. . . .

The thought was almost intolerable, it was with difficulty that he restrained himself from jumping to his feet, muttering some sort of excuse, and fleeing to the smoker. But Gil was saying:

"Careful, Blom! Here's Noni now."

Not like the deadly nightshade, no, beautiful as that was—but the narcissus!

"Noni, you're late!"

"Don't you envy me? I overslept! Positively."

"I don't believe it. I suppose you and Gil know the one, speaking of all the train stories we know, about the fellow who was too tall for a sleeping car berth, and had to open the window and put his feet out?"

Noni's blue eyes were naughty with delight, she was already beginning to laugh.

"No," she said, fascinated. "No, you can tell us!"

"Well, when he took his feet *in*, in the morning, he found he had two red lanterns and a mailbag . . ."

"Fie! I don't call that a story at all! Did it happen to *you*, Blom?"

The bland Negro waiter interrupted her glee; they sat back while with swift legerdemain he moved water bottle and sugar bowl to spread the new cloth, flung down and arranged his handful of bright silver. How well she looked, despite the ever-so-slight flush, and with what perfect unselfconsciousness she managed things! She sipped her water, looked over the glass brim to inspect their fellow voyagers, looked out of the wide window, studied the breakfast menu with delight. Then, with her hand on Gil's sleeve, she said:

"It's a *lovely* book!"

"What book, darling?"

"The one Nancy brought. *The Cloud Messenger*, it's called, it's a Hindu poem, very old——"

"Ah!" Gil said; "too highbrow for me. More to Blom's taste!"

"Blom, you would love it. You *must* read it! So refreshing in this wasteland—a lover separated from his sweetheart who sends a cloud to her with a message—isn't that nice? isn't it lovely?—and the message is the poem——"

She broke off, her own eyes clouding, clouding even as she looked at him, the glass of water held before her: it was as if she were reading the poem, the message, watching that passage of symbol-bearing cloud, in his own eyes and face, retreating magically to another time, another life, another language. Strange counterpoint; for somehow he felt that while she thus held fixed before her, embodied in himself, the past, and explored it lovingly and deeply, she was also aware of the rushing and violent present, fluid beneath and around them, and the future, toward which the train was speeding, unknown but already as fixed and marmoreal as the past. A sibyl—she was like a sibyl. Was it the prospect, the terribly real prospect, of death, which now gazed with such manifest divination out of the grave eyes and gave the fair face such a wonderful stillness? The sunlight touched her hair, to which a slight untidiness lent an additional charm; he noticed with pleasure the copper color in the little braids that crossed the top of her head, as against the slighter gold of the light wind-stirred fibrils at the temples. The cloud messenger—the Megha Duta—he had seen the title as they stood in the South Station, talking with Nancy, and had then wondered what it might be. And now there seemed to him to be something curiously and esoterically appropriate, a sort of obscure fatality, in Nancy's choice. For Noni was herself a kind of cloud messenger, and so was the train, and so was all motion, whether it was a going-toward or a coming from: a vanishing signal, of fleetingest poignancy, like the blue shadows that flew away over these empty fields under the flying smoke. Impermanent, impermanent! she seemed to say; and then suddenly the blue eyes were laughing above the glass of water, laughing at Gil and his passion for detective magazines—and the conductor was coming down the aisle—and she said, between sips of ice water, "Now I suppose he'll be taking *another* yard of ticket——"

And then the Great Divide; in no time at all, in a single flash, they had come upon it—after the interminable dull landscape, featureless as the arid and somehow so bloodless and soulless people who dwelt on its surface, but with something dreadful and eternal about them, too, a melancholy defeated persistence—after this sad land what a relief to foresee this symbol of power and magnificence, in all its rank majesty. It was odd; they had waited at the windows, all three of them, for a half-hour or more, feeling as if by some queer terrestrial empathy that it was near, and that when they at last saw it they would experience something very definite, a sort of secret baptism in the holy waters of their own land.

"It's only then," said Noni, half kneeling, half standing, by the window, "that we shall become really indigenous. Really belong. Don't you feel that, Gil? Don't you feel that, Blom? *Indigenes!*"

"*Indigenes*," Gil said. "What words you do think up, Noni."

"Noni reads the dictionary for fun."

"And with profit, I assure you! Did I tell you about the worm?"

"*What* worm."

"The earthworm, Blom. Just the earthworm! But according to Mr. Webster—you'd never believe it—he's a 'burrowing, terrestrial, *megadrilic* worm.' And the megadrilic, I think you'll admit, is something to think about. And have you noticed, you two——"

She broke off, looking more intently at the swift landscape, a flock of starlings swooping low over a cornfield, spreading out flat like a wave on a beach, then as quickly mounting again in cloudform. Her hand was against the glass.

"Have you noticed that we've come straight into summer, already? This year we shall have no spring. We've come through it, overnight. . . ."

Blom stared, amused.

"It's true. Wonderful observant Noni! And a fascinating idea. We've dived right through it—as if the train were a swimmer, and spring a northward-breaking wave of flower and leaf, a surf of blossom, across the whole continent——"

"Yes, the corn is half-grown. And in Boston, and the Berkshires, the leaves were only beginning——"

"No spring for *us*, this year!"

"It's a little sad . . ."

They were all silent, watching the changing land, the land which now rapidly divulged itself in long, parallel hollows, as if at some time channeled and flood-swept. Shacks, shanties, tiny Negro settlements. And then what was unmistakably a levee—and the ramshackle huts of squatters, on the foreshore—rowboats in gardens tied to shabby porches, rowboats riding the lush inland grass—and suddenly sure enough, the river——!

"Ah," said Noni, "the Mississippi—the father of waters—now we can go home!"

"Go home——?" said Gil.

Her hands on the sill, looking downward from the bridge at the wide brown water, and as if somehow extraordinarily at peace, Noni gave a little sigh.

"Yes, Gil, go home. Go *anywhere*, I mean—go where we've *got* to go! *Do* you see what I mean?"

Gil shook his head, amused. He was himself gazing down at the river, entranced.

"She's off again!" he said.

"Go to Mexico, for instance—or even back to Boston! I feel as if in the twinkling of an eye—or while, in fact, we were crossing that bridge—my soul had shot under water all the way down to New Orleans, even into the Gulf of Mexico, and back again. And now it *belongs* to me. . . ."

In a wide slow circle the train turned southward, bent its course parallel with the river, and the somber walls of the city came to meet them. East St. Louis, St. Louis—already the train felt empty, a little desolate and abandoned; its sounds were becoming subdued; the little cries from the trucks and wheels, as they slipped from one switch to another, one track to another, jolting slightly, were minor and musical; they had almost arrived, they were almost there. Almost there? No such thing, nothing so simple as that. They were only beginning! But if Noni could feel—or was it an incomparable piece of acting?—this astonishing sense of peace—or begin, as she seemed to be doing, to *let go*——

He looked ahead, as they assembled the bags and coats once more, to the days to come; allowed them to flow forward into the present, and to mingle with the immediate; and now it was Little Rock and Texarkana, Palestine and Troup and San Antonio, Laredo and Monterey and Mexico City, the mountains and the jungle, that came alongside with the bobbing and running caps of the Red Caps, the rumbling trucks, the roar of steam against the grimed glass roof of the great station. They were walking with the future. The future joined them as they checked the bags at the kiosk, as they drank cold beer out of tall glasses and ate lunch in the station restaurant, as they inquired about the train, to make sure, and as they walked through the wind and dust of the St. Louis streets toward the river. Fantastic city, down-at-heel jumble of romantic past and shoddy present; skyscrapers, Parthenons, monoliths, and then the old quarter of tumble-down but somehow dignified and beautiful red-brick and clapboard houses, somber or florid, where once the life of the city had flowed fastest. Meretricious, the whole thing—streets that were spacious, but without beauty, buildings that were massive and elaborate, but nevertheless looked as hollow and impermanent as the cream-puff fantasies of a world's fair, something indescribably dreary and provincial and—yes, Noni found the word —*temporary*, about the whole place. The wilderness would come back—the wilderness had never really been defeated, here; it waited around the corner, waited for the dark. . . . A beauty parlor, with wide window, from which fixed doll-like faces stared at the pedestrians outside, while a bedizened beauty, with heavily enameled mouth, stood grinning at the open door and beckoned them in . . . "*Specializing in Photos for Chauffeurs.*" Shabby little shops, dreary shirts and socks, taverns and beer parlors. In one of these, on a corner, they stopped for beer and to ask their way to the river —over the radio a baseball game was coming from Shibe Park. *And remember, folks, this broadcast comes to you by courtesy of—and now somebody's down there warming up, I'll tell you who it is in a minute— yes, just as I thought——!*

"You're sure you're not too tired, Noni?"

"No, Blom, I want to go. I want to put my hands in it."

"Well, you two are certainly romantic!"

Gil was peevish; Gil disliked the wind and dust, the long walk, proceeded with lowered head, his felt hat pulled down on his forehead. But the slum streets, the decrepit old buildings on the dingy slope to the river, broken windows, crumbling walls, old gray stone and brick, shutters hanging awry, cheap lodgings—ten cents a night, five cents a night—in houses which a century since had been the city's best—this was extraordinary, deeply exciting. Here the past became vivid, became rank and real; like a conch shell held to the ear these ruins gave off an echo of the south and the sea: deep south, deep sea. And inland two thousand miles! The south had crept up the river, that was it, there was a foreign feeling here, and something mortuary too: it was like a dead seaport of the south, maritime but defunct. And sinister, also; a gangsters' paradise, smelling of beer and brothels. The sloping streets of cobbles were almost covered with tin beer-bottle tops. Here and there, an old ruin which had once been a thriving river hotel, full of violent life, the life of the Mississippi. Here Mark Twain had walked.

And under the iron-dark structure of the elevated railroad, the very
viaduct over which they had themselves slowly entered the city, they came
to the wide granite-paved beach of the majestic river, walked slowly down
to it. Like tide marks left by the sea, lines of gray and withered flotsam—
driftwood, barrel staves, empty bottles, tin cans, slivers of wood silvered
with age, peeled branches polished like horn, eggshells, orange peels—
marked the many levels at which during the winter the great river had
stood. An enormous beach; against which the dark water slid with sleepy
power, the brown eddies moving swiftly downstream as they coiled
sparkling in the sunlight. A little way upstream, two river boats rotted at
a landing stage, twin-smokestacked—the smokestacks with coronetted tops.
Noni dipped her hand in the water.

"It's the Natchez and the Robert E. Lee," she said.

"Ol' man river," said Gil.

"Now I'm baptized, Blom, in this continent. Now I've got Indian
blood."

"And in the old days they used to say that some of those boats drew
so little water that in a heavy dew they could sail right across the point of
land between one bend of the river and the next!"

"Mark Twain. Mark two!"

"I wouldn't mind taking a boat all the way down——"

Gil was peevish; perhaps he was tired, but indeed all three of them were
tired; a curious feeling of unreality was beginning to affect them, like a mild
fever. He said:

"Well, it looks just like a river to me! But I admit it's a kind of a big
one."

"Now, Gil, you stop worrying about your affairs in Boston! I've told
you they'll *be all right.*"

"Oh yes, they'll all run themselves."

"Probably much better."

"I'm not complaining, Noni——"

"I know, dear. It's all right. Life gets very sudden, sometimes, but isn't
it *fun! Isn't* it, Blom?"

"It's a three-ringed circus, Noni, and I wouldn't have missed it for
worlds. My God, Gil, look about you. You never saw anything like this in
your life. It's crazy."

"Crazy?"

"Sure, crazy. Look at these people, with their withered faces and
scrawny necks, their dead eyes and dead souls——"

"Oh come, Blom dear. It's not as bad as all that!"

"Damn near. They've gone to seed. There's nothing left. No juice in
them, not a particle: this infernal vampire continent has sucked them dry.
They'll blow away like tumbleweed. I've never been so impressed—and
depressed—in my life: it's given me a new and not so very attractive, I'm
bound to say, picture of America. Think of those pathetic Hoosiers on the
train—those bleached and weather-worn countryfolk, animated scraps of
skin and leather—good God, their eyes were a quarter of an inch apart,
they'd never felt anything or seen anything in their lives. Why, you could
as soon expect understanding—*understanding*, illumination, awareness, call

it what you want—of an ox or goat. No mind, no spirit, not a spark . . ."

Gil was amused. He said slowly:

"Blom, you sometimes become really biblical. By the waters of Mississippi we sat down and wept; yea, we wept, when we remembered Boston!"

"Oh no, we laughed!"

The profound river, the strange sad city—what a pair these made, with their so casual conjunction of the magnificent and the trivial, the fecund and the sterile! A whole continent pouring itself out lavishly to the sea, in superb everlasting waste, an immense creative giving, power that could afford to be careless both of means and end—and mankind beside it become as spiritually empty as the locust, and as parasitic. Surely the Indians had been better than this, and the Frenchmen, too, who had first explored these savage waters: in either had been a dignity, a virtue, now lost. And the Mexican Indians, to whom they were going—what of those? Lawrence said—and all the psychoanalysts said—and the guidebooks said——

It was as if he had heard a bell, suddenly, from a deep valley, a jungle valley, inviting to the sacrifice, whether pagan or Christian: there, there were still gods. But here, in this melancholy wreckage of a meager past, in this sloven street, spangled with tin beer caps, which they were climbing slowly again, past stinking cellars and boarded windows, here there was no longer even a true love of earth. This people was lost. . . .

"It's ommernous," he said aloud, grimly; "every bit of it is ommernous."

"Blom's saying it's ommernous again, Noni!"

"I guess we all need another drink. Is it Friday or Tuesday? And after that, Gil dear, I'm going back to the station for a good *wash*."

The Opera House, closed and boarded up, ancient home of burlesque, the silver gilt peeling from its baroque façade of garlands and bosomy nymphs and cracked cornucopias, and a little farther on a café. Gil led the way in, past the bar, at which one man and four waitresses lolled, to a small table at the back. Beyond this a large room, or rather a Cimmerian gloom, unlighted, in which gilded columns were barely visible. Into this, and out of it, mysterious figures went and came, some male, some female. One of the waitresses half lay across a table, in a dark corner, at which a man was sitting. Another led a newcomer into the back, somewhere, and disappeared entirely. Noni said:

"If I weren't tired, I would say we had picked out a very peculiar place!"

"See no evil, speak no evil, drink your beer!"

Palm trees and silver spittoons. A radio, muted, crooned from a corner of the front window. Noni was looking really tired: she ought to lie down. He could tell by the way she tried, without attracting attention, to rest first one shoulder, then the other, and without success, against the uncomfortably small chairback; crossed her knees and then uncrossed them; leaned her elbows on the table, her fists against her cheekbones, the blue eyes bright with sleepiness. He said:

"Guess I'll stay here and write a letter. You fellers go on back to the station when you want to, and I'll meet you there."

Gil seemed pleased. He excused himself, for a moment, wandered off

into the gloom at the back. Noni turned the blue wings, turned the sleepy
eyes, and said:

"How is it, Blom?"

"It's all right, Noni."

"Are you sure?"

"Quite. He asked some questions this morning, fishing a little to find
out if I knew more than *he* did——"

"Do you think he really thinks so?"

"I think he did, a little. But now I think it's all right. You're doing
wonders, Noni—keep it up."

"Thank you, Blom, dear. So are you."

"But now be sensible and take it easy; and try to get some sleep. It's
going to be worse before it's better! The trains might be crowded, you never
know. And maybe hot."

"Yes."

"Is there anything special I can do."

"Do you think he's jealous?"

"No. No more than Gil ever is; no."

She sighed, relaxed, looked at him gratefully.

"That's good. He's been a little silent."

"Just upset by the whole thing, that's all."

"I guess so."

"Here he is."

"Okay. Suppose I meet you at five, then. Or ten to? At the station
bookshop."

"Right!"

She rose to join Gil, took his arm; and he sat still, watching them go
out into the bright street and turn to the left. Then he took out the folded
sheets of paper and began to write, half listening to the voices at the bar.

❲ III

"What is man that thou art mindful of him? What is time, and what is
reality? And what on earth ever put it into the mind of man that any god
or gods *were* mindful of him? As you see, Clint, I'm on my way; and
as you doubtless also observed, I didn't get to Cambridge to see you before
I left. As you can imagine. And I was sorry, too, for, among other things,
I wanted to ask you a favor. Key, as you will surmise as soon as you see the
St. Louis—or wherever—postmark, came across with a hundred dollars,
and made it possible. But only barely possible; that's the point. Now, if
things go wrong, or it takes longer than we had thought, or anything of that
sort, we'll need *more* money; and I'm afraid Key is the only chance. So,
if I should wire you from Mexico just the one word 'Key' would you be an

angel and do what you can? Another hundred, for a guess—but if I have any more definite idea of our exact needs I'll perhaps add the figures. I hope you don't mind—and in fact I'm sure you won't or I wouldn't ask it. It's only that we may really need a watchdog in Boston when we get way off there in the wilderness. . . . Wilderness—my God, as if we weren't already in a wilderness! You must come and see this country of ours—it's a wonder. Talk about your wastelands—it's purely and simply, I'm afraid, a spiritual desert. These faces! They're made of a kind of pale and pasty leather, no ray ever touched or lit them, and the eyes are blind as stones. Arid, dry, withered, there's nothing left of them; they're like old corn shucks hung up in a barn and forgotten. *All* the faces, mind you—and everywhere. There's simply no trace of refinement, or sensitiveness, or subtlety of awareness; and I can't begin to tell you how wonderfully depressing it is. Not, of course, that in a way it's not a godsend, if only as a diversion from the matter in hand! As to that—well, by God, you see me for once not *reading* novels for a publisher, but actually *in* one. It really *is* a novel. Talk about Hart Crane or D. H. Lawrence or whoever, going to Mexico to die, going down to the everlasting dark! What about Blom the embalmer? Blom the undertaker? Blom the best man at the funeral? Blom the chief, if not the only, mourner? No, that's not fair—for Gil does, in his dry wounded way, love Noni; he really does. But just the same he's spared, unlike Noni and myself, the burden of foreknowing, and there are times when in spite of myself I can't help being irritated with him. Poor old Gil! At the bottom of his heart he must simply *hate* my being here at all, and he must certainly wonder himself sick as to why Noni insisted on my coming. But he's a sport about it, I must say, and I admire him for it. As for Noni—well, you know Noni! She's a good soldier. She just marches up against the battery as if it wasn't there; and she hasn't changed her behavior by a hair's breadth. And so far, anyway, she's standing it better than I feared she would. Next to no sleep at all last night—we found out only when we were halfway across New York State that we had to change at a place called Galion, Ohio—think of it—at half past four in the morning. You can imagine what it was like, trying to sleep with *that* hanging over us! Gil really slept—I did fairly well—but Noni was awake pretty much all night. And the change itself wasn't too good, in pitch dark, a hell of a hurry the whole length of two trains, and Noni was in some distress. In spite of which she really seems pretty well today, and has actually been enjoying this odd city very much. And the river. The river moved her deeply—obviously meant something very private to her. You know how she is about such things; I've often thought Noni ought to have been a poet. We took a walk down to see it, through a very fine slum section, much against Gil's will; she insisted she must put her hands in it, *and* did so. It was nice! One of those things you like Noni for. Then we came back and had a drink at a café which looks to me remarkably like a *bagnio*, if you know what I mean, and it's there that I'm sitting to write this. . . . It's funny; half the time I can't really believe a word of it—it doesn't seem actual at all. Of course journeys are a little like that, anyway—but this more so, I suppose, because it all happened so suddenly and with so little time for *thinking* about it. And then, naturally, the situation about Noni makes it all even *harder* to believe. The truth is, I can't admit it to myself; it just doesn't make sense. Things like this don't happen, do they? People don't have to die like that—and we all know that there is a God, and there is justice, and there is beauty—or do we? Noni is here, alive; I saw her stooping to wet her hands in the muddy water of the Mississippi an hour ago. I shall see her again at five, and yet we both know that this is coming to an end, that she will presently—well, vanish. It beats me, Clint! I can't make head or tail of it. How explain such cruelty away? It's enough to make you really hate the whole nature of existence: but then, the joke is, the existence of *Noni*, and the way *she* takes this business, makes me really believe in something *extraordinarily good*—she's herself a sort of proof of the divine excellence of things. A very subtle reversal! . . .

"Next day. I'm finishing this on the train, so forgive the rocky hand-writing. The Sunshine Special is rushing us into Texas, and all day, think of it, we shall do nothing but cross Texas. Noni and Gil are washing— I'm waiting for breakfast. These so-called De Luxe Coaches aren't bad: but none of us did much sleeping, I'm afraid. We were grieved when they took away an extremely nice smoking car, with adjustable seat backs— very comfortable; but damn it, after we'd got our bags into it we found they were going to yank it off during the night. Almost the best thing so far was coming down the river from St. Louis—really magical. I wish there'd been more of it. We followed the river for about half an hour, at dusk—very fine—it's an astonishing river—dark little bayous with flat-bottomed row-boats tied up under tropical trees—nice old farmhouses with lawns going down to the shore—levees, islands, ragged trees sticking up out of deep water where islands or points use to be—the general impression of some-thing marvelously untamed. Noni ate it alive. Here come Noni and Gil now—— I'll finish this, and put it off at the next station—Arp, or Troup, or something. And I'll of course drop you a line when we get to M. Re-member, please, Clint, all this under your hat. Yrs., B.

"If any of this letter doesn't make sense, remember, too, that I haven't had any sleep to speak of for two nights. We're all beginning to feel very odd and vague—as if we'd somehow stepped right out of time. Damned funny! It's a sort of dream state you get into, everything telescopes and foreshortens—something like a fever. Not unpleasant, in a way, either, for in some respects your faculties actually seem sharpened—perhaps only fitfully, and perhaps it's an illusion! . . ."

Dream state. The dream state of Missouri, or Arkansas, or Texas. . . .
The dream state of Mexico. . . .

In the smoking car Gil talked about Little Rock. He was not sure whether he had really seen it, in the middle of the night, or had only had a dream about it. On the deserted platform, talking to a man with a broom, a Negro porter had taken his visored porter's cap out of a paper bag, re-placed it with the straw hat which he had just been wearing. Then there had been stately buildings of marble, a glowing capitol on a hill, palladian lamplit walls, miles of lights, along a river, and the train turning west. . . .

"It sounds like a dream."

"The town does. But the porter with the paper bag——?"

"And anyway, at least we didn't have to change. We were left alone to *not* sleep."

"Yeah. To *not* sleep. . . ."

They closed their eyes and opened them again; again closed them, again opened them. Thou hast nor youth nor age, but, as it were, an after-dinner sleep. The rich country divulged hills, the hills divulged an oil-derrick or two, then others; suddenly like a blond angel in the bright sunlight, unbelievable, the tall fierce flame of a natural-gas well blazed pale yellow in the morning, and another, and a third. The fantastic landscape of skeletal derricks, singly or in groups or rows, stretching away as far as one could see in the broken country, had a sort of natural beauty, it was like something which had actually grown out of the earth. Of some, the pumps were motionless; of others they worked slowly, at the bottom of the derrick, like the lazy kicking of a grasshopper's leg. Oil lands. The surface of the ground looked brown and rusty here and there, as if oil-soaked; pools of shallow scum lay among blighted trees and bushes; junk-heaps of scrap metal, oil tanks like immense mushrooms, bright ugly little towns as new as varnish. And Gil was reading aloud, his ascetic face wrinkled with amusement:

"The picture is a reproduction of William Harden Foster's famous painting——"

"Famous——?"

"Yes, famous painting, 'The Sunshine Special.' The floral border combines the State Flower of each of the eleven States——"

"It's very pretty, all except the chu-chu."

"The Apple Blossom for instance—listen!—is a beautiful pink and white flower chosen by Arkansas because of its outstanding value, both commercial and esthetic. It is described by the legislature as a delight to the eye that ripens into a joy to the palate."

"Just the same, my darling, I think it's a very pretty plate."

"The Wood Violet was chosen by Illinois because of its great beauty and appeal, its modest retiring nature—like Noni—and because it grows so profusely in the State."

"It's *very* beautiful English!"

"And you may not know it, but the Passion Flower, or Maypop—don't you like Maypop?—was selected by the State Horticultural Society of Tennessee as its representative flower. It bears a fruit as large as an egg and very sweet, whose taste pleases exceedingly or repels very strongly."

"Well, which?"

"And surely the sunflower can't be, as it says here, the only genuine American flower——what about goldenrod, Noni? what about Indian pipes? what about the lady's slipper——?"

"Just the same, it's a very pretty plate, and I like the magnolias, even if they *do* look like water lilies——"

She was smiling down at the plate, her two hands laid at either side of it, she was smiling, but now she was looking very tired, very white, and it seemed odd that Gil should not have noticed it—or had he? It was absurd, the whole thing was crazy, saving money like this—sitting up all night for three nights—just in order that she might die, and perhaps even hastening it by the very economy. It was cruel. And it was not the less cruel for being self-imposed by Noni herself. He said:

"And now it's San Anton. And then it's Laredo. And then it's Mexico. All I can say is I hope to God there'll be a letter from Hambo telling us how to get there, and all about the lawyers. And gosh, how I wish we spoke Spanish! Noni, if you'd only spent less time on Bach and more on education——"

They finished the Scotch: they finished the bourbon. The paper cups leaked, even when doubled and trebled, they fell from the window sills and rolled on the floor, to be swept up by the porter with a reproachful eye. "The Megha Duta is throughout in the measure called Mandakranta, from the word 'Manda,' slow, and 'kram,' advance; in fact, it may be rendered by 'Slow Coach' in English. The following is the extract above alluded to: 'If the four first syllables at the beginning of the verse (O thou sweet lotus-smelling little flirt), then the tenth, eleventh, and afterwards the two which come after the twelfth, and the two others which are last, are long, with a caesura after the fourth, sixth, seventh syllables, the best poets (my plump little darling), call it a MANDAKRANTA.' " A *Mandakranta to Mexico*, Noni said, *a winding Mandakranta. And what sentences!* "The women there are with the lotus in the hand. . . . In the locks is interlaced the new-blown jasmine; the beauty of the face is colored a pale white with the pollen-bearing Lodra; the fresh Kuravaka is twined in the luxuriant hair; behind the pretty ear is placed the Sarisha; and, at the hair-parting, the Nipas, which spring up at thy approach. . . . Where, having women for companions, the Yakshas revel on palace terraces inlaid with precious stones, so bright with stones indeed that they look as if they were paved with flowers; where, in the starlight, they grow drunk on the aphrodisiac juice of the kalpa tree, while drums, soft and deep as thine, are gently beaten; there—O Cloud!—by the Mandara blossoms fallen from the hair in agitation, by the golden lotus broken in pieces and dropped from the ear, by the pearls on their bright breasts, and the necklaces, at the rising of the sun are disclosed the nightly ways of loving women. . . . In vain do they, covered with shame, throw a handful of *churna* on the jewel lamps with lofty flames. . . ."

"When you take a taxi in Mexico City, you say *toston* to the driver and you get it for half price——"

"Must be a superstition——"

"And the Hotel Canada, or there's another cheap one, near the station——"

"Maybe they'll meet us——?"

"In the month of the diminishing of waters! Isn't that nice? The month of the diminishing of waters. A procession of priests with music of flutes and trumpets, carrying on plumed litters infants with painted faces, in gay clothing, with colored paper wings, to be sacrificed on the mountains or in a whirlpool in the lake. It is said that the people wept as they passed by; but if so——"

"Mounted the stairs, breaking an earthenware flute against each step——"

"Then seized by the priests, his heart torn out, and held up to the sun, his head spitted on the *tzompantli*——"

"*Tzompantli?*"

"*Tzompantli.* My God, what a people; the whole land bathed in blood——!"

The flat lands, the cotton lands, mule teams on the long flat roads, cotton gins and cotton warehouses, and the interminable fields, stretching away to the sea, the gulf, the waters of the barracuda and the sea trout— time became a meaningless embroidery which unfolded and folded again its gliding greens and grays, a bizarre arrangement of light and sound. Noni was asleep with her cheek against the windowpane; Noni was awake, and holding a book, but without seeing it; Noni was coming back slowly along the littered aisle with a paper drinking cup held steadily in her hand against the lurch of the car. At San Anton, when they crossed the platform to the funny new little train, with its Jim Crow car, she walked painfully, slowly, with her hand against her side; she was biting her lips. At Laredo, after dark, he turned again, as they carried the bags forward to the Mexican car, to see with what careful slowness she followed them, the feeble ceiling lights emphasizing the hollows under her eyes, her hand resting on each chair back in turn as she entered the new world. Mexico! And then the sudden squalling and chattering rush of Indians into the dirty car, the slamming of bags and boxes, the overturning of chair backs, the human uprush as of a dark current from the underworld, inimical, violent, and hot—and Noni lying back indifferent and inert in her corner, but as if somehow really pleased—her face now a little flushed again—and after a little the inspection of the Tourist Cards——

Whoooo—whoooo—whoo—whoo——!

The train cried as it climbed, its voice whirling through the brown and blood-soaked sierras of this dark nocturnal Spain. At every station— *Anahuac—Lampazos—Villaldama*—the lighted platforms were crowded, swarming, violent with fruit vendors, vendors of cakes, trays of green leaves on which were small messes of food, trays of little pottery jugs, trays of drinks; the aisle of the car became jammed with purposeless going and coming, suitcases and boxes were shoved out of hastily opened windows, dramatic and feverish farewells were taken, tearful farewells, groups of soiled men hurrying forward to the crowded car ahead, where drinks seemed to be sold, and then the prolonged shrilling of the conductor's whistle, the sudden laughing stampede of visitors out of the car, vying with one another to see which could be the last to get off, as the train once more gathered speed for its climb into the mountain darkness. Sleep was out of the question—sleep was the last thing any of these Indians would think of, when they had the good fortune to ride on anything so exciting as a train. The conversations on all sides rose at times positively to a scream, as if the idea were to dominate, if possible, the sound of the train itself, or at any rate to assist it in conquering the dreadful silence of the wilderness that lay outside. Derisive and demoniacal laughter, full of fierce and abandoned hatred, the pride of pridelessness, the arrogance of the self-condemned; and the often-turning reptile-lidded eyes, which slowly and malevolently scrutinized the three strange Americans, the *gringos*—with

what a loving and velvety pansy-darkness of murderousness they glowed at
these natural victims! How they laughed for pure hate of this helpless and
comical and so naked but nevertheless so dangerous awareness! They
looked and laughed, looked and laughed again, openly, softly, mockingly,
with every hope of reducing the interchange as quickly as possible to that
level of frank enmity in which the more quickly and absorbedly animal of
the two natures would have all the advantage. Gil was already angry and
distressed, he blushed and stared back, he had become acutely self-conscious. Ah, the advantage of being a Jew, dark-skinned and impervious, as
inscrutable in its way as this Indian darkness——! More so, in fact; for it
was a fluid and directible thing, could flow around and into any other
kind of awareness, like the starfish on the oyster. But what about Noni?
What about poor Noni? This violence of life, this sheer violence——

The Indian girl who sat stiffly beside him, in her pink cotton blouse,
with her hands folded on the dirty wicker basket, was careful not to touch
him, leaned carefully away from him, and pretended elaborately not to
be looking, but nevertheless eyed the timetable (which he had opened
once more) with obvious fascination. And especially the outline map,
which gave in profile the altitudes from Laredo to Mexico City. They had
already, it seemed, been climbing mountains; but this as yet was nothing,
absolutely nothing. Nobody had warned them about it—not a soul. At
Monterey they would be almost half a mile up; by morning, they would
be a mile. As drawn on the little map, the ascent from Monterey to
Saltillo was practically perpendicular, it was up a precipice. And Mexico
City itself a mile and a half above sea level—but wasn't this bad for a bad
heart? Had nobody warned Noni? Not even the doctor? It seemed impossible that no one should have thought to tell her. But then, perhaps
everybody, like himself, had simply not stopped to think. One thought of
Mexico as a jungle; and if one thought of mountains, too, one didn't think
of them as anything very formidable. Or, if high, as not having the ordinary
attributes of height. . . . Was that it? . . .

At Monterey, the car half empty—everybody having rushed out to
the platform to eat and drink, and the Indian girl gone with her basket,
after a last long inquisitorial stare for the purpose of storing her memory—
Gil came wearily, sat sidelong, turning the unshaven blond face, the heavy
eyes. It was like a dream; he must have been asleep; for a moment he
couldn't listen to what Gil was saying. A half starved dog hurried along
the aisle, foraging. A pretty blonde girl, a Mexican, had sat down opposite,
and the smart young man with the cowboy hat had quite obviously and
unnecessarily taken the seat beside her to pick her up.

"—a little alarmed!"

"What?"

"—frightened. Had you known of anything? . . ."

"No, Gil! What do you mean?"

"Just after we changed at San Antonio, she said. I knew there was
something—she was such a long time in the lavatory—and perhaps you
didn't notice—I think you were in the smoking car—but when she came
back she looked like the very devil, she was white as a sheet, and she
seemed to be weak and in pain. And ever since, have you noticed——"

"I thought at Laredo she walked—when we were coming from the other car forward to this one, you know—in a rather odd way——"

"Yes."

Gil's face was drawn, tired; he was nodding quite unnecessarily, without meaning; suddenly it was impossible not to feel very sorry for him. The fatigue had somehow emphasized the essential goodness of Gil's face; he had time to think, vaguely and quickly, that of course it was this that Noni loved, this essential helplessness. He was like a child.

"But I don't suppose it could be anything serious? Have you talked to her about it, Gil?"

"I asked her if there was anything wrong; yes."

"What did she say?"

"Frankly, Blom, I thought she was a little evasive. It's that that scared me. She just said she was tired, and that perhaps it had upset her a little——"

He stopped, as if himself so tired htat he could hardly remember what he was saying, or give it the importance he remembered its deserving. He was frowning down at the fingernails of his left hand, and the onyx signet ring on the fourth finger.

"Has she been sleeping?"

"Yes, a little."

"I daresay she'll be all right. You know, we're climbing very fast, and that might affect her—it does some people."

"Oh. That might be. I hadn't thought of that."

He looked unconvinced. A little.

"Well, don't worry. It won't be long now!"

"No, it won't be long now."

And he was gone again, smiling faintly; and the train was once more pouring itself through space; or no, not that, but climbing, crying and climbing, climbing snail-like up the face of the rock of night, climbing moonlike up the smooth mirror of the sky. The blonde girl had withdrawn as near to the window as she could get, shrinking angrily away from the young man in the cowboy hat, who was looking down at her knees. Behind them, in the two corner seats, facing each other, three Indian women with babies talked in a steady birdlike rush of Spanish, a shrill and endless flood of sound, punctuated now and then with screams of laughter. Nobody wanted to sleep, there would never be any sleep again. He tried his legs to one side, then to the other, the feet wedged down against the footrail, his forehead pressed into the corner of the windowpane, the vibration of the warm glass deep in the bone, deep in the very brain. *Whoooo-whooooo-whoo-whoo*—the powerful oil-burning engine was shouting again for a crossing—but what crossing, save the eagle's, could there possibly be here? Or the cloud's? Or the buzzard's? The blonde girl had said something: very short and severe. The young man had said something: very ingratiating and suggestive, apologetic. The sleeve of Noni's blue jacket was dangling over the edge of the rack, empty, like the sleeve of a one-armed man, a mute protest at horror and injustice, and Gil's fair head was just visible, the top of it, over the back of the seat. The man with the tray of beer bottles again: he seemed to be semiofficial. The young man bought one, drank the beer out of the bottle: the blonde girl stared out of the window with fiercely averted face. Monterey to Saltillo—a half mile straight upward, as the crow flies; and after that it was practically child's play, of course, to get to Mexico City. And with all these sinister looking Indians, too, these lynx-eyed cut-throats, looking at Noni like that, with that look that stripped a woman down to sex and nothing else, exactly as you'd flay a fox! Jesus! What madness it had been, how in God's name had they ever dreamed they could do it, and what an astonishing thing that as if by a sort of instinct Noni should have projected herself—with her consciousness of death, death as immediate as a hand at the throat—into a scene of such basic fertility and filth and cruel vitality! There was something terribly right in it; it was a marriage. A marriage of what? The beer man again, he seemed now a little drunk, or was it the train only; and then he was gone and back again, and again gone. . . . And Noni was saying, close at hand, her voice so close to his ear that it might have been, but wasn't, a dream:

"Are you awake, Blom dear?"

She was leaning toward him, her two hands (one on top of the other) resting in the arm of his seat, the gold braids across the top of her head shining in the pale lamplight. For a moment they looked at each other without a word, motionless, Noni still leaning on the arm of the seat, himself turning his face from the corner where his head still rested against the window; an exchange oddly serene and unsearching, as if they had not bothered even to assume expressions, expressions of any sort. There was no guard up between them, there never had been; and it was like Noni, now, to let him see, for all her serenity, and the faint beginnings of an affectionate smile, the trace of beginning tears as well.

"Yes, Noni," he said, "sit down."

"I will, for a little. Gil's fast asleep. I'm glad."

"Yes, he was looking all in. And what about you, my lamb?"

"Oh, I'm all right."

"No, Noni."

"Yes, Blom."

Sitting beside him, with her fair head turned calmly toward him, she smiled as if with an extraordinary and quite deliberate sense of security, and put her hand on his. How ill she looked, he thought—he noted all the physical signs, one after another, at the same time thinking how little it matters, when one loves, whether the known face looks ill or well. That she looked ill, in fact, even perhaps deepened his feeling for her, sharpened his feeling of what was essential in her. The bracelet of bright hair about the bone! He said, firmly:

"You're a bad liar! Gil told me."

"What did he tell you?"

"That you were ill after the change at San Antonio."

"It was nothing."

"Noni!"

"No, really, Blom, it was nothing."

"Noni, you aren't telling me the truth."

"It was all right, Blom, dear, it was only a *little* one—and I have something I can take—no Blom, *truly*, it wasn't bad——!"

She had clutched his hand, she was shaking it almost fiercely, as if it were of passionate importance that she should convince him. And she was laughing a little in a way that he didn't like at all, hurried and anxious, breathless, a little insincere. He said:

"Tell me, please, Noni—was this the first?"

She drew back a little, was still for a second or two, her eyes all the while on his—he noted now how wide and dark were the pupils—then very slowly, and almost imperceptibly, she shook her head. She withdrew her hand, folded it with the other in her lap. At once, awkwardly, he patted her knee, smiling, and said:

"All right, darling; that's all I want to know. I don't want to know a thing more about it, or a thing more than you want, of course, to tell me; all I want to feel sure of—and *absolutely* sure, confound you!—is that you'll let me and Gil take all the strain off you that we possibly can. That's understood."

"Yes, of course."

"Okay?"

"Okay."

"And now what about holding my hand, like the naughty gal you are, and trying to get a little nap. And if I snore, I give you permission to leave me flat."

"That would be lovely. Yes."

"Incidentally, I told Gil——"

"What?"

"That it was the altitude. Quite forgetting that at San Antonio there *wasn't* any altitude! And incidentally, what *about* the altitude?"

"It doesn't matter. It won't matter."

"Sure?"

"Sure."

"Okay, go to sleep. In two hours, we'll be at Saltillo. And in the twinkling of an eye——"

"At Mexico City!"

"How'd you guess it! Sleep tight!"

"Good night."

She gave him her hand and settled herself, leaning just a little against his arm and shoulder, he saw that she had put her head back and closed her eyes, her other hand lay relaxed and half open on her knee, stirring a little with the everlasting motion of the train. Time with a hundred hands, time with a thousand mouths! The blonde girl had again said something short and severe to the young man in the cowboy hat: the young man in the cowboy hat had again said something apologetic and insinuating to the blonde girl. Blah—blah—blah—blah. What is man that thou art mindful of him? And was it today or yesterday that he had written to Clint? Far away and long ago; way back there in Arkansas. And now Noni was in Mexico, Noni was climbing the great circle to the mountain altar, Noni was trying to sleep in this infernal clamor of confusion and speed, while her hand lay in his, warm and alive. What was she thinking? She lay at peace beside him, of that he was certain; she was happy with Gil and himself, happy to be doing what she was doing. And perhaps that was all that mattered. But did she think about it at all? Did she take the trouble or the time to formulate it? No, she was allowing herself, simply—he felt absolutely sure of this—to be carried like a leaf down the torrent, lost herself in the last swift rush of living, without terror or gratitude, as also without forethought: with nothing, in fact, but a kind of pure acceptance. She was living—and the thought made him tighten ever so gently his hold on the hand that lay in his own—she was living—as how few people dare! —her death. She was living her own death. . . .

And abruptly, almost as if she had known what he was thinking, she was saying, with sleepily turned head, her cheek pressed against the chair-back:

"You don't regret it, Blom, do you——?"

"Of course not, darling. I never was so happy in my life."

"Neither was I! And now you must be very nice to Gil."

Her eyes were wide open again, and still; again they exchanged a leisurely look of unhurried understanding, in which all the future lay between them like a long-familiar landscape, every beloved feature of which was wonderfully known to them. It was all there, every bit of it: the years like seed, the years like furrows, the years like sheaves. Noni at Nonquitt, freckled, sailing an eighteen-footer; Noni in Boston, bringing back a basket of daffodils and music from Faneuil Hall, or standing in line for the symphony concerts; Noni climbing the dark mountains of Mexico. Noni with himself and her devoted Gil, and then—Gil and himself alone, looking back. . . . And as they gazed at each other, motionless, save for the quivering of arm against arm, or hand in hand, with the everlasting vibration of the train, it was as if, in that wide landscape of all life, they could see themselves, now here, now there; now in one part of the landscape and now in another; by the rocky shore of a sea, on a hillside, in a park, in a dark street; walking quickly side by side, walking always in swift unison, their faces turned towards each other, their hands now and again touching, but always, where ever they happened to be going, with perfect knowledge of a shared purpose and view, a known and accepted destiny. This was their life. This had been their life. . . . And then, quickly, the Norse-blue eyes were laughing in the tired face, and he himself was laughing, and they shook their heads at each other for rebuke of such silliness, and Noni once more composed herself for sleep, gave a little wriggle for comfort, and turned her face away.

Whoo-whoooo-whoo-whoo——!

But he was not awake at Saltillo, although he thought he had been awake all night; he could have sworn that he had known each separate time that each of the babies had cried, and the voice of each, and the voice of each of the mothers; but when he awoke, and saw the great gray fan of dawn behind and over the mountains, and the brown twilight close against his window, it was to find that the train had stopped at a tiny little station, a mere adobe hut, white-walled and deserted in the wilderness, and on its front, painted in large black letters, the incredible name: Encantada. Encantada! Enchanted, the Enchanted Town. It was the enchanted mesa of Krazy Kat. He turned quickly to tell Noni, but of course she was gone, she had gone back to Gil. In the profound stillness of early morning, the

train then began to move, glided away from the forlorn and deserted station, where not a soul was to be seen. A little mud-walled town was now
visible, on the dark scrubby slope of the mountain, as forlorn and deserted
as the station; and then, standing alone in the desert, his back to the sharply
outlined mountains in the east, a solitary shrouded figure came into view,
an Indian, wrapped closely in his sarape, standing immovable and secret as
a rock to watch the passage of the train. It was incredible; it was a dream.
It was exactly, to be sure, what he had just been dreaming—that landscapes
are like states of mind, like feelings, like apprehensions. The little town
called Encantada, deserted by all save that brooding and inscrutable hooded
figure—and at this, of all hours, the morning twilight of a desert among
mountains—all this was obviously much more intimately a part of himself
than a mere geographical section of a continent. . . . He had known it
before; as now, too, he felt that he had known before the miles and miles
of sagebrush and mesquite, the straggling rows of broken prickly pear beside
the railway line, the Spanish bayonet, the iron and copper-colored mountains saw-toothed against the cloudless and burning sky. It was no surprise
to see a wolf loping unhurriedly away towards the foothills, nor the citadels
of prairie dogs, nor the buzzards sailing in pairs, sailing and wheeling, their
wide moth wings almost motionless. It was a dream, a continuous dream;
all day it unfolded in identical character; and at breakfast and at lunch,
in the peculiar Mission dining car, with its black oak beams and gaudy
Mexican pottery, they agreed that it was something they had *all* dreamed,
all three of them, long ago, and many times.

"And those date palms, walking up and down the hills like sad little
families," said Noni.

"Or like men charging a hill in open formation."

"But so attitudinizing, so tragic and comic! And so compassionate!"

"Yes. They're really absurd."

"The little ones, especially!"

It was all a dream: and in it now, too, were the manifest distortions of
fatigue; the rocks too angular, the soil too red, the Indians too many and
too sullen, the train too crowded. The suave violinist from San Luis Potosi
gave Noni cards to his maternal "ont" in Mexico City: she ran a *pension*.
They must go to see Roberto Soto, the Charlie Chaplin of Mexico; and a
bullfight; and a cockfight. He had learned his English in school; he had
played in the symphony orchestra in Mexico City; he knew Chavez. The
Spaniards despised the pure-blooded Spaniards of Mexico. *Pulque* was the
ruin of the *peons*. Pulque? Yes, *pulque*. And these desert stretches, with the
maguey, and that other gray brushlike bush, from which it was possible to
make rubber—but farther south the country would be more beautiful. Yes.

The blonde girl had joined the three married women with their babies:
the young man with the cowboy hat sat alone in the seat, sulking. He was
listening, but pretending not to listen, to the loud conversation, the sallies
of wit, the screams of laughter, behind him. Parrot laughter: cold and
fierce. *Monterrrrrey*, the blonde girl was saying, rolling the *r* brilliantly and
mercilessly, Monterrrrrey, something about Monterey, and they all rocked
with uncontrollable and malicious laughter. She was punishing him now;
she had become the life of the party: the demure young thing whom he had

tried to seduce was keeping the whole train in an uproar. The conductors—
there seemed to be two of them—came and joined them, so did the beer
man; so did an Indian woman with a hen in a basket. And always they
were coming back to that everlasting *Monterrrrrey*.

Sure enough, the landscape had changed, was changing; and while the
mountains still kept their indomitable stations, color of slate, color of
bronze, stained with dark blood, the valleys opened outward and downward
in richer greens, in corn fields, in grain fields, and here, too, were mountain
streams, the land was no longer waterless, and now a small river running
and sparkling, where before were only dried beds of rock. Pink churches
stood among the trees, and yellow churches; far below the turning train the
wide-hatted white-clad little figures of laborers could be seen, stooping in
the rich fields. And here, by the tracks, grew goldenrod, already in bloom,
strayed all the way from New England. . . . It was in the dusk that Noni
discovered it, with her hand on the pane—Noni looking down into the
purple valley below them, where now the lights had already begun to
twinkle. Time with a hundred eyes, time the star spider!—the train had
increased its speed once more, it was on the last stretch, it was hurrying
home.

"Do you suppose he'll meet us? Do you suppose Hambo will be there?"

"God knows, Noni; I suspect the train's already late——"

"Quite a lot, I think——!"

"And we don't know how far Cuernavaca is——"

"No. I suppose, at this hour of the night—it's unlikely?"

"And this day of the month, and this year——"

"Where are we anyway? I wouldn't be in the least surprised if I woke
up in Boston——!"

"Yes, it doesn't exist. . . ."

Gil tried to read the detective magazine: Noni nodded over the Megha
Duta. Noni tried to read the detective magazine: Gil nodded over the
Megha Duta. *I Cover the Death House. Guns, Blondes, and Speed.* Burning legs, burning lips, the singed smell of the executioner! And gilded Lil,
tossing off nickel beers in the bar, after her farewell visit to her condemned
husband! *Guns, Blondes, and Speed.*

"Well, I hope he's there. Otherwise we've got to try to get into a hotel."

"O God, our help in ages past."

"And I wonder what kind of a house he's got—did you say he was
Bohemian, Gil?"

"Bohemian? No, I wouldn't say Bohemian. I met him on a ship."

The echoes of the past came around them briefly, with faint evocation;
Noni was looking at her hands, her fingernails, with fatigued amusement;
Noni came back from the lavatory a little distressed (for it was filthy), but
making a weary joke of it; Noni lay back with her hand over her eyes, tired,
while Gil gazed beyond her at the darkening landscape. Nightfall, nightfall;
the train falling around the curve of the world——

And in fact the train had now become positively suicidal. It was at last
rushing downhill, hurling itself precipitately down the mountainsides, down
gorges, down tunnels and valleys, lurching in breakback fashion around
screaming bends, falling and then checking momentarily in the pitch

darkness, only to resume its headlong disastrous plunge to Mexico City. It was unbelievable. Noni was a little frightened: so was Gil. So for that matter was himself. Gil said:

"And when you remember how that rail at Queretaro bent down *two inches*—you saw it, Noni—you just kind of wonder."

"They might as well jump straight down and be done with it!"

"Just about."

"It's as good as Coney Island! . . ."

But abruptly, and as if with purpose, the blonde girl had come back to her seat, had put on her hat with firm fingers, was getting down her bag; the train was slowing; passengers were rising, peering out of windows; another train passed them going north, at a switch point; there were rows of lights, there were buildings. Could it be? . . . Half past eleven; they were an hour late. And now the tolling bell, melancholy and slow, *ylang—ylang, ylang—ylang*, and the slowing train still slower, and the long platform with running figures; and suddenly Gil was exclaiming—as he stared down through the window——

"It's Hambo—look, it's Hambo—Noni—with a stick as tall as himself!"

"He's come to meet us—isn't he a darling?"

The round red face glared up at them affectionately, the fat fist lifted a forked stick towards them in signal; he was walking slowly alongside the train, grinning. So this was Hambo; and now everything would be simple. . . . And this familiar world, this train, would be lost forever.

(IV

"Ommernous, that's what it is, ommernous, every bit of it is ommernous!"

And not least the alien sky, with those gizzard-colored thunderheads already piling up, as Hambo said they always did in the evening, now that it was the rainy season; and not least the smells of these filthy little streets, if streets they could be called; and not least the stinking green-gray water that flowed down the gutters. The landscape, with its great red and brown mountains, everywhere visible round the sprawling white-walled mountain town, was all very handsome; and so—when it came flashing out through the clouds—was Popocatepetl; and so were the savage unfamiliar trees and flowers. It was everything that Hambo said for it. Yes, indeed! But also, it was ommernous. As for Noni——!

He had been walking a long time; exploring, with an indifferent eye, the sights of Cuernavaca; getting himself lost in the narrow streets, and finding himself again. Twice he had arrived at the same odd little church, apricot-colored, its stiff little façade framed (as if parenthetically) by two tall curved cypresses. Twice he had stumbled down to the bridge—and this was indeed fantastic!—which crossed that incredible tree-filled gorge. The fernlike trees were so interlaced across it that one thought of course it must be very shallow; only when one looked a second time did one glimpse—far below—and with a sudden contraction of the heart—tiny rocks and ripples in the filtered sunlight, knotted roots on the dank sides of the narrow little canyon, and the sinister suckers of the creepers, venomous and dark, hanging down hundreds of feet in search of a foothold. The *barranca*. To turn away from that was a relief; but what was there to turn to? The streets were all alike, the Indians were all alike; the truth was that he hated everything, everything was wrong. The market bored and irritated him; so did the sound of a foreign language, Spanish; so did the rows of stalls and barrows in the two little squares that formed the center of the town. Who the devil wanted pots or laces or belts or bead necklaces, or those dreary little messes of food—a few beans, peppers, peanuts, pods, squash seeds—on a tray? Or ears of corn simmering in little pans—so, anyway, it looked—of hot axle grease! . . . No, it was all hateful. And to come upon that sign, that mysterious sign—*Quo Vadis? Inhumaciones*—and to wonder what it meant, and to *find out*—that had been the last straw! For when he had reached the open door of the little shop, and had peered in, it was to discover that it was an undertaker's. A tasteful display of coffins—all sizes and colors— neatly stowed on shelves—and a young man in the act of tacking gray satin, very tenderly indeed, to a small kite-shaped coffin lid. And the cynical question, "*Quo Vadis?*" . . .

The truth was, they never should have done it. The midnight drive out over the mountains, immediately after getting off the train—the abrupt changes in altitude, so that even Gil and himself had been quite deafened —this had been absolute madness; they should never have listened to Noni and Hambo. Never. Though of course nobody had thought it was as far as all that, or as high; and Hambo had been in entire ignorance of the situation, and he himself powerless to speak. It was a trap. Nothing but a trap! "Only an hour," Hambo had said, grinning and patting the steering wheel; but Christ, he hadn't mentioned that you had to climb over the backbone of the continent to do it! And suddenly then, in the dark car, to feel Noni stiffening beside him, stiffening and gasping, thrusting her hands out desperately as if to find something to hold on to, then turning her face fiercely downward against his arm, lest the look of agony be seen, be seen by Gil—the terrible strong shudders of the body, in its powerful instinctive struggle against the enemy within—and all the while the pathetic heroic effort to minimize the convulsion, and to protect poor frightened Gil. "No," he said aloud; "no, things can't be like that, no. . . ."

Turning a corner at random, he stumbled a little on the cobbles, saw the square with the fountain once more before him, and decided he might as well go to Charlie's at once—where he was to meet Hambo—and wait there. It was nearly time anyway—or wasn't it? And besides, his teeth were chattering—which was damned funny, as it was very hot—and a drink would do him good. Charlie's, anyway, was unmistakable—you could see the sign a mile off, a little corner café with open stone arches and red- covered tables, facing the palace square. Cafés, in fact, were everywhere. There was another one next door, and outside this was a crowd of Indians, in their white and pink cottons, trying to get into—or out of, it was difficult to say which—a ramshackle bus. The driver was racing the engine, which rose to a shattering but somehow decrepit roar, a bell began clanging rapidly in the porch of the café, a bird, a really extraordinary bird—at that moment he saw it in its cage, over the gunny sack partition between the two cafés—began simultaneously to scream a contrapuntal and Bachlike thing, which ascended by concealed half tones, and suddenly the bus shot away around the corner of the square, on two wheels, two young men running after it and swinging up on the rear step as it went. The astonishing bird song had stopped as abruptly as it had begun—after a brilliantly complicated climb of perhaps half an octave—and the entire separate uproar attending the departure of the bus had ceased. He ordered his whisky and sat down.

An enormous white butterfly—preposterous—went by, on soft, slow wings—it was like the leisurely waving of a handkerchief. These tropics certainly did things in a big way. Over the red palace of Cortez, on the far side of the square, the clouds had become of an unbelievable purple—there could be no doubt that they meant business, and soon. Not that anybody minded. The hubbub went on just the same; Indian boys on shiny new bicycles rode round and round the square, bumping in and out of the dusty holes, and displaying a positive genius for falling off. A blind beggar, with white slits for eyes, and as evil a face as he ever had seen, was led into the café, and out again, by a frightened little girl. A starved dog with a broken back, the hind quarters twisted, dragged itself crookedly to the little parapet of flowerpots by the entrance, and lay there, mutely begging. No attention was paid to it. The eyes, tender and trusting, beseeching, were enough to break one's heart; and when at last it gave up hope, and began to drag itself away, it heaved such a sigh of pure and beaten despair as ought rightly to have ended the world. He watched its pitifully slow progress all along the side of the darkening square, towards the palace, and then out of sight round a corner. He felt quite sure that it was going away to die; that sigh could have meant nothing else. And it was an indictment of mankind. Or of God? It came to the same thing. . . . Meanwhile, the Bach-bird had again broken out into song, fought its way up that furious contrapuntal cataract of glittering and savage semitones, made once more the final leap of triumph. And just then, round the very corner where the little dog had disappeared, Hambo came into sight, in the dusk, walking slowly with his tall forked stick, for all the world like St. Christopher. The swimming pool had given him lumbago; and the forked stick had been borrowed from one of the rose trees in the garden. Good-natured and solemn, the fringe of blond beard making the round face look a little odd, he approached self-consciously and shyly.

"It's going to rain like hell," he said. "I see you found it."

"Yes, I found it."

"I'm not sure we oughtn't to get back pretty soon, you know—it's late, and it goes dark suddenlike, and when it rains here, it rains. Not to mention lightning. Also, I didn't as a matter of fact like to leave Gil and Noni alone in the house, not speaking any Spanish—Noni doesn't seem very well, does she? It seemed to me that Gil was a little worried. And there's this goddamned fiesta on, you know, San Manuel, with a marimba band in the house across the road, and everybody drunk—they're making a *hell* of a

row, and usually it means trouble. Christ, yes, the gardener's woman—
Pablo, the gardener, you know—just came reeling up the drive and flung
her arms around my neck and kissed me. She was drunk, of course."

"Has Noni got up yet?"

"No, she's still in bed, I think. I haven't seen her. I was thinking, you
know, that if she's ill, that row must upset her. And they'll keep it up all
night. They always do. And Pablo will get pretty drunk, too."

"Is there a good doctor here?"

"There's a funny little Mexican fellow, who's quite good—he mostly
treats the soldiers in the barracks for syphilis, you know—an army doctor,
but good. I hope it's nothing serious?"

"I think I ought to tell you that it *is*, but that Noni doesn't want Gil
to know. It's her heart."

"Oh."

"Which makes it very awkward."

"It does! Yes."

"So that about all we can do is wait and see. I don't like to send for a
doctor, or urge Noni to let me send for one, until I get my cue from her—
but of course, if things took a turn for the worse, I would."

"I see."

Hambo protruded his lower jaw, bared his lower teeth in a grin of
embarrassed preoccupation, hissed through them softly. He tipped the little
glass of pale *tequila* into the tumbler of cracked ice, squeezed half a green
lime into it with awkward fingers. He said, sidelong:

"I'm afraid, by Jesus, I haven't been very helpful. I bring her the glad
news that the divorce is going to take months instead of weeks, and cost
twice as much as she thought—and provide a house full of scorpions, with
beds that not even a Chinaman could sleep in. And worst of all, I drag her
over the mountains at midnight, after she's been three and a half days
without sleep, instead of taking her straight to a hotel. I really thought, you
know, that you fellows would like to get it over with, get out here and get
settled, instead of having the trouble of digging yourselves into a hotel and
then out again. Besides, the hotels in Mexico City are god-awful holes, and
there's nothing to see there anyway. Only churches. But I guess I was a
damned fool. . . . Will you try a *tequila?*"

"It wasn't your fault at all. It was nobody's. . . . Yes I will."

He had a tequila, and another, and a third; he thought they tasted a
good deal like prohibition alcohol. The approaching storm had formed an
immense purple-black canopy over the city, and against it now the electric
lights showed an uncanny and brilliant white. In the tall eucalyptus trees
over the illuminated fountain—or were they a kind of laurel?—hundreds
of large birds were quarreling and screaming, darting to and fro as meaninglessly as the small boys on their bicycles. Hambo was talking about the
niño—an insect like a cricket, he said, only paler in color—Pablo, the
gardener, had brought him one, holding it up by one of its antennas, and
tickling the sting in its tail with a stick—and it was so deadly poisonous, yes,
that there was no known antidote for it. Your throat swelled up until you
died of suffocation. Suffocation, yes. The scorpions were quite easy—
though every night it was as well to have a look around, knock them off
the ceiling. Then there were the *salamancescas*, the little lizards with red

pouches under their throats; beautiful little things; you would see them sitting on the rosetrees—deadly poison too——

"My God, *everything* here seems poisonous!"

"You never said a truer word, Blomberg. Nature red in tooth and claw. The ants here would as soon as not pick your eyes out while you sleep. And as for the Indians—here comes the rain."

A surge of wind over the tall trees announced its coming, a quick wrinkle, of lightning, succeeded almost instantly by a stinging crash of thunder, and at once the rain was falling in a massive downpour, as if it had been raining forever. Across the little side street, the cannon-shaped waterspouts along the eaves of the Café San Marco poured solid round streams of water in a series of loud cataracts on to the sidewalk. The proprietor, in shirt sleeves, a toothpick in his mouth, stared gloomily across at them from his table, very cross-eyed; he looked like a brigand. Hambo nodded towards him, and said:

"Quite a nice chap, though he doesn't look it. His daughter was one of the waitresses here, until she got pregnant. And even then! In fact, I began to be worried about it. . . . If we stand at the entrance, we can signal a taxi. I don't think we'd better walk. There's a taxi *sitio* just up the line, and they may see us."

He stood on the step, waving his ridiculous stick, and grinning, and sure enough in no time at all they were in a smart and glittering but dripping taxi, had plunged down the precipitous road towards the bridge over the gorge, but instead had then turned to the right below the palace, and had slowly crept along the bumpy road which led out of town into the wilderness. They had passed the row of little shops; a bare wooden dinner table set out in the street, covered with empty bottles; a tethered goat; a drunk leaning back helplessly against a white wall.

"*Pulque*," said Hambo, significantly. And then after a while he added: "I'm afraid there's only a cold bite of tongue for supper—Josefina's been in a bad temper today, and is frank about not liking company. But at least she doesn't drink."

"I'm afraid we're rather a handful."

"Oh gosh, no, it's fun. I'm only too glad. But I certainly hope poor Noni isn't going to be——"

He broke off, to lean forward and say something in Spanish to the driver. Presently the car swerved to the left, the headlights lighting brilliantly a white wall hung with bougainvillia—Blomberg had time to see that the two houses on the other side of the road were brightly lighted—and then they had come to a stop. Now, above the steady sound of the rain on the taxi roof, they could hear loud laughter, and then the marimba band, behind them. Hambo was studying the loose silver in the palm of his hand. The headlights rested on that extraordinary little tree, outside the gardener's shed—the little tree which was covered with inverted lilies. He had never seen anything like it in his life. It was quite unreal, a sort of dream—but so, then, was everything; and he found himself wondering, while he waited for Hambo to figure out the change, whether indeed the whole strange expedition, and their presence here, and even Noni's illness, were not just as improbable as this lamplit tree. It was the first thing he had seen, in the morning, out of his window—with hummingbirds flexing their sensitive little bodies for entrance to the hanging white blossoms—and then, too, as now, he had been inclined to read into it some esoteric meaning. Something wildly improbable, the kind of thing one thinks when in despair, or the last stages of exhaustion: as, for example, that the little tree simply meant that Noni would not die. And not only that, but also that Noni, and himself, and Gil, had never, any of them, existed at all. Everything, in short, was all right—the tree proved it.

An electric flashlight had come jerkily up the path towards them; it was Gil with an umbrella—good old Gil! But then Gil was saying to Hambo, through the swung door of the taxi—leaning forward, and rather white—

"I'm damned glad you've come—there's something wrong, something's happened—they've been shouting their heads off——"

"*Who* have!"

"Josefina and Pablo."

The taxi door had slammed, they were running down the slippery path in the welter of rain toward the open dining-room door. In the dining room the table was set, and beyond this, on the long verandah, they could hear the steady, angry shouting of the two voices. They were at the far end of the verandah—Josefina leaning her back to the wall, her hands folded behind her, Pablo rocking before her, very drunk, with pools of water on the tiles round his bare feet. Hambo, stick in hand, approached them slowly, his voice rising; suddenly he had shouted them down. Pablo stared sullenly, swaying; his eyes were bloodshot, he was breathing heavily. Josefina turned her bland, wrinkled face, smiling with a sort of polite cunning, the neat black braid hung forward over her shoulder. She began a long, deliberate, unexcited explanation, always smiling, her hands always clasped behind her: now and then Pablo interrupted with a violent interjection or drunken gesture, began to address Hambo, "Señor!" only at once to give in. . . .

It was money—his wages—but it was also his woman. . . . After he had gone, pocketing the few *pesos* Hambo had given him, and muttering to himself angrily as he lurched away among the slatting banana trees toward the English Consul's badminton court, and the *barranca* beyond, the confused story was partially cleared up. But only partially. He was so drunk—Josefina made this very apparent—that he was incoherent. But he wanted his back wages, for he wanted to leave, he was in trouble. He couldn't remember—Josefina told Hambo in Spanish—whether or not it was so, but he thought perhaps he had drawn a knife on his woman; the police would be after him; it might be better if he went to Mexico City for a few days. He had a cousin there, but he needed the *pesos* to get there, and for food. . . .

It was while Josefina was saying this once more, with glee, and just as Hambo had explained it to Gil and himself, and just, too, as Noni, with the back of one hand against her mouth, had come to the door of her room, behind them—Hambo was repeating that in all probability Pablo, being full of *pulque*, had simply imagined the whole thing—it was just then that they heard him coming back. They heard him still cursing, saw him stagger toward them up the dark slope of irrigated earth under the banana trees, the white figure looking very insubstantial, almost as if it drifted, and then he half fell up the tile steps, and they saw that in his hands he held a knife.

Josefina screamed: Noni stood exactly as she had before, quite still, with her hand against her mouth: Hambo took a step forward. But Pablo was merely explaining—he just wanted to see his knife in the light—that was all—turning it, he moved towards the open door of Hambo's room, he lowered it so that it might catch the rays of the lamp; and it was then that they all saw two things: one, that his trousers had been slit all the way down one leg, from waist to ankle; two, that his knife was covered with blood. While they were still standing speechless with astonishment at this, Pablo himself had already turned and gone down the steps, stooped for a moment to wipe the long blade in the grass by the path, talking to himself, and once more vanished under the banana trees towards the *barranca*.

"By God, I believe he's killed her!"

Hambo turned to Gil, grinning, as he said this; and it seemed to Blomberg that he said it too loudly, too much with an air as of some symbolic meaning. The sort of theatricality he seemed rather given to—though certainly the scene itself had lacked nothing of the theatrical. The attitude, too—the forked stick held upright in the air, for all the world like a druid's wand—seemed a shade overdone, and the characteristic embarrassed grin. A pity, almost, that there couldn't have been a flash of lightning just then, a particularly bright one, to make the thing more spectacular still; and still further to emphasize Hambo's obvious implication that it was all very trivial, very commonplace, and that even if he *had* killed her it didn't much matter. It was life in the tropics, life in the jungle, nature red in tooth and claw! Of course. It was the heart torn from the victim's breast, the head spitted on the *tzompantli*, the dark underworld current of destructive and creative blood—just as simple as that, no more complex than that. Damned funny!

And he did think it funny; until, beginning to smile at the dark current of his own thoughts, and turning his head towards Noni for an exchange of the unspoken, he saw her, with her hand still against her mouth, but her eyes now closed, start to slide down the edge of the doorjamb in a queer, hesitant, slowly *freer* way, which he couldn't for a fraction of a second understand. He caught her just as her head fell forward, lifted the slight figure in his arms. The beloved golden braids shone in the lamplight immediately under his eyes. But no sooner had he touched her than he knew that her heart had ceased to beat; and he read a swift confirmation of his own surmise in the stilled faces—where the same surmise seemed to be frozen—of Hambo and poor Gil.

⟨ V

It had rained in torrents all night—or so, at any rate, it had seemed. To the slatting and slapping of the banana leaves in the wind, the reverberations of the thunder, and the intermittent roar of rain on the pantiled roof, had been added as well the cruelly exultant accompaniment—it seemed almost like a conspiracy—of the marimba band. There was something diabolic in this—something devilish. That steady pulse of ecstatic animal passion, throbbing in the darkness, seemed to him to have an absurd and out-rageous finality in its comment on the defeated body which now lay on the cot, unlistening, in Hambo's lamplit room. My god, what a comfort to be able to pray, as Josefina had done—to fall frankly and loudly on one's knees, there and then, weeping, offering one's grief and humility to that evidence of divine agony! But no such assuagement for himself and Gil; only, in-stead, as they looked incredulously, and as if betrayed, at Noni, or at the reflection of her in the great gilt-framed mirror which hung over the head of the bed, a sense of loss which already was widening and deepening with the winged swiftness of time itself. The reflection of the still body, in the tilted mirror, foreshortened a little in the dim light, had reminded him of some religious picture—perhaps it was the Mantegna Christ. It was a votive offering: there could be no doubt about that: it was, as he remem-bered now, a throwing of flowers into the sea: and that a life should have been so beautiful, and so devoted to good and beautiful things, in the face of the uncompromising principles of impermanence and violence, came to him as a fierce renewal of his faith in the essential magnificence of man's everlasting defeat. As Noni herself, even now, would be thinking. . . .

And the indifferent violence of this night she would herself, also—gratefully, and with delight—have praised. Just the sort of fruitful and un-foreseen counterpoint, nature's wild multiplicity, which she had always passionately loved! Thunder, and a marimba band—what could be better? Music to hear, why hear'st thou music sadly? And the lightning, too. . . . Once, in the night, after hours of vivid sleeplessness—he had lost all sense of time—he got up and went to the window to watch the lightning. So continuous had it become that in its light he could watch the advance of a ragged black edge of cloud right across the sky: the whole sky was quivering with it: and against this palpitant radiance came unceasingly the fierce downward stroke of vermilion or violet. As for the marimba band—it was unremittingly merciless. All night long, over and over again, the same two or three tunes, coming in sudden bursts through the lashed and drenched jungle of the garden, hot and quick, like flashes of sound; dying away for a little, amid a confusion of stampings and laughter, or sinking in a calculated languor, only to be once again savagely revived. He would know those tunes for the rest of his life. And henceforth, they would belong to Noni.

At daybreak, after the rain had stopped, he heard Josefina's cough in the garden, her slow footsteps on the gravel path, the sharp slap of the screen door. Water began to rush loudly along the irrigation channel just outside the window—he could smell, too, the unwholesome dankness of it—and that maddening bird, the one which Hambo called the jitter bird, began his everlasting repetitive hypnotic phwee-phwee-phwee-phwee-*tink*, phwee-phwee-phwee-phwee-*tink*, lost in the top of one of those tall dark trees. In no time at all, then, it was light; Josefina was cautiously sweeping the verandah; the tap of a stick on the tiles announced Hambo. . . . He took his clothes to the bathroom and dressed.

When he emerged on to the verandah, it was to face a world which overnight had been brilliantly re-created: everything flashed and sparkled: in the dazzling east, once more visible, the great volcano sunned its shoulders of ice. He sat on the verandah parapet, watched a brown lizard proceeding along the path below him in a series of short straight dashes, and then, apparently alarmed, scurry back to his hole in a single continuous rush. The morning was still—the wind had dropped—the banana leaves hung limp and unstirring. He noticed that the lower leaves, the older ones, were ragged, split in parallel fringes, or fingers—they had a longer knowledge of the wind; the upper and younger leaves were still smooth and in one piece. And that scarlet dragonfly—it had a favorite observation post, it returned always to one rose-tree tip, and sat there always facing exactly the same way, toward the swimming pool. Hambo's stick tapped behind him, and Hambo was saying gently:

"Good morning!"

"Good morning!"

"I don't know whether you would care to join me; I was just going for a little turn down the road, towards the *barranca*."

"Yes, I'd like to."

"It's the coolest time of day, and the nicest. . . ."

They were silent, a little embarrassed, as they passed the gardener's shed, the little lily-covered tree, the hedge of hibiscus, the bamboo grove. Turning to the left as they emerged from the drive, they stood aside for a moment to allow a small herd of goats to pass—five goats, one sheep, and a boy. The heavy smell hung in the air after they had gone. He said, awkwardly:

"This is very unlucky for you—platitudinous, I'm afraid, but true."

"Nonsense, Blomberg. I'm only too glad if I can be of any help. As soon as the post office is open, we'll buzz down and send off your wire. Not much else we can do till then."

"No."

"I suppose your further plans you can't, as yet, know. Neither you nor Gil."

"Personally, I think I shall go right back. But first I'll find out what Gil wants—if he needs me, and wants to stay here, of course I'll stick around. One of those things it's not too easy to find out! I *suspect* he would like to stay here alone with you—but he may feel shy about saying so. Once I feel sure about it, I'll shove off. Perhaps today."

"Yes. I see. I can understand that."

"Not much point in it!"

"No."

They were silent again; he noticed for the second time the bright yellow little flower by the gutter's edge, candid, wide open—it reminded him of something else—yes, it was like the periwinkle. And that little blue flag—he hadn't seen it since his childhood. Brilliance everywhere—as they turned a bend in the road, and looked downward into the extravagant richness of the valley, with its cornfields, its terraced groves of papayas and bananas, and the morning sunlight already hot as honey over everything, he couldn't help, for just an instant, thinking it was all an outrage. Brilliant, yes, but meaningless! As meaningless as a tomb. Would Gil want to stay and face that——? He found himself reflecting that nothing of this could really be discussed with Gil—nothing at all. Years must pass before that could happen, if indeed it *ever* could happen. Probably never. The realities must be concealed, Gil must be protected.

A tiny donkey came up the muddy road toward them, almost completely hidden under its burden of grass, head downward, walking with neat quick little feet. Hambo gestured with his stick, pointing ahead, where below them lay the little stone bridge in a clump of trees.

"That's the *barranca*, there," he said. "Where Cortez crossed. Shall we go down and smoke a morning pipe? Have you got your pipe?"

"Yes—let's have a morning pipe."

"Right! But watch your step, it's slippery."

He led the way down the narrowing path, and Blomberg followed. . . . That absurd figure, with the forked stick—and such a damned good fellow——! He began shaking his head from side to side, slowly, as he took out his pipe; it was all too much for him, too much altogether. He wanted to laugh at Hambo—wanted to laugh out of pure misery. "And, Christ," he thought, patting his pocket to see whether he had any matches, "Christ, but I'm a long way from home!"

Conversation

or Pilgrims' Progress

([I

Tirra-lirra, tirra-loo, tirra-lirra, tirra-lee—"

"That doesn't make sense, daddy."

"Neither it does. But what does it matter? What's the difference between a loo and a lee? And now then, young woman, how about getting out of that there bath. It's late! Look how late it is! It's autumn! The leaves are falling off the trees! It's going to be cold, you'll catch your death of cold!"

"Oh, but it's so nice in here. Can I do just one handsquirt, just one?"

"Just one. And the leaves came tumbling down—"

"Why do the leaves come off the trees, daddy?"

"Now out you get. Up—!"

He loved to feel the firm small wet body, the compact little chest, between his hands, the legs wriggling and thrusting for the bathmat as he put her down: it was as good as eating, as good as drinking. As good as singing, as good as autumn. The round face, the blue eyes, emerged from the rapid towel to say:

"But *why* do the leaves tumble off the trees!"

"Listen to them scuttling like mice in the pathway, listen to them blowing!"

"But why, but why!"

"I'll tell you what it is, Buzzer, it's a mystery."

"A mystery!"

They gazed together, turning, out of the little groundfloor window of the bathroom, watched the poplar leaves floating down, streaming on air, wafts and drifts and chains of them, golden and endless—like a kind of music, he thought, as inexhaustible and without origin as music.

"But of course you wouldn't know what a mystery is, would you?"

"A mystery, a mystery, a mystery—"

"It's a nice word, and a very important one. It's one of those words as big as a barn door, as big as a circus tent, as big as a railway station, as big as a hollowed-out mountain, so that you can drive anything you like into it—herds of sheep, flocks of cattle, horses, trucks, armies, wagons, cannons, ideas, stars, worlds, moons—in fact, anything you like. See?"

"Now my hands!"

"Did I forget those hands—? Foo! But you see, my pet, it's like this. Once a year the trees all get very tired, and very sleepy, and they want to go to bed."

"To bed! Ho ho, how silly, as if a tree could go to bed! Ho ho!"

"Yes, sir, to bed. They want to go to sleep, and so what do they do? They do just exactly what *you* do, they take off their clothes."

"And the leaves are their clothes! But *we* don't have leaves for clothes, daddy!"

"Ah, that's just where you're wrong. Didn't you ever hear tell of Mother Eve?"

"Of course! Eve and Adam were the first man and woman in the Garden of Eden. Anybody knows *that*. Now my *toes!*"

She lifted one foot, waggled the toes at him.

"Quite right. And you see, Eve wore a fig leaf, that's what she did—"

"And took it off in the autumn, when she wanted to go to sleep?"

"Well, I daresay. Anyway, that's what they *say* she wore—you'd think it must have been a little bit chilly, wouldn't you! Tirra-lirra, tirra-loo—"

"And then do the trees go to sleep?"

She put her hands on the window sill, to look again at the falling of the leaves, automatically raised them as he lowered the little nightgown over the curled head, and worked them skilfully through the sleeves, the face with primmed mouth once more emerging in triumph, like a seal from a wave.

"The trees, bless their hearts, go to sleep. All winter they just dream and rest, exactly, for all the world, as if they were in their beds. After all, you have *flower* beds, you know!"

"Ho ho—and who'd like to sleep in a flower bed! Not me!"

He turned her around, opened the door, smacked her small bottom, guided her toward the hall with a firm finger planted in the middle of her back.

"Well, off to your own, then, if you like that better. Quick! March!"

Ahead of him, she scrambled barefoot up the painted stairs, straddling a little to do so, and he followed smiling. Wind-borne and uneven, he heard the church clock striking seven, and listened, as always, for the queer quavering stammer of the final stroke. The Unitarian Church, the village, the main street, the post office, the evening mail—already the loquacious line would be forming in the shabby little post office, the towns-folk would be there for the evening inspection of each other, the evening spying into each other's affairs. And there might be a letter—his heart be-gan to beat more quickly—he mustn't think of that. And yet, why not? It *ought* to seem particularly naughty—just now, just here—with Buzzer reaching up to trip the latch of the dusk-filled bedroom—but it didn't. No morals in nature, none!

"Tirra-lee!" he said, "and into bed with you."

"Why did you give me my bath? Why didn't mummy give me my bath?"

"Because mummy was very tired, see?"

"Well, then, you must tell me a story."

"I'll tell you a story about John McGlory—"

"Not *that* one!"

"I'll tell you another about his brother—"

"No, no, no, no, *no!*"

"There isn't time tonight, my pet. The world's coming to an end any minute now, and daddy must be there to see it. In with you!"

He threatened her comically, with raised hand, and, pretending alarm, she skipped into the little cot, whipping the pink feet under the blue coun-terpane, with its embroidered birds.

"Ho ho," she said, "you can't fool *me!* It *isn't* coming to an end! Good night."

"Good night."

He stooped to kiss the still damp cheek; the blue eyes looked abstract-edly past him, she was already dismissing him, she had already begun to sing her night-song. Good lord—he thought—how quickly they do it, how quickly they swoop from one world into another! If it was only as easy as that! Patting her knee idly, and straightening up, he looked through the screened window into the little garden, saw Chattahoochee, the cat, in the act of sitting down demurely under the poor bare-armed little plum tree —if ever a tree had committed suicide, *that* one had—and beyond it, be-yond the low white fence, Mrs. Purington moving about in her kitchen next door. A motor boat was chugging in the river, probably Mr. Riley, the fisherman, back from scalloping, the dirty blue boat, foul with fish scales, approaching the Town Landing—maybe it would be a good idea to go and see. On his way to the post office? Afterward? In case there should be a letter—? He frowned as he turned away and closed the white door behind him, frowned as he hesitated at the top of the stairs. But there was Enid, there was Endor, there was Ee—he could hear her in the kitchen now, the clink of a saucepan on the stove, or the sink—and resentment was unmis-takable in the sound, it had been piling up all day. Odd, how one knows— just as one knows a storm is approaching, feels it in the air—the distant mutter even while the sky is still hot and cloudless, the first little sinister breeze turning the silver seams of the poplar trees, a chill draft from the southwest, and then the mounting purple of the clouds, and the Unitarian church steeple turning—suddenly—a livid tombstone white. He took out the watch from the pocket of his khaki trousers—how ridiculous, he knew perfectly well what time it was—and replaced it without looking at it. And now, on top of everything else, this unfortunate business of Jim Connor—

He rattled down the steps, to let Enid know that he was coming—and coming cheerfully—paused at the entrance to the cluttered little studio living room, looked in. The last of the autumn sunlight slanted across the unfinished picture which stood on the easel—the colors jumped out awry, glowed, he felt himself flowing into that shape of ruin, that shape of an old barn on a tangled hill, amongst wild grass, wild lilacs, wild apple trees —but at once the current reversed itself, flowed back on itself, for once more it was unmistakably a failure—a dud, a flop. Impotence, impotence —the hand powerless to shape the actual, the vision powerless to purify its own shafts of light—what was the trouble, what the devil was it? Deep and perhaps inoperable as a cancer, the fine roots untraceably spread and wound in the unconscious, in his whole life—it was perhaps the life itself which was all wrong, wrongly rooted—what was needed was a giant sponge, a new start. But where? Not here. Not with this hall stove which must soon be laid and lit, the coals fetched in from the woodshed in the garden, the ashes dumped on the rain-gutted road that led down to the Town Landing —and yet, why not? Why not indeed! This was rich, real, rank—as rank as the snarled nasturtiums on the river wall at the foot of the garden, as rank as marsh and seaweed, the crawling mudflats at low tide, or the winter, which would presently howl its snows and bitter stars about the small wooden houses of the village, freezing the pipes, sending icy drafts up through the cracks between bare floorboards, chilling the rooms with white light through frosted windows. Real enough, Christ, yes! And as real too as the sound of running water which now came from the kitchen sink.

In the dining room, two silver candlesticks on the table, which had not been set, and Buzzer's porringer on her own little white table under the window—he picked it up, for it would be an ambassador for him, and went down the two steps into the kitchen lean-to.

"Here's these," he said.

"Well, put them down!"

Dark curls turning on the pink smock, the small stubborn head half turning, the liquid green eyes—lovely!—flashing toward and past him, but on a level lower than his own, not meeting his, lowering again to the bright collander in which she was shaking potatoes. The potatoes were very important; she was humming to herself, preoccupied, a cloud of steam rose softly from the kettle on the stove.

"All bathed and abed," he said, "and went like a lamb."

"Did you give her a quilt? It's going to be cold."

"No, I didn't think of it."

"Never mind, then, I'll do it myself."

"I thought I'd go for the mail."

"It couldn't *possibly* wait till after supper, I suppose."

"My dear Ee, you know it would be closed."

"And is there any such important mail that it can't wait till morning?"

"Just the same, I think I'll go, if you don't mind. . . ."

She made no answer as he let himself out through the garden door. The screen clacked behind him, he walked slowly around the back of the house, and looked down over the sloping lawn towards the river and the Town Landing. Mr. Riley, on the cabin roof of the blue motorboat, was in the act of stepping across, rubber-booted, to the rotten piles of the wharf— tomorrow there would be scallops—and a car could be heard kicking up the loose boards of the bridge, rumbling and rattling as it came, then accelerating swiftly as it shot up the sandy road past the Bank, scattering dead leaves lavishly to left and right.

Leaves everywhere—the road that led to the Town Landing was ankle-deep with them, they lay in loose golden drifts on the field where Mr. Riley's nets were spread out to dry, from the tall poplars even now they floated down in lazy parallel chains and curves, they clung about the fading stalks of the chicory, whose last blue flowers glowed like pale stars. Another night, another frost, and the trees would be bare—summer was over. Tirra-loo-tirra-lee! "Shadows rising on you and me"—shadows *rising* was good, one could imagine the shadows rising like water, like a tide, like these full-moon tides. Coming up about one's feet, climbing, deepening—but it was no joke, it was all too true! No letter from Nora, not a word in two weeks, and this on top of her refusal—unwillingness? inability?—to see him last time, and the time before that the unfortunate meeting at the hotel in Boston, and now, as if that wasn't enough, this damned Jim Connor business, and Enid—

Mr. Murphy, getting out of his Ford, just back from the evening train with the mails, waved from his yard, and on the piazza of the Murphy boarding house the old loony was sitting, Miss Schermerhorn, rocking herself intently in a rocking chair, her eyes fixed brightly on the road. She beckoned to him, leaned forward, said mysteriously:

"Did *you* hear anything, mister?"

"No?"

"It's the water running, the water running in the cellar, they forgot to turn it off!"

"Oh!"

"Yes, they'd ought to be told, they went away and left it running!"

"Very well, I'll tell them."

She looked unconvinced, but also as if it didn't much matter, and resumed her rocking. What a village! Every other person cracked or feeble-minded—gone to seed. Dear old Mrs. Chandler, the seamstress, stopping everybody in the streets—of course, it was the only trace of anything wrong with her, otherwise she was perfectly normal—to talk about underclothes, and apropos of absolutely nothing. The weather, the news, the children, the yacht races, the taxes, the church supper—and then suddenly the vital, the burning, question, toward which she had been cunningly working all the time, the dark and precious secret. Yes, I *like* silk, I *like* silk, but then don't you think there is something *really* nicer, *really* cleaner, about *linen*? I change sometimes nine or ten times a day! And Mrs. Kimpton, the washerwoman, with her obscure passion for corsets! Always poking about in the town dump for new specimens—no matter in what state of dilapidation— going there day after day—and then putting them up all round her living-room, as one might put flowers, or pictures! What the devil was *that* all about? A mystery, as Buzzer had said, a mystery, a mystery! But no stranger, perhaps, than wanting to paint.

Two men were standing outside the post-office door, talking, and when he went into the post office, now empty, and peered into Box 67 in the slant light, that too was empty. Nothing. Not a word, not a scrap—nothing. He turned, walked out slowly, paused on the little triangular corner of gravel outside, looked unseeing to left and right.

"When was that, that it became that amount?"

"Just before I went into the hospital."

"And what did you do, did you tell her about it before you went into the hospital?"

"Sure I did. What do you take me for!"

"Well, I don't understand it, and that's a fact."

He crossed the street, took the long way around the block, scuffed the dead leaves with dusty shoes. Empty again. Empty! But it was himself who felt empty: a slow and hollow pang, a queer mixture of guilt and suffering. But why feel guilty *now*, if—as it appeared—she had decided to end the affair, to drop him? It didn't make sense. Understandable enough that he should feel ashamed when he *got* a letter, to read it and carry it about in secret, or burn it slyly in the fireplace—but why *now*, when perhaps the whole delicious exciting thing might be over, and his integrity (willy-nilly) restored? Of course, he had seen it coming—it had begun when he moved to the country, and couldn't see her so often, or *thought* he couldn't. She hadn't reproached him, but just the same you couldn't blame her! *Thought* he couldn't! Ah! of course! The truth was that he *could* have seen her, and even oftener, if he had then really wanted to; but that he himself had definitely not felt like it. Yes. He had been a little bored, a little depressed, by the continuous necessity for secrecy and furtiveness, had simply wanted a rest. And Nora had seen through it.

Oh, well, maybe it was all for the best. It would certainly simplify things, makes things easier with Enid? . . . The slow pang hollowed itself out in his breast again—dear delightful humorous Nora!—but he quenched it, looked away from it, looked down through the Puringtons' garden at the river and the dismasted hulks which lay on their sides on the farther shore—rotting, like so many other things in this sleepy little town—and then, with quicker steps, and a clear sense of relief—or no, not quite that, not quite, but at any rate a sharper sense of detachment and singleness with which to face Enid—he entered his own garden. He walked past the house, toward the back. Terence's blue wagon stood there, looking very large in the twilight, the horse pawing at the grass, and Enid and Terence were talking at the kitchen door.

"It's the lilacs," Enid said. Her arms were folded across her breast, across the pink smock, and she addressed the remark rather to the wagon than to himself.

"Guess you got plenty of 'em, too, Mr. Kane, judging by the looks of those boxes!" Terence took out his clay pipe, grinned, spat.

"A hundred, Terence—ninety-seven plain, and three fancy! What are we going to do with them?"

Enid turned and opened the kitchen door.

"And when you've finished—" she looked down toward the river— "there's some one in the sitting room, the studio, waiting to see you."

The door clacked shut behind her—why the devil couldn't she say who it was!

"Well, Mr. Kane, guess we'd better get 'em in tonight. 'Twon't do 'em no good to lay around here in the frost!"

"You think there's going to be a frost?"

"A good one. I'll come over after supper and bring a shovel."

"Okay, Terence. Let me know and I'll give you a hand."

"They sure packed 'em up good. Quite a weight, too. I thought I'd bust a gut!"

The three boxes lay like great coffins on the grass, the torn grass, the sand showing where the box corners had gouged through the thin topsoil, and Terence kicked one of them affectionately with the toe of a heavy boot.

"And where did you have it in mind to put them?"

Together they looked along the sloping garden, now growing dark, the bare little garden which led down to the river. The river gleamed almost unnaturally in the queer light—bat-light, he thought, betwixt-light, the hour of the mosquito—but later, of course, there would be the full moon.

"Wants two nights for the full moon," Terence added. "Guess we can make out to *see*, all right!"

"All along both sides, Terence—right from the street on that side and from the back of the kitchen on this. And then a few across the middle there, halfway down, leaving just a sort of gateway through to the lower terrace. Where you built the wall."

"Never will I forget those fleas!"

"Yes, that was funny."

"It was all them rats. Yes, sir, it was from them rats they come; foh, I never saw such filth in all my life, no, sir! Why, there was millions of them, that soil and muck and seaweed was full of them, and I begun scratching, and old Bill he begun scratching, we didn't know what it was. But we found out, all right! Gorry! When I got home, I stood up on the middle of a blanket, without nary a stitch on, and a bucket of water beside me, and hoo didn't the little buggers hop! It was all right for me, but poor old Bill, he was half blind, he couldn't see much, and they sure did make him miserable! He was in a torment."

"I remember those rats; they lived in the cellar-hole, and down in the corner where the pigsty used to be. . . ."

Terence chuckled, they both chuckled, then Terence took the reins of the horse, and began backing and turning the wagon.

"I'll be in later, then," he said.

"All right. Give me a shout. Sure you don't mind, Terence?"

"Glad to do it. No good putting dead lilacs into the ground, is there?"

"No!"

The reflector lamp had been lit in the kitchen, on the shelf behind the coal stove, and in the dining room the candle flames rose pale and tall on the table, where Enid sat witchlike, her elbows on the polished walnut, her cheeks on her fists. The yellow light narrowed and brightened the green gleam of her eyes, but he couldn't be sure whether they quite looked at him. She was waiting, visibly waiting, and at once it was as if some obscure current had stiffened and frozen between them.

"Who is it?" he said.

"George."

"Why couldn't you have said so!"

"Was there any necessity? He's got something of considerable interest, you'll find, to say about your friend Jim Connor."

"Oh, he has!"

"Yes. And might I remind you that dinner is ready? I think he could have chosen a better time to call. He knows perfectly well what time we have dinner."

"Very well, you needn't wait for me."

"Thank you, I'll wait!"

"I don't think you'd better."

"What do you mean by that?"

"Oh, nothing. But it might take some time!"

He made this remark as if humorously, over his shoulder, looking back from the doorway. She still sat unmoving, but now the green eyes were subtly lifted and turned towards him, with an expression, however, which he hadn't time to fathom. Good lord, he thought quickly, how lovely she is, it isn't fair! Not fair to man or beast. Nobody has a right to be as beautiful as that, or if they have, they shouldn't be allowed to sit in candle light.

The studio was half dark, and George stood tall and white as a ghost by the fireplace, his striped palmbeach suit immaculate as always, the Panama hat in his hand. He was on his dignity, a little formidable and formal, the man of property come to uphold his rights.

"Hello, didn't Enid give you a light?"

"Ah, I'm afraid I've come at an inconvenient moment, Tip, but I thought as you'd be going up to town tomorrow I mightn't catch you—"

"Not till the day after. Mondays, Tuesdays, and Fridays!"

The bright blue eyes twinkled mischievously behind the black-corded glasses, the magisterial headmasterly head, with its close gray curls, inclined just perceptibly forward in the ghost of a bow. He slapped his hat, as if irritatedly, against his knee, turning slowly towards the struck match, the lighted candle on the mantel, the piled pine logs and pine cones in the wide fireplace.

"Forgive me, old fellow—how stupid of me. Of course."

"Sit down. What's on your mind?"

"Didn't Enid tell you?"

"Well, she murmured something about Jim Connor—"

George motioned with his hat towards the picture on the easel, as he sat down.

"Looks kind of familiar," he said. "Charming, my boy! Weir Village, isn't it?"

"Large as life."

"And twice as natural!"

He crossed his long legs, first carefully pulling up the exquisitely creased white trousers.

"Well, what about Jim Connor?"

"That's what *I* want to know. What we *all* want to know."

"Who is 'all'?"

"I won't mention any names, if you don't mind, but I've talked it over with several people—"

"The town fathers, I suppose?"

"No, not yet. Of course not, Tip. I wanted first to see you."

"Very kind of you."

"Not at all. And you needn't be sarcastic!"

"All right, go ahead."

"Perhaps you could tell me something about him. I think we have a right to know a little more—unless, of course, you want to be responsible for him, which personally I wouldn't recommend! There *is* such a thing as being an accessory before the fact, you know—you'd be conniving!"

"How so? I don't know a thing."

"You know he's a thief! And we hear that he's going to *continue* being a thief while he's living *here*."

"You know more than *I* do then!"

"I judge merely from what Enid said."

"Enid's only source of information, as far as I am aware, is myself."

"Well, my dear fellow, you *must* realize what we feel about it. We can't allow thieves around, you know—there is such a thing as law, after all! Just the same, I don't want to be unreasonable, and as he's a friend of yours, I thought it only fair to give you and him warning."

"Warning?"

"Exactly. It will be my duty as a citizen to notify the police."

(Damn! So that was what they were up to—! And Enid too.)

"Now look here, George—"

He broke off, gave an angry little laugh. It was funny—it was really too funny. The upright but misguided Jim—and yet, *was* he misguided?—causing all this fuss. And the idea of notifying poor old bewildered Uncle Cy William, the Town Constable, who had never made an arrest in his life! But George was leaning back in his chair, smiling cynically, his curled leonine head outlined against the open window—he was going to be difficult, he was going to be truculent. The defender of the faith—confound his impertinence! And the worst of it was that, within his limits, he was perfectly right.

George was saying, twirling the Panama hat round a raised forefinger:

"How long exactly have you known him, by the way, Tip? It isn't as if he was really an old friend of yours, is it?"

"I think I told you. He came up to town with my friend Karl Roth, the painter—that was last spring. I liked him. He struck me at once as one of the few honest people I ever met."

"Honest!"

"Yes. I mean it. The stealing is only an idea, a protest—he's an anarchist and unlike most anarchists he practices what he preaches—doesn't believe in trade for profit or in property being used for profit by barter. And so he steals merely in order to redistribute goods which he thinks are unjustly divided—he doesn't make anything out of it himself—not a cent—gives it all away to the poor and deserving. With a special weakness for helping starving painters and poets."

"And you believe that!"

"Of course I do. He's perfectly candid about it—he even notifies the police himself, sometimes in advance, when he's planning a haul, so as to get himself arrested and air his views in court. Sends the district attorney a picture postcard! They're tired of him. They'd much rather look the other way, I can assure you! And he's actually done a lot of good—he's helped some of the poor creatures a great deal."

"The whole thing's a fake, my dear Tip, and I'm surprised you don't see through it, I really am! Why, those dingy little poets and painters are nothing but parasites, it's just a dishonest and easy living for the whole lot of them. Mind you, I don't care what he does in New York or Greenwich Village—let him do it all he likes down there! But, by gosh, it's another thing when he comes up *here*, and takes the most expensive cottage in town with his ill-gotten gains, and proposes to use *this* as his center of operations! That's too much, yes, sir, that's a bit too much."

"You're quite safe. He doesn't rob houses, and you won't miss any of your silver. You can reassure Mabel!"

"It doesn't make any difference, as far as I can see, *what* he steals."

"Only department stores. He specializes in robbing big department stores. I think it's kind of nice, at that!"

"You've got a right to your own opinion, but, my dear boy, I *beg* you to consider your position very carefully. I don't want to see you get into any trouble."

"Who's likely to make trouble?"

"I am! And you can tell him that from me. And you can tell him he'd better keep out of my way. I don't want to meet him. Nor his houseful of very peculiar-looking friends."

"There'll be no occasion, I assure you."

"They *all* look like crooks to me!"

"They're quite harmless, they're just a little crazy."

"Every man to his own taste, said the farmer, as he kissed the pig! Anyway, you tell your friend Connor that I've warned him, and that I reserve the right to inform the police without further notice. I trust that's quite clear?"

"Quite, my dear George. I'll take Connor your tender message. Not that he's really a friend of mine—I hardly know him!"

"If you've got any sense, you'll drop him. But I must be going."

"I'll walk down to the bridge with you."

Good old George—so well-meaning, but such a righteous idiot! Hopeless to expect anything else of him, of course—one had only to look at the beautiful suit, the hat, the suède shoes, the neat black spectacle cord—but how damned exasperating. And what had he been saying to Enid? Or she to him? The thick was plotting, and with a vengeance, it looked like being a first-class mess. The property instinct—this was what came of owning a colonial mansion and a Pierce-Arrow car, by god! You couldn't blame him, but all the same he was somehow less pleasant to consider than poor honest Connor, for all his crack-brained confusions and inconsistencies. Connor was at least generous.

They walked down the Town Landing lane in the dark. The big moon was just rising over the pine woods across the river, the crickets were chirping like mad, faster and faster, doubtless in a last passionate effort to keep themselves warm. Already the night smelt of frost. He turned his head, saw the dim light between the dining-room curtains—a shadow moved briefly across them, Enid must have decided to begin without him. But no—she was playing the piano; the little Brahms Op. 39 waltz came plaintively into the night, across the rustling of the trodden leaves and the iterated *zeek-zeek-zeek* of the doomed crickets—it was, of course, a protest. He smiled, and said:

"A pity you won't meet them, though—Roth would amuse you. And those gals are a scream. *Gosh,* what a night!"

"Jove, yes! My dear fellow, of course there's nothing personal in it, and I'm thinking as much of your good, yours and Enid's and even Buzzer's, as mine. A fine sort of scandal to get your family mixed up in! But never mind. . . . I hear your lilacs have come."

"Yes. Terence is coming over to put them in before the frost."

"You'll have to get a move on. They'll look well, all along that wall— you know, I often think of that little plum tree—wasn't that the strangest thing you ever saw? *Covered* with blossom, not an inch of branch that wasn't covered with blossom, and then dead so soon after—a week, was it?"

"One week. A suicide, if there ever was one. Why the devil should it want to commit suicide?"

"Oh, well, my dear boy, there are more things in heaven and earth— a good way to die, though."

A little smug, a little suave—but sincere, too, it was old George's attempt at amends, and had better be accepted as such. A car was rattling over the loose boards of the bridge, the headlights shot up the sandy rise of the road, throwing the heaped leaves into brilliant relief. Yes, the little plum tree—how beautiful it had been and how touching—he remembered just exactly how it had looked, remembered it with a pang, for now it must be uprooted, thrown away. Poor little thing.

"Well, good night, I must turn back. Ee will be waiting."

"Good night, old man, and don't take it too unkindly of me."

"Of course not. I'll be seeing you!"

"Good night."

The tall white figure was gone, swerving quickly round the corner of the tumble down tollhouse, the thicket of rusty sumacs growing from the cellar holes, the clutter of rotting boards and shingles—he would be walk-

ing across the moonlit bridge, looking down at the dark swift water where
the red sponges grew on barnacled rock, walking importantly in the moonlight, swinging the beautiful Panama hat, his errand accomplished. Smiling to himself a little too, no doubt, as he prepared the phrases for Mabel
and turned up Chicken-coop Lane towards the pine woods and the cranberry bog and the cluster of houses on the Point. Snob's Village, the na-
tives called it—and with some justice, by god. They wanted everything
their own way. Even to choosing the tenants for empty houses.

Tirra-loo—tirra-lee! Mr. Riley's fishing nets lay like a mist on the grass
and leaves, a ghostly blue, a milky blue, chicory-color, blue reticulated with
silver, semined with silver, and he walked carefully round them, admiring
the cork floats. Leaves on them, too, a fine catch of yellow leaves for breakfast, which at daybreak Mr. Riley would shake out in the frost. And Chattahoochee would be there, hoping for fish.

At the edge of the lane he paused, stood still on the bouldered wall,
listened. The piano had stopped; except for the crickets, everything was
silent. How small the house looked under the moon-charmed poplar trees
—like something at the bottom of the sea, he thought, a sunken ship, something lost and forgotten. But Enid was somewhere there inside it, like a
mermaid, and Buzzer asleep under the silver-gray shingled roof, and
through a chink in the dining-room curtains he could see the warm glow of
the candlelight, the gleaming corner of the piano. A strange and different
reality it had, something safe and solid and enclosed, and yet wasn't it
actually less real, less permanent, than the unfathomable sea of moonlight
in which it lay, the appalling emptiness of night and space? The terror of
space would endure; but some day the house would be gone, and Buzzer,
and Ee and himself—the bare earth turning frozen under the stars. . . .
He shivered, smiled, jumped down into the road, where the gray ashes lay
in the half-filled ruts, and ran up the wooden stairs into the kitchen.

"I do think," Enid said levelly across the dinner table, as he sat down,
her eyes and brow barely raised between the paired candles, "you might
have been a little more considerate!"

"My dear Ee, how can I help it? If old George *must* come bumbling
in just at dinner time—as you yourself pointed out—"

"That's all very well. But you needn't have gone out with him, knowing as you did that dinner was on the table, and everything getting cold. I
should have thought—"

"I'm sorry, darling."

"You'd better eat your eggs, they're quite cold as it is! Besides, I should
have thought that you'd have wanted to discuss it with George of your
own accord, beforehand, and gone to see him."

The half-smile she gave him was a little nettled, a little firm and cryp-
tic, a slight frown went with it, and the grave eyes, barely touching his
own glance for a moment, wavered sidelong, gazed preoccupiedly into the
corner behind him. Her elbows on the table, in the pink-smocked sleeves,
she was eating a biscuit in very small quick bites, the silver butter knife
held lightly in her other hand. He noticed that her chair was drawn crookedly to the table, which gave her the effect of not quite facing him. Or of
being poised for departure.

"Discuss what, dear."

"Oh, come, Timothy!"

She was looking straight at him—for the first time, it seemed to him, in hours—and in a sense this was a relief. A challenging look, the beautiful eyes brilliant under dark eyebrows faintly lowered, the wide white forehead smooth in the soft light. And the richly modeled Botticelli mouth, so firm and lovely—what a disadvantage a man is at, he thought, in having, even at moments like this, to pause and pay tribute! Poor devil, he has to face treason in his own citadel.

He smiled and said:

"Well, I suppose you mean Jim Connor—especially as it appears you've been having quite a heart-to-heart with George on the subject yourself."

"Is there any reason why I shouldn't?"

"Is there any reason why you should?"

"Well, why not?"

"It seems to me it's my affair. It's to do with my friends, isn't it?"

"Friends!"

"I should have thought you could have left it to me."

"I don't agree with you. It seems to me to concern me and Buzzer quite as much as it concerns you. But, of course, you wouldn't think of that. You never do. Any more than it occurred to you to consider George."

"Why the devil should I have considered George! What business was it of his?"

"He's your oldest friend here, isn't he? I should have thought it would be only natural."

"Natural, my foot! It's none of George's business. For that matter, it's really none of my business either. If Jim Connor takes a fancy to this place, and wants to have a holiday here, and give some poor half-starved devils of Greenwich Village poets and painters a rest and change, who the devil is George, or who the devil am I, that we should take it upon ourselves to kick him out! Have a heart, Ee—and don't live *all* your life on County Street, New Bedford, or Beacon Street, Boston! Besides, I didn't ask Jim Connor to come here, remember, and if I like Jim, and he likes me, that's a mere accident. And in many ways a very fortunate one."

"I don't think the sneer at County Street becomes you."

"Sorry, Endor!"

"And say what you will, respectability has its uses. It's all very well for adolescents to want to live in slums—"

"Adolescents!"

"But when it comes to bringing up children, I draw the line."

"So we're bringing up Buzzer in a slum! Really, Ee, you're losing your sense of humor a little. I haven't noticed any slums around. Go out and look at the moonlight, my gal, and those lilacs waiting to be planted, and tell me it's a slum! It's lovely, and you know it."

"No, Tip, I know all that. But it isn't only this, it isn't only Jim Connor, who is after all nothing but a jailbird, and those very nondescript young women he's brought with him—"

"Nondescript! Ho, what an adjective."

"Will you let me finish? Please? It's the whole tendency, I mean, it's your whole leaning towards this kind of thing. It simply isn't fair to me."

"I see. So you took it upon yourself to talk it all over with old George. Discussing my affairs with him behind my back."

"Not at all! George brought it up himself."

"Even going so far as to tell him—what you don't know to be true—that Jim is going to continue stealing while he's living here. May I ask how you knew that?"

"I thought it was assumed."

"Nothing of the sort. You don't know anything more about it than I do, and I know nothing. As far as I'm aware, Jim himself is still undecided. It seems to me a little reckless of you, not to say mischievous, to make statements which have no basis in fact, and to George of all people! I think you might have asked me about it first, at least, and taken the trouble to corroborate it."

"Your usual tactics, I see, of putting me in the wrong. On a minor point!"

She rose before he could reply, began piling the dishes, very carefully, very precisely, her small hands white under the candlelight, the proud head turning quickly and angrily. Imperious, imperial—yes, even the full throat, which showed through the V-shaped opening of the smock, was imperial and intimidating, for all its mature splendor, and the dark curls, as she turned away and went toward the kitchen steps, themselves turned on the pink collar with a sparkling arrogance which seemed to sum up all vitality. He pushed back his chair, reached a hand to the piano, and struck a note, softly, with one finger. Her voice came to him again, from the door—she had paused, with her cheek half turned, as if she were looking out into the garden towards the little dead plum tree.

"The water, by the way," she said, "is very low."

"Why didn't you tell me?"

"I thought you knew."

"Of course not! I suppose it was Buzzer's bath—"

"And don't forget, either, that I did a whole morning's washing! The cesspool was flooded again."

"The devil it was!"

"Yes. I called up Binney. He's coming in the morning. He says we'll probably need to have an extra one put in."

He struck the one note again, listened to it idly, wondered for a moment if the candle flames could feel the vibration—but no, they were perfectly still, rose motionless in the quiet room, as steady and beautiful as peacock's eyes, and the room around them as attentive—with its chairs arranged demurely against the walls of white wood, the lustrous mahogany lowboy, the Chinese embroidery of birds and dragons—as if it existed for them alone. Peace—peace—peace—the crickets were singing in the moonlight outside—the rhythmic incantatory sound was everywhere, came into everything, saturated everything, like a mist. Another night like this, poor devils, and they'd be singing a different tune. Was it love? Was it defiance? Or just a sort of mesmerism, a subtle electric response—or spiritual, even—to the earth itself? Exactly like himself and Enid. A mere sidereal response.

In the kitchen, under the luminous whitewashed rafters, Enid had turned on the tap, was rinsing the dishes, shaking the water off her hand. He pulled the screen door towards him, caught it against his foot, and said:

"Well, for goodness' sake, why so secretive, Ee? Why not tell a fellow!"

"Your door was shut, so I assumed you were painting."

"Damn. And just as I've finally got some grass to grow."

He stepped into the bright sea of moonlight, feeling for all the world as if positively it might lift him off his feet, float him up over the roof top, over the trees, and went slowly to the white-shingled pump house behind the kitchen. The old w.c. A good idea, that had been, moving it from the back of the yard, and turning it into a pump house—one more example of the unwearying adaptability of nature. After all, too, the function was roughly the same, if a shade more refined. And those squashes that he had grown on the former site, the former unsavory site—those man-eating squashes—by god, would anybody ever forget them? They hadn't been squashes at all, they had been saber-toothed tigers. And leaves the size of howdahs, or palanquins, or something. . . . In the cool dark, he stooped toward the compact little engine, fitted the crank handle to it, spun it, spun it again. It caught, coughed, wheezed, then gave three barks in rapid succession and was off.

"Like a lamb," he said. "Like a lamb!"

The pump shaft groaned musically in the bricked well below him, he heard the first chuckle of flowing water from underground, the indicator over the kitchen sink would be beginning to fidget and dance; but averting his eyes from the thought of the new cesspool, as from the three ghostly boxes of lilacs which lay like coffins on the lawn, he averted his attention from all this as well. Damn. And doing a whole morning's washing. And not bothering to tell him about it, just ordering Binney herself. And George. And Nora. And Jim Connor. And the bills—the next thing would, of course, be the bills. The butcher, the baker, the candlestick maker. It was all becoming a colossal, an overwhelming joke, a sort of decuman wave of joke, which was piling up to sweep away everything—himself, Enid, Buzzer, the house—everything. In fact, it was ceasing rapidly to be a joke at all. *Peace—peace—peace*—sang the crickets. Peace? The hell you say, he thought. We ask for peace and they give us a stone. If indeed even a stone. They give us nothing.

"I suppose you couldn't *bear*," Enid said as he opened the door, "to lend me a hand with these few dishes."

"I don't know whether I can *bear* it, if you choose to put it like that, but I will."

The challenge again—her eyes flashed handsomely at him, with something that was almost like admiration, and returned to the steaming dishpan, the Himalaya of soft suds in which she was waggling the dish mop. She was humming a little, under her breath, as she always did when she was preoccupied, or tired, or annoyed—tonelessly, tunelessly—a charming and pathetic sing-song which always tickled him, and endeared her to him. No ear for music at all—or was it that she was practicing the Chinese whole-tone scale? Very modern and polychromatic, he had often told her, and written, as it were, without signature. The indicator danced in its dial

over the sink, from the pipes came the regular half-musical *joog—joog—
joog* of the pumped water pressing its way everywhere, to every corner of
that elaborate arterial artifice of pipes, to every tap, and into the cold heart
of the great tank buried underground. But no, of course not, it was the
engine that was the heart.

"And is that all?"

"That's all. I'll be in in a minute. And thank you."

"Don't mention."

Her pink sleeves rolled back to the elbows, she reached bare-armed to
toss a checkered cloth over the clothesline which stretched across the
kitchen, and almost simultaneously, as he entered the dining room, he
heard something thump heavily on the floor overhead, in Buzzer's room.
He stood still and listened.

"Something must have fallen, upstairs," he said.

"Probably the doll."

"She didn't have a doll."

"Well, why don't you go and see! For heaven's sake, Tip, why do you
have to be so helpless!"

"Helpless!"

Helpless. . . . He lifted a candle from the dinner table, shielded it
with one hand, and went quietly up the narrow stairs to the second floor.
The upper hall was ablaze with moonlight. A great splash of it lay on the
rugless floor and halfway up the wall, it poured through the low window—
and to stand there, with his embarrassed candle, was exactly like being
inside a camera during a time exposure. Must be what a film feels like, he
thought, when you open the shutter: a sensation of flooding. Every cranny
indecently exposed: or is it the world that's exposed—? *Helpless!* He said
it aloud as he opened Buzzer's door; and there was Buzzer, standing bolt
upright in the middle of the floor beside her bed, her eyes closed, her hands
still crumpled against her cheek in the attitude of sleep. Yes, how extraordinary, she was fast asleep. She swayed a little, gropingly, as if trying to find
something to relax against—how lovely, like something growing at the
bottom of a stream, rooted among pebbles, wavering but tethered! He put
the candle on the chair.

"Well, of all the nerve," he said. "What do you think *you're* doing,
floating round in the moonlight like this! Aren't you ashamed?"

"Mmm," she said.

"I should think so. I suppose you fell out, eh?"

"Mmm," she said.

"And had the sense not to wake up."

"Mmm."

"Well, I congratulate you. Now just stay asleep, and I'll put you back,
and you'll never know the difference, see?"

She murmured against his neck, his cheek, as he lifted her back into
bed, but she was already receding, she was already gone, and the firm little
face, on the pillow, instantly averted itself into its chosen dream. What
shape did she make of it? What shape was her world? What shape did she
make of himself, his hands that touched her, the night sounds, the moon-
maddened crickets? Ah, they were all there, in her dream, as a wonderful

and forever-sustaining music, an unfailing love—it was the world as it should be, but as it so seldom, or so briefly, remains. Or were there terrors as well—? Yes, even here there were terrors. But fleeting, already dissipated, gone. *Peace—peace—peace*—sang the crickets, and here, at any rate, they were quite right. But downstairs—!

He heard Enid crossing the dining room—perhaps she was going to play the piano again? That melancholy and tender little waltz, with its series of murmured unanswerable questions. But no, she had gone on, had crossed the hall, he heard the two-toned squeak of the studio door, she was in the studio. Lighting the fire, perhaps, drawing the brown curtains, settling herself with her knitting; but, whatever she did, studiously ignoring the latest picture on the easel. Adolescent, of course! It was the old cry, the old war cry. Why don't you grow up, Tip? Why not, indeed! Damn.

The doors to his own and Enid's rooms were open, and he went into Enid's to look for a moment from the north window toward the lagoons at the head of the river—he knew in advance how they would be sheeted with moonlight, as in winter they would be sheeted with ice. A single green light twinkled at the Point—somebody must be in Paul's boathouse, probably Paul himself going out in his canoe. A tiny ticking sound reached his ear—it was Enid's wrist watch, lying forgotten on her pillow, the small radium dial glowing faintly and hopefully in the dark. Why should there be something so moving, so touching in that—why, suddenly, did it make him think of death? Ridiculous. He straightened up, glanced through the open door beyond, which led into his own adjoining room, then returned into the hall, blew out the candle, and went slowly down the stairs.

In the studio, Enid was already sitting before the fire, her knees crossed, her back to the easel. The firelight flickered rosily on her face, her throat, her hands, flashed along the moving steel needles, twinkled in the buckles of her sandals. The bare white walls danced with light, the whole room seemed to be breathing flame. He went around her, turned the easel away, towards the bookcase, then approached the hearth and pushed back a log with the toe of his shoe.

"Besides, what I don't see is," she spoke without looking up, frowning prettily, the green flame-washed eyes lowered to the narrow strip of jersey which dangled from her needles, "what you can possibly get out of it."

"Oh, for heaven's sake, Enid—!"

"What I don't see is what possible good it can do you. I could understand your sacrificing yourself, and even me and Buzzer—"

"Sacrifice!"

"—if there were any real *use* in it. If they were useful connections, I mean. You *won't* live in New Bedford or Boston, where you might pick up portrait commissions, or steady teaching—"

"I don't want to do portraits."

"—you throw away chances like that, and the connections I could have given you, for which I should have supposed some sacrifices *might* have been justified, and then live in this dreary little village where there's no life at all for me—"

"It's the first time I'd heard of *that!*"

"Well, it's high time you did hear of it, for it's true, and if you'd had any consideration you'd have thought of it yourself. And then, as if all that wasn't enough, Tip, you make life more difficult still by associating with these *really* shabby and dreadful people. What *earthly* use can Roth be to you—or those dirty little females—"

"Really, Ee—!"

"Yes, *dirty!*"

"Roth's a little cheap, and I know it, but he's a good painter. Or interesting, anyway—by gosh, he's at least *alive*, which is more than you can say for those Boston mummies! What's more, it seems to me this is a question for *me* to decide. Not you. I must take what's good where I can find it, that's all. I'm afraid I don't find it in the pure waters of County Street—give me the adulterous Greenwich Village sewers any day! And as for picking out my friends merely because they might be useful, good god, Ee, I never heard anything so revoltingly cynical and selfish and utilitarian in my life! You ought to be ashamed."

"I suppose it's selfish of me to ask you to consider the futures of Buzzer and myself! Is that it?"

"It isn't as simple as that."

"Oh, yes, it is. That's exactly what it is. There *are* limits to what you can expect a wife to give up. This notion of living like your noble pioneer ancestors, without help, without maids, doing all our own work, is all very well, but you ask any of your friends what *they* think of it! Ask Paul, ask George, ask Mabel! I happen to *know!*"

"I see. So you've been crying on the public bosom."

"I haven't. They've made their feelings only too abundantly clear. And I can assure you it's very humiliating."

"Ah. So they've been crying on *your* bosom."

"Not at all. They've merely been rather tactlessly sympathetic. And I assure you I haven't enjoyed it in the least. It's not exactly pleasant to have Mabel heavily hinting that you don't properly provide for us—"

"Mabel! Well, of all the damned impertinence! And do you mean to say you *listened* to her?"

"Why not?"

"You ought to have turned your back. It's none of her damned business. That spoiled, empty-headed, card-playing, prattling sybarite! Well, for the love of mud! Really, Enid, there are times when I have to blush for you. And this is certainly one of them."

"I think you might do a little blushing for yourself."

"No, thank you!"

She was silent, except for the steady clicking of the needles, her face had hardened (he noticed), with a sort of hard serenity, and he felt that his own face had hardened too, as if in answer. He sat down for a moment on the stool by the fire, but jumped up again, thrust his hands into the pockets of his khaki trousers, went abruptly to one of the front windows. Drawing the curtain a little aside, he looked out across the moonlit street, at the white picket fence of the Rileys' house. The Riley garden, beyond, was drowned in a sort of milky penumbra, lay entranced in the great cone of pure space-light, the elm trees still and ghostly; and beyond these again, farther off, the white steeple of the Unitarian Church was achieving a lunar brilliance of architecture that made it seem positively to soar. A white night, with a vengeance! *Nuit blanche.* A light winked on, in an upstairs room of the Riley house, showing a square of yellow curtain, then winked out again. Behind him, from the distant kitchen, he heard the final click, the sighing moan, with which the pump had shut itself off. Enough water till morning. It would serve as an excuse!

He turned back to the room and said:

"I just want to look at the dial. I want to see what the pressure is. If you don't mind."

"I thought it was always the same?"

"It's taken to varying. And sometimes gets too high."

"Then perhaps you'd better tell Binney about it in the morning."

"I'll see!"

"And you might have a look for the cat while you're there."

"Oh, *he* won't be back all night—it's the wrong season. He's away—as Paul so felicitously puts it—*ramming!*"

There—that would hold her! He couldn't help chuckling to himself, as he crossed the dark dining room, guided by the path of light from the reflector lamp in the kitchen—dear innocent Ee, how Paul's quaint vulgarisms always annoyed her! But possibly it wasn't the best moment he could have chosen for it. . . . The indicator on the dial was still quivering a little, steadying itself down—thirty-four. Two points too high, there must be something wrong with the shut-off. What next! Temperament in everything, even in pumps, by god! He watched the needle until it finally came to rest, smiled, then turned on the water in the sink. Yes, it gushed too hard, the pressure was obviously too high—another job for Ratio Binney, and another bill. As if a new cesspool wasn't enough.

Returning, he began to whistle, then stopped, touched one note on the piano as he passed—perhaps that would mollify her. But no. She had laid her knitting aside, was sitting forward with her elbows on her knees, her flushed cheeks on her fists.

"Two points too high," he said.

She made no answer for a moment, then leaned slowly back in the wicker chair, clasped her hands behind her head, and raised her eyes, now full and searching, to his. Her lips were slightly parted, but she was not smiling, though almost—he felt that she was looking, as it were, from one to the other of his eyes, and he waited, smiling a little himself.

"Don't you think," she said at last very deliberately, "you ought to come to some decision about it?"

"Good gracious, Endor dear, what *is* this! A decision about what."

"I assume George told you he would refuse to meet Jim Connor, or to have anything to do with him?"

"Yes, he did."

"It seems to me you might find that worth considering?"

"George doesn't know Jim, and I do. It doesn't affect George one way or the other—which makes all the difference."

"Does it?"

"Of course, it does."

"I'm afraid I fail to see it."

He leaned over her, leaned his face close to hers, took the point of her elbow in his hand, and wagged it affectionately.

"Please, Ee, let's be sensible about this—Jim Connor is really a very nice fellow."

She withdrew her elbow from his clasp, lowered her hands into her lap. It was a deliberate separation, a rebuke, and he straightened up.

"What you mean is, that you won't consider me at all. And in *that* case—" she smiled very brightly up at him, her head tipped a little to one side, the whole attitude charmingly defiant—"I shall of course have to consider what I shall do myself. Not only about this, about everything. It's bad enough having Buzzer bullied in the streets by these little village toughs, knocked down and hurt, and learning to speak in the awful way they speak here—"

"What *are* you talking about, Ee—come to your senses!"

"Oh, no. I mean every word I say. I'm afraid, Timothy, you'd better think it over."

"I see. It's a threat."

"It isn't a threat. I'm just suggesting that for a change you think of *our* interests a little."

"I've never done anything else! But if you think I'm going to throw over Jim Connor just because of this silly business you're very much mistaken. . . . That's Terence at the door—I'll have to go."

"Very well. If that's more important—"

She had spoken the word "important" with a curious and disturbing emphasis, a subtle but somehow pervasive air of finality, and in the silence that followed, broken only by the spurt of a resinous flame, a shrill jet from the imprisoned gas in a pine log, and farther off the sound of Terence's hammering at the boxes in the garden, he suddenly found himself remembering—how absurd!—the random phrase he had used when putting Buzzer to bed, the bantering remark that the end of the world was at hand, and that he must be there to see it. Why the devil should he think of that? Or why, too, as if it were a no less sinister part of the same thing, did he think again of Enid's watch, lying alone on her pillow, ticking and glowing in the dark solitude of her empty room? It had made him conscious, for some obscure reason, of death; just as the falling of the leaves, the sound and sight and chill smell of them, the feeling of hurry and departure, had produced suddenly, from his unconscious, his feeble little joke about the end of the world. "Ho ho—" Buzzer had said—"you can't fool *me!* It *isn't* coming to an end!" But wasn't it—? Or what then had been in his mind, when, from the top of the wall by the lane, looking at the forlorn little house in the moonlight, he had had again a precise vision of precisely that, the end of everything that was precious to him? All this was subjective, no doubt—but it was easy enough just to say that, it was the old fallacy of trying to dispose of things simply by naming them, giving them pretty names—it really got one nowhere, explained nothing. The garment without a seam—good lord, yes, one's conscious life was like that, there were no joins anywhere, everything flowed into everything else, flowed out of everything else, and the end must be—there seemed to be no escape from it whatever—either in admiration or despair. But not despair

—no, not despair, not that, not that! Admiration certainly—wonder—even idolatry; or something, for example, like Buzzer's pure astonishment. There was plenty of room for death, in this—plenty. Yes indeed. But did it really make finalities any more acceptable? He felt a little breathless, the familiar feeling of confused helplessness with which he always began a new painting—always, always—the panic of impotence! The world was always thus getting away from him, going too fast, whizzing off before he had time to shape it, or even—damn the luck—time to see it. It was always as if he were trying desperately to get hold of it before it was too late.

"Endor, darling, listen—"

"You'd better run along, Terence will be waiting for you."

"Will you listen? No lilacs in the world, not a hundred, not a hundred million, are as important, you know that. They can go to hell, the whole damned galaxy and parade of them, and all of them with frozen feet, from here to kingdom come. Don't you know that?"

"You made it quite obvious—"

"Nothing of the sort, Ee. It's simply that they've got to be done—"

"Very well, why not run along and do them."

"They can wait."

"So can I, Tip—I'm quite used to it."

"Don't you think you're being a little bit difficult about this?"

"You mean mulish, I suppose? Why not say it?"

"I didn't mean that at all. It won't help matters to put words into each other's mouths—"

"I've told you what I think—"

"Why don't you listen to what *I* think—"

"—and you've apparently refused to consider it. That seems to me final."

"I didn't mean it to be as final as all that. Damnation, Ee, you can't split up the world into blacks and whites as easily as all that! Try to see it, please—I'm in a very difficult position, painful on all sides, and I *really* want to do what is best."

"Yes, Tip, you find it very hard to give up anything, don't you? Even for me, or Buzzer!"

"I don't think that's deserved."

"Don't you?"

"No, I don't."

"Then that's all I've got to say. Except to repeat what I said before, that I shall of course have to consider what I shall do. I suppose I've got a right to do that!"

"Of course, darling."

"Run along then and attend to your lilacs. I suppose you'll be late—I shall probably be in bed. And would you mind *trying* not to disturb me—? I'm very tired."

The green eyes flashed up at him, a cold and lovely dismissal, flashed up and away; for the barest perceptible instant their eyes met; but no, they hadn't really met at all, it was rather as if her own glance had slid through his own, through and inward, striking it aside—he felt exposed, he felt plumbed! Beautiful, yes, but he was dismissed.

"Very well," he said. "But I may not be as late as all that—sorry you're tired!"

Damn—her bedroom door would be closed—that was what she probably meant—the pressure was to be maintained overnight, she was going to be implacable. Admirable, too, when she was like this—that was the unfairest part of it; for anger so extraordinarily suited her particular sort of beauty, the fierce, small, pseudo-witchlike thing which he so loved. Green flame, cold flame, flame-in-ice—the narrow hard intensity of the sibyl—but with something disarmingly childlike as well. What a demon of a little girl she must have been, and how beautiful! Like Buzzer. But with less sense of humor—she was always a prey to his sense of humor; and he couldn't resist, as he passed through the dining room, touching the one note of the piano once more, for final comic comment: it would infuriate her. And he allowed the kitchen door to clack behind him with unnecessary violence. . . .

Terrence, in blue overalls, grinning among the dismantled boxes, the disheveled clusters of lilacs, looked like a part of the moonlight himself. It was a scene from a ballet, blue-lighted, mysterious—nymphs, or naiads, or dryads, would materialize at any moment, and dance to an orchestra of blue-coated, man-sized crickets. The shouting of the crickets was positively outrageous. And the moon, the all-but-round moon, over the Puringtons' shed, looked down at Terence as if it were about to make some very special and secret use of him.

"Gorry," Terence said, holding up leafless lilac bushes in either hand, "there's thousands of 'em. All labeled, too—pinks, whites, and purples. Not so much root as you might think, either—won't be much trouble. Don't have to dig the holes so deep! How you going to mix these colors, Mister Kane?"

"Not many pinks and whites, Terence—only a sprinkling—so just stick them in where they come. It will be all right. Have you got a shovel?"

"Oh, sure, I got the old faithful. I'll begin up by the road there. Put 'em about a yard apart, I reckon—"

"All right—I'll start behind the kitchen. No use trying to keep the top-soil, I suppose—!"

"No, you can't help it. A little fertilizer will put that right. A little prime horse manure. I'll fetch you over a nice wagon load, come Monday —what's the good of feedin' a horse, if she don't give you manure? Yes, sir, I'll dig it in around 'em so you'd never know the difference, the sand won't hardly show at all!"

"Will they want water?"

"No, they won't want no water. Dry as a bone is the best, and stomp 'em in firm with your foot, that's all."

"Okay, Terence! I'll be seeing you!"

Terence struck a match, lit his clay pipe, the humorous face wrinkling in the intermittently sucked flare, the brown eyes shrewd, warm, and earthy, then stooped for his shovel and an armload of lilacs. The polished shovel blade burned blue as he turned it.

"Yes, sir, and they say plantin' in moonlight is always lucky."

"The better the night the better the deed!"

The Unitarian Church clock began striking—ten o'clock. Or could it be eleven? or nine? . . . But time, in such moonlight as this, obviously ceased to exist, became, by any ordinary human standards, incommensurable. It poured, it flowed, it was all at one level, like a sea—it was simply space, and to be measured, if at all, only by distances, as wave from wave, hand from hand, face from face. A moon, moons, half a moon—one elmtree tip to another, frosted with pure light—the creeping diagonal of dense shadow, like enchantment, along a white picket fence—the slow tide of silver mounting up the still slope of a shingled roof, and then pouring soundlessly away over the rooftree to leave it again in primordial darkness —good god, when you stopped to think about it what a terrifying and unearthly business it was. It was enough to give you the shivers. And when you thought of the whole world, or half of it, revolving in space through this lethal and ethereal light, itself looking dead and frozen, with its cold barnacles of houses—what *must* it look like, seen from the moon? Dreadful no doubt; like a vast skull; or worse still, like an exposed and frozen brain. And that mackerel sky, up there, those shoals of silver fish swimming softly away over the moon, momentarily touching and dimming it, but not obscuring it, themselves brightening or darkening in serried and evanescent rows, yet so orderly and precise—and the bare dark trees reaching upward towards them—yes, the whole thing, he thought, was exactly like a quick cold shiver over the very top of the brain—frost on the eardrums, frost on the eyeballs, frost on the nerve ends! It was a taste, in advance, of the marrowy and foul bitterness of death. . . .

His shovel rose and fell; cutting the soft topsoil, cutting the gritty sand, hacking through the stretched vital roots of the poplars. As fast as he dug the holes, the moonlight filled them; exactly as the holes scooped on a beach fill with the sea. Cold roots, cold soil, cold sand—his hands, pressing down the lilac roots, disentangling and spreading the living radicles, clawing the mixed sand and loam over them, became themselves cold and earthlike, harshly imbrued in the stuff they worked in; they took on something of the coarse violence of earth; so that it was unpleasant, even unnatural, to touch his clothing with them. A time, times, half a time—the upright lilacs began to look like a hedge along the wall above the lane, it was beginning at last to be impressive, and he jumped down into the lane, among the dead leaves, to admire his handiwork. Yes, already the garden had changed, was changing. It had suddenly become organized. A slum! What on earth had made her think of that. Really, the extraordinary things Ee managed to think of! With a river like that, and a house and garden like this, and a moon like the end of the world! A lunar slum, a slum all compact of mercurial magic, a shape of silver vapor—the sheer impudence of it! Typical of the sort of thing one says when angry—the straws clutched at by the madman, clutched at in his own hair. Good old Enid. Or was she perhaps partially right? It was so difficult, sometimes, to distinguish between the simple and the shabby, between the plain and the merely dreary. But a slum!

A purple, a white, a purple again, a pink. Who ever heard of a pink lilac? Must be a *façon de parler*. By god, what a sight they would be when they all blossomed! The House of a Hundred Lilacs, they could call it, with engraved purple notepaper. *Then,* at any rate, Enid would like it—*that,* at any rate, she would like! Or would there be no "then"? Of course—how ridiculous. She hadn't meant it as seriously as all that, it was because she was tired, a good night's sleep would put everything to rights again, everything would be all right in the morning. A whole morning's washing. The cesspool flooded. Old George butting in and messing up the Jim Connor business, as if it wasn't already bad enough. Poor Ee, no wonder her nerves had been on edge. But in the morning, with the sunlight bursting in through the kitchen window, shining into the kitchen sink, silvering the tall upright cylinder of the boiler, and Buzzer singing upstairs, and himself rumbling the carpet sweeper over the dining room rug, and the kettle squealing on the stove—yes, it would probably be all right; this blasted moonlight, with its uncanny unreality, would be gone; and all these obscure pressures and shadows with it. She was probably already asleep, and lying, as she always did, with one hand reversed above her head, her elbow on the pillow, the neat small face, closed and serene, turned a little to one side. But suppose she was awake! And suppose she was still awake, when he himself went up to bed, lying awake there, but with her door closed—? Ah, that stretched and conscious silence, the taut and agonized silence as of eyes staring in the darkness, the silence as of carefully withheld breathing! And would you mind *trying* not to disturb me? Damn. . . .

"Yield to me, lilacs," he said aloud bitterly, "and ye shall bear!"

He straightened up, for his back was beginning to be tired, heard an upper window rattling open in the Purington house, behind him, and then voices.

"Gladys?"

It was Mrs. Purington's voice, remote, sing-song, whining.

"Yes, mother."

"Have you got enough bedclothes? It's going to be cold."

"Yes, mother, enough clothes to sink a ship!"

"*That's* good."

Cold: it was going to be cold. In fact, it was cold already. And it must be late. But they were nearly finished, thank goodness, he turned and saw that Terence had reached the bottom of the garden and come back, had begun putting in the few that were to stand along the terrace wall. A dozen more, or a dozen and a half, at most. He thrust his shovel into the dark pine-smelling woodshed, closed the door.

"I'm knocking off, Terence," he said, standing at the top of the terrace wall. "I'm going to walk down the road a bit. Do you mind finishing it by yourself?"

"Won't take me about another ten minutes, not that."

"By gosh, if I stooped just once more, my backbone would snap right out of me! Like a spring. How do you do it."

"Guess it's all in being used to it! I was born with a shovel in my hands. But it's work, at that."

"It is. Thanks a lot, Terence. How do you think it looks."

"Looks fine. Yes, sir, in about two years it'll make a fine show. Not much blossom next spring—"

"No?"

"No, they'll want about a year's growth of wood first, and to make some roots too—but then, by gorry, they'll give you blaze enough—it ought to be a pretty sight. Got 'em in just in time, too—I can feel the frost in my sciatics already!"

They looked together along the row of lilacs by the Purington fence, as orderly as if they had been there forever. A patch of white sand glowed dimly at the foot of each, like a little circle of phosphorescence, and the dangling labels, too, shone white in the moonlight. Terence shook his head.

"A hundred!" he said.

"Felt more like a thousand! . . . Well, good night, Terence, and I'll see you Monday."

"Yes, I'll be over Monday with a nice load of manure, and put 'em to bed good. . . . Good night!"

"Good night."

He heard the shovel strokes resume behind him, heard them still as he turned to the left to pass the Purington house, and then, as he stepped into the moonlight-stenciled street, he was engulfed abruptly in an astonishing silence. The crickets, all but a few, were still, now—their slower *zeek—zeek—zeek—zeek* was merely the moonlight made audible, the thin threnody of the moonlight itself. Peace be with you—*pax vobiscum!* Lucky little devils, just to crawl into a hole in the ground, freeze quietly into sleep, and forget everything until another year, another summer! Another summer, another love. He walked quickly, the leaves rustling under his feet, retracing the steps that he had taken only a few hours before, when he had come back empty-handed—empty-hearted?—from the post office. Nora, silent, was a different, an unknown Nora, it wasn't like her to be silent, it could mean only one thing. Perhaps she had finally decided to marry that architect chap from Clark College and settle down—perhaps he never would see her again. Would he mind? It had been good, it had been merry: a comic genius—the muse of comedy—had presided over the affair from the very outset: never, in all their clandestine meetings, had they had an unhappy moment—not even when she had been so sick that time under the ailanthus tree in the moonlit back yard. Another summer, another love! *Had* they been in love? Was he in love with her now? Not as he was in love with Ee—odd, too, how they had never once called each other by their Christian names, or even by any nicknames— nothing but "you," "you." On the telephone always—"Hello? Is that 'you'?" "Yes, it's 'me'—is that 'you'? And who is 'you'?" " 'ME!' " . . . And then her delicious giggle, muffled and averted as she turned her face away from the telephone, the so characteristic half-checked giggle, as if it were all so dreadfully naughty, the whole thing—so dreadfully and delightfully naughty, but so dreadfully nice too, and himself and herself the naughtiest of all naughty people in a naughty but enchanting world! Enchanting, yes—the word was like a pang. . . . But had he really been in love? For the oddest thing of all was the way in which the first few months of the affair, so gay and light-hearted, had actually given him back something precious and lost in his relationship with Enid. The something that had been lost, or overlaid, after the birth of Buzzer; as if some kind of bloom, or illusion, had vanished, or been obscured, on the sudden intrusion of that so different reality. Yes, childbirth—who could have foreseen the effect of childbirth? That butcher-shop and meaty reality—as Paul so brutally put it, and quite right too!—was something for which love's young dream hadn't at all been prepared. A loss of belief! And Nora—dear delightful humorous Nora!—had somehow magically restored it. How the devil did such things happen? And why the devil weren't they admitted! Shams everywhere, shams in love, shams in hate, shams in marriage or divorce, shams deeply bedded even in the secret self. The eye loving before the heart or hand admits, the heart hating when the hand delights. It was all a mess. . . .

BAKER STREET: TOWN LANDING.

He turned under the silver-gray signpost, proceeded down the sloping sand road towards Jim Connor's house, which stood high and dark at the river's edge. One light in an upstairs window, one light downstairs—somebody must still be about. A figure detached itself from the shadows of the porch, came uncertainly down the wooden steps into the moonlight—it was Jim, wearing the perpetual cap, pulled down over his eyes, a cigar tip glowing under the sharp visor. The cap that was never off, even indoors.

The half-shadowed prison-blanched face was smiling, the effect was oddly as of a secret smile existing by itself—only when one came nearer could one see the kind eyes in the shadow of the cap-visor. Typical, too—the watchful kindliness always a little in retreat, a little on guard. He remembered, suddenly, the time when Jim had come down from Taunton to spend the night, and when, trying to wake him in the morning, he had had to touch his shoulder—the poor devil had jumped half out of bed, terrified.

"Hello, Jim?"

"Hi, Timothy, old kid. What are you doing round here so late? Pretty late for you domestic fowls, isn't it?"

Old kid—that absurd favorite phrase of his.

"Domestic—what about yourself!"

"Oh, no, not me! I guess I was feeling a little depressed by it. I thought I'd just get a breath of this nice sea air before I turned in."

The voice sounded a shade sad, a shade tired, the gray-sweatered figure turned slowly, they walked down past the house to the beached canoe—it looked like Paul's—at the water's edge. In the shadow of the house, they stood still, the water lapping softly, sibilantly, on the sand, quarreling against the stone piers which supported the moonlit verandah above them.

"Yes, the sea air smells good after all this sheer domesticity."

"Anything wrong?"

"Well, I guess the girls don't like it much. I have a feeling they don't like it much. You'd think they'd at least know a little something about cooking, wouldn't you, or be willing to try? We haven't had a decent meal in two days. You get tired of sardines! And Kitty picking on Karl, and neither Kitty nor Lorna wanting to do any of the housework—yeah, this sea air smells good!"

He smiled again under the visor, but the smile was melancholy and explanatory, he looked tired.

"Maybe they'll get used to it. Sometimes I think you expect too much of human nature, Jim—"

"Do I? Maybe I do. I hadn't thought of it. Lorna has a lot of talent, you know, she ought to be practicing, this is her chance to practice, with a good piano—if only Kitty would just try to take hold of things—but she's not much like your Enid. No, old kid, you've sure got a jewel there!"

"I'm glad you like her."

"A wonderful girl, a real woman—and beautiful, too. I'm sorry she doesn't like me—"

"So am I, Jim; but you know how women are."

"Sure. Don't I just? . . . Did you have anything on your mind, Timothy? I haven't seen you much."

"Yes, I know. And I can only stay a minute now. But there *is* something I thought you ought to hear, and I hoped I'd catch you by yourself. I thought it wouldn't do any good to let Karl and the girls in on it."

"Yeah?"

"May be nothing serious, either; but old George Pierce, across the river, has heard about you, mostly I'm afraid, from Enid, and got on his high horse, and of course he might make trouble."

"I get you—the civic spirit."

"I'm afraid so. Incidentally, I don't want to know what you don't want to tell me, but have you got any plans yet?"

"No. I haven't. But don't worry, kid—don't you worry. I'll be all right."

"I just thought I'd better tip you off, anyway."

"Sure. Thanks. And I appreciate it, Timothy. But I'll be all right. . . . By god, isn't it a wonderful night? Doesn't this make you want to paint? If I were only a poet, now, with a lot of succulent polysyllables—what's the word, sesquipedalian? I have a fondness for long words, you know— it's supposed to be a symptom for something—that's what *Paul* says!"

He dropped his cigar into the dark water, where it went out with a faint *pssst*, stared downward in amused silence for a moment, then added:

"But it was left out of me, I guess—the best I can do is help the ones that *have* got it. You know, I'd like to give you a hand, Tip—you oughtn't to be sweating at teaching, you ought to go abroad."

"Abroad! Don't make me laugh. Damned nice of you, Jim, but as a matter of fact I'm a lot better off than most."

"Well, artists ought be supported by the state—"

"In Utopia, yes!"

"In Utopia. Look at those shells there, on that rock—what are those, kid?"

"Those? Mussels."

"Are they good to eat?"

"Sure they are—delicious, you steam them like clams."

"We'll have to try them. If those girls could even learn to build a fire—this morning they damned near smoked the house out!"

He gave a bitter little laugh as they turned, they were both silent till they had reached the steps to the front porch of the house, emerging once more into the moonlight. The short grim smile under the sharp visor again, the detached smile under the hooded but kindly eyes—he was putting out his hand.

"Well, thanks for coming over, kid—you're honest, the way I like people to be honest. Will I be seeing you tomorrow?"

"I'll try to drop in, in the afternoon."

"I wish you would. It might help me out. You never know."

"Okay, Jim, I'll try. . . . Good night."

"Good night, Timothy. . . . This Pierce guy, is he a friend of yours?"

"Yes. He's a good fellow, too, you know."

"Yes, I guess I know. Good night!"

"Good night."

He watched the tired figure go slowly up the stairs, disappear into the heavy shadow of the porch, heard the door shut behind him—he had gone back into his Utopia, his singular dream of Utopia. Gone back to Karl, to Kitty, to Lorna—to the cynical Karl, who used him and sponged on him, to Kitty who hated him, to Lorna who perhaps loved him, perhaps didn't, perhaps only used him too—Christ, what a tragic joke it all was, what a hell of a Utopia *that* was! He stood still, listening, for a moment—he thought he had heard a sound as of angry voices from one of the open windows upstairs, a sound of quarreling, two voices, male and female, in brief sharp interchange—but if so, everything was again silent. Utopia, by god—! It was more like a crucifixion.

And this gaunt blazing-eyed woman, Lorna—where the devil had *she* suddenly come from, how the devil had *she* got hold of him—with two children, according to Karl (who thought it was all a wonderful joke), and a tubercular husband in the New York Customs House—and she planning to be a concert pianist!

It was cold, he walked quickly—looking up, he saw that the moon was now almost directly overhead, swimming rapidly, dizzily, like a spun silver coin, through a shoal of silver mackerel. It gave to the whole night a sense of ominous hurry, a sense of finality, of falling, of impending end. The downward-going vortical swirl of everything, of all nature, the swirling and inward-funneling death, like those marvelous late Van Goghs, where all shapes seemed to be centrifugally or centripetally self-consuming —trees burning spirally on whirling and burning hillsides, burning their own doomed intensity, the hillsides themselves an exhausted flame of grass and bushes, the very rocks exhaling fiercely away in the final ecstatic "Ahhhh—!" of creative death. If one could only get hold of that—strip one's vision nakedly down to that—

The familiar feeling of breathlessness again, of defeat, of closing one's eyes, lest one see too clearly the very limitedness of one's own vision, the trembling ineffectiveness of one's own hand, the fumbling quick makeshift which, at the last moment always, and in a panic, one had to substitute for the real thing! He entered by the front door—the lilacs could wait till morning, to be a surprise—and stood still by Enid's empty chair in the disordered studio. The three half-burned pine logs, glowing and hissing, to be up-ended against the sooty sides of the brick fireplace—the lamp on the bookcase to be blown out, with its little cold after-smell of kerosene—the two-toned squeak of the hall door—his hands to be scrubbed in the small bathroom, with the nailbrush, to get the grit and sand from under his fingernails—the everlasting toothbrush, the everlasting voracious w.c.—and then the quick climbing of the stairs, taking his candle, the quiet undressing, lest he wake Ee—or was she still awake, lying awake?— and the noiseless getting into bed in the small moon-flooded room . . .

Ee's door was closed.

The house was silent.

⟨ II

"In the morning, (16th November,) as soon as we could see the trace, we proceeded on our journey, and had the track until we had compassed the head of a long creek, and there they took into another wood, and we after them, supposing to find some of their dwellings; but we marched through boughs and bushes, and under hills and valleys, which tore our very armour in pieces, and yet we could meet with none of them, nor their houses, nor find any fresh water which we greatly desired and stood in need of, for we brought neither beer nor water with us, and our victuals was only biscuit and Holland cheese, and a little bottle of aquavite, so as we were sore athirst. About ten o'clock we came into a deep valley, full of brush, wood-gall, and long grass, through which we found little paths or tracts, and there we saw a deer, and found springs of fresh water, of which we were heartily glad, and sat us down and drank our first New England water with as much delight as ever we drank drink in all our lives. . . . There grew also many small vines, and fowl and deer haunted there; there grew much sassafras. From thence we went on and found much plain ground, about fifty acres, fit for the plough, and some signs where the Indians had formerly planted their corn. . . ."

—Journal of the Pilgrims

Blue, blue-bright, gray-bright, gray—the fog-bright sun, the sun-bright fog —there had been a change overnight, a sea change, the sea had come rankly inland and upriver, the small screened window was pale with it, the fine wire screen hung softly luminous with sea dew. Sounds of dripping, too; the heavy patter, irregular and slow, of fog-drops from the poplar trees on the low roof overhead; and the thud of a fallen twig; or the sliding scrape of a dead leaf. But the change was not only this change, the change of weather—it was also something else, there was another change as well—older and stranger shapes hung in the softened light, melted into it, came out of it, were a part of it—and as he looked, or half looked, listened, or half listened, the dream and the actuality seemed but indivisible aspects of the same thing. The indiscreet dream about Nora—! Sharply and deliciously the slow bright turmoil of obscure shape swam upward out of the shadow, as if one glimpsed, through dark water, the turning and involved rondures of a sculptured group, a hand, a face, lifted, lifted as if alive, and then gone. Gone, but the emanations, the meanings, the thrust of the hand, the dark look of the face before it turned downward and under, hung, sang, vibrated, shone, in all shape and sound, ticked with the watch under the pillow, dripped with the sea fog, gave form to the window, extended themselves in and out of the fog-soft, fog-bright room, seemed even co-dimensional—like an aura—with himself. An aura? But which was aura and which was reality? This body—which jumped from bed, hurried down the stairs, shaved its blond face in a small dull square of mirror and plunged itself into the deep green-cold bath—which listened, as it pulled on its socks, to Buzzer singing in her room, or, as it pulled on the khaki trousers, to the church clock striking—was this, after all, only an aura for the dream? Was the whole world only an aura, a sort of Saturn's ring, for the strange and delicious dream, and the dream itself the only reality—? Was that sculptural dream the real core of the world, its only true meaning?

"Tirra-loo—tirra-lee—shadows rising on you and me—"

The lilacs, in the morning fog, were a hundred years old already, they stood orderly and precise and hard in the sun-bright fog, sharply outlined where they stood on the terrace wall against the gray river, like sticks in snow. Sand was scattered on the grass, too, which would have to be raked gingerly, or brushed back into the borders, and the deep crescent hoof marks of Terence's horse, which would have to be filled in and patted down. Shadows rising on you and me—very true, as one looked down from an autumn window; but where did they rise from, what was their source? From the dream? Like fog from the unconscious? Lilacs in sea fog, lilacs standing knee-deep in a dream?

The indiscreet dream about Nora went down the stairs with him like a suppressed radiance, like a dulled singing; the cat shot past him on the stairs—*Skippity-skap!*—he said, flicking at the striped tail with his hand, and in the dining room, over the little round white table, Buzzer's round face opened a round mouth for the tilted spoon of porridge.

"I'm eating porridge," she said.

"Porridge! No."

"Yes, porridge."

"And *why*, may I ask, didn't you come to wake me this morning?"

"Mummy wouldn't let me. She said you were sleeping."

"Foo! How could you *wake* me if I wasn't sleeping? Answer me that!"

"And Chattahoochee was out all night, the naughty cat, and came in hungry as a bear and all skedaddlish—"

"Skedaddlish—who ever heard such a word—"

"And he drank his milk like anything, *slup—slup—slup—slup*."

"Quite true. He always drinks his milk four tonguefuls at a time—just the way you ought to eat your porridge."

"I shouldn't either! Ho ho, how silly! As if I was a little cat!"

"A red-haired cat."

"It isn't red—it's gold!"

"Red."

"Gold! And I saw the lilacs, too—"

He kissed the golden, corn-silk golden, curls, pushed the freckled nose solemnly with one finger, went quickly down the gray steps to the kitchen, but Enid, standing at the blue-flame stove in the far corner, didn't turn, merely said, thus checking his impulse to go to her and kiss her:

"Your breakfast's ready. I'm not having any."

"Not having any! Why not, Ee?"

"Thank you, I don't feel very much like it. You can take the toast and coffee. I'll bring in your egg in a minute."

"Didn't you sleep, darling? Coffee might do you good."

"I slept *quite* well, and I won't want any coffee! Will you take it, please?"

Ah—so it was going to be like that. The preoccupied little hum again, the curved lips compressed a little, the dark curled head turning curtly and quickly—the shadow of the quarrel again, the closed bedroom door. They hadn't slept together, she hadn't allowed him to come and sleep with her! He took the coffee percolator from the table, hesitated.

"I think I'll just take a look at the lilacs first."

"Couldn't they wait till after breakfast? I've got a hard morning ahead of me, and we're late as it is."

"Very well, Ee. Have you looked at them yourself?"

"I'm afraid I've been much too busy!"

The quick oblique smile, intolerant, the oblique green flash of the eyes—lovely!—she was wearing the pale green smock, with the gold threads, the one that was his favorite—but was it a concession or a challenge? It went well with the soft-sheened silver-gray of the corduroy skirt, gave an added brilliance and liquidity to the eyes—as, of course, she well knew. Ah, these cunning, vain, merciless wenches!

"They look marvelous," he said over his shoulder, "but Terence says no blossom till spring after next."

Spring after next. The dream came like a fog between himself and the shining table, the poured coffee, the silver cream pitcher; it filled the morning-bright, fog-bright room, seemed to set everything at a distance. If Enid had allowed him to kiss her—that would perhaps have broken through the strange dull weight of it, the richly haunting burden—perhaps she too would then have shared in it! Or did she anyway? And did all things, even Buzzer? Perhaps. As it was, it was also as if she had somehow divined his infidelity, and as if her hostility were by a miraculous instinct directed precisely to that. And a hard morning ahead of her, and Binney coming, and himself probably delegated to look after Buzzer—instead of working on his picture—

"Can I go waving this morning, daddy?"

"Not waving, wading!"

"No, *waving!*"

"Well, you'll have to ask your mummy about that. Maybe it's too cold."

"Well then, we can go and look at the fiddler crabs."

"We'll see. Perhaps it's too cold for the fiddler crabs, too. How could they dance if their feet were cold? And come to think of it, young woman, what do you mean by walking round in your sleep the way you did last night? What about that?"

"I didn't either!"

"Didn't you, though! I heard a bang on the floor, a thump like an elephant jumping, or an elephantelope, or a rhinocerostrich, or a camelephant—"

"How silly! There *aren't* any such animals!"

"—and when I went up to see what it was, there were you, standing in the middle of the floor, fast asleep, with your eyes tight shut."

"Mummy, isn't daddy silly, he says I was standing up in my sleep! Was I *really?*"

"Cross my heart and hope I die! And all you would say was *mmm*. I asked you what you were doing there, and you said *mmm*; and I asked you if you were asleep, and you said *mmm*; and I asked you if you wanted to go back to bed, and you said *mmm*. That's all you could say, *mmm*. You must have thought you were a humming bird."

"Ho ho! I was a humming bird! But did I *really*, mummy?"

"Yes, I guess you really did. Now have you finished, my pet? I'll untie your bib. And you'd better run along to the bathroom. And when you're ready, you can call me."

"No, I don't *want* you to come—I can wipe myself."

"All right, darling. Aren't you clever! But call me if you need me."

"Yes."

The bib untied, she ran quickly, on tiptoe, from the room, flapping her hands like fins against her thighs. A humming bird. Or a goldfish. Enid, her arms folded across her breast, one foot swinging, had perched herself on a corner of the piano bench, watching him eat his egg—the attitude was temporary and provocative.

"I suppose," she said, "you haven't thought any more about the bills. But hadn't we better discuss them?"

"What is there to discuss, Ee? I thought we had decided—"

"We're very much behind with them. We owe Mr. Paradise for **two** months."

"Ah! The whistling butcher!"

"And he'll be coming this morning. We ought to pay him."

"Damn the butcher. All right. Why don't you make him out a check? How much is it?"

"Twenty-nine dollars."

"Holy mackerel. *That* won't leave much."

"No, it won't. And there's the milk bill, and we still owe Homer for the last ton of coal we had in the spring, and we'll be needing some more in a week or two—"

"My god. All right, pay Homer, too. Or I will."

"I'm afraid something will have to be done. I shall need some winter clothes, and so will Buzzer, and now there's this new cesspool—just how are you planning to manage, may I ask? We can't go on like this, always getting more and more behind. It's really getting to be too much of a strain. It really is!"

"Damnit, as if I didn't know it! Well, I'll see. I'll ask old stick-in-the-mud for some extra work. Or maybe I could get an afternoon's work at the new women's school in St. Botolph Street—"

"I see! An extra day in town every week. I knew there'd be a catch in it somewhere! As if it wasn't bad enough already."

"Good heaven, Ee, you can't have it both ways! You might at least *try* to be reasonable! If you want more money, I'll have to do more work—money doesn't grow out of the ground, you know."

"No, and it doesn't grow out of part-time teaching at second-rate art schools either! The whole arrangement is bad. I should have thought—"

"Second-rate! Perhaps you should have thought before you married me!"

"Indeed, yes! Perhaps I should!"

"Now, Endor, darling, listen—"

"I should have thought, if you don't mind my saying so for the hundredth time—"

"Make it the thousandth, why not—?"

"Will you please listen to me?—that a whole-time job in town was the only possible solution."

"Oh, my god. *Must* we go into that again? You seem to be forgetting that I've got my own work to do. Or to try to do!"

"Your own work. Of course! I suppose you still think that must come first. It doesn't matter if we have to go without proper clothing, does it, or have all the shopkeepers dunning us month after month—"

"You needn't exaggerate—and there's no point in being melodramatic about it either."

"I'm afraid it's the *facts* that are melodramatic, since you choose the word, and not me. Oh, no! But this is where discussion always ends with you, isn't it? In an accusation. I'm in the wrong, as usual! But I think we've reached the limit, and I think you'd better consider what you'll do."

"Ee darling, you know I'll do anything I can, but you *can't* expect me just to give up my own work, offhand, like that! You can't!"

"If you'd wanted to do portraits—"

"I don't want to do no portraits, no, *ma'am!*"

"The upshot seems to be that *I* do a great deal of your work *for* you."

"*That's* a new view of it!"

"It's true. You'd better think it over. And if you don't mind too much, will you take Buzzer out this morning? I've got all the ironing to do."

"I thought Mrs. Kimpton was coming to do it."

"We can't afford it. And besides, as I've told you before, she's not clean."

"Not clean! How can that *possibly* affect ironing!"

"I won't have her in the house with that dreadful feather boa round her neck."

"Very well. When I've laid the studio fire, and carpet-swept this room, and made my little bed, my little solitary bed, and carried in the wood—"

She was just rising, just saying her ironic "thanks!", her eyes widening and brightening as if to let him see better the intensity of her unspoken anger, when the sound of bird-note whistling came cheerfully from the garden, the bird-fluting of Mr. Paradise, the butcher—Paradise, absurd name for a butcher!—and the white-coated figure went quickly past the dining room windows to knock at the kitchen door.

"All right, Endor. And there goes our twenty-nine dollars. And if Ratio Binney comes about the cesspool while I'm out, you'll have to deal with it yourself. That's all *I* can say!"

Dispersed, interrupted for a moment, disturbed, whirled aside like the morning fog on a current of air, in idly glistening and lazy convolutions, the indiscreet dream about Nora was turned away only to return again, all-surrounding, all-entering, all-coloring: its hands were his own hands on the rumbling carpet sweeper—the sweeper carpet, Buzzer called it, trotting behind him, pretending she was a horse—it maneuvered with him under the dinner table, bumped the gate-legs, rattled out from the faded Chinese carpet onto the bare black floor boards at the sides (for Buzzer these were oceans, very dark and cold and deep) and followed sinuously every familiar curve and slope of the ancient uneven floor. It licked up the breakfast crumbs—it *was* the breakfast crumbs. It was the Chinese embroidery of motionless birds and dragons, the silent but alert piano—ready at any moment to burst out in the C-sharp minor Prelude, or the *Cathédrale Englouti*, or the little Brahms waltz—it was the all-too-eloquent thump of Enid's iron on the ironing board in the kitchen—it was the whole house, himself, everything. Strange—very strange—he must be hallucinated. Why should a dream be so damned persistent? It *was* everything, but also, subtly and dangerously, it *changed* everything. The near at hand, certainly—but the remote no less, too. The fireplace in the studio, with the wood ash neatly brushed back from the brick hearth, to make a soft ashen wave under the andirons; the red scaly pine logs, brought in from the woodshed in the fragment woven-wood basket; the crisp pine cones tucked under the crossed logs for kindling, the bright brass jug of the Cape Cod fire lighter standing as if expectantly in its corner—it was in all these as he touched them, watched eagerly by Buzzer, her hands flapping excitedly, but it was also just as importantly discoverable and discernible in the far-off or merely imagined. The river, moon-tide brimmed, hurrying down to the Sound, past the sand dune and the derelict breakwater (ah, what a wonderful nocturnal fire that had been), and then, beyond the iron-framed lighthouse, joining the sea in the quarrelsome tiderip—it was there, too, tossing Paul's canoe, spanking the under bow of George's catboat. It was the sea gulls screaming over Mr. Riley's nets and bobbing lobster buoys, offshore; or, inland, at the head of the river, the harsh *har-har-har—har-har-har-har* of the crows, the high bright circling of the eagles. Somehow, through that luminous and all-permeating dream, Nora, who had never been to the Cape, never even seen this little village, had taken complete and magical possession of it. Possession—of course, the very word for it—it was possessed, *he* was possessed—it was a kind of witchcraft, a sort of effluence from the unconscious, a psychic wave which had washed over the world and given it a new and astonishing brilliance. Everything, in that current, looked suddenly more alive, glowed importantly in its own light and right, seemed to have taken on an added and peculiar significance: the grains of wood, the texture of the linen sheet as he smoothed and folded it, the pillow as he patted and plumped it, the fluttering and sucking of the muslin curtains against the fog-bright screens. And the lilac trees, as he looked down at them from the bedroom window, resting his hands on the low sill, the lilac trees in the fog, which Chattahoochee was now investigating with tolerant curiosity, were already as good as in blossom. It was June of another year—another summer, another love.

Another summer, another love. The slow pang, melancholy, delicious, recapitulative, filled his breast, extended down his forearms, even to his fingertips—it was a physical thing, as actual as pain or fear. In the Purington house next door someone had put on that everlasting record, the worn-out record, and the blurred magnified words added themselves satirically to the odd and exciting theme, the threat of a crumbling world.

> In the morning,
> In the evening;
>   Ain't we got fun?
> Not much money, but, O honey,
>   Ain't we got fun?
> The world was made, dear,
>   For people like us—

The words followed him, fading, as he went down the stairs, became a meaningless gabble, then reappeared stridently as he entered the studio again and turned the easel for a look at the half-finished painting.

> The rich get richer and the poor get children.
> In the meantime,
> In between-time—

No, it was not a success; and now more than ever, in the light of the dream about Nora, it lacked the intensity, the intense simplification, at which he had aimed. The effulgence of this sun-blasted, blue-burning, ragged Cape Cod landscape, invisibly but passionately ablaze between the cruel reflectors of sun and sea, as if set on fire by a vast magnifying glass, was not really there, was only hinted at—and yet, if he could feel it so vividly, live into it so hard, and with all his senses, so love it, in all its roots and ruin, how was it that it could still continue to escape him? Where, exactly, was the failure? He looked, and looked again, stared through it, while the gramaphone squawked and ran down, and Enid's iron, in the kitchen, clashed on its metal rest, and he found himself suddenly seeing the whole Cape Cod landscape as one immense and beautiful thing, from Buzzard's Bay to Provincetown, from shoulder to sea tip, every detail clear, still, translucent, as in a God's-eye view. The salt marshes rotting in powerful sunlight; the red cranberry bogs; the sand-rutted roads through forests of scrub pine and scrub oak, and the secret ponds that existed on no map; thickets of wild grape and bull-briar; fields of blueberry and hot golden-

rod; grass-grown wind-carved dunes, inlets and lagoons, mudflats bedded
with eelgrass, bare at low tide, haunt of the eel, the bluecrab, the horseshoe crab, the fiddlers; and the blown moors, too, with high headlands
and dwarfed cedars and junipers, the dry moss and the poverty grass
crumbling underfoot, the wild-cherry trees glistening with the white tents
of the tent caterpillar under the dome of August blue: he saw it all at a
glance, sun-washed and sea-washed, alive, tangled, and everywhere haunted
by the somehow so sunlit ghost of the vanished Indian. The Indian names
—and the English names—these, too, were a vital part of it—Cataumet,
Manomet, Poppennessett, Cotuit, Monomoy—Truro, Brewster, Yarmouth,
Barnstable, Shoot-Flying Hill, the King's Highway—they ran through it
like a river, ran gleaming into the past, ran too into the future. And the
houses; the cottages of the sea captains—a mile of them in Dennis, the
sea captains who had known St. Petersburg and Canton as well as Boston
—or the porticoed and pagodaed mansions of the China traders; and the
ruined farmhouses and barns, silver-gray ghosts, the sad shingles and clap-
boards smokelessly consuming, among wild apples and wild lilacs (like
Weir Village) back into the burning earth from which they had risen—yes,
it was all of a piece, all in one vision, it was in his blood, his eyes, his
bones, he shook and lived and died with it. Christ, yes! But why, then,
could his mystical and ecstatic vision of it be put to no better use? Ecstasy
—someone had defined ecstasy as "farsight," with the overcoming of the
sensual perceptions of space and time." As in El Greco—as in Van Gogh.
But it wasn't wholly true, for the sensual perceptions of space and time
must be there, too—rarefied and essentialized, perhaps, but there. He could
see that, he knew it deeply, it trembled in his hand just short of the canvas,
and someday, god helping, he would get it. Someday—but, in the meantime, if there were only someone he could discuss it with, shamelessly! If it
didn't have to be so damned *secret!* Enid—impossible. Roth—too cynical,
too urban, too superficial. Paul—too analytic, too much from the outside
looking in. Jim Connor—well, perhaps!

In the meantime,
In between-time—

He turned the easel back to the wall, and suddenly, for no reason at
all, felt light-hearted, felt gay. The whole thing was too ridiculous, it was
all a vast joke, a gigantic hoax of some sort, and if only one saw through
it and refused to be hoodwinked, everything even now would come out all
right—just as it always had before. Keep a stiff upper lip—that was it—
and sing like the very devil. Whistle among the tombstones!

The world was made, dear—for people like us!

He half sang, half shouted, the absurd words, hoping they would
reach Enid, added a "ho ho" of his own to them, *sotto voce*, and then
walked quickly through the dining room to the top of the kitchen steps. It
was time for the morning mail, time for the newspaper, time for the walk

with Buzzer—time for escape into the blue. Enid's cheeks were flushed with the ironing—it had the effect of making the cheekbones look higher, the eyes narrower and deeper. She put up one hand to brush back a moist curl from the moist and lovely forehead.

"And another thing," she said.

"Yes, darling?"

She paused, frowning, to wriggle the bright point of the iron along the white hem of a shirt, flattening it as she went, then round a pearl button —how fascinating, how skillful!

"Since we're on the subject of money—"

"Oh, yes?"

"There's the little matter of Buzzer's education. We can't send her to the public schools here. They're very bad, as you know—the children aren't at all nice. It would be impossible."

"But, Ee dear, aren't you being a little premature?"

"Not at all. We can't keep her out of school indefinitely—even with the help of doctor's certificates—which would be dishonest, anyway—she'd be *made* to go, sooner or later. You can't just put off thinking about it! And there are no good private schools within miles."

"Public schools were good enough for me!"

"Yes. Timothy—yes, perhaps they were! But it's another matter with girls, as you'd have known if you'd had any sisters."

"An oversight. Of course, I'd probably have been a lot more refined in my tastes if I'd been sent to the Friends' Academy in New Bedford, or Miss Nonesuch's Nunnery for Beacon Street's Best."

"I'm afraid there's no doubt about it. And you'd be a good deal more intelligent about this, too. It's just what's wrong with you, with your whole outlook! It's simply not fair to Buzzer, that's the whole truth, and you've *got* to think about it, whether you like it or not. And plan for it. At your present rate of earning—"

"There you go again!"

"Will you allow me to finish?"

"Endor darling, you know I'm entirely in agreement with you, except for my hatred of these damned little snob-schools, where they turn out scatter-brained little one-design nincompoops, with social registers for brains and cash registers for hearts—"

"Nonsense!"

"—but I fail to see the hurry."

"I see. You want to put it off—just as you always want to put off holidays for me and Buzzer, or getting a maid, or any of the other things that might make life a little more agreeable for me here—while *you* have everything you want! Is that it?"

"If that's the way you want to see it, certainly! But perhaps if you've got some brighter plan you'd be so kind as to tell me."

"George and Mabel—"

"Oh, it's George and Mabel again, is it? How nice!"

"They're very good friends of yours. Better than you know, and I think you might at least be grateful when they go out of their way to be kind!"

"Go out of their way! Don't make me laugh. I suppose George was going out of his way last night, when he came butting in here about Jim Connor."

"To be kind, exactly. And this was kind too. They suggested that we ought to take out education insurance. Which seems to me a very good idea."

"I see. So that's where the money comes in."

"Exactly. How clever of you!"

She smiled at him, a smile that wasn't a smile at all, added the neatly folded shirt, with a sort of unnecessary emphasis, to the little pile of freshly laundered linen on the corner of the kitchen table, then turned, before he could speak, and presented the pile to him, one hand on top (the wedding ring, and the pearl), the other at the bottom—it was of course the mute but eloquent evidence of her slavery. Her eyes looked up at him with cold amusement—but, no, not amusement, they were too hostile, too beautifully feline for that—it was almost hate. Good old Enid!

"And would you mind," she said, "taking these up and putting them on my bed? And I think there's someone at the door. It's probably Mr. Peterson with the vegetables, and we don't need any."

"All right. I'm going for the mail."

"In that case, perhaps you could take Buzzer along with you for a walk, if it isn't too much trouble. I think it's too cold for her to go in wading."

"Oh, no trouble at all!"

"Thanks."

He looked steadily into the level eyes for any sign of a relenting, but none came; the exchange between them was hard, unflinching, motionless, almost unbreathing; and in the pause before he turned away he felt that even as he looked at her, with his love for her still intact and vivid, she was being borne backward and away from him by her own will—exactly, he thought, as if she were the figurehead of a ship, swept dizzily away from him, and with just that look of sea-cold inscrutability. Or the stone eyelessness of a statue.

Damned handsome, he thought—dropping the laundry on the bed, and giving it a pat—damned handsome, even when she was angry—but jumping Judas, was there to be no end to it? No end to it whatever? Better an explosion than this everlasting smoldering, better a pitched battle than this guerrilla warfare, this merciless sharpshooting and sniping—and, good god, what a sharpshooter she was! She did him credit, she certainly had blood in her eye, she was the very devil!

"No vegetables today, Mr. Peterson. No, nothing today! Is it going to rain?"

"Well, kind of hard to say. *Seems's* if it might burn off, but you never know, with the wind in the east!"

"No, looks kind of dark."

The green truck with its piled boxes of cauliflowers, crates of pumpkins, crates of cranberries, was gone around the far corner at the turn of the street, under the bare dripping poplars; fog spat on the stone doorstep at his feet, fog dripped on the heaped leaves; and into the garden, as he went around the front of the house to enter it in search of Buzzer, the indiscreet dream about Nora once more slyly accompanied him.

The indiscreet dream—the fleshly, the sensual, the whirling, the Rubenslike— But a strange figure was standing at the foot of the garden, by the river wall, had just come up the steps there from the Town Landing, a little man with a shovel over his shoulder—a tramp, a gnome, a furry-faced gnome, who hobbled forward in trousers much too big for him. The trousers were held up by a string tied round the waist, the short shapeless coat had apparently been made out of a dirty piece of gunnysack, even the little eyes, above the dirty whiskers, looked dirty—obviously the creature had come straight out of the ground, out of the earth, with the caked earth still on him. In the middle of the lawn he stood still, appeared to be mute, darting furtive glances, weasel-like, to right and left, then jerked a quick thumb toward the pump house.

"I clean 'em out," he said.

"What?"

"Name's Pepoon, they all know me. I come to clean 'em out. Want yours cleaned? I live over the river, go 'round to all the houses regular, Bill Pepoon."

He jerked his hand again toward the pump house, an animal-like gesture, blinked the gray eyes under rusty eyebrows.

"Want me to clean it? I got bags to take it away."

"Oh, I see. But I haven't got one."

"Y'ain't got one? What's *that?*"

Letting the shovel fall easily from his shoulder, he pointed with it once more toward the pump house, incredulous.

"It's a pump."

"A pump?"

"Yes, a pump. Come and see it."

He opened the door, showed the little motor on the oil-stained floor, gleaming, motionless, an oilcan beside it, the red wooden pump shaft upright in its groove. The gnome stared at it, unconvinced.

"Oh. Y'ain't got one."

"No, it's a pump."

"Well, if y'ever want me, name's Pepoon, over the river, let me know. Know anybody else wants one cleaned?"

"Thanks—no, I don't."

"Cracky, a pump. And it looks just like—! All right."

"I'm sorry."

"No trouble at all. Good-by."

"Good-by."

He hesitated for a moment, casting an appraising eye at the Purington house, as if estimating his chances there too, but now a little skeptical, then shouldered his shovel again, and was gone almost at a trot around the corner of the woodshed and down into the lane that led to the Town Landing, where presumably he had his "bags." His "bags"! Good god, what a conception. He was all of a piece, an earth-god, and an earth-god of the very lowest—and best!—order. A miracle, no less, and probably inspired by the lilacs. *Willed* by the lilacs! A terrestrial empathy.

"Who was that funny man?"

Buzzer, squatted by the woodshed door, had arranged her collection of white quartz pebbles in a neat circle, like a crown, on the grass.

"Well, you know, Buzzer, I sort of think it was a god. I think it must have been an earth-god, just popped up out of the earth, like a jack-in-the-box!"

"He *wasn't* a god! *How* could he be a god! He was too dirty. . . . Did you see my pebbles? *This* is kingy, and *this* is queeny, and I've got the king and queen of the toenail shells."

"So you have. And what about a walk, my pet, to get the mail."

"The mail?"

She raised the blue eyes, questioning, abstracted, looked beyond him, to the ends of the earth, as if considering the ultimate of all ultimate problems, then scrambled quickly to her feet, flapping the small hands, fin-like.

"All right, but don't you *touch* them, now!"

"No, I won't touch them."

"And can we walk to the golf-links road and go to the secret place?"

"Yes, perhaps, if there's time, we can go to the secret place."

"And eat a checkerberry leaf?"

"And eat a checkerberry leaf."

"And look for Indian Pipes?"

"And look for Indian Pipes."

"You *mustn't* just say everything *I* say!"

" '*Blueberry, bayberry, checkerberry, cherry—goldenrod, silverrod, jack-in-the-pulpit-berry—*' "

" '*Mayflower, columbine, lady's-slipper, aster—which is the flower for your mistress, master?*' Ho ho—and milkweed pods full of silk—"

"You can make a silk bed for kingy and queeny. "

"If they aren't all gone. Do you think they'll be all gone?"

"I don't know, my pet. It's pretty late, you know, and all those seeds have to get busy, and find homes for themselves before spring comes—ha, and *this* is something you didn't know—I read it in a book."

"What, daddy?"

"That seeds have hearts. Did you know that?"

"Hearts that *beat?*"

"Well, I'm not so sure about their beating, but they're hearts, just the same. A little teeny tiny heart, and it's called a corculum—"

"A corculum! Ho ho! What a funny word!"

"Yes, it means 'little heart,' see? So I guess you've got a corculum."

"Don't be silly, *I'm* not a seed!"

"I wouldn't be so sure. I might try planting you, you know!"

Amused, intent on this entrancing world of bright images, images like pebbles to be arranged in rows or circles, to be strung like beads, the small blue homespun-clad figure, with doubled fists and lowered golden head, galloped ahead of him like a little horse. She ploughed through the drifts of fog-dampened poplar leaves, yellow and brown; kicked them, trampled on them; alternately raised and lowered her face, singing; half closed the blue eyes to feel the cool fog-drip on her cheeks, in her hair, the hands outspread—good lord, how wonderful, she was living in a world of her own, a burning and secret world of her own. The same world? a different world? A *new* world—that was it—the world of the poet, the *first* poet, the poet who saw simultaneously, for the first time, the sea and a flower. What! Dogs *and* horses in one and the same world—! It was a miracle. . . .

The letter, when he opened Box 67 with the thin steel key, the blue envelope, addressed with the clear delicate handwriting—the bold T and K, the open-eyed "o's"—how very odd that her handwriting always made him think of her eyes, as if the blue eyes looked up at him frankly from the envelope itself—the letter, carried in his hand, became at once a part of the indiscreet dream—and not merely an extension of it, but perhaps its very center. The letter, on its way from Boston, pernoctating, keeping its open-eyed vigil, had itself brought the sea change, the soft inland-going sea fog, and had brought, too, the obscure and all-troubling delicious dream, the half-seen sculptural shape of involved struggle, the hand lifted and vanishing, the face darkening as it turned away. Pernoctate—yes, the letter had kept a vigil, its blue eyes open all night, and it was this that had projected the whole thing—its influence had preceded it, even to bringing into his very sleep the half-guessed presence, the half-happy and half-unhappy joining and sundering, the ecstatic but broken embrace. Broken!

The familiar sensation of breathlessness, the heart contracting on itself—and yet it was good, too—whatever the outcome, it was good. Joy either way, freedom either way. Enid had come nearer, she already stood nearer, this was the important, the essential, change; and this would be true even if Nora hadn't herself yet made any decision. Or even if she had decided *not* to decide.

"And *that's* our old friend the Quaker burying ground," he said quickly, feeling a little breathless, "with all the little headstones exactly alike—see? —and exactly the same size."

"*Why*, daddy?"

"Well, it's really rather nice; it's to remind people not to be too proud, to be humble—no matter what they've done, or who they are. Not to boast. You see, the Quakers thought to put up a huge great pompous marble tombstone was like a boast, was like saying, 'Ho, look at me, how grand I am! Ho, look at me, but don't pay any attention to that little *Smith* fellow down there, with that measly little stone of his, like a school slate. Why, you've only got to look at his stone to see how unimportant *he* is!' See?"

"Yes, but suppose you were a king. *Then* couldn't you be proud?"

"Foo! A king. I'm afraid not many Quakers were kings. Or, no, come to think of it, perhaps they *all* were! And perhaps they *all* were proud!"

"Well, if *I* was a king, *I'd* be proud, and *I'm* proud *any*way!"

"You look out you don't have a fall, like old doctor Humpty-Dumpty. And all the king's horses—!"

"Ho ho, don't be silly. Humpty-Dumpty was nothing but an egg! And now come on. And shall we go along the little path by the rope walk and into the woods? To the secret place?"

"Yes, all aboard for the secret place."

The morning had perceptibly darkened, the sea fog lay close and smothering above the oak woods, the pine trees, the leaf-strewn wood path; above the fog there must be clouds; it looked like rain. A pungent smell of burning leaves rankled in the air, too, the smudge fires of autumn, smoke of the consuming world. On this path, in the snow, in winter—Buzzer on her little red sled, the leggined legs stuck out stiffly before her, going to the golf links—he must remember tomorrow to get the sled out of the cellar, and take a look, too, at the jugs of elderberry wine on the top of the cellar wall. And Paul's dandelion wine. And the snow shovels. . . . The woods were silent, dripping; a chickadee chattered angrily, a catbird wailed; and at the secret place—the little hollow of pine needles and pine cones under a solitary great boulder of granite, green-lichened, surrounded by pines— while Buzzer built a house of pine twigs, and stood pine cones around them as trees, he opened the blue letter.

No salutation—no signature. A single sheet closely and neatly written, written calmly and unhurriedly, too, as one could see by the care with which the margins had been kept, the text precisely balanced on the page. The longest letter she had ever written to him—which could have, of course, only one meaning—perhaps it would be better not to read it at all—? The burden of it was already manifest in the sudden closing of his heart.

I think I know how it is with you, I think you will know how it is with me. Do you remember how we met, that first time in Washington Street, after we had come out of the vaudeville theater? I suddenly saw you again on the sidewalk, looking down at me, and I said, well, where did you come from, and you, without even so much as taking your hat off, said Oh, I fell from heaven. As casual as that, and of course if I hadn't had too many cocktails for lunch at the Touraine there'd never have been any meeting at all. We've been very happy, haven't we? Maybe because it was all just as casual and light as that. And I never felt that I was taking anything away from Enid, or any pangs of conscience, until I began to feel that you were beginning to have pangs of conscience. You have begun, haven't you? And it's funny, but I don't really mind that at all, in fact I like it, for it makes me like you better—not that I didn't like you anyway—and makes me like Enid better too. And Buzzer. But I expect we both knew it was bound to happen some day, and both kept a little something in reserve, so that when the time did come it wouldn't hurt too much—isn't that it?

So, I think you'd better not come to see me any more. And I think you will like to know that I'm going to be married, next month, to the man you talked to on the telephone once, by mistake—remember?—and whose little painting of the Concord River you liked. I hope you'll be happy, all three of you—I'm sure I'm going to be happy myself—but it was fun, wasn't it? I shall always be glad it happened, and grateful.

Grateful! Dear delightful Nora *grateful!* He began to read the letter again, but found he couldn't. The words were too good, too true, too tender, the direct and rich honesty was more than he could bear, so much more than he could ever possibly have deserved; and abruptly he felt that if he didn't shout, or do something violent, he would burst into tears. He sat quite still for a moment, looked up through the red boughs of a pine tree into the gray fog, then suddenly he put out a hand, seized Buzzer by one ankle, pulled her to him, and hugged her passionately.

"She's grateful!" he shouted. "She says she's *grateful!*"

"Daddy, you put me down this *instant! Look* what you've done to my house!"

"I can't help it, my pet, she says she's *grateful!*"

"*Who's* grateful! Now put me *down!*"

"Mother Nature, that's who. Did you ever have a pine tree tell you she was grateful? *Did* you? No, I'll bet you didn't."

"Don't be *silly!* And you're scratching me, too. You didn't shave!"

"I did too shave, you wretch—you and your houses!"

"You've spoiled it, see? *All* those trees knocked down, *and* the house. Now you'll have to help me fix it up again!"

"You give me one kiss, and I'll help you fix it up again."

"There. Now put me down. You ought to know *better!*"

"All right. We'll fix your palace up, my pet, and surround it with a grove of cedar of Lebanon and shittim wood, and put the Queen of Sheba in it, and King Solomon, too, and a lot of angels and archangels and cherubim and seraphim, and we'll have a procession of kings for them, and music of dulcimers and cymbals and shawms and—sub-tone clarinets. And then, when we've done all that, what do you think—before the rain comes, which might be any minute now, we'll go skulking like Indians by the secret trail down through the primeval forests to the river, and then we'll prowl all the way home along the shore, keeping invisible, with our tomahawks in our hands."

"Where are our tomahawks?"

"Here, this is a likely looking tomahawk, and here's another."

"And nobody will see us?"

"Shhhh, we mustn't talk, you know. We must be *stealthy!*"

"Shhh! Are we ready?"

"Not a sound now—and be careful not to step on twigs! I'll go first, to blaze the trail, and you follow. Come on!"

From the wet sand bluffs by the river, when they emerged into the wide peace of fog, they could just make out the pale yellow sand bluffs of the golf links, opposite, and a solitary figure stooping to pick up a ball on the ninth green, solemnly replacing the metal flag in the hole. They slid down the slope of sand, filling their shoes; sat for a moment on the matted eelgrass, sea-smelling—the curled stiff wave of eel grass which everywhere lined the shores of the river—to empty out the sand; then resumed their prowl over alternate stretches of beach and tangle. The tide was out, the water waveless, leaden, fog-stilled; through the fog, in the direction of Paul's lagoon, came the chug-chug of an invisible motorboat, and the cawing of crows. Bayberry and beach plum, mussel shells, clam shells—carapaces of horseshoe crabs, the little ones golden, the larger ones almost black—their footsteps crunched and snapped and crackled amongst these. They were in the wilderness—tomahawk in hand they were revisiting the Indian wilderness, the wilderness unchanged since the beginning of time. Unchanged? Unchanged save by a dream, perhaps—the dream threading the thickets, the fog, the beds of bubbling eel grass, the hushed and overcast noon, exactly as his own world, all morning, had been threaded and changed by the indiscreet dream about Nora. But now, subtly, that had altered again—it was as if, now, through the fog, a single beam of soft light had plunged downward to that obscure shape of shifting and involved struggle, had quickly lighted and lightened the sinister intricacies of the unknown, lighted the lifted hand, brightened the dark face before it turned away—so that suddenly the delicious embrace, the air-borne embrace, had shed all its burden of sorrow and pathos, all pang and pain, and become wholly benign. The secret was suddenly sunlit, the Rubenslike sensuality was sunlit, and the face, which was half Nora's and half Enid's, no longer reproached him in desolation as it turned away, but instead— or so it seemed—looked up at him almost merrily before it vanished. Had the dream changed? But how could a dream change *afterwards*? He must simply have been mistaken about it, not at the time seen it quite clearly— just as he had not known after all that the ecstatic and anguished face was as much Enid's as Nora's. Had Nora's letter done this? *I think I know how it is with you, I think you will know how it is with me.*

From the indiscreet dream about Nora—strangely, obscurely, like the rayed light from a slowly opening door or window—or like a flood, too— or even, in another sense, like the blood pouring from a freshly reopened wound, releasing and thus ending the pent pain—the sense of the past came thickly and richly, the faces, the words, the mornings, the evenings. But not Nora, or Nora only briefly, for it was as if that first meeting in Washington Street—when he hadn't even taken off his hat—had itself become the door, which, once opened, readmitted a world which had been obscured or lost. It was Enid, it was the first two years at the Frazer School of Fine and Applied Arts, the first two years in Boston, with Christmas holidays in New Bedford, the snow on the terraced lawns of County Street, the Chicken Hops, the sleigh rides to Buttonwood Park: and it was the motor-paced bicycle races—the first expeditions to the art galleries of New York, the steamer along the freezing Sound—the shabby unheated gas-smelling little hall bedroom of the West Eighth Street rooming house, where he had first met Karl Roth and Kitty, and plunged at once into the new and exciting world of Greenwich Village, with its cafés, its drinking parties, its freak poets and painters—male, female, and neuter—but above all its sense of adventure and freedom. Yes, that, and the sharp sense of reality which it had brought him for the first time, painting as a reality, with a real function in society, and life too as a reality, in a far richer and fiercer sense than anything in his childhood in New Bedford had prepared him for; but along with all these things, behind and beneath them, and lending a fresh vividness and iridescence even to the powerful ambition which they had suddenly quickened in him, was Enid. Iridescence—yes, exactly that; she had brought instantly an astonishing iridescence into everything that surrounded him. It had seemed far away, until Nora had somehow sprung it all back into focus again—but now his first meeting with Enid Severance, at Cousin Anna's dinner party, and the drive to the dance in the snow, seemed actually more recent than his first meeting with Nora. Adolescent? No doubt. But there had never been such a first meeting before—there could never be such a first meeting again. White magic, all of it—the silver tissue of the shawl drawn by the lifted hands over the young shoulders, and the clear green eyes, young and candid, looking into his own, across the glittering table, between the candles, with a disturbed be-wilderment of intensity and question, secret but unconsciously declared, which demanded to be probed even while it suffered and refused—the eyes that could listen, as it were, to nothing else, and turned away only to be turned back again, or after an interval to be found covertly watching —no, there could never be anything like that again, that lovely and naïve surrender, which had, at one stroke, drawn him into a completely new world. And then the first "call," at the absurd and ornate Victorian house, with the fretwork gables, the iron deer standing alert on the lawn in the snow, the wide piazza above the terrace (where later, in the summer, were to be tubs of blue and pink hydrangeas, and the enormous rubber plant)— the first stiff "call," and meeting Enid's silent and so obviously disapprov-ing mother, watchful and nervous above her ceaseless knitting, glancing now at himself, now at the black marble clock, which ticked secretly, re-finedly, on the mantel. And, after that, the uninterrupted chain of ever more frequent meetings, designed or fortuitous, their eyes everywhere seeking each other out, at every party, in every street, morning or evening, for the delicious renewal and deepening of contact, the exploration of the sense of touch, of which it had seemed so impossible that they could ever have enough. Physical? Metaphysical, rather. Their tangents had been universal, and everywhere—in the vibrations of texture and tone, in the aliveness of light—they had come together very slowly, without other bodily meeting than in the waltz, at a dance, or the gloved hand lightly held at the crowded skating rink, and in that sublimated intoxication, apple blossom and peach blossom, chestnut blossom and the tiger-throated nasturtium, the solemn bells of the Catholic church in the evening, or the far whistles of the tugs in the Bay, had seemed a sufficient bridge, a sufficiently corporeal language—it had been months before they had first kissed. Adolescent, yes—certainly. And perhaps this had been the initial mistake, if anything so profoundly beautiful could ever be a mistake: the poetry had been too pure a poetry, its further implications (of all that the body, and passion, could exact, or time and diurnal intimacy dishevel and destroy) had been too little understood; and when the prose followed, it had inevitably seemed only too ingrainedly prosaic. The realities had come too quickly and harshly, one after another—lack of money, doubts about his career, the interferences and disapproval of Enid's mother, whose social "ambitions" for Enid had been so cruelly thwarted (good heavens, how she had been shocked at their going to live in a Boston boardinghouse!)— and then, later, the wholly unknown Enid who had cried out quickly with pain, in pneumonia, her eyes animal and unseeing—Enid pregnant—Enid in childbirth—yes, Paul was right, the shock of that "meaty and butcher-shop reality" had been too much for him, it had changed everything. Changed, or only *seemed* to change? Had the disenchantment been real, or only theoretical—a self-induced and half imagined thing? Had he been disen-chanted (if indeed he *had* been) merely because he had *expected* to be, faced with these so many and so different realities, and was disenchant-ment itself therefore only a romantic fiction, or a fiction of the romantic? And how then had Nora so magically managed to give the whole thing back to him? Ah, perhaps because she had instinctively restored to him his belief in the illusion, his belief in the illusion as the only reality. Or, more simply, taught him that the real world was illusion enough!

Yes; for this all-releasing dream, this dream of the pure embrace, air-borne and wind-blown, this whirling and halcyon love, in which the beloved face had become one with his own, the white shoulders and breasts and clinging thighs and knees as if his own body, the throbbing embrace hung ecstatically in sunset light—this ever-clearer dream, as it glowed creatively down from plane to plane of memory, through trapdoor after trap-door, like a lantern casting down its light through successive floors of a dark house, touched now his childhood too, brought that back as near and clear as Enid, and with precisely the same fresh and vernal significance. Like those tiny Japanese folded flowers, made of desiccated wood and tissue, no bigger than seeds, which open out, when put in water, to become irises or almond blossoms, or dark leaves, these images now opened to join the others. The intense and radiant reality, above all, of a girl's face, a hand, a hard green acorn on a branch, the sunlit iris of an eye, the hairs on a grasshopper's leg, the swimming colors of a wet stone, the intricacy of ordinary grass, or the inexhaustible mystery of the simple dust that lay in a country road, this dust that was warm and friendly under one's naked foot, and between one's toes, this extraordinary stuff that was the earth's substance, the very *earth*—suddenly he knew these things again as vividly as he had known them in his childhood in New Bedford, and as vividly as Buzzer—who followed him intently, silently, oak-branch in hand—knew them now. It was like coming alive again. He was alive again, and the whole blazing world alive with him, everything belonging to everything else, and everything with one and the same meaning.

He stopped, stood still, stared down at the beached dory which lay on the sand before him, its galvanized iron anchor, sea-gray, half-buried in the sand, then, drawing his feet together, jumped neatly over it, brandishing his tomahawk in the air.

"Tirra-lirra, tirra-lee!—" he said.

"Daddy, you were supposed to be *quiet!* They'll know we're coming!"

"*Let* them know. That was my war cry, see? And now they know that every Indian, every man-jack of them, must bite the dust!"

"*That* wasn't a war cry. You said that yesterday."

"Did I? Well, perhaps I did. But it doesn't matter. It's as good as fee fie fo fum."

"Ho ho! That was what the *giant* said, silly!"

"So it was. But it was a *kind* of a war cry, just the same, to let the Englishmen know he was coming. Shall we go for a sail in this dory? An imaginary one, you know, with imaginary oars and an imaginary sail, on an imaginary river. Hmm, I see it's got a name, too, it's called *Catfish*. Now why do you suppose it's called *Catfish*? Doesn't look like a cat, doesn't look like a fish, doesn't look like a catfish—"

"What does a catfish look like, daddy?"

"Well, you see, a catfish has whiskers, like a cat—"

"Ho ho, does it really? But it couldn't miaow like a cat, because fishes haven't got any voices."

"Foo! Don't you remember the fish that talked in the frying pan?"

"That was only in a story. It couldn't *really* talk. Shall we go for a sail?"

"Well, I'm afraid not, my pet. It's late, and I think maybe we'd better get a move on. Let's see how quickly we can get there—you run, and I'll walk with my seven-league boots, and we'll be across the road and past the blacksmith shop in a jiffy, and then over Mr. Riley's nets in a single leap—come on now, a little speed! And it's going to rain, it's going to pour pitchforks—"

He clapped his hands and she was gone at a gallop, scrambling up the sand path by the beach plums to the bridge road—the bridge loomed gray and ghostly in the thinning fog, a car came rattling over the loose boards, kicking and rumbling, and when he emerged on to the road, under the dripping poplars, the small blue figure was already halfway across Mr. Riley's field. In another moment she had gone down out of sight into the lane that led to the Town Landing, reappeared bustling up the steps to the lilac hedge by the pump house, and then finally vanished around the corner of the kitchen. Extraordinary child—where the devil had *she* come from? Extraordinary to think that this was Enid and himself, Enid and himself conjoined!—That summer, before she was born, when day after day, waiting, they had played three-handed bridge, Enid and himself and Enid's mother, fanning themselves in the stifling heat of the County Street house, drinking iced lemonade out of tinkling glasses, listening to the four-noted clink of the well chain in the garden through the opened windows—that summer, she had not existed. The ripening pears hung heavy among hot leaves in the garden, the box hedges smelled dustily of the sun, the cherries had long since been gathered and eaten, the green clusters of the grapes, under the broad laves, were beginning to redden, to purple. And New Bedford, with its old wharves and stone warehouses, the Point Road leading to the Fort, and the wide hot Bay, which one could see from the little hexagonal cupola at the top of the house, all the way to the blue islands, was complete and alive, as it had always been. But there was no Buzzer. And then the terrifying reality of the childbirth—Enid walking to and fro, her hand pressed to her back, the beautiful mouth curved and tense with pain and apprehension; Enid holding on to the banisters, desperate, her whole body arched and taut like a bow—and at last, late at night, the animal throe in lamplight, the quick and sickening divulgence of the blood-stained little animal, with its cry of misery, which was Buzzer, which was to become Buzzer! Astonishing, that out of such horror, and a chrysalis so ignoble and so violent, such beauty and brightness could have emerged—how the devil was one to explain it? And nevertheless, now, in the light of the all-exploring delicious dream of Enid and Nora, perhaps one could at last *accept* the bloody roots—the roots were no longer to be reprehended, they had their own dreadful and lightninglike beauty, they were oneself, one's hand, one's heart, one's god. . . .

Yes, but there was Ee still, this ominous attitude of Ee's—

The thought checked him, as he went up the wet wooden steps to the garden, the house was silent except for the irregular fog-drip from the trees on the kitchen roof—*spat-spat-spat*—and as he passed the kitchen window he looked quickly in, over the sink, but Ee was nowhere to be seen. The ironing must be finished, perhaps she had gone out. The pump-house door was open, and out of the pump house, bareheaded, the inevitable yellow foot rule in his hand, stepped Ratio Binney. The shrewd Yankee face, the quick gray eyes, the narrow smile, the corduroy trousers.

"Oh, good morning, Mr. Kane! I was just taking a look. I couldn't raise anybody from the house—"

"Morning, Ratio. You couldn't? Guess Mrs. Kane must have gone out—"

"Yes, I rang and rang, and knocked on your kitchen door. Mrs. Kane said something on the telephone about the cesspool—?"

He pointed, with the yellow rule, towards the foot of the garden, the new lilac hedge.

"Yes, I know."

"What seems to be the trouble."

"Well, I guess we just use too much water. And the cesspool seems to be overflowing. The water stands there, down in the corner—seems to be a sort of little cave-in starting. Come and see it."

The broad circle of sand, in the angle made by the new lilacs, still showed where the cesspool had been dug, the deep well of bricks sunk in the ground—in spite of repeated reseedings the grass above it was still sparse. Damn, and this would mean a further delay! At the edge nearest the terrace wall Ratio kicked with the toe of a scarred shoe at a small subsidence, where the sand was wet and smooth, as if just washed up from below.

"Hm. That's what it is. Been spilling over on this side, see? Too much flow to be carried off at the bottom. You've got to remember you're not much above sea level here! And that's always liable to make trouble. I see you've been putting in some bushes. Looks very nice."

"Lilacs, yes."

"Yes, sir, that's exactly the trouble, seem's if! Too bad, too."

"What do we do about it, Ratio?"

"Only one thing to do. That's what I said to Mrs. Kane, if that was what it turned out to be. Put in another cesspool. An off-set. Won't need to be so big, say a little more than half the size, and a drain into it from near the top of this one. Yes, I guess that's about all we can do, but that'll fix it. That was a big cesspool, too. You folks sure must use a lot of water!"

"I guess we do. How much is it going to set us back?"

"Can't tell, Mr. Kane, not till I know how much brick we'll want. Not much labor in it, though. We ought to do it in a day, easy. Guess it won't cost you too much."

"Okay. I suppose we'd better have it. Not too healthy, having this happen!"

"Oh, it won't do any harm about *that*, but of course if it goes on falling in it won't improve your garden much, and it might even take to backing up."

"I see."

"Yeup. Well, I'll send the boys over in a day or two. Too near sea level, that's what it is. There was only ten feet of water, remember? when we drove that well up there. No time at all."

"Yes, I remember. And will you take a look at the shut-off, while you're here. It shoves the pressure up a little too high—about thirty-four."

"*Oughtn't* to be more than thirty-two. I'll just set the valve back a mite. Pity to dig it all up just when you've got it looking so pretty, but that's what life is, just one durned thing after another. And as they say, one man's sorrow is another man's cash!"

"Okay, Ratio, and ain't it the truth! . . . What's it going to do, rain?"

"Looks like being what these Cape Codders call a tempest. I suppose you've lived here long enough to know that almost anything here is called a tempest? But I don't guess it'll amount to much. A chuckle of thunder, maybe. But you never know with these sea fogs, it might burn off. Well, I'll set that valve for you, and send over the Rollo boys."

"Thanks, Ratio!"

"No trouble."

The engine began its alternate wheezing and barking—three, five, three, two—as he opened the kitchen door, the kitchen pipes were ringing with the remote pump-strokes underground, the indicator danced over the kitchen sink, but the house was silent. The ironing board had been put away, there was no fire in the blue-flame stove, no indications of cooking, and in the dining room the table had not been set for lunch. He stood still by the piano, listening—in the gray stillness of the room he could hear the watch ticking busily in his trouser pocket—Chopin's Preludes were open on the music rest—under Buzzer's little table by the window lay the saucer of milk, apparently untouched, for Chattahoochee—it was all very odd. Like a deserted ship. No Enid. And what had become of Buzzer? She might be upstairs—or she might, of course, have gone over to Mrs. Murphy's kitchen, looking for cookies. Mrs. Murphy's special supply of cookies, with holes in the middle—very likely. But what about lunch? He struck a triad on the piano, softly, and another—thought of Paul's remark about Puccini's use of consecutive fifths—and then went through the little hall, past the stove—which would soon have to be started, damn it—and into the studio living room.

A newspaper lay in Enid's chair. He saw with a start that it was today's. Good lord, how extremely unfortunate, he had totally forgotten it. Ee must have gone shopping at Foster's and been told that he hadn't come for it! Damnation—Nora's letter had put it clean out of his head. He glanced at the headlines without really seeing them, put the paper down again, decided to go upstairs. No use trying to work till after lunch. Always supposing there was going to *be* any lunch! It was all very peculiar.

Enid's door was open at the top of the stairs, and in the little north-lighted room, she was lying motionless on her bed, her arms limp and straight at her sides. Her face was so turned that her eyes, without having to move, were already looking at him, obliquely, endlong, but with a disinterested detachment, a narrowed indifference, that was at once disturbing. He stood still in the doorway, and for some reason suddenly felt himself to be growing angry.

"Oh," he said, "I was *wondering* where you were."

She made no answer for a moment, no move, merely looked at him. Then she said:

"Is it so very surprising that I should want to lie down for a few minutes?"

"Of course not, Ee, but I *was* surprised at not finding you anywhere, or apparently any preparations for lunch!"

"You couldn't trouble to remember that we *always* have a cold lunch on ironing days, I suppose!"

"Oh. Of course. I'd forgotten. Has Buzzer been up here?"

"She has not! I thought *you* were supposed to be looking after Buzzer?"

"I can't be in two places at once, can I? I found Ratio Binney waiting in the garden, and had to discuss the cesspool with him. He said he'd been here for some time, ringing the bell and knocking on doors. I had the impression that *you* were supposed to be attending to *that*. I think you might have taken the trouble to answer the door, especially as we were expecting him, and as it was you who had taken it upon yourself to ask him to come!"

"I see. I'm to be reproached for that! It makes no difference that it was a simple necessity—just as it makes no difference that I felt really too tired to go down. Really, Tip, your egotism is sometimes a little staggering!"

"Egotism! I think you might at least have conferred with me about it!"

"Would you mind leaving me alone now please? I've got something I want to think out by myself."

"Time out for thinking! All right. But you could have chosen a more convenient moment for it, it seems to me!"

"If you're so desperate for your lunch you'll find the cold tongue and potato salad in the icebox. And it would be a help to me if you could set the table and find Buzzer."

"Very well. Come down when you feel like it."

He turned angrily from the angry eyes, went slowly down the stairs, his heart beating, his hands clenched in his pockets. So it was going to be like that again, the pressure increasing—and how infuriating of her just to lie there like that, relaxed, pretending she was tired, listening indifferently to Binney ringing and knocking, punishing Binney merely because she wanted to punish himself! Just the sort of thing that always most enraged him about her, that damned female habit of venting her spleen on every Tom, Dick, and Harry, advertising it to the entire world—like an octopus. And egotism! Merely because he expected to be consulted about his own affairs! Well, she could go to blazes. And if she could keep it up, so could he. Two could play at *that* game. And if she wanted to sulk, and go into a silence, for her damned thinking, by god he'd show here what a real A-number-one brassbound steel-riveted silence could be. A silence with velvet knobs on it! Hmm—yes. But the trouble was—and he suddenly found himself grinning, despite everything—the trouble was, as he knew only too well from long experience, that she could outlast him. *Pour rendre le silence en musique, il me faudrait trois orchestres militaires.* But maybe this time—

The twirled doorbell rang harshly—*zring, zring*—at the front of the house. Just as he was entering the dining room, it rang savagely again. Blast it, what next? Couldn't be Binney—the engine had stopped, and he must have gone. Retracing his steps through the hall and into the studio, he opened the front door into the gray, dripping street, and then stood staring. It was a taxi. A real honest-to-god yellow taxicab, complete with its little metal flag—standing there in front of the house, under the fog-drip from the poplars, in this defunct village, where no taxicab had ever been seen before. The driver was in the very act of clinking down the flag, and turning to the very odd-looking young man, pale and unshaven—or was it a little blond beard?—who was grinning and counting out a huge roll of bills. The black velours hat and the dirty blue flannel shirt were all too eloquent of his occupation. A cardboard suitcase stood on the gravel sidewalk.

"Twenty-eight, thirty. You said thirty, didn't you, buddy? You know, I wouldn't want to cheat you, after a miraculous expedition like that."

"Thirty bucks is right. Say, where's the nearest hotel from here, where I can get some grub?"

"Maybe this gentleman can tell you. I'm a stranger here. Is this Mr. Timothy Kane?"

"Yes. About a mile down the shore road, toward the Point—the Naushon. You can't miss it."

"Okay, thanks. And come again some time when you got nothing to do."

"I'll be seeing you!"

The young man, grinning and showing his bad teeth, dismissed the departing taxi with an effeminately wagged finger, looked after it with a sort of lascivious pride until it had turned the corner and gone out of sight, obviously pleased with his exploit—whatever it was—and then said: "All the way from Fall River, what do you think of that! Thirty iron-men worth of taxi! I suppose you never had a taxi here before? Did you?"

"No, I doubt it. It's a little out of the beaten track."

"The beaten track, eh? Ha ha. I guess you're right. So this is Mr. Timothy Kane! Jim gave me your address here. My name's Louis Bucholtz."

"Glad to meet you. And what can I do for you?"

"Well, you see, I overslept on the boat. We had a party last night to see me off, so I missed the train at Fall River. Too bad! And no other connections for the Cape practically all day. I couldn't wait all day in Fall River, could I? Fall River! My god. Have you ever seen Fall River? Have you ever seen the dump? Nothing doing. So, as I was Jim's guest, so to speak, on a liberal allowance—the only thing I could do was take a taxi. Thirty bucks—*boy*, what a taxi ride. That driver was a nice feller, too. He enjoyed it. He said he'd never been out in the country before in his life. I guess he made a good thing out of it! Where's Jim?"

"He lives up the road a little. I'll show you."

"You'll forgive this spectacular intrusion, Mr. Kane? Jim told me the easiest way to find him would be to come to your house, as you were known here."

"Sure. It's only a couple of minutes' walk. Come along."

"Okay. So this is Jim's little hideout—with trees and bushes and everything. Is that the sea? You know, I couldn't believe it when he wrote me that he was going to live in the country. How do the girls like it?"

"Kitty and Lorna?"

"Yeah."

"Not a hell of a lot. I get the impression they don't take much to cooking."

"Now, Mr. Kane, you wouldn't kid me! Neither of them ever saw a stove before in her life, except maybe on the stage—or in a shop window—what do you expect! If you ask me, I think it's a scream."

"Yes, but you may not think it's so damned funny when you don't get any meals. I think Jim's a little depressed."

"Depressed! You're killing me."

"Are you a painter?"

"Me? No. I'm an artist. There's a distinction. I write, and I paint, and I've done a little stage designing, and a little art criticism, but I haven't decided yet what I'll do. What's the rush? I've got my ideas, but what can you do without a patron?"

"So that's where Jim comes in. He's a wonderful fellow."

"That's your opinion?"

"Isn't it yours?"

"Are you being a little sly, Mr. Kane? A little oblique?"

"Not at all."

"I get you. Yes, Jim's all right."

"There's the house, down there—at the foot of the road. By the river."

"House! My god! It's a palace."

"I've got to go back, but will you tell Jim for me that I'll try to get over this afternoon?"

"Sure. Why not? Anything else?"

"That's all."

"Sure. And thanks for the good guidance!"

The ironic effeminate voice turned away, the shabby and spindling figure, with its shiny blue suit and cracked patent-leather shoes, sauntered down the road, looking as conspicuous as a crow at a garden party, and somehow sinister, though lacking the *strength* to be sinister. Good god, how could Jim be so completely blind? The creature might be amusing, but that he was a fake, a first-class typical Greenwich Village fake and poseur, there couldn't be the smallest doubt in the world. And obviously sponging on Jim—as, of course, others had done before him—without even the redeeming virtue of believing in him. An artist! Nothing so simple and honest as a painter. Naturally. One of those artists who would scorn to learn such humble essentials as the rudiments of drawing and perspective, and dismiss them as old-fashioned. The short-cut, every time!

And that houseful of Jim's, with *this* addition, and Kitty and Lorna not getting on with each other, and no food!

And now this little twirp riding all morning in a taxi, thirty dollars' worth, at Jim's expense, and then just smirking about it, as if it were all nothing but a joke—which in a way, of course, it was!—and already thinking of nothing but his little boast about it, the exploit which could be reported to his epicene friends in New York, on a postcard, or more likely by telegram! Regarding the country, too, as a mere subject for the obscene pleasantries of the cosmopolitan lounge lizards and lounge Lizzies of his dirty little cafés, his dives and ramshackle studios—good god, how sickening it was, if it wasn't all somehow so dreadfully inevitable! Exactly what would, and must, happen to Jim—the just fate of the generous and misguidedly good. Damn!

He went in by the kitchen door, from the garden, not greeting Chattahoochee, who blinked up at him amber-eyed from under the dead plum tree. Enid went past him, ignoring him, carrying two plates up the steps to the dining room. The table, he saw, had already been set, and Buzzer, at her own table, was busy eating her lunch.

"I'm sorry," he said. "I was interrupted."

He sat down opposite her, and as she made no answer, merely frowned down at the potato salad which she was serving, he added, smiling: "By a visitor."

She sat back in her chair, looked at him quickly and fully, dropping her hands in her lap.

"Yes," she said, "I'm afraid I saw your visitor!"

"Oh. I suppose you looked out of the window. And *what* exactly do you mean by 'afraid'?"

"I *happened* to be looking. I didn't look."

"And I suppose of course you listened?"

"I couldn't very well help it, could I?"

"Well, just what do you mean by '*afraid*'?"

"*Need* you be so hypocritical?"

"Hypocritical!"

"You know quite well what I mean."

"Do I?"

"I mean that this is the last straw. Absolutely the last straw. When it's got to the point where our house is to be used as a convenience, and a sort of accommodation address for loathesome objects like that, and criminals, I draw the line. I've waited all morning for you to come to some decision of your own about this, Timothy. I've waited very patiently, but as you apparently prefer simply to evade your responsibilities I've had to come to a decision myself."

"Mummy—"

"Yes, Buzzer, *what* is it?"

"Daddy and I went to the *secret place!* And then we were Indians, with tomahawks—"

"Wasn't that fun."

"And I built a house, too—"

"That was lovely. Now eat your lunch like a good girl."

"I *am* eating it!"

"Ee, dear, I'm as sorry about that as you are, and I didn't like the young man at all, and I regret as much as you do that Jim's taste in friends is so peculiar; but even so, is there anything so very terrible in it?"

"Nothing terrible in it! To have our house and name known in criminal circles in New York—"

"Criminal circles! Good heavens, Ee—"

"Criminal circles. Are you so afraid to face the fact?"

"Of course I'm not afraid to face the fact. I simply see it in a different light. You're wildly exaggerating the importance of the whole thing. Merely because a harmless little character drives up to our door in a taxi— what's so awful about that? I think it was rather funny!"

"Oh, you do."

"Yes, I do. *Damned* funny."

"Then I take it you're not going to do anything about it."

"Do anything about it? Why should I?"

"I see. It doesn't matter to you that the neighbors should see these criminals coming to our door, or know that we're associating with thieves, and those appalling women—"

"Ee, darling, I regret some aspects of it as much as you do, but can't we be a little more flexible and humane about it than that? Surely, we haven't got to take our opinions from our neighbors!"

"So that's how you see it?"

"It seems to me that view is not without its importance. We can't model our lives according to what the Puringtons or Rileys think. Or is that what you propose to do?"

"I simply propose to safeguard our good name and position, mine and Buzzer's, that's all—"

"Of course. Even if you have to sacrifice my integrity to do it. Or my friendships."

"Integrity!"

"Mummy—?"

"Buzzer, darling, you *mustn't* interrupt when Mummy's talking—"

"But I've *finished*. I've eaten *all* my potato, see?"

"Have you, darling? All right then, come here and I'll take your bib off, and then you can go upstairs and have your nap."

"And can I take kingy and queeny?"

"Yes, you can take kingy and queeny if you like, but remember to be nice and quiet, won't you?"

"I'll be as quiet as a *mouse!*"

"That's right. Run along, now."

She tiptoed quickly from the room, the shells tightly clasped in her hands. They listened with averted eyes to the footsteps slowly climbing the hall stairs, hurrying over the floor above, then Enid rose from the table. The preoccupied little hum again, the eyes hurt and angry. She took up her plate and went halfway to the kitchen with it, stopped stiffly, a little awkwardly, but with a kind of angry grace, too, turning her head curtly toward him, the green eyes flashing at him over the held plate, the plate held like a challenge.

"I've come to *my* decision," she said, "if you'd like to hear it?"

"Well?"

"If you don't give these people up, while they're here, I shall go back to New Bedford, and take Buzzer with me."

"Oh, an ultimatum."

"If you want to call it that?"

She smiled brilliantly, triumphantly.

"You're going to force me to give them up."

"As long as they're living here. I have no choice."

"And after that? Am I to be permitted to see them in New York? On neutral ground, so to speak?"

"I think we can consider that later."

"Oh, we can, can we! That's very kind of you."

"And I think you'd better come to your decision today. Otherwise I shall plan to go to New Bedford in the morning. I think it would be as well if you would come to your decision *now*. It seems to me you've had quite time enough!"

"*You* think—*you* think—*you* think—!"

The bitter words, bitterer than somehow he had expected them to be, were addressed to the vanishing green back, the slight green shoulders, the self-consciously upright head, as she went down the steps to the kitchen. He was sitting rigid in his chair, the knife and fork held hard in his hands, and for a moment, staring towards the doorway through which she had just gone, it was as if he had suffered an eclipse, he saw nothing. So she had beaten him, had she—she was going to beat him, was she—she thought she was going to beat him! With that triumphant exit, too, that self-righteous all-conquering know-it-all air, that air of bristling virtue, in every line and feature of her! He felt ashamed, stifled, it was as if something in his breast had suddenly curdled, but as if, too, he must quickly find something to do, something for his hands to do, something violent. The shadow of defeat—it would be impossible to accept it like that, it would be unendurable, the whole shape of his life would be forever wrong and unbearable. Somehow, even now, today, some dark twist must be given to the shaping of the event, some neat knifelike turn, which would at least salvage for him a scrap of pride, a vestige of dignity and power. She must be hurt—she must be injured. And if he was going to be defeated in this, he must see to it—was that it?—that in other respects he was vindicated, justified. He would make her pay for it, by god, he would make her see that *he* wasn't the only offending party. He would give her something to think about for the rest of her smug little life! Beautiful, yes, but there were limits!

He sat still, staring now across the gray room and through the little window towards the Puringtons', past the little dead plum tree, heard Enid pouring the hot water from the kettle into the dishpan, refilling the kettle under the tap, replacing the kettle on the oil stove with a clash. It was her clear suggestion to him that she was waiting, that he was late and delaying her, that he was sulking in defeat, or doing it deliberately to annoy her. Well, let her wait. He finished his potato salad meticulously, angrily, precisely, taking unnecessarily small bites. Yes, let her wait. But the oppressive ring closed in on him, he must do something, say something, or go somewhere—to sit here any longer would put him subtly at a disadvantage. He got up, carried the salt and pepper to the china cupboard in the corner—the silver-gilt salt cellar, the sworled silver pepper shaker—replaced the unused silver in the top drawer of the mahogany lowboy, and the two soiled napkins, looked slowly around the dining room to see if there was anything else he might do, then picked up his plate and tumbler and went down into the kitchen lean-to. The low-ceilinged whitewashed room was dark in the overcast light that came from the one window over the sink, and Enid, already washing the few dishes, looked up at him as if almost amusedly from the steaming dishpan, but he avoided her eyes, merely put down the plate and tumbler on the drainboard.

"You're in rather a rush, all of a sudden, aren't you?" he said.

"I wasn't aware of it. It seems to me that it was *you* who were in a rush, until of course it suited you for reasons of your own to change your mind!"

"Need that have prevented your staying at the table until I had finished?"

"Why should I? Are you by any chance aware that I've had to eat my last *three* meals practically alone? You're hardly the one to complain."

"Was that any fault of mine?"

"Of course not, you're never at fault, are you? You certainly didn't need to go out with George last night—"

"Oh, no, one *never* must be polite—"

"To one's wife, no! You can leave *her* alone as much as you like."

"Of course. That goes without saying."

"And are you going to help me with the dishes?"

"I don't think I will, if you don't mind. I'm afraid I don't feel very much like it, in the circumstances."

"Oh! So you're going to be ungenerous, too, into the bargain!"

"Ungenerous! Do you know I haven't had five minutes today for my own work? Not that *you* care about it. And tomorrow and next day in town —don't make me laugh."

He smiled bitterly, opening the garden door, holding the screen door open with his foot. She turned towards him, her wet hands held up before her, her eyes wide, handsome, fiercely satirical.

"And may I ask," she said, "where you are going, then? I suppose you're going to work in the garden?"

"I'm just going *out*. It doesn't seem to me to matter much! And if I want to work in the garden, or anywhere else that suits me, I certainly will!"

She stood still, her hands still held oddly up before her, as he turned away and went out, letting the screen door clack sharply shut behind him, he was aware as if through his back that she had not moved, still stood glaring contemptuously after him, her whole attitude one of helpless rage —and it gave him a kind of base satisfaction, as of a blow struck and not replied to, to turn towards the pump house and simply leave her there, entranced by her own fury. Let her stare, let her glare, let her rage. He had met her halfway long enough, it was her turn to worry now, the shoe would be on the other foot! If she thought he was as easy as all that, at the mercy of her beauty, or his love for her, to be whistled to and fro like a servant, a shadow, she would have another think coming. He opened the pump house door, looked down at the neat little engine, unseeing. But, of course, Binney had run it, no water was needed. Still, he could pretend to be examining the shut-off valve, for she would now be watching him from the window, watching for any sign of weakness—and after a moment he could saunter down to the foot of the garden, look at the lilacs, the site of the new cesspool, the river, the weather.

Buzzer's little garland of pebbles still lay on the wet grass by the woodshed door, and on the floor of the wood-shed, just inside the open door, the box of toenail shells, the box of pink boat shells; and beyond these, by the empty, or all but empty, coalbin, the rainbow-hued sawhorse, on which Karl Roth had squeezed out his remnants of tubes. Long ago, far away, a year ago—and if Karl hadn't come then, and hadn't, half as a joke, asked Jim to run down for the night, none of this would have happened. Jim would never have fallen in love with this village, these marshes, would never have come here again on his so peculiar mission, everything would still be at peace. Or would it? There was a perverse fate in these things, perhaps it all would have happened anyway, and the whole business of Jim was only an accessory—had it all really started with Nora? *I think I know how it is with you, I think you will know how it is with me. . . .*

He stood still; for a moment it was as if he had stopped breathing. He had a sudden sharp vision of Nora, so sharp as to make him feel empty-armed, empty-handed—blue-eyed shameless Nora, lying on the couch in the half-darkened room, and laughing as she lifted one leg in the air to pull on a stocking—looking at him out of the corners of her eyes, and laughing, the garter clasp bright silver against the whiteness of her skin. But suppose Enid really left him—suppose it came to the worst—would he really want to marry Nora? No. There was no question of that, there had never been any question of that. It was a different thing, as they had both known from the outset, and wholly without illusions. A different thing. He had always loved Enid—as who could better testify than Nora herself, who had always accepted the fact? By god, what a wonderful irony *that* was, if only Enid could be told! The supreme immorality—or was it a supreme morality? No, no morals in the bloodstream, no morals in hand or claw or mouth—it was a shambles. Fidelity—there was no such thing, or only relative. . . .

He lifted down the shovel from its nail on the woodshed wall, scooped a little earth from the lilac border, sprinkled it tenderly in the crescent-shaped hoofmarks on the lawn, where Terence's horse had stood pawing, filled them in and patted them down. There—the lawn would be all right even if nothing else was. The house might collapse and everything else with it, his world be blown to smithereens, but the hoofmarks of Terence's horse on the lawn would be obliterated. What the hell did the grass care? The uncut hair of graves.

He was hanging the shovel up again, when he heard her steps behind him, the heavy soft swish of the corduroy skirt. She stood on the grass before the open door, facing him, dark against the darkening afternoon, her arms jauntily akimbo. He made to go past her, merely allowing his eyes to slide unperceptively over hers, but she moved as he moved, turning, pivoting, and said:

"And another thing. I think it would be only decent—"

He went past her without any answer, walked slowly to the top of the terrace wall, stooped there to examine the subsidence of wet fresh sand where the new cesspool was to be. He felt of it with his hand, as if idly, appraisingly, and saw, out of the corner of his eye, that, after a moment's dismay, and an awkward balance of hesitation, she had decided to follow him, was coming very slowly towards him, her hands still on her hips. The

steps gingerly, self-conscious, on the wet grass, like a slow kind of dancing.
Graceful, but infuriating. And standing above him, looking down at him,
she repeated:

"I said there was another thing."

"Well, I heard you!"

"I think it would be only decent, when you inform Jim Connor, if you
will be loyal enough not to try to put the blame on me. I think it ought
to be put to him as *your* decision."

"Oh, you do."

"Yes, I do."

He stood up, smiling grimly.

"I'll do absolutely nothing of the sort! And aren't you taking quite a lot
for granted? I haven't said yet, have I, that I would inform Jim Connor of
anything. Put *that* in your pipe and smoke it."

She was silent, the flecked green eyes faintly narrowed, the lips barely
parted. For the first time she appeared to be a little taken aback and a
little shaken; she was trying to fathom him. She had folded her arms
across her breast, stood slightly swaying.

"And now," he added, "if you don't *too* much mind I'll try to get in
the daily ten minutes' work that is allowed to me. Or five. If you can spare
me that much!"

He went past her again, smiling. Her lips were now pressed tight, the
mouth beautiful and hard, and for the merest fraction of a second, as he
passed, their eyes, engaging, locked in the purest and cruelest hate—it was
an exchange of ice. There! Let her laugh *that* off. Let her work *that* out, in
her bedtime thinking! And write to mamma about it. And go around crying on the public bosom. And put it in the papers. And tell Mabel and
George and Paul. Let her stand there, like a statue of protest, under the
dark sky, waiting for rain—it was not for nothing that she had a sense of
the dramatic, and knew how damned handsome she was—but for once,
by god, what a good thing it would be if she got her belly full of it! Let it
pour.

In the studio, he turned the easel to the light, laid out the palette and
the neat row of brushes—but what was the use. Impossible to concentrate
now, to steady one's nerves in this turmoil, to peel one's eyes of anger and
hate—it was like a red film over everything.

"Van Gogh," he said aloud, "my *hat!*"

The church clock was striking—Terence's blue wagon rattled past
along the street, Terence standing upright in it, the reins easily held, like
a charioteer—old Mr. Fosdick, the town librarian, trudged by on his way
to the library, an apple in his hand—thinking no doubt of his lost career
in Rio de Janeiro, the twenty years sacrificed for nothing, looking after a
shiftless bedridden brother—the phonograph in the Puringtons' squawked
its "*In between-time, in the meantime*" for the thousandth time, and then
was silent, for the resumed dripping of the fog from the trees—it was all
hopeless.

When at last the hall door opened, with its two-toned squeak, and
Enid, still calm and implacable, asked him, in the blandest of voices,
"Well, have you made up your mind?" he could stand it no longer. He

merely said, over his shoulder, putting as much venom into it as he could possibly concentrate:

"Will you please *get out?*"

It was like a new voice between them. Nothing like this had ever happened to them before. And in the second before she turned, he saw in her eyes, her mouth, her whole face, even in the queer gesture of her hand on the glass doorknob, a something new and unknown, something hurt, which he had never yet seen there. It was as if a gulf had opened between them, and as if she had become a stranger.

⟨ III

". . . *The houses were made with long young sapling trees, bended, and both ends stuck into the ground. They were made round, like unto an arbour, and covered down to the ground with thick and well wrought mats, and the door was not over a yard high, made of a mat to open. The chimney was a wide hole in the top, for which they had a mat to cover it close when they pleased. One might stand and go upright in them. In the midst of them were four little trunches, knocked into the ground, and small sticks laid over, on which they hung their pots, and what they had to seethe. Round about the fire they lay on mats, which are their beds. . . . In the houses we found wooden bowls, trays, and dishes; earthen pots; hand baskets, made of crab shells, wrought together; also, an English pail or bucket, it wanted a bayle, but it had two iron ears. There was also baskets of sundry sorts, bigger and some lesser, finer and some coarser; some were curiously wrought with black and white, in pretty works, and sundry other of their household stuff. . . . There was also a company of deer's feet stuck up in the houses, hart's horns, and eagle's claws, and sundry such like things there was; also, two or three baskets full of parched acorns, pieces of fish, and a piece of a broiled herring. . . . Having thus discovered this place, it was controversial amongst us what to do touching our abode and settling there. Some thought it best, for many reasons, to abide there. . . .*"

—JOURNAL OF THE PILGRIMS

"I'm going out," he said into the darkened room, through the half-opened door. "I'm going over to Jim Connor's. To deliver your tender message."

She made no answer. She was lying on her bed again, this time with her elbows raised, her hands above her head on the pillow, and her eyes (though in the obscure light he couldn't be sure) turned up towards the sloping ceiling. Was there a handkerchief in one of her hands? Had she been crying?

"Did you hear me?" he said.

"Yes, I heard you."

Her voice was averted, flat, stifled. She hadn't moved.

"All right. And I don't know when I'll be back. If they should ask me to stay for supper, I think perhaps I *will*—just this once!"

He waited a moment for an answer, leaning against the doorjamb, but, as he got none, he went slowly down the stairs, through the studio, and into the tiny entry hall, where he took his oilskin hat and slicker from the wooden peg.

Ratio Binney's chuckle of thunder—it was a murmur, rather—for a second time ran softly from the southwest round the sky, a continuous but stumbling sound; and when he stepped out into the street he found that it had already begun to rain a little—a drizzle so gentle, however, that its sound, even on the heaped leaves, was barely audible. The afternoon was no brighter, for if the fog had at last really lifted, the clouds had taken its place. The omens were all for a soft, settled rain, an all-nighter—in some ways the best of Cape weather. It would be good for the lilacs, bed the roots down, wash off the sand. They would settle, take their permanent place in the garden, their permanent place in the earth, and get themselves ready for the spring.

The spring! But would there be such a thing as spring?

He shut his teeth bitterly on the unspoken phrase, as if indeed he were biting the words, biting them to shreds, and walked slowly, unseeing, or only automatically seeing, past the white house, the red house, the house with the cupola; the house with the little cement-lined garden pool; the cottage with the catalpa tree (now naked) and the painted swing. Deserted, autumnal, resigned—the deserted village. The Scudders' windmill yawed and moaned, a sad minor note, on top of its red wooden tower; he looked up at it and away, kicking the sodden leaves on the path—in no time at all it would be winter, there would be snow. Catching the early train, too, on pitch-dark mornings, Mr. Murphy coming over with a lantern to ring the doorbell, shout up at the window—standing there with his lantern in the snow, the collar of his sheepskin coat turned up, wearing a cap with earmuffs. And then, at the forlorn little station in the woods, the brightly lighted train coming slowly round the bend, its voice crying mournfully over the frozen trees, the bell clanging and steam hissing as it stopped by the frost-rimed unlighted boards of the platform: the dirty little train with its early morning card-players, heavy-eyed businessmen, high-school children on their way to school, and the Boston papers. Crawling through the winter morning twilight to Boston, to the gray slush-filled streets of Boston, the subway, the smelly crowds, and the everlasting school, the Frazer School of Fine and Applied Arts. Another winter of it, another year of it, the time for his own work always becoming shorter, perhaps at last vanishing entirely. Good god, what a vision.

"If you can't do it with your eye, use a plumb line."

"Miss Shea, why *will* you try to fill up every corner with extraneous objects?"

"Fine feeling for form and rhythm in that one, yes, but look—the color is so heavy it kills it."

"My dear girl, exaggerate only for emphasis. Won't you try to remember that?"

"All right now. Jump your eye down from the shoulder blade to the patella. You can see then how much your figure is out of balance. If you can't draw, Miss Casani, how in god's name do you expect to paint? Draw with the brush, draw with the brush."

"Retouching varnish might help *some* of those dead spots, but remember you can't paint a picture with *nothing* but varnish!"

"Empathy, empathy, empathy—"

"Miss Bloom, that brush of yours needs a shave. Can't you see what it's doing? Try a razor blade on it, cut those crooked hairs off."

"And for goodness' sake, hold your brush as if it were something more than the stub of a pencil!"

The dreadful roundelay of trite phrases, over and over again, day after day—plastic form, linear perspective, volume, weight, mass, tone—solidity, color-rhythm, luminosity, the Chinese vertical perspective—kinetic, static, calligrapher—balance, proportion—in Christ's name, when you got right down to it, what the devil did they all mean? A pitiful pettifogging dishevelment of a process which must *be* a process, and an instinctive and automatic one, a fluid and unanalyzed action, or nothing. Paint, on a square of canvas—or a vision, which had somehow extended itself through the hand. And in between, the muddied sty of the teacher.

But where, exactly, did a picture come from?

BAKER STREET: TOWN LANDING.

He turned down the wet lane, his slicker rustling, the oilskin hat in his hand. The tall house, with its weathered shingles and heavy stone porch, stood gray and forbidding against the leaden river, the porch was deserted, save for a single rocking chair, bright red, tilted against the wall—not a soul, not a sound. He stood listening at the foot of the steps for a minute, heard inside the house a rising murmur of voices, then walked softly down to the water's edge and Paul's canoe. The ribbed floor of it, usually spick and span in its bright varnish, was extraordinarily muddy—something very peculiar must have happened to it—certainly not Paul's doing. A sodden cushion, too, which they had neglected to take in. How disgustingly typical. It reminded him, for no reason, of old Pop Amos and his newly painted boat, beside which he had sat all summer on the shore, in a kitchen chair, reluctant to put fresh work to use—horrified at the thought of that exquisite sheen exposed to the ravages of salt water and mud. Not like this! He pushed the canoe before him down into the rain-pricked water, took the wet paddle from beneath the rear thwart, stepped in and shoved off. The tide was coming in, nearly full, he could drift up to the bridge, and then paddle back. Time to think.

Yes, I heard you, she had said, *yes, I heard you.* And with what a voice, too—that stifled and averted voice, pity-demanding. Yes, by god, now that she was going to have her way, she wanted to be pitied, too—was that it? Well, let her look for it. Let her go and look for it!

But where did a picture come from?

From a dream perhaps: from the bloodstream perhaps: from memory perhaps: an observed trifle which touched down quickly and magically into the unconscious, like the rain-ringed water, the rain-seethed water, round the drifting canoe—its varnished yellow stem, like the stem of a gondola, nodding and notching against the deserted hulks of the fishing boats on the opposite shore, against the sand bar, against the granite pier of the two-spanned bridge. That curved stem, brightly swaying in the gray light, and beyond it the red iron girders of the bridge—to what did they not invite, to what did they not lead? To the bright open hand of childhood, the rain-filled eye of childhood—or tear-filled? A nucleus smaller and brighter than a tear; and how astonishingly more fecund and powerful—the infinitesimal droplet of wild rain, wild water, growing, whirling, expanding, until it should become an all-containing sphere of creative and whirling light, a microcosm of living shape! Yes, a *feeling*, first—more tenuous than shadow, tenderer and more elusive than light—less substanital far than tentacle or palpacle—softer than an ache, vaguer than a longing—the seed of a design that should be, or become, oneself, as if one's heart were to begin all over again, from the very beginning of the world, and seek for itself a better and stranger, but at the same time more *intimate* shape, a shape deeply truer to oneself—was it something like that? And one's love too, was that not there also? *Must* it not be there? As of the first leaf that one ever loved, the first sunbeam one ever saw on a wall, or on the coarse bark of a tree, the first rain that one ever walked out into alone. And the terrifying maternal dark, which filled so much of the world—that echoless or almost echoless dark, fathomless, tunneling everywhere, even through sunlight, tunneling between hour and hour, between one minute and the next, so that at last nothing at all seemed to remain solid, not even oneself: yes, it came out of this, or went into it, or both—the first leaf was seen against that dark, separate from it, and it was to the brilliant and beloved, and so isolated first leaf, that one attempted to return. It was a celebration, at one and the same time, of love and terror.

The piled granite blocks of the central pier were right before him, rough, whitely barnacled, the swift and silent current had borne him close, he could see through the deep clear water, green-wavering, the red fronds of sponge that grew at their base, combed by the tide. He remembered Buzzer's extraordinary discovery, by the sea wall at the foot of the garden, that the barnacles were feeding, combing the tide with quick minute thread-like filaments, licking in their tiny morsels of sea food—he must turn back. He dipped the wet paddle, the flat blade cleaving the water with a powerful swirling chuckle, a slow skirling eddy of vortical sound, swung the canoe round and shorewards, careening, out of the main current and into the shallows. The Indian stroke, the hands turning inward and downward, so that the bow was driven straight—good lord, how long ago he had learned that, on the Assabet River! Now he could look up from the river to his own sea wall, and beyond this the terrace wall, the new lilacs, the white wood-shed, the dormered windows of the cottage itself. The little wet garden was deserted. Not even Chattachoochee. Buzzer was still lying down, sing-ing to herself over her shells. And, of course, Enid—

A car rattled quickly over the bridge behind him, going down the Cape; in the silence that followed he could hear again the faint whisper, the delicately needled seethe, of the fine drizzle on the water. Thunder, for the third time—Ratio Binney's chuckle of thunder—ran somewhere behind the sullen clouds in the southwest, to which he lifted his eyes, but there was no lightning. It might rain all night, but there would be no "tempest." The bare boughs of the silver-leaf poplars, above the low roofs of the village, were yellow, yellow-green, lizard-green—something might be done with them. They suggested something, reminded him of something—something urgent and lightninglike, but slow and cancerous, too. Was this the first leaf again? The first hand seen in the dark? The first grasp, first clutch, in the maternal nothing? Hands against the sky, claws against the sky. . . .

Karl Roth was standing on the fringe of beach, waiting there by the stone arches under the verandah, a dirty raincoat flung capelike over his round shoulders, the white face already sneering, the queer yellow head bare to the drizzle. He stood silent, disapproving, as the canoe rustled up past him on the sand, driven by the last powerful stroke, then said:

"Well, if it isn't our Mr. Kane. And just when we thought he'd ratted on us."

"Meaning what?"

"Oh, nothing. Nothing, *gat*-all, Mr. Kane! I just like to sneer."

"Yeah? Well, you'd better save up your sneers, Karl, till you've got something to sneer at. You'll have plenty. Is Jim inside?"

"Yes, sir, just when we thought he'd weaseled on us! Sure Jim's inside. Where else would he be? It's old home week, didn't you know? And we're having a housewarming."

"I hope that means those gals of yours have got you a meal."

"A meal! Don't make me laugh. If you want to see something funny take a gander at our kitchen. Just take a peek when nobody's looking. I'm not squeamish, but—! No, the girls have gone on strike. We're having a stinko of a row. You're just in time to give us a hand. Come on in, the water's fine."

Kitty's voice, wailing, had just risen to a shrill "No!" as they opened the door. She faced them with open red mouth from the dinner table in the middle of the big room, where she was sitting—her black hair was disordered, the small dark eyes swollen as with weeping, she looked pale and distraught, harrowed. The sound of a piano came briskly through the open door from the room beyond, the verandah room—Lorna, no doubt, ploughing through a Chopin Etude—and Jim, obviously very tired, sat in a rocking chair by the littered fireplace. The cap was pulled morosely down over the brown eyes, he was smoking a cigar. He waved the cigar, without getting up, and said wearily:

"Hello, kid. I'm glad you came."

"Sure, you are. Ain't we all? Mr. Kane's come slumming, he wants to see how the other half lives. He wants to see our kitchen."

Kitty turned fiercely to Karl, shaking her hair, and said:

"Shut up, will you? Until you've got something to say."

"Shut up yourself! It's about time *you* cut the yammer. And telling me won't make me, either."

"Would you like a drink, Tip? There's plenty of gin, and plenty of glasses there—all dirty. Take your pick."

The combination living room and dining room was cold, and incredibly disordered—a fire of miscellaneous fragments burned sadly in the fireplace, a heap of wood from a broken box lay on the green-tiled hearth at Jim's feet—newspapers and cigarette ends littered the floor, dead matches, a hairpin—and the dinner table, with the oil lamp standing in the middle, was covered, simply covered, with dirty dishes, stacked or single, except for a small space before Kitty, which she had apparently cleared. There, between her arms, she had placed—for no apparent reason—a sheet of paper and a pencil. She stared down at these, her sallow cheeks on her fists, her eyes almost closed. The piano in the next room stopped; for a moment they were all silent.

"Where's your new friend?"

"Who? Louis?"

"Yes."

"Aw, he's gone for a walk. He said he wanted to see the sea!"

"He's welcome to it! If I never see the sea again—"

"He's probably hungry by this time."

"Was that a crack?"

"Sure, it was a crack. Christ, if two females between them can't start a fire without burning the house down, or think of anything to eat but canned corned beef—you're a couple of dumb clucks."

"Shut up! It was your idea, wasn't it? You're the one that wants to stay here, aren't you?"

Karl, the raincoat still wrapped round his shoulders, stretched himself out on the wicker sofa at the other side of the fireplace, opposite Jim, and crossed his knees. The pale unshaven face, the lashless eyes, chicken-lidded, were turned long sufferingly toward the ceiling. He looked sick.

"Yes, kid, you certainly came at the psychological moment."

"In the nicotine, as they say!"

"You'd think, Tip, with a nice house like this, and all these comforts, and the river, and this nice peaceful countryside, and even a canoe—"

"Yeah, tell him about the canoe!"

"—that four people could be happy, wouldn't you? The nicest house in the town, with nice furniture, a real home—"

"How does it feel, Mister Kane, to be in a real home? Tell him about the canoe, Jim."

Karl with his head back on a pillow, cackled obscenely.

"But I never expected anything like this. No, sir, I never expected anything like this. Look at it. Look at us. We no sooner get here than we start fighting. We come for a nice holiday and rest—"

"Who's supposed to get the rest? Who, Jim Connor, I'd like to know? If it's a fire in the fireplace you want, that's all right, you can start that, but if it's a fire in the kitchen stove—"

"That isn't the point. We're supposed to co-operate."

"Co-operate! Co-operate! Oh, my gard—"

She laughed shrilly and briefly, reached for the half-filled gin bottle, poured gin rashly into a tumbler, added a little water to it, and took a drink. She set down the tumbler rather hard, and a little at random, and at the same moment the piano began again in the next room. This time it was a succession of scales, too fast, imprecise—the effect somehow viscous and slimy. A concert pianist! She certainly had a long way to go. Like

Bucholtz, she probably regarded herself as an artist, not as a pianist—nothing so simple and straightforward as that. Did she and Jim occupy the same room? Perhaps that was the explanation. Poor Jim.

"Co-operation. Where do you get that stuff, Jim? You may have noticed, Mister Kane, that our friend Mister Connor is sometimes just a little naïve."

"I mean it. Co-operation."

"Yeah. And did you ever know women to co-operate? Since when. Women have only one idea. And that is—"

"What do you know about women, I'd like to know!"

"Plenty. I haven't lived with you four years for nothing."

"Lived *with* me! You mean *on* me. If I hadn't worked my eyes out as a stenographer to support you—"

"You knew what to expect, didn't you? You haven't got any kick coming. You can quit any time, as far as I'm concerned. I got along all right without you, didn't I? You give me a pain."

"Women, women, women! You mean slaves, you and your theories about women. Somebody to work for you and go to bed with, that's all you mean."

"You get a position out of it, don't you?"

"A position. Would you listen to that. Yes, the position of admiring your genius, I suppose. That's all the position I get."

"You thought that was good enough when you married me. You knew what the chances were. Why don't you stick to your bargain? The trouble with you women is that you're nothing but receptacles."

"Receptacles! Oh, my gard—"

"Did you ever notice that, Jim? Nothing but receptacles. Yeah. You give, but you don't get. You put things in, but you don't get nothing back. No matter how you dig your toes in, you can't satisfy *those* babies! No, sir, by god, you can't. What's their idea? Just security, just safety. And to get themselves all dressed up like a plush horse. Jesus Christ, they give me the pip."

"Oh, cut it, Karl. Kitty means all right. I know how she feels about this—"

"If you do, why don't you do something about it!"

"You see, Tip, old kid, I'm afraid the girls are a little upset by your friend's warning. That's what the trouble is."

"It isn't that at all."

"Yes, and I'm damned sorry, Jim."

"How is your conscience, Mister Kane? How does it feel to be carrying such a burden of responsibility. I hear that exquisite wife of yours has been blabbing where the blabbing does the most good."

"Shut up! And you leave Enid out of this. Don't pay any attention to him, Tip, Enid was perfectly right, he's only looking for an excuse to start a quarrel. Maybe he'll start something he can't finish. Like the time the Hudson Dusters beat him up. Oh, my gard, will I ever forget it. The way they dragged him out of that bar by the feet, looking like a sick rabbit—a lot of fight you showed then, didn't you? Like hell you did. It's all right bullying women—"

"Take it easy, Kitty—"

"And, oh, boy, what a pair of black eyes! It did me good—and carrying on like a baby about it, afraid to go outdoors for a week. Oh, my gard, I wish I could get out of here, I'm so sick of this place. What is there to do here? I'm so tired of listening to these damned sea gulls and blackbirds—"

"Them ain't blackbirds, you mental giant. Them's crows."

"And this sea gets on my nerves. I'm going to get out, I tell you—I'm going to get out, I've *got* to get out of here or I'll go crazy. I can't *stand* it!"

She pushed her chair back suddenly, jumped to her feet, the tears starting from her eyes, dashed a tear from one cheek with the back of her hand, then went quickly, hysterically, across the long room, and ran up the stairs in the far corner. A moment later a door slammed. The piano, undisturbed, continued its remorseless inaccurate scales, slurred, uneven, repetitive. There was a sort of vicious eagerness in the ascending notes, an ugly greed, as of an unappeasable appetite for sheer noise. The fire snapped and flung out a spark, all three were silent, listening, and then Jim Connor said:

"That's the way it's been, Tip. That's the way it's been all day."

"I think you were a little hard on her, Karl."

"Yeah, I know, I know. I was a little hard on her. But it's the only way to treat her when she goes hysterical. And don't I know it. She'll get over it; she always does. You just have to spank her, and then she has a good cry and gets over it. She'll come back as sweet as pie."

"Maybe. But I think this is a little different. Maybe you'd better go up and talk to her."

"No. Let her have her cry first."

"By god, I'm so hungry! I wonder if there are any of those sardines left?"

"There was one in the kitchen, by the sink—I saw it with my own eyes. But Lorna may have got it, I wouldn't be surprised. One little sardine. First come, first served in this house. What we need is the miracle of the loaves and fishes. I wish to god there was a delicatessen in this dump. What couldn't I do to a *wiener schnitzel!* Boy. Or a nice big plate of spaghetti."

"That's what it's been like all day, Tip—first Lorna, and then Kitty. They want to go back to New York. And I've got this place for six months, I've paid the rent for six months. And now your friend Paul's sore about his canoe—"

"Tell him about the canoe."

"Well, what about the canoe. I noticed there was a lot of mud in it."

"Mud! You call that mud, Mister Kane? You can't ever have *seen* any mud. You amaze me. Tell him about it, Jim."

"I don't really think it was our fault, kid, I don't really think it was, but Paul seems almost to think we did it on purpose."

"Yeah, and is Paul burned up! Is he frying! Go on, tell him the whole story."

"What happened?"

"Well, kid, we were supposed to go up there yesterday in the canoe. Paul asked us to come up, and told us how to get there. And it seems there was a misunderstanding."

"A misunderstanding! Am I laughing?"

"We don't know anything about boats—so he gave us directions. He said when we got up to the place opposite the golf links—you know, where the lagoon begins—there would be a little narrow place in the river, and then it would broaden out again. He said it would be too shallow on the left, or too much eelgrass—is that it, eelgrass?—or something, and so he told us to keep the canoe as close as we could to the right-hand shore. And then follow that shore till we got to his boathouse. See? Well, we did exactly as he told us—"

"I'm afraid Mister Kane will be a little contemptuous? I'm afraid he'll think we're just a pair of landlubbers—eh, Mister Kane?"

"We did exactly as he told us. But when we tried to keep as close to the shore as all that, well, there wasn't enough water even for a canoe—so we had to get out."

"You had to get out!"

"Yeah, we had to get out. We ran aground on the mud. So we had to get out and push it."

"Push it! Good lord."

"Yeah, push it. Karl took the front and I took the back. But we didn't realize there was so much mud, that it would be as soft as that—gosh, we sunk in up to our knees. We had to pull off our shoes and stockings, then, and put them in the canoe—it took us over an hour. I should think it must have been damned near two miles."

"Yeah. Two miles as the mud flies!"

"At the end, we finally got to some deep water again, and got back in, but by that time the damage was done. And your friend Paul was pretty sore. It seems we had misunderstood him—"

"*And* how. Oh, boy, this is killing me!"

"—and that he didn't mean us to stick as close as all that to the bank, but just to follow it, for guidance, you see? But how could we know that? He said the other side was too shallow or something—by god, kid, but it certainly was a mess! And then we stuck our feet in the kitchen oven to dry—"

"And did Paul like that? Did your exquisite friend Paul like that? He *did* not. You'd have thought we were desecrating the place. I fear your friend Paul is just a shade dainty, if you know what I mean?"

"Dainty! I never knew it."

"Yes, and it seemed to me too that he was just a *little* too curious, and asked just a *few* too many questions. He was exceedingly inquisitive. Did you notice that, Jim?"

"No, I didn't."

"You mean to say you didn't notice that?"

"What sort of questions?"

"Oh, he was very cagey, your friend Paul was. He wanted to know all sorts of things. I'm afraid Jim is a little naïve, he fell for it. Questions about his profession, questions about his technique."

"His technique?"

"Sure, his technique. What you and I do with a camel's hair brush, and Jim does with legerdemain. Do you get me? The technique of redistribution. Oh, boy, oh, boy, oh, boy, oh, boy—do I amuse myself to death! Am I burned alive! And you sure had him fascinated, Jim— Yeah, he was all hopped up with the idea that at last he was seeing life in the raw. You'd have thought he was entertaining a couple of Apaches. I think, Mister Kane, he was even a little frightened. And that reminds me—don't you sometimes feel a *little* out of your element with us, a *little* out of your depth? You Bostonians are so godawful refined—"

"Don't be a damned fool, Karl. Why in hell should I feel out of my element? I always take my own element *with* me!"

"Ah, very neat, very neat. But a little unconvincing?"

"Not at all."

"Yes, I've occasionally felt that you were just a shade self-conscious with us, just a shade uncomfortable. I've noticed it when you were in New York. How is it you Bostonians keep so exquisitely innocent. Or is it a refined kind of hypocrisy, Mister Kane, and are you keeping things up your sleeve? Maybe that's it. Maybe we'd be surprised if we really knew you."

"Maybe you would. Maybe you will."

"But don't let's be unpleasant."

"Were you being unpleasant?"

"Ah, perhaps I wasn't. Sometimes I don't know my own subtlety."

"Yeah. I prefer your subtlety when it's on canvas! It isn't quite so ignoble."

"Ignoble! Ouch! I led with my chin, that time. Yeah—you should never lead with your chin—or with your heart. Never lead with the heart! Well, I guess I'll go up and see if I can calm Kitty down—why don't you tell Mister Kane about your technique, Jim. It might amuse him!"

He got up slowly, indifferently, the dirty raincoat still held shroudlike over his shoulders, blinked the lashless blue eyes, smiling, with an affectation of cynicism which couldn't wholly conceal the essential beauty— though a wasted beauty—of the pallid ascetic face, and then went quietly, the raincoat rustling, across the room and up the unpainted pine stairs.

"Karl gets my goat when he talks like that."

"I think this place and Kitty have got on his nerves. He's been crabbing everybody and everything. Don't pay any attention to him, kid. When he sees you don't mind, he quits."

"Yes, I know. If only he weren't such a damned good painter—"

"You think he is, don't you?"

"Brilliant, yes—a real poetic genius for it. Too soon to say what'll he do, of course, and he certainly ought to work a lot harder—"

"Yes, Kitty spoils him, of course—"

The piano paused in the next room, they heard Lorna coughing, and Jim half turned his head—across the front windows of the house, the long room, a gust of fine rain flew with quick needle-sound from window to window, stinging and darkening them—the soft sound then lost in the sudden resumption of the music. This time it was Gershwin's Rhapsody in Blue—played languishingly, sentimentally, heavily, the rubatos hanging and dripping like sirup, like treacle. Jim's eyes, hooded and solemn under the cap visor, looked toward the open door, he was listening intently, listening proudly.

"She sure can play, can't she?" he said.

"Yes, she sure can. What was this about your technique, Jim?"

"Oh, that. I guess that wouldn't interest you much, would it, kid? I always thought it wouldn't interest you much."

"Sure it would. I never asked you, because I thought maybe it was something you didn't want to talk about."

"Not at all. As you know, Tip, I've always tried to be the reverse of secretive about it, about every aspect of it. That was very important!"

"Yes, I know."

"The same with this. It's better to be frank about it, isn't it? But it might interest you, at that. I think it's pretty good."

He smiled, and there was evident relish in the way he spoke of it—evident enjoyment. Was this the weak spot in his "case," perhaps—in the case he made out for himself? Was it perhaps, after all, a kind of compulsion, and the anarchistic theory merely a delayed rationalization? Perhaps the stealing came first?

"I'd like very much to hear about it."

"It's really quite simple, but of course it took some working out. I made some mistakes. But now it's pretty nearly foolproof. You know I always specialize in furs?"

"Yes, I knew that. Karl told me."

"That was the first step, you see. I got to know everything I could about furs—quite a lot. Well, now, suppose I'm going to start out on an expedition. I'd pick out two or three big cities—only big cities, Chicago and St. Louis one time, Cleveland and Detroit the next—and go to just those two or three. All right, and suppose I go to Boston, say."

"Did you ever actually try Boston?"

"As a matter of fact, kid, I did, and I could tell you the name of the store, but I won't, because that might make you a kind of accessory, see? All right now, suppose I go to Boston. I spend the first two or three days just going round to the big department stores, and looking over the layout —finding out where the fur department is, and the other departments, all the arrangements, the stairs, the lavatories, everything like that—and what time they open in the morning and what time they close at night."

"Yes, I see."

"Okay. Well, I pick out what seems to be the best one, and get to know it pretty well. And then I go in some afternoon just a little before closing time. I'm wearing a cap—like this—and inside my coat, buttoned up, I've got a couple of big paper bags, folded small—just ordinary coarse paper bags. Well, I go to the men's lavatory, in the basement, into a w.c., and stay there quietly till maybe half an hour after the store is closed. Then I come out—but first I take my cap off, see, and put it inside my coat, or in a pocket—you get the idea?"

"No?"

"That's so I'll look like some sort of employee. If I meet anybody I'll look like an employee; and I can just say I'm a furniture polisher going up to the furniture department to do some polishing."

"Sounds simple enough!"

"It is. There's hardly ever any trouble about that. Well, then, I go upstairs, without trying to hide myself at all, and maybe in this store we're talking about the fur department is on the way to the furniture department

—which makes it easier. I go to the fur department, and by this time, with any luck, it's deserted. If it's not, I keep on going, of course, and come back later. But if it's deserted, and no one around, then I pick out a couple of small but good furs—small, see, because they're easier to handle. And that's where the paper bags come in. I put them into the paper bags, and tie them up with heavy string, so as to make them sort of clumsy-looking parcels, the sort nobody would think was of any value—just ordinary bundles. But I don't take them out with me. No. Oh, no."

"What do you do?"

"This is where the real technique comes in, kid—I think it's pretty good! What I do is this. I take the two bundles into the furniture department, and that's deserted, too, if I'm lucky—and then I go to a chiffonier or chest of drawers, probably one I've picked out beforehand, because it's a little out of the way, in a corner, or behind other stuff—you'll see why in a minute. All right, I open one of the drawers, and put in the bundles—but I don't *quite* shut the drawer again. I leave it about a half an inch open— just so that the edge of the drawer is sticking out a little—and then I take a broken match, a very small piece of broken match, and put it on the edge."

"Good lord, Jim."

"Yeah. And that's all. Then I go downstairs again and go out. The watchman is at the door, of course, but *that's* easy. I've got nothing on me, and if he asks any questions, well, I'm just a new furniture polisher; and so there's usually no trouble, he lets me out. . . . Well, that's the first stage. The second comes next day. This is a little more ticklish—and now is where the broken match comes in. What I do is wait till the rush hour is on—say, about twelve o'clock, see?"

"Yeah."

"And then I go in and go straight up to the furniture department. This time, of course, I'm just an ordinary shopper; just somebody looking at furniture; sort of sauntering round. Well, I don't want to go too close, in case there's been a slip-up, or the bundles have been discovered—that happened to me once—and maybe I pretend I'm looking at something else, walking slowly by, but I manage to take a look at that drawer, from a little way off, to see if that small piece of broken match is still there. It has to be pretty small, of course—about a quarter of an inch, so as not to be too conspicuous, and put kind of at one side, too—otherwise one of the salesmen might spot it, and look in. All right, I take a quick look, and see it's there, or not there. If it's not there, I don't take any chances—I go while the going is good. It means that drawer has probably been opened. But if it's there, and in exactly the same place, which I can easily tell, then the chances are fifty to one it's okay—and of course, too, if the drawer, and the other drawers, are all just the way I left them. You can notice those things—there was once, in New York, when at first it looked all right to me, but there was just a little something that made me hesitate—it just didn't seem quite right to me, god knows what it was—so I hung round a little way off and waited, pretending to be looking at things; and pretty soon along came a guy with my two bundles in his hands and put them *back* in that drawer—"

"Good lord, setting a trap!"

"Setting a trap. So, of course, I beat it. But suppose it's all right—well, then, it's pretty easy. All I do is wait till there's nobody much round there, or everybody busy, and just quickly take out the two bundles—and that's all there is to it. Once I've got them in my hands, I'm safe as a church. Everybody else in a store has bundles—so what's the difference, see? I walk out with maybe a thousand dollars' worth of furs, and that's that—it's as easy as rolling off a log."

"Well, I'm damned."

"Yes, kid. Now you know. I think it's pretty good."

"It's the most extraordinary thing I ever heard. My god, I should think it must be terrifying! Was it your own idea, Jim? How'd you ever think of it?"

"Yes, I just sort of worked it out. I started with the idea of the second day, you see, coming out with the bundles—and then just worked back. It was really very simple. You could have done it yourself, kid."

"Not me, by god. I wouldn't have the nerve."

"Oh, it doesn't take any nerve."

"Oh, no! Of course not! I can see that!"

"No. It's just sort of exciting."

"Exciting! Good god, I should think it would be like a nightmare. I wouldn't be able to move hand or foot."

Exciting—yes. Again there was that evident relish in the way he spoke of the excitement, a distinct gleam, a distinct glee—it was as obvious, wasn't it?—that he intensely *enjoyed* the whole thing as that he was extremely proud of its ingenuity. Yes, but was it fair to assume from this that the whole thing was nothing but a compulsion, as Paul maintained it was? After all, the use to which he put his profits, the idealistic use, even if sometimes misguided—as witness Bucholtz—was good; and granted that his premise was tenable, and that property should be at the free disposal of all, and not used for private gain, it was difficult to find any flaw in it. It all came down to the question of motive, of course, and of *priority* of motive. If the mere *pleasure* in stealing came first—but did even that make any difference? There could be no question, anyway—none at all—of his honesty: his sincerity was unmistakable. The circle of logic was complete.

Jim had stooped to fling a couple of broken boxboards on the fire, kicked some cigarette butts over the hearth towards the bed of ashes, then straightened up, smiling, with a kind of melancholy amusement.

"Of course, kid, your friend Paul—"

"Yeah. What about his friend Paul!"

Karl was coming down the stairs, walking slowly, the raincoat still over his shoulders—Kitty preceded him, almost at a run, as if in fact she were running from him. She rushed straight across the room, walking jerkily, and flung herself in her chair again. Her eyes were squeezed almost shut, one cheek had been powdered roughly, but not the other, one side only of her mouth had been lipsticked—evidently she had been interrupted in her attempt to repair the ravages of crying. She picked up the pencil and began rapidly drawing with it, or writing, on the sheet of paper. In the next room, Lorna paused to cough, then started the Rhapsody in Blue all over again.

"Won't she ever stop? Has she got to sit in there in that damned dressing gown and play all day?"

"She's practicing. Let her practice, Kitty, it's what she came here for."

"Yeah. And what about Mister Kane's snotty friend Paul?"

"Nothing, Karl, nothing. I was just telling Tip about my technique."

"Your technique! So we've got to hear all about *that* again!"

"You haven't got to hear anything at all, Kitty. I was just telling Tip about it, that's all."

"Well, for gard's sake, why don't you tell the police about it, and be done with it! I'm sick of this suspense. I'm sick of it!"

"Hold your horses. I'll tell the police when I'm ready to tell them, and not before."

"Maybe Mister Kane's dear friend George will save you the trouble, Jim. Maybe Enid will."

"I think we ought to get out of here. I want to get out of here. And so does Lorna, you ask her! The whole thing's crazy. Buying that expensive camping outfit, too, tents and everything, and all for one night in the woods, freezing to death and getting bitten by mosquitoes—"

"Oh, baby, was that funny!"

"I think we ought to accept Mrs. Murphy's offer."

"What offer was that? I never heard about any offer."

"You did too! I told you. But of course you never listen to anything *I* say!"

"All right, spill it, bird-brain, spill it—what offer?"

"She said if we didn't want it any more she'd take it for her kids, and give us vegetables for it—"

"*Vegetables!* Well, for crying out loud—"

"Yes, vegetables. And what's funny in that. It's no good to *us*, is it? The idea of you trying to camp out, trying to paint in a tent! You *did* look like a fool. We might as well take what we can get for it. If we've got any sense we'll fill those suitcases with vegetables and go right back to New York."

"Okay, okay. What's stopping you? Go on, take your carrots and get out of here. It'll be a lot better than listening to you shooting off your face—"

"Shut up!"

"I won't shut up."

"Oh, for god's sake, Kitty and Karl—"

"For god's sake, yes, for god's sake—and you're supposed to be the god!"

"Pipe down, Kitty."

"Yes, the little tin god."

"Now is that a nice way to speak to Jim? After all he's done for us? I ask you. You poor dumb dope, you don't know what's good for you!"

"Oh, don't I?"

"No, you don't."

"Cut it, you two, will you? Quarreling isn't going to do you any good. Tip didn't come over here just to listen to you two fighting."

"Yeah? Well, what *did* Tip come over for. Spying, I suppose, Mister Kane?"

"I don't think that's very nice of you, Karl. I thought we were better friends than that. But just the same I'm glad you asked the question, for as a matter of fact I came over for a damned unpleasant reason."

Kitty turned sharply in her chair. She was suddenly rigid, rigid with apprehension—her mouth was a little open, she had sucked in her breath quickly, the terrified eyes looked at him as if begging him to deny their terror. She sat quite still, continuing to stare, while Karl, with a labored assumption of sardonic indifference, once more stretched himself out on the wicker couch.

"There's rats in them words," he said. "I smell rats in them words. What did I tell you?"

"What is it, kid? What's on your mind?"

"I've never hated doing anything so much in my life, Jim—"

"We'll pass that up, *Mister* Kane!"

"—but I'm afraid it can't be helped. It's Enid. To put it briefly, she's threatened to leave me, if I don't stop seeing you while you're here. She means it too. She said she'd go tomorrow if I didn't come over and tell you. We've been having a row about it ever since yesterday, and I've argued the whole thing backwards and forwards, but it's no use, she's got me in a hole, and she knows it. I'm sorry."

"I see. I'm sorry too, kid."

"They're *both* sorry. That makes two."

"I wish to god it hadn't happened. You know *I* haven't got any feelings about it, one way or the other—"

"Of course not, kid. But don't you worry, it'll be all right. Enid's got a right to her own opinion, hasn't she?"

"Sure, anybody can be a Judas, can't they?"

"Oh, gard, oh, gard, oh, gard, what's going to happen now—I knew something like this would happen."

"Yeah. Mrs. Exquisite Blueblood Kane. A knife in the back from Mrs. Exquisite Blueblood Kane. Just as I expected. That's what you get for mixing with the upper classes, a knife in the back."

"Sorry, Karl. I assure you I don't like it any more than you do. Of course, this'll only be temporary, I hope. We can meet in New York later on, and I hope without hard feelings—"

"Oh, sure. We'll forget all about it, won't we, Jim? Don't give it a thought. What's a knife in the back between friends?"

"It won't make any difference to me, kid."

"So you're going to take it lying down!"

"There's one thing I thought I'd suggest, though."

"Listen to this, this is probably going to be good."

"Shut up, Karl, will you? Let Tip say what he wants to say."

"It's simply this, Jim. If you'd agree to suspend your operations while you're here, and not use this as a center for operations, I think maybe I could persuade Enid to reconsider."

"Well, for the—! Isn't that just too sweet of Mister Kane? Go on, Jim, *tell* him! Seems to me I smell the cloven hoof."

"Well, that's very nice of you, kid. And of course it goes without saying that I'll miss not seeing you, and all our good philosophical talks. That's one of the main reasons I came here, as you know, and it won't be the same thing without you—yes, I'm sorry about that. And I see how you're fixed—you can't do anything if Enid feels like that about it. I wouldn't expect you to, and I don't want to be the cause of trouble between you—I like you both much too much for that, you know that, Tip. And the same way, I can honor Enid's principles about all this, even if I can't agree with them. I like Enid, she's honest, and she isn't afraid of sticking to her guns. She's a damned fine girl. But no, I'm afraid, kid, I couldn't do that, I couldn't promise to do that."

"Yeah. Maybe Mister Upright Kane will try to realize that it isn't only the upright Bostonians and upright snobs that have upright principles—"

"Well, yes, that's it. It's a matter of principle with me. It's what I believe, see, kid? And you wouldn't really expect me to give that up, any more than I would expect Enid to, would you?"

"*Why* can't you—oh, gard, oh, gard—why don't you have some sense for once, and let us have a little peace here, instead of just sitting round waiting for the police to come. And it won't be only you they'll come for, either, it'll be you too, Karl. It'll be all of us—they'll arrest us all. Oh, gard, what's the use—"

"Will you shut your damned fool wailing, weakwit? You wouldn't know a principle if it hit you in the face."

"As if *you* had any principles! As if you were doing anything but sponge! As if you were doing anything—"

"Shut up!"

"Yes, by god, Karl, I'm damned if I don't think Kitty's right! I don't believe you give a hoot in hell for Jim's principles, or care a damn what happens to him—so long as you get your share of the money. That's what makes me feel really sick about *all* this business, Jim. I don't think Karl or this Bucholtz, for instance, really believe in you for a minute—oh, I know, they think it's all very amusing and original, it makes a good story, doesn't it? It's nice and spectacular, and they can share in the glory—from a safe distance! But they'll use you for their own selfish ends, and then sacrifice you when the time comes. Look at that cheapskate riding all the way up here in a taxi at your expense—he'll be the first to run out on you when the trouble starts—"

"Yeah? And *would* he be the first to take a run-out powder round here? You make me sick."

"No, kid, I don't believe that."

"Oh, of course not, you're too holy to believe anything like that, aren't you, you and your Messiah idea—"

"Who said anything about a Messiah idea, Kitty?"

"Oh, no, you never posed as a Messiah, did you?—you never thought you were another Christ, did you?—why, he's crazy, that's what he is, and anybody can see it—he's crazy as a bedbug, he ought to be in a hospital, even Lorna admits that, she feels the same way I do about it—"

Suddenly she began wailing again—grotesquely, tragically, as if in an absurd kind of accompaniment to the badly played jazz from the next room, that glucose rhapsody—but as abruptly she stopped again, pressed a stained handkerchief hard against her mouth, and began feverishly writing once more on the sheet of paper which lay before her on the disordered table. Tears were running down her cheeks, she was audibly sniffling, she was obviously on the verge of hysterics—and it was as if this sudden manifestation of the depth of her misery had brought them all up short, they were all silent, they all watched her and were silent. A needled flight of rain, swift and light, a gust of blown drizzle, pattered across the windows of the long room, stinging and darkening them; the fire smoked; Lorna interrupted her playing to cough once more, and then resumed stolidly, stubbornly, almost as if angrily; the *putt—putt—putt* of a motorboat stuttered from the river, a detached and ironic reminder of the sea, of the outer world—but they were all silent, as if somehow bewitched by Kitty's unhappiness, and as if it had mysteriously emptied them of all power to act or speak. What more was there to do? What more was there to say? It was time alone that remained, and as they listened to the hectic scribbling of the pencil, moving rapidly on the paper, by a tacit agreement they avoided each other's eyes. Was it shame? Embarrassment? Despair? Jim, moving very carefully, very slowly, leaned over to strike a match on the tiles at his feet, drew it crackling and spurting towards him, to relight the blackened stump of his cigar. Karl lay sideways on the wicker couch, the blue eyes looking at nothing, the thin mouth fixed in a defensive half-smile, the soiled raincoat drawn over his knees. And in that stillness the disorderly room, with its unswept floor, the piled dishes, the tumblers, the gin bottle, the dead matches and lipsticked cigarettes, looked inconceivably forlorn. How could they ever be happy here? How could anybody possibly be happy here? Newspapers—a rocking chair, with one rocker broken, shoved out of the way against the corner wall under the stairs— the one sardine, too, in the kitchen—and Lorna, in "that damned dressing gown," playing the piano tirelessly, badly, as if nothing else in the world existed—no, they could never be happy here. But would they, in fact, *be* here much longer? For the little Utopia was already broken, and even now above it hovered the invisible wings of departure. The mistake was coming to an end.

"Well, I guess there's not much else to say, Jim."

"No, I guess there's not much else to say."

"Except to say that I'm sorry, again."

"Yes, Mister Kane, you said that before. I suppose you plan to leave the rest to your friend Mister George Pierce?"

"I don't think you need to worry about Mister George Pierce."

"Yeah? I thought he was threatening to notify the police?"

"You don't know the police here, Karl. The police consists of Uncle Cy William, who boasts that he never made an arrest in his life. It's a fact. Once they heard him yelling late at night to some thieves he'd been set on, 'Run, boys, run, or Uncle Cy William will get you!' No, his only vice is cutting off the heads of dogs."

"*What*, kid?"

"Yes, one of his jobs is to see that all dogs are licensed. Dog licenses cost two bucks, and the money goes to the town library for books—it's the library's only support. They say, if he finds an unlicensed dog, he takes it out to the woods and chops its head off with an axe. But I don't know. Besides, I feel pretty sure George Pierce was only bluffing. You don't need to worry."

"Thanks for them few kind words. And here's your hat, what's your hurry? But don't try to reach for that one, it's over your head."

"Very clever of you, Karl. Your magnanimity overwhelms me."

"Keep the change."

"And if I might be allowed one personal observation—"

"Oh, sure. And why not?"

"It seems to me, in a matter that's after all none of your business, that you're behaving damned badly."

"Yeah?"

"Yeah. I've got nothing but respect for Jim. I've got none at all, I'm afraid, for you."

"Thanks. I appreciate that. Coming from you—"

"Don't pay any attention to him, kid. Just let him sulk. He'll get over it."

"Okay. Well, I guess I'll be going."

He got up and went to the table to shake hands with Kitty, but she sat with lowered head, as if blind, desperately absorbed in her writing, and he merely patted her shoulder instead. Even as he touched the stooped shoulder she continued to write—and looking down he saw at last what it was. The torn piece of paper was almost entirely covered with the words *Jesus Christ*. And while he watched, fascinated, the hurrying hysterical pencil added yet others—*Jesus Christ, Jesus Christ, Jesus Christ, Jesus Christ . . .* It was her final comment on the Utopia.

"Good-by, Kitty," he said.

"Good-by, Tip. I think you've been swell."

"No. I'm damned sorry. Good-by, Jim."

"Don't say good-by, kid. We'll be seeing you in New York."

"Not if I see him first, he won't!"

"Okay, Karl, if that's the way you feel about it—"

"That's the way I feel about it."

"All right. That suits me."

"Forget it, kid. He's just got a grouch on. And give my best to Enid. And shall I tell Lorna about it? *For* you, I mean, as she wasn't here?"

"Sure. And give her my best, too."

"All right. Good-by for the present."

"Good-by for the present."

Jim was standing by the fireplace, smiling—Karl lay unmoving on the couch, with his eyes now closed, as if he were endeavoring to imitate the death mask of a saint, but nevertheless looking more than ever like a dead hen—Kitty continued to scribble her Jesus Christs. The ceaseless piano, the intolerable piano, was the only sound as he let himself out, closed the door behind him, went down the steps into the light rain, and started up Baker Street. The Rhapsody in Blue—

Under the silver-gray signpost, in the rain, he hesitated for a moment, and then turned to the left, towards the sea. Impossible to go home—

impossible—the mere thought was unbearable. Let her wait. It would do her good to wait! He would walk to the sea by the mile-long shore road, perhaps take the little footpath through the wet pine woods, where always, under the soft needles, the first Mayflowers were to be found, the first pipsissewa, the whitest Indian Pipes. And then the stone jetty, the skeletal iron light house, and the sea. The unpotable sea, the all-smiling sea, which was driving Kitty mad.

❡ IV

"... *the wind was south, the morning misty; but towards noon warm and fair weather. The birds sang in the woods most pleasantly. At one o'clock it thundered, which was the first we heard in that country. It was strong and great claps, but short; but after an hour it rained very sadly till midnight. . . . This day some garden seeds were sown. . . .*"
—JOURNAL OF THE PILGRIMS

"So you wouldn't wait for me, eh? And you had your supper without me, eh? And at the Murphys', too, with doughnuts! And I have to give this lummox of a girl her bath, and go without supper, or eat a cold sad sardine, all because I'm a little late, and walk to the sea! Fie upon you, and out upon you, and fie. That's all *I* can say. Now shut your eyes."

"And did you walk *all* the way to the sea?"

"Yes, I walked *all* the way to the sea. And I stood on the breakwater and looked at it—"

"And what did you see, daddy?"

"I saw nothing. I saw lots and lots and lots of nothing."

"Ho, how silly, as if you could see lots of nothing!"

"Well, that's what it was like, see? There was a gray, cold, miserable rain, filling all the air as far as you could see, and falling on the water, and rustling on my slicker, and running in beads off my oilskin hat, and there wasn't a single ship, nor a motorboat, not even so much as a dory. There was only the little red bell buoy, in the middle of the channel, bobbing up and down like a jack-in-the-box—"

"Not like a jack-in-the-box—!"

"Well, sort of. And ringing its little sad bell, *cling-clang, clingity-clang, cling-clang, cling-clang,* so dolefully and pitifully to itself, with not even a sea gull listening to it—"

"And then what?"

"Well, then, after looking at all that nothing, I came back. I came back by the pine wood path, the Indian Pipe path, and it was all wet and silent and juicy and dripping and solemn and mysterious—"

"A mystery, a mystery!"

"Exactly—a mystery."

"Yes, and go on."

"Well, I guess that's about all. Now, out of that bath!"

"All right. But you must tell me about the starlings."

"Foo! Why, you saw the starlings yourself!"

"Yes, I know, but I want you to *tell* me about them. *You* saw them *first*, daddy, you *know* you did!"

"Well, so I did. Now, out you come—heave, *ho!*"

"So what."

"Well, first of all I heard a great chittering and chattering, and a squeaking and a squawking, and a dithering and a dathering—"

"Ho ho, what funny words!"

"Like a thousand mice all squealing and squeaking—"

"*Mice* in a *tree?*"

"Ha, but I didn't say they *were* mice, did I? That was before I knew *what* they were. Of course, it would have been very funny if they *had* turned out to be mice, up in a tree—perhaps that would have been better! Shall we have it mice instead?"

"No, let's have it starlings. Besides, daddy, they *were* starlings!"

"So they were. Anyway, that's what I *saw* they were, when I looked up at the tree to find out what all that uproar was about. And there they were, a thousand starlings—or maybe a thousand and one—"

"You couldn't *count* them, silly!"

"Approximately. Now give me that foot."

"You've already *dried* that one!"

"Well, then, the other."

"And now go on—"

"I saw them all in the big poplar tree at the corner by Mr. Murphy's house, that's where they were first, and they were all fluttering and flapping, as if they were quarreling. They would dart down into the middle of the tree and then up again, whistling and screeching and shrieking at the tops of their voices, as if they were dreadfully angry about something; and then it seemed to me that there was some sort of fight going on, right in the middle of the tree, where most of the flapping was—"

"And that was where the poor starling was."

"That was where the poor starling was. Of course, he may have been very naughty—"

"Well, and then what."

"Suddenly they all went scrambling, the whole thousand, to the tree across the street, by the Bank, in Mister Riley's field, all still chittering and chattering, and I was just getting back from my walk to the sea, and I watched them, and then I saw that they were all fighting with that one poor starling, pecking and pecking at him—"

"Do you suppose they really meant to *hurt* him?"

"Well, perhaps not, Buzzer—perhaps they just meant to punish him a *little*, see?"

"Yes, if he'd been *really* naughty—and go on!"

"And that was when I saw you, and told you to come and look at them. And we rushed into the garden then, just in time to see the whole great black cloud of them fly straight into the Puringtons' poplar tree, right over our beautiful new lilac hedge, screaming and flapping, and then suddenly—"

"Yes, suddenly!"

"—that poor starling fell like a stone; with hardly so much as a flutter of a wing; on the wet grass right at our feet. And at first we thought it was dead, didn't we?—"

"Yes, and you clapped your hands at all the other starlings, and they flew away—you were very angry, weren't you, daddy? Because it *was* mean of them to all fight against just one—"

"—and it didn't move, and its eyes were closed, and it lay there on its back, with its claws in the air, and then I picked it up and held it in my hands, and it was quite still—"

"But it wasn't dead? Ho ho! It wasn't dead at all! Was it!"

"No, it wasn't dead at all. For suddenly it opened its eyes, and looked at us, quite calmly, first at you and then at me—"

"*Did* it, daddy?"

"Well, it just looked *around*, perhaps—perhaps to see where the rest of the starlings had gone to. And then, just as if *nothing* at all had happened, it up and flew away—lippity-lippity-lip!"

"And it was alive all the time!"

"It was alive all the time."

"But why did it lie so still, and fall down out of the tree like that!"

"Well, Buzzer, I think maybe it was playing 'possum. Maybe it was *pretending* to be dead, so that the other starlings would all go away. And so it pretended to fall, like that, as if it couldn't fly any more, but all the same managing not to hit the ground *too* hard, you see—it just waggled a wing once or twice, when it saw the ground coming up pretty fast, so as to keep from being hurt, and then it lay still with its eyes shut—but of course it hadn't expected *you* and *me* to be there! That was a surprise."

"Ho ho! And what do you suppose it thought when you picked it up, daddy?"

"Hmm, I don't know, my pet. That must have given it rather a shock. Maybe it thought the other *starlings* were picking it up—goodness knows! But when it opened its eyes, and saw that it was sitting in my hand, and saw a little girl staring at it with eyes as big as lollipops, or marbles, or cannon-balls—or umbrellas—"

"Ho, how silly, they weren't either!"

"—and her mouth wide open, like the wolf in Little Red Riding-hood—"

"Do you suppose it thought I would *eat* it?"

"Ha! You never know. I daresay you looked pretty frightening, my lamb! And *much* bigger than a lion. And now, up the stairs!"

"And do you suppose it's gone back to its friends, now?"

"Very likely. Perhaps when they saw what a *fearful* danger it was in, actually right in the hands of one of those dreadful, dreadful men—they'd be sorry for it, and think it had been punished enough, see? Now up you go, no more dillydallying. *March!*"

She skipped out of the bathroom, her hands flapping excitedly against her sides, and scrambled barefooted up the darkening stairs ahead of him.

He followed slowly, already feeling how that gaiety fell from him, fell away like something false—or could it be that it was actually truer than the other? No, they were both true—they were both true. The unhappiness with Enid was certainly no truer than the happiness with Buzzer—not a bit. It was only that the *shadow* of that made this so difficult. And as for the dreadful news about poor Miss Twitchell, which Terence had stopped the wagon to tell him—found drowned in Indian Pond—absent for two days, too, without even being *missed*—lying there in three feet of water for two days before anybody had so much as noticed that she was gone—

"And wasn't it *lucky*, daddy, that Chattahoochee wasn't there!"

"Yes, very lucky. I should say so. Now, in you hop—"

"And tell me a story!"

"Foo! What nonsense. And besides it's late. Didn't I tell you that the world was coming to an end? Well, it *has*—and with a bang. It's burst into a billion, billion, *billion* little pieces."

"It hasn't either. I know better! If it *had* burst, how could you *stand* there!"

She skipped into the little cot, drew up the counterpane with its embroidered birds, holding it snug against her chin, gave a quick wriggle, and then suddenly lay still. The blue eyes softened, dimmed, looked farther and farther away past him, and as he stooped to kiss the wet golden curl on the forehead, she was already beginning to sing her night song—that odd tuneless little sing-song, so like Enid's rhymeless humming, with which she always magicked herself to sleep.

"Good night, my pet."

"Good night!"

"Sleep tight."

"Sleep tight!"

"Hope the bedbugs don't bite."

"Mmmmm!"

"And have a nice dream."

"Mmmmmm!"

"And I'll see you next year."

"Mmmm."

He touched the tip of her nose with one finger, straightened, went slowly back to the upper hall, and stood there under the sloping roof, listening to the gentle slithery sound of the rain on the shingles, the soft continuous patter mixed with the heavier occasional drip from the trees. Almost dark—the river barely visible, visible only as a dull gleam—mercury-colored. Diffused moonlight, of course—through the clouds, through the rain: the moon was all but full. *Cut all things or gather, the moon in the wane; but sow in increasing, or give it his bane*—where did that come from? A superstition? But it might be true, and if so the lilacs—

Yes—and the lilies of the valley, which Miss Twitchell had promised to give them, from her garden, only two weeks ago—for the shaded corner at the front, by the street—the lilies of the valley, which now they would never have! Taken with her into the shallow waters of Indian Pond, the pickerel weed and pond lilies—what had happened, what in god's name had happened? Lying face down, drowned, only a few feet from the rocky shore, bareheaded—and waiting there two days to be found by small boys! What could it possibly mean? Maybe Ee would know—she had been Ee's friend, rather than his—or acquaintance, rather—but, in the circumstances, how could he tell Ee about it? Had it been money? Cancer? What *could* move a middle-aged spinster—and apparently perfectly happy—to such a thing, and so suddenly? An orphan, they said she had been, and adopted, living alone in that big house, with the beautiful pine trees, and the Tree of Heaven, and liked by everybody, and kind to everybody. It had been so characteristic of her to come and offer the lilies of the valley, noticing that dark little corner of the garden where nothing would ever grow—he could remember just how she had pointed, with those rather odd-looking chalky hands of hers, the quick and diffident gesture, and said, "Yes lilies of the valley, I'll bring you some roots." And now, dead for two days without anyone, not a soul, even noticing her absence! Ah, that was human nature for you, that was brotherly love!

He felt a soft pressure against his leg, heard a little chirp—it was Chattahoochee, curling a striped tail ingratiatingly round his knee, and looking up at him with his slightly dishonest but very affectionate cat-smile.

"So it's you," he said.

"*Prtrnyow*," said the cat.

"And what, might I ask, do *you* want? Food, I expect."

"*Prtrnyow*."

"And I suppose the weather's too much for you, so that the ramming is off, eh? Is that it?"

"*Prrrrt*."

"Well, I'm afraid I can't do anything about *that*. I've got troubles enough of my own!"

The idea amused him, and he found himself grinning at it, in spite of everything—how shocked Ee would be, by god! The cat padded stiffly away round the corner, tail in air, towards Buzzer's room, towards his favorite counterpane (it was Buzzer's theory that he liked to sleep among the embroidered birds) and as he turned from the low window to go down the stairs he heard the first snapping of the fire in the studio—Ee must have come back. She must have come in quietly, without telling him, without saying a word—it was part of the silent treatment, of course. As dining at the Murphys' had been. The silence before the storm.

The fan of yellow lamplight fell across the hall floor from the half-opened door to the studio, and he found Enid crouched on the hearth before the fire, matchbox in hand. She looked up at him inquisitively, but otherwise without expression—except perhaps that the mouth seemed a little rigid, a shade too controlled. And perhaps she was pale.

"That was ingenious of you," he said.

"I beg your pardon?"

"Going to the Murphys' for supper, like that, so that I would come back to an empty house!"

"You said yourself—"

"And then sending Buzzer over for me to put to bed as soon as you saw me arriving! That was a neat touch, too. How did you manage to keep the house watched? Or did you get the Murphy kids to do it?"

"You said yourself you wouldn't be back."

"I said I *mightn't* be back."

"And I'm supposed just to wait and see—"

"You had no intention of going to the Murphys' until it seemed to you to offer just one more chance of punishing me—had you?"

"That has nothing to do with it. If you go out for supper, why shouldn't I!"

"You went there simply and solely to give me an empty house to come back to, and whether or *not* I stayed out to supper, didn't you! The idea of the empty house, when you'd been blackmailing me with threats of leaving—"

"I had a *perfect* right to do what I did."

"It was one of the *meanest* things you ever did—and I may say you've certainly been excelling yourself lately! Think it over. And perhaps, when I've finished foraging for the cold supper which you've so kindly not left for me, you'll be ready to apologize."

Turning too quickly, lest he give her time to answer, he tripped over the hall rug, stumbled, kicked it from him violently—damn! And then in his haste to retrieve himself, miscalculating in the dark, struck his right shoulder, painfully, against the doorjamb of the dining room. How disgusting—how grotesque. To give her, on top of everything else, *that* opportunity! He reeled, the pain sickened him, he pressed his hand hard against the bone, and it was not till he had reached the dark kitchen, and was groping for the lamp chimney on the shelf behind the stove, that he realized how completely the two little accidents had changed his plans. He had meant to go first, a little ostentatiously, to the dining room, light the candles, lay out the silver on the table, make his preparations with every appearance of leisure and formality—he might have to dine alone, but, by god, he could at any rate dine in state, wife or no wife! Yes . . . But instead, the unforeseen shock had driven him straight out to the kitchen, as far from her as he could get, so that he could hug his pain in secret. Just the sort of unpredictable accident that ruins everything—the little element of last-minute comedy that turns a tragedy into a farce. Like accidents on the stage—as when the tree trunk parted of its own accord, and Siegfried's sword fell clattering out, before he had time even to get his hands on it. Yes. Damned funny! If one was on the right side of the curtain! But as it was—

As it was, the kitchen had its points: it was nice in a rain, anyway, for the rain on the thin, low roof sounded so loud and so near, one felt so exposed, it was almost as if one were outdoors: and the shadows, cast across the peeling whitewashed rafters, were so spectacular: and besides, in the circumstances, the whole notion was perhaps agreeably forlorn. He found in the cupboard—sure enough, what a joke—a tin of sardines, miraculously complete with a key, and opened it—he found a box of crackers. He forked out the dovetailed metallic sardines with a leaden kitchen fork, laid them neatly across the white crackers, and perched himself on the corner of the kitchen table to eat.

Dining at the Murphys' like that—!

And then pretending that she had no ulterior motive—!

And knowing all the while that he would really be back for supper, anyway—

He rubbed his shoulder and listened to the persistent rain. He remembered that tomorrow was Friday, and that Mr. Murphy would be calling for him early with the Ford (which meant no breakfast either, not till he had reached the South Station in Boston), and he was just thinking how extraordinarily a silence can put *distance* between people, or turn a small house into a big one—as now, for instance, with positively an Atlantic Ocean spreading its screaming wastes between the studio and the kitchen—when the front doorbell rang. *Zring—zring*—it rang twice, loudly, and he heard Enid opening the studio door, and shooting back the bolt of the front door, and a voice, a male voice. Who the devil—!

He stepped up quietly into the dark dining room and listened.

"No, I'm afraid I *don't* know where Timothy is."

"Oh."

"I'm sorry."

"Well, I'm very sorry to disturb *you*, Enid—"

(It was Jim Connor—the voice broke off, hesitating.)

"—but I just thought I'd like to bring these little things over, these little toys, for Buzzer—if you didn't mind—"

"Oh! I see."

"They're not very much. A couple of small things, all I could find here —Shall I put them down on the floor?"

"Yes. That will be all right."

"Okay. There! Just a little pink cart—I thought, as we might be leaving for New York soon—"

"Oh—"

"—I'd like to give Buzzer something for her birthday. And to say good-by, Enid, and tell you how sorry I am about this mix-up."

"Yes. That's all been settled, *hasn't* it?"

"Settled? Yes, I'm afraid it has! Well, good night, Enid, and no hard feelings."

"Good night."

"Good night!"

The door closed firmly on the melancholy voice, the bolt shot sharply in its socket, and then there was silence. Was she looking now at the little pink cart? Standing there and looking at the pink cart—and perhaps belatedly discovering, and feeling, her shame? Good god, what a scene. There was time, and plenty, to run after him, of course—he could walk back with him, walk up to the post office with him—across the bridge, even—but what was the use? To do so would solve nothing, alleviate no feelings. The rehabilitation with Jim could well wait, couldn't it? till next he went to New York, and met him on "neutral" ground—and meanwhile it would only serve, of course, to complicate still further the dreadful tangle with Enid. Or was it cowardice to look at it like that?

Cowardice—yes.

He sat down on the piano bench, in the half-dark room, struck a match, lit the green bayberry candle that stood on the piano, in the green-wax-smeared mahogany candlestick, and looked up at the Japanese print which hung on the wall above and behind it. *Famous Place to See Moon*. The dark, nocturnal mountain torrent, among black rocks, rocks hooked and horned, zigzagged its way downward under the moon, and in every pool, on every stone shelf where the night-blue water had gathered to spill, a full moon was reflected—it was a chorus of moons, among the dark mountains, to praise that other moon which sidled out from a frond of cloud. *Famous Place to See Moon*—he remembered when they had bought it in Boston—seeing it in the window—he remembered how they had looked at it then, how much they had seen in it, how magical it had seemed. And now, suddenly, it struck him that he had not looked at it in the same way—looked at it like this, with care, with love—for years. Yes, that was true. And it was true of other things, too. One forgot them, one took them for granted—but how could it be otherwise, how could it possibly be otherwise? The first leaf, again—yes, it was exactly like that, the freshness of the first vision—the freshness of the first love—and manifestly it would be absurd to expect that first freshness to last. As if an ecstasy could be permanent! How absurd. And yet, the *thing itself* was as beautiful as ever: the leaf, the Japanese print, or the woman one loved: it was only oneself that failed. The eye became fatigued, ceased to see—ceased to look—and instead of love, by god, marriage settled down to being just the terrible bed of habit—callous, careless, indifferent—but how else could it be? And all the w.c.'s—!

Comic, yes—and an act of divination as well—for just as he was amusing himself with his own sudden vision of life, as symbolized in an endless vista of w.c.'s, which receded parabolically into the infinite, Enid went quickly across the hall, into the bathroom, and shut the door. At the same instant, too, a light switched on in an upper room of the Purington house, and he turned around just in time to see Gladys Purington, black-haired and handsome, reaching up to pull down the window shade. Intimacy—yes, how was one to compromise with intimacy? Now with this print, *Famous Place to See Moon*, it was just as obvious that a prolonged familiarity was in some degree deadening as with a person. He had forgotten how lovely it was, forgotten its precise virtue of naïve magic, its tenderness, its—yes, above all—*love*, and could not now, perhaps, so much love it again himself had he *not* forgotten it—it was all very odd!

He struck a chord, and another, and a third—tried, angrily, to remember Schoenberg's "mystic" chord, and what Paul had said about it—began to play Debussy's Arabesque and stopped; and was beginning a fragment of a Bach toccata when Enid came and stood in the doorway. Her arms were folded across the green smock, she was lightly biting her lower lip. She looked angry, but unhappy as well. There was a curious awkwardness, half of aggression and half of retreat, in the way she leaned slightly against the doorjamb. Her head, tipped a little to one side, was just perceptibly swaying, and the steady green eyes—beautiful—looked for a long moment into his own before she spoke.

"Don't you think we ought to discuss this?" she said.

He smiled cynically up at her, tapped a note, tapped it again, felt with his fingers for a little chord, and then suddenly hardened his gaze and looked beyond her, into the dark garden where the dead plum tree stood in the rain.

"Why?" he said.

"Why not?"

"I'm afraid I'm becoming a little indifferent."

"Indifferent? To what?"

"To you. I don't think you can blame me if I feel a little bruised!"

"I see. You become indifferent to me when I dare to stand up for my rights!"

"Work it out for yourself—however you like! I don't really much care, that's all!"

"Oh. And you just propose to let things go on like this?"

"Why not? You started it, didn't you? Can't you finish it? *I* don't mind, if *you* don't. And as long as you intend to treat me in this fashion I'm quite happy without your society. A woman who can behave as you did just now to Jim Connor doesn't interest me. Or only pathologically!"

"There was nothing else for me to do."

"Nothing else for you to do! You could have been human. But that's not your long suit, is it?"

"Human—! What is there to *make* me human, in *this* life—!"

"Oh, have you got to be *made* human? And I'm supposed to do it, I suppose—?"

"You're very clever, you can twist my words—"

"I damned well need to be. If I'm clever, you're *hard!* My god, the things you've been doing—how *could* you do that to Jim Connor, when he was actually bringing presents for Buzzer! Not to mention lying to him, and telling him you didn't know where I was!"

"I *didn't* know—I thought you might have gone out."

"I don't believe you."

"Very well—I can't make you believe me. I was abrupt with Jim partly because I was embarrassed—naturally I was surprised to see him when I thought the whole thing was finished—"

"Embarrassed—I should think so! You ought to have been sick with shame. And I'd think a lot better of you if you *had* been. It's not enough, is it, that you drive my friends away, cut me off from them, from the few people I find interesting and stimulating—you have to insult them on my very doorstep—"

"I didn't insult him—"

"Not in so many words, no! But did I hear any thanks for what was really an extraordinarily nice thing of him to do? Did you even offer to *take* the things from him? Oh, no—you just stood there and let him put them on the floor. Where I suppose they still are! And this on top of everything else—driving him out of town, dictating that we aren't to see each other— my god, and then you have the *gall* to turn around and try to pretend that it's all in self-defense!"

"Which is exactly what it is."

"Oh, yes, let's hear all about *that* again—it's bad for our precious names and social positions, and Buzzer's future will be ruined, and all the rest of that snobbish silly nonsense—"

"Do you *ever* think of anybody but yourself? For one moment?"

"Never."

"I thought not. You never think, for instance, of the difference between a woman's social position and a man's—"

"Oh? Let's hear about it."

"It's true. It's the woman who stays at home, who has to face it, not the man—the man doesn't know about it, and doesn't care—he's got his own separate life—but what about the woman? It's all very well for you, with half your life spent in town, or on trips to New York—"

"Trips to New York—!"

"Yes, trips to New York. And about half the week at home, and most of that shut up in the studio—but what about me, the rest of the time? Does it ever occur to you that people *talk?*"

"How wonderful."

"It's not wonderful at all. It's very natural."

"Well? And what do they talk about?"

"They begin by pitying me. Just like George and Mabel. Oh, if you'd known the times Mabel has asked me if I didn't get lonely—"

"Yes—I know—one of those sweet little services that women *love* to do for each other!"

"And then, because they're afraid of showing their pity, if they're nice, and embarrassed by it, they begin to stay away. Do you realize that nowadays, when you're in town, George and Mabel practically never come to see me? Or anybody else, for that matter? Oh, I'm kept in cold storage, all right. They come to see me when you're here, but apparently it's beginning to be thought not quite respectable to call on me when I'm alone. Or as if it wasn't respectable for me to be *left* alone."

"Aren't you being just a little imaginative?"

"Oh, no. You ask your friend George—ask your friend Paul, too. If you can get an honest answer out of them, which I doubt! The truth is, they're ashamed *for* you. And the neighbors, too—they shun me as if I were the plague. Even Mrs. Murphy is always hinting, saying it's such a pity, isn't it, that my husband has to be away so much, as if it implied either that there was something wrong with you, or something *terribly* wrong with *me!*"

"Yes. And what else?"

"Well—naturally, it all leads to gossip."

"Oh. I see. How nice."

"It isn't at all nice."

"Well, let's hear it!"

"They think—"

"*Who* thinks?"

"They *all* do."

"Oh. And they *all* told you?"

"No. It's not necessary to go into that!"

"All right, let's have the gossip."

"They think, when you go to town, or to New York—"

"New York! I haven't been there for six months!"

"No matter. When you go to town—when you go away—they think you wouldn't go so much, or stay so long, if there weren't some other reason. Some reason other than your work. They think you're having an affair. They can't imagine that you wouldn't have arranged things better— so as to spare me so much work and so much loneliness—if there weren't some other reason."

"I see."

"Yes."

"By god, I—and *who* are the saintly people who told you this?"

"Would any useful purpose be served by telling you?"

"They ought to be faced with it, the damned mischief-makers—and I suppose, of course, *you* didn't—!"

"On the contrary, I *did!*"

"You shouldn't have permitted them to raise the thing at all."

"How could I help it? They merely said, besides, what everybody else is *thinking.* So what does it matter!"

"*Any* loyal wife can prevent that sort of thing being said to her. You know that as well as I do. The truth is you've been *looking* for causes of complaint—"

"I have not!"

"—for the past six months. Oh, yes, you have. And if you can pick up a dirty little piece of gossip to fling in my face—"

"I did nothing of the sort. I've done nothing of the sort."

"It looks very like it, doesn't it? You complain about my friends, even compel me to drop them, you complain about my work, about our poverty, you complain about living in the country, you complain even because you have to do a little work yourself—"

"A *little* work! You try doing a morning's washing!"

"—and now you complain because the neighbors gossip. Good god, Enid, what next? Oh, yes, and the schools, too—I'd forgotten about that— the schools aren't good enough for Buzzer, and the children speak with simply atrocious accents! Is there anything else, while we're on the subject? We might as well get right down to it. And when you've had *your* say, maybe I'll have mine."

"I've got plenty to say—I've had plenty to say—if you'd ever take the trouble to *listen.* And when I say listen, I mean *listen.* But I might as well be living alone, living in a vacuum, as far as getting any understanding is concerned—!"

"Ah, the old classic. So I don't understand you any more."

"If you even paid me as much attention as you pay to Buzzer—or gave me a little of the kind of imaginative sympathy you give to her—"

"Good god almighty, do you mean to say you're going to be so low as to be jealous of your own *child*—?"

"It *isn't* jealousy. I wouldn't take it away from Buzzer, it's very good for her, and it's very lovely, too, it's the nicest thing about you—but why couldn't you give a little of it to me?"

"As if I hadn't! And why the devil should I? What in hell do you give me? What? You do nothing but interfere with my life, my work, my career, my friends—the whole blasted business—and then you come running to me for understanding! Why don't you run to your *mother*—it seems to be what you need!"

"Perhaps I will!"

"*She* ought to understand you—you get more *like* her every day! You're turning into a complete prig."

"Oh."

"Yes. A damned prig."

"If you're going to have recourse to swearing, simply—"

She had suddenly flushed, the high cheekbones were beautifully flushed, the green eyes widened as if deliberately for contempt, and she turned abruptly and went out, went through the hall and into the studio. He heard the two-toned squeak of the door, the clink of the tongs in the fireplace, the soft rustling thud of a pine log on to the other logs in the fire— that familiar, scaly, bark-scabbing sound, the red bark flaking and peeling —and he waited then for the creak of her wicker chair, but none came. She must be standing—she must simply be *standing* there—looking at the fire, looking out of the window—looking even at his pictures? Not likely! But standing in the intensity of her thought, standing and waiting. Yes— and implying too, by her departure on that particular note, that it was New Bedford she was thinking of, and the now twice-threatened return to her mother. Good god, how extraordinary, how simply grotesque—that actually, after all this time, they should now find themselves in *this* situation! Home and mother—how preposterous! He struck a chord at random, and looked up again at the Japanese print, in the dim candlelight. But that business of the "gossip," and so ridiculously just *now*, as the affair with Nora was coming to an end, and especially in view of the fact that it had *begun* coming to an end precisely *because* they had decided to move into the country, to live in this village—how ironically and infuriatingly unfair *that* was, how typically silly an injustice! And Ee herself apparently disbelieving it—

But did she?

Or had it been a skillful tactical bit of probing?

No, probably not. But just the same the mere *suggestion* of a suspicion—whether hers, or George's and Mabel's, or Mrs. Murphy's—shook him and made him angry; and all the more so because while in *fact* it was right—or partly—in *principle* it was wrong. Yes, there was something definitely mean about it, that was it—that they should suspect him of going to town—or even to New York, good heavens—in pursuance of a love affair; and abandoning poor Enid for that reason; when in truth the very opposite was the case, and it was *Nora* who had been abandoned—this was simply a piece of wanton invention and mischief-making. It was sickening. And without a shred of evidence or motive for it, either! His mere *absences* had led their imaginations to this, that was all—and the absences had been innocent. Not only innocent, but hard work, too, by god, and increasingly at the cost of what he had hoped to make his career! Yes, this was a genuine meanness, and of a sort that surprised him in George and Mabel. So *that* was the way their minds worked. Ah—and *there* was human nature for you, again—always suspect the worst, and whisper it where it will do the most good! By all means. And by all means separate a wife from her husband if you can, it's very likely the kindest thing you can do! And drive the idealists, like Jim Connor, out of town— and forget the Miss Twitchells till they are dead. . . .

He started to strike a chord, but decided not to, and allowed his hands to lie relaxed on the keys. It would be better to be silent. Yes. *Her* silence in the studio, *his* silence in the dining room—and the battlefront, of course, halfway between, in the hall. But the finest irony of all, and the most infuriating part of the whole thing—if it hadn't also been really damned funny—was that after *having* an affair, and in entire and success- ful secrecy, he should now be suspected when he was innocent. It was ridiculous, it made him feel helpless. In fact, what he really wanted to do was to go straight to them and *tell* them about it. "Look here, you blankety- blank fools and idiots, you low-minded suspicious imbeciles—do you think if I ever *did* have an affair I'd conduct it in such a way that simpletons like yourselves would entertain even the shadowiest ghost of a suspicion of it? Of course not. As is proved by the fact that when I was living in Boston I *did* have an affair, which none of you ever guessed for one minute. And now, you poor prunes, when I merely go to town three days a week, to *work*, your feculent little fancies have nothing better to do than this! Go crawl into a cesspool, will you? where you belong. Or into one of Mr. Will Pepoon's bags!"

The visual image amused him, he half-smiled, involuntarily struck a note on the piano, then got up and went down into the rain-sounding kitchen for a glass of water. Amusing—yes! But the whole thing was now too complex, too difficult—and the feeling of insecurity, too, was begin- ning to be oppressive. Unfair, that he should have to bear the extra burden, just now, along with all this, of knowing about little Miss Twitchell—un- fair, also, that into the same day should have come not only Nora's letter, but that subtly disturbing dream as well. Why in god's name had they had to quarrel *now*, when—

When what?

He averted his eyes from the thought, from the memory of the walk with Buzzer, in which the sun-bright fog and the queer dream and the letter had all been so deliciously and magically woven together. It was as if he had winced; and instead he turned the cold water tap quickly on and off several times, in the kitchen sink, to watch the indicator in the dial drop down and then shoot up again. Twenty-eight. He could go out and start the engine, of course, and run it for five minutes, just to test it—but actually there was water enough for two days. And besides, there was the "tempest," Ratio's tempest, it was raining. Tempest! These absurd Cape Codders! Like calling the ceiling the "wall," and the walls "side-walls."

He turned down the little fishtail of yellow flame in the reflector lamp on its shelf behind the stove, walked slowly into the dining room, and blew out the candle on the piano; then proceeded, slowly again, his hands in his pockets, to the studio. It was exactly as he had foreseen. Enid was standing—simply *standing*—in the middle of the room, behind her wicker chair. Her fists were on her hips, and she was facing, but not looking at, the fire—the narrowed eyes were looking downward at nothing. For a second they lifted to meet his—a curious and remote look, as if it came from far beneath, far below, quickly and blindly tipped upward and then tipped down again. There was something doll-like in the movement, something inhuman and mechanical, but also pathetic. Then, addressing the fire, she said slowly:

"Well, what are we going to do?"

"That's up to you!"

"Why is it up to me?"

"You started the whole thing, it's all your creation, your action, your aggression—I haven't done anything—"

"You persist in that, don't you?"

"Certainly."

"I wish you could see that my aggression, as you call it—"

"Oh, call it anything you like!"

"Will you let me finish?—is simply a symptom. Of the deeper grievances that I've tried to tell you about, and that you won't face. When I try to talk to you about them, you merely take to abuse and swearing."

"What nonsense!"

"It's true. As just now when I *presumed* to suggest that a little of your imaginative sympathy with Buzzer might well come to me—and all you could do was accuse me of jealousy."

"And wasn't it?"

"No!"

"Oh. I beg your pardon."

"And besides, what you were *really* doing, was evading the point. Exactly as you always do. You didn't want to face the fact that you *don't* any longer give me that kind of imaginative sympathy. Do you."

"I wasn't aware of it. Perhaps I don't. But if I don't, is it any wonder? You don't make yourself very attractive when you do this sort of thing, you know—you can't drive me with a whip and *then* expect me to come to you with imaginative sympathy! Good god, I never heard anything so idiotic. Yes, and let me tell you another thing, while we're on the subject—one that I wouldn't have supposed a woman would *ever* have to be told by a man, either—and that is this: the one thing you *cannot* do in a marriage is *demand* love, or understanding, or sympathy, or whatever you want to call it, at the point of a pistol. You *cannot* do that. It's fatal. There is nothing so calculated to freeze every spark of feeling—the mere demanding of it kills it. Feelings can't be probed and bullied like that, you've got to leave them alone. And it's bad enough, by god, to have you make the mistake—without my *then* having to *explain* it to you! Where does *that* leave me? A hell of a long way off, I'm afraid."

"You're very clever, aren't you?"

"There's nothing clever about it—it's the unfortunate truth."

"I see. So if I'm unhappy, of course it's a mistake to say so. I mustn't complain, on the penalty of making things still worse by alienating you. It's a very ingenious little system, isn't it? Oh, very. I'm just supposed to eat my heart out in silence. And if I hate this life here and hate all these people and hate being alone so much and hate the work and the dirt and the dishes and the everlasting social drabness and boredom of it, not to mention only seeing you half the week, and even then being pushed off by you because you want to work—"

"Go on!"

"I *will* go on. If I hate all this until I'm sick, and feel wretched day in and day out of the days on end when I'm alone, worrying about the money and how to make ends meet, or to keep up appearances, I'm just expected by you to say nothing. Why? Why? What do *I* get out of it? Oh, I know, all that nonsense of yours about plain living and high thinking, about living the natural and honest life of our Pilgrim ancestors, and being independent—but it's no good for a woman, I can't stand it much longer, I'm being starved, I warn you, Timothy."

"I see. So it's like that. You won't stick to your bargain."

"There *was* no bargain."

"There was an agreement."

"An agreement to *try* it, yes!"

"And certainly for a longer period than this. Long enough for me to see how my own work would go, to see what I could do."

"But what *have* you done? Nothing."

"Nothing! That's what you always say, isn't it? The truth is, and for me it's a damned bitter truth, that you never even bother to look at my work, you don't take any longer the slightest interest in it, except insofar as it might make some money, you don't know what I'm doing. Things have changed a lot in five years, haven't they? By god, yes. It makes me laugh. I can remember when you used to *ask* to see what I was doing, in the first year or two—and when we were engaged you could think of nothing else. But nowadays all I get from you is the old parrot cry of why not do portraits, why not do portraits—"

"Well, I'm sorry—"

"*Sorry!* Good god almighty."

"Besides, if you're not altogether sure of yourself, how can you expect *me* to be sure of you?

"You were sure enough when we were engaged, weren't you?"

"Yes, yes—I was. But don't forget that we were both very young."

"Of course! And now we're grown up, aren't we? And must put away these childish things—is that it? I suppose you think my career is finished? I suppose you think I ought to give it up entirely, and do nothing but teach —is that it? Come on, let's hear you say it!"

"Will you *please* stop twisting my words? I merely meant that it was natural enough, when we were both young, that we should feel confident."

"Ah. And natural enough *now* that we should be disillusioned. You *are* disillusioned, aren't you?"

"No—but disappointed! It hasn't seemed to me—"

"Yes, go on, let's have it."

"—that your work has matured much. It seems to me to be still young and unformed."

"Oh, yes, I know—adolescent. Why not stick to your favorite word!"

"In a way, yes."

"Gosh, what a comfort *that* is! Unformed and adolescent—which I suppose by implication applies to me too. After eight years of work and sweat and passion—by god, it's too funny. It's funny either way—funny as the devil if you're right, funny as hell if you're wrong. And if Karl sees power in it, well, then, Karl is adolescent too. We're all adolescent, the whole lot of us—which is just what you've really been maintaining all along—as, of course, so conspicuously in the Jim Connor episode!"

"Candidly, yes!"

"Very well, then, Ee—we've come to a definite parting of the ways. That's flat. From now on, my work will be private. I don't want you to know a thing about it, or to inquire about it, or to *look* at it. It's going to be none of your damned business. If you have no faith in it, as has become increasingly clear, then you can have no part in it. And all the more so because of the very fact that I *do* myself feel unsure about it. It's bad enough to have to fight my own self-doubts, but I can't have an additional enemy in my own house—and that's what you've become. So from now on, as far as my career is concerned, I'm going my own way."

"Is that fair? You asked for my opinion and I gave it—"

"The first law of life is self-preservation!"

"I see. So you're going to separate yourself even *more* from me, as if you hadn't already separated yourself quite enough, with this arrangement of living in the country and working in town. And that's all right for *your* precious career, but what about mine?"

"Yours!"

"Yes, mine. *That* surprises you, doesn't it? To think that *I* should expect a career? And that's funny, too. Women don't really exist, do they? Not for you, they don't! It never occurs to you that nature intended *us* for something, and something beyond just being your slaves."

"Slaves. Don't be an ass!"

"Aren't you being rather an ass yourself? I *hate* you when you talk like that."

"You can hate all you like, but I won't listen to such damned silly nonsense."

"Why not? Are you afraid of it? That's it, poor Timothy, you're afraid of it, aren't you? You can't really face a woman, can you? You can't face or understand her necessities, and so therefore you simply deny them. Absurdly simple for you, isn't it? Much too simple. And it won't work. *I've* got to live, too—whether with or without you—and there's a minimum of love and happiness and well-being without which it's impossible. I'm a woman, I was made for those things, I *need* them—oh, it's no use your laughing—it may sound like platitudes, but it's true. And I want more children while I'm *young*, I want and need babies, I *want* them, but I'm not allowed to have them because of your wonderful career, and the necessity of living economically for it, and without servants—"

"May I remind you that we agreed about that—"

"Oh, we agreed about it, all right."

"Then I fail to see what you're kicking about?"

"But I was a fool to agree, I was signing my own death warrant, I ought to have known better than to do it—I did it only because I loved you, and wanted to give you a chance—and anyway I thought it might somehow work, and that if you were happy you would be more generous—"

"More generous! What more could I possibly have given you!"

"Oh, I don't mean only money, and servants, and the obvious things, like that—I mean the intangibles, too, I mean affection, I mean companionship—being talked to, for instance, you *never* talk to me any more—"

"That's not true."

"It *is* true. It's been true almost ever since Buzzer was born. You've increasingly left me alone by myself, it never even occurs to you to have a *conversation* with me, in the evening, unless other people are present, or to take me for a walk, as you do Buzzer."

"Why, I never heard anything so ridiculous and untrue in my life! What on *earth* are you talking about—a *conversation!*"

"Oh, it's true. You stop and think about it. From the time Buzzer was born, and the next six months, when I was so tied down, and couldn't do things with you as much—that was the beginning, and it's got steadily worse ever since. When do you ever talk to me? What do you ever discuss with me? Oh, no, it's your old superiority complex, I suppose, your feeling that the female isn't your intellectual equal—"

"What absolute nonsense—you simply don't know what you're saying! Good lord, what do you think marriage is? Do you think two people can go on indefinitely, day after day, year after year, holding set-piece conversations, polite little discussions, with each other—is that your idea? Heaven forbid—it would drive me mad. You *can't* do things like that. Life isn't *like that*. We may not have any beautiful highbrow Platonic dialogues at breakfast, or while we do the dishes, but to say that we don't have any talk at all is simply an outrageous and thumping lie. We talk all the time—morning, noon, and night—it may be casual and fragmentary—of course, it is—but when two people are as intimate as we are that's what talk naturally becomes. Good god, Enid, you really are becoming impossible. What's the *use* of discussing anything with you if you're going to misconceive and misconstrue every mortal thing like this?"

"You're very glib—you can always defend yourself, can't you? By turning your back on the facts. You know what I'm saying is true. And it's deeper than that, it's more than that—it isn't only your not talking with me, it's *everything* of that kind. It's your never thinking of taking me anywhere, or planning anything *with* me, any more. I don't mean anything important, I mean just *little* things. How many shared pleasures do we have any more? Precious few, and you know it. And it's because you've turned away your affection, and companionship, partly because you've turned them on to Buzzer (and you needn't stare at me like that, it's true, and it's perfectly natural! I felt it at the time, and I've felt it ever since)—you've more and more separated yourself, withdrawn yourself—but where is it going to lead us? We can't go on like this, I *can't* go on, it's drying me up, it's making me mean and hard and selfish—"

"I see. It's all going to be fathered on me, is it? No, Enid, that won't work. I'm not going to swallow that, not by a damned sight. You get *this* into your head and *keep* it in your head, that the real trouble has been your constant and increasing interference with *everything* connected with my work and career. From the moment Buzzer was born, you've ceased to co-operate with me—from that very moment. That was the signal for the beginning of the pressure, and you've never relaxed it for a second. Oh, no! You evidently made up your mind that a possible artist was all very well, but that a breadwinner was much more important—so you went to work in every conceivable way, trying to wean me from my friends, or to give me new and 'better' ones, and to change subtly the whole mode of our life in a direction you thought more suitable. And with mother's help, too—*that* was clear enough, that heavy and priggish hand from New Bedford! We had to live in the right street, and know the right people, and do the right things—and so, of course, more money was needed—and so the vicious circle had rounded on itself. And then it began to be suggested that perhaps my *work* had better be changed—or perhaps I could do something *else*, like society portraits. Pretty damned cunning! And the *whole* of my original idea, my ambition, my career—**good** god, it just makes me rage to think of it—was to be scrapped, and for what? For financial security and social ambition. And that being so, what it comes down to is this: that you married me under false pretences. You were keen enough on my being a painter beforehand, weren't you? And you swore you would help me in every possible way. Well—*now* look at it. If it's blown up, it's your own silly fault. And I'll tell you this right now—that I'm not going to be driven a *single step farther*. My surrender today about Jim is the last I'm going to make. From now on I'm going to stick to my own notion of how to run my career, and I don't want any interference from any one—you or your mother either!"

"I see—and *you* complain about lack of co-operation! You intend simply to dictate, is that it?"

"In matters vital to me, I certainly do. I've learned my lesson."

"And what about me? What about the things that are vital to me?"

"Well—what, for instance?"

"Well—love, for instance."

"Love! What do you know about love!"

"And what exactly do you mean by that?"

"It was a flat enough question, wasn't it? What *do* you know about love? *Can* you love? Have you ever really loved me for a minute? I very much doubt it. If you had, how could you *possibly* have done all these things to me!"

"So you think I don't love you."

"Well—do you?"

"I think I'll leave that to you. You seem to know everything, don't you? So perhaps you'll tell me."

"Well, I think I will. I think perhaps for once I will."

"Do."

"And it goes for all of you—the whole New Bedford and Boston lot of you—the whole cold-smoked egotistical lot of you. There's really something wrong with you, you New England women—something esthetically wrong with you, something wrong with the pulse, you're not quite human. And it was summed up, I think, quite well, by a Greenwich Village poet who evidently knew what he was talking about. He said: '*I have eaten apple pie for breakfast in the New England of your sensuality.*'"

"Oh!"

"Yes. Very pretty, isn't it?"

"That's the *cruelest* thing—"

"*Cruel*—!"

She spun suddenly on her heels, turning her back, flashing a hand towards her face, but not before he had seen the quick tears starting, the lovely mouth quivering and arched with pain. Her shoulders were trembling, she was biting the back of her hand and trembling, but she hadn't made a sound—and then (as suddenly as she had turned away) she turned back again, went quickly, blindly, past him into the hall, and across it and into the bathroom. He heard the door close, heard the sound of running water—she had turned the taps on, to drown out the sound of her crying. She was standing there crying—and as he waited irresolute, half wanting to listen and half not—for he had never heard Ee really crying before—it seemed to him that something very queer and profound had happened to him in that instant when she had turned away, with the tears starting on to the back of her hand, on to her rings, and her mouth taking that extraordinary shape of unhappiness. For one thing, her mouth, in that moment, had seemed to him more beautiful than it had ever seemed before—as if, suddenly, it had taken on a new and deeper meaning. *All* of her, in fact, had changed startlingly in that instant. She had become tragically different, a separate and unknown, an unhappy and perhaps somehow *doomed*, person—and a person. moreover, who might already have resumed her liberty of action! What would happen to her—what *wouldn't* happen to her— what would become of her? Shapes of disaster, misery, death—the feeling of catastrophe again—but now immediate and dreadful: and himself perhaps powerless and exiled. The distance between them had become immense; and yet at the same time it seemed to him that he had never before seen her so clearly. He remembered thinking of her as a ship's figurehead, borne backward away from him by her own will—but that had been nothing, that had been a mere pretense—this was real. It was as if she had gone.

But *had* she resumed her liberty of action?

Was that what it meant?

Had he at last hurt her *too much*? Hurt her so much that now there would be no going back—no bridging of the gulf that had fallen between them?

He stood still and listened. He stepped softly into the hall and listened. He could hear nothing—nothing but the sound of the running water in the basin. That and the rain—and then a car rumbling over the loose boards of the bridge, coming nearer, its Klaxon skirling angrily as it shot up the road into the village. And then the silence again, for the gentle persistent sound of the rain, the sound of running water.

He went back into the studio, walked twice round it, circling the wicker chair, avoiding the tripod legs of the easel—paused to press back the front log in the fire with his shoe—then pulled one of the window curtains aside and looked out at the street. Nobody—nothing—it was deserted: nothing but the sad autumnal rain, the rain which would probably last all night and all day. The Rileys' house was dark—but, of course, Mr. Riley had turned in early, tomorrow was a fishing day, he would be down at the Town Landing, with his bait boxes, at four in the morning. Going down the river in the rain, the dirty blue boat stuttering loudly past the sleeping houses, past the moored yachts at the lower village; and then down the channel, past the breakwater and the bell buoy, to the Sound, the open sea, a mile of lobster pots along the sandy shore. How simple, how good, how solid—how reassuring, if life were always as well arranged as that! Yet he had been a friend, hadn't he, of Miss Twitchell—Miss Twitchell had often called there with her basket of flowers, standing there on the porch, Mrs. Riley's white, sharp, New England face peering around the half-opened door, the door which she always held tightly clutched in her hands—he and his wife had been her friends, but what good had *that* done her? She had lain for two days in Indian Pond without their even knowing it. . . .

He let the curtain fall back into place, opened the door to the little front hall, with its wooden hat pegs on the white paneling, and there on the floor, as he had foreseen, was the pink cart. A doll, too, squatted against the wall, its china arms upraised, the dead blue eyes half-closed, and a level fringe of brown hair showing under the bonnet's edge. *"Just a little pink cart"*—Jim Connor had said: the typical, the eternal, pink cart of childhood, with the yellow tongue, the bands of silvery metal round the wheels, and the crude bright floral design on the hubs. How she would love it—how she would love the doll, too, and take it for rides round the garden—and how good of Jim! How good of him to think of it, and *do* it, in the middle of his own troubles—to go to a shop and *find* these things! A Messiah, as Kitty had said? Perhaps not. But there were times when he was very like.

He picked them up, and carried them slowly through the studio into the hall, where he put them down on the window seat. It was odd—but it seemed to him, for some reason, that he was noticing everything, every detail. As he passed through the studio it was as if he enumerated each thing that he saw. The wood basket, of pale woven wood, and a pine log with silver moss on it; the brass Cape Cod firelighter on the brick hearth, with a splayed red reflection of the lampshade down its side; the black iron rosettes, like black pond lilies, of the firedogs; a wavering comb of flame, fine-toothed and golden, just beginning to play up, and retreat, between the uppermost logs of the fire; and Karl's little etching in the corner—his first—of a Mexican adobe hut, round-doored, in snow-bright moonlight: he had observed each of these things in turn, and subtly as if out of some deep necessity or purpose. Or perhaps simply to be reassured, to be given back his confidence?

But *why?*

How ridiculous!

Just the same—

In the hall, standing by the stove again—the stove in which perhaps he ought to lay a fire—he listened, swaying slightly in his effort to remain still. He heard nothing, nothing beyond the running of the water—and then it seemed to him *wrong* to listen, or *only* to listen—wrong to be there *in secret*, listening—so he went hesitantly into the dark dining room, and

down into the kitchen, and back into the dining room again. He struck a
match and relighted the candle on the piano top—for it would be absurd
to be found just standing there in the dark, doing nothing—and looked up
once more at *Famous Place to See Moon;* but this time without seeing it.

—*Famous Place to See Moon! Christ!*

He said it aloud, with surprising anger and bitterness, stressing ironically
each word in turn; swung about, his hands in his khaki pockets, to stare
towards the dark Purington house; and then found himself, without having
made any decision about it, knocking at the white bathroom door.

"Enid," he said.

The water was still running—he listened with averted face, breathing
rather quickly. Perhaps she couldn't hear him? He knocked again.

"Enid, please!"

There was no answer.

"*Enid!*"

"Will you please go *away*, Timothy?"

The voice was muffled and distant—the water seemed to be running
louder.

"No, I *won't* go away. Will you please let me in?"

"I don't want to see you."

"Ee, dear, listen—I'm sorry I said that, *terribly* sorry—"

"It doesn't matter—any more, Timothy."

"Of course it matters, darling. Darling, don't be absurd."

"It doesn't matter; nothing matters. Timothy, will you please *go away?*"

"No, Ee. I won't go away. I'm going to stay right here till you open the
door. Now, darling, don't be silly—"

The sound of water seemed to have diminished—perhaps one of the
taps had been turned off. But there was no answer, no other sound. He
listened, his cheek against the door—he tried pressing it, but it was latched.
He rattled it again.

"Ee, dear, did you hear what I said? *Please!*"

There was again a long pause, and then Enid's voice, now a little clearer:

"Yes, I heard you—"

"Are you all right, darling?"

"Yes, I'm all right."

"Darling, *do* forgive me. I didn't mean it, I was just too angry—and *let*
me come in, won't you, please?"

"No, Tip—"

"Please, darling—"

"No."

"Why not?"

"I couldn't, Tip—not now. I look too dreadful—"

"As if *that* mattered—but we *can't* leave it like this, darling, it was all
so wrong and bad—are you still listening, darling?"

"Yes, I'm listening—"

He grinned, privately, at the door, and said:

"You're running *much* too much water, you know!"

"Oh!"

"In every sense of the word. And I'm *very* much ashamed of myself, and I love you *very* much. And if you don't come out *this minute* I'll break the door down. See?"

"But I *can't*, looking like this—"

"Oh, yes, you can."

"Well—"

There was a pause, the water was turned off, a little interval of silence; and then he heard her footsteps coming towards him, the obstinate resonant little click of the door hook, and the door swung slowly inward. She was pale, she was trying to smile, there were still tears in her eyes, she was shy—she was as shy as she had been when he had first told her that he was in love with her. Her hands held behind her back, her mouth trembling a little, she looked up at him, the pupils of her eyes very large and dark, very hurt, but very tender, too. The arrogance had gone from her—and in the moment before either of them moved it was as if he heard, high above them somewhere, the swift wingbeats of hatred, flashing past and away— and then he put out his hand and took the green-smocked elbow in it and drew her towards him. She didn't offer to kiss him—she merely leaned her cheek against his breast.

"Darling, will you forgive me—"

"Of course, Tip, dear, if you'll forgive me, too—"

"No, I'm afraid *I* was the naughty one—but *oh*, what a relief—!"

"Isn't it *heavenly*—!"

"Just to be *together* again, after all these days and days—"

"I've been very hard and mean and selfish, Tip, I'm so dreadfully ashamed, but I'll do better—"

"No, darling, no. It's only that things have been difficult for us—"

"Do you think so? But aren't we silly to hurt each other so much!"

"I didn't mean any of it, darling. I didn't mean a single word. Don't you believe a thing I said—"

"And you too, Tip dear, I was demented—"

"Not a single word. I didn't know what I was saying. I don't know what got into me, I just wanted to hurt and hurt you, and said anything I could *think* of that would hurt you—"

"That's just what *I* did, Tip. It's as if a demon had got hold of us, isn't it, and jangled us—do you suppose for some purpose? It's all so *meaningless!*"

"I know. Good god, what a pair of fools we are—you'd think after all this time together we'd have a *little* more sense, wouldn't you?"

"We *mustn't* do it again, we must promise not to do it again—"

"No, Ee darling, we won't—and isn't it absurd—"

"What, dear?"

"—that it's really because we love each other so much that we can hurt each other so, and perhaps feel we have to—I wonder if that's it? And I do love you so much, Ee, I simply adore you—all day, in spite of everything, I've been adoring you, you don't know how much—"

"*Really*, Tip?"

"*Really*, Ee—like anything. Even in my *rage* about things I couldn't forget it, it seemed to me I'd *never* loved you so much. It was all really damned funny—what with that blasted cesspool, and Jim Connor, and that dreadful little 'artist' in the taxi, and everything—and all the time I was simply *bursting* with love—"

"Darling, how sweet and funny you are!"

"And *you*, darling, what a cold and clammy cheek you have—aren't you *ashamed* of crying like that? Were you crying?"

"Yes, I was crying— It was funny, it's a long time since I've cried—I guess maybe it took *you* to make me cry—perhaps it's a good thing! Anyway, it's a testimonial to your power!"

"*What* a thing to say to your husband!"

"Oh, dear—!"

She sighed, smiled, looked up at him quickly, then began rubbing her nose rabbitlike against his coat. It suddenly occurred to him how comic the whole thing was, their standing here in the bathroom door, for such a purpose, but then, abruptly, he remembered—

"Listen, darling," he said.

"Yes, Tip, dear."

"No—I don't know. Perhaps I'd better not?"

He shook his head.

"What, dear—what is it!"

"My *lovely* Endor, it's nothing to do with this—but I suddenly thought of it, it's been so much on my mind all evening. It's a terrible thing that Terence told me tonight, I met him down at the lower village—"

"Ought I to hear it?"

"Yes—it will shock you, darling—but as a matter of fact it ought to do us both good. Maybe at least it will remind us to come to our senses! Miss Twitchell was found drowned this morning in Indian Pond."

"Oh, *no*, Tip—!"

"Yes. Some small boys found her. And they now think she'd been dead for two days. I wanted *so* much to tell you, Ee—I thought it might even bring us together—but I couldn't, somehow, with things so unhappy between us—"

"Oh, the poor, *poor* creature—! But *why*, Tip, *why*?"

"Nobody seems to know. It was suicide, though. There doesn't seem to be much doubt about that."

"And I meant to call on her, and didn't—or to have her to tea—and she was so nice, remember, about those lilies of the valley—"

"Yes, I know—those lilies of the valley have been haunting me. I've been thinking about them ever since, and about how typical it was of her."

"Oh, how awful, how simply awful. Oh, *Tip*—"

"Yes, darling—"

"Don't ever stop loving me. Don't ever let me stop loving you, will you? Don't believe the dreadful things I say!"

"Of course not, darling, of course not—"

"Poor, *poor* little Miss Twitchell, all by herself. What *could* have made her do such a thing?"

"Now, Ee, darling, I didn't mean to start you crying again—you've done enough for one day—and in the bathroom of all places!"

"It's a very *good* place—! But, yes, I mustn't. Can I dry my eyes on your sleeve?"

"Of course!"

She gave a quick smile, a last tear fell as she closed her eyes to rub them against his shoulder, and as he held her he felt the suppressed shudder rise in her breast and then slowly subside again. She sighed, leaned her head on his shoulder, and relaxed sleepily, her eyes still closed. He kissed the white forehead, ran a fingertip along the curve of one eyebrow—but then he thought he heard an odd little sound from upstairs. He turned his head to listen. The Unitarian Church clock began striking at the same moment, he would have to wait till it was finished (—and an early start in the morning, good lord—) *eight! nine! ten!* And then, yes, the same obscure sound again—

"Listen," he said.

"Yes, darling?"

"I think it's Buzzer—I'd better go up and see. And I *suppose*, my darling, we ought to go to bed— It's Boston for me in the morning!"

"Oh, of course! Well, if you'll go up to her, Tip, dear—unless you'd *rather* I did—"

"No, I'll go, if you'll put the house to bed. There's a light I left in the kitchen—"

"All right then, darling, run along!"

He took the candle from the top of the piano, and went lightly, swiftly, up the stairs into the smell and sound of night, the smell and sound of rain. And cold, too—the upper hall was damp and cold, a little cave of autumnal rain-sound—good lord, it would be winter in no time. The room whirled as he moved the candle, above the sound of the rain he could hear Buzzer's low continuous crying, and when he stooped through the low door he found her sitting up in her bed, and crying with her eyes closed, the backs of her hands pressed to her cheeks.

"Why, Buzzer, what is it, my pet? Did you have a bad dream?— There, that's right, you lie down, you'll get all cold—and tuck these hands in— Was that what it was, my pet? Did you have a bad dream?"

"Mmmmmm!"

"I guess so. But don't you worry—everything's going to be all right now, see?"

"Mmmmmm."

"Good night. And go to sleep."

He stooped and kissed the already sleeping head, stroked the small forehead—once, twice, thrice—heard the breathing pause and deepen. What had she been dreaming about—what truth, what terror, what despair? Perhaps the dead starling—the starling which *hadn't* been dead? Or perhaps, was it possible—for children had such extraordinary divinations in these things, a sort of sixth sense, like cats—perhaps she had somehow *known?* How dreadful—if so, how dreadful! He must tell Ee about it— they must never do it again. . . .

His candle uplifted, he waited at the head of the narrow stairs—he wanted to see her come up the stairs. When at last she came, holding her own candle before her, he said:

"Would you mind standing still, right there, till I tell you something? Till I ask you a question?"

"Why, what is it, Tip? *Was* it Buzzer?"

"Yes, it was Buzzer. *She's* all right—it was only some funny little dream she had."

"Well—!"

She looked up at him, from halfway up the stairs, one lovely knee in the silvery corduroy skirt advanced above the other—her face candlelit, smiling doubtfully, a little puzzled.

"It's only that I thought it would be nice to ask you from a *distance*, just to *see* you when I ask it—these things are usually settled at such close quarters, see?"

"Yes, darling, go on—"

"Well, it's only this. How would you *feel*, my darling, if I was to say that I thought it would be nice if we were to have a son."

"Oh, *Tip!*"

"And if a woman can look as lovely as that, it's high time, too!"

"What nonsense! Darling!"

"No nonsense at all. Besides, there's an omen. I had an omen!"

"*What* was your precious omen?"

"*Cut all things or gather, the moon in the wane—*
But sow in increasing or give it his bane.

Two lines I suddenly remembered out of an old book."

"But what do they *mean?*—Tip?"

"What do they *mean?* You just come up and go to bed, my darling; and I'll go down and brush my teeth; and then—well, we'll just see!"

"But, Tip, have you considered—I mean, all the things—"

"There *aren't* any things—and I *have* considered. And to hell with considering anyway! I want a *son*, see? Even if he's born, like me, with a cleft palette in his hand!"

"How *ridiculous* you are, darling!"

"Yes, I guess maybe I am—I guess maybe I am! But being ridiculous isn't always such a bad thing to be. . . ."